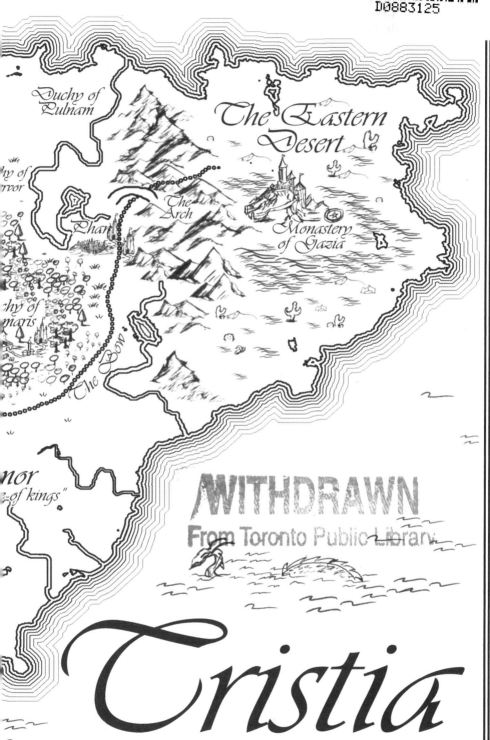

Duchy of
Pulnam

The Eastern
Desert

...hy of
...rvor

The
Arch

Phan...

Monastery
of Gazia

...chy of
...maris

The Bow

...nor
...-of kings"

Cristia

KNIGHT'S
SHADOW

THE
GREATCOATS
BOOK 2

KNIGHT'S SHADOW

SEBASTIEN DE CASTELL

VIKING

VIKING

an imprint of Penguin Canada Books Inc.

Published by the Penguin Group
Penguin Canada Books Inc.,
90 Eglinton Avenue East, Suite 700, Toronto, Ontario, Canada M4P 2Y3

Penguin Group (USA) Inc., 375 Hudson Street, New York, New York 10014, U.S.A.
Penguin Books Ltd, 80 Strand, London WC2R 0RL, England
Penguin Ireland, 25 St Stephen's Green, Dublin 2, Ireland
(a division of Penguin Books Ltd)
Penguin Group (Australia), 707 Collins Street, Melbourne, Victoria 3008, Australia
(a division of Pearson Australia Group Pty Ltd)
Penguin Books India Pvt Ltd, 11 Community Centre, Panchsheel Park,
New Delhi – 110 017, India
Penguin Group (NZ), 67 Apollo Drive, Rosedale, Auckland 0632, New Zealand
(a division of Pearson New Zealand Ltd)
Penguin Books (South Africa) (Pty) Ltd, 24 Sturdee Avenue, Rosebank,
Johannesburg 2196, South Africa

Penguin Books Ltd, Registered Offices: 80 Strand, London WC2R 0RL, England

Published in Viking hardcover by Penguin Canada Books Inc., 2015
Simultaneously published in the United States by Quercus, A Hachette
Company, 1290 Avenue of the Americas, New York, NY 10104

1 2 3 4 5 6 7 8 9 10 (RRD)

Manufactured in the U.S.A.

LIBRARY AND ARCHIVES CANADA CATALOGUING IN PUBLICATION
DATA AVAILABLE UPON REQUEST TO THE PUBLISHER.

Print ISBN 978-0-670-06999-6

eBook ISBN 978-0-14-319695-2

American Library of Congress Cataloging in Publication data available

Visit the Penguin Canada website at www.penguin.ca

Special and corporate bulk purchase rates available; please see
www.penguin.ca/corporatesales or call 1-800-810-3104, ext. 2477.

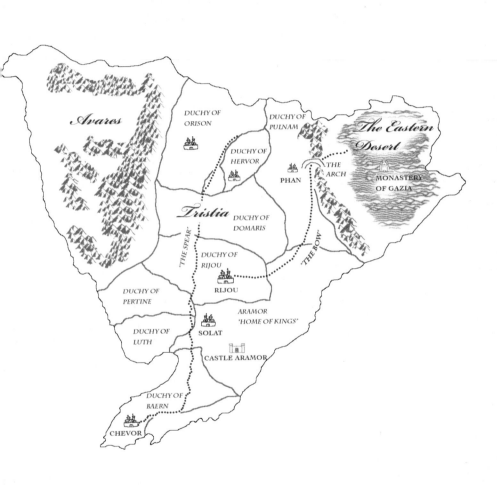

Avares

DUCHY OF
ORISON

DUCHY OF
PULNAM

The Eastern
Desert

DUCHY OF
HERVOR

THE
ARCH

PHAN

MONASTERY
OF GAZIA

Tristia

DUCHY OF
DOMARIS

"THE SPEAR"

DUCHY OF
RIJOU

"THE BOW"

RIJOU

DUCHY OF
PERTINE

ARAMOR
'HOME OF KINGS'

DUCHY OF
LUTH

SOLAT

CASTLE ARAMOR

DUCHY OF
RAERN

CHEVOR

CONTENTS

PROLOGUE

If on a winter's night a traveler like you finds shelter in one of the inns that line the trade roads of Tristia, sitting close to the fire, drinking what is quite likely watered-down ale, and doing your best to stay out of the way of the local bully-boys, you might chance to see a Greatcoat wander in. You'll know him or her by the long leather coat of office, weathered to a deep brown and tempered by a hint of dark red or green or sometimes even blue.

He or she will do their best to blend in with the crowd. They're good at it—in fact, if you look over there to your left, sitting alone in the shadows you'll see a second Greatcoat. The one at the door will almost certainly walk over and sit with the first one.

If you sidle over (carefully, now) and listen in to their conversation, you'll hear snatches of stories about the cases they once judged in the cities, towns, and hamlets throughout the countryside. They'll talk about this Duke or that Lord and which crimes they perpetrated on their people this time. You'll learn the details of how each case was decided and whether the Greatcoat had to fight a duel in order to get the verdict upheld.

Watch these two long enough and you'll begin to notice the way that they check out the room every so often. They'll be gauging the other patrons, looking for potential trouble. Look closer at those coats and you'll see a faint pattern in the leather: that'll be the bone plates sewn into the lining, hard enough to withstand arrow, blade, or bolt, and yet the coat itself moves as naturally as the one you yourself might be wearing. If you ever got the chance to reach inside, you'd find hidden pockets—some say a hundred of them—all filled with tricks and traps and esoteric pills and powders designed to give them an edge, whether fighting a single man or a mob. And while the swords hidden beneath the coats aren't fancy, you'd find them well oiled, well honed, and more than pointy enough to do the job.

Legend has it the Greatcoats began as duelists and assassins-for-hire, until some benevolent King or Queen brought them under the command of the monarchy to ensure that ancient laws were preserved in each of the nine duchies of Tristia. The Dukes, quite naturally, responded to this unwanted intrusion by devising the most painful deaths they could imagine for any Greatcoats their Knights defeated in combat. But for every Greatcoat killed, another would rise up to take the mantle and continue the job, going around the country annoying the nobility by enforcing laws that the nobility found inconvenient. That was until just over a hundred years ago, when a group of the wealthier (and more determined) Dukes hired the *Dashini*—an order of assassins who never failed to spread corruption, even in a place already as corrupt as Tristia—to provide them with a more enduring means of discouraging dissent. They called it the Greatcoat's Lament.

I will not bore you with the details, gentle traveler, for they are unfit for conversation between folk of good breeding. Suffice it to say, after the Dashini finished giving the Lament to the last Greatcoat they'd managed to catch, no more came forward to take up the mantle . . . at least, not for nearly a century, not until an overly idealistic young king named Paelis and a foolhardy commoner named Falcio decided to push back against the tide of history and recreate the Greatcoats.

But that's all done with now. King Paelis is dead and the Great-coats have been disbanded these last five years or more. The two you are watching risk death and worse any time they attempt to fulfill their traditional duties. So instead they will simply finish up their drinks, pay their tab, and wander off into the night. Perhaps you'll catch a glimpse of their smiles as they reassure each other that the Greatcoat's Lament is just one of those stories told by travelers in front of a warm fire on a cold night; that even if it had once existed, no one alive today would have the faintest idea of how to inflict it. But they—and you—would be wrong. For you see, I have it on extremely good authority that the Greatcoat's Lament is very real, and that it is even more painful and terrible than even the most hor-rifying stories made out. I would tell you more, but unfortunately, the "good authority" I mentioned is me.

My name is Falcio val Mond, one of the last of the King's Great-coats, and if you listen very carefully you might still be able to hear me screaming.

1

THE WAITING GAME

I can count on one hand the number of times in my adult life when I've awakened peacefully and happily, without either fear of imminent death or sufficient annoyance to make me want to murder someone else. The morning four weeks after Patriana, Duchess of Hervor had poisoned me was not one of those times.

"He's dead."

Despite the fog clogging my head and dulling the sounds in my ears, I recognized Brasti's voice.

"He's not dead," said another, slightly deeper voice. That one belonged to Kest.

The light thump-thump of Brasti's footsteps on the wooden floor of the cottage grew louder. "Usually he comes out of it by now. I'm telling you, this time he's dead. Look: he's barely breathing."

A finger prodded at my chest, then my cheek, then my eye.

You might be wondering why I didn't simply stab Brasti and go back to sleep; first, my rapiers were ten feet away, lying on a bench next to the door of the small cottage we occupied. Second, I couldn't move.

"Stop poking at him," Kest said. "Barely breathing still means *alive*."

"Which is another thing," Brasti said. "Neatha's supposed to be fatal." I imagined him wagging his finger at me. "We're all happy you survived it, Falcio, but this lying about each morning is highly inconvenient behavior. One might even call it selfish."

Despite my repeated attempts, my hands refused to reach out and wrap themselves around Brasti's throat.

The first week after I'd been poisoned, I'd noticed a slight weakness in my limbs—I moved more slowly than usual. Sometimes I'd try to move my hand and it would take a second before it would obey. But instead of getting better, the condition had gradually worsened and I found myself imprisoned in my own body for longer and longer each morning after I awoke.

A hand on my chest pressed down with a great deal of pressure: Brasti was leaning on me. "But Kest, I think you have to agree that Falcio is *largely* dead."

There was another pause and I knew Kest was considering the matter. The problem with Brasti is that he's an idiot. He's handsome and charming; he can outshoot any man or woman with a bow, and he's an idiot. Oh, you wouldn't think so at first; he's a fine conversationalist and uses many words that sound like the sort of words smart people use. He just doesn't use them in the right context. Or even the right order.

The problem with Kest, though, is that while he *is* extremely intelligent, he thinks that "being philosophical" requires giving any idea due consideration, even if it's utterly nonsensical and being uttered by the aforementioned idiot.

"I suppose," Kest said finally, and then redeemed himself marginally by adding, "But wouldn't it be more correct to say he's somewhat *alive*?"

More silence. Did I mention that the two fools in question are my best friends, fellow Greatcoats, and the men I was counting on to protect me in case the Lady Trin picked that precise moment to send her Knights after us?

I suppose I should get used to calling her *Duchess* Trin now. After all, I'd killed her mother, Patriana (yes, the one who'd poisoned me)—in my defense, I was trying to protect the King's heir at the time. I suspect that's the real source of Trin's grievance with me, as the presence of a genuine monarch gets in the way of her scheme to take the throne for herself.

"He's still not moving," Brasti said. "I really think he might be dead this time." I felt his hand brush a rather private part of my body and realized he was searching my pockets for money—which proves yet again that hiring a former poacher to be a traveling magistrate had not necessarily been one of the King's best ideas. "We're out of food, by the way," he said. "I thought those damned villagers were supposed to be bringing us supplies."

"Be grateful they're letting us hide here in the first place," Kest said placidly. "Feeding more than a hundred Greatcoats is a heavy burden for a village this small. Besides, they did bring food—from their winter caches in the mountains, just a few minutes ago. The Tailor's managing distribution."

"Then why don't I hear brats running around screaming and annoying us, asking to borrow our swords—or worse, play with my bows?"

"Perhaps they heard you complaining? They left their families in the mountains this morning."

"Well, that's something anyway."

I felt Brasti's fingers pulling the lid of my right eye back, and white light blinded me. Then the fingers went away and the light disappeared.

"How long until Falcio's *mostly* alive and no longer *entirely* useless? I mean, what happens when Trin's Knights learn about this? Or Dashini assassins? Or anyone else, for that matter?" Brasti's voice was growing more anxious as he spoke. "You name any group of people out there who know how to kill a man horribly and I'll bet you good gold that Falcio's made an enemy of them. Any one of them could—"

I felt my heart moving faster and faster, and tried to force my breathing to slow down, but panic was beginning to overtake me.

"Stop talking, Brasti. You're making him worse."

"They'll come for him, Kest, you know it—they might even be coming now. Are you going to kill every single one of them?"

"If that is what's required." You can hear a coldness in Kest's voice when he talks that way.

"You might be the Saint of Swords now, but you're still just one man. You can't fight an army. And what happens if Falcio's condition gets worse, and he just stops breathing? What happens when we're not here and—?"

I heard the sound of a scuffle and felt the bed shake a bit as someone was pushed up against the wall.

"Take your Gods-damned hands off me, Kest! Saint or no, I'll—"

"I'm scared for him too, Brasti," Kest said. "We're all scared."

"He's . . . By all the hells we've been to—he's supposed to be the smart one. How in the name of Saint Laina's left tit did he let himself get poisoned *again*?"

"To save her," Kest said. "To save Aline."

There was silence for a few moments and for the first time that morning I couldn't envision Kest and Brasti's faces. It was troubling, as if perhaps my hearing had suddenly gone away too. Fortunately, silence is a condition Brasti's never been able to abide for long.

"And that's another thing," he said, "if he's so damned brilliant then why is it that all anyone has to do to get him to risk his life for a girl he's never met before is just name her after his dead wife?"

"She's the King's heir, Brasti, and if you talk about Falcio's wife again you'll discover there are worse things than being paralyzed."

"I'd take the chance if I thought it would bring him out of this," Brasti said. "Damn it, Kest! He *is* the smart one. Trin's got armies and assassins and damned fucking Dukes on her side and we've got nothing. How are we supposed to put a thirteen-year-old girl on the throne with Falcio in this condition?"

I felt my eyes begin to flutter some more, and empty gray started flashing to bright white and back again, over and over. The effect was a little disconcerting.

"I suppose you and I will have to try to be smarter," Kest said.

"And just how do you propose we go about that?"

"Well, how does Falcio do it?"

There was a long pause, then Brasti started, "He . . . well, he figures things out, doesn't he? You know, there'll be six things going on, none of which seem all that important, and then all of a sudden he'll jump up and declare that assassins are coming or a Lord Caravaner must've bribed a City Constable or whatever."

"Then that's what you and I need to do," Kest said. "We need to start figuring those things out before they happen."

"How?"

"Well, what's happening right now?"

Brasti snorted. "Well, Trin's got five thousand soldiers on her side and the backing of at least two powerful duchies. We've got about a hundred Greatcoats and the tepid support of the creaky old Duke of Pulnam. Oh, and right about now she's probably having a nice breakfast and going over her plans for taking the throne while we sit here starving, hiding out in this shitty little village watching Falcio do his best impression of a corpse. And I *am* starving."

There was silence again. I tried to move a finger. I don't think I succeeded, but now I could feel the rough wool of the blanket on my fingertip. That was a good sign.

"At least you aren't having to listen to screaming children," Kest said.

"There's that."

I heard the sound of Kest's footsteps as he approached me and felt a hand on my shoulder. "So what do you suppose Falcio would make of all that? What does it all mean?"

"It means . . ." There was a long pause before Brasti finally said, "nothing. It's all just a bunch of unconnected details, none of which have anything to do with the others. Do you suppose that maybe Falcio just pretends to be clever and no one's caught on yet?"

I wanted to laugh at Brasti's frustration, then I felt the small muscles at the edges of my mouth twitch, just a bit. Oh, Gods, I'm coming out of it. *Move*, I told myself. *Get out of bed and go and help the Tailor defeat Trin's army. Put Aline on the throne, and then get out of this business of politics and war and go back to judging land disputes over whose cow farted on whose field, and chasing down the occasional corrupt Knight.*

A tightness in my stomach made me aware of how hungry I was, and I realized Brasti wasn't the only one ready for a hearty breakfast. *Food,* I thought, *then figure out how to save the world.* I was glad I wouldn't have to do it while the villagers' screaming brats ran around wanting to play at being Greatcoats with us, demanding our swords and trying our patience.

Which was odd. Why didn't the villagers bring their children? There wasn't much danger to the village—the Tailor had sent out scouts and none had reported sighting anything more than a few handfuls of Trin's men—not enough to cause us grief. Come to think of it, where were the rest of Trin's men? They might have been on missions, but surely they'd have been recalled as soon as anyone knew we were here. And the children . . .

"Swords!" I shouted.

Well, "shouted" is a bit optimistic, given my tongue was still thick in my throat, and I could barely move my lips. My eyes opened, though, which was good.

Brasti ran over to me. "Whores? What are you talking about?"

"Do you suppose he means that woman from Rijou? The one who saved his life?"

"You might be right," Brasti said, awkwardly brushing a hand across my head. "Don't worry, Falcio. We'll find you another whore just as soon as—"

"Swords, you damned fools," I mumbled. *"Swords!"*

"Help him up," Brasti said. "I think he said 'hordes'. Maybe we're about to be attacked."

Kest put his arm around my shoulders and helped me off the bed and onto my unsteady feet. Damn it, I was moving like an old man.

Brasti picked up my rapiers from the bench and handed them to me. "Here. You should probably have your swords ready if we're going to get into a fight, don't you think?"

I would have killed both of them, were it not for the fact that I was fairly sure someone else was about to do it for me.

2

THE NIGHTMIST

I stumbled out of the cottage, barely able to keep a grip on my swords. The sunlight irritated my eyes and turned the row of mud-brick cottages into a red-brown haze the color of dried blood.

"What's going on, Falcio?" Kest asked.

"The children," I said, almost coherently.

"They're not here, didn't you hear?" Brasti said.

"That's the point—the villagers left their children in the mountain. Why would they do that unless they knew something was coming? We're about to get hit."

I stepped on a small rock and lost my balance, but Kest's hand on my shoulder kept me from falling over. "You should go back inside, Falcio, let Brasti and m—"

To my left a villager was puttering about in one of the small front gardens. "Where's the Tailor?" I asked. My mouth was still largely numb from the paralysis, and I probably sounded like something between a simpleton and a madman.

The man looked confused and frightened until Kest translated, "He's asking you where the Tailor is."

The villager rose and pointed to another cottage about fifty yards away, his hand trembling just a bit. "She's in there. Been there the last day and night with the girl and a couple of them other Greatcoats."

"Get your folk," I said. "Get them out of here."

"You all should have left by now," he said, his voice a mixture of indignation and anxiety that would have struck me as odd had I had the time to consider it. "Ain't good for us to be seen sheltering Greatcoats."

"Where are your children?" I asked.

"Safe," he said.

I pushed the man out of the way and started running toward the house. I managed about three steps before I fell flat on my face. Kest and Brasti knelt down to help me, but I screamed, "Gods damn it, leave me and get to Aline!"

They took me literally, dropping me to the ground and pounding along the path to the other house. As I pushed myself back up to my feet I looked around again, expecting to find enemies on all sides, but all I saw were the same villagers I'd seen before, and here and there, some of the Tailor's Greatcoats. Could there be enemies hiding among them? Most of the men were doing no more than tending to their gardens, as they'd done every time they returned from the mountains.

I hobbled awkwardly after Kest and Brasti and arrived just in time to see the Tailor storm out of the cottage, her steel-gray hair flying in the wind and her craggy features displaying her foul temper. She looked nothing like the mother of a King—I suppose that's how she'd kept it secret for so long, even after Paelis had died. "What in the name of Saint Birgid-who-weeps-rivers are you about, Falcio? We're trying to make battle plans here."

I felt a momentary annoyance that she had chosen to exclude us from her strategy sessions, but set that aside, for now at least. "The children," I panted, "the villagers didn't bring their children . . ."

"So? Perhaps they got tired of Brasti teaching them to swear."

"Your scouts," I said, pointing to two Greatcoats who stood nearby. "You told me they couldn't find any of Trin's forces anywhere for fifty miles."

The Tailor gave a nasty grin. "That little bitch may think of herself as a wolf, but she knows better than to attack us here. We've bitten her heels at every encounter. They'll not try to engage us again unless they want to see more of their men litter the ground."

"Saints! Don't you get it? That's the point: it's something else. The villagers have betrayed us!"

The Tailor's expression soured. "Watch yer tongue, boy. I've known the people of Phan for more than twenty years. They're on our side."

"And in all those years have you ever known them to leave their children behind in the mountains when there wasn't any danger coming?"

The anger on the Tailor's face was replaced by suspicion and she looked around again, then shouted to one of the men tending his garden, "You, Cragthen! What are you about?"

The man was in his middle years, balding, with a fringe of brown hair and a short beard. "Just looking after my verden roots," he said.

The Tailor started walking toward him, pulling a knife from her coat. "Then what are you burying in the dirt, Cragthen, when we're so close to the harvest?"

The man rose to his feet, his eyes flitting between us and other villagers who were beginning to gather around. "You weren't supposed to be here this long—it's our village, damn you, not yours. We have families to think of. The Duchess Trin—"

The Tailor reached forward with her left hand and grabbed Cragthen by the shirt. "What fool thing have you done, Cragthen? You think you're scared of Trin? Cross me and I'll give you something to fear that's a lot worse than an eighteen-year-old whore who beds her uncle for his armies and fancies herself a Queen."

At first Cragthen looked cowed by the Tailor, but then he managed to pull away and shouted, "We have children, damn you!" as he turned and fled toward the far end of the village.

"Stop him!" the Tailor shouted.

It took only moments for two of her Greatcoats to catch up with Cragthen. As they hauled him back he said urgently, "Let me go!"

His voice was low but full of terror. "Please, please, no! If they see me talking to you they'll kill her!"

The Tailor bent down to look at what Cragthen had been planting and I joined her. "Hells," she grunted, looking at the mixture of black earth and a dark yellowish-green powder.

"What is it?" I asked.

"Nightmist—the damned fool is setting nightmist!"

I looked around at the rest of the villagers, at the other men who had also been busy working their gardens, and saw some were lugging over-full pails from the pump, water spilling over the sides.

"Don't let them pour that water on the ground!" I shouted, but as soon as the village men saw the Greatcoats coming toward them they dumped the contents of their pails onto the freshly turned earth.

"Too late," the Tailor sighed as the first drops of water hit the nightmist and gray-black smoke thick as bog water began to fill the air. Even a handful of the mixture—sulfur and yellowflake and Saints-know-whatever-else goes into it—can fill a hundred yards with smoke so thick you couldn't see your hand in front of your face. The villagers had put down bucketfuls.

I turned to the Tailor. "Tell me where Aline is—now!"

"She went for a walk to see that giant damned horse of hers," she said, pointing down the path. "Don't just stand there wobbling: go!"

Kest and Brasti ran ahead of me, and as I followed, we began to hear the heavy thumping of marching men and the raucous clangor of metal on metal.

Had we guessed what was going on even a few minutes sooner we might have been better prepared, but instead, I had been lying in bed paralyzed like a broken old man. Now our enemies were about to launch an attack that could only have one purpose: to kill the daughter of my King.

The billowing black fog overtook me before I'd gone ten paces down the path. Though the sun still shone above me and the sky remained clear and blue, down here on the ground the world was shadows painted on top of other shadows.

I pointed my rapiers out in front of me and waved them around like the feelers on an ant, moving in smooth arcs high and low, quiet as I could: I needed to find my enemies before they could find me, and before they found Aline. I longed to call out for her, to hear her voice and know she was alive so that I could make my way to her, but to do so would just make her a target for Trin's men.

A dreamlike chaos settled over the village: one moment the night-mist would dissipate enough for me to make out figures in the distance, fighting and dying, the next it closed in on me, suffocating me while it revealed only glints of light reflecting from steel swords clashing in the distance like fireflies flitting in the night air.

I hate magic.

"Falcio!" Brasti called out.

His voice sounded far away but I'd run only a few feet before I saw him fighting two men dressed all in dark cloth with masks covering their faces. For an instant I froze, thinking, *Dashini! Trin has sent the Dashini for us.* In my mind I envisioned hundreds of the dark assassins, fighting in pairs to kill us one by one. I had barely survived facing two of them in Rijou, so if Trin had managed to—

"A little help?" Brasti shouted, breaking the spell, and I got to him just as one of his opponents swung a warsword down in a vicious arc that would have taken Brasti's head off if I hadn't crossed my rapiers above his head and blocked the blow, my still-unsteady legs feeling the weight of my opponent's attack. Brasti dived and rolled out of the way—a dangerous move when you're holding a shortsword—but he kicked out with one foot at the back of the man's knees and drove him to the ground.

The other one turned to me and beckoned teasingly with his sword. "Come, *Trattari*," he said, his voice thick and resonant in the mist. "Amuse me with your Greatcoat tricks before I break you—or better yet, show me to the one who calls himself the Saint of Swords. I'll happily take that title from him."

It wasn't like a Dashini to bluster in a fight. They say creepy things like, "You are tired . . . your eyes wish to close . . . let peace come to you . . ."—that sort of thing. And a warsword? No, they fought with long, stiletto-like blades, not military weapons. *So not Dashini then. Someone else.*

I stepped forward and flicked the point of my rapier in his face, but he didn't try to parry, instead using his forearm to swipe the blade aside. I heard a clang of metal against metal. *Aha. That's a metal vambrace*, I thought. *You're wearing armor under that dark gray cloth.*

"Shouldn't you introduce yourself, Sir Knight?" I asked.

He took a swing at me with that great big sword of his. I was still moving too slowly and barely leaned back in time to watch it sail by; when I tried a thrust for his right armpit I missed by a good inch, hitting steel plate instead of flesh: I definitely hadn't fully shaken off the vestiges of my temporary paralysis. Had Kest been there he would have reminded me, in that way he has, that a good swordsman would adjust for the stiffness.

The problem with fighting Knights is that they tend to wear a great deal of metal, which means you either have to bludgeon them to death, which is hard to do with a rapier, or find the gaps in their armor and strike there. The dark gray cloth my opponent was wearing made it harder to find those spots, and the nightmist wasn't helping either. Brasti and his opponent had already disappeared from view.

"Hardly sporting," I said, goading the Knight by moving clockwise around him, counting on his plate-mail to make it hard for him to turn gracefully. "Aren't Ducal Knights required to wear their tabards and show their colors in combat?"

"You'd lecture me in honor, Trattari?" the Knight asked, his tone mocking me, and to add injury to insult, he tried to drive the point of his sword through my belly. I shifted on my heel so it went by me on the left and drove the pommel of my rapier against the flat of his blade, knocking the point down toward the ground. He stepped back before I could take advantage of his lowered guard.

"Well, I don't like to brag about honor," I said, "but I shouldn't have to point out that I'm not the one sneaking in under cover of nightmist to murder a thirteen-year-old girl. In the dark. Like an *assassin*. Like a *coward*."

I thought that would send him into a rage. I'm usually very good at making Knights want to kill me as quickly as possible. But he just laughed. "You see? That's why you Greatcoats can never become Knights."

"Because we don't kill children?" I flicked my point at him again but he batted it away with his hand.

"Because you think honor comes from actions—as if a horse who stamps his feet three times when you show him three apples is a scholar." He began attacking me with quick, vicious swings of his warsword, turning the momentum of each attack into the next as I slid and skipped back and forth to avoid the blows. As I stumbled backward, I was praying to Saint Werta-who-walks-the-waves that I wouldn't hit a rock or tree root and fall down. I long ago gave up hope of living to an old age but I still had aspirations of dying with slightly more dignity than a Knight's warsword removing my head while I was stuck on the ground with my ass in the mud.

"Honor is granted by the Gods and by a man's Lord," the Knight said, continuing his attacks as well as his lecture, "not earned from learning some litany of children's verses. What is sin for you is virtue for me, Trattari." His blade came down at an odd angle and I was forced to parry it with both rapiers and the force of his blow nearly knocked them from my hands. "Nothing will come from the noblest act of your short life," he said, "but the Gods' blessings will come to me when I squeeze the life from that little bitch . . . that . . . bi—"

He stopped talking then, perhaps because the point of my rapier had found the opening of his mouth beneath his mask. I kept pushing the blade until it found the back of his skull and stopped at the steel of his helm. The Knight sank to his knees, his body twitching: not yet dead, but well on his way.

Kest sometimes makes fun of me for talking too much during a fight, but unlike some, I've had enough practice to keep my focus while I do it.

I withdrew my blade and took a moment to catch my breath as my opponent fell back to the ground. Only a Tristian Knight would make the argument that to be honorable doesn't require behaving honorably; that murdering a young girl is justified so long as your lawful Lord demands it. But there you have it. That's the country of my birth and the place I'd spent most of my life trying to defend from itself. If that meant I had to kill a few Knights along the way, well, I thought, as I took in deep breaths and tried to slow my heart, I could live with that.

"Brasti?" I called out.

There was no answer and I feared he might have been struck down. He'd been carrying his sword and that wasn't his best weapon, even in close combat like this. I needed to get to him and Kest so we could find Aline. I'd taken too long with the Knight . . .

Hells. We never should have stayed in the village. I know they were hoping I would get better rather than worse—so was I, but you don't need to be a grand military strategist to know that when you're fighting a force fifty times your size you don't stay in one place too long.

As I ran through the mist, filled with ever-growing anger and frustration, I tripped over a body on the ground. As I caught myself, I looked down and through the smoke I saw the still-bleeding corpse of a young girl in a bright blue dress, her arms crossed over her face as if she were still cowering from the blow that had already killed her.

3

THE DEAD GIRL

The harsh sound of my own ragged breath filled my ears as I stood over the girl's body, trying to steel myself for what I was about to see. *Saint Zaghev-who-sings-for-tears, please, no, not now . . . Let it not be her.* I knelt down and pried the girl's arms away from her face.

As I forced the arm aside, I saw the child's wide eyes, her mouth frozen in a distorted mixture of fear and agony from the blow of the blade that had cut so deeply into her skull, the blood seeping from the wound staining red hair to a deeper crimson.

Red hair.

Thank the Saints. This girl had curly red hair, not the straight mostly-brown tresses that Aline had inherited from her father. The rapture of unexpected relief soon turned to a grinding, sickening guilt. This girl whom I had so easily consigned to irrelevance had done nothing—less than nothing—to deserve this end, this way, alone. When the blade had come for her, had she cried out for her mother, or her father?

A choking scream reached my ears and I turned to see a figure running toward me, the nightmist clinging to his outstretched arms. It was one of the village men—Bannis? Baris? All I could remember was that he grew barley in a small field and made beer with it. The locals liked it.

"Celeste!" he screamed, ignoring my swords and pushing me out of the way. He fell to his knees and cradled the girl in his arms. "I told her to stay in the mountains!" he cried. "I *told* her . . . I went back but she was gone—she must've followed me. You—! This is because of you and your damned Greatcoats . . . your damned . . . damned . . . Trattari!" He sobbed as he yelled at me then, accusing me of terrible crimes, saying the things a man says when his child is dead and he needs someone to blame. I wanted to shout right back at him: to scream at him that if he and his thrice-damned friends hadn't betrayed us, his child would have had a chance, but I couldn't bring myself to do so because he was right, in a way: had we not been here, he wouldn't have had to betray us, and maybe then none of this would have happened.

On the other hand, this is Tristia.

I clenched my hands tightly around the grips of my rapiers. Grief passes faster than it should when there are still enemies in the field, and rage provides its own kind of clarity. I would find Trin and make her pay for this: not just for the men, women, and children dying in villages and towns across the Duchy of Pulnam as she kept up pressure on Duke Erris to swear his support for her, but for the murder of Lord Tremondi, and most of all for what she was trying to do to Aline.

The sounds of steel-on-steel broke through the mist and guilt gave way to fear. *Move*, I told myself. *Don't sit here wallowing. Aline is out there, alone, waiting for you to find her.* I ran toward the noises in the mist. *I will find her*, I promised myself. Aline's a smart girl and she can be brave when she needs to be—hadn't we survived together for nearly the entire Blood Week in Rijou before we'd been caught? She was hiding now, I was sure of it. She'd've found a place to wait for me, and now I would find her before Trin's men did and I would pick her up and get to my horse and take her fast and far from this place. The daughter of my King wouldn't die because of me.

* * *

I found Brasti some fifty yards away, near one of the village's two wells, nursing his hand while sitting on the corpse of his opponent, which was lying facedown in the mud.

"The son of a bitch got me," he said, showing me a wound barely deeper than a shaving cut.

"You'll live," I said. "Get up."

"It's my hand, Falcio," Brasti complained, rising to his feet. "I'm an archer, not a swordsman. My art requires finesse and skill; it's not just swinging a pointy bar of metal around like a doddering old man waving a stick."

"Remind me to kiss it better for you later," I said, hauling him up by the shoulder.

We took off at a run and headed into the mist, ignoring the bodies of villagers, Greatcoats, and Trin's warriors littering the ground. There was still no sign of Aline, so I gave a short prayer to Saint Birgid-who-weeps-rivers that one of ours had found her.

"Where's Kest?" I asked suddenly.

"I'm not sure. He took off after some spectacularly big armored bastard who'd just made short work of two of the Tailor's Greatcoats. I told him we needed to stick together but he started glowing red and ignored me." Brasti's expression became grim. "He's still doing it, Falcio. He just—"

"I know," I said. Ever since Kest had defeated Caveil-whose-blade-cuts-water and taken on the mantle of the Saint of Swords, something had changed in him. Whenever we got into trouble he went straight the strongest fighter, *only* the strongest fighter, as if compulsion had overtaken reason.

"Falcio, we need a plan. We don't know how many of Trin's men there are here. They could outnumber us ten to one, for all we know—and they're wearing armor."

There was something shockingly unsettling about the fact that Brasti Goodbow, a man who'd never met a plan he fully understood, never mind liked, was the one reminding me we needed a strategy. But he was right: as Greatcoats we were trained for dueling, not facing armies, and the dark gray cloth Trin's Knights were wearing combined with the nightmist made it even harder to find the weak spots in their armor. We needed an advantage: a trick that could surprise them when the moment came . . .

"Brasti, I need you to get Intemperance and get up to the rooftops."

"That won't work. It might be clear up there but I can't make out friend from foe in the mists—I'm just as likely to hit one of ours as one of theirs. Why can't they run around with their armor all shiny like they usually do?"

I reached inside my coat to a tiny pocket—one of the dozens that held a Greatcoat's tools and tricks—and found three pieces of brittle amberglow. "Leave that to me," I said. "You just make sure you've got those damned long ironwood arrows of yours and get up top."

"Fine, but if don't blame me if I end up shooting you by mistake," he said, and turned to ran back the way we'd come, toward the center of the village.

I resumed my search for Aline, and a few moments later, the mist shifted again and a figure appeared in front of me: a woman with dark hair, too tall to be Aline. She was looking off to the side and I could make out the elegant, sensuous lines of a face for which most men would do just about anything.

Trin.

Hate and fear mixed inside me like the ingredients of nightmist, filling me with swirling desire. I tightened my grip on my rapiers. *She hasn't seen me. She hasn't even drawn her sword.* Part of me wanted to call out her name, to hear it drip from my lips, to see her face as I finally put an end to her. But I kept silent. Capturing Trin would have given us a huge strategic victory but if I challenged her or tried to take her alive there was too great a chance of her men being close enough to hear me and I couldn't risk a dozen Knights swarming over me before I'd dealt with their mistress. Great heroics are nice, but when you're still partially paralyzed and terrified, a dirty win works just fine. *It won't be assassination if I simply kill her, will it? This is a battle—we're at war.* Even the King would have understood that. Wouldn't he?

I let the point of my rapier drift into position and began the three steps it would take me to reach Trin and take her from this world. All the rage and frustration I'd felt these past weeks ignited inside me like a bonfire. A few seconds more and she would join her damned mother in whichever hell was reserved for those who would murder children. The skin on my face felt tight, and it took a moment to realize I was smiling.

Just as I was in striking distance of her, she turned to see me. Her eyes went wide as the light glinted off my rapier, but when she saw my face the look of fear changed instantly to relief. "Falcio!" she said.

I barely stopped my blade in time, stumbling to a halt and barely keeping my balance. *Valiana. It's Valiana, you idiot!* She and Trin looked enough alike that in the fog my hunger for revenge had overtaken my senses.

"What are you doing here?" I demanded. *Damn you! Damn you for not being her.* "Get inside one of the cottages and hide before you get yourself killed." My rebuke was harsher than she deserved, and aimed at the wrong target.

"I'm . . . I'm a Greatcoat now," she said, with as much defiance as an eighteen-year-old girl who'd never fought a duel in her life could muster. "I've got to find Aline and protect her."

Valiana's determination was the only thing that was truly her own. Her life as a princess had been a ruse, a cruel joke perpetrated by Duchess Patriana, devised not just to amuse herself with that cold, calculating cleverness that only the very rich and very evil find amusing, but also to hide Trin, her true daughter, in plain sight. Now Valiana had a sword in her hand and a Greatcoat made for her by the Tailor in exchange for her vow to throw herself in front of any blade coming for Aline. *And your name*, I reminded myself. *You gave her your name. She's Valiana val Mond now and as close to a daughter as you'll ever have.*

"I need you to get inside one of the cottages," I said, more gently this time. "I need to know that you're safe."

"I swore an oath to protect her," Valiana replied, her voice stronger now, and more sure than she had any right to be. "If I die doing so, then so be it."

I considered knocking the sword out of her hand and dragging her to safety. She'd been trained in fencing the way all sheltered nobles were: as if it were all a game, with points scored and style applauded. Out here in the real world it was a recipe for a quick death.

"Falcio!" she screamed.

I've learned over the years—often the hard way—that if the face of the person in front of you suddenly fills with terror and screams your name, it generally means something unpleasant is about to happen. I ducked even as I spun around and saw the spiked iron ball of a flail fly past the spot where my head had been an instant before. I brought my rapiers up in front of me just as the man wielding the flail prepared his second strike.

I've never understood the flail as a weapon: it always feels slow and cumbersome (and aptly named, as far as I'm concerned). But my enemy was quite determined to prove me wrong. His fast, precise swing sent the small spiked metal ball on the end of the chain hurtling toward me: an overhead attack this time. I sidestepped it, expecting to see it hit the ground and pull my opponent off-balance, but instead my opponent used the momentum of the swing to bring the weighted ball back and straight around again, this time on a horizontal axis toward me. I've seen the impact of the spiked-ball end of a flail break the ribs of an armored opponent. The bone plates in my greatcoat were strong, but so far I'd managed to avoid finding out if they could resist a flail and I didn't think now was the time to start. I brought my right rapier up so the point was aiming straight up to the sky and stepping back, leaned away just enough that the ball missed me but the chain wrapped around the blade of my sword. I yanked on it as hard as I could, pulling the man toward me, driving the point of my rapier in the vicinity of his armpit, where the gap in between his armor would be. My thrust missed and once again I cursed the dark gray cloth.

Valiana tried stabbing at the Knight with her sword but she didn't have the training to deal with an armored opponent and her light blade did little but annoy him. For my part, I hung onto his weapon arm for my life and kept stabbing my rapier as quickly as I could, trying to find that damned gap. It was hardly the kind of swordsmanship they sing about in the sagas, but most of those sagas aren't about Greatcoats anyway. After three tries my tip found a spot between his helm and the top of his neck. He dropped the flail and fell to the ground.

Before I could enjoy what a well-earned sense of relief, Valiana shouted and I turned to see a gaggle of Knights coming for us. *Hells!* I thought, *had I been a little faster, we might have been able to escape before they found us.*

Three were brandishing swords and the other two had maces. I couldn't hope to take two opponents right now, never mind five. *Kest could have done it,* I thought. I cursed my black luck and the damned nightmist and the fact that Kest wasn't here when I needed him. "Run!" I shouted to Valiana. "Run and find Kest and stay with him."

She didn't obey but took up a guard position next to me that would have made a lovely painting in the hall of a Duke's castle but wouldn't be the slightest help when our enemies attacked.

"Falcio!" I heard Brasti call out from somewhere behind and above us, "where the hells are you?"

"I'm here," I yelled back.

"I can't see for shit. I can make out shapes but I don't know which ones are you and which ones are the damned Knights!"

"Too bad for you," one of the Knights said. He looked at Valiana. "Duchess Trin will find special favor for the man who brings this one back in chains." There was a hunger in his voice that filled my mind with images of what they would do to her. *No,* I thought, *stay here. Stay calm. You won't win on rage alone.*

An arrow whizzed through the air and very nearly clipped me in the arm before hitting the ground.

"Did I get him?"

"Don't go by the sound of their voices!" I shouted. "The nightmist distorts the way we hear noises." Somewhere in the world lives a God or a Saint who took it upon himself to invent magic. I plan on killing him some day.

"Then how—?"

As the first Knight came for us, I reached into my pocket and took found one of the pieces of amberglow. It's a lightweight, brittle substance that glows just enough when you crush it to let you mark the spot where a piece of evidence is found. I hurled it at the Knight's chest. At first it didn't look like anything had happened, but a few seconds later a small spot on his clothing began to glow, almost as if it had caught fire.

For a moment the Knight looked panicked, but he quickly realized he wasn't burning. "Stupid Greatcoat tricks," he said, and raised his blade.

"What's that?" Brasti shouted. "Falcio, is that—?"

"Aim for the glow, Brasti!"

"Now," the Knight roared, "now, Trattari! Now death comes!" He charged for us.

"You bet death is coming, metal man," Brasti called out.

The Knight had only a brief instant to look up before he heard the loud thunk of a two-and-a-half-foot-long black arrow piercing his chest so deeply that I thought it might come out the other side.

"Cowardice . . ." the man murmured, sinking to his knees.

"That's not cowardice, Sir Knight," I said, "that's Intemperance."

I gave a silent thanks to Saint Merhan-who-rides-the-arrow for having made Brasti a Greatcoat. No matter how strong a Knight's armor, it's not impenetrable to a two-and-a-half-foot-long steel-tipped arrow launched from a six-foot longbow made of red yew and black hicksten and drawn by a man who hates Knights more than any other living thing.

The other attackers were more cautious now and started moving to surround us. I threw a second piece of amberglow at one of the other Knights but before it could shed any light he brushed it off and stamped it into the ground. Well, it's not as if my luck ever lasts longer than a second or two.

The Knight opposite me echoed my thoughts: "Your trick worked once, Trattari. It won't work a second time."

"Falcio, what's happening?" Brasti shouted. "Where's the next target?"

"I'm working on it," I said.

The Knight brought his blade down hard and I skipped back, letting it pass in front of my face and down to the ground. I flicked both my rapiers at him, slicing them across his chest, but he just laughed and didn't even bother to parry. A rapier cut against plate-armor is about as deadly as the soft caress of silk. But I wasn't trying to cut the plate. I was simply cutting the cloth that covered it.

"Something's glinting," Brasti called out.

"That's your target! Hit it!"

The Knight realized what was about to happen and frantically tried to cover the sheen of his exposed armor, but he was too late, and an instant later an arrow pierced his chest.

"Valiana," I said, "take one of the Knights with the maces. Keep out of his reach and don't try to kill him—just cut as much of the cloth covering his armor as you can."

The other Knights rushed us, but this was a fight I could deal with. The two swordsmen tried to outflank me but my rapiers were just as long as their warswords and twice as fast. And I didn't need to aim very well at all.

Brasti's voice called out. "I think I see—"

"Wait until you're sure!" I shouted back, fearful he might mistake the flashing of my blades for exposed armor.

One of the Knights tried to behead me and I slipped underneath and ran behind him. It took just two quick slashes to expose the plate on his back; I doubt he even noticed as he turned back around to face me. The sun overhead was beginning to burn through the nightmist—just enough that its rays gleamed against the Knight's armor and an instant later an arrow buried itself into his body.

I heard another arrow whiz through the air and spun around to see it lodged in the leg of Valiana's opponent. *Good girl. Don't try to expose him for the killing blow—settle for anything you can.* As he went down on one knee she slashed at him again and a moment later a second arrow took the same Knight in the throat.

My second swordsman was trying to stay close to me but this was a fight of speed and agility and even with my recent infirmity I had the edge. I skipped back and slashed three times, exposing a wide area of plate around his belly. Brasti's arrow found it moments later. All I needed to do now was take out the second mace fighter.

I heard a scream and turned to see Valiana, her sword on the ground several feet away and the last Knight readying his mace to strike her down. She would die the instant that blow landed. In my mind's eye I saw her lying on the ground, her skull crushed inwards. I darted toward them, cursing every Saint I could name, already knowing I would be too late. The Knight was still fully covered in his gray cloth and there was still too much mist for Brasti to be able to make out anything but blurred shadows. Valiana slipped and fell to the ground, and I knew that if Brasti shot now he was just as likely to kill me or Valiana as the Knight. But we had no other choice.

"Brasti! Take the shot!"

"Falcio, I can't see—"

"Take the—"

The mist parted and a wild figure emerged, running at Valiana and her opponent, a warsword in his hand. He was glowing red, as if fire was burning just under the surface of his skin. *A demon,* I thought. *Trin's found a way to send demons for us now.* At the last instant the figure leapt in the air, sailing effortlessly over the girl, sword held downward in a reverse grip with the point toward the ground. As gravity pulled him back to earth, he drove the tip of the sword into the Knight's chest with all the crashing force of his momentum behind it. The blade pierced the plate armor and sank deep into the Knight's body. The world froze for a brief moment.

"Never tried that before," Kest said, withdrawing the bloody sword, his voice as calm and relaxed as if he'd just stepped out of a warm bath.

"What's happening?" Brasti called out. "I can't—"

"It's all right," I said, holding my hand out to help Valiana up. "The Saint of Swords finally decided to show up."

Kest raised an eyebrow at me. "I was busy killing seven of them. How many have you killed?"

"Not as many," I admitted.

Brasti emerged from the mist carrying Intemperance in one hand and half a dozen arrows in the other. "I killed eight." I was fairly sure he was lying.

It's hard to describe my sense of relief at Kest's arrival. He was my best friend and the deadliest fighter I'd ever known, and with him and Brasti at my side I felt as if the mists were about to fade. Together we could deal with Trin's men. We could find Aline.

Another figure emerged from the mist. "You!" he called out, and as he came closer I was able to recognize him as one of the Tailor's Greatcoats. His face suddenly became deathly pale and I realized that Kest, Brasti, Valiana and I all had our weapons pointed at him.

"Come with me," he said, doing an impressive job of mastering himself. "The Tailor wants you."

"Where?"

"To the horses—the rest of Trin's Knights have fled and they've taken Aline."

4

THE DECEPTION

In the few minutes it took us to reach the far end of the village, most of the gray-black fog had dissipated, as if the nightmist itself knew that its mission was complete. All that was left were a few wispy tendrils of smoke that made my lungs burn and the chaos that invariably follows a battle.

Bodies were lying scattered along the village paths. I counted four fallen Greatcoats and nearly twenty-five of Trin's Knights, but both sides were vastly outnumbered by the men from the village. Those who'd betrayed us had ended up trapped in the very fog they'd helped to create, caught between two fighting forces. The ground was littered with their bodies. Some were injured, crying out for help; a precious few still had enough strength to provide aid to those less able. But most were dying, or already dead.

I found the Tailor surrounded by a dozen of her Greatcoats, a hundred yards from the rows of uneven posts where our horses were tethered. She wore her own greatcoat and her normally wild gray hair was tied back. Her eyes were bright and clear and she looked like a battle-hardened general rather than the enigmatic, bellicose tailor I'd known for so many years. There was no trace of urgency in her expression, nor in her men's faces, and when I looked at the horses I noticed that none of them were saddled.

"What in all the hells are you doing just standing here?" I demanded. "Do you have any—?"

"Wait," the Tailor said, holding up a hand to keep me silent.

"Are you mad? They've got Aline!" I started to push past her to get to the horses. Two of her Greatcoats stepped out in front to block my way, their hands on their weapons, and Kest and Brasti took up positions on either side of me. I turned back to the Tailor. "Would you try and stop me from rescuing the King's heir? Your own granddaughter?"

"I haven't forgotten who she is," the Tailor said, her gaze moving to the village men nearby. "We have a plan and we're going to follow it."

The calm in her voice—the utter lack of any sign that she shared the panic that was seizing me—made it difficult for me to keep my temper. It made it impossible for Brasti.

"I have a thought," he said. "How about we beat your men senseless, get on our horses, save the girl, and then you can tell us all about your little plan when we get back?"

She looked at the three of us with a kind of disdain that I hadn't seen before, like a teacher who's had enough of coddling a feebleminded student. "Hold your tongue and come with me," she said. The iron in her voice brooked no dissent.

"The hells for that," Brasti said. "Come on, Falcio, let's teach these fops in black leather why real Greatcoats don't bow to anyone."

I wanted to, the Gods know how much I longed to. The Tailor needed to understand that even if she did rule her own little army of men and women who looked like Greatcoats and called themselves Greatcoats, yet behaved more like soldiers and spies than magistrates, she didn't rule us. But something in her expression gave me pause. She knew something I didn't.

"We'll come," I said to her, "but you'd best say something to prove your loyalty to the King's heir very quickly."

She stepped into one of the nearby cottages without replying and I motioned for Kest and Brasti to follow me inside.

A few dim rays of sunshine snuck through cracks in the walls of the room but they barely illuminated the darkness within. As the three of us entered, the Tailor motioned for me to close the door. "You'll keep your voice calm and quiet in here, all of you."

I didn't want to be calm or quiet. I wanted to scream my frustration, but then the Tailor pointed toward the far corner of the room. At first I saw nothing but shadows, my eyes not yet having recovered from going from darkness to light to darkness again. Slowly edges and lines became clearer and the shadows resolved into a figure sitting in a chair. A girl.

I started to shout her name, but Brasti put a hand over my mouth. His vision is better than Kest's or mine and he must have seen her a moment before we did. She rose from the chair and came closer. Now I could see the shoulder-length, messy brown hair, the worn and faded green dress, the pretty face with the features that, like her father's, were just a bit too sharp to be called beautiful. *It's her, thank all the Saints. It's Aline.*

Brasti removed his hand from my mouth and I knelt down and embraced her. *Gods, stop the world from spinning,* I thought, relief washing over me. *Let me feel this happy for just a few moments more.*

"I was scared," Aline whispered in my ear.

"Really?" I asked, my own voice shaking. "I can't imagine what you had to be scared about."

She let go of me and her eyes met mine. "I couldn't be out there with you, keeping hold of your throwing knives for you like in Rijou. I was afraid you'd get hurt without me."

It always surprised me—the way that Aline, despite her keen intellect, could sometimes sound so much younger to me than her thirteen years.

Brasti snorted. "That's a smart girl we have here, Falcio. Terrific survival instincts. Can't wait to put her on the throne."

"All right," the Tailor said, "enough of the lovey-dovey. The girl's safe and we're all friends again. Now let's go back out there and you lot keep your mouths shut. Some of the village men are still alive and we can't trust any of them anymore."

"But who did the Knights carry off?" I asked. "Your man said they took Aline."

"He saw them carry off a girl," the Tailor said, "one they think is Aline. That's all you need to know."

"You gave them a girl they think is Aline? They'll kill her!"

"A few minutes ago you challenged my loyalty to the King's heir. Now you say I do too much for her? Listen to me, Falcio, and listen well. There is one thing and one thing only that matters: Aline must be protected so that she can take the throne. Nothing else can stand in the way of that. Nothing will."

I thought back to the dead girl in the village, her red hair dyed crimson with blood. Had she been another of the Tailor's pawns? Had she died to try to put Trin's Knights off the scent? How far would the King have wanted us to go to protect Aline? *Not this far*, I told myself. He would never have done this. Very carefully I said, "There was a child in the village. She was close to Aline's age. Was she—?"

"I had nothing to do with her. That idiot Braneth knew Celeste hated to be left alone. He should have made sure someone in their mountain hideaway kept an eye on her. The fool reaps the wages of betrayal now, may some forgiving saint guard him."

The memory of the man's grief as he held his child's destroyed body filled me with equal portions of sorrow and confusion. "You prepared for this attack," I said. "You must have. But how could you have planned for *this*? How could you have known they were coming for her?"

"I didn't," the Tailor said as she walked over to the chair Aline had previously occupied and sat down. "But I knew something *like* this would happen soon." She looked over at the small counter and pointed. "Aline, dear, get me a cup of whatever's in that jug over there, would you?"

Aline nodded and filled an old battered metal cup with something that looked like it might have once been beer.

"Trin's weak," the Tailor said, and took a swig from the cup. "For all the vicious brilliance she inherited from Patriana, she's still an eighteen-year-old girl, and more, one who everyone thought was just Valiana's handmaiden, up until a few weeks ago."

"She has an army four times the size of the Duke of Pulnam's," Kest pointed out.

"Aye, she has an army: an army of men twice her age who have no reason to be loyal other than tradition and parentage. When Patriana ruled Hervor she did so with skill and cunning. Her army had won every battle they fought in the last twenty years and the duchy prospered accordingly. But Patriana's dead now and we should all thank the Gods for that."

"And now they have Trin," I said, following the Tailor's line of reasoning. "Young. Untested . . ."

"No," the Tailor said, her voice on the edge of glee, "tested indeed! Nearly a month she's been trying to force the Duke of Pulnam to bow before her, and what has she to show for it? Nothing but the dead bodies of her soldiers!"

If Trin's armies of Hervor ever met the wretched and under-trained forces of Erris, Duke of Pulnam, on the battlefield, I doubted Pulnam would last a day. But the Tailor's Greatcoats had been launching buzzing attacks on her forces that had kept them busy trying to swat us: an army that had not known defeat in two decades was now being delayed from destroying its enemy by a mere hundred Greatcoats.

"She had to attack us," I agreed. "But if the villagers had betrayed us to her, then why not send her whole army?"

"They're still too far away," Kest said, looking as if he were counting odds in his head. "Trying to move that many men so quickly would make them vulnerable to attack from Pulnam's forces."

I imagined Trin, parading her beauty and arrogance before the military generals of Hervor. She could be a masterful actor when she wanted, as capable of simulating innocent and seductive need as she was of committing casual and merciless violence. She'd fooled all of us, playing the shy young girl even as she murdered Lord Tremondi and manipulated everyone around her. *Trin loves games*, I thought. *There must be a way to use that when the time is right.*

"She needs to show her Knights that she's as clever as her mother was," the Tailor said. "She needs them to believe she can lead them to ever-more-brilliant victories. It can't just be sending ten thousand men to crush one hundred. To make an impression, she needed to do us great harm using just a few of her own men: a victory won with little cost to her. Murdering you, in some ingenious and theatrical manner, Falcio, was one of the more likely scenarios."

"Did you have some plan for protecting me?"

She jabbed a finger at Kest. "I figured he'd deal with that."

"You realize I'm here too, don't you?" Brasti said.

The Tailor ignored him. "But the biggest prize would be to take Aline. Imagine Trin, dragging King Paelis's heir through the muck and mud as her generals watched, telling the story of her cunning victory to the cheers of her soldiers before she turned the girl over to them."

Gods, the things they would have done to her before finally slitting her throat. *They'll do those same things to whomever the Tailor has given them*, I realized with a start. "The girl—the one you have masquerading as Aline—"

"The one I sent knows how to protect herself," the Tailor said, cutting me off. "I'll tell you no more than that. She'll leave us a trail and we'll send out the Greatcoats in an hour."

"Why not right now?"

"In between here and Trin's army there will be a smaller force— one sent ahead to support the attack. She'll have taken over one of the smaller villages or perhaps set up an encampment. I want to know where it is. I *want* those men." The Tailor smiled. It wasn't a nice smile. "The little bitch thought she'd play her tricks on *me*? Let her stand before her military commanders and explain how she not only failed to take Aline, but lost a hundred men in the process. See if that doesn't give a few generals some ideas about the ducal succession of Hervor."

"And if they don't wait to reach their camp before they figure out that they don't have Aline? If they decide to . . . use her then and there?"

The Tailor shrugged. "That's the risk we all take. Besides, none of Trin's Knights have ever seen Aline. They'll likely take good enough care of her until they get back to their camp." The old woman rose from the chair and motioned for Aline to take her place. "Now, she's going to stay in here and stay quiet. The rest of us are going to go back out there and keep silent about all of this."

I understood the need to maintain the ruse in front of the villagers, but it seemed cruel to hide the fact that Aline was safe from the other Greatcoats. I'd almost lost my mind when I thought she'd been taken—Gods—!

"We've got to find Valiana! She doesn't know your plan—she still thinks Aline's been captured!"

"Fine. You can tell her," the Tailor said, "but do it quietly. No screams of joy or—"

"You don't understand! She thinks it's her sacred duty to protect Aline. Since she hasn't already broken down the door to find out how we're planning to rescue her, it means she's already gone!"

I ran out of the cottage and looked around, but all I could see were the Tailor's Greatcoats. When I got to where the horses were tethered I saw one gray mare missing: Valiana's.

I felt a hand on my shoulder and turned to see the Tailor.

"Falcio, you can't go after her. You'll endanger our plans. Valiana has made her own choice—"

"She thinks they've got Aline, damn you! She'll be caught—what if Trin is waiting there at the camp?" *Saints, let it not be so.* Trin's hatred of Valiana knew no limits. The things she would do to her would make the tortures I'd experienced at her mother's hands pale in comparison.

"You can't go," the Tailor insisted. "Even if you did, she's too far ahead of you. You'll never catch up. No, we stick to the plan."

"The hells for your plans!" I said, pushing her away. There was only one thing I could do.

I ran to the far side of the barns where a single horse was kept tethered, apart from all the others: a huge, scarred creature made of rage and hate. She was one of the legendary fey horses—or at least she had been, except Patriana, Duchess of Hervor had spent years torturing her, trying to turn her into a tool of war, so now she was a massive, angry beast with sharpened teeth and a fury inside her that matched my own. We called her Monster.

I untied her and she made the strange mixture of neigh and growl that signaled she had no intention of being ridden today.

I braced myself and got onto her back anyway. "Valiana needs our help," I shouted into the horse's ear. "She is of our herd. Dan'he vath fallatu. *She is of your herd.* She will be taken by Trin, the foal of the she who tortured your young. Trin will strip the skin from Valiana's flesh unless you and I go and fight for her."

An explosion of muscle and rage nearly shook me from Monster's back, but I clung on for dear life as her hooves began tearing up chunks of dirt, sending dust and sand in the air as she raced across the burnt grass plains outside of the village and toward the mountains. The Greathorse had murder in her heart.

So did I.

5

THE CAPTIVE

The Knights had made a poor job of covering their tracks. Wherever there was a fork in the wide dusty trails that passed for roads in this part of Pulnam, they'd gone a few dozen yards in the wrong direction before circling back. I wasn't fooled, and from Valiana's tracks I could see that she hadn't been deceived either, which meant she was going to reach them before I caught up with her.

We'd gone about ten miles from the village when I counted five horses off in the distance. I was fairly certain one was Valiana's gray mare, which meant the body I saw in a heap on the ground must be Valiana herself. One of the Knights was holding her down with his foot while his fellows were fending off the sweeping attacks of a young girl wearing a yellow dress made brown by dust. The girl was swinging a blade nearly as tall as she was, which she must have taken from one of the Knights. She wielded it with impressive skill despite its weight, but there were four Knights and I doubted she could keep them off her for long and I was still too far away.

"K'hey!" I called to Monster, drawing one of my rapiers. *Fly*.

The great beast gave a growl that broke through the distance between us and our quarry and I saw one of the Knights turn to us as we bridged the gap. He wasn't wearing his helmet and by this time I was close enough to enjoy the wide-eyed look of fear in his eyes as he caught sight of the creature charging for him. He should have kept his attention on the girl. She swung her stolen warsword and, with a single stroke, the Knight's head flew from his body.

I leapt off Monster's back and engaged with the man who was holding Valiana down, making a thrust for his face that forced him to step back. Valiana didn't rise, and a quick glance told me that she was unconscious. The Knight evaded my next strike, only to be struck down by Monster's hooves. I had to jump out of the way as the beast began crushing the Knight beneath her.

One of the remaining Knights was gaining the advantage on the girl in the yellow dress. Strong as she was, I could tell she was beginning to tire from wielding the heavy blade. As he prepared for a downward strike, I grabbed his sword arm from behind and pulled it back as hard as I could, hoping to make him lose his balance. Knights in armor don't do well on their backs. When he felt the resistance from my hand he struck back with his elbow. I turned my head—just in time—but he struck my collarbone with a force that made me thankful for the bone plates inside my coat.

I struck at his face with the pommel of my rapier—he was wearing a full-face helmet but I managed to ring his bell hard enough for him to stumble. Unfortunately, the girl had moved into position behind him and as he fell she went down beneath him.

"Don't worry about me, you idiot," she shouted as she wriggled a hand holding a dagger out from beneath the Knight's bulk while he struggled to flip himself around. "The other one's getting away! If he escapes with her then the whole plan fails!"

In my peripheral vision a blur passed by me: the remaining Knight had grabbed Valiana and was making for the mountains off in the distance on a black horse.

I ran to Monster. I'd barely leapt onto her back she began racing toward the Knight on his black charger. The other horse was fast, but Monster was all speed and fury and we overtook them in a flurry of hoofbeats. Monster barreled into the side of the other horse, throwing the Knight and Valiana to the ground and reminding me once again that there is always a price to pay for using a creature as dangerous as a maddened Greathorse.

The Knight recovered enough to get to his knees and reached for a mace attached to his waist, but by then the point of my rapier was at his throat, carefully placed above the protection of his gorget and just under his chin. "Yield," I said.

The Knight moved his hand away from his mace. "I yield," he said.

Keeping my point on him I turned to glance first at Valiana, who looked stunned but was now conscious, then back to see the girl walking toward us, dagger in hand. Several yards back her opponent was on the ground with the others, presumably already dead.

"You have to kill him," the girl said. "No one can know what happened here."

"He yielded. He's our prisoner."

She kept walking toward us. I could see now that she calling her a girl was inaccurate. She was young, to be sure—perhaps twenty; no more than twenty-five, certainly—and she was short for a woman, only a little over five feet, no taller than Aline. Her face was youthful enough to make it plausible for her to pass as a teenage girl. But one good look in her eyes removed any doubt of her being a child.

"I said kill him—"

"And I said he's my prisoner. Now tell me your name and—"

The girl walked right by me, so casually that I was surprised when she knocked the blade of my rapier aside and, without so much as a glance at me, drove her dagger into the Knight's throat. She pushed slowly but surely, forcing his body backward until, with a sudden twist, she yanked the blade free. Blood fountained from his neck as he died.

I was horrified by the indifference with which she'd killed a man who'd already surrendered, but I wasn't looking for a confrontation. Not yet. "Who are you?" I asked again. She didn't offer a response and I didn't wait for one. Valiana was sitting up now, but she still looked dazed. I knelt down to examine her for wounds. "Valiana, it's me, Falcio. Are you hurt?"

"My name is Dariana," the woman said from behind me. "And the girl is not half so hurt as you'll be if you ever get in my way again."

Valiana had a bruise on her cheek and looked as if she'd taken a hit to the head but I could see no blood. "You're not half the size you'd need to be to make good on that threat," I said.

I felt the point of a blade at the back of my neck. This Dariana was smart. If she'd reached around to put the blade at my throat I could have grabbed her arm and thrown her over my shoulder. This way she was in control.

"Haven't you heard?" she said. "It's not how tall a man is that matters, it's how long a blade he wields."

"You're working for the Tailor so I assume you're one of her new Greatcoats. Perhaps you should be acting like one."

"A Greatcoat?" I heard the woman spit. "Why would I want to be a fucking Greatcoat?"

If Kest had been there he could have suggested half a dozen ways of deflecting the blade, followed by their respective odds of success, followed by a reminder that I should not have turned my back on someone I had just met in the first place. But I ignored his sage, if imaginary, council and instead reached down to lift Valiana up off the ground. If this woman wanted to kill me, she could. I was tired and sore and angry and sick of being tired and sore and angry. "I'm taking Valiana back to the village," I said. "You can help or not."

The sharp pressure on the back of my neck disappeared. "I'll get the other horses," she said. "Try not to screw anything else up while I'm gone."

6

THE BETRAYAL

Hours later I was back in my cottage, collecting my belongings and preparing for our departure in the morning. The Tailor believed that if we continued to harass Trin's troops we could box her in long enough for Duke Erris to rally his own forces; all we had to do was deny Trin victory long enough for her generals to lose faith in her. From there we might even be able to convince them that a naïve thirteen-year-old girl on the throne was preferable to a psychotic eighteen-year-old murderer with exotic tastes in torture.

I wondered what would become of this small village once we abandoned it. The cries of those few men still alive but beyond saving had all but faded now. Their families had come down from the mountain hideaways to witness the destruction that had fallen upon a place that, until the Greatcoats had come along, had survived border raids and territorial disputes for hundreds of years. The women and children had been so full of shock and fury that I'd feared they might attack us then and there. But in the end, we had the numbers and the weapons, and so they had simply taken their dead and dying and made their way back into the mountains, cursing us all the while.

The memory of their faces had shaken my faith in my King, maybe for the first time in my life. All those years he'd spent planning and plotting, developing strategies and tactics to bring peace and justice to this broken, bitter country, and in the end, what had he left us with? None of us, even those who had been closest to him, knew his plan. Instead, in the days just before losing his throne and his head to the Dukes, Paelis had given each of us a secret and individual command and scattered us to the winds—a hundred and forty-four men and women, dispatched on a hundred and forty-four different journeys—never to know what became of the others.

For five years I had searched for what Paelis had called the "King's Charoites," despite having no idea where they might be, nor, in fact, what a charoite was other than a kind of rare precious stone. Finally, I had found Aline: the King's secret daughter. His blood. His heir. The rarest jewel of them all.

And now what was I supposed to do now?

Put Aline on the throne?

Was that the entirety of your plan, you gangly-limbed, half-starved excuse for a King? We had shared a dream, he and I. At first it was just the two of us, but we'd tricked others into believing it too. Every one of the original Greatcoats could recite the King's Laws by heart; we could all sing them well enough that even a drunken farmer could remember our verdicts word for word a year later. How many of them still believed in all that talk of law and justice and an easing of sorrow? How much did Brasti and Kest and the other original Greatcoats, wherever they were, still believe?

How much did I?

I removed my coat and set it aside on the bench next to my swords. I would sleep reluctantly tonight, as frightened of my own guilty dreams as I was of finding out what Patriana's poison had in store for me when I next awoke.

A soft, tentative knock at my door interrupted my thoughts. It was strange that I immediately knew it was Aline. Maybe it was because of those days we had spent together on the run in Rijou, always quiet, always fearful that someone would hear us and raise the alarm. I opened the door and she came in, still wearing the faded green dress.

"What are you doing here?" I asked, looking outside to see if anyone was watching. "If the villagers—"

"The villagers have all gone away," she said. "Besides, it's done now. Trin will know her men failed."

"You should be asleep," I said.

"I should be dead."

I knelt down and looked her in the eyes. She was more haggard than scared. "What's happened?"

"Nothing."

"Then why—?"

"Nothing, except that someone powerful sent men to kill me. Again. Like they always do. Like they always *will.*"

I stood up and went to pour us each a cup of water from the jug in the small kitchen. "They failed," I said, handing her the cup.

She drank, and I took that as a sign things might not be so bad and did the same.

"Thank you," she said, handing me back the cup.

"Do you want some more?"

She shook her head.

"Did you want to sit and talk?"

Aline looked toward the still open door. "Could we go for a walk outside? I'd like to see the stars."

The Tailor wouldn't like that and nor would her Greatcoats. I was tired and not looking for another fight. But Aline was the heir, not our prisoner, and by now the Tailor's men would have set up a proper perimeter.

Also, as the King used to remind me on an almost daily basis, I'm belligerent.

"Sure," I said. "Just let me grab something." I retrieved my coat and rapiers and found a thick woolen blanket that I wrapped around Aline's shoulders.

We walked down the main path, the flickering candlelight escaping through the cracks in the shutters lighting our way. Occasionally we could hear the sounds of other Greatcoats talking inside.

"Where shall we go?" I asked.

"Can we go up the little hill outside the village?"

That was an awkward request. I really didn't want to take her outside the protection of our camp, but we were unlikely to be attacked again—Trin had made her attempt, and her men had paid the price for it. "All right," I said, "but just for a little while."

Aline took my hand and we made our way down the path, passing a group of six of the Tailor's Greatcoats. They didn't bother to greet us, but I saw they noted our presence. As long as we didn't go far they'd likely not complain. I ignored the soft footsteps not far behind us. They had been there since we'd left the cottage.

We crossed the wide trail that passed through the strange rock formation called the Arch. Beyond it was the Eastern Desert and the curved north–south trade route called the Bow that led to Rijou.

Rijou.

The memories of that place still make me shudder.

"Are you cold?" Aline asked.

"No, just thinking."

"That happens to me too when I think," she said.

"Oh? What do you think about that makes you shiver?"

She looked up. "I like the stars," she said, ignoring my question. "You could see some in Rijou, but never as many as here. It's as if they're right near us. Come on. I want to get closer to them."

We made our way up the hill along a narrow path. At the top the terrain flattened out and we sat at the edge. Small animals scurried about in the dark, not quite obscuring the other sound that trailed us.

"She follows me everywhere I go," Aline said.

I was surprised at first that Aline could hear the footsteps, but then, she was a smart girl and she'd gotten used to paying attention to things around her. "She's wounded," I said. "She should be resting."

"You could tell her, but I don't think she'd listen. She's lost, Falcio."

I looked at Aline's face to find some clue as to her meaning but she was still just looking up at the stars. "What do you mean?"

"They've taken everything away from her," she said. "She spent her whole life being a princess and now she's just a girl. I spent my whole life thinking I was just a girl and now they tell me I have to be a queen. It doesn't seem fair."

"To whom?" I asked.

She turned to me and put a hand on my arm. "I don't want Valiana to die for nothing, Falcio. Will you protect her?"

"What do you mean, 'for nothing'? Saving your life isn't 'nothing.'"

She leaned back on the ground and looked up again. "Can you see this many stars in the Southern Islands?"

"I . . . I don't know," I said. "I suppose so. I think it's mostly a function of how many clouds there are and how much light down here there is—that makes it harder for us to see the stars."

The answer seemed to satisfy her. "So if we weren't in a big city and it wasn't cloudy we should see a lot of stars from an island too, right?"

"Aline, what's this about?"

"Do you think about Ethalia, Falcio?"

That took me by surprise. Of course I still thought of Ethalia—every day. It hadn't been so long ago that she had healed my wounds and saved the last little part of my soul.

"I do think about her, yes," I said carefully.

"That morning when you were in her room—when she sent me downstairs," she started, then admitted, "I didn't go all the way. I stayed near the door and I heard what she said to you."

For an instant I was back in that small room, the smell of clean sheets and simple food, of morning flowers and, above all, of her. *Don't you think it at all possible that you are meant to be happy, that I am meant to be happy, and that our happiness can be found together?*

I had known Ethalia one night and in that short time had fallen in love for only the second time in my life. Minutes after she had said those words I had left her there, alone. Weeping.

"Why are you telling me this, Aline?"

"Do you think she'd still take us to that island that she mentioned? She said I could come too, right?"

"I . . . I'm sure one day, when you're tired of being Queen, I mean you could . . ." I knew I sounded like an idiot so I didn't bother to finish.

"No," Aline said, "I mean, now. If we went back there now—not all the way to Rijou, I know we'd need to get a message to her—but if we could, do you think she'd still take us to that island?"

"Aline," I said, "you're the daughter of King Paelis. You're going to be Queen of all Tristia."

She shook her head. She wasn't crying, though. It was as if she'd played this conversation over in her head and was ready for my objections. "I don't have to be Queen, though. No one can force me to be Queen."

"I don't always want to be a Greatcoat but I do it anyway. Where would you be if I'd stopped?"

"Dead," she said plainly. "I'd be dead. Just like when Shiballe's men tried to kill me, or when the bully-boys found us. Or when Laetha and Radger betrayed me, or when the Dashini assassins came. Or today."

I felt a fool. I kept forgetting how young she was, still a child, and already she'd faced as much death as any soldier. "I've kept you safe, though, haven't I?"

"Yes, you did. You killed Shiballe's men and the bully-boys and those fake Greatcoats and the Dashini. And today you killed more men for me. How many people will you kill for me, Falcio?"

I took her hand. "I'll kill as many as it takes, Aline. I'll kill them until they stop coming for you."

She pulled her hand away and jumped to her feet. "You don't understand *anything*! I don't *want* you to kill people for me! I don't want Valiana to die to protect me. I didn't want the villagers to betray us and then be killed because of it! I'm only thirteen, Falcio, and already I've caused the death of more people than I can count. I don't want it!"

I rose to my feet. "We don't always get—"

"No! It's not the same. I don't want to be a Queen. And you're not a Greatcoat because you have to be, Falcio—you're a Greatcoat because you don't know how to be anything else." She turned and ran off.

She was right, of course. It *wasn't* fair. She deserved better; she deserved to be a child, to laugh and cry and get angry and run off into the darkness and pout. But the world hadn't been fair to her up to now and it showed absolutely no signs of relenting, and that meant I couldn't let her go off by herself to pout in the darkness.

So I ran and caught her before she could reach the path down the hill.

"Leave me alone!" she screamed.

"Stop," I said, taking her arm. "Stop and tell me what it is you want. Do you want me to take you away from here? To take you south, to see if Ethalia would still have us?" Aline's arm was shaking—no, it wasn't her. It was *me*. It was the thought of what might be if she commanded me to take her from this place. *Oh Gods, say yes, and in that yes shake me of the bonds that bind me to your father. You gave me no instructions, my King. You just said to find her, and I did that. If she asks me to take her away I will and to the hells with whatever plans you made but never bothered to tell me.*

But she didn't say yes. It was as if she could tell I would have taken her south that very instant if she asked. Instead, she said, "I want to stop being afraid," not knowing that it was the bravest thing she could have said just then.

"That's not the same thing. I'm not sure that's even possible."

She started crying. "Why do I have to be Queen?"

"You don't," I said. "The country can carry on as it has. The Dukes can keep doing what they've been doing. Trin can take the throne."

"Mattea—The Tailor—she said there were others." Her voice was full of frustration. "Why didn't you find one of them?"

"I don't know. I didn't know they existed, or that you did. But I don't think any of them are left, Aline. Patriana hunted them all down." I thought about that a moment. Patriana had held Aline in her clutches. She had beaten her and tortured her—and yet she hadn't killed her, preferring instead to use her to torment me. And now I thought about it, she'd kept asking, over and over, "Where are the others?" At the time I'd assumed she was talking about the other Greatcoats but in hindsight it was more likely she had been seeking the other heirs, the "Charoites," as the King had enigmatically called them. What if there *were* other heirs still alive?

"Aline, if there was another, would you want them to take your place?"

"I . . ." Tears were dripping slowly down her cheeks and I wanted to hold her, but I knew she didn't want to be touched. So we stood there until she finally looked up at me. "They would have to deal with the same things I do, wouldn't they?"

I nodded. I didn't speak, for I could see that her heart had made its decision and now her mind was catching up to it.

"And . . . and it would be worse for them, wouldn't it? Because they won't have faced the things I have. It'll all come down on them at once."

"I think that's probably true."

She stood there, silent, looking back up at the stars for a very long time. "Then it has to be me, doesn't it? If I don't do this then it will fall on somebody else and it might be even harder for them. They would have to be braver than me."

My voice caught in my throat as I said, "I don't think there is anyone braver than you, sweetheart."

She wrapped her arms around herself. "We don't always get to be who we want to be, do we?"

It took me a minute before I could speak. I hadn't fully understood until that moment how much I'd wanted her to refuse her birthright; to tell me she wanted me to take her away. I'd not admitted, even to myself, how much I longed to go to Ethalia and live out a normal life without the burden of trying to carry on a dead King's fading dream. I remembered back to the day when I had first met King Paelis, and the wild, idealistic insanity that had followed. I thought about Kest and Brasti and all the others: every one of them had their own tale, every one had made the same choice. "I think . . . I think we get to be what the world needs us to be."

Aline sniffed once more, as if trying to take back in the tears she had shed. "Then that has to be enough. I'll be the Queen, then, Falcio, if that will make things better. If that is what the world wants of me."

We stood like that for a little while before she took my hand and we began the walk down the path and back toward the village.

I should have made a vow then, loudly, to the night and to whatever awaited us in the morning. I should have promised to always be there for Aline, to always protect her. I should have made an oath to the Gods and Saints. But I didn't. Aline was a smart and serious girl, and she didn't like it when people made vows they couldn't keep.

I awoke the next day as I had for the previous several days, unable to move or speak. The first time it had lasted only a few terrifying seconds. Now, as I tried to count the minutes in my head, the paralysis felt expected, almost natural.

Someone was in the room with me. The sound of my visitor's breathing was soft and slow, punctuated every few minutes by a moan of pain or fear that wasn't quite breaking through their sleep. *Valiana*, I thought. Only hours from nearly losing her own life and yet here she was, sitting watch over me. I imagined the Tailor had forced her to stay away from Aline's cottage and she'd decided to guard me instead. How much she'd changed from the haughty noblewoman I'd met just a few months ago, served by everyone around her, raised to rule over the country. What must it be like to imagine yourself a princess only to discover you're the child of an unknown peasant woman with no title, no family, no name? I wished I could open my eyes and see her. I wished I could see anything.

I met a blind man years ago, selling fruit along the trade road, being led around by a very old woman whom I assumed was his wife. I'd asked him what it was like to be without sight. *Close your eyes*, he'd said. *Think of a beautiful woman. That's what I see every minute of every day.* His wife had looked over at him fondly. He'd told me the world could be the most lovely place you could imagine, so long as your imagination was fueled by love. I wanted to tell him that when I closed my eyes I too saw my wife, and the sight filled me with pain and sorrow and a rage I could never control. But I feared that if I did tell him I might change the vista he beheld, and so the gap-toothed grin on his old face held me back.

Now, all these years later, I couldn't remember my wife's face. Not really. I could describe her to you—her hair, her skin, the crooked smile when she mocked some silly thing I had said . . . That smile. It promised laughter and kisses and more. I could tell you every detail because I've made myself remember them, but only as words. We had been poor, so there were no paintings or sketches of her. The sight of her was lost to me forever and there was only one way to get it back.

A rough hand grabbed my jaw and the heat of someone's breath brought an uncomfortable warmth to my face. I heard Valiana move in her chair. "Stop!"

I felt the first tingles in my fingertips. I couldn't be sure how long I'd been paralyzed this time, but it felt longer than the day before. My eyes began fluttering open. If ever there was a face I *didn't* long to see at that precise moment, it was the Tailor's.

"Wakey-wakey, First Cantor," she said, her voice a mixture of sarcasm and urgency. "Time to get up and greet the day."

Valiana entered my view as she tried and failed to push the Tailor away. "It's still hours away from when you said we were leaving."

"That was before," the Tailor said.

"Before what?" I asked, the thick feeling in my tongue slurring my words.

The Tailor looked at me and only then did I realize how much anger was in her eyes. "Before the Duke of Pulnam betrayed us."

Outside the cottage the other Greatcoats were making preparations to leave the village. Horses were dragging litters holding the dead bodies of fallen Knights and some of the homes damaged in the fight were being hastily repaired.

"No sense leaving the villagers with broken homes and a bunch of dead Knights to bury," the Tailor said, striding toward the far end of the village just a little too quickly for me to keep up in my current state. "We'll take them out and leave them in a nice pile for Trin and that bastard Erris, Duke of Pulnam, to find."

"I don't understand," I said. "Why did he betray us? I thought you said our raids were working."

She sneered. "The raids worked too well. Trin offered him an armistice. She won't take the duchy away from him, and in exchange he'll give her troops access through southern Pulnam so they can bypass the Duchy of Domaris's defenses. He'll also pay for the cost of her troops' passage."

"He'll pay? For what?"

"Protection," the Tailor said. "Seems there are Greatcoats about."

As we reached the far side of the village I saw Kest and Brasti readying their horses. "Finally," Brasti said. "Falcio, would you tell her to stop ordering us about without telling us why?"

"What is this?" I asked the Tailor.

"You're going south."

"To where?"

"Aramor. Where it all began."

"Saints," Brasti said, rolling his eyes. "You do recall that we're wanted for murder in Aramor, don't you?"

"Trin killed Lord Tremondi," Kest said. "Surely Duke Isault must know that by now."

"It doesn't matter," the Tailor said.

"Why?" Brasti asked. "Because the three of us are expendable?"

"Because we have no damned choice, you fool. Duke Isault's got money and soldiers. We need both and we need them now." The Tailor grabbed a stick from the ground and began drawing lines in the dirt. "Trin's going to go south from here," she said, "to the Duchy of Domaris and its endless forests. Hadiermo, the vaunted Iron Duke of Domaris, is an idiot but he'll fight her. He knows that Duke Perault has become Trin's lover, and that he wants to expand his own duchy's borders. If Domaris falls, Perault will take one half and Trin will take the other and Duke Hadiermo will be left standing out in the cold in his underclothes."

"How long can he hold out against the combined forces of Trin and Perault?" I asked.

"A few weeks. Maybe a month."

Kest, Brasti, and I looked at each other as the magnitude of events came crashing down on us: Hervor, Orison, Pulnam, and finally Domaris—all four of the northern duchies. Trin would hold them all with an army that would sweep the south unless the southern duchies rose united against her, which they never would, not without a King or Queen to lead them.

"Ah," the Tailor said. "It seems light does eventually reach even the dimmest places."

"Why would the Duke of Aramor side with Aline?" Kest asked.

"Aramor has always had a special relationship with the Kings of Tristia," the Tailor replied. "Isault didn't love my son, but he didn't hate him the way the others did. And he's an opportunist. He'll know he can get a better deal from us than from Trin."

I was still dubious. Isault's "special relationship" hadn't done King Paelis much good when he and the other Dukes came for his head. "Let's say we can turn Isault," I began.

"You *will* turn him," the Tailor said. "Make no mistake: if he sides with Trin this is all over and the world itself won't be big enough to hide any of us. You're going to go down there and stroke his ego and promise him whatever you must to get his support."

"Fine. So I turn him. Then what?"

She tapped each of the duchies of the southwest on her map in the dirt. "From Aramor you go to secure the support of the Dukes of Luth and then Pertine. The Duchy of Baern will fall into line behind them."

"Trin will have the north and Aline will have the south," I said.

The Tailor gave me a grim smile as she poked her stick dead center in the heart of the country. "And the final battle will be fought in Rijou, where your old friend Duke Jillard will decide the fate of the world. Still proud of yourself for not killing him when you had the chance?"

"He swore to support Aline's claim," I said. "Besides, there are laws, even in times of war."

"Aye. But you don't seem to have learned the first one: it's the victor who makes the laws." She swept the marks in the dirt away with her foot. "I'll take the Greatcoats to Domaris and we'll do our best to slow Trin down. If she thought our raids were a pain before, she'll be amazed at how much damage we can do once her soldiers have to travel through a hundred and fifty miles of forest."

"What about Aline?" I asked. "You can't mean to keep taking her into battlefields like this."

"You have a better solution?" the Tailor asked.

"We'll take her with us. We get her the hells away from Pulnam and Domaris, take her south where we can find somewhere safe for her until all this is over."

The Tailor smiled. "Perfect. I like your thinking, Falcio."

I searched the old woman's face for signs of mockery. I couldn't believe she'd go along with a plan I'd had all of ten seconds to devise. "You're serious? You'll let me take her?"

She shook her head. "Of course not, you fool. But I'm counting on the fact that you aren't the only one who thinks a woman's place is hiding behind men."

I started to protest, but she held up a hand. "Don't start telling me about all the female Greatcoats you recruited. If Aline were a man you'd say she needed to show the world she was brave enough to lead it."

On the long list I kept in my head of things I hated about the Tailor, second from the top was the arrogant way she presumed to see every one of my flaws. Top on the list was that she was probably right. "If my instincts are so flawed, then why—?"

"Because Trin thinks like a man too. She'll believe we'll send Aline south and she'll be convinced you're the one who will take her. You really are quite predictable, Falcio."

Brasti snorted. "It won't take her spies long to realize we don't have Aline with us. What are we supposed to do, parade Kest around in a sundress?"

"You're not going by yourselves," the Tailor said as Dariana stepped out from behind one of the hitching posts. She was wearing a greatcoat. "Ah, Dari, there you are."

"I've warned you before about calling me that."

"Well, threaten me a few more times and perhaps I'll remember to give a damn one of these days." The Tailor turned to me. "She'll be going with you."

"Looks a bit small for fighting," Brasti said, looking her up and down. "Or much of anything else, really."

Dariana wasted only the briefest of glances on Brasti before she gave him a dismissive little snort and then turned to stare at Kest somewhat more appraisingly. "So you're the Saint of Swords, eh?" She let her gaze drift from his face to his hands to his feet and back again. "I'm finding it hard to be impressed."

"Four moves," Kest said.

"What?"

"You're wondering if you could take me. You'd last four moves."

"Well then," she said, smiling innocently and reaching a hand out to touch his chest. "Suppose I take you in your sleep?"

"I took that for granted when I said four. Did you want to know how long you'd last if you didn't take me by surprise?"

"Oh, great Gods save me from these mad duelists," the Tailor moaned. "Could the two of you compare the length of your swords someplace else? It's time for you to go."

"So that's it?" I asked. "At least let me say goodbye to Aline and Valiana."

"Aline is already in hiding with my men," the Tailor said. "You said your goodbyes last night, even if you weren't aware of it at the time. As for Valiana, you can talk to her all you like on the way south. Here she comes now."

Two of the Tailor's new Greatcoats were hauling Valiana between them, lifting her by the arms as she struggled to break free.

"Stop!" the Tailor shouted, and at first I'd assumed she was ordering her men to stand down, but then I realized my rapier was in my hand. "Valiana's unharmed," the Tailor said to me.

"Which is more than I can say for the rest of us," one of her Greatcoats growled as they dropped her in front of us. "Little twit gave me a cut across the cheek before we got the sword out of her hand."

The Tailor walked up to him and without warning slapped him hard across the face. His eyes darkened. "What's that for?" he asked. "You ordered us to bring her—"

"All that secret training, all your deadly arts, and a fool who barely knows how to draw her own sword without cutting herself nearly takes your eye?"

"He'll lose more than that if he touches me again," Valiana said, rising to her feet and snatching the rapier from my hand.

The other Greatcoat reached for his sword, but Dariana put a hand on Valiana's arm. "There now, pretty bird. How about we teach you how to handle that little pig-sticker of yours and then we can go and kill a few men—and do it properly, eh?"

The Tailor turned from her men and back to us. "Have we done with the games? Time is wasting and I have more important things to deal with than your petulance."

"I've sworn my life to protect Aline," Valiana said. "I won't leave her."

"Yes, and if we're all lucky, that's just what Trin will think."

"But—"

"You want so badly to be a hero like these fools?" the Tailor asked, pointing at Kest, Brasti, and me. "You want to die thinking you saved Aline; that your life was worth more in the end than it was in the beginning? Fine. Do what I ask and go with them. Go and take the blade in your gut and know that in some small way you've helped protect her. Let's hope Trin's hatred of you will prompt her to waste resources chasing you. You're useless to Aline here, except perhaps to get in the way of those with the strength and skill to keep her safe."

The anger drained from Valiana's face, along with her pride. She'd been clinging so desperately to the oath that she'd made to Aline because she needed to believe she stood for something, for *anything*, so that her life could have some meaning. She was just like I had been, years ago, when I first met the King. He'd believed in me, and he'd made me believe in myself. King Paelis was an idealist and a romantic and a dreamer. But the Tailor was none of those things.

"I'll do what you ask," Valiana said finally. She turned and walked away from us toward the horses.

The callousness of the Tailor's words, the way she discarded all of Valiana's pain and sorrow—all of the pain each of us had experienced in our lives—burned in me. I needed her to know how much I hated this, all of it: her cold, calculating strategies, the way she planned and plotted. She wasn't much different from the Dukes we all despised.

The others were looking at me, waiting to see how I would react. I didn't want to be an angry, petulant child. I wanted to be noble and brave and all the things I'd tried to be since the day the King had shaken me out of my madness. But I couldn't. I simply didn't have it in me. "You're a fucking bitch," I said.

The Tailor smiled. "Aye, I am. I'm exactly what the world needs me to be—what my granddaughter needs me to be. Now go and be what she needs *you* to be. Get me the support of the southern Dukes so we can win this damned war before the girl we've both sworn to protect gets killed."

7

THE MASK

The ancient trade route known as the Bow was our means out of Pulnam. When trade was good, as it had been during King Paelis's reign, hundreds of horse carts and caravans would travel its three-hundred-mile length each year. Roadside inns and taverns had made good business off the success and heady optimism of traveling merchants and those seeking their fortunes in the eastern duchies. Now, five years after the King's death, the cobblestones laid down centuries before were gradually becoming covered in sand and dirt. Hardy desert brush the color of burnt leaves worked its way slowly from the sides of the road, worming in between the stones. Brigands outnumbered honest travelers now, and even they had trouble making ends meet.

We rode hard during the first week, reasoning that a fast-moving target is harder to hit than a slow one. This turned out to be true, and I thanked Saint Gan-who-laughs-with-dice for the good fortune that helped us survive those first few harried hours after leaving the village. Just before we'd reached the Bow we were set upon by six of Trin's scouts. They were armed with crossbows and hiding in the brush, leaving us no choice but to run their gauntlet rather than let ourselves be caught in the open grass and sand. We knew they'd have fresh horses ready to pursue us should we somehow evade their bolts, so the moment they'd finished firing their crossbows, we'd turned on them.

Adding a new fighter to a team is a dangerous business. Kest, Brasti, and I had a kind of rhythm, a flow that allowed us to sense each other's movements. We were fortunate that Dariana fit into the mix so quickly and so well: Kest would immediately identify and attack the strongest fighter of the group, and while Brasti sent arrows flying at those trying to outflank us, Dariana snuck along the edge, slitting throats and stabbing bellies before her enemies knew she was even in range. It took only a few moments for the three of them to kill all six scouts. For my part, I spent that battle, and those that came in the days after, trying to keep Valiana from getting killed.

"You stay at the back," I said every time. "You don't try and engage with the enemy, got it? Not until you're trained and ready."

"When will that be?" she said every time.

"Sometime after I've died peacefully in bed from old age."

We were attacked twice more during that first week, and it became clear that the Tailor's ruse had worked: Trin believed Aline was with us, and her scouts did indeed mistake little Dariana for the King's heir. Her favorite tactic at the beginning of each attack was to put on a show of running in terror, screaming as one of Trin's men pursued her, only to turn and smile as she drove the point of her sword into his neck. Brasti took to calling her "Deadly Dari." She in turn took to threatening to eviscerate him anytime he used that nickname within her hearing.

Dariana's sheer joy in battle unnerved me, but it was Valiana's reck-lessness that terrified me. In one encounter, the last of our attackers, having seen Dariana kill two men, had figured out that she couldn't possibly be Aline, so he went after Valiana instead. She could have run or simply backed away and let me deal with him. Instead, she attacked him ferociously, getting in my way with all her thrusting of her long thin blade, always trying for the kill-shot without bother-ing with any of that old-fashioned parrying of the man's attacks. She fought as if she were in a fencing competition, where the sword tips were blunted and the deadliest outcome was a nasty bruise.

Trin's man wasn't especially fast, but he was sure-footed and used a series of feints to catch her off-balance. Valiana stumbled back and her sword point dropped—which at last got her out of the way and gave me the opening I needed. I slashed the man's exposed sword-arm with my left rapier and thrust the right one into his side. As he slid to the ground I withdrew my blade and readied it in case he had any fight left in him, but he fell unconscious and began the steady process of dying as blood welled from the wound.

"I can fight my own battles," Valiana said angrily.

"No, actually, you can't, not until . . ." My eyes were still on the dying soldier, but then I noticed out of the corner of my eye that she had a hand on her chest. "Hells," I said, and sheathed my rapier so that I could see to her.

"It's barely a scratch," she said, pulling away from me before I could examine the wound. That's when I realized she'd left her coat unbuttoned during the fight.

"You forgot to close your damned coat properly," I said. "You practice your sword-work for hours every day and yet you forget to do the one thing that will save your life!"

Kest and Brasti knew not to get in my way but Dariana came over pushed me aside. She examined Valiana's wound, then announced, "It's not so bad. It'll leave a pretty little scar you can show off."

I pulled a small black jar from my coat and held it out to Valiana. "Just put on some damned salve," I said. "Even a shallow wound can become infected."

"You've only got a small amount," Valiana replied angrily. "What happens if one of you gets hurt? Aline needs all of you alive."

"I imagine she'd appreciate it if you stayed alive too," I said.

"It doesn't matter what happens to me."

Part of me knew I should deal with these feelings of worthlessness she carried with her, coax her into talking about it and find a way to change her thinking, but I wasn't a healer. Hells, my only qualification in even discussing diseases of the mind was the fact that I'd spent a good many years being insane myself. So instead I said, "If you won't do it then take off your fucking shirt and I'll put the salve on you myself."

She grabbed the small black jar from my hand and walked a few yards away toward the brush by the side of the road. "If it's all right with you I'd just as soon not parade shirtless in front of you, Kest, and Brasti."

Damn me, I thought. *I should have forbidden her from coming and to the hells with the Tailor's orders.*

"She needs training," Dariana said, "and she needs it now, not in some imaginary future where you get over yourself."

"I'll train her," Kest offered, kneeling to wipe the blood from his own blade on the sparse brush by the side of the road.

Dariana laughed. "You?"

"He *is* the Saint of Swords," Brasti said, not that he or I—or Kest himself, for that matter—knew exactly what that meant yet.

"He's also twice her size and probably three times as strong," Dari argued. "What good will his methods do her?" She walked over to where Valiana was putting her coat back on. "Come on, pretty bird, I'll show you how you kill a man properly. You need to be able to size up your enemy and find their weaknesses. Every once in a while you need to know how to stay out of trouble in the first place."

Valiana looked uncertain at first, as if she wasn't sure if Dari were making fun of her. Valiana had a coat she hadn't earned and a sword she didn't know how to use, and she knew that everyone else could see it too. It didn't help matters much that the most powerful woman in the world longed to see her dead. "Just teach me how to fight," she said, "I'll figure the rest out for myself."

As she led Valiana out a few yards into the desert I said to Kest, "Somehow the prospect of Deadly Dari teaching her to fight doesn't reassure me."

"Do you think she'll hurt her?"

"I don't know. I don't *think* so. Dariana certainly knows how to fight. But she's so damned *eager* in battle. I don't know how to place it. It's like she's—"

"Fucking insane?" Brasti suggested.

"Something like that."

"Well, if it makes you feel any better, Valiana's going to do a lot better studying under Dari than with her last teacher. She looked up to that man like he was a Saint and yet he completely ignored her."

"Who was that, then?" I asked.

Brasti patted me on the shoulder. "You."

The next day, our tenth since we'd left the Tailor and her Great-coats, started without incident. Despite the Gods and Saints having graced me with a lifetime of advanced warning, I allowed myself to hope that we'd evaded the last of Trin's scouts. The further south we went, the more side-routes and horse-tracks from outlying villages appeared, providing more and more opportunities for us to still get to Aramor without using the main trade route.

I'd been looking for a suitable place to leave the Bow to set up camp when I saw a girl in a pale yellow dress crying by the side of the road.

She was kneeling awkwardly on the ground about a hundred yards ahead of us, and her hands were raised, covering her face. Behind her was a small stone building with a circle of stones laid around it, which I took for an old church. I signaled the others to stop.

"Do you see anyone other than the girl?" I asked Brasti.

His eyes narrowed as he peered across the distance. "No one."

"How old would you say she is?"

"I'd make her to be five feet tall. Maybe twelve or thirteen?" He glanced back at Dariana. "Unless she's stunted."

Dariana stayed silent, her eyes focused on the road ahead of us.

"Any signs of a trap?" I asked.

"Nothing I can see," Brasti said. "There's no evidence of hoof-prints or footsteps going into the trees by the side of the road. She could have swept them, I suppose, but then there'd be some sign of the sweeping itself. There's not much holding the walls of that old church together, either. If there were more than a couple of men inside I could see them from here."

Kest looked behind us along the road. "No sounds of anyone coming from behind."

"No signs of danger at all," Brasti said.

I loosened both my rapiers. "So, definitely a trap, then."

"Oh, absolutely," Brasti said, and motioned for me to go forward. "I imagine you'll want to walk right into it."

"I'll come with you," Valiana said.

"No, you stay here. Brasti, give Valiana your quiver." When he'd unslung it and passed it to her I said, "Your job is to hand him arrows as quickly as he fires them. It sounds simple, but you have to keep up. If there's a horde of Trin's men hidden nearby I'll need him to take out as many as possible."

"What about me?" Dariana asked.

"You stay here too."

"And do what?"

"Try to look helpless. You're supposed to be Aline. If it *is* a trap I don't want to take a chance on anyone finding out we don't really have her."

"The girl's seen us," Kest said, looking toward her.

I looked back down the road. The girl's dark brown hair hung loose and unkempt. She was too far away from me to make out her features or expression, but now that she was facing us I could see a kind of thick oval band that went around her face from the top of her head down to her chin.

"What's that thing she's wearing?" I asked.

"I don't know," Brasti said. "Looks almost like the frame from an oval mirror. Not exactly flattering, but maybe she works for the local cleric and this is the latest in ecclesiastical fashion? You can never tell with religious people."

The girl held up her hand and waved to me. When I didn't wave back she turned and ran into the small stone building.

"She might have some kind of crossbow or even a pistol in there," Kest cautioned.

"Or maybe she's an innocent girl who's been attacked and is now scared for her life," I said.

Dariana snorted. "Do you really believe that?"

"No. I'm fairly sure it's a trap."

"Then why go in?"

"So I can find out—"

"Because that's what he does," Brasti interrupted. "He asks himself what the dumbest possible thing to do would be in any given situation and then he does it."

"Let's go," I said to Kest.

He drew his warsword and followed me. I left my rapiers in their sheaths and pulled a throwing knife from my coat. I'm terrible with the bow but I have good luck with throwing knives now and then, and if the girl somehow did have a pistol, I wanted something that could bridge the distance between us before she fired.

As we neared the entrance to the little church Kest put a hand on my shoulder. "There's something wrong."

"What?"

"I don't know," he said. His forehead was slick with sweat.

"Then—"

"I can't go any closer," he said.

His eyes were wide and his jaw was clenched tight, as if he were trying too hard to swallow. In my entire life I've never seen Kest show fear for himself. "What's wrong with you?"

"I don't know. I . . . I can't go in there."

I looked again at the little stone building. There was nothing special about the tiny church—you could find dozens like it along the length of the Bow. When I looked down at the ground where some of the blocks had fallen I saw the wide circular ring of stones around it were still largely intact. "It's just a broken-down old Saint's temple," I said. "You're not getting religious on me, are you?"

"I . . . I seem to be . . ." He tried to take another step toward it and I saw his leg shaking as he did. With a massive effort his foot finally came down, but then Kest sank down to his knees, his head bowed.

"Kest, get up," I said.

"I can't."

"He's telling the truth," a woman's voice called out from inside the church.

I looked into the small building to see the girl in the yellow dress standing in the entrance. Brasti had been right: she was perhaps five feet tall, her ill-fed body that of a girl no more than thirteen years old. Her face though, was a few years older, that of a full-grown young woman. Big dark eyes looked out at me beneath thick lashes. Her nose was straight and delicate and her cheekbones chiseled like a sculpture of the Goddess Love. The skin on her face had a golden tone to it at odds with the pale arms and legs of the girl's body. Full red lips decorated a mouth that was just slightly wide and yet somehow perfect. Her face held the kind of sensuality that troubadours sing about.

Trin.

I had already pulled back my arm to throw the knife into her throat when Kest grabbed my ankle. "No, Falcio, it can't be her. Trin is as tall as Valiana. This is someone else."

"My name is Cantissa," the girl said, her voice shaking and her hands clasped together as if she were pleading with us for mercy. "I live nearby in the village with my parents."

"Drop the pretense," I said. "I've seen better actors doing penny one-acts outside alleyway brothels." The girl was close enough now that I could clearly see the strange oval frame. It was made of dark wood and went around her head. Thick iron screws with short wooden handles for turning them ringed the apparatus, holding it in place. The effect was unsettling and obscene—it was neither mirror nor mask, but whatever it was, it gave the girl Trin's face.

Magic, I thought. *Saints, how I hate magic.*

For just a moment the girl's lip trembled as though I'd hurt her feelings, then the sides of her mouth began to curve up into a wide smile. "Ah, my lovely tatter-cloak, I never could deceive you, could I? I mean, except for the time I killed Lord Tremondi in front of you. Oh, and those many weeks we spent together on the road as I played the part of the handmaiden. Where is Valiana, by the way? Is that her I saw with you over there? I'd love to see her again."

"I'd bring Valiana over to say hello but I think she'd kill you before figuring out you're not really here."

"Oh my, has she finally grown a spine? When I knew her she couldn't comb her hair without my help. So have you bedded her yet? She was still a virgin when I left her—a terrible state for such an attractive young woman."

"Really? I understand that your uncle Duke Perault solved that particular problem for you some time ago."

"Now don't be jealous, Falcio. I offered myself to you first, surely you remember?" Her hands began to tremble, as if the girl was trying to resist, but after a moment the hands relaxed and moved up to her neck, then began to slide slowly down her body. I think it was supposed to be alluring. "Perhaps with this body you'd find me more appealing? She's about the same age as Aline, after all." She turned her head and peaked out of the entrance. "Is that her you have with you?" she asked, looking down the road. "These roads are awfully dangerous for a young girl. I'm sure Cantissa would agree with me— if she could speak."

"Cantissa can take whatever solace she can in knowing that you will never put your hands on Aline. She will take the throne and become Queen and you will be nothing but a bad memory for this world."

For just a moment the girl's hands shook and I knew then that Cantissa was in there, aware, fighting. I looked again at the screws with their small wooden handles. If I removed them, would the spell be broken? I took a tentative step toward her.

"Ah, ah ah," Trin said. "I don't think you're coming to kiss me, my tatter-cloak, so you'll just stay back, or I'll make Cantissa here pull her own eyes from their sockets."

I backed away. Trin watched me and then frowned theatrically. "Really? Not willing to risk even a stupid little farm girl's life? What if killing her while I'm inside her could kill me as well, Falcio?"

I said nothing, waiting instead to see if there was some sign that what she'd said might be true. Could I do it? How many lives could I save if I killed Trin right now? Would Cantissa understand? Would she even now beg me to do it?

"You really are no fun when you aren't bound to a chair in a dungeon, Falcio. We'll have to rectify that soon."

I saw no value in playing along with Trin's game. What was her aim—to delay us? Was she even now giving her men instructions somehow, telling them where we were so that she could finally send enough of them to kill us? "What's happening to Kest?" I asked.

Her glance shifted down to where Kest was still kneeling. "That's obvious, isn't it? He can't enter holy places." She leaned forward. "You shouldn't have killed Caveil-whose-blade-cuts-water," she said to him loudly, as if she were explaining something to a half-deaf simpleton. "That was very bad. You upset someone I like very much."

"Why wouldn't he be able to enter holy places? Kest is the Saint of Swords now," I said.

"True. But I believe the title of 'Saint' is a bit of a misnomer. They're really more accursed than anything else. Poor old Caveil wandered the world searching for opponents worthy of his blade— nearly killed his own wife and son once, I'm told."

"Why would a Saint be accursed?"

"The Gods don't appreciate humans growing above their station, Falcio. Haven't you figured that out yet? It's the way of all things in the world: we all have a place and a purpose, and there is a cost to defying it."

I looked down at Kest, whose whole body was shaking as he continued his struggle to move, but it was if he were shackled to the ground. Time to take a chance. I stowed my throwing knife back in my coat and put my hands under his armpits and hauled him backward. Once I had dragged him a foot away he put up a hand.

"I can move again," he said.

"Good. Let's go."

He hesitated for a moment, glancing back at the girl.

"I'm not playing her games," I said.

Trin laughed. "Silly man, if you won't play with me then I'll just get someone else." She cupped her hands to the sides of her mouth and called out, "Valiana? Come on, sweetheart! Come and play with your beloved Trin!"

Hells, I should have expected this. "Stay where you are," I shouted, but it was no good. The sound of Trin's voice—the woman who had taken everything away from her—might as well have been a rope pulling at Valiana's neck and she raced to the church.

When she saw Trin's face on the girl, Valiana lunged for her without even drawing her blade.

"Stop!" I said, grabbing the back of her coat and hauling her back to me. "It's not Trin. It's a trick."

"I just wanted to see my beautiful Valiana again," Trin said, mock-hurt. "Besides, who are you to speak of tricks, Falcio? Pretending you had Aline with you and making me send all those men to chase after you? Now that I've finally captured little Aline myself, I'll have to instruct my men to be especially harsh with her."

My heart sank. How had the Tailor failed so soon? If Trin had Aline, then the Tailor and her Greatcoats were likely dead—and yet if Trin had won, why bother with this entire performance?

Trin held a hand by her ear as if listening to something off in the distance. "Can you hear that? I think our little Aline has just become a woman."

Anger threatened to overtake me but the saner, smarter part of me knew something was wrong. I didn't doubt Trin would order her men to do such a thing, but I knew that she'd want to be there when it happened. *A ruse. It's a ruse.* Too late I understood why she'd called out for Valiana.

"Don't you dare touch her!" Valiana screamed, as if her voice could somehow reach through the wooden frame to Trin's men. "You will *not* touch her! Do you hear me? Don't you dare touch her!"

Trin smiled at me. "See, now was that so hard?"

Valiana turned to me, confused.

I shook my head. "She doesn't have Aline," I said. "She wanted to know if we did."

"Oh, don't be angry with Valiana. I would have found out eventually. Besides, it hardly takes a master strategist to know the old woman has sent you to get support from the southern Dukes, and one of them would have sent word to me eventually that you didn't really have the girl." She paused for a moment. "Which Duke are you after first, I wonder? Roset in Luth has the most soldiers. But Isault has more money. Or perhaps grouchy old Meillard in Pertine? It might make sense to start with your own duchy, wouldn't it?"

"You're really not as good at this as you think you are," I said.

"It hardly matters; none of them will trust the Greatcoats and if you're smart you won't trust any of them. It's really a very cold world we live in, Falcio."

"Made colder by your presence in it," I said. "A problem that the Tailor will soon rectify—if your own generals don't do it first."

"Now, don't be mean with me, darling. I went through a lot of trouble to be here with you." She looked down at the ground and made a coquettish expression, as if she were a young maid about to ask a boy to dance. "I have a gift for you, Falcio."

The girl's hands opened for the first time. Cupped inside them was something that looked like a small, yellow-white piece of stone half the size of a fingernail. She held it out to me.

"I had it polished just for you. It was quite brown and ugly when we found it." When I didn't move Trin said, "Come. Take it. It cost me a great deal of time and money to acquire it. It's from your wife Aline."

I felt the air in my lungs grow cold. Trin *knew*. She knew about Aline, and how the King had named his heir after her. I'd been a fool to think that Trin or one of her people wouldn't find out about my past eventually. Despite the risk, I took a small piece of black cloth from my coat, one I used for cleaning my blades, before reaching out and taking the tiny thing.

When I held it close to me and looked inside the cloth I saw that it was a tooth. *She's given me one of my wife's teeth.*

"I'm told it was found inside a tavern where it's been for—oh my, I suppose it must be fifteen years now. I thought about putting it on a little chain for you but that seemed old-fashioned."

My hand squeezed around the cloth and the tooth so tightly I thought either my fingers would break or the tooth would crumble to dust. Kest's hand was on my arm. He knew how close I was to drawing my sword and stabbing Trin through the neck. But of course she wasn't there and all my rage and frustration would serve only to kill the poor girl Trin was using.

Very slowly and very carefully, I opened my hand and took the tooth from the cloth. Then I turned and threw it as far as I could into the desert.

Trin made a *tsk-tsk* sound. "Now is that any way to treat a gift? And especially one so rare? Never mind. I have another. I'll keep it safe for you so that it's ready when the time comes."

I started to speak, but then noticed something was happening. The skin of the girl's face began to grow paler and her eyes became unfocused. A tear slipped from Trin's eye down her cheek. "Oh, stop, you simpering child, it's almost over." She sighed. "It seems my little Cantissa hasn't long left. The magic is very hard on such a frail young body."

"Fine. You've made your point. Let the girl go."

"Have I made my point, Falcio? I'm not sure I have, and it's so very important for you to understand: Cantissa is like Tristia itself. She's foolish, underfed, and exists only to die in whatever service her betters require. This is the world we live in, Falcio—a place where even an innocent girl has no hope of a life free of the machinations of Dukes and Knights and Saints. Honestly, why would you even bother fighting for such a terrible place? Better to leave it behind. Better to leave it to me. I have armies and influence and more money than you can possibly imagine."

"If you have so much power, then why are you so concerned about me?"

"Silly man. It's not about you—it never has been. It's about what other people do *because* of you. You inspire people to take foolish actions, Falcio—actions that could become bothersome for a new Queen."

"The only throne you'll take is the basest seat in the lowest, darkest hell I can find for you."

The girl's hands moved to her hips as if she were about to scold me. "Well, if you're going to be like that, my tatter-cloak, then I'll just have to say goodbye!" Trin's smile widened and her hands reached up to the wooden handles of the screws pressed at each side of the girl's temples. Before I could reach out she gave them a full turn.

"Stop!" I screamed. Valiana and I both ran toward the girl, but before either of us could reach her she stumbled back into the church and I saw her turn the screws twice more. She fell to the ground and her body began to twitch.

I heard someone running toward us: Brasti was behind me, bow in hand. "What's happening?" he asked. "What's wrong with the girl? Who is she?"

"Leave it," Kest called from outside, but I walked inside the church. The girl's face was her own now. Cantissa had the plain features of a farmer's daughter: small round eyes above a slightly flat nose. Those eyes were wide and full of fear now. Blood seeped out from the sides of her head where the screws had pushed through her skull and her body trembled in little spasms. I knelt down and held her to my chest and tried to quiet her shaking until Cantissa finally let go of the world.

8

THE ROAD

The landscape became greener over the next week as we made our way through from the southern edge of Pulnam to the northern tip of Aramor. The desert to the east kept watch on us even as the brown brush and sand that bounded the wide road was gradually replaced by the thick fields of grain and barley that signaled Aramor's age-old prosperity.

Each morning I awoke unable to move, unable to speak, and unable to see, and each morning I told myself that the time I spent in that condition wasn't getting any longer, that this was like a fever that would pass on its own some day soon.

For the first few mornings, I imagined that Cantissa was there with me, her hands reaching but never touching the iron screws topped by short wooden handles that were slowly being driven into her skull. Sometimes I imagined her face changing into Aline's.

There was nothing I could do for my King's daughter now. I had to hope the Tailor and her Greatcoats were keeping her hidden and safe. My focus had to be on Aramor, and Duke Isault. Only by securing his support could I give Aline the chance she needed to become Queen. The Tailor's words echoed in my ears: *"Aline must be protected so that she can take the throne. Nothing else can stand in the way of that. Nothing will."*

When we finally crossed into the northern edge of the Duchy of Aramor I signaled a halt. "We should let the horses drink," I said, bringing one leg over the saddle and stepping down to the ground.

"I don't care what you say, Falcio," Brasti said, dropping down from his own mount and walking over to join me, "I'm sleeping in an inn tonight. I've had enough of the cold desert wind chilling my balls."

"Your balls could do with chilling," Dariana said, still on her horse.

Brasti looked up at her with a disgusted expression. "Have no fear, Dari, my dear. You chill my balls plenty as it is."

His words rang false. Dariana was quite pretty in her way, though I could never quite bring myself to call her attractive—she reminded me a little too much of the Tailor. Brasti, on the other hand, had more—well, *cosmopolitan* tastes in sexual partners. During our time on the road he'd been making frequent and increasingly elaborate overtures to Dariana, most of which included a recitation of his virtues that, if true, would have stretched the boundaries of natural laws. For her part, she obviously found him repugnant, and she took every opportunity to remind him of that—which, to me at least, was her most endearing quality.

"Someone's coming," Brasti said, pointing down the road.

"Where?" I asked.

"About two hundred yards."

Valiana joined us, her hand on the hilt of her sword. "I don't see anything."

"Listen."

After a few seconds the rest of us could make out the sound of a horse cart, its wheels making bumpy progress along the trade road.

"Hide, fight, or flee?" Kest asked.

I looked at Brasti. "Are there other horses with the cart?"

"No, I doubt it's anything more than a merchant."

"Keep close to the horses," I said.

A minute later an old man rode along, sitting on top of a wagon pulled by two sorry-looking mules. "Greatcoats, eh?" he said, pulling to a stop.

I nodded.

"Got redweed," he said. "Good for sore gums." He peered at us as if trying to see our teeth.

"Thanks, but we're fine," I said.

"Got lots of other things. Stems from jackroot; that'll help with joint pain. Give you a little boost with the ladies in the bargain, or so my customers tell me."

"Again, no."

He let go of the reins and pulled the blanket up from the back of his wagon. There were dozens of jars and boxes there. "Can't tell me you don't need anything for healing," he said. "Fellas like you? Must get into all kinds of scrapes. How about some black thelma? Does a fine job on bruises."

"I . . ." A thought occurred to me. "Have you got anything for neatha poisoning?" I asked.

"Neatha? You sure you got the right name?"

"Yes, neatha."

The old man shook his head. "Might as well ask if I've got a cure for rain. Stay out of it, that's the cure. Neatha's lethal, son. One whiff and you're gone. Not a bad way to go, or so they say. Not sure how 'they' would know though."

"All right. Have you ever heard of a man being paralyzed in the morning, after his body's been still for a few hours?"

"How long does it last?" he asked.

"A few minutes. Maybe as much as an hour. Followed by stiffness in the limbs."

"I think they call it old age, son."

"It's not that, it's—"

"Doesn't make a difference either way," he said. "Neatha's fatal. A man's exposed to it and he dies. It's that simple."

"I was exposed," I said. "And I'm still moving."

The old man took up the reins of his mules. "If you got hit by neatha then you're dead, son. Your body just needs a bit of time to figure that out, is all."

"Cheerful old bastard," Brasti said. He looked at the sun starting to slowly set in the sky. "I need a drink. Hey, old man," he called out. "Is there a town with an inn close by?"

"Shalliard," the man shouted back. "Three hours the way you're headed. Assuming you don't fall off your horse and die first."

Brasti grinned. "Well, I think at least some of us can manage that, can't we?"

We spent that night in a small inn called the Golden Bell, and the following morning I awoke to the sight of my King, which was remarkable, since he'd been dead for more than five years. His form was blurry and dark, which made sense seeing as my eyes were still shut. I couldn't make sense of his features nor his clothing, yet there was something so distinctive about that thin, bony frame and the ungainly posture that always made me think he was about to tell a dirty joke.

White light began ever so slowly to fill my vision and I realized that my eyes must be opening. I was coming out of the paralysis. Oddly, my hallucination became sharper, and for a brief moment I could see King Paelis as clearly as if he were just inches away from me. He looked just as he had the last time I'd seen him, in that cold tower above Castle Aramor where he'd spent his last hours. His gaze was gentle and he opened his mouth. I was surprised that I could hear his voice so clearly. He said only four words before my eyes opened fully.

What he said was, "You will betray her."

The harsh rays of morning light banished my vision, and the King's face was replaced with that of Kest.

"Can you move yet?" he asked.

"I think so," I said.

"Rest a minute."

Sound advice. "What are the others doing?"

"Brasti went hunting. He said there's some kind of wild pheasant in these parts that's prized by the nobles of Pulnam. I think he misses being a poacher."

"What about Valiana?" I asked.

"Same as always—practicing. Dariana's a good teacher, despite her odd fencing style. I still can't quite place it."

"A mystery for another day," I said, leaning on my elbow and pushing my way unsteadily to my feet.

Kest gave me a hand. When I was standing he looked at me and said, "It was twelve minutes this time."

"What are you talking about?" I already knew the answer; I just didn't want to think about it right now. The first time I'd awakened trapped in my own body, the paralysis had lasted just a few seconds. Then it was a full minute. Now it was twelve.

"What are you going to do?" Kest asked.

"Nothing. We make our way to the Ducal Palace of Aramor and knock very softly and politely at the gate. If all goes well, we'll secure Isault's support and then move on to Luth and Pertine and whomever else we need to put the King's heir on the throne."

"And then?"

"Then? Then we get me cured and find something else to worry about," I said, grinning.

Kest shrugged and helped me pack up my bedroll. In my mind I imagined an island I'd heard of just off the coast of Baern in the warm southern sea, and a woman with dark hair and a pretty face with tiny wrinkles around her eyes who had given me respite and hope when I'd needed it most. *Let me see Ethalia once more before the end*, I thought. That's all I ask.

"Let's go," I said. "Aramor awaits. Saints willing we can do this without screwing up the entire world."

In case I've never mentioned it before, in Tristia the Saints only answer the calls of the very rich, the very powerful, or those blessed by the Gods. I had never been any of those things.

9

THE DUKE

By midday we'd arrived at the Ducal Palace of Aramor and knocked politely at the gate to give the guards the papers that ensured that we'd be brought in to see Duke Isault unharmed. So much for courtesy: before we'd really had a chance to take in the palace sights we were surrounded by two dozen Knights in full armor, their swords drawn in a singularly unwelcoming manner.

"Brasti, the next time you feel it necessary to put an arrow through a Knight's chest," I said, my voice as calm as I could make it, "try not to do it in front of twenty of his fellows."

"Or at least kill more than just the one," Dariana suggested.

The five of us stood face-out in a tight circle inside a massive stone courtyard, looking at what I was pretty sure was a detachment of Ducal Knights. They gripped their two-handed warswords and began close in on us, step by step. Sometimes they would stop, as if waiting for an order from their captain, and then invariably one of them would say something threatening and advance toward us, just an inch or two, and the others would follow. From above I imagined we must look like a troupe of dancers not yet sure when to begin the performance.

"For the record, Falcio, that particular piece of advice is best delivered in advance of the action in question. Also, he was about to kill you."

"You don't know that."

"He had his sword out and was aiming it at your neck."

"He might have just been trying to make a point," I said.

"Yes, the point being that a man's head can indeed be separated from his body with a single stroke."

He was right, of course: The Knight who'd had his sword on me had shown no inclination toward conversation other than to keep repeating "Trattari scum" over and over. In his defense, he'd clearly been standing in the hot sun all morning and looked as if he were baking inside his armor. I hadn't had time to draw my rapiers so Brasti had made a judgment call. It wasn't a bad one, except in so far as we were all going to die now. The Knights keeping us penned in were just waiting for the order from their Knight-Captain before they overpowered us.

"You need to reconsider your next move," I warned the Knights in front of us. "No one else needs to die today."

"Do you Greatcoats always talk this much when you should be fighting?" Dari asked.

"Always," Brasti and Kest said together.

"I'm starting to see how the Dukes managed to kill off the King so easily." Her voice betrayed no sign of fear. She kept her left hand on Valiana's arm. I wasn't sure whether this was to reassure her or to keep her from charging headlong to her death.

I scanned the tabards of the Knights surrounding us. Each bore the silver steer of Aramor on a green field. One of the Knights had three stars above his steer.

"Knight-Captain!" I called to him. "We came here to meet with Duke Isault in good faith—"

"What value is a Trattari's faith?" he asked from behind a steel helm.

"Apparently more than a Duke's, these days," Brasti said.

"You're not helping."

The Knights were still edging forward, but why hadn't they attacked already? I turned toward Kest. "What are our chances of winning?"

He looked around at the twenty Knights surrounding us in the courtyard, at the large gate that had been closed behind us, then up at the high interior walls, probably looking for places to climb if we could break out of the circle. "No chance whatsoever," he said.

"Really?" I'd been expecting something bad, but nothing quite so final.

"Twenty to five, and they're wearing full armor. We must have caught them on training exercises or during a troop review," he said. "Possibly there's a parade later today. Is it a holiday in Aramor?"

"Perfect," Brasti said. "We're about to die and the Saint of Swords is busy trying to figure out if there's going to be a feast later."

"All right, but what if we break through the circle?" I asked.

"Look up on the walls," Kest said.

I'd been so determined to talk our way in and avoid bloodshed that I hadn't taken notice of the multitude of men with crossbows hiding in the ramparts. "Ah, hells," I said.

The Knight-Captain saw my reaction. "There is only one way out for you, Trattari. It leads through a river of your own blood. Come and meet the fate you have earned a hundred times over."

"You break faith with the laws and traditions of Aramor and dishonor your Duke!" Valiana shouted, holding her sword out in front of her.

The Knight-Captain laughed. "And what would you know of a Duke's honor, whore?"

"I—"

"Nothing," I said. "She knows nothing of these matters, Sir Knight. Let her and the other woman go. They are merely travelers seeking entry into Aramor and have nothing to do with this."

"Then why are they wearing greatcoats?" the Knight asked.

I heard Dariana snort behind me. "Is he always this brilliant a strategist?"

The Knight-Captain laughed again. "I'll leave the first move to you, Trattari."

I caught Kest's eye, then Brasti's and they nodded to me in turn. We all knew what was to come next. Every duelist one day meets his better. The day you begin to learn the sword is the day you start to ready yourself to feel its point driven into your own belly. But Valiana wasn't a Greatcoat, not to me, anyway. She was an innocent young woman who'd never had the chance to prepare for a death like the one coming for her. She deserved better.

I whispered to Dariana, "When the fighting starts, we'll try to break their circle. When we do, you grab Valiana and the two of you make for the guardhouse next to the gate. There's only one man there and you can use his door to get around the gate."

She looked at me with a smirk. "Are you trying to save my life or my soul? You think I'm not ready to die fighting these bastards? You think I'm afraid?"

"Dariana, I think you're utterly insane. I think you're eager, if not desperate, to die fighting. But Valiana's not like us. She's not—"

"She may be a pretty little bird but she's got the heart of a lion, First Cantor. You shame her by treating her like a child."

"Fine. She can hate me for it later. For now, do what I'm telling you."

She looked at me questioningly for just an instant before nodding. Smart. She knew when a fight couldn't be won.

I turned back to the others.

"So it's over then?" Brasti asked.

"It's over," I said, and was surprised by the strange calm that came over me. There's a serenity that comes in knowing you've got only one thing left to fight for.

"Fine," Brasti said. "If today's the day then, well, fine. But if I have to die then I'm taking some of these fucking Knights with me."

"Which ones should we kill?" Kest asked. "We can take six—no, you've got your fast bow, haven't you? So eight."

The Knights inched forward again. They were less than ten feet away now. Another step and they'd launch their attack.

"Excuse me?" Brasti called out. "We have a bit of a dilemma here."

"I'd say you do, Trattari," said one of the other Knights, laughing.

Brasti ignored him. "You see our friend here, the Saint of Swords? He reckons we can kill eight of you before you kill us. Now, I'm sure some of you are perfectly nice people, though why a perfectly nice person would ever choose a career as a Knight I don't know, but everyone makes mistakes. One time I even—"

"Get to the point, Brasti," I said.

"Right. Well, if any of you are wife-beaters, child-killers, perhaps murderers of old people? Could you just sort of raise a hand or nod? It would make it a lot easier for us."

"Brasti, that's ridi—"

But to my utter amazement, one of the Knights started to raise his hand, just for a moment before he saw his fellows look at him. No one ever said you had to be brilliant to wear armor.

"Right," Brasti said. "So which was it? Wife-beating, child-killing? Did you—? Ah, I suppose it doesn't matter." He pulled an arrow and let it loose. It pierced the man's gorget and he went down, blood spouting from his neck. "All right. Who's next? Anyone mean to animals?"

The Knights roared as one and moved to close the gap between us. I'm not as good as Kest at working out how a battle will go, but I guessed we had just under a minute before we were overwhelmed.

"Go!" I screamed to Dari, and turned my attention to our enemies. The key, when there are far, far too many opponents, is to try to get them in each other's way, and the best way to do that is to move in as close as you can to your enemies—but that means exposing your back to them. Another way is simply to try to get them to want so badly to be the one who kills you that they literally jostle each other out of the way. It's easier to do than you'd imagine. In fact, we have a song for it.

I pulled out my rapiers. "Every Knight I meet is a sickening fool," I sang.

Kest chimed in immediately, "He's cowardly, vain, he is ugly and cruel—"

"He'd gladly rape his own mother," Brasti harmonized cheerfully.

"His sister and his brother," Kest added.

"But most days he'll settle for his own damn mule!"

The Knights barreled into us, which turned out to be helpful as it made it hard for the crossbowmen on the walls above to hit us. A warsword was coming straight down at me; I lifted the guard of my right rapier, keeping the point down, and let the blow slide along the blade, sparks trailing after it. Another Knight swung his sword in a straight horizontal line so I slipped past the first Knight and let the blow hit him in the belly. Better his armor took the hit than my coat. A quick glimpse showed me that the girls were still with us. I cursed the Saints, but I had no time to do anything about it.

We tried to stay inside the mass of Knights to make it harder for the crossbows to hit us. Our greatcoats can withstand a bolt or two but the impact would be jarring enough to make us lose concentration, and even a moment not focusing gives someone the chance to jab something pointy into us. I glanced up briefly at the crossbowmen above and to my surprise saw they were standing stock-still, restrained by their own Knight-Captain, who had his right arm held high, apparently holding his men back. Something was wrong here. Why was one group of Knights trying to kill us while the other wasn't?

Brasti was swinging his bow in a wide horizontal arc, keeping the Knights at bay, but the tactic wouldn't work for long. Kest had already engaged three of the men and I could see two others trying to get behind him. It was over for us. *So soon?* I thought. I don't think time slows down when death is coming; I think our minds, realizing they have only a few moments left of life, simply work more quickly. Brasti would get two arrows off before he was overcome. Kest would keep his attackers off, only to have crossbow bolts from above pierce his head. Me? Well, there was a tall man holding a very pointy weapon that looked destined to meet my left eye in the very near future.

A horn, loud as a hundred eagles screaming, broke through the chaos.

Most of the Knights pulled back almost instantly—the man thrusting his sword at my face didn't manage to stop in time, but he was distracted enough that I was able to parry the blow myself.

The horn rang out again, this time three very short bursts, and the Knights withdrew from the fight and formed up in four lines. The two we'd killed before the fight were still on the ground and five more had joined them.

For a brief moment there was silence as the dust slowly began to settle on the courtyard, then a voice broke through. "Knight-Captain Heridos, report."

One of the Knights in the front row took two steps forward, as if he were about to address Kest, Brasti, and me.

"Knight-Commander, sir," he said.

I heard footsteps from behind the soldiers and a taller man, bigger than the rest of the Knights, walked toward us, his armor gleaming in the sunlight. His tabard showed the steer of Aramor, but this one had four stars around it. He stopped in front of his Knights and faced us as if to prove that he didn't need to see his men to know they would follow his commands.

"Report, I said."

"We—" Brasti began.

I elbowed him. "He's not talking to us."

"Sir Shuran, these *Trattari* attacked us—"

The big Knight, Sir Shuran, still facing us, said, "Oh? Was one of them dressed as Sir Kee? Because I do believe I watched from above as Sir Kee tried to sever this man's head from his body before he'd even drawn a blade."

"I told you," Brasti whispered.

Heridos shifted uncomfortably. "Sir—"

"What instructions did I leave you with this morning, Knight-Captain Heridos?"

"Yes, sir, but—"

"The *instructions*, Knight-Captain. What were they?"

Captain Heridos's eyes narrowed, a seething disdain for the Knight-Commander visible in his expression. "Sir Shuran, sir, your instructions were to await the arrival of three envoys sent by the Pretender."

"And?"

"Your orders were not to engage the envoys, regardless of provocation."

Sir Shuran removed his helm. Short-cropped black hair sat atop square-jawed features. He looked to be in his early forties, though it was hard to tell because the left half of his face bore the leather texture and heavy scars of severe burns. "I have learned, Knight-Captain Heridos, that responding to provocation can lead to unpleasant results."

The Knight-Captain hesitated for a moment, then said, "But, sir, even after Sir Kee was slain and before we attacked, the bowman slew Sir Retaris. And five more of ours lie dead on the ground."

Shuran walked over to the corpse of Sir Retaris, the man Brasti had killed. He pushed at the body with the toe of his boot. "Which do you suppose it was?" he asked.

"Sir?"

"Wife-beater, child-slayer, or murderer of old people—which one do you think he was agreeing to?"

I was starting to like Sir Shuran. Then I reminded myself that he was a Knight and the problem went away. "Sir Shuran, my name is Falcio val—"

He held up a gauntleted hand. "A moment, please. I am not quite done with my men. Knight-Captain Heridos, you allowed Sir Kee to attack the men I *specifically* instructed you to not to engage. You then surrounded them and made it clear you intended to capture or kill them." The big Knight shielded his eyes against the sun and looked up at the ramparts. "You will take note that Sir Nemeth kept his own men on the ramparts in check as instructed. Finally, I feel I must point out that, with twenty of the finest Knights in Aramor, you succeeded in killing precisely zero of your chosen enemies while they have taken the lives of eight of my men."

"Sir?" the Knight-Captain asked.

"Yes?"

"They only killed seven of ours."

Sir Shuran left the corpse and took a position in front of the Knight-Captain. "Thank you for reminding me. Kneel and remove your helm, Sir Heridos."

The Knight-Captain looked from left to right for a moment, as if hoping someone would speak up for him. Then he knelt and removed his helm, revealing long blond hair and a youthful face.

Sir Shuran pulled out his sword. It was a simple thing, without any ornate elements or inscription on the blade. But I noted that it was exactly the right length for a man of Sir Shuran's height, of whom there couldn't be many, and broader than a normal sword, as if it were weighted for someone of his obvious strength. This was a custom blade, well made and expensive, despite its simple appearance. This man placed a high value on his weapon but hadn't the vanity to have it decorated.

Sir Shuran took the sword in both hands and held it above the Knight-Captain's neck. "Are you prepared, Captain Heridos?"

"Yes, Knight-Commander."

"Do you require a moment to give prayer to your gods or instructions to your men on any disposition of personal items to your loved ones?"

"No, Knight-Commander. I am ready to die."

"Here, in the dust of the courtyard? For no better reason than I require it?"

"Yes, Knight-Commander."

"Very well," Sir Shuran said. "Foolishness has cost you your life, Knight-Captain. It's only fitting that obedience should buy it back." He replaced the blade in the sheath at his left hip. "Remain where you are until the sun has set and risen again." He left the man kneeling there and walked over to me. "I am Sir Shuran, Knight-Commander of Aramor and loyal servant to Isault, Duke of Aramor." He removed his gauntlet and extended his right hand to me.

I stood there like a statue for a full minute. I have met more than a hundred Knights in my time. Not one has ever asked to shake my hand, or that of any Greatcoat.

"Falcio val Mond," I said, taking his hand at last and shaking it awkwardly. "First Cantor of the King's Greatcoats."

"Forgive me for saying this, but how are you the 'King's Greatcoats' when the man himself is dead?"

"It's mostly an honorary sort of thing," Brasti said. He extended his hand gleefully, waiting for the Knight to refuse it. "Brasti Goodbow."

To his surprise, Sir Shuran shook his hand as well. The big Knight looked past me and said, "Ladies, I apologize for the discourtesy of my men."

I turned and saw Dari and Valiana standing behind me. "Door was locked," Dari said.

"And you," Sir Shuran said, turning to Kest. "Am I correct in saying that you are the Greatcoat known as Kest Murrowson?"

"I am," he said.

"There is a story going around that you claim to be the greatest swordsman in the world."

"I find I rarely have to claim it," Kest said.

"He's a Saint," Brasti said. "Just not the Saint of Humility."

Sir Shuran smiled. "I wonder, sir, if you might favor me with a bout, should we have the time?"

Kest looked over the Knight appraisingly, then he looked past him at the man's footprints on the ground. "You have a heavy left-footed stance," he said, "keeping your right side to your opponent, perhaps to shield the burned side of your face from attack?"

"Perhaps," Sir Shuran replied.

"Or is it because your left eye is somewhat damaged and you don't see as well as you need to?"

The Knight smiled. "That, too, is a possibility."

"You'd last ten strikes with me. Perhaps twelve if the sun were in my eyes."

"Well then, not much point in a bout if you have it all—"

"I do."

"Still though, if we get the chance, I'd like to find out firsthand. Can you defeat me without actually killing me?"

Kest thought about that. "Fourteen strikes."

"Sir Shuran," I said, "I realize that the idea of being beaten half to death by Kest might be highly diverting to some people but we—"

"Forgive me, you're correct," he said. "I'm a competitive man at heart. But that's not why you're here. Let me take you to the Duke. He's eager to meet you."

As we walked the length of the courtyard and into the palace proper, I tried to make sense of this big Knight who appeared to hold no antipathy toward me or the Greatcoats. It's not as if there was a law commanding that all Knights despise us—well, not one I'd seen with my own eyes, at any rate. And yet something was bothering me. "You ordered your men to await our arrival," I said as we walked up a wide set of stone stairs.

"I did."

"How did you know we'd arrive today?"

"I didn't. They've been waiting for you since we received word you were coming."

"How long ago was that?" I asked.

"Six days."

I stopped at the top of the stairs. "So you told twenty Knights and twenty crossbowmen to stand out in the hot sun every day for a week and wait for three Greatcoats."

"Is there a problem, First Cantor? I also ordered them not to attack you."

"Yes, yes, you ordered them not to attack us. But you knew they would, didn't you? On a good day, with a purse of gold, a full cask of wine, and after fucking Saint Laina-who-whores-for-Gods, a Knight would still find an excuse to attack a Greatcoat. These men—"

Sir Shuran started walking again and we followed him down a long hallway past red and green tapestries. "Those men should have obeyed their orders. A Knight needs discipline above all things. But most of the time, following orders is easy for a Knight. We ask them to do things they expect. Things they even like to do."

"So you thought you'd take advantage of the opportunity to see just how well trained your men were."

"Yes," Sir Shuran said. "And now I've learned."

"And what if they'd managed to kill us before you intervened? Wouldn't your Duke have found that a bit of a pain?"

"First Cantor, my understanding is that you three are the best of King Paelis's Greatcoats." He smiled at Dari and Valiana. "No offense to either of you; I'm sure you're both stout fighters. But if the stories are to be believed, Falcio escaped a Ducal prison, tamed a fey horse, defeated Dashini assassins—something that's supposed to be impossible—and slew the Duke of Rijou."

"Which is not nearly as impressive as the fact that he brought him back to life," Brasti said.

"Quite so. Therefore, First Cantor, I can only conclude that if my men had killed you before I intervened, Duke Isault would have no use for you."

We reached the end of a hallway wide enough to drive a caravan through. The two guards standing outside the imposing entrance saluted Sir Shuran and opened the great double doors in tandem. Inside was a large room with a throne at the far end. Sir Shuran pointed toward it. "Go ahead," he said. "The Duke will see you when he's ready."

The five of us spent the next hour standing like statues in the hereditary throne room of the Dukes of Aramor. "What are we doing here, Falcio?" Brasti asked for the third time.

"Shut up," I said for the fourth. The first time had been an unsuccessful attempt to preempt the others.

The room was pretty much a perfect match for every other Ducal throne room I've ever found myself in over the years, which is to say that it looked much as you might expect a King's throne room would. Tapestries hung from the wall showing scenes of various battles (one had to assume they didn't bother with any in which Aramor wasn't victorious). Swords and shields adorned the square columns spaced out along the length of the room, each one bearing the Ducal crest, but with enough individual details to delineate particular members of the line of Isault. There was just enough sparkle of silver and gold to reach for royal elegance without quite achieving it.

It must have been hard for a man like Isault to live here, knowing Castle Aramor was only thirty miles away and was both grander than Isault's palace and completely vacant since King Paelis had been deposed and killed. To be so close to the seat of Tristia's power and yet unable to so much as walk through the front door without setting off a war with the other Dukes must have annoyed him no end.

Eventually an old man entered through the same door we had, followed by four pages carrying heavy silver trays. Two tables were set, one on each side of the throne, each laden with food and wine, and then the servants left and the old man took a position by the door. I wondered whether the food was set there as a test to see if we'd eat it before the Duke arrived.

"You realize that you ask Falcio that question quite frequently?" Kest said.

"What?" Brasti asked.

"'What are we doing here?' You ask him that question wherever we go."

"And?"

"By now you should assume he doesn't have an answer."

Thanks, Kest. I looked back at the door where we'd entered. Sir Shuran was standing there. He nodded to me. I nodded back. The old chamberlain stood next to him. He didn't grace me with a look of any kind. I would have been offended, but I wasn't entirely sure the old man was awake.

"Just keep your tongues," I said to the others. "Shuran's been more polite than we could've hoped for thus far, and I don't want to offend anyone."

"They tried to kill us, Falcio," Brasti said.

"The Ducal Knights always try to kill us. At least these ones are polite. Nine duchies in the Kingdom—there has to be at least one where people respect us."

"Ah, there they are," came a deep, rumbling voice from behind the throne. "The whoresons of King Paelis, their tongues still brown with the dried crumbs of his defecation."

I had never met Isault before, so I watched closely as he entered the room from a door set in an alcove a few feet behind the throne. He was a man of average height and middle years with a substantial belly; his clothes, green and gold, made of silk, or something like it. They weren't especially flattering. Neither was the wooden crown with gold inlay and a large green jewel in the center. Only in Tristia do Dukes get to wear crowns.

"Your Grace," I said, without bowing.

"Shit-eater," he replied, and walked the two steps leading up to the throne. He sat down heavily. "There's food if you want it. But eat from that table," he said, pointing to the one on our right. "The other one's for me."

Yes, because you never run into trouble eating food that's been prepared just for you when the other guy has his own food. "We're fine, your Grace. We ate earlier."

The Duke reached down, nearly tipping from his throne. His crown fell from his head and clattered on the ground. He didn't seem to care. Instead he grabbed a leg of meat that had once belonged to some type of large bird. "Chicken," he said, biting into it. I wasn't clear who he was referring to. "I see you brought whores. Which one of them is for me?"

Dariana said, "That would be me, your Grace."

Isault saw the disturbing grin on her face and turned to me. "Why do I get the feeling that this nasty little creature has things other than my pleasure in mind? Perhaps she would enjoy it more if I bound her hand and foot first?"

Her expression changed instantly. "I would delight in your attempt, your Grace."

I put a hand on Dariana's sword arm. Her eyes went from my hand to my face. She looked much more angrily at me than she had at the Duke.

"Rude little thing. I see she wears a Greatcoat too, which explains it. The problem with you Greatcoats is . . . ah, hells. Beshard!" he shouted to the old man at the back of the room, "What was I saying the problem with the Greatcoats was? You remember, the other day?"

"They're full of themselves, your Grace," the chamberlain shouted back.

"Right! Quite right. Full of yourselves. That's what you are." His Grace leaned toward us and whispered theatrically, "Beshard is a saggy old queer who dreams of buggering me in my sleep but he's as loyal as a pit-terrier." Isault tossed the chicken back at the plate on the table. He missed. "Really, you should try attacking me. I swear old Beshard will get here before Shuran does."

"Duke Isault—" I began.

"Now you're probably wondering why I summoned you here," he said.

"Umm . . . you didn't summon us, your Grace. We came on orders from the Tailor on behalf of Aline, daughter of—"

"Yes, yes . . . Aline, daughter of somebody, ruler of something, heir to the throne of somewhere. It's all shit, though, isn't it?"

"I don't quite follow, your Grace."

"I said, it's all shit."

"Yes, your Grace, I heard the words coming out of your mouth. I just don't understand them."

Duke Isault reached over and picked up another piece of the bird—a wing this time. "Who cares who anyone is? You don't know me—for all you know, I was born the son of a pig herder and some washerwoman confused me with the real Duke's son. For all you know the real Duke of Aramor is out there pouring swill into a trough right now."

Looking at Isault, his face already covered in no small amount of grease, I found the idea increasingly plausible.

He wiped his mouth on his sleeve. "Patents of nobility, Heart's Trials, City Sages . . . it's all of it a bunch of shit. But you've got those swords of yours, don't you?" he asked rhetorically. "Now *those* matter. A hundred Greatcoats go and kick the ass of five hundred of Jillard's men? That *matters*. Now, mind you, pull that trick more than a few times and you'll find an army of thirty thousand in front of you. That's what's coming, you know that, don't you?"

"What's that, your Grace? I'm still somewhere back at the washerwoman."

He laughed. "Hah! That's the one thing I like about you. You Greatcoats. You've got . . . damn it! What was it I was saying those Greatcoats have, Beshard?"

"'Balls', your Grace," Beshard shouted from the other end of the room. "You said they have . . . balls."

"Balls! Great big balls," Isault chortled, holding out both hands to give us a sense of both the estimated size and weight of the afore-mentioned balls. "You're all half-crazy to begin with, what with your 'the law says this' and 'the law says that'. Add a little war into the equation and soon enough you'll all go rushing headlong into an army no matter what the size." He shook a finger at me. "Thirty thousand men, boy. That's what the Dukes could field against you if they banded together. Thirty thousand. Think you and your hun-dred Greatcoats can take on an enemy of that size?"

"No, your Grace. We couldn't defeat thirty thousand." I thought about my next reply very carefully. "But we'll never have to."

"Oh?" Isault asked, "and why is that?"

"Because you don't trust each other," I said. "You all talk about wiping out this opponent or that, but in the end you all fear the expansion of any one Duke's power more than almost anything else. Your changeling pig farmer will sit on your throne long before the mythical army you're describing ever sees the field."

Isault started laughing: a big, uproarious laugh. "Ha! Now that's the other thing I like about Greatcoats! Remember Beshard, what was it I said the other day?"

Beshard started to reply but I held up a hand. "Our sense of humor. Your Grace, forgive my impertinence, but could we get to the point?"

The Duke stopped laughing. "The point? The point, which you'd know if you weren't quite so full of yourself, without that big pair of balls on you and that sense of humor you hold up like a shield, the point is that the Dukes should never be able to unite."

"Then—"

"Unless you scare them enough. We united once before, did we not, Falcio val Mond, First Cantor of the Greatcoats?"

"Yes, you did," I said, my voice cold.

"Oooh, Shuran, you better come and bring that big sword of yours over here. The boy's giving me a dirty look. Oh, my!" Duke Isault started wiggling his fingers in the air.

There wasn't much point in responding, so I didn't.

Isault watched me for a moment and then said, "Good. You're not as stupid as you look. Who designed those coats, anyway? You look like . . . well, it doesn't matter. The point is, the King made all of us more scared of him than of each other and that was a mistake. He united us. We had no choice but to take him down. He had to go."

Again I felt a dark heat inside me begin to rise. Duke Isault stared into my eyes, then he got up off his throne and walked down the two steps to stand right in front of me. "Give me that look again, boy, and I'll go and grab my own sword and give you the beating you deserve. Think I can't do it?"

"You'll last two strikes," Kest said. "Falcio will let your first blow pass and then—"

"The question was theoretical," Brasti whispered, so loudly that I imagine the Duke's dead ancestors heard it.

"I think you mean 'rhetorical'," Kest replied.

I held up my hand. "Leave it."

"Smart," Isault said. "Now be smart again. If you want to put your little girl on the throne, you'd better find a way to keep us fighting each other and not you and your traveling troupe of madmen."

"You seem rather determined to see us find a way to beat the Dukes, considering you're one of them, your Grace."

He walked over to the table on the right; the one he'd told us to eat from. He picked up another leg from the bird. "Aye, I suppose I am."

"Might I ask why?"

"I've some of my own reasons, but the most important one is that we need a King. Or a Queen. Or a fucking goat for all I care. Hells, even one of your little ladies here would do. But we need someone on the throne in Castle Aramor. We need King's Laws." He held up a finger. "Not a lot—not as many as Paelis wanted. But some. Enough. A man's got to be able to work his land and raise his family and not fear that some shit-eating lordling will come to call to rape his daughters and steal his money. The whole economy suffers that way, you know that don't you?"

I'd never thought of it in quite those terms, but . . . "Yes, your Grace, I do."

"And what happens if those barbarian piss-drinkers in Avares come over the mountains one day? They'll tear us apart. Thirty thousand men, I told you, didn't I? That's what all the Dukes could field if we banded together. Well, boy, Avares could put a hundred thousand in the field if they wanted." He bit into his chicken.

Isault's words made sense. His assessment of the state of the country was true and though I couldn't be sure about his estimate of the size of any potential Avares army, the numbers wouldn't surprise me. On the other hand, I still remembered the day the Ducal army had come to Castle Aramor. The army wasn't particularly large, but it had troops from every duchy, including Aramor. "So why didn't you support the King when you had the chance? Why not take a stand?"

"Take a stand?" He threw the half-eaten leg at me and it bounced off my coat leaving a little trail of grease. "Don't call me a coward, boy. I told you: your damned King Paelis was pushing too hard and too fast. That bitch Patriana had us all up in arms, claiming the Greatcoats were going to start taking over the duchies. He'd've gone after Duke Jillard in Rijou first; he'd've had to—and then guess who sits between the armpit of Hervor and the asshole of Rijou?" Isault pointed a thumb at himself. "Aramor. That's who."

"The King never sought to take over the duchies," I said. "Not one. There isn't a single order ever issued nor any decree ever written. He just wanted to make the lives of the common folk more bearable."

Isault gave a snort. "Really? Is that the lie he told you?"

I heard the sound of a Knight's warsword being pulled from its sheath across the hall. "What—?"

I felt Kest's hand on my arm. "You drew first, Falcio," he said, his own right hand on the grip of his sword. I looked down to see it was true. I'd half-drawn my sword.

"Forgive me, your Grace," I said. "I lost my head."

"Aye, boy, you nearly did. Look, I'm not saying the King was a bad man. I'm saying that he too knew of the danger from Avares. He knew we have to become a more prosperous country if we ever hope to be able to field an army to defend Tristia from invaders." He put up a hand. "I can see from the look on your face that we're not going to agree on this point, so let's leave it be. Let Paelis be the common man's hero in your eyes and the cunning and self-serving strategist in mine. Perhaps we're both right. Either way, Tristia can't be strong without a ruler on the throne."

"Then you'll support Aline?"

He let out a breath through his nose and looked me in the eyes. "Is she really the best you can do?"

"I don't understand, your Grace."

"A thirteen-year-old girl with no training in how to rule: that's our best hope?"

"She's the King's heir."

"And the others?"

I kept my expression as neutral as I could as I tried to decide how to answer that question.

"Ah," he said. "So you don't know if any of the others lived. Well then. Maybe we'll both be surprised one day."

"But for now?" I asked. "Will you support Aline as Queen of Tristia?"

"Aye, I will."

The tightness in my chest released. Aramor wasn't a particularly strong duchy but it had wealth and a good food supply and it was a damned good start: it would give others a reason to consider supporting us. We could—

"For a price."

"I'm sorry, your Grace?"

He picked up the plate of chicken from the table and carried it with him up to his throne. "Don't play the fool with me, boy. The old hag didn't send you here empty-handed, did she?"

"No, your Grace. In exchange for your support, Aline is—"

"The Tailor, you mean."

"I—"

"Aline doesn't have shit to offer, boy. She's a girl—she probably couldn't read a tax levy even with two scribes and a large magnifying glass. The old woman is the one pulling the threads. We're all just damned lucky she isn't in the line of succession—I'd hate to see a world with that old hag on the throne."

"*Aline*," I said, emphasizing her name, "is willing to set the Crown's tax rates at ten percent lower than they were when Paelis was King. She will also promise to keep the rates at that level for ten years."

"Well, I'm paying next to nothing right now, so that's not much of an offer."

"That's not entirely true, your Grace," Valiana said.

"Eh?" he said, looking her up and down. "So she talks, too? Delightful! What other things can she do with her mouth?"

Valiana ignored the comment. "You pay substantial fees to the Ducal Concord each year."

"Still only half of what I paid to Paelis in taxes."

"Most of the taxes you paid to the crown went back into maintaining the roads and ensuring the trade that is so vital to your duchy's economy. How much of the fees you pay now come back to Aramor, your Grace?"

"I think I liked you better when you were quiet and I could imagine you—"

"Imagine all you want," Valiana said. She smiled and, just for a moment, I saw the haughty noblewoman I'd first met. "Meanwhile other Dukes swallow lands in the north and look south toward the fields and herds of Aramor. What do you suppose *they're* imagining, your Grace?"

Isault looked singularly unhappy at the thought, and I took that as a good sign. "Aline will ensure your borders and trade routes are secure. She'll also press the Lords Caravaner to lower the tariffs and exchange rates across the Spear and the Bow."

"Oh?" Isault asked. "And how will she do that?"

"She'll use some of the tax levies to repair the roads and place guard-stations along the trade routes."

"Smart," Isault said, "and might even work. But it's not enough."

"She'll also agree to no new laws infringing on the duchies for a period of five years."

"So, just long enough for her to grow up and learn what the current laws are? Fine. Still not enough."

"Forgive me, your Grace. What else do you want?"

Isault held out his plate of chicken at me. Not knowing what else to do, I took it and placed it on the table.

"See that, boy?" he asked. "Ten minutes ago you'd never have taken the plate from me. Now you can smell a deal and you'll happily debase yourself."

"That's not—"

"Oh, I'm not criticizing. In fact, I'm glad to see you've got a shred of sense in you. Because what I want, your little girl can't offer me."

"What is it you want, then, your Grace?"

He pointed a finger. "You."

"Me?"

"You. The Greatcoats. You're supposed to enforce the laws, aren't you?"

"We are, your Grace."

"And a Duke has the right to tax a man living in one of his villages, doesn't he?"

"He does, so long as the tax—"

"'So long as the tax is neither so onerous it cannot be fairly paid nor the penalty so heavy, and hogswash and horseshit and so on and so forth . . .' Whatever. Point is, if I haven't done any of that, they have to pay, right? Well, I want you and your boys there to go to the village of Carefal about three days from here on my western border."

"Your Grace, I don't understand. Are you saying you need us to travel to this village because a man refuses to pay his taxes?"

"Not quite," Isault said. "I want you to go there because the entire village of Carefal has refused to pay their taxes. You're going to go there, do your little Greatcoats dance and sing some song about the law and make them do their duty."

"But don't you have—?" I looked back toward Shuran.

"I'm not sending my Knights and soldiers to oppress some little village. I'll either lose men or taxpayers. No, boy. You want to put your little girl on the throne? You want to be the law of the land? Fine. Go and prove to us you can administer the law for everyone."

"And if we do this?"

Isault got off his throne, walked down the steps, and held out his hand. "I'll put the full weight of Aramor behind your little girl. We may not have a large standing army, but the Knights of Aramor are the deadliest in the country. I send Shuran out there to stand in front of Trin's soldiers and I'll bet you half of them defect on the spot."

"I . . ." I looked at the others. Kest looked uninterested; his eyes were focused on the shields and swords in the room. Valiana looked disappointed in me and Dari smirked as if she'd just won an argument. Brasti simply looked troubled. I knew how he felt; I was too. But I couldn't see I had much choice. There was no way we could ever put Aline on the throne without the support of at least some of the Dukes, and no Duke was more likely to help than Isault. "Very well. I'll go to Carefal. If the people there are refusing to pay their taxes, as you say, then I'll judge in your favor."

We shook hands.

"Go then," the Duke said. "Shuran will go with you with some of his men to keep you from being killed if it comes down to it."

As the five of us walked toward the exit at the other end Isault called out to me, "That girl?" I stopped and turned back to look at him. "I said I'd help you put her on the throne, and I will. But she'll never last, Falcio. Thirteen years old? She'll be dead a week after she's crowned."

10
THE TROUBADOURS

There's a hundred-mile stretch of road between the Ducal Palace of Aramor and the farming village of Carefal. It's a nice two-day ride if you like listening to the sound of horses grunting up and down rolling hills, in between periodically slipping on the broken gray shale that peels off from the narrow mountains like the scabs from a leper's arms.

"Your roads could do with some repair, Sir Shuran," I called back to the Knight-Commander riding close behind me with his men. He had taken the time to introduce me to all nine of them, but since none had been willing to shake my hand I'd decided to reciprocate by instantly forgetting their names.

"The state of the roads in Aramor isn't exactly a Knight's responsibility," Shuran replied. "Was it the practice of the Greatcoats to sweep the stairs and mop the floors at Castle Aramor?"

"Give him time," Brasti said, leaving Kest's side and riding up next to me. "I'm sure Falcio will get to it once he's done doing the rest of the Dukes' dirty work for them."

"Be quiet, Brasti," Kest said, more out of habit than from any evidence that his admonitions did any good.

If you find a hundred miles on horseback fighting nausea passes too quickly, one solution is to bring along a man who, nominally at least, is supposed to be your subordinate, and have him carp at you like a fishwife the entire way.

I'd hoped that Dariana might save me by subjecting us all to one of her elaborate polemics on the quality of Brasti's manhood. Unfortunately, she and Valiana had chosen to ride behind us and all I heard from them were occasional spurts of laughter. It shouldn't have bothered me that the two of them were forming a bond, but it did. Dari was an effective enough instructor for Valiana and she could even be affable in her own way (although that usually involved talk about maiming people), but beneath her Saints-may-care demeanor she was a blood-soaked killer who slaughtered her opponents without a second thought. My horse slipped on a piece of shale and nearly threw me off, reminding me to keep my eyes focused on the road ahead.

One of Shuran's men said something I didn't quite catch, which was followed by a loud snort. It took me a moment to realize the Knights were still enjoying Brasti's barb. Knights apparently derive a great deal of entertainment from listening to Greatcoats insult each other. I suppose watching us beat each other to death would amuse them too, and that was looking more and more like a distinct possibility.

Shuran looked at me as if he were about to broach a sensitive subject, then finally spoke up. "I confess, First Cantor, that I'm not sure I understand your chain of command. If one of my Knights spoke to me in such a manner he would face a severe reprimand."

"I'll get to it when I have time."

"Perhaps you could simply dock his pay?" Shuran offered helpfully.

Brasti's laughter was so sudden and high-pitched it bordered on giggling. "There has to be pay for someone to withhold it."

Shuran looked surprised. "You don't pay your men?"

"Do I look like a King?" I said. "What, do you pay your men?"

Shuran turned to the Knight who had laughed earlier. "Sir Elleth, who pays your weekly wage?"

"You do, Knight-Commander."

"And should you be wounded, who pays the healer?"

"You do, Knight-Commander."

"If you should fall in battle, who will pay the pension to your family?"

"You will—"

"Hold on a second," I said. "Doesn't he work for the Duke?"

"He *serves* the Duke," Shuran said. "We all do, but it is the responsibility of the Knight-Commander to pay his men." Shuran's voice became noticeably pious. "It would sully the sacred bond of our service to the Duke should our lord be required to pay us compensation. It would be like asking the Gods to give us a salary in exchange for living our lives well."

"Finally! A religious doctrine I could support," Brasti said. He held his horse's reins between his hands as if in devout prayer. "Oh great Goddess Love, I shall walk the long and lonely roads of this country bringing your message of compassion to anyone who needs it. I will bow my head at every sign of beauty and sing your praises morning, midday, and throughout the night." He turned to us with a wicked grin on his face. "In exchange I'd like a weekly salary of twelve silver stags with a bonus of two stags on market days. Also, a small cottage would be nice. Nothing too grand, you understand, just—"

"Be quiet, Brasti," Kest and I said together.

The Knights were having a grand time of it, and Brasti didn't seem to mind. He liked being the center of attention, even if that attention came from Ducal Knights, each and every one of whom he despised, just on principle.

The idea of the commander paying his men from his own pocket struck me as odd. And expensive. "Wait a second. If you have to pay every Ducal Knight under your command, who pays you?"

"The Duke, obviously," Brasti said.

"But would that not sully the service he provides?" Kest asked, finally taking an interest in the conversation. In addition to being the best swordsman in the world, Kest has an unnatural fascination with bureaucracy.

"It would indeed blemish my service were I to be paid," Shuran said. "We are holy men, after all."

Brasti started to say something rude, but Kest interrupted him. "So am I right to assume that it does not diminish your service should the Duke, on occasion, grant you a gift in admiration for your noble character?"

Shuran gave a small smile. "Such a gift would be an affirmation of my fulfillment of my God's will."

"And should such gifts happen with some degree of regularity—?"

"Well, I do try to be noble on a weekly basis." His smile widened. "I am known to be especially noble on Wednesdays."

I tried to calculate in my head what kind of gift was required to support the pay of more than a thousand Knights, but sums have never been my strong point. Eventually I gave up. "So you pay your men from the Duke's 'gifts'?" I asked.

"That's part of it, but that would only cover the barest salary and expenses of my men."

"Then where does the rest come from?"

Shuran signaled the others to slow and pulled back on his horse's reins. "That," he said, "is a matter that requires a lengthier conversation."

Valiana brought her horse up close to ours. "Why are we slowing down?"

Shuran pointed to a two-story wooden building about a hundred yards ahead, nearly hidden by trees. "There's an inn up ahead. They don't have much for rooms, but we can get food and drink and make camp nearby."

"I've traveled this way before with my mother . . ." She shook her head as if trying to clear it. "I mean, with the erstwhile Duchess of Hervor." There was a note of sadness in her voice. It had only been a few weeks since Valiana had discovered in singularly unpleasant fashion that she wasn't the daughter of a duchess. "Anyway," she continued, "I'm fairly certain there's a much better inn ten miles down the road that would have rooms for us."

"Forgive me, my lady," Shuran said, "but it's getting late and I prefer not to work the horses too hard. We'll stay here tonight and make for the village of Carefal in the morning."

"If they haven't got rooms for us, then what's the point?" Brasti asked.

"There'll be food, for us and the horses, and they're known to have entertainment that I suspect you'll appreciate."

"And the Duke's hammer came down," the storyteller said. Despite his youthful appearance, his voice deep and resonant, as if Saint Anlas-who-remembers-the-world himself were channeling his words through the man. The light of the fire cast shadows about the large room, illuminating his handsome features as if he were some creature born of magic. Straight dark hair reached down to his chin, and he sported the short mustache and beard common among troubadours. They probably think it makes them look wise. Or dashing. Actually, I'm not sure why they do it. He wore a blue shirt under a black waistcoat that matched his pants; I noted that they were patched in several places.

The woman sitting on a stool next to him plucked at the strings of a short traveling guitar in accompaniment to his story. She also wore blue and black, but she was in every other way a contrast to him: sandy-brown hair framed a round, plain face, set atop a thick body that showed neither curves nor sensuality. But the music that came from her instrument, mostly simple arpeggios performed expertly, made the storyteller's otherwise banal performance enthralling.

"But did our hero fear the Duke's power?" the storyteller demanded of his audience. "Did he move even an inch as the Duke's soldiers came for him?"

The thirty or forty farmers and tradesmen who currently filled the tables of The Inn at the End of the World were far too rapt—by either the story or their drinks—to respond, and the troubadour took this as license to continue, waving his hands through the smoke emanating from patrons' pipes. "He feared not, friends, for his sword arm was strong, yes, but his voice . . . his words—they were mighty indeed. You might say he was something of a troubadour!"

That got a laugh, mostly from Brasti.

"What'll you have, Trattari?" the barman asked, quietly, so as not to disturb the story being told at the other end of the common room. "We've got beer at three black pennies per, or a decent wine for five. We've got some beef for dinner at only one silver steer."

I let the "Trattari" slide. Half the people in the countryside don't even know that it means tatter-cloak, or that it's an insult. Or maybe they just don't care.

"We don't get beef around here so often," the barman went on, leaning in as if he were letting us in on the deal of the century. "It's nigh as rare as mutton."

"Possibly because we're 'at the End of the World'?" Kest asked.

"Uh, well, aye, I suppose."

"We're not actually at the end of the world," Brasti said. "I mean, it's certainly not far from the south, but it's not the end of the world by any means. And if it was, pretty much every inn from Baern to Pertine would have to be called 'The Inn at the End of the World.'" Brasti looked around. "Come to think of it, this isn't actually an inn so much as a tavern, is it?"

"It's got a room," the barman said tersely. "That makes it an inn."

"Where's the room?" Brasti asked.

He pointed outside. "Over there. It's got a bed 'n' everything."

"Isn't that a barn?" Kest asked.

"There's no horses in it," the barman replied.

"Yes, but still, it's not actually—"

"Look, Trattari," the barman said, "if you and your little company don't want a room, you don't need to pay for a room. If you want to call this a tavern instead of an inn, you're welcome to do so. So what'll the three of you have? The beer at five pennies per, the wine for seven, or the beef for a silver and three pennies?"

"Wait a second, you said—"

"Those were inn rates. These are tavern rates. Happy?"

I reached into one of my pockets for five silvers, feeling for the ones with the silver steer of Aramor embossed on them. I put them on the bar one by one. "We'll have five beef dinners," I said, "and you'll throw in the five beers."

"What? That's not near enough. What're you doin', robbing me now, Trattari?"

I pointed to some of the shabby-looking patrons at the tables eating their dinners. "Those men didn't come in here with silver and they seem to be eating just fine, and drinking, too. Neither beef nor mutton is rare in these parts, perhaps because Aramor is known for its livestock," I said, pointing a finger at the steer imprinted on the silver coin. "And finally, if the next phrase out of your mouth includes the word 'Trattari' I'll pay you your extra black pennies but you'll have to shit them out in the morning, along with your front teeth, to count them."

The barman looked less aghast than annoyed. "Fine. Fine. Five dinners for five silvers."

"And ten beers," Brasti reminded him.

"Aye, and five beers. I'll pour them into ten cups if it pleases you." As he turned away from us, the barman muttered, "You might be Greatcoats, but you're no Falsios, I'll tell you that much for free."

Falsios?

Brasti pulled me by the shoulder toward the last empty table in the common room, where the girls were waiting for us. It was in the far corner, away from most of the other patrons and deep in the shadows, which suited us fine. Shuran had taken food from the inn (which the Knights, apparently, weren't expected to pay for) and gone back to the camp where his men were setting up for the night. Apparently the entertainment here wasn't all that interesting to them.

The female troubadour was strumming her guitar so smoothly it was almost impossible to tell where one chord changed to another, even as her little finger plucked a melody over the top of her partner's song.

"She's incredible," Valiana said, watching every movement of the musician's hands.

Dariana shrugged. "She stays in tune. That's more than I can say for the singer."

"No, you don't understand. When I lived in Hervor we often had troubadours come to perform in the palace. They were skilled, all of them, or else my moth—the Duchess would never have allowed them to play. This woman, she's something else . . . her fingers are like water gliding over river rocks."

"Well, I've no ear for such subtleties," Dariana said. Then she winced. "Though I may well have to kill her partner if he goes flat again."

I turned my attention back to the performance, listening both for the masterful guitar playing and the uneven singing.

And lo, the light broke through the dark,
The wolf's howls stayed by the song of the lark,
His words, once spoken, forever would stand,
And make their way 'cross this troubled land.

The singer stopped but the woman continued to strum softly, easing the audience out of the performance. "And thus ends my story, friends and countrymen. May it warm your hearts and give you courage when the darkest nights are upon us. If you think it might, perhaps you would give a coin or three to a troubadour long absent from his home and hearth."

One of the patrons shouted "Coin? For a story? This beer's all the courage that'll do for us!"

"Aye," another said, "keep your silly girls' songs."

The man next to him punched him in the shoulder. "Leave be, Jost, there's nothing wrong with a story now and then. T'aint the point t'were it true or not."

"Ah," the storyteller said, his voice still smooth, "but I'm one of the *Bardatti*, my friends." He looked around as if that revelation should produce a reaction in the audience. It didn't. "The tales I tell are more real than that moon you see outside, and more honest than even the strong trees in the forest."

At this point Jost stood up. "You're tellin' me that whole thing is true? That some fool managed to rile up the Duke hisself, what? And the people all just stood up and saved some little girl just on his say-so?"

Jost swallowed his remaining beer and looked as if he might be thinking of throwing the cup at the bard.

"Don't you go makin' trouble now, Jost," the barman said as he laid down plates in front of us. I noticed the beef was severely outmatched by the onions and potatoes. A lithe young woman with red hair set down our beers and gave Brasti a smile. Brasti smiled back and was about to speak, but I jabbed him with my elbow.

Jost threw up his hands. "Ah, leave me be, Berret, ah'm not doin' nobody no harm. Just don't like people what lie to me and then ask for coin, that's all."

"Then you're in the wrong tavern!" someone else chimed in.

"Inn," Berret said angrily. He turned to me. "See what you've started?"

"Friends! Friends!" the storyteller said, standing. He looked nervous, realizing his chance at coin was slipping away. The woman with him paid no attention, just continued picking out a low, sweet tune. "Pay me or not, it's your choice. But question not the word of a true Bardatti"—and here he made his voice deeper, as if it might terrify the crowd into tossing him their money—"for it's ill luck to slight a man of Saint Anlas-who-remembers-the-world. I tell you the story is true, and only I know it so well, for I was there that day." He put one foot up on the stool and pointed southwards as if he were captaining a ship. "Aye. I was in Rijou that very morning. I saw him speak. I was one of his twelve. And here, if you need more proof." The troubadour raised his fingers and a coin appeared between them. It was gold and had the King's symbol on it—a seven-pointed crown, along with a sword behind it. My mouth went dry. It was a Greatcoat's coin, the ones we give jurors who risk their own lives to uphold verdicts. A single gold coin could feed an entire family for more than a year.

There was a kind of gasp that emerged from the audience. "So it's true . . ." Jost said, his hand reaching out of its own accord toward the coin.

The troubadour made it disappear again. "Every word."

"Well then," another man said, standing up and looking around at his tablemates to see how much support he could drum up, "seems to me a man with a gold coin can afford to buy all of us a round, eh?"

"No," the storyteller said, "a true juryman would never part with his coin. And I would sell my very soul before I gave up this one, given to me by the Greatcoat himself."

"Then where is he now, this hero of yours? Lives in some castle with a dozen wives, does he?"

The storyteller looked over at us and for a moment I thought he might point us out to the crowd, but the woman with the guitar hit a slightly discordant note and the man turned back to the crowd. "That I don't know, my friend. No one does. But wherever he is, I pray Falsio is somewhere warm, eating a fine meal and enjoying good beer tonight." Then the troubadour lifted his cup high in the air. "To Falsio Dal Vond!" he said.

The crowd raised their cups. "To Falsio Dal Vond!" they said in unison.

I looked at Brasti, who was staring at me with a ridiculous smile on his face. "Put down your damned cup, you fool," I said.

"What's the problem? We're famous! And not for the usual things like, you know, murder, cowardice, and treason." Brasti glanced around the room, probably looking for the redheaded waitress.

"I'm not sure how Falcio's fame extends to us," Kest said.

"Don't you recall? We were right there with him—twenty, no, *fifty* ducal guardsmen came rushing for him when you and I stepped up and saved Falcio with my bow. I killed fifteen of them in the first few minutes."

"And how many did I kill?" Kest asked.

Brasti pursed his lips and looked up as if he were counting sums in his head. "Two," he said finally. "Maybe three."

"That's—"

"Enough," I said.

"Now, now," Brasti said, "no need be so—"

"Shut up." I thought through the details of the troubadour's story, wishing I'd listened more carefully from the start. I didn't know whether he'd been in Rijou or not, but he wasn't one of the jurymen, that I would have remembered. What was really bothering me was that Brasti was right. It had been years since any of us had heard a tale about the Greatcoats that didn't involve accusations us of cowardice and betrayal. I was surprised the troubadour dared say anything good about us in public—and yet the audience had applauded. They appeared willing to believe I was some kind of hero, standing up to the Dukes. I couldn't imagine such a story would find favor with a man like Isault. *Ah, hells.*

"What is it?" Kest asked.

"I know why Isault sent us to deal with this village uprising."

"Because of the troubadour? It's just one story, Falcio."

"It won't be just here," Valiana said. "If such a ballad's made it to a little backwater tavern like this, it's being told all over. Falcio's right. Word must be spreading that the Greatcoats are coming back and Isault is afraid that the common folk are starting to admire all of you again."

Admire all of you *again.* I heard it in her tone and saw again that sadness in her eyes that told me that she considered herself an outsider. I considered saying something, but right now I had more urgent matters to deal with than Valiana's feelings. Behind her I saw Dariana's eyes catch mine, and she mouthed the word "idiot."

"Admire *us*," I said and clapped her on the shoulder. "Don't think you're getting out of this mess. We're all in the same soup."

She smiled, just a bit, and Dariana mouthed *better* at me.

"Fine," Brasti said, still trying to attract the attention of the pretty waitress. "We're all in terrible, terrible trouble. People like us again. Whatever will we do?"

"You don't understand," I said. "This is why Isault wanted us to come out here. It's not to prove we can be trusted to enforce the laws. He wants us to put down the village rebellion and then he's going to make sure the whole world hears about it. He's using us to destroy our own reputation."

Brasti gestured to the redheaded waitress, who was now standing near the door, and when she smiled back at him, rose from the table. "Well, you worry about it if you want, Falcio. But don't spend too much time on it. It's just a story, after all."

Brasti never did understand how powerful a story could be.

11

THE VILLAGE

"Is there any way we could go back to inhaling the Dashini dust?" Brasti asked. "Because while that involved being scared out of my wits and mumbling like a madman while pissing and shitting myself, I swear this is worse."

"What? What are you talking about?" I asked. When no sound came from my mouth I realized it was morning and I was hallucinating from the paralysis again. *How long will it be this time?* I wondered.

Despite my eyes being closed, I could see a large room in front of me, the bare stone flags a stark contrast to the purple and silver hangings on the walls. It was hazy, of course, as hallucinations always are. Yet it still felt as if I were there, with two dozen Greatcoats, men and women I hadn't seen in years, sitting on the floor next to Kest and Brasti. We were back in Castle Aramor, training in one form of combat we'd never expected to study.

Salima, the troubadour the King had hired to teach us to sing, struck an angry chord on her guitar. I swear it gave me a pain in the back of my head whenever she did that.

"If you open your mouth again and I do not hear music coming from it," she said, her voice dark and rich, "I will play such a song that will drive you to run off a cliff to your doom."

Brasti looked troubled for a moment, then grinned and opened his mouth and in a sing-song voice said, "If you keep making me sing, I'll run off the cliff without any further prompting."

Salima started plucking single strings on the guitar, fast and furious notes that never seemed to find a melody. Each one sounded ever so slightly off-key, though I'd heard her retuning only moments before. The notes got faster and faster, and as they did, my mind struggled more and more to make sense of them. But it couldn't, and what began as a mild annoyance soon turned to a fearsome anxiety that threatened to overcome me. It suddenly occurred to me that the old stories of the Bardatti being able to drive a man mad with their songs might be true. Through the haze of pain and uncertainty I began, very slowly, to try to unsheathe my sword.

"Saints, are we under attack?" The King's voice shattered the spell instantly—or at least his arrival in the room got Salima to stop playing. "Troubadour? Are we engaging in experimental melodies this evening?"

She smiled up at him from where she sat cross-legged on the floor. Bardatti never appeared to be too concerned about offending the nobility. "Merely chastising them, your Majesty. These 'Greatcoats' of yours have very little discipline."

The King agreed, apparently. "A problem I have yet to rectify. And yet I find your solution equally painful to me, and I can assure you, I have no issues with my own level of discipline."

"Your Majesty," Brasti said, standing up, "will you not put a stop to this? I can't imagine I'm going to sing my way out of a duel, nor will my voice ever make a Duke accept a verdict he doesn't like."

"It's not for the Dukes, Brasti, and it's not for you, either."

"Then forgive me, Sire, but I'm lost as to the point. It's not like I'm going to launch a career singing for farmers and blacksmiths in inns and taverns, is it? So why are you making us all do this?"

The King didn't answer. He had a habit of making us do things without giving us the reason. His argument was that a lesson you had to be told seldom stuck as much as one you had figured out on your own. The King always did have an overly ambitious impression of our skills as students.

"It's the melodies, isn't it?" Kest asked. His eyes had a faraway look, as though he were trying to do sums in his head. "We need people in the towns and villages to remember the verdicts we issue, but most of them can't read and none of them will remember our words."

"But everyone remembers a good bar song. Right, Brasti?"

Brasti grinned. "I know a good many, your Majesty. Have I ever told you the one about the maiden who woke up to find diamonds in her—"

"Shut up, Brasti," I said.

"'The Maiden's Diamonds'," Salima said. "The melody is called 'The Traveler's Third Reel'. It's the same as is used for 'Coppers & Ale' and for 'The Old Man's Bite'."

I thought about that for a moment. I'd heard "The Old Man's Bite" a time or two, and "Coppers & Ale" was sung in half the taverns in Tristia. "You're right," I said. "I'd never noticed that."

"And do you remember the words to those songs?" the King asked.

I nodded, and so did everyone else.

"Good," King Paelis said. "Then you'll learn 'The Traveler's Third Reel'. And the first and second and fourth, and however many others we need. Then you'll learn to set your verdicts to them. That way—"

"That way every farmer and blacksmith will remember the verdicts we issue," I said. "They'll remember them long after we leave. Hells, they'll probably end up singing them whenever they get drunk."

The King smiled. Sometimes he was a very clever man. When he noticed me staring he stopped smiling. "And then you will betray her, Falcio," he said, and he turned and walked away from me.

"What? No!" I tried to rise from the floor but I couldn't move. The sensation of paralysis brought me back to myself and to the hard ground on which I slept.

"Easy," a voice said, and I felt a gentle pressure on my shoulder.

My eyes opened reluctantly and let in the morning light. Kest was watching me. "You're awake now," he said.

I tried to say something clever but couldn't quite get the words out yet.

"The others are getting ready to leave," Kest said. He rose and reached down a hand to help me up. "It was nearly an hour this time, Falcio."

We traveled that day in silence. Even Brasti knew enough not to make me any more angry than I already was. If I failed to deliver what the Duke asked for, he would never support Aline. If I did, he might still break his oath, and either way the Greatcoats would once again be seen as traitors to the people of Tristia. *You will betray her.*

"We'll be in Carefal soon," Shuran said, pulling his horse up to mine.

I didn't reply. I didn't feel much like talking to the Knight-Commander of Aramor that day.

After a few awkward moments Shuran said, "Maybe another mile."

"What happens when we arrive?" I said at last.

"We'll meet a man named Tespet. He's the Duke's tax collector for this region. He and his clerk will brief us on the current state of affairs with the villagers."

"Fine," I said.

"You're quiet today, Falcio."

When it became clear he wasn't going to leave me alone, I asked, "Did you know?"

"Know what?"

"The story that's been going around about me and what happened in Rijou? And that Isault made this deal with me so that the

Greatcoats would be seen to have broken faith with the common people."

"*Duke* Isault consults me on many things, Falcio, but politics is seldom one of them."

"And still, somehow I think you knew," I said.

"Oh? Why would you say that?"

"The 'entertainment' you mentioned yesterday—did you have us stop at that inn just so I could hear the stories? Did you know what the troubadours have been saying about me?"

Shuran looked at me, his expression betraying nothing. "I'm a Knight, Falcio. I don't have much time for stories and songs. They rarely serve my cause." He flicked the reins and his horse pulled ahead.

Brasti stood up in his stirrups and peered ahead. He has the best distance vision of any of us—I suspect being an archer makes good eyesight something of a requirement. "The village is half a mile ahead of us." He shaded his eyes from the sun with one hand. "And there's something outside the village. Two things, actually."

"What are they?"

"It looks like a pair of cages."

"Cages? Can you see what's inside them?"

He sat back down on his horse. "I can't be sure, but if I had to guess, I'd say people."

"Are they dead?" Shuran asked.

The two cages were made out of the trunks of saplings. Inside each one was a man, crouched on the ground.

I got off my horse and reached toward one of the bodies to feel for a pulse but stopped when I saw the chest move in and out. "No, just knocked out." I turned to the big Knight. "If I find out your tax collector Tespet put these men here we're going to have a very big problem."

"He did not," Shuran said.

"How can you be so sure?" Dariana asked, coming closer to see for herself.

He pointed to the man in the cage on the right. "That's Tespet. The other is his clerk."

I got a whiff of the man's breath, then went and knelt down by the second cage. Both men were very drunk.

"Falcio," Kest said, "company."

As I rose I saw nearly forty men and women emerging from the trees lining the road. Some had bows; others carried rudely fashioned clubs. Some were holding swords, and I wondered how they had acquired proper steel weapons.

Sir Shuran's men drew their swords and one of them called out, "On your knees."

"On yours," a woman's voice replied.

"Everyone calm down," I said, holding up a hand in a peaceable fashion. "We're not here to cause trouble."

The woman came closer. "You'll cause us no trouble, travelers, if you turn back around and go the way you came." She had short brown hair and a sturdy frame. She might have been forty, but then again, she could have been in her twenties; village life in Tristia was not easy. She pointed a sword at Shuran. "The Knights will stay as our hostages."

"I don't think that will be possible," Shuran said. "I'm fairly sure my orders include not being captured."

The woman ignored the Knight and looked more closely at me. "Are those Greatcoats you and your company are wearing?"

"Why do they always assume he's in charge?" Brasti asked Kest.

"Shut up, Brasti," Kest replied.

"These are Greatcoats," I said.

The woman grimaced. "Then you'll be staying too. We don't take kindly to those who steal greatcoats."

Valiana took an imprudent step closer to the woman. "You'll not take from us what is ours by right," she said. "What makes you think we're not Greatcoats?"

An old man awkwardly holding a longbow, his arms shaking on the bent string, making me worry he'd end up killing one of us for no better reason than that his arm got tired, said, "Whoever heard of a Greatcoat mucking about with Knights?"

Brasti looked at me as if this somehow proved his point.

"My name is Falcio," I said to the woman, "First Cantor of the King's Greatcoats. These are Kest, Brasti, Dari, and Valiana. The Knights with us are—"

The woman's laughter cut me off. She turned to her men. "Look, boys, Duke Isault decided to put on a show for us. He's sent actors to put on a play. 'The Hero of Rijou and the Slayer of Saint Caveil'!"

"Oh, aye," one of the men said, waving a pitchfork in the air. "Falsio himself, here to liberate us! Come on, Vera, quit playing around. Let's kill them and be done with it."

"Wait," Brasti said, "what about me?"

"What about you?" Vera asked.

"I'm Brasti Goodbow. Haven't you heard of me?"

"'fraid not."

"Don't worry though," the man with the pitchfork said, "we'll kill you just as if you were famous, too."

Sir Shuran put a hand on the pommel of his warsword. "I think you'll find us difficult to murder."

"There's more of us than there are of you," Pitchfork said. He motioned around at the other villagers. Few among them looked like warriors; they were simply farmers and merchants. A young girl with a knife in her hand brandished it defiantly, and for an instant I mistook her for Aline. *Saints, don't let me start hallucinating while I'm awake.*

A few of Shuran's Knights laughed aloud and Vera looked at them through narrowed eyes. "Giggle all you want, *Sir Knights*, but some of us have heard enough of your laughter to fill a lifetime." She nodded to one of her men on the other side and then the two of them pulled on ropes I now saw were looped around the branches of two trees lining the sides of the path and a set of crudely fashioned spears held together with more sapling trunks rose up from the ground. At the same time, twenty more villagers appeared behind the others, all carrying a bow or a sling or a sword or even just handfuls of rocks.

I looked at Kest, who shook his head. I agreed; there wasn't an easy way around this. All the time we were trying to navigate around the spears to reach our opponents, the villagers could pepper us with arrows and rocks.

"What's the matter, *Sir Knights*? Not laughing now?"

"You're making a mistake," I said.

"Really? Because it seems to me that capturing the men sent to kill us and holding them hostage could hardly be a mistake."

"If we'd come to kill you," Sir Shuran said, "we would have brought thirty Knights and you'd all be dead by now. I am Sir Shuran, Knight-Commander of Aramor. Duke Isault sent us to settle your dispute in good faith."

The villagers looked wary. A lifetime spent trying to survive under the weight of the nobility and their greed hardly made for a great deal of trust.

Vera turned to me. "You say you're a Greatcoat. Prove it."

"How would you like me to do that?"

"Tell me the Seventh Law of Property."

I was about to answer but Valiana was ahead of me. "There is no Seventh Law of Property."

Vera tried in vain to stare Valiana down, and watching them, I realized that the two weren't as far apart in age as I'd thought. What differentiated them was that Valiana had spent her eighteen years living in security and luxury and Vera hadn't.

"Fine. What's the Sixth Law then?"

She didn't hesitate. "'The taxing of a thing can never be more than a quarter of the yield it creates.'"

I shouldn't have been surprised that she could quote the King's Laws from memory. It made sense—after all, she'd spent most of her life training to be Queen. No doubt she'd learned all the laws of Tristia, even those the Dukes would never have allowed her to enforce.

Vera eyed Valiana suspiciously. "Anyone who can read *The Book of the King's Laws* could know that."

Valiana frowned. She really could look like the epitome of the arrogant noblewoman when she set her mind to it. "Then why did you bother asking?"

"If you hadn't known the answer I might have saved myself some time," she said.

I looked out at the villagers who'd come ready to fight. I doubted even one of them knew the King's Laws of Property, or any other laws for that matter. "Well, it doesn't seem to have worked," I said. "Do you even know why the King wrote the Sixth Law of Property?"

"So that the Dukes wouldn't be able to deprive us of what we earn through our labors."

"That's part of it," I acknowledged.

"That's the only part that matters."

"Not to a monarch," Valiana said. "If the Duke overtaxes your land here, it creates shortages of supplies of food, lumber, and other resources for you to trade, and that then causes shortages in other goods, and eventually the whole system falls apart. The reason for the law is to prevent an economic collapse."

"Why are you telling me this?" Vera asked.

"So that you know that the King wanted you to pay your damned taxes," I said.

Vera snorted. "You're funny. When you're dead I'll mount your head on a spike and perhaps it'll help me laugh when I've had a hard day working the fields."

"He's not that funny when he's dying," Brasti said. "He gets quite preachy."

I heard the sound of an arrow flying and felt the air shiver near my left cheek as it passed and landed in a tree just behind me. The old man's arm had finally given out. Before I could react, one of Shuran's men had brought his blade up and taken a step forward. "The penalty for attacking one of the Duke's envoys is death, old man."

"Stop!" I yelled, pulling my left rapier from its sheath.

"The Trattari betray us!" one of the other Knights said, and shifted position, ready to attack me.

A moment later ten Knights were facing the five of us, two of the Knights holding suddenly loaded crossbows, while we were stuck between the sharpened logs the villagers had set all around us.

"Falcio . . ." Kest began.

"I know the odds, damn it. Put down your swords," I said to the Knights. "This isn't why we came here, Shuran."

The Knight-Commander hadn't drawn his weapon. "I agree. That's why I need you, your men, and these villagers to put down their weapons. I can't have people drawing on the Duke's own Knights."

Vera sneered. "The incentive for killing all of us is considerably higher if we're not holding weapons."

"Put down your weapons," Shuran repeated, "or I'll have no choice but to order my men to fight."

"You give that order," I said, "and I'll order Brasti to kill you first."

The old man who had started all this leaned heavily on his bow, apparently unconcerned. "Now, see, this is more what you expect with Knights and Greatcoats."

One of the villagers started spinning a sling.

"Brasti, keep an eye on that man. Vera, keep your people in check."

"Falcio?" Brasti said.

"I'm busy."

"It's just that it would be helpful to me if you could let me know who I'm supposed to kill right now."

"I'm still trying to work that out."

A crashing sound came from the woods, nearly setting off the battle right then and there. A thin, awkward-looking young man emerged, out of breath and carrying a rapier in his hand. Few men other than me carry rapiers. I had met this one before.

"Cairn?" I asked incredulously.

Guileless brown eyes beneath a mop of brown hair met mine. "Falcio?" He ran up to me and dropped to his knees. "First Cantor! I can't believe it's you! Here in Carefal! Did you come to find me?"

"Get up," I said. The last time I'd seen Cairn was in Rijou, where he'd proven to be almost as eager to be a Greatcoat as he was unsuited to the role. I could tell things hadn't changed since then.

"I merely—"

"First of all, you're not a Greatcoat, so you don't owe me any fealty, and second, Greatcoats don't bow to anyone."

Brasti leaned forward and whispered as loudly as he could, "Except Dukes, as it turns out, when we want our lips to more comfortably reach their asses."

"Shut up, Brasti."

"Cairn, is this true?" Vera asked. "Is this man really who he says he is?"

Cairn stood up. "I don't know who he says he is, but I know him to be Falcio val Mond, First Cantor of the Greatcoats." The boy reached into his pocket and pulled out a gold coin. "He gave me this. I was one of his twelve jurors when he called an end to the Ganath Kalila. This is the Hero of Rijou—the man who inspired our rebellion!"

I winced. Cairn's voice was all pride mixed with religious fervor and to me at least, he sounded like a halfwit who'd just discovered a Saint's face in his cottage cheese. But looking around at the villagers I saw their expressions change, just a little, and understood just how badly they wanted to believe that there were heroes out there coming to save them. For the first time in a long while it looked like they were even willing to believe those heroes might be Greatcoats.

Vera stepped forward until she was less than a foot away and looked into my face as if she were inspecting a coin to see if it had been forged. "Well then, 'Hero of Rijou,'" she said, "have you come to save us, or to betray us?"

12

THE TRIAL

Carefal was a large village, as these things go. Perhaps two hundred people lived there in as much comfort as peasant farming ever allowed. It had a long main street, not paved but well enough maintained that a horse and cart could go down it without breaking a wheel. The thatch-roofed homes were modest, but looked reasonably weatherproof. I noticed not one but two churches, one to Coin, who was called Argentus in Aramor, and the other to Love, whom they referred to as Phenia—the two Gods who best represented the simple desires of simple folk. Mostly what struck me about Carefal, though, were the faces of the people lining the street. Men, women, elderly folk, and small children all watched us go by, and I felt as if we were on parade, except that no one was smiling and waving flags.

When we reached the central square Cairn stood up on the plinth of a stone statue nearly as tall as one of the houses behind it. The figure represented was fat and looked ill-made for war, despite holding a war-ax and being improbably well dressed. I assumed it was meant to be either Duke Isault or one of his predecessors.

"Friends of Carefal!" Cairn shouted. "You know I am not a man for speeches."

Responses from the crowd ranged from "then shut up!" to "thank the Saints for that" to "since when are you a *man*?" So apparently Cairn was held in roughly the same regard here as he had been in Rijou. To his credit, he ignored the jibes. "There, my friends," he said, pointing straight at me, "there stands Falcio val Mond, First Cantor of the Greatcoats. There stands the Hero of Rijou!"

For a moment the crowd was silent. Then a small boy said, "I thought he was called 'Falsio.'"

Then they all went mad.

The people of Carefal swarmed over me. Had Shuran's Knights had the slightest real concern for my safety they would have attacked, but the Knight-Commander kept his men well back from the crowd. Hands touched me, not always in places I deemed entirely polite, and people shouted my name. Some asked questions that I couldn't answer because I was too busy being pulled at by others. Eventually, though, the crowd's voices coalesced into a steady chant of "Falsio! Falsio! Freedom for Carefal! Freedom for Carefal!"

Vera and her men began pushing the others out of the way. "Enough!" she shouted. "Are you all mad? Can you not see that ten Ducal Knights stand here? Can you not see that this man, this 'Falsio' or 'Falcio' or whatever he calls himself, has come here *with* them? Will you fawn over this trained dog while our village is seized by the Duke?"

A few of the villagers continued to shout my name as if it were an answer, but eventually they settled down. I felt a hand on my shoulder and turned to see Kest looking at me. "What is it?" I asked.

"I just thought you might like to know that this is the part where you calm the crowd down before a riot starts and everyone is massacred."

I turned back to the villagers. Saints, but Kest was right: there was a smoldering need in the way they looked at me. It'd been five years since the King died: five years of gradual decay—the steady, day-by-day loss of faith in one's rulers and one's country and ultimately, oneself. Who wouldn't seek out the first strong voice that made sense to follow? And if the only option for self-worth was reckless and doomed rebellion, well, at least it was something, wasn't it?

"My name is Falcio val Mond," I said, and resisted the urge to add, *pronounced Fal-key-oh*, "and yes, I am the First Cantor of the King's Greatcoats. I *was* at Rijou—" The crowd roared. "Yes, well, like most stories you've heard it's probably grown substantially more heroic and noble in the retelling." That bought me a laugh, thank the Saints. "I'm not here to start a war. I'm here to stop one. Those Knights aren't wearing armor for show. If you attack them, they will fight back. If you overwhelm them, others will come and they'll kill each and every one of you. And the only heroic thing I or my fellow Greatcoats will be able to do is die right alongside you. Look to your families. Look to your children. There's nothing noble about falling under the footsteps of an army and leaving the corpses of young ones behind."

The crowd began to settle down, though the looks of hope and admiration were quickly changing to despair and disgust.

"I'm curious," Dariana said. "Is this the same speech you gave in Rijou? Because if it is, I have to say, I think the troubadour told it better."

"Falcio's right," Valiana said, turning to the crowd. "If you don't back down now, you're going to be killed. Every man and woman in your village will die, and for what?"

"They'll die too," Vera said, pointing at the Knights. "And once a few nobles go hungry because there's no one to harvest the crops, well, let's just say I think Isault will put his stomach above his pride!" She drew cheers with that last line.

"You're wrong," Valiana replied. "I know something of the way the Dukes think. They will never allow rebellion to persist in their duchies. Their rule is too precarious for that."

"But that's good, ain't it?" the old man with the bow asked.

"No. It's not good. The fragility of ducal rule means they can never be seen as weak—they would rather burn their duchies to the ground than lose face in front of their rivals."

"Then what's left for us but suffering to please their egos?"

Some of the peasants looked at me as if I might contradict Valiana's words. Part of me wanted to: when a tree is rotten to the core, what's left but to cut it down?

"The Law," I said aloud. "What's left is the Law."

"What would you have us do?" Vera asked. "Set down our weapons and starve to death? Is that what your Law gives us to look forward to?"

"Have you had a bad harvest?" I asked.

Vera snarled, "We've had one of the best harvests in ten years," she said.

"Then what—?"

"They're taxing us to death!" she snapped. "Your armored friends over there and their fat Dukes are pushing us to starvation."

Shuran stepped forward and for a moment Vera looked like she might attack, but blessedly the big Knight held his hands up. "If I may?"

Vera nodded acquiescence, but didn't give an inch. I had to admire her.

"I believe the dispute has to do with where this town sits."

"You mean geographically," I asked, "or politically?"

"Both, as it turns out. Carefal lies on the border between Aramor and Luth. There have been . . . well, disagreements as to which duchy it belongs to."

"In other words, they both tax us!" Vera said.

Cairn stepped forward as if he was going to try to make an effort to speak on behalf of the village, but Vera pushed him back. Apparently the glow of my reputation didn't extend down to him.

Valiana confronted Shuran. "You're saying these people pay taxes twice? There's no precedent in Ducal law for such a thing."

"No," Shuran corrected her, "after a number of border skirmishes the Dukes of Aramor and Luth came to an understanding; Aramor collects the tax in even years and Luth in the odd."

"And both tax us past what is fair," Vera said.

"As it happens, both Aramor and Luth tax at the rate set by the old King: one quarter of the yield."

"That's why you asked us about the King's Sixth Law of Property," I said to Vera.

"Aye, but that's not what we've been charged. Collector Tespet demanded a full half of our yield this year."

"Is that true?" I asked Shuran.

The Knight looked uncomfortable. "There is a legal exemption during times of war. Duke Isault has invoked the exemption this year."

"War? What war?"

"It hasn't started quite yet, but with some of the radical shifts happening in the political landscape the Duke's advisers are quite certain that there will be conflict."

"What 'shifts in the political landscape'?" I asked.

"Well, for one thing, you killed the Duchess of Hervor. You turned the people of Rijou against their Duke and ended the Ganath Kalila." He looked at Valiana. "You also brought down the Ducal Concord's plans to put Patriana's daughter on the throne, which—"

"Does Duke Isault *want* Trin to take the throne?" Valiana demanded.

Shuran spoke calmly. "The Duke wasn't fully aware of her true nature at the time. Like the other Dukes, he thought that you, my lady, were the true-born daughter of Duchess Patriana of Hervor and Duke Jillard of Rijou. The true depth of her conspiracy was hidden from almost everyone."

"Trin will never sit the throne," Valiana said, her hand on the hilt of her sword. "Aline will be Queen."

Shuran turned to me. "You yourselves have come to request Aramor's support against the duchies of the North, so does it not follow that we will soon be at war, and so does the Duke not have the right to gather the resources needed for such a conflict?"

Brasti turned to Kest and whispered theatrically, his voice carrying loud enough for all of us to hear, "Is it just me, or does it look like Falcio has pretty much broken the country?"

Kest looked uncomfortable. "I . . . Actually, Falcio, it does. A bit." He turned to Shuran. "Although it's worth pointing out that the Duke's actions in overtaxing his people will almost assuredly start a war even if none were coming."

"A fair point," Shuran said. "But now this must be resolved. The people of Carefal cannot simply refuse to pay taxes."

"Make us pay if you can!" Vera said. The crowd cheered. They'd had enough of standing around yakking; they were ready for violence. As with any other large group of people, they vastly overestimated how much good being in a crowd would do them.

Kest and Brasti were looking at me. *Damn it. Why am I the one who always has to drop a noose around his own neck?*

"All right," I said at last, "the Duke asked me to resolve this, and resolve it I will." I held up a hand. "Peacefully." I turned to Vera. "Pick whomever you want to argue your side." Turning back to Shuran I asked, "Will Tespet represent the Duke's position?"

"I suspect he is still too drunk. I can speak for the Duke's case. Though I make no promise of agreeing to your verdict. You are here as the Duke's envoy, not as an arbiter of the Law."

"I'm here trying to keep the bloodshed to a minimum. We'll see where this leads, but I suggest you remember that."

Shuran spread his hands. "As you say, let us see where this leads."

I've presided over hundreds of trials in my time as a Greatcoat. I've listened to disputes over sheep-grazing, contracts of marriage and declarations of war between duchies. I've had to enforce verdicts by summoning juries from the townspeople, threatening local rulers with reprisals from the King, and on more occasions than I can count, by dueling a Duke's champion. Never before have I wanted so badly to slit my own throat.

The townspeople had found a large and surprisingly uncomfortable wooden chair for me to sit in while Vera and Shuran stood in front of me and rehearsed the same arguments they had for the past three hours. It all came down to the same question: did the Duke have the right to impose wartime taxes even when there was no actual war? If he did, what stopped Luth from coming and asking for wartime taxes as well? In fact, it wasn't entirely unforeseeable that the people of Carefal might find themselves paying taxes to both Aramor and Luth as the two sides fought each other.

Not that Vera's solution was any more sound. From her perspective, the Duke had voided his right to collect any taxes at all. She came perilously close to demanding that the Duke pay back all the tax he'd taken from them in the previous years.

"Enough," I said at last. "I'll need a few minutes to confer with my fellow Greatcoats." I rose from the chair. My backside was sore and I had a pounding headache—not only from the unwavering rancor from each side, but as much from the way this bitter feud illustrated how badly Tristia was coming apart at the seams. Even if I could get Aline on the throne, how on earth could she ever mend this broken country? Duke Isault's words kept playing themselves over and over in my mind: *she'll be dead a week after she's crowned.*

Brasti sensed my discomfort. "We're not going to let them starve these people, are we?"

"No, but . . . but we do need Isault's support. We can't put Aline on the throne without him. Nothing we do here will achieve anything until there's a monarch on the throne and—"

"Don't start up about politics, Falcio. You've been letting the Tailor lead you around by the nose for weeks now and it's gotten us nowhere. The Duke of Pulnam betrayed us, the Duke of Aramor is manipulating us, and now you want us to turn our backs on these people because you're so desperate to put a thirteen-year-old girl on the throne that you've forgotten that the whole point of the Law is to make peoples' lives better. I like Aline, Falcio, and it really was a miracle beyond any I've heard in story or song that you managed to keep her alive during Blood Week. But she's not my Queen. Not yet."

"You swore an oath to King Paelis," I started.

"Yes: I swore to uphold the laws of Tristia."

"The law says they have to pay their damned taxes."

"Not if it means they starve," Dariana said, crossing her arms and leaning against a post. Her expression made it clear she cared little for the outcome but wasn't going to miss the chance to point out my hypocrisy. "What happens if Knights from Luth come calling tomorrow demanding their war levies as well?"

I started to reply, but Kest stopped me. "Falcio, have you ever considered that maybe this is what the King had in mind?"

"This?" I asked, pointing to the crowd. "Armed villagers declaring themselves independent and starting wars they can't win?"

"Maybe they can win," Kest said. "Not now, not today, but in the future. Maybe this is how it starts."

Kest's words caught me off guard. *Maybe this is how it starts.* The King had no love for the Ducal system. He spent his life trying to find ways to bring the nobility to heel so that the average man or woman could live their lives in some semblance of freedom. But if he'd wanted chaos and civil war he could have done it when we Greatcoats were at our peak—he chose not to. He'd allowed the Dukes to depose him, rather than have us fight them head on. "No," I said, "he wanted his heir on the throne. Aline—"

"You can't let that factor into your judgment," Valiana said.

"Oh? Since when are you ambivalent about Aline's future?" I asked.

"I'm not. She's the King's heir, and I'll die to put her on the throne. But the King's Law is the law only if it's applied without prejudice. You can't decide one way over another simply out of convenience."

It irked me that Valiana should be scolding me about the need to live up to the ideals of the Greatcoats, but she was right.

I looked back at the crowd, standing a hundred yards away, and Shuran's Knights, much nearer. If I found in favor of the Duke, these people would either starve or they would continue to rebel and so die faster. If I found in favor of the villagers, how could I uphold the verdict? I thought back to a conversation I'd once had with the King one late night as we'd debated the finer points of some obscure law we'd found in one of his old books. "When there's no right thing to do, the Gods command that we follow the letter of the law," he'd said. I'd asked whether the Gods would smile on us for doing so. "Smile on us? No, Falcio, I'm quite sure that following the letter of the law will get you smited even faster than breaking it."

"What?" Brasti asked.

"Hmm?" I said.

"You chuckled. Or coughed. Maybe you were about to sneeze, but it was something. Have you made a decision? Do we side with Isault or with the villagers?"

"The Law," I said. "We follow the Law."
Come, you Gods, I thought. *Come and get me.*

My verdict had exactly one virtue: no one liked it. Shuran's Knights called me a traitor and a coward for failing to fulfill my promise to the Duke (which, in their minds, obviously meant shutting up the villagers and getting back in time for supper). The villagers called me a traitor and a coward (in fairness, by their logic anything other than killing the Knights with my bare hands was a betrayal).

"The law says one quarter of the yield," I repeated for the third time. "There is no lawful declaration of war, therefore wartime levies cannot be imposed. There is also no cause for rebellion, which, I should point out, will mean a great deal more starvation than paying the taxes. The monies levied thus far by the Duke's tax collector, who needs to be released as soon as he's sobered up, by the way, will count toward this year's taxes."

There were a number of arguments, counterarguments, and outright insults, most of which were directed at me. When I'd had enough I let them know I'd be leaving momentarily and they'd be free to kill each other if that was truly what they wished. The villagers grumbled, but eventually even Vera agreed. "Marked," she said at last.

I thought the Knights were going to be trouble, but Shuran silenced them and said, "Marked."

"Really?" I asked in near disbelief.

"It's not a perfect solution," he said, "but it's not a perfect world, either."

"Knight-Commander," one of Shuran's men called out. He was young, maybe twenty, with black hair and a sparse beard that looked a trifle ambitious for him.

"Yes, Sir Walland?"

"These people must turn over their weapons, sir."

Shuran frowned. "Sir Walland, I did not ask for your opinion."

Sir Walland stiffened his shoulders. "Begging your pardon sir, it's the most ancient of Ducal Laws: a man may possess an iron-forged weapon only if he be under the direct service of the Duke. Sir."

Shuran was tight-lipped as he looked at his overzealous junior Knight, but after a moment he sighed. "He's right. These people must disarm. The forged weapons must come with us."

I'd known this since the outset, but Knights are often ignorant of the specifics of the law, even those set by their own Dukes, and I'd hoped that would be the case here. However, it appeared that Sir Walland was a more astute student of Ducal Law than most. I turned to Valiana, just in case she might know of any exception I could apply.

But she shook her head. "He's right," she said. "Every duchy in the country has a similar law."

"Why?" Brasti asked. "What do you care as long as they pay their taxes?"

Shuran's annoyance transferred to Brasti. "Because we can't have armed peasants ready to attack the Duke's representative the next time they decide they don't like his policies."

Dariana barked out a laugh. "See, I think armed peasants are exactly what the Duke needs to make sure he keeps his representatives in check."

"On this we will have to disagree." Shuran kept his tone light, but there was no doubt in my mind that he'd not brook any further incitement.

A stoop-backed man raised a sword. "Well, what if we don't care much for what you think, Sir Knight?"

"Then," Shuran said, his hand moving to the hilt of his sword, "we will have to find a different way to resolve the question."

"What compromise will you accept?" I asked Shuran.

"Any that ensures the people of this village follow the Duke's Law and are not in a position to attack him or his representatives."

"What guarantee can you give me that these people won't be punished after we leave?"

"So long as they do not take up arms again, they will not be harmed. On this, you have my word."

A woman with a farmer's strong build and gray in her hair stepped forward and spat on the ground between us. "A Knight's word. A Knight's *honor.*" She lifted her arms to show the backs of her hands. Lines of scars riddled skin that was a singular leathery brown. "Ten years ago my husband died trying to fend off Knights from Luth when they claimed we owed them taxes. They took everything we had. When the tax collector from Aramor came a week later with his own two Knights and heard my story they said I owed the taxes anyway. They said that if my husband couldn't protect our land then we didn't deserve to hold it. I slapped the bastard once—just once, mind you. They dragged me to the smithy and held my hands against the furnace. But they held the backs against it, not the front, see? They wanted to make sure I could still work the land the Duke claimed to pay off my debt. To the hells with Knights' words and Knights' honor!"

As Shuran took a step toward her Brasti nocked an arrow and I pulled my rapier, but the big Knight raised a hand to us. "Abide," he said.

"I was not always a Knight," Shuran said, removing his helm and revealing the burnt left side of his face. "I wasn't born to a noble family. My father was no more a Knight than any of you are."

The farmer stared dumbfounded at Shuran's face. He reached out and took her hand and gently placed the back of it against the skin of his face. "We are not so different," he said.

The farmer withdrew her hand. "Except that I fight to make things better and you fight to keep them the same."

I admired Shuran's attempt to bridge the gap with the villagers. He was a natural leader—more so than anyone I'd met other than King Paelis himself. I also admired the farmer and the way that neither threats nor flattery could sway her sense of right and wrong. But in the end there wasn't much that any amount of courage could do about the fact that peasants weren't allowed to keep proper weapons, not unless they were in the Duke's service.

"The steel-forged weapons must go with us," I said. Several of the Knights began to smirk. "But you have to buy them."

One of Shuran's men nearly drew, but the Knight-Commander stopped him with a wave. "How much?" he asked.

"Ten—no, twenty stags a piece," Vera suggested.

"Marked," Shuran said.

She looked surprised by how quickly he agreed.

"What about our tools?" the pitchfork man said.

Shuran smiled. "You can keep your tools. We can't very well collect taxes if you can't work your farms."

"Bows are for hunting," Brasti said suddenly. "They need them for deer to help get through the winter."

For a moment I thought Shuran would argue the point but instead he nodded and said, "Fine. Bows are needed for hunting and after all, are not a proper weapon anyway." He turned to the crowd. "But I saw three crossbows among you. Those come with us."

There were complaints and small efforts at hiding weapons, but in the end, everyone did their part. You wouldn't be able to say the Knights and the villagers parted as friends but at least no one died in the process.

An hour later we left the village. I urged my horse forward to ride parallel with Shuran. "Will the Duke be angry?" I asked.

Shuran turned to me, a quizzical expression on his face. "What cause would he have for displeasure?"

"Because the villagers will be paying less tax now than before. And you're coming back with your coin purse significantly lighter."

The big Knight started laughing.

"What's so funny?" I asked.

"I'm sorry," he said, "I meant no disrespect. It's just that—"

"What?"

"Well, you set the rate of taxation at one-quarter of the annual worth."

"And?"

"It's just that the Duke empowered me to go as low as one-fifth to settle the uprising. And these swords? They would cost me fifty stags apiece if I had them forged in the smithies of Aramor, so I'll be making a tidy sum when next we need to replace our weapons."

Hells.

Shuran clapped a hand on my shoulder. "You're an excellent negotiator," he said. "You should ask the Duke for a job."

13

SAINT'S FEVER

We found rooms in a small inn twenty miles from Carefal. The others passed the evening in the common room downstairs, but I didn't feel much like company. So the first person I spoke to after leaving Carefal turned out to be my dead King.

The red brocade robe he was wearing this time had been a gift from the emissary of one of the small impoverished countries beyond the Eastern Desert. The robe was far too long for a man of the King's modest height, and its decoration was far too elaborate for his plain looks, so Paelis only wore it—when he was alive—when he felt the need to annoy some noble who'd demanded a private audience.

"It throws them off their guard," Paelis said, or rather, I hallucinated him saying.

"It doesn't throw anyone off their guard," I imagined myself saying back. "It just makes them think you're half-witted."

He grinned. "So what's the difference?"

That stumped me for a moment. The King always did that: he turned insults aimed at him into backhanded proof of his own cleverness. In my own defense, the neatha was probably addling my mind in addition to paralyzing my body. "Maybe you should have worn it when the Dukes came to kill you," I said at last.

"That wasn't the plan. I—" The King started coughing, as he often did, being prone to colds and agues.

I took advantage of his momentary disability. "Oh? Getting killed was all part of the plan, was it? And what about after you died? Is this the plan? Sending me off to try to find your heir without ever even telling me you had one? What if I'd never found her?"

The King continued to cough. I waited for a moment but he didn't stop, and for some reason that annoyed me.

"What if I'd never found her?" I repeated. "What if Patriana had managed to kill *all* of your so-called 'charoites'? And who in all the hells calls their bastards 'charoites' anyway? Was it really that important to make sure I had no damned idea what you'd sent me to do? What about the other Greatcoats? Are they all wandering the country trying to make sense of the last command you gave each of them?"

The King was smiling, but still coughing. He drew a red handkerchief from inside his robes and wiped at his mouth. When he pulled it back I couldn't tell if there was blood on it or whether it was simply spit darkening the fabric. And still the King continued to cough.

"And what am I supposed to do now?" I ranted on. "Look at me!" And since the King wasn't paying attention to me, I began shouting, "Look at me! I'm paralyzed! A few minutes here, a few minutes there, what does it matter? Do you think I'm stupid? Do you think I can't tell that it's getting worse every day? The neatha won't leave my system—I'm going to die!"

King Paelis was coughing louder than ever now, filling my ears and my mind, drowning out the sound of my words. "What if I can't get Aline on the throne before that happens, then what? What do you want me to do?"

My throat felt raw from screaming at him, which was odd, since I was only imagining it.

Finally the King stopped coughing. "I thought I told you," he started, and a trickle of bright red blood slipped out from the left side of his mouth. He reached up to dab it with the handkerchief, but then he stopped and instead carefully folded the handkerchief into a neat square and tucked it away inside his robes. He straightened himself up and looked into my eyes. "You will betray her, Falcio."

"Why do you keep saying this to me? Why would I betray her?" I tried to pound my fist on something, but I couldn't. Reality was slowly imposing itself on my hallucination.

The image of Paelis began to fade as my eyes flickered between light and darkness. But even in a hallucination he lacked the propriety of a decent King. "You're asking the wrong question again, Falcio."

"Then what is the *right* question, damn you?"

He smiled and pointed at me. "The right question is, 'Why is there a knife at my throat?'"

My eyes flickered open just in time to see the blade of a dagger withdraw from my neck.

"Ah, I wondered if that might do the trick," Dariana said.

I didn't take the bait, but only because my tongue was still numb and I didn't want to embarrass myself further. The sight of Dariana standing over me was unnerving. How long had she been in my room? More importantly, why would Kest and Brasti allow someone we barely knew to be alone with me when I was paralyzed?

"You probably want to know why I'm here," she said. She rose from the bed and walked over to the small window that was the only redeeming feature of the tiny room that Kest, Brasti, and I were sharing in the inn. "Shuran had a visitor."

"Who?" I croaked.

"A Knight. Well, he was wearing armor, anyway. He arrived early this morning and demanded to see the Knight-Commander. The other Knights didn't appear to know him. Shuran came out of his room and spoke to him in private. Then the man left and headed down the main road. Would you like to know which direction?"

"Just—"

"To Isault's palace."

I shook my head to try and clear away the fog. Why would Shuran be sending a man ahead of us when we were on our way back to the palace anyway? We'd fulfilled our part of the bargain . . . unless Isault had never believed we'd be successful in putting down the rebellion. Was Shuran even now preparing to betray us?

I looked around for something to help me haul myself out of bed and finding nothing, rolled myself onto the floor—at least the numbness dulled the pain a bit—and then crawled around in a little circle so that I could use the footboard to pull myself to my feet, cursing the Saints all the while, and not just because of my ungainly rising: I had been stupid enough to take off my clothes last night and now I had to stumble around trying to dress myself in front of Dari.

"The other Knight left an hour ago," she said. "Kest and Brasti went to talk to Shuran to find out what's going on because apparently you need to sleep all morning. You do seem rather helpless a good deal of the time—I can't help but wonder why you're the leader of the three, *First Cantor.*"

"Luck," I said, trying out one word to see how close I was to being functional. I was pleased with the results—which showed how low my expectations were these days. I very carefully and awkwardly reached for my pants and shirt on the floor only to realize halfway down that if I kept going I was going to fall over again.

She turned and looked at me. It was the first time I'd noticed that her eyes were a beautiful rich brown. I didn't like her smile, though. "Really?" she asked. "As I've heard it, you were abandoned by your father, your wife was murdered, your King was executed as a tyrant, your Greatcoats were scattered and now they're either dead or turned to banditry. The country is a corrupt black pit and the only reason it isn't overrun by devils is likely because they'd find it too unpleasant here. You've been beaten, tortured, and poisoned, and now you lie around half-dead. I could have killed you in your sleep and I doubt anyone would have minded. So what is it exactly that keeps you going?"

I tried once again to reach down for my pants, leaning my back against the wall to keep from toppling over. I had to admit I probably wasn't an impressive sight, swaying wildly and periodically grabbing at the edge of the bed to keep from landing back on the floor. "You're forgetting something," I said, hoping she'd pay more attention to my speech, which had mostly returned now, than my lack of balance.

"Oh? What's that?"

"The people who did those things—Yered, Duke of Pertine; Patriana, Duchess of Hervor; a dozen corrupt city constables, enough wife-beaters, child-slayers, rapists, and bully-boys to fill a castle, two Dashini assassins and more than fifty Ducal Knights—"

"I take it those are people you've killed?"

"Yes."

"All right, so you've killed all those people. They're dead. What is it that keeps you going now?"

"There are a few left I haven't gotten around to. Yet."

She smiled and walked over and kissed me on the cheek. "See? Now that's something I can get behind." She reached down and picked up my clothes and handed them to me. "You should get dressed. If we're about to fight Shuran and his men you won't want to do it half-naked."

"Why would we have to fight Shuran?" I asked. "Has he—?"

"He hasn't done anything, yet. I just don't trust him."

"Is there anyone you *do* trust?"

"Not really. But your real problem is that the Saint of Swords doesn't trust him either. Looks like Shuran is preparing to leave ahead of us, and Kest thinks that means Isault is going to betray Aline. I suspect he's going to do something reckless."

I had a good laugh at that. Kest was the least reckless person I'd ever known. He was invariably reasoned, cautious, and patient. I supposed he might try to convince Shuran to wait until I was able to move, but he certainly wouldn't start a war over it. "Kest will find a way to keep the peace," I said. "Where is he now?"

"Last time I saw him, the Saint of Swords was headed down to the courtyard to confront the Knight-Commander of Aramor. Tell me, does his skin always glow red when he's planning to keep the peace?"

* * *

"Why in all the hells did you wait so long to warn me that Kest and Shuran were preparing to fight?" I demanded of Dariana as I hobbled into the inn's courtyard. Morning sunshine blinded me, compounding the blurry haze that still haunted my vision.

"Who says I want you to stop the fight?" she asked.

On one side of the courtyard stood Shuran's Knights, their swords drawn. On the other stood Brasti, his short bow raised, an arrow nocked, and Valiana, her sword drawn but the point kept low so as to not set off an attack. It would have been a horribly mismatched battle—but neither the Knights nor the Greatcoats looked at all concerned with each other.

Between the two sides stood Shuran in full armor, his helm fastened and his massive sword held above him in a high guard, a position suited to making a fast and deadly first strike, the very picture of the chivalric ideal: strong, determined, unwavering—despite how difficult it is to remain still while standing in heavy armor. Opposite him, Kest waited impatiently in nothing more than his pants and shirt. His greatcoat lay discarded on the ground. This wasn't the Kest I had known since childhood, the man as patient as still water under a lake of ice. The man I knew didn't circle like a restless wolf waiting to attack: no, the man I'd stood side by side with in a hundred fights was silent as the night air when his sword was drawn. The man I knew didn't shout incoherent threats and jeer loudly at his opponent. The man I knew didn't have skin that burned red against the morning mist.

"Come on, you coward," Kest shouted, his voice strained but mocking, like a madman trying to contain his own laughter. "You dare draw a sword in my presence? In front of the Saint of Swords?"

"I do not seek to challenge you, Kest." Shuran's voice was calm and reasonable, his words carefully measured. "You drew first. I acted only to protect myself. There is no cause for conflict here. Let us both withdraw and talk this through before blood is spilled."

If I hadn't already known something was very wrong indeed, Kest's complete nonreaction to Shuran's words would have told me so. Even if Kest had true cause to duel, he should have immediately agreed to parlay or at least offer terms of surrender. Instead, Shuran's reticence just made him angrier. "'Talk'? Why? So you can seize your chance to slit my throat in my sleep? Do you think you'll take it from me that way?"

Shuran shook his head. "There is nothing I want to take from you."

Kest started laughing. "Really? You think I can't tell how much you want to be the Saint of Swords, Shuran? The hunger is written all over your face!"

"Even if I did want it, now is not the time. You and I both have greater matters to contend with than the question of which one of us is the better swordsman."

"You fool," Kest said, shaking his sword in the air, "this is the only thing that matters. *This*: blades slicing the wind, the sound of tempered steel cutting air and skin and bone, the flesh yielding like paper, the blood flooding the ground like rain. This is all there is!"

"What in all the hells is going on here?" I asked Brasti.

He turned at the sound of my voice. "Falcio! Thank whichever Gods aren't arrayed against us yet! You've got to get Kest to stop—he's lost his mind."

"What happened?"

"Shuran said he'd gotten orders from Isault to return immediately and he started getting ready to leave ahead of the rest of us—then Kest found out and went completely berserk. He started snarling and taunting Shuran and challenged him to a duel—in fact, I'm not entirely sure he didn't challenge me to one as well."

"Hells! Why didn't you calm him down?"

"I *did* try—oddly, he wasn't persuaded by my charm." Brasti pointed to what looked like a pair of broken short wooden staves on the ground joined by a string. It was one of his bows, sliced neatly in half.

"Kest!" I shouted, taking a couple of steps toward him. The air glinted in front of me and I felt something as soft as a child's breath pass lightly under my chin. When I looked at Kest he had already returned to his position. His eyes were still fixed on Shuran. *Shit, I* thought, *he nearly took my head off and he didn't even bother to look at me.* "Kest, withdraw. Now!"

"Shut up, Falcio. Your turn will come soon enough."

"Have you lost your mind? I'm your friend!"

This time he favored me with a look—the briefest of looks—and all I saw was the red of his eyes and a sneer. "Don't waste your words on me, Falcio. I know you think you're better than I am. You're wrong."

"Kest, I don't—"

Before I could even finish my sentence Kest leapt at Shuran, bridging the distance between them in less than an eye-blink and aiming a devastating thrust at the Knight's chestplate. Shuran brought his sword down in a fast parry intended to knock Kest's blade out of his hand, but it didn't work. Kest's own sword moved like water, slipping out of the way of the parry and returning to its target. The only thing that saved Shuran's life was that the big Knight managed to stumble backward, just out of reach of Kest's point.

Kest grinned. "I told you that you put too much weight on your back leg."

Shuran regained his footing. "Again, I do not dispute your superiority with the blade at this time, Saint of Swords."

Before Shuran could even get his weapon back into guard, Kest struck again, whirling his blade in and out of the line of attack like a snake. Filling the air with the mocking sound of steel against steel, the point of his sword struck once, twice, thrice: Shuran's wrists, his knee-joints, his elbows.

Hells, how could anyone, *even Kest, be that fast?*

Shuran, despite his size, moved swiftly and with deadly force. As a swordsman, it's almost impossible when watching a duel not to wonder if you yourself could take either of the opponents. Watching the way he moved, I doubted very much that I could beat Shuran in a fair fight—and yet I could see his heavy-footed stance was holding him back. Whatever injury had resulted in the burns on his body had also kept him from being anywhere near Kest's equal and Kest knew it. He used Shuran's weaknesses against him, laughing all the while, relentlessly forcing the big man to rely on heavier and heavier swings to parry Kest's blade. It felt like hours were passing by with each pass, and yet they had been fighting for just a few moments. The fight would not last much longer.

"I told you when we met that I would take you in twelve moves, Knight-Commander," Kest said. "You've got five left."

"I believe we settled on fourteen," Shuran replied, his breath coming in heavy bursts.

"Fourteen was for if I wasn't planning to kill you."

"Kest, stop!" I shouted. "That's a fucking order!"

But Kest ignored me, instead focusing all his gleeful attention on Shuran. Watching the way he went after the Knight-Commander was sickening. He was using his greater speed and skill to bind Shuran's movements, reminding me of a man using needle and thread to sew a shroud around a still-moving body. Kest was about to kill the Knight-Commander of Aramor right in front of his own men and destroy any hopes we had for an alliance with Aramor. Shuran stumbled back again and fell hard on one knee.

"Get up," Kest said. "Get up one last time. Or yield, and I will mercifully separate your greedy head from its shoulders."

Shuran kept his sword out in front of him even as he struggled to rise. "Think, man! Is this really what you want? To start a war between the Duke of Aramor and the girl you want to make Queen?"

Kest didn't answer; he just grinned and motioned again for Shuran to rise. There was no way in all the hells we were all destined for that the Knight-Commander was going to survive this next attack. *Saints forgive me*, I thought, and drew a throwing knife from my coat.

"What in all the name of Saint Laina's left tit are you doing?" Brasti hissed, his hand on my shoulder.

"Preventing a war," I said, drawing back and throwing the small blade at Kest's shoulder.

He barely turned toward me as his blade whipped up and dismissively knocked the knife out of the air. But I knew Kest better than anyone else in the world, and of course I knew what he was capable of doing with a blade—that's why I'd drawn and thrown the second knife the instant the first one had left my hand. There was a small *thunk!* as my second knife pierced his thigh. If he'd been wearing his greatcoat it would have protected him. *Had he left it off intentionally? Did some part of Kest want me to stop him?*

"Clever," he said to me, and grinned as he reached down to pull the knife out.

Oh shit . . .

I flipped up the collar, turned, and crouched down, just in time to feel the blade strike at the bone plates sewn inside my greatcoat. The impact was only mildly painful, and yet it hurt me deeply. Had Kest known for certain I'd be able to protect myself in time? Or was he so far gone that he was really willing to kill me?

I turned back to the two men to see Shuran trying to use Kest's wounded leg to turn the tide of the fight. But it was too late—the big Knight had been struck so many times by Kest that I was surprised he could still hold his sword. Shuran gave a great roar and tried one last sweeping attack, only to have Kest catch the blow on the crossbar of his sword and twist hard in a sudden counter-clockwise motion that spun the blade out of Shuran's hand.

Kest grinned. "Only one move left, Sir Knight."

Shuran dropped to his knees, his hands at his sides. His Knights looked like they were ready to attack Kest, but the Knight-Commander held up a hand. "No! We are Ducal Knights. We are men of honor. When this is done, fly, all of you—take separate roads. Whoever reaches the Duke first, tell him that the Greatcoats have betrayed us."

"Kest!" I shouted again, "*stop*! For the love of the King, you must stop!"

He turned to me and for an instant he looked like himself again, as if victory was quieting the madness inside him. The moment didn't last. "I'll be with you in a moment, Falcio," he replied and turned back to Shuran.

Kest was more than a brother to me. I'd known him since we were children and I'd loved him every day since. But I couldn't let him destroy the King's dream. I slipped off my greatcoat and drew my rapiers. I turned to Brasti. "If this doesn't work, you have to shoot him."

"You want me fire an arrow at Kest?"

"Not just one, as many as it takes. You keep firing until he stops moving."

"He can't parry an arrow, Falcio."

"Yes," I said, "he can." I walked toward Kest. "You just keep shooting until he stops moving."

Kest kept his sword on Shuran as he let his gaze drift toward me. "Why did you take off your coat, Falcio?"

"If you kill him, I'm next. Give me your sword, Kest, or else fight me."

Kest's eyes narrowed. "You think you can beat me? Without even the protection of your coat? Falcio, I think you might be going a little insane."

"Let's find out."

His expression changed, just a bit, as if he were suddenly confused about where he was. He was close to coming back to us; I just wasn't sure if he was close enough. I took another step forward.

"Falcio, stop . . ." Then he said, "I don't want to kill you."

"Nevertheless, those are your options." We were almost in range of each other now. Damn me, of all the deaths I'd ever envisioned for myself—and I have a *very* inventive mind—this wasn't one of them.

Kest looked at me and then at Shuran, his lips moving as if he was talking to himself, and I could see them forming the word "no" over and over again. Suddenly he brought his sword up high in the air and tilted the point down, toward Shuran's chest. The angle would allow him to use his tremendous strength to drive the blade straight through Shuran's chestplate.

"No!" I screamed and, cursing myself, I leapt toward him in a long lunge.

Kest beat away my rapier effortlessly and tossed his own sword lightly in the air, flipping it over so that he could grab the blade and aim the pommel at Shuran. He brought it down on Shuran's chest like a farmer trying to drive a stake into the ground. A sound like the clanging of a church bell filled the courtyard, and when I looked back at Shuran he was still on his knees, but reeling mightily from the blow. There was a small circular indentation the size of Kest's pommel on the left side of Shuran's chestplate. Kest had marked exactly where his point would have gone: straight into Shuran's heart.

My best friend looked at me, his mouth quivering and his eyes uncertain, then he turned to the Knight-Commander of Aramor and said, "I yield!" before falling unconscious to the ground.

A considerable amount of chaos followed. The moment Kest fell, Shuran's men took up positions in a circle around the two opponents, with five men guarding Shuran while the others stood over Kest's body. I ran to him, but several of Shuran's men made it quite clear that I wasn't going to get through them. Brasti, Valiana, and Dariana joined me and together we faced off with the Knights.

"Stop," Shuran said, breathing so hard he could barely get the word barely out. He removed his helm and I could see sweat dripping down his forehead, giving an unnatural sheen to the burnt side of his face. "It's done. No one is dead and no one needs to be."

"Step aside and let us see to our man," I said.

The Knights moved closer together. "This mad dog of yours is our prisoner now," one of them said. "He tried to murder the Knight-Commander of Aramor."

"There's something wrong with him," I said. "He'd never—"

Shuran cut me off with a wave of his hand. "This was a duel, fairly fought," he said to his men.

"But Knight-Commander," one of the Knights said, "this man—"

"First positions behind me!" Shuran barked and the Knights, moving in perfect unison, shifted from a circle around Kest to a line of men standing four feet behind Shuran. The Knight-Commander took a step back to give me room and I knelt down next to Kest. When I felt for the beating of his heart I found it slow, slower than mine by far. But was that normal for Kest now? I had no idea, never having had a Saint for a friend before. He had an unworldly look to him now. The red glow of his skin hadn't so much disappeared as turned inwards, as if he'd been standing out in the sun for several days. His skin was dry, almost burnt.

"What in hells is wrong with him?" I asked.

I hadn't been expecting a reply, but to my surprise, Shuran spoke up. "It's Saint's Fever, I think."

Brasti came forward to join me. "What is that, a joke? Saint's Fever is just redberry sickness—it's a child's ailment!"

"Parents call it Saint's Fever because the symptoms are similar, but there really is a Saint's Fever, and it's named that for a reason. There aren't that many written sources dealing with the nature of the Saints, but I've read something that speaks of a kind of ailment that builds inside them. How long has it been since Kest last bound himself in a sanctuary?"

"I . . . I'm not sure I even know what you're talking about," I admitted. We'd not exactly had the leisure for researching Kest's new condition since he'd taken on Saint Caveil's mantle.

Shuran looked at me as if he doubted my words for a moment. "You're telling me he hasn't *bound* himself? Not since he murdered the previous Saint of Swords?"

"It was no murder but a duel, fairly fought," I pointed out. "Caveil was trying to kill *us*."

"Still, why has Kest not—?"

Brasti stepped forward. "What we're telling you, metal man, is that we have no fucking idea what you're talking about."

The Knight-Commander looked back down at Kest, his eyes wide. "Gods! No wonder the madness was upon him. I can't believe he managed to hold it back as long as he did—"

"What is this sanctuary you're talking about?" I asked.

"A church—any church. He has to spend three nights inside until—"

"He can't go into a church," I said. I wasn't likely to forget our last encounter with Trin any time soon. "He couldn't pass the stone circle."

"That's how it works," Shuran said. "You need to go to a church and ask the cleric to remove one of the stones, then Kest will be able to pass through. The cleric will replace the stone and reconsecrate the circle—"

"Won't that trap him inside the church?" Brasti asked. A pertinent question, I thought.

"That's the point: he'll be bound inside the sanctuary. The force that burns inside him must be held in check. A Saint must be humbled by man's church to be saved. If the stories are true, after three days the cleric can remove the stone once again and the Saint will be able to walk the world, once again able to control the divine madness."

"You know an awful lot about Saints," I said.

"Doesn't every man who aspires to become something greater than himself?"

The almost dismissive answer didn't sit well with me, but looking down at Kest's face reminded me we had more pressing concerns. His skin was returning to a more normal pallor but there was something thin and worn about him. "What do I do now?" I murmured, almost to myself.

"Nothing," Shuran said, stepping back from us and sheathing his sword. "I'm no expert, but from what I've read he should be fine for a while. When the fever strikes it is . . . well, *pronounced*, but its passing should leave him in control for some time. However, I would advise that once your business with Duke Isault is complete, you should find Kest a sanctuary."

"Shit," Brasti said. "Doesn't sound like being a Saint is all it's made out to be in the stories."

Shuran smiled. "Few things are. And yet I imagine for those called it's hard to resist."

I thought back to what Kest had been shouting at the beginning of his fight with Shuran. *You think the hunger isn't written all over your face when you look at me?* "And you, Sir Shuran? Do you feel the call to become the Saint of Swords?"

"Right now the only call I'm heeding is the one to return to my Duke," Shuran said. "Sir Lorandes, if you wouldn't mind?"

One of the Knights broke out of formation and walked over to the horses. Without a word he took the reins of Shuran's steed and led him back to us.

"The rest of you will travel to the Ducal Palace together," Shuran said. "I'll see you when you arrive, tomorrow or the next day." He turned and looked at his men. "On my honor, not one of my men will seek to do Kest—or any of you—harm."

"But why is it so important that you leave right now?" I asked. "Why are you going ahead on your own?"

"Because I have been summoned by my lord and instructed to proceed with all speed. I can reach the palace a good deal faster if I'm traveling by myself. I follow the Duke's commands, Falcio. That's how it works."

I was standing close to him and he towered above me. I kept my focus on his eyes. "And what if the Duke decides to betray us?"

To his credit, Shuran didn't blink. "Duke Isault is the ruler of Aramor. If he decides to go back on his agreement with you then there's nothing I can do about that."

"So you'll betray us if he asks."

"You really don't understand Knighthood, do you, Falcio? If the Duke commands it, it won't be a betrayal."

I had no small amount of admiration for Shuran, and in another life, who knows, perhaps we would have been friends. But at that moment the only thing running through my mind was, was, *Saints, how I hate Knights.* "So you expect us to just waltz into the palace and hope it's not a trap? If Isault's planning on selling us out to Trin, what's to stop him from capturing us or killing us to seal the deal?"

"Duke Isault would never do that," Shuran said firmly. "If he changes his mind and decides to back Duchess Trin instead of Princess Aline he'll tell you to your face and send you on your way. He won't order me to arrest you, not unless you attack him first."

I looked around at Shuran's men. There were five of us and ten of them, so decent odds. We could take them if we had to—assuming, of course, that Kest awakened from his current slumber.

"I'll swear this much," Shuran said. "If you come to the palace, I will personally guarantee your safety."

"And what if Isault orders you to attack us? You'll—what? Refuse?"

The question was pretty obvious to me, and yet Shuran was clearly troubled by it. Eventually he said, "Then I'll renounce my Knighthood and do what I must to ensure my promise to you is upheld."

"What about your precious honor then?" I asked.

He put his foot in the stirrup and mounted his horse. "If the Duke tells me to attack those he's sworn to treat with fairly, then my honor won't be worth a black penny anymore."

He kicked his horse and left me standing in the inn's small courtyard feeling somehow both betrayed and yet ignoble. That was quite a feat.

14

THE BETRAYAL

A few hours later found the five of us back on the road, riding along-side Shuran's Knights in deathly silence. We'd been halfway through constructing a litter for Kest—all Greatcoats learned a variety of useful knots for such eventualities—when he'd awakened from his fever. The red glow was completely gone now, but it had been replaced with a gray pallor; it might have simply been exhaustion, but I couldn't help but worry it might be something more deadly. He sat astride his horse—you couldn't even call it riding—and stared at the ground passing below like a hungover man reflecting on the wages lost in a drunken game of dice.

Sometimes I slowed my own mount so that Kest could catch up, each time hoping he would talk to me, help me understand what was happening to him. But each time he just held up a hand and muttered, "Not yet."

And so we continued on our way.

A steady rain began to fall and the roads, ill-maintained since the King's death, became slick and dangerous, forcing us to slow even more for we could not risk the horses.

The drudgery of our pace affected us in different ways. I was thankful for the watchful eye Dariana was keeping on the Knights riding ahead of us, though none of them had yet decided to disobey Shuran's order. Brasti had sunk back into a black mood, still brooding on what he saw as a betrayal of the villagers in Carefal.

Only Valiana saw fit to speak to me. "We did the right thing, you know." She pulled her horse up next to mine. "In the village, I mean."

"'The law is the law,'" I said, though the words sounded more like a taunt than the comfort they were supposed to be.

She reached out and rested a hand on my arm. "People will only believe in the laws if they see them enforced."

"We just enforced the law on a group of brave women and men who wanted nothing more than fairer treatment from their Duke."

"That's just the point," she said. "The Dukes were wrong, but so were the villagers. They acted as they did because they saw no other choice. That's what's wrong with this country, Falcio. People see no other choice than to take as much power as they can and use it for themselves."

"Says the girl who not so long ago planned to make herself Queen."

I instantly regretted my words; she had done as she'd been raised to do and none of this was her fault. I was about to apologize when I realized she wasn't as hurt as I'd expected.

"If I had been made Queen, I would have found a way to bring the Law back to Tristia—that's what the monarch is supposed to do. It's what King Paelis did, isn't it?"

"Until the Dukes had him killed, yes."

"And what has it brought them? The country is poorer now, the roads more dangerous. The Dukes are no richer than they were before, but now what part of their fortune they don't lose to brigands they spend on spies to keep watch on each other and more Knights to fill out their armies, and all the while paying their men less and less."

"Knights don't get paid, remember? They serve for honor."

Valiana ignored my sarcasm. "Look at Shuran's men, then think back to those we saw back at the palace. Did you notice that several of them were greybeards, well past their prime? Knights used to be given gifts of land after their years of service so they could retire and live in peace and prosperity. Isault's not doing that, is he? And neither are any of the other Dukes, not now. They all keep adding more Knights to their rosters, but without rewarding the ones they have."

I hadn't considered that before now, but she was right. Despite all the stories of Knights and their honor and brave deeds, to us Greatcoats, Knights were nothing more than hired thugs with pretensions to nobility. It had never occurred to me to think of them as men who had hopes and dreams of a life outside the confines of their armor. I supposed it was probably easier not to think of them at all, given how often I'd had to fight them. I shook my head to clear the thought from my mind. "If you're asking me to feel any sympathy for the Ducal Knights—"

"You should have sympathy for anyone who suffers," she countered. "In Rijou you told me that nothing is worse than sitting back while evil prospers. Shouldn't you be able to show some pity for these men, too?"

I thought about Aline, and how impossible it was going to be to make her Queen, and about Trin, who was out there somewhere merrily creating chaos in the world. I thought about the rest of the King's original hundred and forty-four Greatcoats who were scattered to the winds, alone or dead, or worse, turning to banditry to survive. I thought about Kest, who was even now suffering under this sainthood that had turned out to be a huge curse. And I thought about the fact that when I laid my head down on my pillow tonight, I had no idea if I would ever move again.

Then I looked at the ten Ducal Knights of Aramor in front of us. Each of them would happily turn on us right then and there and slit our throats for no other reason than we were Greatcoats, were it not for the command of one man.

"Fuck the Knights," I said.

Three more days and enough rain to convince me that every God in Tristia had taken this opportunity to piss on my head brought us back to the courtyard of Duke Isault's palace. We were soaked to the bone as we waited in the never-ending downpour for one of the watchmen to seek out Sir Shuran.

"You've arrived safely," the big Knight said, striding toward us from the wide arched doors to the palace. His freshly polished armor gleamed, in studied contrast to our sodden, grimy coats. "I understand you made it back without incident."

I noted that Shuran had been followed by the usual coterie of heavily armed men who were now standing around him with their weapons drawn. Kest stepped forward, his hands held out to show that he wasn't holding a weapon. "Sir Shuran, I behaved . . . inappropriately. The actions were mine and no one else knew I would—"

"What? Call me a coward and a traitor? Challenge me to a duel for no particular reason and then do a remarkably good job of trying to put a sword through my heart?" He tapped a finger on the indentation in his chest plate. He had done an amazing job of polishing his armor to a mirror-shine, but he hadn't bothered to beat out the dent. "You've given my enemies an awfully precise target, Saint of Swords."

Kest nodded. "I will accept any punishment you deem necessary, so long as my friends—"

"Enough," Shuran said. "I might be fascinated by the Saints but I've got a low tolerance for martyrs. You were beset by the Saint's Fever at the time—and besides, technically I did accept your challenge."

"Still . . . I would make restitution."

Shuran grinned. "Good. Let the price be that some day you'll give me a fair bout when I'm not busy trying to stay alive to do the Duke's business and you aren't in the middle of a fucking red rage."

Kest nodded, and the matter seemed done with, for the moment at least.

Shuran turned to me. "I'll have someone take you to your rooms. The Duke knows what transpired in Carefal. I'm sure he'll want to see you in the morning."

The thought of spending the night here made me uneasy. I had no doubt that even now Shuran's Knights were telling their fellows the story of how close the Greatcoats had come to killing their leader.

"No," I said, "I need to finalize things tonight. We won't be staying at the palace."

"Tonight isn't a good time," Shuran said. "The Duke is busy this evening."

Lightning flashed ever so briefly to the north of us and a moment later the boom of thunder reached my ears. Water was dripping from my hair into my eyes and all I could think of was a fat, arrogant Duke sitting on his throne, enjoying whatever amusements pleased him. I wasn't looking for trouble, but I'd had just about enough of being under Isault's thumb. "I don't care. Tell him he's going to see us tonight."

Shuran's voice grew quiet, as if he didn't want his men to hear. "I'm afraid it doesn't work that way, Falcio. The Duke decides when he sees you, not the other way around."

"Then tell him that one way or another, with or without his support, Aline is going to be Queen, and she's going to be making all kinds of decisions about taxes and laws and the boundaries between duchies. Tell him I have saved her life—several times—and there's a very good chance I may use that fact to punish those people who've irritated me over the years."

Shuran looked at me as if he were trying to see whether or not I was serious. After a moment he said, "All right, Falcio. I'll tell him. Whatever happens after that is on your head."

Half an hour later I was back in the Ducal throne room, this time alone—at Duke Isault's insistence. I suppose he wanted to make me nervous. "Your Grace," I said, tilting my head so the water dripped onto his floor.

"Shit-eater," he replied, "there's a story going around that you— Beshard, what was it Shuran was saying earlier? He said the shit-eater here—"

"Demanded to see you, your Grace."

"That's right," Isault said, "you *demanded* to see me. But there was something else, too. What was that again, Beshard? What was that other thing the shit-eater did?"

"He threatened you, your Grace?" Beshard offered.

Isault clapped his hands together. "That's right: the Greatcoat *threatened* me. Now, Shuran's known to be a big fat liar, right, Beshard?"

"No, your Grace, I've never heard that said of Sir Shuran, begging your pardon."

"No? Oh, so then it's true, is it, Falcio val Mond?"

"I suppose my words could fairly be interpreted as a threat," I agreed.

Isault smiled and took a long drink from the goblet sitting precariously on the arm of his throne. He wiped his mouth on the sleeve of his green silk robe. "Excellent. I've been having accommodations prepared for you. In my dungeon. Lovely place—mind you, you've had a lot more experience at being chained up and tortured than I have so I'll be keen to get your opinion of it. But I was afraid I'd gotten my information wrong and my admittedly hasty preparations might be in vain."

I put my hands in the pockets of my coat, not wanting the Duke to see them shaking. It wasn't that long since I'd spent several days being tortured in the dungeons of Rijou and unless I tried very hard, I could still feel the manacles that had held my wrists, and the pain in my shoulder sockets from hanging suspended by my arms for days on end. I had barely survived the experience once, and the thought of repeating it terrified me. "I wouldn't want you to go to any trouble," I said casually.

"Oh, I assure you, it's no trouble at all."

"Still, I think there's a more expeditious solution, your Grace."

"Really? Well, we in Aramor are all in favor of expeditious solutions. What's yours?"

"Give me the decree you promised swearing support to Aline and then I'll be on my way and we need never see each other again."

I'd expected an insult or some kind of threat; instead, the Duke just scratched his beard. "And you think you've earned that, do you?"

"I did what you asked," I said. "I put down the rebellion."

"I suppose that's true, isn't it?" The Duke gave a little giggle and looked longingly at his empty goblet of wine. Evidently it hadn't been his first that evening. "Wish I'd been there to see it: the great Falcio val Mond, First Cantor of the King's Greatcoats. The Hero of Rijou. You did just exactly what I wanted you to do."

The tone of his voice softened. He was no longer mocking; now he sounded . . . disappointed?

"You take orders surprisingly well, Falcio," the Duke went on. Then he shouted across the room, "He'd make a good Beshard, wouldn't he, Beshard?"

"If your Grace says so," the chamberlain replied.

"Yes, I do." Isault turned his attention back to me. "Maybe you secretly want to bugger me, just like old Beshard does." He held up a hand as if to stop any expostulation I might make. "Or no, not like Beshard. Maybe you just want so badly to be loyal to your dead King that you'll do anything just to prove yourself. Maybe we should make you a Knight, eh? Like Shuran? Would you like to be a Knight, shit-eater? No offense, you understand. Just curious."

"I'd rather marry one of your torturers and spend the honeymoon in the darkest cell in your dungeon than become one of your Ducal Knights," I said. "No offense."

Isault laughed then, not at what I'd said, but at something else: a private joke between him and himself. Both looked inordinately pleased. "Do you want to hear something funny?" he asked.

"I'd—"

"I often think about your dead King Paelis."

"He was your King too," I said reflexively.

Isault waved his fingers in the air. "Details. Just like a magistrate to focus on the details and miss the point."

Beshard, responding to a cue I hadn't noticed, walked up to the throne carrying a silver jug. He refilled Isault's goblet before bowing and turning to begin the trek back to his allotted position at the other end of the long room. The Duke drained his goblet almost immediately and tapped it with one finger and a moment later Beshard once again started the journey from the back of the room.

"Perhaps it would be more efficient if Beshard and the wine stayed here," I suggested.

"No, no; this is my last one. Where was I? Oh yes, I think about King Paelis sometimes. In fact, occasionally I like him being right here in front of me. We talk about things, he and I. Do you ever imagine yourself talking to the King?"

"I try to limit the number of conversations I have with the dead, your Grace."

"Ah, see, that's where you're wrong. It's an entirely sensible activity. I talk to King Paelis about the Law and the country; about securing borders and negotiating agreements with my fellow Dukes."

"Does the King talk back?"

"No—that's the best part, in fact. In life all he did was talk, but in death, he's a mercifully good listener. I ask him questions sometimes, but of course he doesn't answer, just stands there with that stupid lopsided smirk of his. I hated that expression when he was alive. Made me want to slap him. But now, strangely enough, it just makes me think and think some more, and wouldn't you know it? I end up coming up with the answer all by myself. A much better King in death than in life is our Paelis. I could do with only ever having dead monarchs."

"I'm glad you finally worked out a productive relationship with the King."

Isault waved a finger. "But there is one thing I sometimes ask Paelis, and when I do, sure enough, he gives me that stupid smirk of his, only with this question I never do come up with the answer myself."

Isault drank again from his goblet, but this time it was a small sip and he kept his eyes fixed on me the whole time. Since it was obvious he wanted me to ask, I did.

"And what question is that, your Grace?"

The Duke threw his goblet at me—it was so unexpected that it hit me in the cheek and soaked me in red wine. "What the fuck was your plan?" he shouted. He stood up from his throne and for an instant I thought he might attack me, but he just stood there, yelling at the room, "You made all your damned promises to the country and you gave us your damned useless Greatcoats and when we came to gut you, you just sat there like a lamb awaiting the shears! All the while I thought you had some brilliant strategy, some inspired scheme that was going to change the world—but it's been five fucking years and still I don't know what your plan was! Was it simply to drive us all mad as we waited for it to unfold? Is that it? It's nothing more than a grand joke to stand alongside all the other jokes you played on us?"

The Duke was getting hysterical, but when I looked back at Beshard at the other end of the room I saw the old chamberlain wasn't reacting, either because he'd seen this before or because he really was that good at standing there quietly and not reacting.

"Your Grace," I began, but then I stopped, because I really wasn't sure what to say next. Fortunately, I didn't have to say anything because Isault sat down heavily on his throne.

"Enough. That's enough," he said. "Go to bed, First Cantor of the Greatcoats. You did what you promised and I shall do the same. In the morning we'll do a little ceremony and I'll sign the decree."

He sagged deeper into his great uncomfortable seat and I felt as if I were intruding on the man's most private grief.

Beshard gave a polite cough behind me, signaling that it was time for me to go.

"I'm sorry, your Grace," I said, "but I can't leave until you've given me the decree."

"I told you, shit-eater, in the morning. At the ceremony. There'll be cakes."

"I'm certain I'll enjoy the cakes, your Grace, but I really do need the decree now."

The Duke looked up at me, his eyes heavy-lidded. "Do you question my honor, Falcio val Mond?"

I knew I was treading on dangerous terrain now, but I couldn't take a chance on the volatile Duke changing his mind. "We had an agreement, your Grace and it seems to me that any questions regarding your honor are now for you to resolve."

The Duke's face turned red and I thought he might leap up and try to strangle me. But a moment later the anger drained from him and he reached into the folds of his green silk robe and pulled out a rolled-up piece of parchment. He tossed it to the floor in front of me. "There are the wages of your sins, Falcio val Mond."

I knelt down and picked up the parchment, not quite sure if I dared pull open the narrow green silk tie that bound it.

"Go ahead," Isault said. "It's not as if you'll offend me any more than you already have."

I gently untied the silk ribbon and read the decree. It was as simple and straightforward a document as I'd ever seen, with no evasions, no equivocations: Isault simply acknowledged that Aline was the rightful Queen of Tristia and that Aramor would perform all traditional duties owed her. At the bottom was his signature. "Thank you, your Grace," I said. "I regret I'll have to forego the cakes in the morning as we need to leave tonight."

Isault snorted. "No, I don't think you will be leaving tonight."

I looked around quickly, expecting to see his Knights coming to arrest me, but Beshard was still the only other person in the throne room, standing there as placidly as ever.

"I expect to get some small benefit from your otherwise worthless presence here," the Duke said. "Showing my lords and margraves that I've made an alliance that gives preferential status to Aramor keeps them in line."

"Your Grace—"

Isault pulled out a second parchment from his robes. "If you aren't here in the morning, First Cantor, I'll sign this second decree revoking the first one."

I looked down at the parchment still in my hand. "What value is your decree, Duke Isault, if it can so simply be overridden by another, and what value is your word if you can change it so easily?"

Isault looked to his chamberlain. "You see that, Beshard? The shit-eater isn't half so stupid as he looks."

Beshard led me up the stairs and down a long hallway to my room, pointing out as we passed where Kest, Brasti, Valiana, and Dari had been accommodated.

"I'll return for you in the morning," the old man said as he unlocked the door.

"How long have you served the Duke?"

"I served his father, and for a brief time, his father's father."

"Would you say he's an honorable man?" I asked, anticipating an angry retort from the old man. Hells, I probably said it just to elicit one.

"In his own fashion," Beshard said, entirely calmly. "We live in dishonorable times, in a corrupt country. I suppose one could say the Duke is as honorable a man as such a world allows."

The statement was so candid and plainly logical that I couldn't think of a reply, but apparently none was needed. The old man put a hand on my shoulder—an oddly intimate gesture—until I realized he had a tiny sliver of a blade held between his old fingers and its point was touching my neck. "That said, I have looked after Duke Isault since the day he was born. I have loved him since he first opened his eyes and farted. If, after you speak to him in the morning, you attempt to do him harm, be aware that you will soon be looking up at the ceiling, your life's blood draining from the wound in your throat where an old man's blade severed the artery." He took his hand away and gave me a crooked smile. "I should imagine that would be terribly embarrassing for such a capable young man such as you."

He handed me the key to my room and said, "Sleep well, Trattari."

I spent the next few minutes trying to stop myself from shaking. Between Isault's threats and Beshard's little blade my nerves were on edge. *Taken like an amateur by an old man barely able to lift a serving tray.* There were a hundred ways I could have bested the chamberlain and yet I'd allowed him to get close enough that he could have slit my throat with the barest effort: all my training and experience voided by a single moment of inattention.

Once I felt I could speak without stuttering, I went about quietly knocking on doors and assembling the rest in my room. I explained the situation with Isault and showed them the decree, and then I told them my plan.

"I have a question," Dariana said after I was done. She was sitting cross-legged on my bed, quite unconcerned that the dirt on her boots was rapidly transferring itself to my blankets.

"What?" I asked.

"Do you have any plans that don't involve telling Valiana and me to run away and hide somewhere while you—?"

"—while he tries to get Kest and me killed?" Brasti finished. "No. That's pretty much the crux of all of Falcio's masterful stratagems, so you might as well get used to it now."

"It's not what you think," I said, handing the scroll to Dariana. One glance made it very clear what Valiana thought of my master plan. "Look, we need to get the decree into the hands of the Tailor. Even if Isault signs a second one, we might be able to use this one to Aline's benefit. Dariana, you're the one who knows her plans and where she's most likely to be, so unless you would like to share that information with the rest of us—"

"I don't."

"—fine. Then you need to get out of the palace tonight. Wait for us at the inn we passed, two days back—hells, what was it called?"

"The Inn of the Red Hammer," Kest offered.

"Right, that's the one. It's on the edge of the Spear, and that will be the fastest way to travel north to Domaris. If we don't show up in the next three days, go and find the Tailor and let her know we've failed."

"Sounds perfectly logical," Dariana said.

"Good, then—"

"So why are you sending Valiana too? I can travel faster by myself."

I kept my gaze on her until her eyes met mine. "Because I don't trust you. That's why."

She grinned. "See, now that makes sense."

"Good. There's a window at the end of this hallway. If you wait until—"

"Please don't start explaining how to break into and out of buildings to me. You'll only embarrass yourself."

"Had a lot of experience sneaking in and out of Ducal palaces, have you?" Brasti asked.

"I've had excellent tutors," she replied.

"Good for you," I said. "Now everyone get the hells out of my room. If all goes well, the Duke will hold true to his word and the worst thing that will happen is Kest and Brasti and I will be forced to listen to more of his insults while we eat his cake and drink his wine."

I was about to fall down on my bed when I realized Brasti had his hand up.

"Do you have a question?"

"No," he said. "I just wanted to call first strike on Duke Isault."

"What do you mean?" Kest asked.

"Well, when we show up in the throne room in the morning and Isault betrays us and Shuran and his Knights surround us and Falcio is jumping up and down giving speeches about the Law and staying true to one's word and the other rubbish he spews at times like these, I get to stab Isault first."

"Are you always such a pessimist?" Dariana asked.

"Believe it or not, I used to be quite cheerful."

"What happened to make you so cynical?"

Oddly, it was Kest who said, "He joined the Greatcoats."

The four of them left me then, and as I removed my coat and outer clothes I stood shivering for a moment standing on the cold flagstone floor. I looked at the warm covers on the bed, longing for sleep, but knowing I couldn't afford it. Days on horseback had made me stiff and I needed to stretch my muscles—and I also needed to make sure my weapons were all oiled and sharpened. Above all, I couldn't risk sleep: if Brasti was right and the Duke really was preparing an ambush for us in the morning, then I couldn't afford to wake up paralyzed, then groggy and slow.

Get to work, I told myself, reaching for my rapiers and oiling cloth. *You can rest when Aline sits on the throne and Trin lies at the bottom of a grave.*

Two hours later a knock at my door proved Brasti had it all wrong.

"It's a bit late for visitors, I'm afraid," I called out, standing to the side of the door in case whoever was on the other side had a pistol ready to fire through it. Kest and Brasti and I have different knocks we use to communicate all manner of things—who's outside, what's occurring, why we're there . . . We even have a knock for those rare occasions where one of us has a knife held to our throat and is being forced to entrap the other.

This knock wasn't any of those so I kept my rapier at the ready and waited.

"It's Knight-Commander Shuran. Open the door." After a brief pause he said, "And I'd advise keeping the point of your sword aimed at the ground."

The fact that he'd used his full title told me there were men with him and the reference to my sword told me he was expecting violence. "I'm warning you, Shuran, if the Duke has decided to go back on his word, I'll make it an expensive decision for everyone," I said.

"Open the door, First Cantor. This is a poor time to make threats."

"Where are Kest and Brasti?" I asked.

"I came to you first."

I thought about that. If he'd come to me first he thought the other two would attack first and he wanted me to keep them from starting anything. With no better solution in mind, I opened the door.

"Thank you," Shuran said.

I could see half a dozen Knights behind him, in full armor.

"What's happened?" I asked.

"Duke Isault has been murdered," he said.

15

AN INELEGANT CORPSE

Isault, Duke of Pulnam, made an inelegant corpse. Even under the green silk sheet that had been placed over him, the dome formed by his prodigious belly made him look more like a mound of dirt than a man.

The body was lying in the center of the room, surround by twelve Knights in full armor clenching their swords. When I reached down to pull away the sheet covering Duke Isault, all twelve swords pointed in my direction.

"First positions," Shuran said, his voice betraying neither anger nor anxiety, only absolute certainty that his order would be instantly obeyed.

His confidence was not misplaced: the Knights moved like a well-oiled machine, returning at once to their former stance, the blade of their swords pointed upward and resting against their shoulders, ready to attack at will.

I reached forward again and pulled back the sheet. Isault's expression was frozen in a snarl, reminding me of the outraged face of a dead bear mounted as a wall trophy. I removed the sheet entirely and saw his arms, folded across his chest, were covered in cuts. He had fought back, taking a dozen thin slices on his forearms as he tried to protect his body. It wasn't until I pulled his arms apart that I saw the small wound that had been thrust into his heart and ended his life.

"Precise," Kest said, standing over me. "The assassin could have disabled him more quickly had he not been so determined to kill him with a single thrust."

The sounds of heavy boots echoed in the room and a Knight with long blond hair came striding toward us: Heridos, the Knight-Captain who'd ordered the attack on us when we'd first arrived in Aramor the previous week.

He ignored Shuran completely and spoke directly to the Knights surrounding us. "Arrest those men," he said.

"Belay that order," Shuran said.

"You would allow these murderers to defile the Duke's body?" the Knight-Captain demanded. "Did you help them do this?"

Shuran's gauntleted hand struck out and the Knight-Captain fell back. "Keep your wits about you, Sir Heridos, or you'll lose the head that obedience so recently bought back for you. I am still Knight-Commander of Aramor."

Sir Heridos didn't look pleased. Or scared. "A man cannot hold the post of Knight-Commander if he commits treason."

Sir Shuran took a step toward him. "Think back, Sir Heridos, to the most dangerous moment of your fool's existence: the one in which you thought you were within a hair's-breadth of losing your life. I assure you, you are much closer to death now than you were then."

"These men are assassins!" Sir Heridos said.

"Our own men were standing guard outside their rooms all night. How could they have committed the murders?"

Murders? I'd seen two dead guards outside the throne room when they'd brought us here, but somehow I doubted Shuran was talking about them.

"Then they are accomplices!" Sir Heridos insisted. He held up a piece of parchment. "Look here. The Duke had a decree disavowing his agreement with the Trattari. Had he signed it, their plans would fallen apart."

"Which does not alter the fact that we had their rooms watched all night."

"And what about the two women?" Sir Heridos asked, "Or were you not aware they fled the palace last night?"

"Indeed I am aware, Sir Heridos, and I had them followed." He turned to me. "The ladies have not been harmed. My men followed them for several hours until they were outside our border before they returned. Neither would have had time to come back and murder the Duke."

"And the other one?" Sir Heridos asked.

What other one? Sir Shuran looked at me and then back to his Knight-Captain.

Kest nudged me. "Falcio, something's wrong."

"What do you mean?"

"They know we couldn't have done it, so why is Sir Heridos determined to believe it was one of us?"

"Because they're Knights and we're Greatcoats," Brasti said, "and that's how these things work."

I looked at Sir Heridos. The hatred in his eyes was genuine and it was specific. He truly believed we had murdered his Duke. Brasti was right.

"Who stands to benefit from the Duke's death?" I asked Sir Shuran.

"His enemies," Sir Heridos said, "and who hates the Dukes more than the Trattari? Boot-lickers to a tyrant King bound to revenge themselves on those who restored honor to the country these five years past!"

I thought back to all the times over the last few years when I had stood in the shadows outside a Duke's home in the cold and rain, the blood in my veins so hot and itchy I had to stop myself from tearing my skin as I wondered whether murder was still murder if the intended victims bragged to each other at their annual celebration marking the day they came with an army and killed my King. Yet Paelis had made us swear oaths that we would not seek revenge. Instead we wandered the countryside trying desperately to fulfill the final enigmatic commands he had given each one of us. I didn't know how many of us were left now besides Kest, Brasti, and me.

"Shut your mouth," Sir Shuran said. He turned to me. "To answer your question, the Duke was well liked by the people of Aramor, as far as that goes. The rebels in Carefal were the first I've ever known to try to cause trouble. Roset, Duke of Luth, had cause for grievance over border disputes, as did Jillard, Duke of Rijou; however, attacking a fellow Duke would put either man in a great deal of jeopardy from the Ducal Concord."

"Who becomes Duke of Aramor after Isault?"

"His son, Lucan, is sixteen and next in line. After that, Patrin, who at twelve is too young, so the Duke's wife, Yenelle, would act as regent. Finally, there is the daughter Avette. She is six. But the killer wasn't one of the Duke's family, nor anyone who would hope for more favorable treatment from them."

"Why not?" I asked.

Sir Shuran's eyes were on mine for a long while.

He knows something and he wants to see if I know it too.

After a moment he turned to Sir Heridos. "Tell them to come in," he said.

"The clerics—"

"I gave you an order," he said.

The Knight-Captain walked back to the entrance of the throne room and opened the door. He motioned to a group of Knights in the hallway and they entered, each one bearing something large wrapped in green cloth in their arms. They gently placed their burdens one by one next to the Duke.

Sir Shuran lifted the silken covers from them one by one. The first was a woman in her middle years with curly reddish-blond hair. "Her Grace Duchess Yenelle," he said. He pulled the silk cloth from the second. A teenage boy, tall for his age. "Her son Lucan." The next was smaller and his face was smeared in blood. "Her second son, Patrin." He reached down and lifted the silk cloth from the final body, this one very small, her bright blond hair in ringlets. Her face would have been pretty had it not been frozen in terror. She wore a yellow dress stained dark red from the collar down where the slit in her throat had let the blood flow out from her body. "Avette," he said. "She liked to paint pictures of dogs. She thought that if she could make one beautiful enough it would persuade her father to give her a puppy for her birthday."

Sir Shuran was looking at me, measuring my reaction. He had held this back to see what we already knew. Whatever he was looking for, I don't think he found it.

"The assassin," he said to Sir Heridos. "Show us."

"You've caught the killer?" I asked.

"Yes, but I don't think it will help matters much," Shuran replied.

"But then why are we—?"

"It's easier if we show you," the Knight-Commander said, and motioned to Sir Heridos again. The Knight-Captain turned on his heels and began walking toward the other side of the throne room with such eagerness that it took me a moment to realize he was expecting us to follow him.

He led us into a small office or private library, with shelves of books and a desk that took up the whole of one wall.

"Here," Heridos said, pointing to the body lying with a bloodied broadsword next to it. "Here is the assassin you sent to butcher the Duke of Aramor and his family."

This corpse wasn't covered in a sheet. It was lying facedown on the floor and it was wearing a leather greatcoat.

Sir Shuran knelt down and turned the body over, revealing a tall woman with light brown hair, her blue eyes set wide, the sharp features of her face drawn into an angry smile.

"How did she die?" I asked Sir Heridos. "Did your men kill her?"

"No, the Duke himself took her before he fell. He thrust his dagger into her black heart."

"Do you know this woman?" Sir Shuran asked.

She was beautiful, in her own way: fierce and foul-tongued and always looking for a good fight. There were lines on her forehead that I didn't remember, but it had been several years since I'd last seen her.

I looked back at Kest and Brasti to make sure my eyes weren't deceiving me. Brasti let out a curse. Kest peered at her closely, as if examining every detail of her face. He looked at me and nodded.

"Yes, I know her," I said, my mind drawn back to a day many years ago when she, like me, first received her greatcoat. She had looked up at the King and smiled, tears streaming down her face, as they were streaming down all of ours. I had never seen her cry before or since that day. "Her name was Dara," I said, "called the King's Fury, Third Cantor of the King's Greatcoats."

When I looked back at the others I saw that Sir Heridos had finally found something to smile about.

Watching Sir Shuran argue with his Knight-Captain for the next hour was oddly disconcerting. It wasn't simply the fact that Sir Heridos was advocating so forcefully for our summary execution that bothered me; that was to be expected given the circumstances. Rather, it was the fact that Sir Shuran, who was as powerful a commander as I'd ever met, appeared to be unwilling or unable to shut the other Knight down. Every time Heridos spoke, Shuran would glance at the Knights and clerics assembled in the throne room, almost as if they were a panel of ducal magistrates sitting in judgment rather than soldiers who would instantly follow whatever order he gave. I was pretty sure that Heridos had managed to ensure the Knights guarding the room were loyal to him before anyone else.

"Duke Isault's murder cries out for justice!" Heridos shouted again. He walked to the bodies of Isault's family. "His wife deserves justice! His children cry out for justice! And two of our own, Sir Ursan and Sir Walland, they too are dead—struck down no doubt by the Trattari whore. Their souls, too, cry out for justice. Though perhaps their pleading sounds *foreign* to your ears, Sir Shuran."

"Indeed? Do you hear their voices, Sir Heridos?" Shuran asked.

"I do! I hear them scream from beyond." Heridos opened his arms wide. "And so does every man here who loved the Duke."

The energy in the room seemed to flow into Heridos. Sir Shuran's rank, his reputation, and his relationships with his men were like memories from another time now. The way Sir Heridos kept using the word *foreigner* in reference to Sir Shuran clearly resonated with some, if not all, of the other Knights, and I began to wonder how long it would be before Sir Shuran found himself in irons. There was simply too much at stake to consider loyalty now. Power, previously so rigidly allocated and controlled, was now spilling everywhere in the duchy of Aramor.

And there it is, I thought, *the fragility of Tristia laid bare in front of us*. With the Duke and his family dead, who ruled Aramor now? Would one of the region's Margraves or Lords take power and form a new ducal line? What if one of them had engineered the assassination? But no, the Ducal Knights could never allow that possibility, which meant they would need to take control until the Duchy Council could be convened, otherwise all would be chaos and blood. So that meant that Sir Shuran, Knight-Commander of Aramor, had the power now—but only if the Knights followed him. They had looked so loyal, so disciplined, only a week ago, but since then, Shuran had come with us to Carefal and the Duke had been murdered. Now he was defending the Greatcoats—those very bastards who had, at least as far as the rest of the Knights were concerned, killed their Duke. In its own way, Aramor was at war, and politics would come swiftly on its heels.

"Cleric!" Shuran said at last.

There were several men in green robes standing together in the room, but none stepped forward. Shuran's gaze fell on one in particular, a young man with thinning black hair, who muttered, "Knight-Commander?"

"To whom did the Duke pray?"

"I'm sorry?"

"It is a simple enough question: to which God did Duke Isault pray? You were his personal cleric, were you not?"

"I was, Sir Shuran."

"And did he not confide in you to which God he gave fealty? I wonder how you could provide him with spiritual guidance if you did not know whether he prayed to War or to Love."

For a moment, there was murmured laughter in the room, but it didn't last.

"To Argentus, God of Coin, Knight-Commander," the weaselly little man said at last. "All the Dukes of Pulnam have followed the teachings of Argentus."

"And the Duke's family? Did they pray to Argentus as well?"

"Of course," the cleric said.

"Good," Sir Shuran said, "now we're getting somewhere."

"I don't see how," Sir Heridos muttered.

Sir Shuran ignored him. "And when a faithful servant of Coin dies, where does he go?"

"Why, into the arms of Argentus himself," the cleric said, "to feast and walk in joy throughout the heavenly manor he creates from his wealth on earth."

"What?" Shuran asked. "Are you saying a faithful servant of Argentus does not spend all his time screaming in pain and tortured regret at the manner of his death?"

"Of course not, Knight-Commander. Only a faithless man would suffer such a . . ." The cleric caught the look in Sir Heridos's eyes and stopped.

"Enough," Sir Heridos said.

"Do you still hear our Duke's voice, Knight-Captain?" Sir Shuran said.

"This is not the time for—"

"I asked you a question, Sir Heridos. Do you hear the Duke crying out?"

Sir Heridos looked around the room, but seeing no strong support, he said, "What I *meant*, Knight-Commander, is that the people of Aramor deserve vengeance for what has happened here. It is our duty to serve them in this."

"Ah," Sir Shuran said, "now perhaps there is something we can agree on."

"Good, then—"

"But not in *vengeance*, Sir Heridos. The people couldn't care less about vengeance. Or if they do care, that will soon be outweighed by other concerns."

Heridos looked as if Shuran had suddenly tossed him a sack of gold coins. "What other concern could take precedence over punishing the murderers?"

"Finding them would be a nice start," Sir Shuran said.

"They stand there," Sir Heridos said.

I couldn't even blame Sir Heridos. Dara was one of us, after all, as true a Greatcoat as there had ever been, though I could not see how it was possible that a Cantor could have turned assassin. Dara had no love for the Dukes, certainly—and neither did I, or Kest, or Brasti, or any of us—but she followed the King's Laws with diligence. What could have made her turn? My mind slipped back to my days in the dungeons of Rijou with Patriana, Duchess of Hervor laughing as she oversaw my torture, and laughing hardest of all as she told me that half the Greatcoats were hers already, and the other half had turned to banditry. The thought of those hours bound and hanging by my wrists made me shudder; the memories still fresh of those cuts made in my skin and the ointments applied to my wounds that burned flesh and boiled skin.

I shook my head. *You're dead, you old snake. Stay out of my soul.*

"I will be happy to behead these men myself," Shuran said, "if we have evidence of their involvement, but since they were under our own guard when it happened, I think it would be hard to convict them."

"You think it a coincidence that they arrived here and six days later the Duke and his family are murdered?" Heridos cried. "They want to put their little bitch on the throne!"

"Which would be a lot easier to do with the Duke alive to deliver the support he's promised in his decree."

"Silence, Trattari," Sir Heridos said. "Would that my men had killed you when you arrived."

Sir Shuran took a step toward Heridos. "Had they done so, Knight-Captain, they would have disobeyed a direct order from your superior. Shall I remind you of the penalty for disobeying a direct order from the Knight-Commander?"

Heridos wasn't cowed. "Is it the same as the penalty for treason? You weren't born in Aramor, were you, Sir Shuran? An odd thing, that, since every other man here was born and bred in this duchy. You rose quickly for a man who has been here for only a few short years."

Now we had come to the point: Heridos was trying to convince his fellow Knights and the assembled clerics that Sir Shuran was a traitor; he'd keep reminding them of his foreignness and see where that might lead.

"I rose in the ranks, Sir Heridos, because the Duke ordered it so."

"The Duke was ever a generous man," Heridos said.

Sir Shuran smiled. "Yes, that is so. In fact, I can't even remember why I was first raised to the rank of Knight-Sergeant." He looked around the room. "Can anyone here remember why? I seem to have quite forgotten."

There was an awkward silence.

"I know," Shuran said. "It must have been because it was my birthday." He walked over to one of the Knights, an older man with broad shoulders and a fringe of brown hair around his otherwise bald head. Shuran stood inches from the man's face. "Was that it, Sir Karlen? Was I given the rank of Knight-Sergeant as a birthday present?"

I watched his performance with admiration: this was a man who knew how to play his crowd.

"No," Karlen replied.

"No, Sir Karlen?" Shuran said. "Then why do you suppose? Was it perhaps because of my pretty looks?" He gestured at the burns along the left side of his face.

"It was for the Battle of Brantle's Peak," Sir Karlen said.

"The Battle of what? Are you quite sure, Sir Karlen?"

"Yes, Knight-Commander. You saved the Duke's life that day."

Sir Shuran turned around and looked at the rest of the Knights. "Really? What an odd thing for a *foreigner* to do." He walked over to another Knight, this one almost as tall as he was, but much younger. "Then why did the Duke make me Knight-Captain, Sir Belletris?"

"The brigands," the young Knight said. "We were set upon by them as the Duke's family was coming back from Hervor in the north. You saved them—you saved all of us."

I thought I heard a little hero-worship surfacing in the younger Knight's voice and demeanor.

"I did? How remarkable of me. Well then, surely my rise to Knight-Commander must have been just some kind of jest—the Duke loved a good jest, did he not, Sir Heridos?"

Shuran walked over to the Knight-Captain and stood in front of him.

"You've made your point," the other man said.

"No, I don't think I have. Why was I raised to the rank of Knight-Commander, Sir Heridos?"

"The attack from Luth last year."

"Attack from where, did you say?" Shuran asked.

"Luth: the attack by Duke Roset's men at the border—they outnumbered us three to one and you led the charge that won the battle."

Sir Shuran looked thoughtful. "You know, now that you mention it, I do recall something about that day. But you were there as well, weren't you, Sir Heridos? We both held the same rank—remind me, why didn't you lead that charge?"

Sir Heridos muttered something.

"What's that? Forgive me, Sir Heridos, I'm a little hard of hearing. Could you repeat that?"

"I was incapacitated."

Someone among the Knights gave a small laugh.

"Yes," Sir Shuran said, "it can be particularly hard to get back up when you've dropped your sword and then slipped and fallen in the mud while trying to retrieve it."

Now the laughter spread. Evidently the assembled Knights had reached a consensus. Shuran turned his back on all of them and faced Kest, Brasti, and me. For a moment I thought he was about to say something else, but instead he just stood there as laughter filled the room.

Move, you fool, I thought. *You're giving Heridos the perfect target!*

"I'll not be under the thumb of a foreign traitor!" Heridos shouted.

But even then, Shuran didn't move. Sir Heridos rushed at him, warsword in hand, and I began to draw my rapier, even knowing I wouldn't have time. Some of the other Knights could see the attack coming, but none of them moved. Why? This was a dishonorable attack—a coward's gambit. But then, once Shuran was dead, would anyone care? I watched as Heridos's blade came up in preparation for a blow that would crush Shuran's skull. But just as the blade began its descent, I watched in awe as Shuran, in one smooth, perfect motion, spun around, drawing his own warsword and using the momentum to slice through Sir Heridos's neck.

The head of Knight-Captain Heridos flew through the air and then bounced on the ground, once, twice, and a third time, before rolling halfway to the door that led out of the throne room.

"Shit," Brasti said.

I heard Kest exhale next to me and turned to look at him. His eyes blinked repeatedly, as if he were watching the attack over and over again. "He's better than he let on," he said finally. "It's going to take me nineteen moves."

"Only if you have to fight him again," I said. "Let's hope that's not necessary."

Sir Shuran slid his blade back into its sheath. "Is there anyone else who desires my death?" he asked the assembled Knights in a voice barely above a whisper.

There was no answer.

"I said, is there anyone else who would challenge me?" He slammed a gauntleted fist against one of the square pillars in the room. "I am the Knight-Commander of Aramor," he said, his voice suddenly very different than it had been before; now it was bold, definitive; *commanding*. "If the lot of you want me to step down, speak now. You get one chance. I'll lay down my sword here and now and you can even clap me in irons if you like. If you think another can do a better job of leading us through the dark days to come, then say the word."

No one spoke.

"Think carefully," he said, "for if I am to remain Knight-Commander of Aramor then this will be the last time—the *very* last time—that I entertain this sort of foolishness. The next man who questions my honor or my rank or tries to attack me, I will break in two and send the pieces north and south to the ends of the world."

He walked along the line of Knights and clerics. "Well, I await your answer. Am I the leader of the Knights of Aramor?"

"Yes, Knight-Commander," they said as one.

I thought their voices were as loud as could be, but it wasn't enough for Sir Shuran.

"I said, am I your leader?"

"Yes, Knight-Commander!" they all shouted.

"As I told Sir Heridos, I'm hard of hearing these days. Speak up, if you would have me hear you."

"Yes, Knight-Commander!" they screamed, their voices so loud I heard the metal swords mounted on the pillars clang. They continued to shout Shuran's title and it was as if the room was being struck by lightning over and over. Shuran had turned the situation around so completely that men who minutes before had been ready to betray him were twice as loyal to him now as they had ever been before. He no longer simply *led* the Knights of Aramor. He *ruled* them.

Shuran turned to the cleric. "Prepare messages for the Margraves and Lords. You will not send even one of them until I have read the words. Knights, prepare the castle guards and the rest of the troops. No one leaves here without my say-so. I'll have no word of this go out until I'm good and ready. Oh, and have someone bury Sir Heridos with honors."

"But sir," said the cleric, "what of the Duke and his family? We must prepare them for the funeral."

"No," Shuran said, "you make what preparations you need, but leave the bodies here. I need the day to try to make sense of what happened."

"And them?" the cleric asked, pointing at Kest, Brasti, and me.

"The Greatcoats?" Shuran turned to me. "They have a great deal of training in these matters. They will assist me in piecing together what took place. If they give me what I need, then they will have the gratitude of Aramor."

He glared at each of us in turn. "And if not, I'll kill them myself."

16

THE INVESTIGATION

"The girl died first," I said to Kest, who was kneeling beside me next to the bodies. Brasti was looking out of the east-facing window; he had no taste for this kind of work. Violence, especially murder, brings a chaos with it that resists explanation and wears on the soul. I had to turn away from Avette's face every few seconds. She was younger than Aline, with softer features, but my mind kept interposing Aline's features on the body of the girl on the throne room's cold floor. *Look at her,* I told myself. *You'll do Avette no good by pretending she isn't dead.*

A Greatcoat needs to be able to make sense of the wounds on a body as well as the tearing of clothes and the scuffmarks on the floor. There can be no justice until the story of what happened is uncovered.

"How do you know?" Shuran asked, his voice echoing in the now mostly empty room. The rows of metal-clad Knights and silk-robed clerics all giving instructions to confused and weary servants had all filed out and now there were only the three of us and the Knight-Commander. And the dead, of course.

"Here, where her throat was slit, the cut is heaviest at this side, see? She has small bruises on the side of her face"—I placed my own fingers in roughly the same position so he could see what I meant—"and they were made by a man's fingers. Did she share a room with any of the others?"

"Her mother—she sometimes had nightmares . . ." His voice dropped away.

"The killer likely held her like this." Kest held his left arm out, his hand gripping an imaginary girl's head. "Look at Duchess Yenelle here: the stab wound is in the back of her neck. She was ordered to kneel, then the assassin dragged the girl behind her mother, slit her throat, and then pushed the blade straight through the back of the mother's neck."

"What about the boys?" Shuran asked.

I moved to Lucan, the elder of the two. "He has wounds on his arms, you see here? Not just on the outside of his forearms where you would get cut trying to cover your face"—I held up his left arm, revealing two deep gashes—"but here on the inside, from trying to grab at someone armed with a blade. He tried to fight."

"They might have died first," Shuran said.

"Look at how deep and jagged these gashes are," I said. "Was Lucan a reckless boy?"

"No," Shuran replied, "he was ever a studious child."

"To get this many wounds and for them to be so deep, he must have rushed in close, like a wild man: he saw the bodies of his mother and sister, if not the murders themselves."

Shuran looked at Kest and me then, his eyes a little wide. I'd seen that expression many times before, especially from Knights. Most people see the world in such simple terms—honor and dishonor; right and wrong, alive or dead—and it takes them by surprise when they have to start seeing things as we do, as pieces of a story built up from the tiny echoes of events past.

A part of me wanted to stop there, despite the urgent need to prove that a Greatcoat hadn't been the killer. It's one thing to see a child dead, but quite another to force yourself, step by step, to envision the moments up to their death. It felt wrong, cruel. Perverse, even.

I had told the King as much, once, during one of those many late nights he forced us to pore over the corpses of men and women and children whose deaths we already knew from witnesses. "They're dead," I'd said. "Let them rest."

The King had turned to me then, those inquisitive eyes of his probing at me as though he were investigating me too. "A murdered man gets no rest, Falcio. He either serves the living by revealing his killer or serves the murderer by concealing his identity. Which would you rather be?"

"Falcio? Are we to continue?" Shuran asked, shaking me from my memories.

I met his gaze and found a kind of sickened fascination there. He walked over to the smaller of the two boys. "Tell me about Patrin."

"He came last, I think."

"Why do you say so?"

"The killer would have started with the more dangerous opponent: Lucan was older, and taller too, so he would be killed first. I think . . ." I had to pause. The depraved logic of murder was sticking in my throat. "I think Patrin saw his mother and older brother being killed."

"How can you tell?"

"I can't," I said, "not for certain, anyway, but look here: he has only one wound, a thrust to the heart like his father suffered." I pulled the green cloth down to the boy's knees. There was a darkened patch on his nightclothes, at his groin.

"He pissed himself," Shuran said. His voice held neither judgment nor sympathy.

"The lad would have been terrified," I said, a little defensively.

The Knight-Commander rose and walked over to Duke Isault's body. "And you're positive the Duke died after his family? How can you be so certain?"

"Two reasons," I said, covering Patrin back up before joining Shuran. "First, the killer clearly wanted the whole family dead. The

Duke would be the most closely guarded, so there's a far greater risk of the body being discovered and the alarm being raised."

"And the second reason?"

"Look at his face."

I watched as Sir Shuran peered into the face of the man who'd given him everything. "He was mad," Shuran said, and now his voice betrayed a deep sadness. "His eyes . . . they're almost feral."

Sometimes the dead speak to us in a language so plain it needs no words, I thought. "This is the face of a man who has just been told his family has been killed."

Sir Shuran left the bodies and walked over to the throne, staring at it as if he expected the Duke to appear on it at any moment.

"Can you tell me how this could happen, Falcio? Why would your woman—Dara—have done this?"

"She wouldn't," I said. This was the part we had left for last. Somehow it felt important to tell the story of the other dead first: those who would be forgotten as soon as the struggle for power in Aramor began.

He turned to me. "I can understand how you wouldn't want to think ill of your fellow Greatcoat, but she is here and her blade took the Duke's life."

That part at least was true: Dara always fought with a broadsword, with a blade that widened slightly just before it angled sharply to its point. The thrust into Isault's heart had been made with that very sword.

"It might not have been the same weapon used on the Duke's family," Kest started.

"They were killed with broadswords as well," Shuran said.

"Yes, but it's not clear that it was the same weapon. These could have been done with any broad-bladed sword."

"Including hers," Shuran insisted.

He nodded.

"Then, forgive me, but it appears to me that we have the killer."

Before I could say anything else, the doors to the throne room burst open. A Knight with dark hair flecked with gray walked in hauling an old woman, her hair tied back and wearing a dirty apron.

"What is this, Sir Chandis?" Shuran asked.

Sir Chandis pulled the woman over to Dara's body. "Is that her?" The old woman took sight of the six corpses in the room and shut her eyes.

"Is that her?" Chandis demanded, shaking her.

"Aye, it's her," she said, crying. "It's her."

"What is this?" I asked. "Who are you?"

"I'm Wirrina, Knight-Commander," she said, looking at Sir Shuran and ignoring me. "The head cook."

"Of course I remember you, Wirrina," Shuran said, his tone kindly. "What do you have to tell us about the Duke's death?"

"Oh, nothing, sir, I know nothing of that, only . . . the woman? Tessa?"

"Who?"

"She means the assassin," Sir Chandis said. "Wirrina told one of the guards that a servant had gone missing, and she matched the description of the Greatcoat so I brought her to see the body."

Wirrina held her hands together and shook her head, over and over. "It's her, Knight-Commander, I swear it, though I never seen her dressed that way before."

"Did she know the Duke?" Shuran asked.

"We all know the Duke, sir, him bein'—Oh, but you mean, know him better'n other people?"

"Yes, Wirrina, I mean other than that."

The old woman looked down and chewed her lip. She shook her head left and right, as if she were having an argument with herself.

"Speak, woman, you're in the presence of the Knight-Commander of Aramor," Sir Chandis said.

"I suspect she knows that already, Sir Chandis," Shuran said mildly. "Wirrina, it will be helpful if you tell us everything you know."

"Well, sir, I . . . I don't want to get into no trouble, not for somethin' I couldn't—"

"You'll be fine as long as you tell us the truth."

"She—well, the Duke sent a boy to fetch her once in a while. I think he . . ." She trailed off and looked at the floor.

"You think he had a relationship with her?" Shuran asked.

"I'm sure I couldn't say, not for true, but he did send for her sometimes."

A silence filled the room briefly as we all tried to work through the implications of that simple statement. *He did send for her sometimes.* The Dara I had known was hardly likely to give her body away, and most certainly not to a man like Isault. Her own husband had been murdered shortly before she'd joined the Greatcoats—it was his murder and the failure of another Duke to prosecute the crime that led her to join us. So what did she do at those times when the Duke sent for her?

"Beshard," I said suddenly. "Where's Beshard?" If there was any man in the duchy who would have known of Isault's relationships, surely it was Beshard. Hells, Isault probably made the old chamberlain watch.

"Beshard is dead," Chandis said.

"What—? When?" Shuran asked.

"We just discovered him in his room, in bed. His throat was opened." Sir Chandis was watching Shuran's expression. "Knight-Commander, isn't it obvious? These men killed the chamberlain to cover up the harlot Trattari's secret. She wormed her way into the castle kitchens as a maid, she caught the Duke's eye, and when the time was right, did the business she was sent to do." The Knight pointed at us. "By the child, Aline, the one *they* want to put on the throne."

Sir Shuran raised an eyebrow. "I can believe this woman—Tessa or Dara, or whatever her name was—committed the crimes, but I hardly think it the plan of a thirteen-year-old girl, Sir Chandis."

"Thirteen?" Wirrina interrupted. "Oh, I think that's impossible, sir."

Chandis sneered. "Are you an investigator now, old woman?"

"Oh, no, sir, not that, it's just that—well, this Aline, whoever she is? Well, she'd've had to've hatched the plan when she was eight. Tessa's been with us for nigh on five year now."

Five years? Dara had been hiding out as a scullery maid for five years? And doing what all that time? Sleeping with the Duke of Aramor?

"None of this makes any sense," I muttered.

Sir Shuran looked to me and then back to the head cook. "Thank you, Wirrina. Sir Chandis will take you back to the kitchens now. You need not fear for you or yours; of that I can assure you. I'll need to talk to you again soon, and in the meantime, Sir Chandis himself will bear full responsibility for your safety."

Sir Chandis looked properly chastened, and after a moment he saluted and left with the old woman in tow.

"This certainly sounds like a plot, First Cantor," Sir Shuran said to me.

"It does," Kest said, "but not a very good one."

"And why not? It has succeeded admirably." The Knight-Commander's voice was beginning to show distinct irritation.

"The assassin sneaks into the family's rooms, knocking out but not killing the guards, and murders the Duke's wife and children. Then the assassin goes to Beshard's room and murders him. Finally, the assassin comes here, kills two guards, takes the time to inform his Grace that his entire family is lying dead, then kills him too. Eight dead in total."

"Forgive me, Saint of Swords, but that sounds perfectly logical to me," Shuran said.

"Why not kill the other guards?" Brasti asked. "The ones outside the family rooms? Why knock them out? It's a greater risk."

"Elegance?" Shuran offered. "Perhaps this Dara of yours wanted to kill the nobles but not the guards who were just doing their jobs? Then when she got here, she found she had no choice but to kill Isault's guards—"

"What about Beshard?" I asked. "He wasn't a noble, and yet you say he was killed in his bed."

"She would have had to have killed Beshard if he knew of her relationship with the Duke." Shuran spread his hands to indicate the bodies on the floor. "I realize this may be hard for you to believe, Falcio, but the simplest and most logical explanation is that your woman, Dara, murdered the Duke and his family."

"But *why*?" I asked.

He shrugged. "Perhaps out of revenge for his part in the death of the King."

"Five years later?" Kest asked.

"Or for some more recent slight. If they were lovers, perhaps the Duke tired of her. Or perhaps she discovered that Duke Isault was not going to give you the decree supporting Aline and was instead going to support Trin."

"Was he?" I asked.

"I don't know," Shuran said. "When I spoke with the Duke last night he was quite drunk. He switched back and forth, first swearing he would back Aline, then cursing the King's name and vowing to support Trin. When I pressed him on the matter he sent me away."

"Which way did you press him?"

Shuran gave a weary smile. "I asked only that he tell me which way he was going to go so I could prepare my men for whatever we needed to do next."

What he really meant to say was, *If Isault was going to betray you, I needed to ready my men to arrest you or kill you.* I wondered if he even knew whether he would have followed through on his duty to the Duke or his promise to me. There are times when honor sucks.

We stood there in silence for a few moments more, trying to make sense of what had happened. "She's a bloody mess," Brasti said at last. He'd been silent all this time and so the soft, sorrowful note in his voice surprised all of us.

"What do you mean?"

"Here," he said, pointing at a wound on her thigh. "Look at how messy this wound is. It's like the Duke stabbed her three or four times in the same place."

"The Duke was enraged," Kest said.

"Sure. So why is the one in her chest so clean? It's a single strike. Have you ever seen a man driven mad by rage who stabs someone repeatedly in the thigh and then gives them a single thrust to the heart? Why didn't he butcher her?"

"Probably because he was dying," Shuran said. "They struggled for a while, she gave him the fatal thrust, and then before he died he thrust his dagger into her heart."

Brasti snorted. "Just like the old stories."

"There is a dark symmetry to it."

"Except a man with a sword through his heart isn't going to have the strength to do what you say Isault did. Falcio, someone else killed Dara."

I looked at Kest. "Surprisingly," he said, "Brasti is right. The chances of all this being due to one woman, even Dara, is nearly impossible. And to then be killed by a fat, drunken man mad with rage? Even seriously wounded, Dara would have dispatched him easily."

"I agree: there's another killer," I said. "Whatever else happened here, it wasn't all between Dara and Duke Isault. Shuran, you need to let us go after him. Kest, Brasti, and I have experience with this. We've tracked killers before."

"I can't do that, Falcio. You know I can't. Releasing you would show weakness to the very nobles and clerics who will be vying for power."

"Who'll take the throne?" I asked.

"No one. There hasn't been a case of an entire ducal family murdered in . . . Actually, I can't think of a case. I'll need to have my Knights establish control over the local guardsmen across the duchy until the Ducal Concord can be called."

"You mean the other eight get to decide who takes over?" He nodded.

"Who benefits in the meantime?"

Shuran was silent for a few moments. "Me, I suppose, for a while. But it's not as if the other Dukes would ever elevate a Knight."

"What about Isault's enemies?"

"Duke Roset may try to use the opportunity to extend his control over the border between Aramor and Luth. I imagine Carefal and the other villages like it will slip into Roset's control."

"What about Trin?" Brasti asked. "Without Isault to support Aline doesn't that mean things get easier for her?"

"Not really," Shuran said. "If suspicion falls on her then it's highly likely the Dukes of Pertine, Luth, Baern, and even Rijou will band together. Assassinating a Duke is not considered good form for a putative monarch."

"Good, then," Brasti said. "So all we need to do is go find proof that she's responsible for this and then we can put this whole mess to bed."

Shuran stepped forward and put a hand on the hilt of his sword. "I told you, I can't let you leave. I know you're not responsible for these deaths but I'll have enough trouble establishing control without having the nobles accusing me of letting the Greatcoats get away with murder."

Kest stood in front of him. He hadn't bothered to draw his own sword, and nor had the Knight-Commander. "We've fought once, Sir Shuran. On the best day of your life, do you believe you could win?"

Shuran gave a wry smile. "I don't know." He let go of the hilt of his sword and it slid back down into its sheath. "Certainly today is unlikely to be my best day." He turned to me. "You want me to try and take control of Aramor while being known as the man who let the Greatcoats free?"

"It's either that, or be the man who let the assassin escape justice. I doubt there's anything that would please the murderer so much as you detaining us now. You'll have to decide how best to serve Duke Isault."

Shuran looked at me, at Kest, at Brasti, as if he hoped for some sign in our expressions that we could be trusted—or perhaps, that we were guilty—anything that would make his decision easier. My hand was close to my rapier. I didn't really think he would let us go.

He knelt down in front of the Duke's body. "Isault was kind to me, you know. I think he liked the fact that I was a foreigner, that I was different. He used to make fun of my scars. Everybody else pretends not to see them, but the Duke, well, he always told the truth as he saw it."

The big Knight rose. "Go," he said, still looking at the body. "If there was another assassin, he or she will have used the passage behind the door near the throne. It leads out of the castle. If you're telling the truth, then you're my only hope of finding whoever did this. If you're not, then be very sure you understand that I too can find people if I need to."

The passageway that began behind Isault's throne wound its torturous way through the inner walls of the palace. It reminded me of the trail left by a snake that had eaten its way through the stone. It took us to empty hallways near the outer walls, then wove its way deep into the heart of the castle itself.

"Saints," Brasti said at last, "which drunken architect designed this mess?"

"There's a pattern," Kest said, as he pointed to one of the narrow doors that periodically interrupted the path. "The main passageway winds its way around the castle, while these side passageways gave the Duke access to nearly every other room in the place."

"So he could spy on his own people."

"Better that than the reverse, I imagine," Kest replied.

I spotted a small bloody smear on the wall again. "The assassin went this way," I said, pointing to another side corridor. "Why didn't the damned guards follow the trail?"

"Perhaps they were too busy assuming it really was us," Kest suggested.

"No," Brasti said as he knelt down to examine tracks along the dusty floor. His former life—as hunter and poacher—had given him eyes for following a trail that Kest and I lacked. "Look, you can see where some of the guards have followed the trail."

"Any chance they caught the assassin?" I asked.

"No, see here? The trail looks like it heads to the inner circuit, but that's only because the assassin wants us to go that way. He's tried to mask his tracks in the dust but he's favoring his left leg. What he actually did was to head straight out the passageway to leave the castle."

"How do you know?"

Brasti carefully brushed some of the dust out of the way. At first I saw nothing amiss, but peering closer, I could just make out the dark red drops on the floor. "He's been covering up his blood with dust, and then wiping some on the walls to show him going the other way—but in fact he always backtracks toward the outer passage. Look at the way he's favoring one leg."

"Dara always did prefer to go for a leg wound first," Kest said.

It was a good strategy, and one that had served her well in the past; when it works, it throws the opponent's balance off and slows them down, giving the swordsman time to concentrate on the killing stroke.

"Too bad someone played her at her own game this time," I said. "Come on."

We picked up our pace, all the while keeping an eye out for any overzealous guards who might be continuing their own search. The passageways wound their way around the entire palace, sometimes sloping upward at a ridiculously steep angle to get up to the next story, other times proceeding downward by precipitously narrow stairs. Eventually, despite our best efforts, we lost the trail.

"How far back did he fool us?" I asked Brasti.

"A long way, I think," he replied angrily. "Damn it. I should have caught on. If we go back now—"

"—we'll likely end up getting caught by the palace guards."

Hells. Whoever had done this was better at sneaking than we were at tracking them.

"What now?" Kest asked.

"There's the way out," Brasti said, pointing to a circle of white light off to the right of us.

The path became steadily more uneven as we approached the exit. Outside was a sheer cliff dropping a hundred feet to a rocky riverbed, but on closer inspection we spotted a vague excuse for a trail that led away from the castle.

"That's one hell of an escape route to have to take in the dark," Brasti said. "I doubt it would have done Isault much good if he'd ever needed it."

"The assassin made it down," I said, "I'm sure of it. He or she led us all that way around the entire fucking palace, but I bet they got here hours ago."

"Then how did these tracks get here?" Kest asked.

"He must have planted them last night," Brasti said. "The assassin knew this would be the best escape route so he must have set a trail long before he committed the murders."

Kest looked unconvinced. "That would be a rather large risk to take for someone whose own life depended on not being seen."

"Not really," I said. "I'll bet Isault didn't let many people use those hallways—what good's a secret spying network if everyone knows about it? If the assassin knew the way in, he or she probably had the passages all to themselves."

"That all makes sense," Kest said, "but something is still bothering me."

"Other than the obvious fact that we're completely screwed?" Brasti asked.

"Yes: it's the timing of the murders. Why kill the Duke's family first?"

"Because the Duke kept the better guards for himself?" Brasti suggested.

"Except he didn't. Two guards? He had far more men in the family wing protecting his wife and children."

"It's likely he wanted to keep whatever relationship he had with Dara a secret," I said.

"Fine," Brasti said, "so he was fucking Dara—which completely confuses me by the way. She never so much as laughed at my jokes— but that aside, it still makes more sense to kill him first. If someone had seen the assassin going in and out of the family rooms, they would have sounded the alarm and the killer would never have reached Isault. No, there had to be at least two assassins: someone killed Isault, and someone else killed his family."

"That doesn't stop Dara from being the one who killed the Duke while an accomplice killed his family," Kest said.

"Not possible," Brasti said, his voice echoing with absolute certainty.

"So you agree with Falcio?" Kest sounded surprised.

"Of course not," he replied. "Falcio's an idealistic idiot when it comes to Dara and the others, the same way he is about the King. He's forgotten that Dara was a fucking lunatic."

"Then—"

"That's the point: if she'd wanted to murder Isault she wouldn't have waited five years to do it. And she wouldn't kill him with some poet's thrust to the heart, either. Do you remember what she was like in a fight? Shit, if Dara had decided to kill Isault she would have decapitated him and all his guards, spent the next hour arranging their heads on spears around the throne room, then drunk whatever was left of his wine before leaving. There's no way Dara did this out of some kind of desire for personal revenge."

"There is another possibility," Kest said. He turned to me. "But you won't like it, Falcio."

"What is it?"

"Perhaps we should get out of here first. We've got a long walk down that gully and then we're going to need to get to a village to buy new horses and gear."

"Tell me," I said.

He paused for a moment, then said, "You've been saying all along that the King must have had a plan; that he wouldn't have simply left all this to chance. What if this was his plan? What if—?"

"No," I said, "there's no way the King would sanction murder. Even if—"

"Hear me out. Aline's birthright has just been uncovered. Word is spreading that she's going to try to take the throne. Isault may or may not have been planning to betray us, and suddenly he turns up dead?"

"It's no—"

"Kest is right," Brasti said. "Look, Falcio, I know how much you loved the King. Most of us did. But this is war and politics, it's not sipping wine in the library at Castle Aramor and swapping old books about stoic philosophy. This is about *Aline*, the King's own daughter. If you had a child and you knew what would happen to her after you were dead, wouldn't you do *anything* to protect her? And if you knew you weren't going to be around to do it, wouldn't something like this make perfect sense? Send Greatcoats out, ready to kill the Dukes when the time came—get his stroke in before they can attack her?"

"There's a flaw in your theory," I said.

He threw up his hands. "Yeah, you don't like it."

Kest looked as if he were trying to work through the theory in his head again, and then again. At last he asked, "What's the flaw?"

"The three of us are probably the best choices for a mission like that," I replied, "but he didn't order us to do any such thing, did he?"

The two of them were looking at me, their eyes a little wide with disbelief. It occurred to me for the first time that neither of them had ever revealed the last command the King had given each of them.

But then Brasti said, "Saints, Falcio. You really can't see it, can you?"

"What?"

It was Kest who answered, and his voice was quiet, gentler than usual. "The King loved you too much to ask you to commit murder. He knew something like this would kill you, Falcio."

I leaned a hand against the cliff. My chest felt tight and it was hard to breathe. There was a small part of me that couldn't help but believe that there was truth in what Brasti and Kest were saying. The King and I had always been close, and I'd always believed that the two of us had shared the same ideals. But in his darkest hour, with the Dukes marching toward the castle with an army at their backs and intent on taking his head . . . could Paelis have gone back on those ideals? In the name of his own daughter, could he truly have commanded my fellow Greatcoats to commit murder? I felt my legs become unsteady, as if the neatha paralysis were taking over again. In my mind King Paelis's words repeated over and over again: *You will betray her.*

17

THE TAILOR

Even before we had left the palace chaos had already begun taking over Isault's duchy. City constables were roaming the streets, weapons drawn, though they had no clue what they were looking for. Along the outlying country roads small contingents of Shuran's Knights patrolled in a more disciplined fashion, though there too it looked to be more for show than for any real purpose. We avoided them all. Our journey would have been easier if Shuran had given us traveling papers, but I could understand why he'd preferred the freedom to decide later whether he'd let us go free or that we'd escaped.

So we made our way through the back roads of Aramor, trading its wide, well-traveled routes for muddy cart tracks and forest paths. Word of the Duke's murder was spreading slowly outside the capital, and most of those who noticed us just ignored us and went about their own business.

Despite Shuran's assurances, I was anxious to see for myself that Valiana and Dari were unharmed, but by the time we arrived at the Inn of the Red Hammer late on the second evening, they were already gone.

The innkeeper was a young man with sandy blond hair named Tyne who was sufficiently mystified by the simple business of signing the ledgers that I suspected he'd not long held the job. After a fair amount of flipping pages back and forth along with a good deal of mumbling, he finally said, "They left two days ago."

"Two days?" I asked. "That would have been only a day after they'd arrived. Check your records again."

He did, looking genuinely concerned that he'd gotten it wrong, and then said again, "Two days."

"Are you sure you aren't mistaking 'departure' with 'arrival'?"

Tyne gave a nervous giggle. "No, see, it says right here in the arrival column, 'two beautiful women' and the day they arrived. Then over here"—he flipped the page over and pointed with his finger—"right here under departure, the day later, 'the two beautiful women'. Simple, see?"

"Why 'two beautiful women'?" Kest asked. "Why wouldn't you take their names down?"

The innkeeper shrugged. "'m not good with names, really. Besides, no one ever stays here long. It's easier to just write 'three burly soldiers' or 'crazy old man'."

"You realize that Ducal Law in Aramor means you're required to keep track of guests' names in the register, don't you?"

Tyne looked like he'd swallowed something too big for his throat. "Please, sirs . . . I didn't know! I'm not . . . I mean, I'm still new at this job. My uncle only bought the place a month ago—he told me I was to run it and then he buggered off again back to Pertine."

"Your uncle owns a lot of inns, does he?" I asked.

"Nah, he's a Knight. Runs around fighting border wars with other Knights. Stupid job, really."

"And yet he earns enough money to buy an inn?" Kest asked.

Tyne shrugged again. "I guess his Knight-Commander rewarded him for his service. Not that Uncle Eduarte ever seemed very reliable to me—Mum always says—Say, you're not going to fine me, are you? I mean, I just work here. I don't—"

I took advantage of his momentary panic to take the book from his hands. There were the two entries listed, separated by a single day. "Why would they arrive one day and then leave the next without waiting for us?" I handed the book back to the innkeeper. "Did they leave a message for us?"

"Who're you?"

"Falcio," I said. "Falcio val Mond."

The innkeeper grinned. "That's funny. Anyone ever tell you your name sounds a lot like Fal—"

"Just check for messages."

"Don't need to," he said, pointing to a wooden box sitting on the counter behind him. "There ain't none in the box."

"Then why did you bother to ask my name?"

The innkeeper's forehead furrowed. "Didn't you just say I should be takin' names?"

Kest pointed at the entry showing the next arrival at the inn. "Falcio, look, here. I suspect this explains why they're not here."

I looked down at the entry. The price was half what the innkeeper had told us we'd have to pay, but when I read the line that was supposed to hold the guest's name, I forgave him.

Brasti looked over my shoulder and read the entry. "Shit."

"Do you know where the 'angry old woman' is now?" I asked the young innkeeper.

"In her rooms, like as not. Hasn't stepped out of here since she arrived, so far as I can tell. It's upstairs, last door on the right. We usually keep that suite for nobles but, well . . . she sort of . . . and I just didn't want—"

"I understand," I said, and gave him my best sympathetic smile.

Kest, Brasti, and I straightened our shoulders and brushed ourselves down before walking up the stairs and down to the end of the hall. The last door was of stout oak planks, smoothed and bound in brass, decorated with proper brass fittings and with a brass door-knocker. I was about to use it when I heard a voice from inside growl, "Just come in, you fools."

I opened the door and the three of us entered what was obviously the inn's most palatial rooms, which is to say the receiving room was a little larger than the others, and there was a separate sleeping room behind a closed door at the far end. Oh, and there were large rugs on the floor and actual curtains at the window. The Tailor was sitting at a chair by the window with needle and thread in hand, sewing something that looked like a large handkerchief.

"How did you know it was us?" Brasti asked.

"I know where every thread starts and where every thread ends," the Tailor replied without looking up from her sewing. "Besides, I could hear your footsteps coming down the hallway. The three of you walk like a cross between a drunken three-legged horse and a family of ducks."

I sat at the end of the wide bench a few feet away from her. A quick lift of her eyebrows told me this irritated her, but I considered it a small advance on the annoyance she was probably planning to cause me. "Why did you send Valiana and Dari away?" I asked.

"I had things for them to do."

"Care to elaborate?"

"If you like. I had *important* things for them to do."

I sat there for a minute, unwilling to engage in the Tailor's game. She had always liked to begin every conversation by establishing that she knew more than I did, that she had more power than I did, and that she alone would decide exactly what we would and would not discuss.

"What are you doing?" the Tailor asked.

I thought she was speaking to me but her eyes were focused over my shoulder and I turned to see Brasti halfway out of the door. "I'm going to find something to eat," he said. "I'll be back in an hour or two. Maybe by then Falcio will be done letting you cuckold him."

"I don't think cuckold means what you think it does," Kest said.

The Tailor chuckled.

"Brasti has a point, though," Kest said. "Duke Isault is dead and a Greatcoat's been implicated in his murder. There's at least one other assassin out there and we have no idea what this is about. This isn't the time for games."

"Well then," the Tailor said, "since you know nothing, perhaps you could keep your mouths shut while I'll tell you what you need to know."

"You'll tell us what you think we need to know," I muttered. "What's the difference?"

Brasti leaned against the doorjamb with his arms folded. "You know what I've been thinking about lately, old woman? I've been thinking that maybe you never got over the fact that you were once wife to a King, with servants and retainers and all those 'thees' and 'thous' and the rest. I think you miss it. I think the closest you can get to all that now is to treat the rest of us like servants, and Falcio keeps letting you do it."

Brasti's tone was light, almost whimsical, but his eyes betrayed a deeper resentment than I'd seen before.

"Let it be," I said. "We're all allies here and—"

"That's what you 'think', is it?" the Tailor asked, still staring at her sewing. "Because what I find interesting is the idea that a former poacher with a mind the size of a pea is under the illusion that what he *thinks* matters one bit to the world. You're nothing but a wayward bastard, Brasti Goodbow. You're a hanger-on to better men, hoping some kind of meaning will rub off on you from one of these other two fools."

"Enough!" I shouted. "Brasti is a Greatcoat. He's one of us and you will address him with the respect he deserves."

The Tailor stopped her sewing and looked at me as if I were an errant puppy who'd taken to barking at her. "You would think that men who'd come close to death so many times would grow wary of it."

"You would be wrong," Kest said.

The creak of a door being opened rather tentatively interrupted us and a voice whispered, "What's happening?" from the sleeping chamber.

In the crack between the door and the frame was Aline's face.

"Falcio," she said, her voice excited and yet muted at the same time, and she pushed open the door the rest of the way and ran clumsily toward me. "I was sleeping," she said, her arms wrapping around me.

"I'm very sorry to have woken you," I said, kneeling so I could embrace her properly. "We were playing a game."

Aline took half a step back. "Don't you all have much more important things to do than play games?"

My eyes caught those of the Tailor. "You know something? You're absolutely right. We don't have time for silly games."

The old woman let out a small chuckle.

I looked back at Aline, trying not to let my growing sense of horror show on my face. Her skin was pale, almost ashen, and she didn't look as if I'd awakened her from sleep—she looked as if she hadn't slept at all, not for weeks. She was even thinner than when I'd last seen her, and her eyes had a sunken quality to them, and dark circles that had no place on the face of a thirteen-year-old girl. She fiddled with her hair, which looked thin and brittle. Her fingernails were chewed.

"What are you looking at?" she demanded, a little indignantly.

I forced a smile on my face. "A very unkempt young woman with her father's gangly limbs and a nose that's too thin and bony to make a proper Queen."

"Well you don't look like a proper Greatcoat, either," she said, her hand rising self-consciously to her nose.

"That's true," I said, and hugged her to me once again. "But we're all the world has to work with, so I suppose we'll just have to do our best, won't we?"

She gripped me hard for a second and then pulled away once again. "I'm very happy to see you, Falcio. But if it's all right, I'm going to go back to sleep for a little while. I'm very tired today."

"Sure, sweetheart."

"You'll wake me before you go, though, right?"

Aline's hand was in her hair again, unconsciously tugging strands of it free. I reached out and pulled her hand away. "I'll see you before I go. Get some rest now."

When she smiled, it was as if all the energy had drained out of her. She turned and walked wearily back into the sleeping room, pulling the big oak door closed behind her.

I looked back at the others. I imagine the expression on my face matched theirs.

"She's been drugged," Kest said, his voice calm but still bearing the edge of accusation.

"Just to make her sleep," the Tailor replied. "Or try to, anyway."

Brasti looked as if he were about to explode. "What in all the hells is—?"

"Keep quiet," the Tailor said. "Don't make things any worse than they already are."

Brasti's fists clenched at his sides and he seemed to master himself. His voice became a whisper, lower in volume but no less fierce than before. "Saint Zaghev-who-sings-for-tears! What's happened to Aline?"

I shared Brasti's fear and frustration, but I already knew the answer. "War," I said. I turned to the Tailor. "The battle in Domaris goes poorly, doesn't it? That's why you're here."

The Tailor nodded.

"How long?" Kest asked.

"Duke Hadiermo's forces are close to being routed. My Great-coats have been hitting Trin's soldiers where we can, but all we can do is slow them now, not defeat them. Domaris will hold for another week, maybe two at best. Then Trin will move her forces south to the border of Rijou."

"What does any of that have to do with Aline? Was she injured?" Brasti asked.

"Not by any blade."

"Then what's wrong with her? She talks like a child of seven, not a future queen coming into womanhood."

"It's exhaustion, you fool," the Tailor said. Her voice was so angry and brittle that I realized she too was living under the weight of having failed Aline. "She's a thirteen-year-old girl."

"But it's only been a few weeks!" Brasti's voice was almost pleading, as if he was trying to negotiate for a better answer.

"No," I said quietly. "For her it's been months. This all started in Rijou, where she only narrowly avoided being burned alive along with the Tiaren family—the family she believed to be her own. Then we found her and immediately we went on the run. We were hunted by every killer the city had to throw at us until the Blood Week was over—and let's face it, Rijou has never been short of murderous killers, has it?"

"And then we had to flee from Duke Perault's Knights," Kest added, his gaze far away, "all the way through Pulnam."

I remembered my one meeting with Perault, Duke of Orison, and his barely subdued glee as he anticipated taking Aline and Valiana for his own sick pleasure.

The Tailor snickered. "If it makes you feel any better, Falcio, it turns out that Perault was insufficiently entertaining for Trin. She had her new lover kill Perault while he was enjoying his last ride with her."

"None of this helps Aline," Kest said.

The Tailor picked up her sewing. "And nothing can. She's a good girl, our Aline, and a brave one. But she's a thirteen-year-old, and there is only so much the mind of a thirteen-year-old girl can take before—"

A creeping sickness filled my belly and throat. "She's going mad from fear."

The Tailor kept her eyes firmly on her sewing but her lips pinched together for a moment. "Aye, that's as true a way to see it as any."

"But what are we going to do?" Brasti demanded. The fingers of his right hand were twitching as if they were trying to feel for an arrow. "We keep wasting our time with all this war and politics, and meanwhile the girl we're supposed to save is fading away! How is she supposed to take the throne in this state?"

The Tailor's hands moved the needle deftly through the fabric, back and forth. She remained silent. No angry retorts, no clever jabs, just the desperate stillness of a battlefield after the fighting is done.

"Tailor, are you telling us it's over?" I asked. "Is there no hope of putting Aline on the throne?"

No one spoke. Kest looked around the room, his gaze flitting from wall to wall as if he were trying to find a pattern in the grain of the wood. Brasti's eyes were filling with tears of frustration and sorrow, and I suspected mine were too.

"It's over," the Tailor said finally. She put her sewing on the windowsill and rose from her chair. "To answer your earlier question, the girls should be back later tonight. A dozen of Trin's men caught our trail in Domaris and followed us all the way through Rijou, so Dari and Valiana are leading them on a merry chase right now."

"Why not more?" Kest asked. "Why not send a hundred or a thousand, to get you once and for all?"

"Jillard has made it clear he won't allow Trin's forces to march through his duchy, so Trin can send only as many men as can sneak through the border."

"So he's holding up his end of the bargain?" I asked, a little surprised. "The Duke of Rijou is honoring the agreement with Aline?"

The Tailor snorted. "You should know better than anyone that using the word 'honor' in the same sentence as 'Rijou' is like handing wool to a sheep and asking him to knit you a coat. He's just doing what all the rest of them are doing: holding out until Trin offers him a deal he can live with."

"And when she does?" Kest asked.

The Tailor's expression didn't change at all, but we could all see the rage and frustration that boiled beneath the surface of her skin. "May every Duke in Tristia find themselves in their own personal hell," she said. "That's all I ask of the Gods now."

"We have the decree," Brasti said. "Can't we use that to—?"

"To what?" I asked. "If it was just Isault who'd been killed, then his eldest child would have taken the ducal throne and he'd be bound by the decree, but—"

The Tailor's eyes narrowed. "What are you talking about? Someone killed Lucan as well as Isault?"

I couldn't stop myself from taking some small pleasure in the fact that, for once, the Tailor didn't know everything.

"Not just him. Isault's entire family was taken out."

"Damn this country," the Tailor swore, peering into each of our faces in turn as if to see if we were lying. "How is that possible? Were they with Isault?"

"No," Kest said, "they were in their separate rooms when the assassin came for them."

"Saint Laina-who-whores-for-Gods! What a mess." The Tailor turned to me. "There's a story going around that a Greatcoat was found in Isault's throne room when he was killed. Is it true?"

I nodded. "Dara."

The Tailor's expression grew thoughtful. "Why in all the hells was she there?"

That was a question that had been burning a hole in me since we'd arrived, but I wasn't sure if I was prepared for the answer.

Hells, I thought, *will it really make things any worse if I know for sure?* "Did you and the King ever discuss a plan to have Greatcoats assassinate the Dukes?"

"Paelis would never condone such a thing. You know that."

"What happens now?" Kest asked. "If we can't win a war against Trin, how do we proceed?"

The Tailor opened a cloth bag sitting on the windowsill next to her sewing. She pulled out three smaller bags and handed one to each of us.

I opened up my bag and saw a pile of small gold coins inside— more than thirty, I reckoned at first sight. "What are we supposed to do with these?"

"Retire," she said.

"I don't understand."

"Go to Merisaw; it's just outside the capital of Rijou."

"I know where Merisaw is—but why would I go there?"

The Tailor's voice softened. "Because *she's* there," she said. "She's waiting for you."

Brasti threw his hands up in the air, nearly losing hold of his bag of coins. "Will one of you please tell me what you're talking about?"

A woman's face came into my mind: dark hair framing pale white skin, blue eyes with tiny wrinkles on each side that you could only see if you were close enough to kiss her. A smile that promised the stars. "Ethalia," I said. "Ethalia is there."

The Tailor smiled. "Look at that idiot expression on your face, Falcio. I swear, in a better world I'd find it endearing. Take the back roads and make your way there. From Merisaw you can join one of the caravans going south; when you get to Baern you can get yourself a little boat. Go and spend your days in the Southern Islands. Trin will have little interest in them."

"But what about us?" Brasti said.

"You? Take your money; go and live your life. There's enough there to keep you in whores and ale until you get so drunk you shoot yourself dead with an arrow from your own bow."

"I have no use for whores nor ale," Kest said.

The Tailor walked over to him and put a hand on his face. "Ah, Kest. Your love may well be the noblest thing I've ever seen. It's certainly the most pathetic."

Before I could ask her what she was talking about, a more pressing thought entered my mind. "But what about Aline—what happens to her?"

"Aline will come with me," she said. "I'll keep her hidden. Trin will take the country and drive it into chaos and civil war, which is probably for the best."

I started to object but the Tailor held up a hand. "Tristia can't be saved, not as it is, and not with Aline too young to survive the throne. No, Trin will take power and ruin things even more, and before long she'll find herself looking down at her headless body from the top of a spike. The Dukes will likely fall right alongside her and the country will be ready for a sane monarch. Until that day, Aline must be protected."

I thought back to my conversation with Aline on the top of the little hill outside the village of Phan. "Aline comes with me," I said.

The Tailor's eyes were as flat and hard as black rock. "No. She does not."

"I kept her safe in Rijou."

"This is easier. I can—"

"You weren't dying in Rijou," the Tailor said quietly.

"What are you talking about?" Brasti asked.

"You haven't told them?"

Kest and Brasti looked at me. They might have suspected, but they were still not sure. They knew I was suffering from the neatha, but I'd kept my thoughts about where the paralysis was leading to myself; insanely, I had still hoped there might be some cure. Now all I could think about was the number of days the journey from Pertine to Merisaw would take, and then how much further down to the Southern Islands.

"How long do I have?" I asked.

The Tailor's expression was full of sorrow and pity, but her eyes were as hard as ever. "If you leave now, you may well get to see a sunset over the Southern Islands."

"So it's over, just like that?" Brasti asked. "Everything we did, everything the King talked about . . . it's over? We don't run or fight or judge. We just—"

"It's over for you, that's all. The world will continue. Aline will survive, I'll see to that. But the three of you have done enough. Go and live out your days with whatever happiness you can find in this corrupt and broken world." She reached over and put her hand on Brasti's chest, a gentle gesture that made no sense to me, not coming from the Tailor. "This was never a land for heroes. The war that's coming will have no place for you at all."

I rose and stood with Kest and Brasti. Somehow it always came back to the three of us. Even when we journeyed apart, we always knew we would come back together again. For nearly fifteen years we had been the arrow and the blade and the heart of the King's dream, but now the Tailor was telling us that we were finished, that everything we'd fought for was going away, that the path of the Greatcoats had been a dream, soon to be forgotten. We were being ordered to walk away from the fight.

Kest and Brasti and I looked at each other wordlessly, and after a moment we each nodded in turn. For one brief instant our minds were joined and we shared between the three of us an inescapable truth. We didn't clasp hands, or hug each other. We didn't say or do anything, in fact, for anything we might have done would have felt like a performance.

"All right, then. Good," the Tailor said. She went over to the door of the bedchamber and opened it quietly before going in. I heard her gently rouse Aline from sleep and pick up her things. When they returned, I knelt down awkwardly by the bench so that the King's daughter could put a weary head on my shoulder.

"The Tailor says we're leaving, but you can't come with us right now. Are you going on a mission?"

At that moment I realized I had never before lied to Aline. "Yes," I said, "and it's a very important mission. I'd tell you all about it, but it's a secret and no one but Kest and Brasti and I know about it."

She giggled for just a moment, then said, "You're such a bad liar, Falcio."

"That's why I never lie to you," I said. "Besides, if I did, Monster would bite my hand off."

Aline's eyes became soft and quickly filled with tears. "I had to send Monster away, Falcio. She was going crazy all the time—she even tried to bite me. She's gone."

"I . . . I'm sorry to hear that." I pulled my King's daughter to me, and over her shoulder caught the Tailor's eye. Her expression confirmed what I suspected: Monster would try to kill *anyone* who hurt Aline—but how could the fey horse fight something as insidious as what was happening to the girl now?

I don't pray often, you mad beast, but I pray you find peace for yourself. Dan'ha vath fallatu, Monster. I am of your herd.

The Tailor's hand appeared on Aline's shoulder and she gently pulled her away. "It's time we go now, sweetness."

Aline looked at me for a moment. "I'm going to smile now," she said. "You smile too, and then we both close our eyes and keep them closed until I'm gone. That way we'll always remember each other like that."

"I . . . All right, Aline, we'll do that."

She smiled at me, and it was as if the whole world became bright, just for a moment. Then I smiled too, and closed my eyes quickly, afraid our smiles might break before I had them tight shut. I kept my eyes closed and a moment later heard the sounds of Aline's light footsteps alongside those of the Tailor. I stayed where I was, leaning against the bench, and listened as they walked out of the room and along the hall, down the stairs and, ever so faintly, through the front door of the inn and out of my life.

Finally I felt Kest's arm around my shoulders, pulling me up.

The three of us looked at each other, and no one was quite sure whether to speak or not.

It was Brasti who broke first. "So," he said. "Do you think the Tailor bought it?"

18

A LAST DRINK

Kest and I found a table near the door of the Inn of the Red Hammer's remarkably large common room. A central fire illuminated a small stage and spread warmth among the two dozen men and women who filled barely a quarter of the tables and benches spread throughout the room.

Brasti returned from the bar with three mugs of ale. He examined each one carefully, then made sure to set the largest mug down in front of me. "I'm sorry you're dying, Falcio."

"Thanks," I said, and reached for the mug, oddly touched by the simple gesture.

"You probably won't need all your coin, will you?" he added. "I mean, what with things being as they are?"

Kest raised an eyebrow. "Would you seriously use Falcio's illness as a way to worm his money away from him?"

"Now wait a minute, I—"

I chuckled. "He did give me the bigger mug, Kest."

"That's right," Brasti said. "I did."

I took a long drink. The ale was good, the room was warm, I was sitting with the two men I loved best in the world and at that precise moment no one was trying to kill me. I felt, absurdly, happy.

Brasti started to speak, but Kest, his eyes on me, held up a hand to stop him. Brasti leaned back in his chair and drank his ale, and the three of us sat together in silence. I felt a small stab of guilt at the thought that Aline now believed I was leaving her forever. *At least I didn't lie to her,* I told myself. Nor had I lied to the Tailor, in fact—not really, anyway.

I understood why the Tailor wanted us out of the way. It would have made it easier for her, for Aline—probably for everyone. If they were going into hiding, to watch and wait as the world fell apart under Trin's capricious rule, it probably wouldn't do much good having Kest, Brasti, and me tearing up the countryside trying to delay it. I understood her reasoning and her logic. I simply didn't care.

There had been a man once who was both brilliant and foolish. He'd seen the darkness of this country and dreamed of something brighter. And even when he'd been killed and his incomplete work had been shattered to pieces, little shards of his dream had lodged themselves inside Kest and Brasti and me. This was something we three shared, in our own separate and sometimes incompatible ways.

But there was something else the three of us shared, too: a belief that there are some fights you don't walk away from, no matter what the cost. That's why I knew, at that moment when the Tailor offered us respite and resignation from our duty, that none of us would take it. We'd stood in that room and locked eyes and without having to speak it aloud, shared a single silent promise: if the world is going to fall apart, then we will go down with it. Fighting.

That was why, in the not overly crowded common room of that dirty little inn, situated on the border of three duchies, I felt a momentary but indescribably precious happiness.

The clerics teach us that pride is a bad thing—it's a weakness; a vanity that leads men to forget their natural humility. They say that only through accepting our place as servants to the greater forces of the world can we achieve contentment. Pride, they tell us, is the gate that stands between us and the Gods.

Fuck the clerics, I thought. *I'll keep what pride I can hold onto for as long as I can.*

I reached the bottom of my mug and set it down on the table. Brasti looked at me and then at Kest, almost as if waiting for permission to speak. Kest rolled his eyes and Brasti gave him a dirty look, then turned to me and asked, "So what's the plan, then?"

"Luth," I said. "We'll stay the night here, but in the morning we'll go to Luth."

"Luth? What's in Luth?"

"Two things. First, despite what the Tailor thinks, it's still possible that Duke Roset will agree to support Aline in order to keep Trin from the throne."

"But Aline's not trying to be Queen anymore."

"Roset doesn't know that," Kest said.

Brasti grinned. "Well, I like the idea of deceiving a Duke anyway, just in principle. What's the other reason to go there?"

"Roset and Isault were often enemies," I said, remembering Shuran's words at Carefal, and again at the Ducal Palace. "Aramor and Luth haven't been the best of friends lately, if all of these little border disputes are any indication."

Kest's expression was wary. "You really think Duke Roset would go so far as to send assassins for Isault *and* his family?"

"Maybe," I said, "and maybe not, but he'll certainly know who Isault's other enemies were. Either way, things will go very badly for him with the Ducal Concord if there is real cause to believe he had a fellow Duke and his family murdered."

"You think you can push him into giving Aline his support? What happens if he decides that with Trin coming he's not worried about the Ducal Concord and calls your bluff?"

I picked up my mug and tried to shake a last drop or two down my throat. "Then I imagine we'll need to escape. Quickly."

Brasti laughed. "So our strategy is go to Luth and blackmail a Duke, and then if that fails, run very fast." He turned to Kest. "People still think he's the smart one, you know."

Kest didn't respond. His eyes were focused behind us, but my back was to the door so I felt the breeze first and then heard the footsteps of a man and a woman entering the inn.

"That's odd," Kest said.

I turned to look at the new patrons. The man was young and handsome, with dark hair and a short beard. The woman, plain and thickset, carried a brown leather guitar-case.

"Saint Gan-who-laughs-with-dice," Brasti said. "What are the odds of them showing up here and now?"

The man, noticing us staring, gave a noncommittal smile and the sort of nod of one who cannot quite recall where he'd seen us before. Then I remembered we'd been sitting in the shadows at the Inn at the End of the World when he'd performed there, so he'd probably not actually seen us at all.

The troubadours walked over to the stage. The woman placed her guitar-case on top of an empty chair, then opened it carefully and moved the chair a little closer to the fire to warm it up.

A waitress came over and set down three bowls of stew in front of us. "That's a stag each," she said. "D'you want me to bring you more ale?"

"We didn't order food," Kest said.

"You stay for the performance, you have to eat."

I reached into my pocket and felt around, not wanting to bring out a gold piece in the middle of a common room. I gave her four silver pieces. "That's for the three meals and another two ales each," I said. As she reached down for the stags I put my hand over them. "How often do those two perform here?" I asked.

"Them? Oh, every month or two, I'd say. They follow the same route around the southern duchies as most of the troubadours."

"When were they last here?" Kest asked.

The waitress looked up as if the answer were on the ceiling. "Oh, about . . . well, just a couple of weeks ago, now that I think of it."

"And their names?"

"How should I know? They're just troubadours. They come, they play, the man drinks a lot and tries to bed me, and then they go." She pulled my hand off the coins and took them.

"How often does he succeed?" Brasti asked.

The waitress gave a sly grin. "Wouldn't you like to find out?"

Brasti returned her smile, and the waitress left for the bar. I felt oddly put out by their immediate, even if largely artificial, sense of intimacy. Ethalia was there in Merisaw, not even five days' ride from here. Was she waiting for me? Did she wake up each morning wondering if this was the day I'd come for her and the two of us would—? No, better to leave those thoughts behind. If there was any justice in the world, Ethalia would give up on me quickly.

"They're about to begin," Kest said, and I turned my attention to the stage just as the guitarist began to play. I marveled once again at the way she plucked out little melodies that intertwined within the chords and subtly changed rhythm of the music. The patrons of the inn were still largely focused on their food and drink and the storyteller was pacing the small stage, stretching his arms and neck as if he were about to begin a boxing match.

I felt a brief rush of cool air as the door opened again, and a moment later I heard a female voice say, "Oh, hells, tell me I haven't spent the last three days racing around the countryside without so much as a hot meal in my belly only to come and have to listen to that idiot gargling out his fool stories again."

I turned and saw Dariana standing behind me.

"Well, now, speaking of idiots," she said with a smile.

"Stop blocking the door, Dari; I'm getting cold," another voice said, and Valiana pushed past her.

Both women looked pretty road-worn, with dusty coats and dirty faces. Valiana's long dark hair was tangled, even though she'd tied it back, and strands were fluttering around her face. Dariana's shorter reddish-brown hair looked as if it'd been blown about by high winds.

The two of them pulled chairs up to our table, and as they undid their coats I could see their clothes were rumpled, and Dariana's shirt was torn from the neck to halfway down her chest.

"Having a good look, are you?" she asked, her eyes on Brasti.

"Just checking for wounds," he said.

The troubadour was telling his damned story again, still mispronouncing my name, which was the least of his inaccuracies. Valiana had placed her chair between Kest and me, and for some reason I leaned over and hugged her. I felt like a fool afterward.

"Ah, see?" Dariana said tartly, "Papa Falcio missed you."

Valiana smiled awkwardly.

The troubadour on the stage continued his story, while the guitar-player did her best to use her music to enhance his mediocre voice.

"Ugh," Dariana said, and she poked Brasti in the shoulder. "Ale, please." He looked annoyed, but when she returned his gaze he either decided it wasn't an issue worth taking a stand over or, more likely, realized he was thirsty himself; he got up and headed for the bar.

"Where have you been?" Kest asked.

"Where haven't we been?" she replied, giving Valiana a wink. "In the past two days we've seen the borders of Aramor, Pertine, and Rijou. We've spun around so many times I think we made some of Duchess Trin's men seasick."

"And?" Kest asked.

"The ones we didn't lose, we killed, of course."

I looked at Valiana, who was grinning broadly. "Dari was amazing! She tricked them into thinking we'd separated, then when they split up she managed to get one group nearly riding into a seventy-foot gully! Then—"

"Don't give out all my secrets, pretty bird," Dariana said as Brasti returned with the beer. She took one and drank deeply, keeping her eyes on him the whole time.

"What?" he asked.

"You know, it might just be the lack of sleep or proper food in me, but you don't look half as ugly as I remember. Maybe it's time I gave you a try. After all, surviving near-death always makes me—"

"I think you have blood on your chin," Brasti said, looking slightly queasy. "And there's something . . . um, *fleshy*—there on your neck."

She reached up and wiped at it with her hand, then held it up in front of her face. "Hmm . . . wonder who this came from? Oh well, I'm sure he doesn't need it anymore."

I expected to see shock and disgust in Valiana's expression, and instead found a kind of grim satisfaction. "What?" she asked. "They came hoping to murder Aline."

Dari reached over and patted Valiana on the shoulder. "Pretty bird took out three of them all by herself, too. Not all at the same time, mind you."

"I'll get better," Valiana said, her chin high and shoulders back. Her look softened as she turned to me. "The Tailor told us . . . Well, she told us everything."

I found myself struggling for something to say, for once not sure whether to be glib or sincere.

Fortunately, Brasti spoke for me, choosing "glib." "Hey, it's not all bad news. You'll be happy to hear that Trin has dropped Duke Perault as a lover and now he's dead, so, you know, things balance out."

Valiana looked neither amused as Brasti had intended, nor relieved as I might have expected. Her eyes narrowed, as if she thought we might be lying. "Why would she end her liaison with Duke Perault?"

"Boredom?" Kest suggested.

"Who cares?" Brasti replied. "Who knows why that lunatic does anything?"

"Trin isn't crazy," Valiana said, "and despite what you may think, she isn't vain or petty either." She looked at each of us in turn. "You all talk about her as if she's some wanton madwoman, but she's not. She's malicious and evil and calculating, but she's no fool. Patriana taught us to treat every encounter and every liaison as a tool, a way to enhance our position in the world. Trin let Perault bed her because she wanted his army—and now you say he's dead? Surely that will make it much harder for her to hold onto his generals?"

"Then why would she do it?" Dariana asked.

Valiana looked anxious. "I don't know. But if she took another lover it's because this new one has something she wants—something that's even more useful than Perault's army."

Brasti looked down at his mug. "Well, that's a fine way to take the warmth out of an otherwise pleasant evening."

"It's a problem for another day," I said, thinking, *Saints, just what my life was missing: more secrets and deceptions* . . .

The music in the room died down and I noted the troubadour was finishing his story and once again brandishing the juryman's coin. *Where did he get that coin from?* I wondered. Turning back to Valiana and Dari, I started to spin a simple story, just enough to make them believe we'd accepted the Tailor's instructions, but then I stopped and leaned back in my chair and looked at these two bedeviling women. They were brave and capable, and neither had given me any reason to doubt them. How many times had I railed against the Tailor for her evasions and deceptions? I was sick of all the lying and manipulation surrounding us, and the dangers we were about to face would be easier met with five than with three.

I caught Kest's eye and then Brasti's, and both nodded their approval. *Saint Olaria-who-carries-the-clouds, the three of us have turned into an old married couple,* I thought. *We'll be finishing each other's sentences before long.*

"The Tailor thinks the war is over," I said. "She thinks there's no point in fighting anymore; no point in trying to save the country from falling into chaos and civil war. Kest, Brasti, and I plan to prove her wrong."

Dariana set her mug of ale down on the table. "You're going to disobey the Tailor?"

I didn't know what her connection to the Tailor truly was, or how strong her loyalty was. *In fact, I really don't know* anything *about this woman,* I thought. *She could be anyone. She could be the Tailor's own damned daughter, for all I know.* The waitress came by with the beer I'd paid for earlier. After she'd gone, I said, "Yes, I'm going to disobey the Tailor. And I want you to disobey her, too."

There was a brief pause, and then Valiana reached for one of the brimming mugs. "I follow the First Cantor," she said. "To the Greatcoats."

Kest picked up his mug and raised it. "To the Greatcoats."

Brasti did the same, and Dariana gave a snort. "To the hells with your Greatcoats," she said, but she took one of the mugs and raised it all the same. "Your way sounds like it's going to involve mayhem and a lot more fighting. So I'm in."

Well, I thought, *that will have to do.*

I raised my mug. "To mayhem and fighting."

That's when the door to the inn broke open and every kind of hell broke loose.

The first sign that we were in trouble was when I saw Brasti's eyes go wide as he looked behind me. I started to turn to look myself, but before I could, Brasti had reached across the table, grabbed me by the hair and pulled my head down. I turned just before my face collided with the wooden surface of the table, feeling the sudden impact in my left cheekbone. All I could see was Kest's body rising from his chair, his hand simultaneously reaching down and drawing his sword and the blade flying in a smooth arc toward me. I felt the sudden rush of air as the blade swung past my cheek and over my body and clanged into something metallic behind me. Brasti released his grip on my head and used both hands to grab the back of my coat and haul me across the table, and we went tumbling over each other as the weight of my body brought both of us to the ground. We landed side by side on the other side of the table.

"I accept your grateful thanks for saving your life," he said as a cacophony of heavy boots and the sound of swords mixed with screams and shouts coming from the patrons in the room. Oddly, I noticed the guitarist was still playing.

"Couldn't you have just warned me?"

Brasti's eyes flickered somewhere above me. "No time," he said, and pushed me hard so that I rolled off to the right. An ax lodged itself in the floor where our necks had been a moment before. Brasti was already on his feet and drawing his sword as I was pushing myself up onto my knees.

"Well, don't just sit there," he said, and with that he leaped over our upturned table and into the fray.

The common room of the inn had suddenly become a lot more crowded; it was now filled with a dozen men or more, all in shiny armor. Most had swords; a few—like the man who'd just tried to take me out—had axes. He'd attacked me first—so was I the intended target? But no, he wouldn't have been able to see my face, not from where he'd been standing, so more likely he'd simply wanted to take out one of us before we knew what was happening.

"Any time now, Falcio!" Brasti shouted, and I drew my rapiers and looked around to see who needed my help first. Valiana and Dari were fighting side by side, their blades thrusting and slashing in a complicated syncopated rhythm that kept the men in front of them from getting any chance to strike. I took a moment to silently thank Dariana for teaching her student so well. Kest had pushed his way into the thick of the mêlée, fighting using a style that Brasti once dubbed *sorendito*, which is an old Pertine word for a rather filthy act that costs extra in most brothels, involving three partners and . . . well, never mind. Kest was striking alternately forward and then backward, first driving the point of his blade at his opponent's belly and then immediately pulling back hard to drive the pommel of his sword into the face of the man stupid enough to try to get behind him. Brasti was going at it hells-for-leather, swinging wildly and trying to keep two opponents with longer swords from backing him up against the wall.

I saw a gap in the armor and drove the point of my right-hand rapier deep into muscle and bone behind the man's right knee. The man screamed and as he turned, his mouth was an enticingly wide opening, so I felt I had no choice but to thrust my other rapier into it. His partner had just grabbed hold of Brasti's blade with a gauntleted hand and was hanging onto it even as he drew back his own sword to strike at my head. This might have been a good idea, in principle, at least, except that Brasti just let go of his own weapon, slipped behind the man's back and pulled hard on his helm, yanking him backward so that he fell to the ground and onto his back. He lifted his foot and drove his heel into the man's face with a gratifyingly sickening crunch.

Brasti reached down and picked up his sword. "I was doing fine."

"Fifteen years and you still swing your sword wildly and jab it in the air like an amateur."

"It's a fucking sword, Falcio. What else do you do with it but swing and jab?"

"Where's your bow?"

He pointed across the room to where his shortbow was hanging next to his quiver on a hook by the open door leading from the common room into the inn proper. I could see a few of our attackers in the way, standing around like fools waiting for a chance to get to Kest, Valiana, and Dari, who were now fighting back to back.

"I'm going for it," Brasti said. "I'll be back."

"The common room's too big," I pointed out. "It works in their favor." I rushed toward the exit, Brasti close behind me, and when we'd fought our way through three men blocking the door— gracefully, on my part, less elegantly on Brasti's—I shouted, "All of you! Over here!" Kest gave a curt nod, otherwise barely glancing up until his two opponents lay writhing at his feet, then he collected Dari and Valiana and the three of them wove their way between the fallen furniture now littering the floor until all of us were on the same side of the room.

"Through the door!" Brasti and I cried together, and we all moved as one.

It was a simple enough plan: if we were on one side of the thick wooden doorway and our attackers were on the other, then they could only fight us one-on-one. At that point I could just point Kest to the front and the rest of us could catch our breath, even have a nap, for all it would matter. We were just about to reach the doorway when the flaw in my plan presented itself: with a look of sheer terror on his face, the young innkeeper Tyne slammed the door closed from the other side, and even as I tried to push it open he dropped the stout oak bar into place. It was obviously used to secure the common room at night; there was no way we'd be able to break through from our side.

We were now completely trapped, and another dozen or so men were pouring into the room through the main entrance. We'd taken out a fair few already—some were dead, some unconscious—but I could still count seventeen standing in a line in front of us. Three

wore travelers' clothes, but I caught glimpses of armor underneath—
Knights could never resist polishing their damned plate till it shone
like the sun, which might be all very well if you wanted to impress
some innocent maid, but it wasn't not much good when you were
supposed to be under cover. The rest of our attackers wore the yellow
and silver tabards of Luth. Most were regular soldiers, but I counted
four Knights among them, one of whom had the double star on his
tabard that marked him as a Knight-Captain. "Place your weapons
on the ground," he said in a light tenor voice that made me wonder
if he might not make a better singer than the troubadour who was
now standing at the far end of the room trying his best to push the
wall down with his back. Those few patrons who had not managed
to slip out the back door were hiding under tables. The guitarist
was still sitting on her chair on the little stage, and now the noise of
swords clashing and screaming was dying down, I could hear she
was still playing.

"I think you can stop now," Brasti shouted to her. I noticed he'd
managed to grab his bow and slide his quiver over his shoulder.

"I'm bored, and there's nothing else to do," she shouted back.

The world is a stupid, stupid place sometimes.

The Knight-Captain took another step forward. "By the order of
Roset, Duke of Luth, I order you to put your weapons down on the
ground and surrender yourselves."

"You realize we're in Aramor, don't you?" I said.

"We've the right to pursue criminals within ten miles of the border."

"How close are we now?" Brasti asked.

"Less than that."

"On what charge are you arresting us?" I asked.

"We'll deal with that in Luth," he said.

I realized what was bothering me about this particular scenario:
it wasn't as if we hadn't been hunted by Ducal Knights before, but we
hadn't even been to Luth yet. Then I saw one of the armored men in
brown traveling clothes whisper something to the Knight-Captain.
He pointed toward us—well, not so much toward us as toward Dari
and Valiana.

"Dariana?" I said.

She looked at me with mild curiosity. "Yes, First Cantor?"

"Is it at all possible that you didn't actually lose all of those men Trin sent after you?"

"You know, now that I think about it, I never did bother to count them all. Do you suppose I should have?"

"That might be something to consider in the future, yes."

Three of the Luthan soldiers had pulled crossbows from their backs and were winding them.

"You shouldn't do that," Brasti warned.

"Do not address my men, Trattari," the Knight-Captain said. "Will you surrender peacefully, or do I order my men to attack?"

"Why are soldiers of Luth doing the bidding of Knights in disguise sent by the Duchess of Hervor?" I asked. "Does your Duke know that you've ceded jurisdiction of his lands to a pretender who seeks to usurp the throne of Tristia?"

The skin of the Knight-Captain's face tightened. "There is nothing dishonorable in Ducal Knights giving each other courtesy in matters involving the apprehension of criminals."

"Except that we haven't committed any crime," I said.

"My fellow Knights tell me the little witch over there has committed a number of murders."

"Falcio?" Kest said mildly.

"What?"

He gave a little sigh.

It was one I recognized.

"Ah. I'm talking when I should be fighting again, aren't I?"

He nodded.

"Let me handle this," Brasti said. He looked to the Knight-Captain and in a loud, commanding voice said, "All right. We surrender."

The Knight looked surprised. "You do?"

"Absolutely."

"Drop your bow, then, Trattari."

Brasti let the bow fall to the floor. It landed on his left foot and he put his hands up in the air. "See? There's no need for further violence."

Kest and I stared at him. Neither of us were quite sure that he hadn't just lost his mind. "What?" he said. "We've never tried surrendering before. I just wanted to see what it was like."

The Knight smiled. It was an ugly smile for such a handsome face.

"Ah, see, now," Brasti said, his hands still in the air, "that look on your face isn't giving me any confidence in your Duke's honor."

Dariana jabbed Brasti in the side with her elbow. "If you were trying to impress me with your intellect, Brasti Goodbow, you've just failed miserably."

Brasti looked from the Knight to Dariana and then to me. "You see what I get when I try to do the smart thing? You always tell me I'm too reckless but when I—Oh, fine, then. Fuck all this." He jerked his left foot up, the bow leapt into the air and in one smooth motion Brasti grabbed the shaft of the bow with his left hand and reached into his quiver with his right, nocking an arrow so quickly it was as if he hadn't moved at all.

"I see seventeen duckies," Brasti said loudly, "seventeen nice yellow duckies all in a row for me. How many do I have to hit to win a prize?"

"There's still a chance to settle this peacefully, Sir Knight," I said. "Withdraw your men and swear me an oath to leave us be and you can return to Luth."

"Those three stay," Valiana said, pointing to Trin's men. "They came to murder the rightful heir to the throne."

Terrific. Because what I really needed was for Valiana to adopt Dari's bloodthirsty tendencies.

One of the three men stepped forward and addressed me. "I'll make you a better offer, Trattari. Give us the two whores who used treachery and deceit to kill true Knights. We'll do with them as we will, and the rest of you can run away with your tails between your legs." He turned to the back of the room. "You! Storyteller!"

The young troubadour took a small, terrified step forward. "Me?" he asked.

The woman with the guitar rolled her eyes.

"Yes, you. Let's make a deal, you and me. How fast can you write one of your stories?"

"I . . . well, it depends on the subject matt—"

"Whatever. I'll do it for you. This here's the tale of Sir Elwyn Arnott. You get that name right if you know what's good for you."

"Not much chance of that," I muttered.

"You tell people what happened here: you tell them that Sir Elwyn faced off with the treacherous Trattari and made them run away, leaving their whores behind."

"I . . . There's more to a story than—" He stopped speaking when the guitar-player jabbed him with the head of her instrument.

Sir Elwyn turned back to us and grinned. "Come on, Trattari. You haven't got a chance in all the hells that the Gods have waiting for you. At least this way you and your friends get to live."

"This is getting boring," Dariana said idly. "You promised me mayhem and fighting."

I kept my eyes on the Knights. "Odds?" I whispered to Kest.

When he didn't reply I looked at him. A red haze surrounded him—for a moment I hoped it was just a trick of the light caused by the brazier hanging by the door, but no, it really was coming from his skin. He turned to me and grinned. His expression was one of the most terrifying things I've ever seen. "To mayhem and fighting," he said, and launched himself across the room toward the men, his sword beginning a lazy circle over his head as he prepared to strike.

"Hells! Brasti, now!" I said, but I needn't have bothered. One of the crossbowman already had the shaft of an arrow jutting from his chest, and out of the corner of my eye I could see Brasti had already nocked another arrow. The rest of us raced across the room to join Kest: five against seventeen, and most of them in armor. But we had Brasti with his bow and a quiver full of arrows and the Saint of Swords burning with a fire that sang out for blood.

To mayhem and fighting, I thought.

19

THE BARDATTI

The five of us fought as a unit with deadly efficiency—some of that was necessity; some a great deal of luck. I imagine to someone watching it must have looked like chaos incarnate, with the steel blade of Kest's sword reflecting the red glow of his skin even as it drowned the glow in the deeper red blood of his opponents. And Brasti was just as deadly, the string of his bow singing in the air as every one of his arrows struck its intended target. When I caught a look at his face, there was just as much anger and madness as on Kest's, which reminded me that for all his good humor, Brasti hated Knights above all things.

Dariana fought like a hummingbird, stealing thrusts at her opponents and then just as quickly flitting outside of their reach.

But it was Valiana who scared me most. Her skills really had improved, and she was holding her own against men with years of soldiering behind them. And yet at least part of why she was so effective was because she ran into the fight without any hesitation at all. I swear I saw her running straight into an opponent's blade and he pulled it back simply out of reflex. When it was all done, she had a grim look of satisfaction on her face.

"Leave her be," Dariana said quietly. "You won't make it better, so at least don't make it worse."

"She fights as if she wants to be killed," I muttered.

"Of course. She fights like you."

"What? Are you mad? I don't—"

But before I could finish she had walked away from me as if I didn't exist. I looked around the room to make sure none of the dead or dying were going to get up for another try. A creaking noise drew my eyes to the door between the common room and the rest of the inn in time to see it open just a hair.

"Saints!" Tyne said. Then he caught my expression and slammed the door shut again.

"Just for that, we're not paying for our rooms," Brasti shouted. He turned to me. "And don't you start up about Greatcoats not stealing. If he wanted his money all he had to do was not lock us in with seventeen soldiers determined to see us dead."

"It's fine," I said. I checked around the room to see if any patrons were still hiding or had been injured, but it looked like they'd all gotten away. Hopefully they were safe in their homes now. Then I realized someone else was also gone. "Damned Saint Olaria-who-carries-the-clouds," I said.

"What is it?" Kest asked mildly. He was cleaning the blood off his blade and looked completely normal again, as calm as still water.

"The troubadours—I wanted to talk to them."

"They snuck out just as things were coming to a close," Brasti said. "I think they were heading toward the barn. Why is it so many inns in Tristia have barns?"

"Most used to be family farms," Kest said. "I read in the third Census from King Ugrid that—"

"Let's go," I said. "I want to talk to that storyteller."

The others followed me out into the night.

"What's the problem?" Brasti asked as we walked across the cobblestone courtyard. "I didn't even have a chance to grab a jug of that ale. You're not still mad about him getting your name wrong, are you?"

"I don't give a damn about that," I said, "but just before things got messy he showed that damned coin again. I want to know where he got it." Stealing a juryman's coin used to be a serious offense, back in the days when anyone cared what the Greatcoats thought. It represented a promise to uphold the verdict; it was a badge of honor—but most of all, it was a payment to the family of the man or woman who risked losing their lives and leaving their loved ones without means. A gold coin like that could keep a family fed for a year, and I didn't like the idea that it had been taken from someone a Greatcoat had given it to.

As we approached the entrance to the barn a voice called out and I looked up to see the storyteller, a bow and arrow in hand, perched in the window of the second floor. The arrow was aimed at me.

"If you've come looking for trouble, I warn you, I'm as skilled an archer as your man there. I can take out all five of you before the first one's blood begins to seep through his clothing. You'll face your Gods with your entrails hanging out like snakes fleeing from a burning ship."

"Nice imagery," Brasti said.

"It's fine, I suppose," Kest replied, "but it's not actually that impressive to kill someone with a bow before they have a chance to run into the barn and up the stairs, when you think about it."

"It's not the physics of the thing that matters, it's the lyrical quality of the phrase. He's a *troubadour*, remember? He's supposed to be *poetic*."

"Are you quite done?" the troubadour asked.

"I think you should come down and talk," I said.

"Give me three reasons," the bard replied, "for if I dislike the first two, that will give you one last chance at life."

"See?" Brasti said. "He's a *poet*."

"Fine," I said. "In the first place, it looks as if that crack on the front of your bow is about to give way. So I imagine you found it hanging on a wall in there which means it's been exposed to cold and rain for Saints know how long. Also, the way you're holding it leads me to believe that the only way you could hit the side of a barn right now would be if you dropped the arrow."

"Oh, that was clever," Brasti said approvingly.

"Perhaps Falcio could be a poet too," Kest suggested.

"I'll wager my bow will hold just long enough to drive an arrow through your chest," the troubadour said.

"Probably not," I said, "for even if you did manage to fire that arrow, and if the bow didn't break, and if the wind picked up and compensated for your poor aim, you'd still find our coats are very difficult to pierce, even with an arrow."

"You'd need a bigger bow," Brasti called up. "A longbow might do it. Needs to be six feet long, ideally. Go for yew, if they have it."

I gave Brasti a look.

"What?" he said. "I don't want to discourage anyone from learning archery."

"I'm unconvinced," the troubadour said. "Any man can get a coat made to look like a Greatcoat's if he has money."

"That seems like a poor use of funds," Kest said, "since it would be more than likely to get the man in question killed."

"I never said you were smart. Give me your third reason or go away and save your lives."

"Fine," I said. "My third reason is that my name is Falcio val Mond. That's right, *Fal-key-oh*. Not Fal-*si*-o. And *val* means 'child of' in the old tongue of Pertine, whereas *dal* isn't a word at all. I won't bother with the rest, except to say that I'm the First Cantor of the Greatcoats, you're holding a juryman's coin, and unless you give me a very good reason for it, I'm going to come up there and beat you half to death with that stick you're holding and then I'm going to shove it up your ass. How's that for a reason?" I drew my rapier. "And while you're thinking on that, tell your friend hiding in the bushes by the barn that if she wants to keep her fingers for playing the guitar then she'd better drop the dagger she's holding."

The troubadour looked aghast. "I . . . find your argument compelling. Wait . . . are you really the Falsio from the stories?"

"That's it," I said heading for the barn. "I'm going to kill him."

Brasti put a hand on my arm. "Yes, he is. He's the Great Falsio Bal Jond. So just come down here, tell us where you got that coin and we can all go back to our barmaids . . . I mean, beds."

The woman came out from the bushes, her dagger held in front of her. "I was making water," she said in a tone that sounded as if she was challenging me to disagree with her.

A minute later the storyteller was down in the courtyard with us, bow still in hand and a look on his face that was somewhere between sheepish and terrified. "It's really you?" he asked.

I nodded.

"I thought . . . it's just you sounded taller in the story."

"So much for Bardatti," Kest said.

"It's really more of an artistic statement," the man said, but I'd noticed the woman's eyes had narrowed.

"See?" Brasti said. "I told you he was a poet."

"What's your name, storyteller?" I asked.

"Colwyn," he said, extending his hand. "And this lovely dear is Lady Nehra."

"Just 'Nehra,'" she corrected.

I shook hands with both of them despite my reservations. I was curious about the relationship between the two but kept to my original purpose. "Well, Colwyn, let's see it."

"What?"

"The coin, damn it."

"Ah." He reached into the pocket of his pants and handed it to me. "You can keep it if you like. For the trouble, I mean."

"You'd give away a gold Greatcoat's coin?" Kest asked, for once actually looking surprised.

"Nah, it's a copper sparrow. From Hervor. If you leave it in yellowberry juice overnight it turns gold-colored. You just need to scratch it up a bit first. See? Looks almost like a crown with a sword through it if you don't look too close."

The troubadour reached into his pockets again. "Look, I'll give one to each of you if you like. I can make ten of these at a time; I just need to get hold of more copper sparrows."

"Why would you need more than one?" Kest asked.

Colwyn held up the coin and smiled. "The women, see? You take one to bed and promise to come back for her. Tell her to hang onto your juryman coin. Makes them feel special."

Brasti took one of the coins, looked at it, and held it up to Kest and me. "Do you realize what I could do with a few of these?" He turned back to the troubadour and hugged him. "You really are a true Bardatti."

"What about the story? About me?" I asked. "Why did you change it?"

"Oh, that. Well, sorry if I offended you—it's just, well, the old one was heroic, but this one is funny, and more laughter means more coins. Say, could you let me know which parts I got wrong? It's hard to get the facts straight and the truth always sounds more, you know . . ."

"True?" Kest asked.

"Right."

"But how did you hear the story?" I asked. "I mean the original one—in Rijou. If you weren't there, how did you hear about it?"

"The story of Falsio at the Rock?"

"Falcio," I said. "Fal–key–oh."

"Right, sorry. Well, I mean it's been going around for weeks now. We don't often get a good Greatcoat tale anymore. Some of these village hicks, you know, they still like those kinds of stories, just have to be careful not to tell it around the ears of the wrong people. Knights and Duke's men and such." He clapped me on the shoulder. "You should be right proud! What you did there, well, whatever you really did. The story's traveling faster than a thief on a good horse. You'll be famous soon!"

"Well, Falsio will be, anyway," Brasti said, grinning.

"What's the point of the story?" I asked.

"What do you mean? It's just a good story is all," Colwyn said.

"Yes, but what's the . . . ? You know, what do people take away from it?"

"Ah, depends on the crowd, I suppose. But for most, I reckon they figure you're going to come along and fight for justice and, you know, kill off all the evil Dukes and such."

"Kill off the Dukes?"

"Well, you did kill the Duke of Rijou, didn't you? Cut his head off with that broadsword of yours."

"Rapier," Kest corrected. "Falcio fights with rapiers."

The troubadour looked confused. "Can't see how you could cut off a man's head with a rapier. It's not heavy enough, is it?"

I grabbed the man by the shoulders. "You're telling me that you're running around the countryside telling people I assassinated Jillard, Duke of Rijou?"

"Not just me—I mean, all the troubadours are telling that story these days. Not in the cities, of course, but out here in the country. Makes the hicks feel good."

"But Jillard *isn't dead!*" I said.

"Who cares? When's the last time you imagine the Duke of Rijou went for a walk through a village in the middle of Aramor? Hells, Duke Isault probably hasn't been here in years and it's in his duchy. I've killed off lots of Lords and Dukes. I even killed off the King himself a time or two back in the day. People like a good story about nobles being murdered and assassinated and whatnot."

"The nobles don't," I said.

"Don't mind Falsio," Brasti said, giving me a sideways grin. "Let's go find a jug of that excellent ale and you can tell me more about these women who love Greatcoat coins."

Colwyn grinned back at him, and for a brief moment I felt as if I'd just witnessed two long-lost brothers reunited. The two of them started walking back toward the inn.

"I'll keep an eye on him," Kest said, and followed a few feet behind them.

Dariana yawned. "Hells. Three days without rest, but I don't suppose we can stay at the inn tonight. Come on, pretty bird," she said to Valiana. "We'd best grab our things and get the horses ready."

The two headed back into the inn, leaving me alone with the woman called Nehra.

"You're a fool, Falcio val Mond. You know that?"

"I do know that," I said, "but why now in particular? Were we supposed to let those men kill us?"

"Not that," she said, "Carefal. Doing Isault's dirty work—just exactly how stupid are you?"

"You know, I'm starting to understand why Colwyn does the talking in your performances."

"Colwyn's also a fool," she said dismissively. "But unlike you, he's harmless. He's not off setting off civil wars."

"I was trying to *stop* one."

She snorted. "Then you—"

"Stop calling me a fool and tell me what you came to say. Saints! I thought the Bardatti were supposed to tell stories, not just hurl insults."

She raised one eyebrow. "And a second time you show your ignorance. Come, give us a third, for the Gods love things in threes."

"Fine. I see one of the Bardatti going around the countryside with a barely competent troubadour telling stories and, I'm starting to think, following me around and spying on me."

"Hmm," she said. "That won't do. It seems you're not entirely without wits."

"What do you mean?"

"The Bardatti tell stories, yes, and you're too quick to dismiss them, by the way. It's stories that inspire people to change. It's stories that make them believe things can be better. But we also *collect* stories. Ours is the job of traveling the land to capture the great changes in the world, just as you Trattari administered the laws."

"Don't call us *Trattari*," I warned.

"You see? You Greatcoats don't even know your own history. *Trattari* isn't an *insult*: it's an old name for one of the great orders. Like the Bardatti, like the Rangieri or the—"

"*Trattari* means tatter-cloak."

"Yes, just as *Bardatti* means 'broken voice': it's our badge of honor. We travel so long and sing so passionately that our voices break with the strain."

And the Greatcoats fight for the Law until their coats become torn and tattered. I'd never heard that explanation before, but it did sound plausible. "So did you stay out here just to give me a history lesson?" I asked.

She shook her head. "No, a warning. You were tricked into putting down that rebellion."

"I already knew that."

"It's not for nothing that Colwyn started changing the story, you know. Word is spreading fast and people will start talking of how Falcio val Mond—and don't worry, this time they'll get the *fal-key*-oh correctly—sides with Dukes and Knights instead of the common folk."

I thought about that for a moment. She was probably right, but it didn't matter. "Those same common folk abandoned us when the King died. They barely supported us when he was alive. How much difference will this make?"

Nehra laughed. "Ah, you see, and there is the third piece of foolishness you promised me. People need *something* to believe in, Falcio. The King is dead, the Dukes are petty tyrants, and the last thing they might have had faith in, the Greatcoats, are proving to be useless. How long do you think it'll be before they start clamoring for someone—*anyone*—to take power? Even Trin. Maybe even someone worse."

"There's no one worse than Trin," I said vehemently.

Nehra shook her head and sighed. "That's the trouble with you Trattari. You don't know your history. There's *always* someone worse, Falcio, and it's usually the last person you suspect."

20

THE DUKE OF LUTH

"I wish you hadn't killed him, your Majesty," I said to a trembling King Paelis as we looked down at the dead man on the floor dressed in one of the royal guard's purple tabards fringed in silver. He'd been my age, or close to it. His blond hair was framed by a halo of blood pooling on the floor around his head.

It was the first assassination attempt on the King—well, technically, it was the second, since I'd been the first—and he'd only been on the throne for a few months.

"You'd rather he had killed me?" Paelis was still holding the dinner knife he'd used to stab the man in the throat when he'd attacked him.

"I'd rather he was wounded but alive—that way we could interrogate him."

"*Torture* him?"

"Ask him forcefully," I said. I didn't like the idea of torture, and anyway, Paelis had forbidden it outright. Whenever the subject came up he would pull out one particular book he kept on hand that argued—quite effectively, I had to admit—that a man subjected to torture will say anything to spare himself pain—anything, *except* the truth. "We do need to know who sent him, your Majesty."

The King tossed the knife on the floor. "Who sent him? Who cares? It was Duke Jillard or Duke Perault, or maybe Duchess Patriana. I hardly think the good God Love would have minded one way or another once I turned up at her door."

I was incredulous at the cavalier way he was acting. "You don't think it matters?"

"Of course it matters, Falcio—but we'll know soon enough."

I thought about the investigation I'd have to start to find who'd sent the assassin: find out who'd spoken with the man, where he had come from, what horse he had ridden to get here, then once I'd traced his movements, I could get back to who'd hired him and then . . . it would take me *months*.

"Ha!" The King laughed at my expression. "Look at you, Falcio. It's as if you think the Greatcoats are the only means I have of getting anything done. Whoever would have thought you were so full of yourself?"

"If not us, then who?"

He walked over to the window. "Spies," he said. "I'll get a report back soon enough on whichever Duke or Lord or Margrave sent this man."

That threw me. "You'd need a lot of spies for that to work."

He turned and clapped me on the shoulder. "Falcio, I have five times as many spies as I have Greatcoats—in every Duke's castle, every Lord's manor . . . I have spies *everywhere!*"

"And the Dukes?" I asked. "Do they have spies here?"

"Of course. Pulnam, Domaris, Orison, even your old home duchy of Pertine—they're all here. I swear it's our national industry."

"Fine," I said, "so then let's find out who did it and then we can—"

"You can what?" The King turned from the window and looked at me.

"Kest and I will go and kill the bastard."

The King shook his head. "No, you won't."

"Are you serious? You won't let us go and punish whichever Duke or Lord sent this man?"

"Duke. It will have been one of the Dukes. Most of the Lords hate me too, but they hate their Dukes at least as much."

I felt myself growing angry. "So you're putting the Dukes above the law?"

"*Of course* the Dukes are above the law, Falcio—and so am I. Do you think you could arrest me?"

"If you committed murder or theft or rape, then yes, damn it, I'd arrest you."

He spread his hands. "And if one of the Dukes committed murder or theft or rape, you could go off and bring them to justice. But you can't arrest them for any act taken in accordance with their office."

"That doesn't make sense."

"It makes perfect sense. If you happen to find a Duke or Duchess who tries to murder me for nefarious reasons, you are free to arrest them. If, however, they are trying to murder me because, as holders of their Ducal office they deem it necessary for the protection and preservation of their duchy, then you can't."

I felt deflated. What was the point of all our discussions about recreating the Greatcoats, creating a new order of traveling magistrates to bring justice to the towns and villages of Tristia, if we couldn't actually bring down the Dukes themselves?

As if sensing my disappointment, he said, "We need justice to be a river, Falcio, always flowing, always wearing against the rocks that stand in its way, not a sword that shatters when you strike it against stone."

"Then perhaps we should outfit the Greatcoats with boats instead of blades."

The King ignored me, which was a little odd, as he usually had a quick comeback, being fond both of wit in general and his own in particular.

"You're scared of the Dukes," I said after a moment.

"Scared? No, Falcio, I'm not scared: I'm *terrified*. The nobles over whom I am laughably supposed to rule are feckless, tyrannical, and relentless."

"You're scared we might fail? You don't think we could take down the Duke who sent this man? Is that why you won't challenge them?"

The King looked at me for a second and then broke out laughing. "Is that what you think? That I don't believe I could have one of them killed if I wanted to?" He walked over to me and put a hand on my shoulder. "Falcio, I could have any one of them killed within the week—hells, I could have every single one of them dead in their own throne rooms any time I commanded it. I could utterly *eliminate* them, Falcio: not just every Duke, every Lord, every Margrave but their wives, their children—their entire lines—wiped from the face of the earth. All I have to do is ask for it."

Suddenly Paelis was no longer the King I'd become friends with, the man with whom I dreamed of a different future for the country. He was a skinny, scared boy, terrified, and angry beyond words. In the months I had known him, I had become awed by his intellect, charmed beyond words by his good humor, and entranced by the depth of his ideals. I had never once been afraid of King Paelis. Until then.

It's a strange thing, switching day for night. We had ridden since midnight, reasoning it was best to get as far away from the scene of the battle as possible. In the darkness we had the luxury of being able to stop frequently to mask our tracks, but there's a weariness that overcomes you after a fight, and eventually the body has to give way. Shortly before dawn we rode into the forest that runs alongside the southern edge of one of the smaller roads. The plan was to sleep through most of the day and then travel again at night before making our way into Luth's capital city.

We all woke sporadically during the first hours of daylight. I could hear the others rising periodically, changing watch shifts or moving away to relieve themselves. It's possible that I heard Brasti and Dariana having sex, though I'd like to think that was simply a nightmare. Sometime around noon, I awoke properly, and couldn't move. For the first few minutes I kept calm, but when it wouldn't stop I began to panic. I tried as hard as I could to open my eyes, to make a sound, but all that happened was that my breathing quickened as a kind of hysteria began to overtake me. Anyone could sneak up on me and slit my throat—or worse, Trin's men might even now be sneaking up on our camp. By the time we took the horses off the road Valiana had been exhausted. She wasn't used to this kind of life.

Damn you, Brasti. Damn you to all the hells you deserve if you've fallen off watch. Damn Dariana and her games and secrets. Damn me for my weakness. Damn me! Anxiety became panic and panic turned into a madness that I thought would swallow me whole. I'm not sure what would have happened if I hadn't felt a warm hand on my chest and heard Kest's voice. "You're safe," he said. "I'm here."

For a while the tremors kept coming, but slowly, steadily, the soft but constant pressure of his hand quieted me. "You've been like this for nearly an hour, if you're wondering. I don't think it should be much longer."

An hour. It had only been fifteen minutes the last time he'd kept watch over me. How many days ago had that been? How long had the Tailor given me? *If you leave now, you may well get to see a sunset over the Southern Islands before it's over.* I felt myself begin to panic again, but Kest, ever the brilliant tactician, began talking to me, about everything and nothing. He described the trees in the forest, and explained his theory on why they were greyer here than in Pulnam, even though Pulnam was drier and closer to the desert. He told me about every insect and animal that had moved around the forest during the hours we'd been there. "Oh, and I'm fairly certain that Brasti and Dariana had sex while he was supposed to be on watch, though I suppose it's possible she was just making sure he stayed awake."

I heard a feeble chuckle that sounded something like my voice, or at least, what I imagined my voice would sound like when I became an old man, though of course that would never happen. White light flecked with the gray-green leaves of the trees overhead flickered into my vision.

"You're coming out of it," Kest said. "Don't try to move yet."

I started crying, reached out numbly with my hand and pulled on his arm. I'd intended to express my gratitude, to tell him how much his friendship meant to me, but somewhere between that first effort to make my muscles work and the time when he leaned over so he could hear me, the weight of the world had sunk back into me. "I want to murder them, Kest. I want to murder every one of the bastards who's trying to kill Aline."

"That might be a lot of people," he said gently.

"Then I'll start with the fucking Duke of Luth and see where that leads me."

Carefully, Kest put his hands under my shoulders and lifted me up until I was now leaning against a tree. He brushed off some of the dirt and leaves that had collected on my clothes. "Is that what the King would want?" he asked.

"I don't know anymore," I said. "I'm not even sure if I still care."

Kest rose to his feet. "I'll get you something to eat," he said. "It's early afternoon and there's plenty of time before dark. We're only a few hours away from Roset's palace. You'll need to decide by then what kind of people you want us to be."

Kest's troubling words turned my mind to thoughts of Roset, Duke of Luth. Had he really given permission to his men to help Trin's assassins? Was the Tailor right, was the world already heading inexorably toward a madwoman taking the throne while the country sank into rack and ruin?

Leave it be, I told myself, and laid my head back against the rough bark of the tree. Whether Duke Roset ordered his men to support Trin or whether he was simply so weak they had chosen to do it on their own, Knights of Luth had tried to assassinate my King's daughter. Soon we would arrive at the Ducal Palace of Luth, and then the bastard would have some explaining to do. For once I didn't question whether he would talk. I was dying—my country was dying— and not only was the girl I'd sworn to protect breaking apart into a thousand pieces, but the last shreds of my own sense of right and wrong were coming apart like old threads pulled too tight. Since leaving the Ducal Palace of Aramor I'd asked myself over and over whether it was possible that Dara, a Greatcoat, could be moved to murder. I wasn't asking myself that question anymore.

* * *

Six hours later we began climbing the sloped south wall of the Ducal Palace of Luth. Though I'm no healer, I'm fairly sure that if one had been present, he would have advised against such an activity for a man in my condition.

"Don't fall," Brasti whispered quietly, waiting for me to catch up to him. He was sitting on a stone corbel that protruded from the wall, swinging his legs in the night air. "You might want to hurry up, though. We haven't got all night."

Saint Marta-who-shakes-the-lion, just grant me enough strength to make it a few more inches so that I can grab onto Brasti's foot and drag him with me to my death. That's not too much to ask, is it?

I reached up to the next gap in the stones, the spiked handgrips (one of the King's more useful inventions) from my greatcoat making what would otherwise have been a suicidal task merely perilous and foolhardy. In the darkness I could make out the shadowy forms of the others above me working their way to the top of the wall. Kest moved slowly but with an effortless grace that made my own awkward progress feel particularly clumsy.

I'd expected to be outpaced by Kest, but it was Dariana who was furthest ahead. She climbed with astonishing ease, often leaping from one foothold to grab onto a mortared gap in the stones, only to swing herself one-handed up to reach for her next handhold, and all at a speed that made even Kest look like an amateur. I would have spent more time marveling at her skill were it not for the fact that my own fingers were growing numb, and I was afraid of slipping.

"No, wait!" Kest whispered.

I looked up just in time to see Valiana trying to duplicate Dariana's jump; the reckless maneuver caused her to lose her grip. *Saints, she's going to fall!* She began sliding down the sloped wall toward me, her spiked handgrips screeching against the stones, and I gripped my own handholds desperately, hoping I would be strong enough to support Valiana when her feet struck my shoulders. Kest managed to sidle over just in time to grab at the back of her coat with his left hand, giving her just enough stability for her to catch herself against the stone wall. A few seconds later she nodded to Kest and began climbing again.

Damned fool! I raged silently, now that the immediate danger was past. *Stop trying to emulate fucking Dariana!*

Fear and exhaustion made my own breath come in ragged bursts and focused my attention: I had to get to the top in one piece myself. Stone by stone I worked my way up to the edge of one of the crenellations in the wall and saw the others all there ahead of me.

"Are you planning on joining us anytime soon?" Dariana asked, her voice a whisper.

"Just enjoying the night air," I replied, reaching out with my now completely numb right hand to grab at the top of the wall. When I couldn't get a grip Kest reached down and took hold of my wrists, supporting me as I pulled myself up.

"Something's wrong," he said, once I had joined the others.

"I'm fine," I said. "Stop being such a—"

"No, not that. We were too slow."

I glanced around, expecting to see a dozen guards coming for us, but found none.

Brasti snorted. "The Saint of Swords is just upset because we haven't been attacked by a dozen guards yet."

Kest shook his head. "That's not it; we took too long—the watchmen should have made it back from their rounds already."

He was right. It had taken us nearly half an hour to make it to the top, but we knew from our earlier surveillance that the guards made the route every twenty minutes. *So where are they?*

"You can report them to their superiors later," Brasti said. "Stop complaining every time we manage to avoid death and destruction."

"Brasti's right," I said. The Duke of Luth could worry about his guards' shoddy timekeeping; we would just be grateful for those extra ten minutes. "Let's go do what we came to do."

We began making our way along the battlement. Duke Roset's home was more like a fortified castle than a traditional palace, a sign of both the man's military pretensions and his anxieties over his security. *Well, I can't really blame you, your Grace, since we're about to threaten your personal safety.*

We were about to descend the stairs leading into the upper floors of the palace when Valiana grabbed my arm. I turned and saw the look of profound shame on her face. "I'm sorry, Falcio. We could have been caught because of me."

Part of me wanted to berate her, to remind her that she was inexperienced and reckless, but while that was certainly true, there was something deeper that struck me. "You didn't scream," I said.

"I . . . I don't understand."

"When you began to slip, you stayed silent. Most people, no matter how experienced, would have cried out once they felt themselves falling. You didn't."

She gave me a grateful smile and turned to make her way down the stairs.

I wondered once again at Valiana's courage and determination. *Saints,* I thought, *she could become the finest Greatcoat of any of us one day.* Of course the chances were I wasn't going to live long enough to see it happen.

Over the next half an hour we moved quickly and quietly through the palace until we reached the wing that held Duke Roset's private apartments, slipping past guards too lazy or too ill-trained to watch for those who know how to move silently and through the shadows. Greatcoats spend a great deal of their lives sneaking into—and out of—various castles, mansions, prisons, and equally well-guarded buildings; that goes with the job. Luth had its own contingent of retainers, watchmen, and guards, both Knighted and otherwise, but it turned out none of them had the training we did, or the experience. Not one of them saw us as we walked into Roset's personal wing. If we'd wanted to, we could have made our way through the deepest hallways in the palace and right to the Duke of Luth's bedroom and stuck a knife in him. It was easy. It was too easy.

"Something's wrong," I said.

"What do you mean?" Brasti asked.

"Kest was right. No one is where they're supposed to be. I'm seeing one man guarding a door when there should be two. I've spotted several retainers running down the halls like chickens with their heads cut off. The Knights are moving in six-man formations. They're looking for someone, but they're not doing it very well. They're panicked."

It became very clear that chaos was beginning to overtake the entire building. We moved silently in and out of corridors and empty rooms, keeping out of the way of the palace's guards, until we stopped inside a small servant's room that looked like it wasn't much used. Brasti kept his ear to the door and listened.

"What's going on?" I asked.

He held up a finger to tell me to be quiet, and only then did I realize there were voices on the other side of the door. My rapier was already drawn but I pulled a throwing knife from my coat as well, ready to throw at the first one through the door. After a few moments, the voices died down and we heard their footsteps as they walked away.

Brasti turned to us. "Well, I've figured out why things are so disorganized."

"What is it?" Valiana asked.

"It looks like we've arrived late for the party. Duke Roset is already dead."

21

THE KING'S ARM

Dariana came in and closed the door behind her, carefully navigating around the stacks of dishes and linens to avoid causing a crash that might draw attention to us even in the din of activity rushing through the hallways of Castle Luth. "It's madness out there," she said, almost gleefully. "I guess now we know why it was so easy breaking in."

"I don't understand how that was supposed to be easy," Valiana said, still massaging her hands. "I thought I was going to fall and die."

"That's what being alive is supposed to feel like, pretty bird." Dari grinned.

"Getting out is going to be the problem," Kest said. "We should leave now—slipping past the guards isn't going to be easy, not now."

"No," I said, carefully retying the cords of my small bag of climbing chalk and stuffing it back into its inner pocket, "we need to find out what happened to Roset."

"Are you trying to get us killed?" Brasti asked, grabbing me by the lapels. "The Duke of Luth ends up dead and the five of us are found in his castle? Do you really think there's going to be another kindly Knight-Commander like Shuran who just happens to take our side?"

"Think about it," I said, pushing his hands away. "The Dukes of Aramor and Luth were enemies, so the most likely person to have assassinated either one of them was the other. And yet now they're both dead? There's something wrong with all of this."

Brasti snorted. "Only you, Falcio, would think there was something wrong with Dukes dying. Let them kill each other off—so what if every Duke in the country dies tomorrow? Who will miss them?"

I'd been asking myself that same question during our journey from Aramor to Luth: who would miss the Dukes? If the country really was falling apart, wouldn't it be better, after the chaos, to rebuild it without the Dukes' venal influence? But the closer we'd come to the castle, the more I'd realized I could never go through with an act of outright political assassination. When I closed my eyes I could almost see King Paelis, with that lopsided grin of his. *But you came close, didn't you, Falcio?* He always did love watching me wrestle with my conscience.

Kest peeked out through the door. "The guards and Knights are rushing all over the place; there's no real coordination. It's like they've all gone mad."

I took his place and looked out at servants and guardsmen alike, all racing up and down the halls, practically running into each other at every corner. Confusion had taken over the castle. The duchies had always been ruled by their iron-fisted Dukes; it was beginning to look like without them, no one knew what to do. Knights in plate-armor and yellow tabards were trying to establish control, but from whom would they take their orders once the dust had settled?

What I was witnessing was the very reason why King Paelis had never considered forcibly removing the Dukes from power when he was alive. I closed the door and turned to Brasti. "What's happening inside this palace right now is only a small fraction of the mayhem that would engulf the country if we lost all the

Dukes: Tristia would be awash in bloody civil war for years to come."

"Perhaps that's what someone wants," Kest said. He started to say something else, then he stopped. "I hear something. Guardsmen are coming."

"They'll pass us by like the others," Brasti said confidently.

"And then what?" Dariana asked. "Whoever the assassin is, you're never going to be able to catch him with that mob of fools in the way."

Valiana caught my eye. "Falcio, what about the family? You said that it wasn't only Isault who was murdered, but his heirs as well."

"You're right—if there was one assassin there could be others—and we don't know who they're after now."

Dariana snorted. "A few hours ago you sounded as if you were ready to murder Roset yourself."

"Leave it," Kest said. He always knew which way I was headed before I did.

But Dariana ignored him. "Think, First Cantor: what have we got to gain here? How is any of this going to help Aline?"

"Everyone shut up," Brasti whispered. "They're coming this way." He took up a position that gave him the best vantage point to fire at anyone who came into the room. Dariana drew a long dagger from her coat and moved to the side of the door.

The five of us stood in silence. I could make out several men on the other side of the door arguing. "Check *every* room," one of them said.

"No one goes in there—besides, there's no way out. You'd have to be a fool to hide here. For Saints' sake, man, you're wounded. Go and see the healer before you bleed out."

"Not yet. We've got to—"

"Fine. Suit yourself if you want to watch your own blood stain the floor, Knight-Sergeant. I'm going to regroup with the others and get the damned search under control."

A few moments later the knob turned and an armored man entered the room carrying a broadsword. I was the first thing he saw. "You! It's you! I damned well—"

Kest's hand whipped out and grabbed the Knight by the back of the neck, yanking him into the room and shutting the door behind him.

"Speak softly, Sir Knight," Dariana said, the point of her blade at the Knight's throat.

The Knight's eyes darted back and forth between her blade and the rest of us. You could almost see his mind working desperately to find a way to hold us all off long enough to get help. Brasti noticed it too, and aimed his arrow at the Knight's stomach. "Make one move, metal man, one small sound, and I'll send this arrow straight through your—" Brasti leaned in closer and after a moment he slackened his grip on the string. "Falcio, I think someone's already done this guy in."

He was right. There was a tiny hole in the belly of the man's chest-plate and blood was slowly dripping out of it.

"You!" the Knight repeated, stumbling backward against the door. "I *knew* it was you. I could tell—"

"We didn't—"

The Knight dropped his sword and reached up to pull off his helm. Shoulder-length brown hair framed a soft face with a short beard. "I knew I remembered that voice, Falcio."

"Who are you?" Kest asked just as the Knight fell to his knees.

"The Knight looked up at Kest and grinned. You don't recognize me? It's—"

"Nile," I said. "Kest, it's Nile."

Nile, the son of a fisherman who took up the sword to fight for the Duchy of Pertine during a brief war with raiders from Avares, who came back to find his family gone and wandered aimlessly until we found him defending a broken old man from being kicked to death by a Lord's nephew. Nile Padgeman, Eighth Cantor of the Greatcoats, called the King's Arm.

"Saints, Nile, what happened?" I asked.

Nile shook his head briefly and winced, and as if in response, the blood began to flow faster from the wound in his stomach. "He got me, Falcio. The bastard really got me."

*   *   *

As we managed to get Nile seated with his back against the door Brasti voiced the question we were all asking. "Saints, Nile, what in the name of Saint Zaghev's bony ass are you doing here?"

We used to call Nile "the King's Arm" because even though he wasn't an especially big man he was so strong he could arm-wrestle men twice his size. The King used to joke that if we could just introduce arm-wrestling as a dueling option into Tristian culture, Nile could single-handedly win the King's peace for all time.

"Oh, hello, Brasti," Nile said, his voice weaker. A thin trickle of blood mixed with the spittle coming from his mouth. "You look . . . older. Wouldn't have recognized any of you if I hadn't had word you were coming."

"I am not—" Brasti began, reaching a hand up to his hair.

Kest slapped him on the arm. "Focus." He turned his attention to Nile. "Who told you we were coming?"

"Got word from Aramor—some little fool of a Knight said the three of you might be coming here. You'll be happy to hear he said there was a reasonable chance you *hadn't* just participated in the murder of Duke Isault."

Nile was reaching for one of the metal clasps near the shoulder of his breastplate. I knelt down and helped him undo it.

"Ah, thanks," he said. "Gods-damned armor. Five years and I still can't stand it. I miss my coat. Should've kept it with me, but I couldn't risk someone finding it. You know I had to bury the thing three miles from here? It's by a lake . . . I wonder if it's still in good shape. Probably should've burned it, but I couldn't bring myself to do it." His eyes looked as if they were going in and out of focus. Then he saw Valiana. "Oh, hello there, my pretty. What's your name?"

"Valiana," she replied.

"You're a Greatcoat?"

"I'm . . ." She hesitated for a moment and looked at me as if asking for permission.

"One of the finest," Brasti said, and for a moment I resented his quick response because it might make it sound as if I didn't believe in her.

Nile smiled and reached out a gauntleted hand to touch her arm. "Don't look so frightened, my lady. I'm dying from a belly wound, not the winter flu."

Valiana knelt down next to him and gripped his hand in hers. "Well, as long as it's not catching."

Nile laughed. "Ah. Hmm. Say, I'd swear I've seen a portrait of you. Gaudy damned thing sent by the Bitch-Who-Shall-Not-Be-Named. Did that foul old woman ever mention me? I caused her trouble a time or two."

Valiana hesitated for a moment, then said, "She spoke of you many times. She said you were one of the few Greatcoats she feared, and that if she could see you dead at her hand she'd end her days a happy woman."

Nile gave a chortle. "Oh, I like this one, Falcio. She knows how to lie with a straight face. Should've been a court lady. Now that I think of it, weren't you supposed to be Queen at some point? So many damned women trying to be Queen these days—what about you?" he said, looking at Dariana. "You want to be Queen too?"

She snorted. "Not fucking likely."

"Smart woman. Terrible job from what I understand. The King seemed to hate it." Nile craned his neck forward a little. "You know, you look just like Shanilla's little girl. Do you remember Shanilla, Falcio?"

I did. Shanilla was one of Greatcoats I'd admired the most. She knew the King's Laws and she knew how to fight, but she always tried to keep the peace when she could. She and Dara had been like sisters. I only barely remembered her having a daughter, though. Was this Dariana's secret? *Focus*, I reminded myself. "What were you doing here, Nile?" I asked. "And don't bother telling me I look older too because I've been tortured and poisoned and I've died at least once."

Nile gave a little laugh that became a cough. I pulled a piece of cloth from one of my pockets and wiped the bloody spit from his mouth.

"Thanks," he said. "Some water?"

We all glanced around the room and I spotted a jug sitting on a sideboard. Kest jumped up and brought it over. Looking inside it and sniffing, he said, "It's wine, I think."

"Even better," Nile said. "Give it here."

Brasti and I supported Nile while Kest poured a thimbleful of the wine into his mouth.

"Come on, Kest," he complained. "You always were a prude. I'm dying here."

Kest gave him a little more, but when Nile tried to reach for the jug, he said, "I'm sorry, Nile, but we need answers and getting you drunk won't help."

"It'll help me—"

"Nile," I said, "whoever did this is out there. We need to find him while we still can."

"He's long gone, Falcio," Nile replied. "You won't find him—not unless he wants you to, and I don't think you can take him."

"Let me deal with that. First tell me what in all the Saints' names you're doing here."

Nile glanced sideways at me. "The King, of course."

"What about him?" Brasti asked.

"It was his command to me. His last one . . . that day at Castle Aramor, when he met with each of us? He told me to come here and guard the Duke."

"How?"

Nile shrugged. "It was King Paelis, Falcio. When did he ever give us enough information? He just told me I had to come and guard the Duke for as long as I could."

"So you just up and joined the Ducal Knights?" Brasti asked.

Nile grinned. "It was easier than you'd think. I had some Patents of Nobility made up—you remember Pimar? That kid who used to wait on the King? Turns out he was a hell of a forger. He swore to me up and down that the King himself had found a teacher for him and ordered him to learn. Gods, King Paelis was a strange man. Why did we follow him, exactly?"

"Because everyone else was worse," Kest replied.

"Ah, right, I knew there was a reason. Anyway, Knighthood's a lot less complicated than they make it out, even with all their rules and codes and 'thees' and 'thous'. Basically, you have to come from a noble family—"

"Or have a good forger," Brasti said.

"Right, or that. Hardly anybody checks anyway, since as far as the Dukes are concerned, the Knights are just a bunch of slightly more effective soldiers. Anyway, once you're in, rank's of no more use except at tourneys and the like. Once I got the hang of the lance and wearing all this damned metal all the time, it wasn't so hard."

"So you became a Knight-Sergeant?" I asked.

"Could've made Knight-Captain if I'd wanted, but that would have meant more travel, whereas the Knight-Sergeants are usually the ones commanding the Duke's guards."

"And you've been guarding him for the past five years?"

Nile smiled. "Easiest job I ever had, Falcio. The food's good, the pay is—well, it's more than a fucking Greatcoat's, I promise you that. Women pretty much flock to you and no one expects you to marry them." Nile looked over to Brasti. "I'm surprised you haven't joined up."

"I would have," he said, "if they weren't so squeamish about archery."

"Fair enough." Nile closed his eyes.

"Help me get him out of this thing," I said to Kest, pointing at the breastplate.

Nile reached a gauntleted hand over and grabbed my arm. "You do that and I'm just going to bleed out all over the place. It's keeping my insides together." He tried to look down at the small hole in the plate of his armor. "Can you believe the bastard managed to get a poignard through that? Thin damned thing, looked like it would break right off. Even if I'd been fast enough, I'm not sure I'd have bothered to parry it. And yet . . ."

"What can we do for you?" I asked.

"Nothing. Reckon I've got about another ten minutes before I pass out and maybe thirty more after that before I go and find Paelis in whatever hell he's in now and beat the shit out of him." Nile looked at me and laughed. "Hah! You should see your expression, Falcio. You never could stand to hear anyone say anything bad about the King, could you?"

"The assassin, Nile, what was he like?"

"He was an assassin, Falcio. They don't exactly make it easy for you to identify them. The room was nearly pitch-black but I think he . . . you know, wore a mask and was generally in dark clothes. I suspect that makes it easier."

"How many times have there been attempts on the Duke's life?"

"Over the past five years? Other than this time?"

I nodded.

"None," Nile said.

"None? No one's *ever* tried to kill him?"

"Who's going to do it? The peasants and townsfolk have been under his heel forever, and none of the nobles would ever dare try it."

"What about other Dukes?" I asked.

He shook his head. "There's no way—hey, d'you know what I discovered over the past five years? Tristia's main agricultural crop is spies—not spies against foreign countries, mind you, but ones who spend all their time right here in Tristia. I tell you, Falcio, every castle in the country is bulging with spies from every other castle. If a Duke ever tried to send an assassin after another Duke, chances are he'd be discovered before he even finished writing down the order."

Nile coughed again, and this time there was a lot more blood. I didn't think he had much longer. "Then who did this? Who could—?" I asked.

"No, tell me how he moved," Kest said, his eyes peering into Nile's.

"Leave it," I said.

"No, I need to know."

Nile looked straight ahead at the wall opposite. "He was flowing, like a river." He waved his hand out in front of himself in tiny figures-of-eights. "It was like trying to outwit an eel. Slippery. Fast."

I'd only once ever encountered men who moved the way Nile was describing. "Nile, are you telling me the assassin was a *Dashini*?"

"You know, at first I thought it might be, but he never spat any of that damned dust at me—you know? The stuff that makes you pee your pants while they kill you? But now that I'm thinking about it, he did move the way the stories tell. Say, is it true you fought one in Rijou?"

"Yes," I said.

"You know people are saying it was actually two of them. Don't suppose that's true, is it?"

I nodded.

"Saints," he said. "You killed *two* Dashini? How in all the hells did you accomplish that?"

"I said some things that threw them off guard just long enough to—"

"Hah," Nile laughed, blood now dripping freely from his mouth, "isn't that ironic? You always did talk people to death, Falcio."

Valiana reached out to wipe the blood from his mouth but he took her hand instead and held it next to his heart, and then, just like that, without so much as a gurgle or a sigh, Nile Padgeman died. Valiana kept hold of his hand. Even though she'd barely even met the man, she hung on until she was sure his spirit was truly gone and then, only then did she let go, and the tears started to roll silently down her cheeks. I loved her for those tears.

22

THE DUKE'S WIFE

"Falcio, we've got to get out of here," Brasti said.

"Just a minute," I said, passing my hand over Nile's eyes to close the lids. "We should take him with us."

Kest looked down at me. "We can't. Chances are we're going to have to fight our way out as it is."

"We can't leave him here," I said. Nile deserved better than to be left soaking in his own blood in a servant's room. He deserved a proper burial, and not in this damned armor but in his own coat. "Where did Nile say he buried his coat? By a lake? We can take him there and—"

Kest knelt down to face me. "We can't, Falcio; you know that. They think he's a Knight here. They'll bury him with full Knight's honors."

Nile would have hated that idea. "Why?" I asked. "Why did the King send him here to guard a damned Duke? Did he send Dara too? Is that why she was in Aramor?" I felt sick inside. *Had he ordered her to become Isault's mistress, too?*

Kest put his hands on both sides of my face, an odd gesture; he only did it on those occasions when he thought I was losing my mind. "Dara is dead. Nile is dead. The King is dead. Falcio, you have to decide if you want us to die, too, because soon—"

"Too late," Dariana said, leaping to the side of the door and readying her blade.

"How many?" Kest asked.

"More than enough," came a deep baritone voice. The door opened and a man in armor with a Knight-Captain's insignia on his livery came into view. Brasti aimed right for the man's helmed head, but the Knight put up a hand. "Loose that arrow and the full might of the Duke's guards will fall on you, Trattari."

"What happens if I don't?" Brasti asked.

"You." The Knight was pointing at me. "The Lady Beytina has asked for you."

"And who is this Beytina supposed to be?"

"The *Lady* Beytina is Duke Roset's wife and, as of about three hours ago, the new ruler of Luth. She is also, for a very short while at any rate, the only thing stopping me from stringing up a rope and hanging the lot of you in the middle of the hallway."

"Why would she ask for us?" Brasti asked.

The Knight snorted. "She didn't." He pointed a gauntleted hand at me. "She asked for *you*, Falcio val Mond, First something-or-other of the Tatter-cloaks."

My blade whispered from its sheath.

The guards outside the room tensed but the Knight stopped them. "Leave it," he said.

"How could she even know I was here?" I asked.

The Knight-Captain glanced back at his men. "You see what I was talking about? These Trattari—they all think they're so damned clever." He turned back to me. "We had word from our spies days ago about what happened in Aramor. Duke Roset knew you'd come here, shaking your fist and demanding some kind of redress for his imaginary crimes."

I considered our options. The doorway was narrow, which would make it hard for more than one of the Knights to attack us head-on, but by the same token, we had no way out. There were men with crossbows who needed only to fire over the shoulder of their captain to get at us, and we were packed into the little room too tightly to be able to take cover.

"What assurances do I have as to the Lady Beytina's intentions?" I asked finally.

"The Duchess wants to talk to you privately. More than that, I don't need to know. Neither do you."

"Aren't you afraid I might assassinate her?"

"Not really," the Knight said. "The assassin got to her already." He pointed to Nile. "Knight-Sergeant Kylen there tried to protect her but the assassin's blade got her in the lung. She's dying."

I could hear Lady Beytina wheezing from the open door to her room.

"Fluid's in the lungs," Kest said. He has always had an uncanny ability to discern any condition that leads to a painful death.

Two guards in yellow livery stood in our way, doing their best not to look nervous, which only magnified the degree to which they seemed terrified of us.

"Stay back, Trattari," the more senior of the two said.

A soft, broken voice came from inside the room. "Let them in, Rasten. They aren't the ones who did this and there's little more they could do to me now at any rate."

The guards stood aside and we were allowed entry into the Lady's room. It was a grand place, with blue and silver trim brightening the dark oak-paneled walls. There were no fewer than three mirrors, two hanging on the walls and one especially ornate one set in a gilded wooden frame carved with elaborate flowers standing near the center of the room. A small door opened to a dressing room on one side; inside, I could see armoires and racks of clothing.

I remembered what I'd heard about the Lady Beytina now. She had married Duke Roset, three decades her senior, very recently. She was only a few years out of her teens, a very pretty, graceful girl likely just becoming used to the trappings of wealth and power.

"Here," she wheezed, "please, come here, Trattari."

I left the others by the door and approached her. Two young women knelt by the Lady's bed, holding her hands while an elderly woman with curly gray hair removed a white towel laden with pale green blades of grass and yellow flower petals from Beytina's forehead. She replaced it with another towel, similarly filled.

"It's called feypurse," Beytina said. "They tell me it will cure me in no time."

She was more than pretty; even now she was a stunningly beautiful woman. Long yellow hair, which should have been damp and matted from sweat and fever, had been carefully brushed and arranged just so on her pillows, framing a face pale and pained, and yet still painted the white of alabaster rather than allowing the gray of imminent death to show through. She had a wreath of small blue flowers around her neck which echoed the shadows of a similar hue around her eyes. She looked like one of those paintings of Saint Werta-who-walks-the-waves that often adorn the cabins of wealthy ships' captains.

I found the whole scene pathetic.

This is how the rich met their ends—neither bravely nor cowardly, but prettily. Such was Beytina's vanity that even as she made her way inch by inch to Death's chamber she insisted on looking as if she would rise from her bed at any moment and lead a company of great lords and ladies in a country dance. I wanted to tell her that she was well dead, even now; that a man had snuck into her castle and killed her without a thought to her beauty or her grace or her manners; that there were no doubt many heavens that awaited the soon-to-be-departed but that in all likelihood none of them would open their doors to her.

"They tell stories of your beauty, my Lady," I said when I reached her bedside. "None of them do you justice."

She smiled at me, and I saw the first tiny blur in her eyes that heralded the coming of tears. She blinked them back. "Thank you, Trattari."

She shook off the hands of the girls keeping her company and waved them away, along with the healer. I looked back at Kest and Brasti who

were waiting at the entrance and they left as well. The guards closed
the door behind us.

"You asked to see me, my Lady," I said. "Is there anything I can
do to make you more comfortable?"

She gave a small laugh that turned into a hacking cough, displac-
ing the carefully arranged hair and causing the towel to slip awkwardly halfway down her forehead. "Please," she said, "no jests."

I reached over and carefully began to replace the towel packed
with herbs.

"No," she said, "get this stupid thing off me."

I lifted the towel from the bed and then thought of how it might
look when the others returned. "Are you sure? Isn't it supposed to—"

"Don't be an idiot. You can't heal an internal bleed with a com-
press of weeds and flower petals," she said.

"Do you want me to tell your men to find another healer?"

"That flittering idiot I just sent away was as good as we have here,"
she said. "The old fool will give you any number of sweetly flavored
tinctures and pleasant-smelling salves but she wouldn't know how
to prepare ginroot if it grew between her toes."

"You have some experience at medicine?" I asked.

"I was training to be a healer myself," Beytina replied. "I was in
my final year, in fact, when the Duke met me by chance and set a
new course for my life." She tried to push herself up on the bed but
failed. Her eyes turned to me.

I helped her to sit up, trying not to jostle her in the process.

"Do you want to hear something funny, Greatcoat?" she asked
while I was still moving her. "The healers who come from the small
towns and villages—the ones who learn from their mothers and their
mothers' mothers; the ones who prepare foul-tasting potions and
rancid-smelling ointments—they actually *cure* people sometimes.
And yet the ones trained to work inside the Ducal houses—the ones
who learn from the great masters—they are largely ineffective. Oh,
they can give you all kinds of very masterful-sounding names for
things, but they don't actually heal you at all."

"It's a wonder any of the nobles survive having a cold," I said.

She smiled wanly. "They—*we*, I mean—eat well and stay out of the cold. We don't get wounded very often and we never suffer from hunger or thirst. But when we do get sick, we have neither the medicines to cure our conditions nor the hardiness to sustain us. We are like very tall, very pretty glass vases: throw one stone and we fall to pieces." She spread her arms out in a beatific pose. "We are full of useless beauty."

It surprised me that she was so conscious of her condition. The nobles had so carefully constructed their world to keep out the rabble that they would never trust a peasant healer or village witchywoman in their presence. They were, as the Lady said, incredibly fragile.

"And yet," I said, "you seem quite determined to go into the next world looking—"

She smiled, though only one side of her mouth rose to the occasion. "Beauty, however lacking in real value, is all the wealth I've been able to count on in my life. It got me admitted into school when I didn't have the money; it earned me a Duke's hand when I didn't have a noble name. I have to assume the Gods are just as shallow as the rest of us. Tell me, do you think I should pray to Orros or to Lepheys before I die?"

"Who, your Grace?"

"Orros is what we call the God Coin in the duchy of Luth. Lepheys is the Goddess of Love, but she is sometimes a jealous deity, or so the clerics tell us. Purgeize, God of War, isn't much better, but surely he will grant me some favor if only I die as pretty as I lived?"

"I'm afraid I have very little experience with the Gods, my Lady."

She nodded as if I'd said something wise. "True. The Gods do not appear for the small folk, do they? My husband told me once that Orros spoke to him, but I'm not entirely sure Roset wasn't making fun of me." She closed her eyes for a moment. "I suppose it doesn't matter. The noble healers are at least very good with opiates. I feel no pain at all now."

Despite the glibness of her words, her eyes began filling with tears again. She talked a good game, but I could see she was not just afraid but terrified, and I felt ashamed at my earlier dismissal of her. Regardless of her husband's actions, she was a young woman about to die for no better reason than that she had accepted an offer of marriage that she could hardly have refused.

"If you ask it of me, Lady, I will go quickly and seek out a better healer. There is a village not far from here. I could be back within a day."

She stared back at me for a moment, then said, "Give me your hand."

I reached out, assuming she wanted to me to help her rise. Instead she took my hand in hers and brought it to her lips and kissed it once. "I like the fact that you would try to save me even though on a different day you would just as likely see me dead. Do you think it's my pathetic situation that sways you, or the pretty flowers in my hair?"

"Neither, my Lady."

"Please tell me it's not out of honor or duty, for I'm quite sure I would never believe you."

"No, my Lady. I . . ." There was no good reason for me to comfort her, and certainly no reason to be truthful with her, but she was scared and hurting, and pain and suffering deserve some kind of answer. "I was married once."

"Was she as pretty as me?" Beytina asked.

I found it an odd question. "She was not half so pretty as you, my Lady, but twice as beautiful."

The Lady gave a small laugh. "Good answer. If I meet your wife in the Afterworlds I will be sure to let her know of both your kindness and your fidelity. But go on, tell me about this woman of yours. Was she especially saintly?"

I thought about my wife, Aline, with her wicked smiles and nasty jokes; the way she'd badger vendors at the market until they would shake their heads in disgust as they looked down at the paltry price she'd paid for their best wares, and then the way she'd come back and give the same man a cake she'd baked as a gift. I remembered the times she would refuse to give even a black penny to the clerics, and how once she'd even stolen from a church, only to use the money to buy meals for the children waiting outside. I remembered the way she would call me a coward if I backed down from our more aggressive neighbors one day, only to beg me not to fight when . . .

"She was sensible," I said. "She disliked waste and meanness."

"And so?"

"And so when I look at you, I simply ask myself what Aline would have told me to do. I think she would have said—"

Beytina gave a little snort. "Husband, go get that prissy rich woman a good country healer!"

"Something like that."

"And how would you have replied?"

I spoke my next words as gently as I could. "I would have told her that a day or even half a day would still be too long. That you have fluid in your lungs and all that's left is to prepare for the end."

The Lady reached for my hand again. I didn't want to touch her but I felt compelled to. *It's just a hand*, Aline would have said. *It's not like being stabbed is contagious.* I gave her my hand and when she squeezed it, I squeezed back a little.

"Would you sit with me a while longer?" she asked.

"I . . ."

There was an assassin out there, possibly more than one, and they had plans and schemes, and I had no clue what they might be. If it really was the Dashini, killing off any Duke who might support the King's heir taking the throne, then we were as good as lost already. "I will stay a little while," I said finally.

"Even though I am your enemy's wife?"

"Even so," I said.

"And will you promise to stay with me for an hour, even though I must say terrible, hurtful things to you now?"

I looked at her. The expression on her face was earnest. "My Lady?"

She took in a breath, a slow, wheezing inhalation that seemed to take forever and yet never quite ended. "My husband made a very bad agreement. One should never make contracts out of fear," she said. She looked into my eyes. "I know who you are, Falcio val Mond. You're the First Cantor of the Greatcoats. You were the Tyrant King's favorite."

I noticed my hand was squeezing hers too hard. "My Lady, it would be best if we do not speak of the King."

"Forgive me," she said, "I meant—well, I suppose it's late to be saying I meant no offense. Regardless, what I wanted to say is that if the troubadours are to be believed, you withstood torture and assassins and an endless number of enemies to save the King's heir."

"They also say I beheaded Jillard, Duke of Rijou, my Lady, but I suspect you'll find him soon returned to his castle, his head still firmly seated on his neck. The troubadours have a propensity for embellishment."

"Did they also embellish the tale that you spoke at the Rock? That you roused the people of Rijou from restlessness? Did they make up the fact that you stopped the Duke from extending the Ganath Kalila?"

"I . . . I suppose, but I was only—"

"You were only trying to save the girl." The Lady shook her head. "What kind of fool are you, precisely?"

"My Lady?"

"We've been speaking about how fragile the nobility is, how insulated and yet vulnerable. Falcio, you went to Rijou and you reached the Rock! Did you know they rioted for ten days afterward? Did you know that many of the lower houses have not only refused to pay increases in their rents but have failed to pay their lawful taxes?"

I thought back to that day—how long had it been? Two months, perhaps? I'd lost track of time and now it was all a bit of a blur. I did remember the crowds, the way they'd chanted at the end: "No Man Breaks The Rock!" they'd shouted. I assumed it would have died down after a good night of drinking.

"It has begun to spread," Beytina said, pulling me from my reverie. "Oh, the cities have enough guardsmen and Knights to bring them to heel, but in the towns and hamlets far from the reach of the Duke's men? They are beginning to hear the stories of your exploits and they are wondering if they really should have to bear the weight of the nobility. We received word that a tax collector was murdered in one of the outlying villages just yesterday."

Carefal, I thought. *She's talking about Carefal.* Was it really just because of me, of one stupid speech given in the heat of desperation as I'd looked for a way to get Aline out of there alive? "My Lady," I said, "what is it you want to tell me?"

"I told you, Falcio of the Greatcoats, the nobility—we are less secure than we appear. What must a weak man with a sword do when those around him begin to question his strength? The weak man with the sword must kill quickly, mercilessly, or else it won't take long before someone decides to take the sword from him. My husband made a deal, Falcio: a terrible deal. He needed to regain control and he let his Knight-Commander decide how to do it. Carefal sits on our border. If the village were allowed to flout Ducal Law, others would do so as well; the duchy would fall into chaos. They have weapons—steel weapons. Duke Roset had no choice, Falcio. You left him none."

"What are you saying?" I demanded.

"The Knight-Commander sent his men to Carefal," she said.

Suddenly the veil lifted from my eyes and I understood what she was telling me. "No—"

"You needn't feel rushed," she said. "It's far too late. I imagine Carefal is already in flames by now."

I let go of her hand and stepped back.

Beytina looked at her hand. "Say what you want about that gray-haired old gasbag, she brews an awfully good painkiller." She held her hand out to me. "I do believe you've broken my hand, Falcio."

I was horrified and disgusted by what I'd done to her. "Why?" I asked. "Why did you tell me this?"

"I'm sorry. You seem like a genuinely decent man and you've been kind to me, so far at least."

"Then why?"

Beytina sighed, a little sadly. "Because I married the Duke and despite everything else I am a loyal wife. He was angered by what he had to do and he would have wanted me to say this to you: every dead body you find in that village, every dead body to follow as other Dukes are forced to put down rebellions with blood and steel—each one is on your head, Falcio val Mond. You have driven us to murder."

She began coughing and wheezing again, and despite my promise to her, I fled the room.

23

CAREFAL

The smoke and stench began to suffocate us almost half a mile before we entered the village; the tale of Carefal's destruction was told long before the bodies themselves came into view. The closer we came, the more our horses resisted, and in the end we dismounted and walked the final hundred yards. We needed to see for ourselves what had become of the people of Carefal.

"Keep an eye out," Kest told Valiana and Dari. "Whoever did this might have left someone behind, just in case."

"What are we looking for?" Valiana asked.

"Knights," I replied.

"There might be children," Brasti said, his voice airy and fragile, as if he were half dreaming. "Sometimes the children go to gather berries."

It was a foolish thing to say. Kest and Brasti and I all came from villages no bigger than Carefal and we all knew full well that the picking season had passed weeks ago; no children would be coming back to the village. But the tightness in Brasti's jaw and the tremor in his voice kept me from saying any of this.

The first visible sign of what had taken place greeted us at the entrance to the village seven corpses, their bodies, charred from the smoke and flame of now burned-out fires, hung from ropes tied to branches of the tall trees. A slight breeze made the bodies spin, ever so slowly, as if some invisible hand were turning meat on a spit.

Why bother burning them if they had already been hanged? I wondered.

Dariana, standing next to me, anticipated my question. "Look at the knots in the ropes," she said, pointing above us. "Those are trunk knots—they don't tighten, not unless you pull against them. So they hung them there and lit the fires and waited until the heat and smoke made them twitch."

The need to retch was almost overwhelming. I had to lean against a tree to keep from falling to my knees. These people had died terrified, in pain, and horribly, torturously slowly.

"Why?" Brasti asked, his shortbow in hand and an arrow nocked at the ready. "What was the point?"

The point is that Dariana isn't the only one who can recognize a trunk knot, I thought. *The point is that others will come here and see what had happened to these people, and the story of Carefal will spread, and everyone will know that there is a price beyond death to pay for rebelling against the Dukes.* I knew all this but couldn't bring myself to say it out loud.

Inside the village the carnage was less staged but far more prolific. Men, women, and children, the very young and the very old, were all lying together, piled in untidy heaps. Some had died from sword thrusts to the belly, some had had their heads taken off. A few showed signs of being trampled by horses. All of them had been burned.

The thatched roofs of the houses had been pulled down onto the dirt pathways between the houses and set fire to, then the bodies had then been thrown on top. I could see the charring of the flesh was patchy, incomplete: some limbs had been burned black while other parts were still pink. In my head I watched the killers forcing the villagers at sword-point to tear off the roofs of their own homes, only killing them after they had built their own pyres.

"How many?" I asked Kest.

"Villagers?" He looked at the piles of corpses. "Close to two hundred, I think."

"No, how many did this?"

Kest looked around the village. "I see hoofprints and boot marks. They worked methodically, going through the streets while maintaining a perimeter around the paths out of the village. So thirty or forty, I'd say."

"Were they Knights?" I asked. A small part of me wished it had been bandits of some kind—it wouldn't have made a blind bit of difference to the dead, but it might have made the bounty on my soul a little smaller.

Kest seldom wastes words, so he didn't bother to answer. The footprints on the ground were heavy; the men were obviously wearing armor. Anyone could see that the killers were Knights. I cursed Duke Roset again, as I had every mile from the palace to this place. There was a sobbing sound behind me and for an instant I hoped there might be someone left alive, someone who could tell us for sure what had happened, but it was Valiana. Tears streamed endlessly down her face even as she wiped her eyes over and over again. For a brief, ignoble moment I wanted to shout at her for her useless tears, but then I realized, *She doesn't look away. She just keeps staring at them.*

"You don't have to—"

"Of course she does," Dariana said, her voice flat. She stood in the shadow of another set of hanging corpses. Her eyes were as black as coal. "This is the world we live in now."

"I don't believe that. I can't believe—"

"Falcio," Kest said, his arm on my shoulder, "you've got to talk to Brasti."

"What are—?"

He pointed a little way down the path to where Brasti was hauling corpses off one of the piles. By the time I got there he was kneeling on the ground and digging at the dirt with his fingers, only inches away from a big pile of bodies.

"Planning to dig your way to the Shan Empire?" I asked, my voice as gentle as I could make it.

"I just want to bury them," he said. "It won't take long. I know we can't stay."

There were thirty, maybe forty, corpses in this heap, their limbs tangling with one another. Like the rest, their skin was crusted and burned black in places. There were several such piles around the village. "Brasti, you can't bury them all. Even if we had shovels, it would take us days, maybe weeks," I said softly. "We can't stay here."

"I know," he said, but went right on digging.

I knelt down and put a hand on his shoulder. "Brasti, this won't work. You can't dig a grave with your fingers."

"Sure I can," he said. "Just watch me."

The wind shifted and the full force of the stench from the bodies hit me again. There was a soft rustle and I looked up, fearful one of the corpses was about to fall on us. Their faces pulled me in. Some of the heads were turned away, as if they were terrified of the living; others were watching Brasti's efforts with a kind of mute terror, their eyes wide-open and mouths gaping. One woman's face caught me by surprise, the anger and outrage making of her expression making her known to me. *Vera*, I thought. The farmer who'd help lead the rebellion. In the end she'd just been stacked on the pile with the rest of them.

I turned back to Brasti and noticed his fingers. They were already bleeding.

"Stop," I said.

"It's not going to take long, Falcio. Just let me—"

"Stop. You've got to stop." I grabbed his wrists and forced them up to his face. He'd broken through the skin and every one of his fingertips was bleeding. "Look at what you're doing!"

He tried to pull his hands away. "It doesn't hurt, Falcio. Just give me time—I can do this."

I thought perhaps he was going mad, but neither the look in his eyes nor the sound of his voice betrayed any hysteria; it sounded as if his actions were the result of calm, collected reasoning. "You're going to rip through your fingers, Brasti."

"Don't need them," he said, and broke free from my grip.

"You're an archer, you fool. You can't very well pull a bowstring if you've worn your fingers to the bone." I kept my voice light, setting him up to make some retort about how he could shoot with his toes if he wanted to. Brasti loves to get the last word in when he can.

But he just went back to digging with his hands again. Then he muttered something under his breath, but I couldn't make out what it was.

"What did you say?" I asked.

"I said, 'The arrow only strikes true when it's pointed in the right direction.'"

"I don't understand. Brasti, *stop digging*—stop, or I'm going to get Kest and the two of us are going to tie you up until you start making sense."

His hands stopped moving and he went completely still, like some old painting of a man mourning at his wife's grave. Then I noticed his breathing was getting faster and faster, and I could hear the hiss of the air coming into his mouth and the whoosh as it left. I was starting to worry that he would pass out, so I reached out to put a hand on his shoulder again, but before my hand even touched him he spun on his knees and faced me. His bloodied hands reached up, and he grabbed the lapels of my coat. "What does it matter if I'm an archer? What difference does it make if I can hit a target when I'm never aiming at the right one? Who would know the difference if I cut my hands off here and now?"

"Brasti, calm down. Let's get out of here and talk—"

"Talk!" he shouted, "*talk*! That's what you do, Falcio! You talk and you talk and you talk, but you never *say* anything. You have us running around the countryside trying to find the answer to questions no one but you cares about! You think anyone really wants to know who killed Duke-fucking-Isault? Or whether the same people also killed Duke-fucking-Roset? Or if someone wants to start a war among the nobility?"

"The King would care. He'd—"

Brasti pushed me so hard I fell backward into the pile of bodies, and arms and legs shaken loose from their position fell over my shoulders and face as if they were trying to draw me into the pile with them.

"Maybe the King wanted it this way, Falcio! Have you ever even considered that? Dara was right there, in Isault's throne room, and she *hated* the Dukes, Falcio, you know that! So she killed herself one—it's that fucking simple. But you? Oh no, you have to believe there's some other *secret* reason. Why does everyone think you're so damned clever when all you do is twist the evidence to fit your own personal beliefs?"

I pushed myself back up to my feet, the feeling of dead flesh still clinging to my skin. "She wasn't there to kill him," I said, trying to make him understand. "Nile said he was sent by the King. He was there to—"

Brasti started laughing hysterically. "Did it even occur to you that maybe Nile was lying to you? Maybe the King planned it this way all along—he told the others to wait until one of his heirs revealed themselves, and then they were to kill off the Dukes and clear the path to the throne. And you know what else? I'll just bet you he told every one of the other Greatcoats, 'Don't go telling Falcio about this. He wouldn't understand. Falcio's a sensitive lad, wants to save the world, don't you know.'"

My skin was growing hot. "I think I knew the King better than you did, Brasti—"

"Really? Is that what you think? Because I think almost everyone in this damned country knew the King better than you did."

"Enough," I said. "You're angry, I get that. What happened here is . . . It's like nothing any of us have ever seen. But now we have to *think*. We have to have a plan." Even to my own ears the words sounded trite.

Brasti dismissed me with a wave of his hand. "*A plan?* The hells with your plans, Falcio. I have my own plan now: I'm going to kill every Knight who walks the earth. I don't care if they're as base as brigands or as noble as your fucking friend Shuran."

"Brasti, if we don't uphold the laws, then what—?"

He spun back to me. "You want laws? Here's a law: *no man wears armor. Ever.* There's only one reason why a man puts on armor, Falcio—because it means he can beat and kill and rape anyone too poor to afford their own." He pointed at the corpses on the ground. "Look at these poor bastards! Some of them even had swords—and what good did it do them against armor, the kind a Ducal Knight wears? You can't get through it unless you've spent your life training for it. Well, guess what: I have a cure for that. I've got Intemperance, and she can send an ironwood shaft through even their thickest steel plates. I can make as many arrows as I need, and I'll keep making them until there isn't a man left alive with the balls to put on another suit of armor." Brasti spat on the ground between us. "You want laws? That's Brasti's Law."

I struggled to find something to say, some way to counter both his logic and his anger, but I couldn't, because he was right, in a way. I looked at the bodies. The skin on the palms of those holding swords had bubbled and blistered from the heat of the flames transferred through the steel.

Kest came down the path toward us, Dari and Valiana close behind. He murmured, "Give Brasti time. This . . . this isn't something he can deal with."

It was true. Brasti loved the simple things in life, especially those simple things which came from being with other people. Kest was driven by a need to master the sword, and me? Well, I was driven by something else. At heart Brasti just wanted to be around people—but somehow that angered me right at that moment. There were people I wanted to be with, too. Most were dead. The few who remained I probably wouldn't see before the neatha finally claimed me. The hells with Brasti and his anger.

The smell from the corpses was overpowering. *Damn you all,* I thought. *Why did people without even minimal training take up swords against armored Knights?* I looked down at the bodies again.

Saint Dheneph-who-tricks-the-gods. "Why?" wasn't the right question. "Why?" didn't matter at all. The question was *"How?"*

"What is it?" Valiana asked.

"The swords," I said. "We took away their swords, remember? Shuran paid for them and brought them back to Isault's palace to ensure they couldn't be used against them."

"You think they bought more?" Kest asked. "With the money Shuran paid them?"

"No—remember what Shuran said? Those weapons would cost him twice what he'd paid for them if he'd had to buy them new. How could they even afford it? In fact, if they'd bought them in the first place, why didn't they know the price of a forged sword?"

"So someone is supplying the peasants with weapons," Dariana said, "but why? Out of the goodness of their hearts?"

"No." Valiana looked thoughtful. "No, this is like something Patriana would've done: arm your enemy's peasants and foment rebellion so you can force the Duke's soldiers to waste their resources. You use three times as many men as there are civilians just to keep the peace and weaken them from inside their own borders—and that makes them easier to defeat on the field."

"Only the Dukes aren't trying to keep the peace, not this time," I said.

"They can't—that woman, Duke Roset's wife? She was right, Falcio. The Knights have to create so much fear that once word spreads no peasant will even *think* about rebelling against their lord—otherwise how will the Dukes be able to resist Trin's armies when they come?"

Beytina's words echoed in my mind. *What must a weak man with a sword do when those around him begin to question his strength?* I turned and looked back down the path where Brasti was walking slowly, looking closely at each corpse, like a painter planning to create a portrait of each one. "Kest, go and get him."

Kest's expression was uncertain. "Falcio, I'm not sure he's—"

"Now," I said. "Brasti can lose his mind later, but right now I need him and his bow and his anger. He wants to kill Knights? I've got dozens for him."

Kest took off at a jog down the path.

Valiana knelt down next to a boy no older than twelve years old, his face cleaved by a single blow. In his hands was a steel sword that was probably too heavy for him even to lift properly. Valiana carefully pried his fingers apart and took the blade, then she drew her own weapon and placed it in his hand.

"That's a lot heavier than yours," Dariana said.

"I'm stronger now, and if we're going to fight men in armor then I'll need something heavier."

"Well now," Dari said, a little smirk on her face, "glad to hear you've finally discovered the virtue of revenge."

"It's not about revenge," Valiana said. "If the southern Dukes are trying to make sure the peasants don't consider rebellion as an option, they're not going to stop at massacring one village."

"Why should they stop?" Brasti asked, leaning on Kest as though his legs wouldn't hold him up any longer. "Why would any of them stop? They killed our King and we did nothing. They took the country and we did nothing." He shrugged off Kest's arm and knelt down next to the body of the boy from whom Valiana had taken the sword, reaching over awkwardly to smooth the child's hair. "Now they've . . . now they've done this. Why would they stop when there's never a price to pay for their deeds?"

I looked at Kest, counting on his support most of all, but even he couldn't meet my eyes. "There are too many of them, Falcio. Trin—the Dukes—the Knights, even the Dashini . . . we don't even know who all of our enemies are anymore. There's just . . . what do you want us to do?"

They all stood there staring at me, their faces as cold as the dead of Carefal. How could I ask this of them now? Valiana was barely trained, holding a sword too heavy for her. Dariana was as vicious a fighter as any of our enemies, and probably just as trustworthy. Kest, the Saint of Swords, could lose himself at any moment. Brasti, the laughing rogue; his mind was even now shattering into a thousand pieces as he cried over the burned remains of the villagers. And me: a dying fool fighting his last few bouts with an enemy I couldn't see, never mind defeat. We were five broken people trying to hold together a broken country. But we were all that was left.

"You're right," I said, "there are too many of them and too few of us. Plots within plots, and assassins coming at us from all sides—but you know what? I don't care anymore. You say we don't know who our enemies are? I say, they don't know who *we* are. Maybe this is a hopeless fight." I looked at Kest and Brasti and, despite the flat looks on their faces, I smiled. "But hopeless fights just happen to be our specialty."

For a long time there was nothing but the quiet breeze blowing against the embers of scorched homes.

It was Brasti who spoke first. "Where would we even start?" He said it cynically, dismissively, and yet that tiny spark of hope was the first shred of warmth I'd felt in a long time.

"We hunt them," I said.

"Hunt who?" Valiana asked. "The Knights?"

"The Knights. Trin. The Dashini. We hunt them all."

Dariana snorted. "And when we find them, then what?"

I smiled, perhaps because I knew it would annoy her, perhaps because, no matter how broken these people were, they were people I loved, or perhaps simply because smiling in the face of death is what you do when there's nothing else left to try.

"That's the easy part," I said. "We teach them the first rule of the sword."

INTERLUDE

In the heart of Castle Aramor sits a small private library known as the Royal Athenaeum (or, as Brasti used to call it, "that funny little round room where the King liked to take noblewomen to show them how clever he was.") Not long after the Dukes took the King's head, they looted most of his books—probably because they too had noblemen and women to impress with their brilliance. However if you search long enough among the refuse that the Dukes left behind, pushing aside the unswept dust and thick cobwebs, you might chance upon an unimpressive-looking tome entitled *On The Virtus of Knights*.

Now, you might suppose that such a book would be one of the very first that any pompous ass of a Duke would desire to see sitting proudly on his mantel. After all, what nobleman doesn't bloviate, self-righteously and to considerable extent, about the honor and loyalty of their Knights? (Not to mention the money spent on them.) Surely such a book so auspiciously titled *On The Virtus of Knights* ought therefore to have been desired and fought over by the Dukes.

Alas, the cover of this particular tome happens to be rather worn and rubbed, its color faded, and its considerably foxed pages imbued with a not-especially-pleasant smell of moldy leather overlaying that of the rotting paper.

Had one of those Dukes chosen to pick up the book, however, he might have noticed that the author was a man named Arlan Hemensis, and even the briefest time spent on research into that name would have yielded the fact that Arlan was a former clerk of a minor noble's household who had spent many of his later years in prison as a result of a dispute with a Ducal Knight. The Knight in question had been aggrieved over the old man's steadfast refusal to pay for a replacement tabard after the blood of Veren Hemensis, Arlan's only son, had stained it beyond redemption. The tabard had been bloodied during the Knight's duel with young Veren . . . it mattered not one jot that the boy, who was only seven and a half years old, thought he had been playing when he challenged the Knight to the duel. After all, the duel is one of the Ducal Knights' sacred obligations.

When Arlan was finally released from prison at the age of sixty-seven, he lived just long enough to write his little book.

On the surface, the book lauds the honor and effectiveness of the Knighthood, though a more detailed study might raise a few questions in the minds of more cynical readers. My favorite passage is the very last one, which reads thus:

So grand is a true Knight that even should one be slain on the battlefield, his armor pierced by, let's say, a dozen arrows, his helmet struck so hard that the steel that once protected said Knight's skull now crushes it, sending brain matter dribbling down the other side of his head . . . even then, Gentle Reader, as the remnants of his broken body fall crashing to the ground, the great clanging sound his armor makes is so rich and noble in tone that one might be forgiven for longing to hear it again and again.

And, too, it must be said that while the deaths of a thousands peasants might pass unnoticed by history, when such perfidious wretches as would attack their betters do, by some chance, take down a Knight, his armored body casts a very long shadow indeed.

24

THE SAINT OF MERCY

We five weary, desperate Greatcoats rode in bitter silence toward the northern village of Luth, chasing after forty Ducal Knights. Kest reckoned they had a full day's head-start on us, despite the great weight of armor they were lugging around. Whenever sleep threatened to overtake me, I pictured the men we pursued as grinning jackals, gleefully tearing innocent villagers to pieces. In truth, the slaughter was likely done quite methodically, dispassionately. These were Ducal Knights, after all: men who were just following orders—oh, and the dictates of what they considered their own honor. I planned to kill every last one of them.

Our enemies were making no effort to mask their trail: every hoofprint was like a smile etched into the dirt, inviting us to follow. Whenever I looked behind us, I could almost see the dead of Carefal following close behind, the men, women, and children staring at me with their flat, empty eyes. I imagined them mouthing the words "coward" and "traitor" over and over, as if by so doing they might force me to greater speed, but we were already riding as fast as our horses and the rough road would allow, alternating between galloping and walking—it was that, or risk the beasts dropping dead of exhaustion.

Dariana and Kest took turns leading, constantly checking for any signs of the Knights deviating from their northern route. That first day Brasti didn't say a word, and he refused to look any of us in the eye. It was Valiana who broke through to him in the end. She'd ignored his silence and ridden alongside him, not saying anything, just being there. The next day she did the same, and after a few hours I thought I heard him mumble something—I couldn't hear what, but she didn't react, whatever it was. I kept my distance, but after a while I could hear Brasti talking, then railing, then sobbing, and through it all Valiana said nothing. She just listened. And when at last he fell to silence, she didn't try to solve his problems or correct his thinking or tell him he was being a fool.

"Go on," she said.

I wanted to join them—to say something clever or funny that would, if only out of reflex, force *our* Brasti to return, to bring back the laughing, arrogant bastard who usually kept the rest of us sane. But I was pretty sure any words that came out of my mouth would just make things worse, so I kept my eyes on the road ahead and my mind on the problem at hand.

Someone was murdering my country.

This can't just be about keeping order, I thought. *The assassinations of Duke Isault and Duke Roset and their families must be connected to the uprisings in the villages.*

It would have been easy to pin this all on Trin: we all knew she was depraved enough to command such a thing, and she'd certainly revel in the results—but if she had that kind of power and influence in the region, why hadn't she taken control of the country already? And if she did drive Tristia into the chaos of a civil war, what would be left for her to rule?

I cursed every single Saint in turn.

I needed more information. I needed to talk this out, to get the jumble of images and words out of my head and see how they sounded to someone else. Valiana had spent her whole life next to

Trin and knew more about her and her ways than anyone else, but her attention was firmly fixed on Brasti. I knew I would need him in the battle ahead so I left them alone.

"I wanted to hate her, you know."

I turned to see Dariana riding next to me.

"I'd heard of her, of course," she said. "Word was that she was quite the stuck-up bitch: the high and mighty daughter of The Damned Duchess, the girl who all her life believed that Patriana was going to make her Queen. And when Trin was revealed, I waited to see this Valiana make herself the wounded Saint. But she didn't."

"No," I said, "she didn't."

"She gets handed a sword and a coat and she just . . . You know, she isn't even angry? I mean, she wants Trin dead, of course, but mostly because Trin's trying to kill Aline." She looked back at Valiana. "How do you figure that? All the trappings of nobility, all that power gets taken away from her and she becomes . . ."

"Noble?"

Dariana snorted. "I suppose." For a few seconds she said nothing, then, "She should be out of her mind with anger! She should be trying to kill everyone who ever . . ."

Her voice faded away and we rode in silence for a few minutes before I said, "It's true, isn't it? What Nile said? You're the daughter of Shanilla, the King's Compass."

Dariana's eyes narrowed. "Would it matter if I was?"

"I only met her a few times," I said, picturing the small, red-haired woman with the deep green eyes. "The King named her to the Greatcoats while I was judging a case in Domaris, so we weren't all that close, but I knew her well enough to respect her."

"And do you see much of her in me?" Dariana asked.

"I . . ."

Shanilla had been one of our best Magistrates. Her mastery of the vagaries of the King's Law was second to none—not even Kest could match her. She'd been a competent swordswoman too, though it wasn't her greatest strength. "You have a little of her look around the eyes. But no, I can hardly imagine two more different people."

Dariana smiled. It wasn't a happy smile. "Good."

There was a fragility in the hard set of her jaw, and it made me feel like I had to try to connect with her somehow. Shanilla had never set out to make an enemy of anyone; she usually tried her best to avoid conflict. And yet some Duke or Margrave or Lord, angered over how she had judged a case or outfought his champion to enforce a verdict, had resented Shanilla enough to send a pair of Dashini assassins to kill her one night, barely a mile away from the safety of Castle Aramor. "You were young when she died, weren't you?"

Dariana nodded.

"What, fourteen or fifteen?"

Again she nodded, declining to be more specific.

I thought about Valiana and how she'd managed to reach through to Brasti. Maybe I could do the same for Dari. "It's all right to talk about it," I said, as gently as I knew how.

"Could I ask you a question, Falcio?"

"Of course."

"Your wife died about fifteen years ago, didn't she?"

"Yes."

"Would you mind describing every detail of the day she died? And perhaps some of the days afterward? Did she scream your name when she was being killed?"

My hands tensed around the reins. "Why would you—?"

Dariana leaned closer. "She was raped, too, right? Have you played out in your mind what they did to her? Every indignity and violation they performed on her body? Do you imagine the faces of each man as he—"

"Stop!" I shouted. "What in all the hells is wrong with you?"

"I'm sorry," she said. "I suppose the memories would only bring you pain."

"They bring me pain every day, damn you."

Dariana leaned in until her face was near mine. "Good. Think on your wife if you want to reopen old wounds so badly. Leave mine the fuck alone."

She gave her horse a nudge and trotted away.

A few minutes later Kest pulled his horse up beside mine. "I don't think she likes you."

"We were just talking," I said.

"No, you don't understand: when she looks at you, there's a fierce anger in her stare—it's maybe even hatred. This isn't the first time I've seen it."

"You think she means me harm?" I asked.

"I don't know, but I'd keep an eye on her."

I thought back to all the fights we'd been in together, from the attack by Trin's scouts in Pulnam to the mêlée with the Luthan Knights in the Inn of the Red Hammer just a few days ago. "She's had plenty of chances to kill me if she wanted to," I pointed out. I hadn't forgotten the morning I'd awakened from my paralysis to find her knife at my throat. "She could've done it when we were alone, too."

"True," Kest said, "and yet . . ."

"I know. She hates me. There's a lot of that going around these days. I'm sure everyone will think better of me when I'm dead."

A normal person might have let that hang in the air a while before speaking but Kest never likes to waste time. "How are you feeling?" he asked, his eyes boring into my face as if he could see through my skin.

"Fine, I guess. I'm a little slower than usual, I think. My mind drifts off more. Mostly, I just wake up so terrified I would piss myself, except even that's paralyzed."

Kest nodded. "So . . . not all bad, then."

A chuckle escaped my lips. "Oh, everything has a bright side, even death by paralysis. For example, I won't have to worry about getting old and wrinkled."

He looked me up and down with a perfect semblance of serious examination. "I do believe you'll make a fine-looking corpse, Falcio."

"Well, see, that's the paralysis: I'm getting plenty of beauty sleep each day."

"I've heard that insomnia and sleepwalking are remarkably common ailments."

"Not for me, they're not." I raised an imaginary glass in the air. "To Duchess Patriana and the many unexpected splendors of neatha poisoning."

He raised his own phantom glass. "Not the least of which is that it killed her first."

Both of us laughed then, ignoring the strangeness of riding out of violence and into violence, moving seamlessly from a massacre to a battle with only the briefest moment of comfort—each other's company—to break the pattern. Still, when these little sparks of happiness break through the darkness, you try your best not to ruin them. That's why I waited a few minutes before I asked the question I'd been avoiding for days. "How long do you think I have?"

His eyes flickered to mine and then to the road ahead. "I'm not a healer, Falcio. I don't know—"

"Come on," I said, "you spend your time calculating the difference between how much longer it takes to draw a sword in the rain than when it's dry. You work out the odds every time a man so much as looks at us the wrong way. Are you telling me you haven't figured out when the neatha is going to kill me?"

"It's . . . I don't know all the factors. Certainly you're longer in the paralysis each time, and the longer you're in, the shallower your breathing gets, and sometimes your throat goes into spasm, as if it can't quite open enough to—"

"How long?"

Kest looked at me and took in a deep, labored breath, almost as if thinking about my symptoms was affecting his own breathing. "Six days, I think. It could be seven." He turned his head away again. He always does that when he doesn't really believe what's about to come out of his mouth. "And there might be medicines which could make a difference. Or the poison could start leaving your system. It might get better if—"

"That's fine," I said. "Six days."

"Maybe seven."

"Maybe seven. So in that time I need to figure out who killed two Dukes and their families, and why two hundred villagers lie dead in Carefal."

"They might not be related, you know," he pointed out. "Nile thought it was a Dashini who killed him—whoever these Knights are, I doubt they're Dashini."

"They could be working for the same people," I said, though the words rang false to my ears even as I said them. "No, somehow that doesn't make sense."

"Why not?"

"The Dashini are precise: they're quick and deadly, like a stiletto blade. They're a tool to be used when subtlety is required—like a whisper in the dark."

Kest gave a curious smile. "A whisper in the dark? Have you taken up poetry in your spare hours?"

"It's that damned Bardatti rubbing off on me!" I complained. "But think about it: Knights are all blunt force and fury: a mace hefted by a strong arm. Using them is a statement, something you shout from the rooftops."

"So the villagers are trapped between the sharp blade of the Dashini and the heavy hammer of the Knights."

"Now who's taking up poetry?" I teased him. "But it's more than that: someone's been arming the villagers—and not just once but *twice*. The first time was before we'd ever even heard of Carefal—and then blow me, they get armed all over again as soon as we confiscate all their steel weapons."

"Someone really wants to drive the country into civil war," Kest said.

"No," I said, "it's already headed that way—it's been going in that direction for years. Someone is trying to speed it up."

"Trin is still the obvious choice."

"But why? She wants to *rule* Tristia, not just sit on a pretty throne and watch the country tear itself apart."

"She *is* crazy," Kest said.

"She's crazy. She's not stupid." I looked down the road, focusing on the tracks of the men we were pursuing. "Kest, someone is deliberately leading this country into chaos. Someone wants to see it burn."

Every hour we rode became its own kind of poison over those next two days. It was making me tired and careless—I spent so much of my time trying not to fall asleep that I'd miss bumps and holes in the road, jerking from an uneasy doze and scrambling to grab the poor horse's neck to keep from falling off. Time was malleable, first shrinking, with half a day disappearing in a blink, then at other times stretching unforgivably as my mind conjured up images of the horrors the Knights who'd massacred Carefal might be planning for their next target.

"There's someone ahead," Brasti said, shaking me from my thoughts.

We reined in, and I lifted my hand to shade my eyes from the sun. "How many?" I asked.

"Just one. A woman," he answered.

"Is she carrying a weapon?" I drew one of my rapiers and squinted at where Brasti was pointing to. I'd always envied him his distance vision, though I supposed it was only fair; I couldn't see a near-sighted archer doing too well in a battle.

"How do you manage with such worthless eyesight?"

"By stabbing people who bring it up. Answer the question."

He leaned forward on his horse, peering out at the road ahead. "I don't see a weapon. She's just standing there. Her hair is blond, almost white. She's wearing a pale dress that . . . I don't know . . . it flows about her like sheer curtains billowing in the evening breeze."

"Saints, is everyone turning into a Bardatti—?" Then my thoughts were suddenly pulled back to that small church on the road from Pulnam, where Trin had used an innocent girl as an instrument of torture, just to torment us. "Brasti, is there anything—?"

But he was already there, shaking his head and saying, "No, there's nothing attached to her head."

I nudged my horse to a slow walk. No sense in creating trouble if none were needed. Within a few moments I could see the woman myself. From further away her white-blond hair made her seem old, but now I could see that she was younger than we were, perhaps twenty or twenty-five.

"Stop," Kest said.

Brasti and I pulled our horses to a stop.

"What is it? What do you see?" I asked.

Dariana made a protective sign in the air. "Is she a witch?"

"No," Kest said. He dismounted.

"What, then?" I asked.

"She's not here for you," Kest replied, and began walking toward her, very slowly, almost warily. "She's here for me."

When Kest was halfway between us and the woman, Valiana asked, "What does he mean, 'She's here for me'?"

"I don't know," I said. I turned to Brasti. "Ready your bow."

Brasti dismounted and pulled Intemperance, the tallest of his three bows, from the saddle and placed the quiver on the ground, leaning up against his leg. He pulled out a handful of arrows and handed some to each of us. "I'll call your name when I want the arrow. You place it in my open hand, with the fletching toward me, the black feather on the left."

"Anything else, *master* archer?" Dariana asked.

"Yes. Don't get in front of me."

Kest was standing with the woman now, and they were talking. I couldn't hear what they were saying, not from this distance, but the way they stood made them look . . . familiar, almost intimate. "Is it possible that Kest knows her?"

Brasti snorted. "A woman? How would that help his sword-fighting?"

The woman shook her head and Kest became more animated—I could see him moving his hands, the way he does when he's explaining a fight or planning an attack. The woman remained still, as calm as if she were just watching waves splash on to the shore.

After a few minutes, Kest stopped and the woman spoke. I couldn't hear a word, but she was going on at some length. After a bit, Kest began to look as if he were shivering.

"What's she doing?" I asked, and drew my second rapier. "Brasti, put an arrow in her leg, will you? Something's wrong with Kest."

I started toward them, but Brasti pulled me back. "Stop," he said. "I don't think she's hurting him."

"Then what's the matter with him?"

"He's crying."

"Kest? *Crying?*" I couldn't recall seeing Kest cry, not since we were ten-year-old boys and even then it was only from the things that make ten-year-old boys cry: falling into the river, being beaten by someone older and stronger—and none of those things had happened for many, many years.

"He's coming back," Brasti said.

Kest walked back to us, his movements slow, awkward, almost as if he weren't sure of the terrain.

"What's happened?" I asked, gripping his shoulder. "Did that woman do something to you?"

"No, nothing," he said. His eyes were red and unfocused but he didn't bother to wipe away the tears. "She wants to talk to you."

"Who?" Dariana asked.

"Falcio. She says she needs to talk to Falcio."

I was about to begin walking toward her—I really wanted to know what was going on here—but Kest put a hand on my wrist. "Leave your rapiers."

"Why?"

Kest held out his hands and waited, and for some reason I felt unable to refuse him. "Why?" I asked again as I placed them into his hands.

"Because you get angry sometimes, Falcio. I don't want you to do anything stupid."

"All right," I said, absurdly hurt by his words.

The woman wasn't looking at me; instead she was gazing past me. Perhaps she was still watching Kest.

"Hello," I said as I approached her.

She turned to me and smiled. I very nearly dropped down to my knees at her beauty.

Greatcoats don't kneel for anyone, I reminded myself.

"Hello, Falcio," the woman said, holding out her hand, palm down. I took it in mine and leaned down to kiss it.

"Thank you for leaving your rapiers behind," she said. "I know you are loath to be without them."

I let go of her hand. "A man in my line of work tends to find too many occasions to regret their absence."

"Perhaps," she said, "but a man who carries weapons everywhere is wont to make such occasions inevitable."

Great, I thought, *as if I didn't have enough problems with poets, now I have to deal with a philosopher.* "I did not come to dance with you, my Lady. Is that why you asked for me?"

She looked at me with a great softness in her eyes. "They would not have helped that day, you know. Even if you had them there, when those men came to call. Even had you all the weapons and skills you have now, Aline would still have died, and you would have too."

"Speak—"

"You needn't threaten me, Falcio val Mond."

"I wasn't going to—"

She put a hand up. "'Speak her name again', you were going to say. 'Say it twice more and see what becomes of you'. You threaten people too much, Falcio, and almost always over the wrong things."

"You appear to know me too well, my Lady."

This time her voice had a tinge of steel in it when she said, "And you know me too little."

I stared once again at the features of her face, looking past the beauty that threatened to overwhelm me, noting the line of her nose and the shape of her lips. A woman might dress or color her hair, but she could not change her face. Yet the more I examined the lady in the white dress, the more certain I was that I'd never seen her before. "We've never met," I said at last.

"You are correct," she said, "but I have called out to you many, many times."

"When? And if we haven't met, what answer could you have hoped for?"

She closed her eyes and brushed a fingertip against each one, and the woman and the road both instantly disappeared from my sight and instead I began to see battles, duels, desperate and angry fights. I recognized the opponents in all of them. They were men I'd killed.

"In the heat of the fight," she said, "I have called out to you, always when the victory was won but before the final blow was struck."

I felt the final push of my rapier's thrust into an enemy's belly, the slash of my blade across a neck. "Why do you show me these things?" I asked.

"You said you didn't know me," she said. "I wanted to show you why."

"Because I win my fights?" I was confused and more than a little irritated, but I knew this—whatever *this* might turn out to be—was important.

She opened her eyes again and there was anger in them. "Because you ignore me when I call to you."

"I'm—" I was going to say that I was tired of this game. I've seen magic before and I hate it. I knew she wanted me to ask her—to beg her to tell me who she was—and I dislike that even more than magic. "She's not here for you," Kest had said. "She's here for me." So who would be here for Kest but not me? That was the first clue. *I know what you are, Lady; now I need to know who.* "You want me to feel pity for men who've tried very hard to kill me?"

"Eventually we all find ourselves in need of a little pity."

"Or perhaps mercy?" I suggested.

She smiled. "I've often thought that mercy is more practical than pity."

"Then I know you, Lady," I said.

"Oh? What is my name?"

"Your name is Birgid."

She curtsied. "I am, indeed, Birgid. It is a common enough name, but still an impressive guess. Do you perform other tricks as well, Falcio?"

"The second part of your name is less common, Lady."

"Then say it, and show the world how wise you are."

"Saint Birgid-who-weeps-rivers: you are the Saint of Mercy, or so some say."

She gave a laugh. "Ah, so it's true what I've heard. You are indeed a clever man, Falcio, First Cantor of the Greatcoats."

I felt something in my chest, as if my heart was suddenly full—of laughter, of sorrow, of anticipation, of regret. "Stop that," I said angrily.

"I cannot help but move you, Falcio. Valor is ever drawn to compassion; it comes with your recognition of me." She put a hand on my cheek. "I regret that I cannot sway you when I need to most."

"And why do you need to sway me?"

She ignored the question. "Do you know where we are?"

We stood at a crossroads: the main road went north, with a side road cutting east and west. "By now we're in the Duchy of Rijou."

"We are," she said. She pointed eastward. "Do you know what lies down that road? Perhaps sixty miles away?"

"Nothing that matters," I said, "given that the tracks of the men we're pursuing continue north."

"There's a town—it's small, but pretty. I believe it began as an encampment for merchants awaiting permits to enter the city of Rijou." She looked at me with those eyes that looked so young and yet felt ancient. "It's said to be a lovely place to visit."

A face suddenly filled my mind: dark hair and red lips meant for smiling. *Ethalia.* "The town is Merisaw," I said. "You're talking about Merisaw."

She nodded.

"Is that why you're here?"

"I'm here for Kest, not you. And yet isn't it odd that your hunt should bring you here, to this crossroads? Do you suppose the Gods themselves are speaking to you?"

"No," I said, "the Gods speak only to the very holy or the very rich."

A small smiled pulled at the corners of her mouth. "And Saints?"

"I have only a little experience with Saints, Lady, but my instincts tell me they function much the same way as the Gods, though perhaps for a lesser price."

"You think I'm trying to push you toward Ethalia? Have no fear on that score, Falcio. I would rather you stay far away from Ethalia."

"You know her?" I asked.

"She is a child of compassion," Birgid replied, "and she loves you. But compassion is ever overmatched by violence."

"That's a rather cynical view, coming from the Saint of Mercy," I pointed out.

"It comes from a woman who has tried and failed to marry mercy to violence. The child of that union is only more violence."

I couldn't help but feel swayed by her: she was as beautiful as the memory of a perfect kiss. When she spoke, it was as if all the best instincts inside me were calling out. But I've learned from experience not always to trust my instincts. "I appreciate you taking the time to tell me what a shit I am, Saint Birgid, but I'm trying to stop a war. So if you don't mind, perhaps you could tell me what you want to say and then get the hells out of my way."

"I already told you, I didn't come here for you." She placed a hand on my cheek. "But even I am drawn to valor. I wanted to meet you in person."

"You're here for Kest," I said, changing the subject to one that made me only slightly less uncomfortable. "Why?"

She removed her hand. "You needn't fear me, Falcio."

"I've rarely found that statement reassuring. Answer the question, if you would."

There was a flicker of annoyance in her expression—not, I suspected, because I was being rude, but because she knew I was being rude in order to break through her saintly demeanor. "I came for Kest because he is new to his Sainthood and there are things he needs to know, things a Saint must learn. Caveil should have told him but their relationship was—by necessity—less than cordial. There is a place—a retreat near Aramor. The cleric there can be trusted. Kest may find respite from his desires there."

"His 'desires'? You mean this 'Saint's Fever', whatever it is, don't you? He doesn't need any sanctuary. He's got the fever under control."

"He does not. When he holds it in, the red fever burns him up inside. When he lets it out, it grows in strength. The red will eat Kest alive." She began to walk along the narrow side-road, but toward the west, not the east. "Come. What I need to tell you now will take only a moment as we walk."

I joined her but remained silent, still determined I would not be forced to beg for answers. I was done begging people for answers.

She obviously sensed my reticence. "Very well, Falcio. If anyone ever asks, I will be sure to say you were stoic during our entire conversation. This is what you need to know: it was for you that Kest took up the sword."

"Me?" I stopped walking. "Because we were friends?"

"Yes," she said, "but such a simple statement doesn't tell the tale."

"What, then?"

"When Kest was young, a woman came to him and she told him your future."

And yet again she was waiting for me to inquire further. This was getting boring. Yet again I refused to play her silly game.

"She told him that you would die at the hands of the Saint of Swords."

"What?"

I thought back to that day, more than twenty years ago, when Kest came to my door and told me he was going to take up the sword. He'd never said why, and I'd never asked; I think I'd known he wouldn't answer. "Then—?"

"She told him that the Saint of Swords must always duel an opponent who might beat him—that's our curse, you understand: we must forever be the truest embodiment of that which we represent. We can resist it; we can try to hold it at bay, but in the end the compulsion will overcome our will."

"So you must always be the most merciful person in the world?"

"Something like that."

"What happens if someone capable of greater mercy comes along?"

"On that day, Falcio, I will be very happy."

I looked over at Kest, who was standing with Brasti, looking away down the road. "So he made himself the greatest swordsman in the world just so that I wouldn't have to fight Caveil."

"Yes," she said. "He always made sure he was better than you." Her eyes were sorrowful.

"But . . . but it worked, didn't it? He defeated Caveil."

"He did. And now he is the Saint of Swords."

"So then—"

She stretched out her hand to place it on my cheek again. "And right now, you, Falcio val Mond, are the second-best swordsman in the world."

"I . . ." I pulled away. "You're playing with me, my Lady. There are many men much faster than I am, far stronger than I am, and most certainly more skilled than I am."

"I didn't say the fastest nor the strongest nor even the most skilled. I said 'the best'. You were the only person who ever beat him in a fight, were you not?"

"It was a tournament," I said, "and I cheated."

"Isn't there an old saying among fencers? The fights that matter most—"

"—are never won on skill," I said, a little annoyed that I couldn't stop myself from finishing the sentence.

"Look at him," Birgid said. "A war wages inside him every second he's with you. How long do you think he can hold on?"

I looked back at Kest, who was standing twenty feet away from us, his head bowed, and now that I focused on him I could almost feel the red heat radiating from him. Was I really putting him through some kind of private hell reserved for Saints who don't want to butcher their best friends? I wanted to run to him and tell him to get out of here, to ride back to Aramor and find himself a nice little church to barricade himself inside—but then my thoughts turned to Aline, with her limp hair and face gaunt from weeks of terror and exhaustion, and I thought about the bodies piled up in Carefal.

"He can hold on a while longer," I said. "I need him. The country needs him."

A look of frustration—no, something deeper than frustration—showed on Birgid's unnaturally young features. "And who do you think you are to speak for an entire country?" she asked a little waspishly.

Something in her tone pushed me too far and a reckless anger filled me inside. "Me? I'm no one," I said. "I'm nothing but a man with a sword in his hand and poison in his veins and far too many enemies out for my head. But I'm *trying*, Saint Birgid. While you stand there and shower your useless radiance on the world I'm giving my life to save it. Who am I? Lady, I'm a *Greatcoat*. Who the hells are you?"

I've stared down Dukes and Knights and every kind of thug, but the look in Saint Birgid's eyes was like staring into an infinite expanse of solitude, and I found myself overcome by a sense of loneliness so powerful my legs began to buckle.

"On your knees, man of violence," Saint Birgid said, her voice still calm, and yet it felt like a wave crashing down on me. "Look not at me with your blind eyes. Look instead upon the ground where you will meet your end if you stay on this course."

No, I thought, *I won't kneel, not before one of you*. When had the Gods or the Saints ever helped anyone but the rich and powerful of this country? I kept my eyes focused on the ground and willed myself to stay standing. *You can kill me if you want, Lady, but I'm not bowing down to you*.

The profound sense of emptiness kept building inside of me, leaving me feeling so insubstantial that I had to stare at the individual stones on the ground just to remind myself I existed at all. I studied the tracks in the dirt, the bits of broken twig, the patterns of dust, the fallen leaves swept across the road . . .

The patterns were *wrong*.

The tracks looked as if they kept going north, but someone had swept leaves onto the road. I turned my head to the left and only then saw the covered tracks heading westward. *The Knights had tricked us after all.* They'd made it so easy to follow them that I'd missed it when they'd laid false tracks going through the crossroads. I would have kept us going northward, oblivious to the fact that the damned Knights had changed course. What was west of here . . . ? Garniol—that would be some ten miles west of here, a village a bit bigger than Carefal but still no more than a few hundred people. The Knights had succeeded in destroying Carefal. Now they were ready to try their tactics on a larger target.

The pressure and the emptiness inside me suddenly faded away and I lifted my head and looked again at Saint Birgid-who-weeps-rivers. There was a deep sadness in her eyes, and I realized what had just happened. She wasn't allowed to help us directly and so she'd goaded me into anger so she could attack me—apparently the Gods don't mind if Saints kill people; they just don't want them *helping* us.

"It is not our place to interfere," she said, and suddenly she looked much younger to me, like a child whispering as if an angry parent was watching over them.

"If it makes the Gods feel any better, I have it on good authority that I'm going to be dead in a week or two anyway."

Saint Birgid turned and walked away from me. "You speak too glibly, Falcio val Mond. Some deaths are worse than others. The one you go to is the worst of all."

25

GARNIOL

My horse was showing signs of exhaustion when the winding road finally reached the hilltop overlooking the village of Garniol. "We can't all be fey horses," I told him, sympathizing with the beast's plight. He'd served me well these past weeks but I wished it was Monster with me. She never tired, especially when in pursuit, and I couldn't deny that Aline sending her away had been nagging at me. There had been a strange sort of sympathy between the two broken creatures and I suppose I'd hoped the one might help cure the other.

"Come on, old man," Dariana said, and I realized that no matter how hard I tried to hide my symptoms from the others, Dariana always took note—and she invariably commented on it.

"Don't tease him," Valiana said. "Falcio's not old. He's battling a poison that would have killed anyone else long before now."

"It's fine," I said, a little annoyed that an eighteen-year-old girl felt the need to come to my defense, and also because "battling" suggested there was a fight that might be won—as if I just needed to try harder to stave off my otherwise inevitable death.

Saint Birgid, If I have to die, please don't let it be in shitty little Garniol. I had been here before, twice, and I remembered it as being a simple place, bigger than most of the villages around and yet still smaller than a proper town, which served only to ensure its residents were poor, insular, and self-righteous. It wasn't just that they didn't take kindly to Greatcoats; they'd never seen fit to forge bonds with the neighboring towns either. Maybe that's why the Knights we were pursuing had chosen to attack it.

"I don't see any fires," Kest said. "It looks quiet."

"That's because you're blind," Brasti said, standing in his stirrups and shielding his eyes with one hand as he peered down at Garniol.

From this distance, I could just make out groups of houses, and little streets that all led into a large central square. The people looked like blurry ants to me, but something was glinting in the light of the sun.

"What do you see?" I asked Brasti.

"I see twenty-five—no, thirty Knights in armor. There are scattered mobs of villagers. The Knights are moving together, in formation. They've got kite-shields." He leaned so far forward on his horse I thought he might tip over. "*Damn*. The damned villagers don't know how to fight. The Knights haven't attacked yet; they're just driving the villagers over to one side of the square."

"How long before they start to clash?" I asked.

"The way they're moving? I'd say we've got maybe ten minutes before the blood starts flowing."

"What are the villagers fighting with?"

"Farming implements, mostly, from what I can tell—no, hold on . . . there's a fair number of proper swords too there. Some spears, and a few people have got hunting bows. Hells—why aren't they fighting together? The archers are firing straight into the Knights' damned shields—"

"They're fools," Dari said, her voice almost mocking. "Never pull a sword if you don't know how to use it."

I restrained a powerful urge to knock her from her horse. "I doubt that the men and women down there would find that to be useful advice right about now."

"They're farmers and plowmen," Valiana said. "Most of them have probably never even held a sword before today."

Where in all the hells were these people getting steel swords? I doubted any of them could afford forged weapons by themselves.

"Sympathize with them all you want, pretty bird," Dari said, putting a hand on Valiana's arm, "but if we run down there into those Knights, they'll kill the five of us in no time and the villagers will still be dead."

"But we beat those soldiers at the inn!"

"That was half as many men, fighting around a room full of tables and chairs. This is a battle formation of Knights in full armor with kite-shields. Five of us won't break their line."

There was a merciless truth in what she was saying, but Valiana was right too: we had to do *something*.

Brasti turned to me, his eyes dark and his voice as hard as I'd ever heard it. "Tell us what to do," he said.

"What—?"

He pointed a finger at me accusingly. "This is what you're supposed to be good for, Falcio. This is why we follow you. Those people are going to be killed, every single one of them. I can see children down there, Falcio, and I . . . I don't know how to do this." His voice cracked. "You've got to tell me what to do."

I looked over at Kest, who shook his head. "We have to break their line, but five is too few, and even Brasti's arrows won't get through their shields. We need to pull that formation apart, and even if there were ten of us, I doubt we'd be able to do it with untrained villagers underfoot."

I shared Brasti's hatred for the Knights. *You're loving this, aren't you, you cowards, so secure in your metal hides.*

There were five times as many villagers as invaders, so the Knights would see this as an honorable victory, even though the villagers didn't stand a chance. They could stand there outnumbered, knowing that the villagers didn't have even the simplest training needed to break their Gods-damned line—and it is simple enough to break such a line with a larger force if you just know the basic principles . . .

I turned to the others. "Listen now. We're going to go down there, and the first temptation is going to be to try to pick off some of the Knights. Don't do it. We won't get anywhere that way."

"What are we supposed to do then?" Dariana asked.

"We're going to start on the outside perimeter, near the crowds of villagers. I want you to shout for those with the longer weapons—spears, old halberds, pitchforks, whatever they have."

Her expression was incredulous. "You want me to get them to form their own line?"

"Exactly. Get those with swords to stand behind them. When the Knights push forward against the spears, have the swordsmen run forward to strike in the gaps between them."

"Half of them will be killed!" Valiana said.

"Half is better than all," I said, my voice sounding horribly grim and cold, even to my own ears. Dariana looked as if she might launch into some sort of diatribe, but I stopped her dead and growled, "Just shut up and do as I say or every extra life lost is on your soul."

"Fine," she said. "Get them into a line, put the ones with long pointy things in front and send the ones with swords to strike in the openings. Anything else, Commander val Mond?"

I ignored the sarcasm. "Tell the bowmen to get to the south side of the village. They can use the paths and alleys, just keep out of the main square." I turned to Brasti. "You get to the southern end and tell those twice-damned archers to hold their fire until we've created an opening."

"What about me?" Valiana asked.

"The children," I said, "you need to get them as far to the west of the village as you can." When I saw her expression I put up a hand. "I know you can fight, Valiana, but the children will be terrified and they're more likely to trust your face than mine."

She nodded and I heaved an inward sigh of relief. *At least she can follow logic even if she's not great on following orders.*

"Do you want me to round up the other swordsmen?" Kest asked.

"No, I'm going to do that. If those Knights are smart, when we charge the line a smaller group will break off to outflank the villagers.

They'll try to create as much fear and panic as they can—I need you to keep them occupied. Kest, when you fight them . . ."

I hated myself for what I was about to say.

"What is it?" he asked.

For a brief instant I thought about Ethalia and how, just an hour before and a few miles back, I had been standing at a crossroads where I could have chosen another road. A different Falcio val Mond might have found rest and comfort, and a few final days of love. Instead, I'd chosen bloodshed once again. I had turned away from the road that led to joy and not violence, and peace for Kest, not fire. *The red will eat Kest alive*, Birgid had said.

And now I hated myself even more as I said quietly, "Kest, when you fight them . . . let the red out."

His eyes widened for just an instant as he realized what I was asking of him, then he dipped his head in acquiescence and started checking the straps on his horse's saddle. But Kest wasn't the only one who felt a red fever burning inside him.

I turned and looked at the others. *No speeches. No promises.*

"For Carefal," I said, and spurred my horse straight down the steep dirt road toward the village.

The moment we hit the village the five of us split apart, each following our separate plans. Dariana went right so that she could sneak around the main body of Knights while Brasti went to rally the scattered archers. Most of the villagers were huddling together in small, incoherent clumps, weapons in shaking hands, no idea how to make any headway against the unstoppable machine of thirty Knights with shields and warswords pushing forward in military formation.

The Knights were wearing black tabards. *This is a war to them*, I thought. *They're here to wage war against their own people.*

I leapt off my horse. "Over here," I shouted to a group of three women and two men crouching nearby. One of the men held a long boar-spear. "You," I said, "get over to the other side and form up with the other spearmen." Two of the women held roughly made hunting bows—the string on one was too slack, but they were something to work with. I pointed to the narrow path between the rundown little houses on my left. "You two, go that way. You'll see a man with red hair and beard, dressed like me. He'll tell you what to do."

"And who are you that we should listen?" one of the archers said, turning and aiming the arrow toward my chest. She had long bright yellow hair and a wide face.

"You know how to use that thing?" I asked.

"What do you think?" She pulled back on the string and I brought up the arm of my coat to cover my face just as she turned and fired one of her arrows toward the Knights thirty yards away. It stuck in one of the shields. "I've used a bow since I was a girl. I just—"

I slid off my horse and grabbed the bow from her hand before she could nock another arrow. "If you know how to shoot so damned well, then why are you wasting your fucking arrows decorating those kite-shields?" I cried. "You asked who I am? I'm Falcio val Mond, First Cantor of the King's Greatcoats."

She spat on the ground. "Never heard of you. People here barely remember the Greatcoats, for all the good you've done us."

I smiled and tossed the bow back to her. "Well, I've never heard of you either, sister. So how about you stop showing off and do what I'm telling you and maybe one day people will remember both our names."

The other woman had hair just as blond, though the lines on her forehead marked her a few years older, said, "Come on, Pol, what we're doing isn't working. Might as well try—"

"Fine," she said.

The remaining man and woman were closer to sixty than anything that might be called fighting years, even in poor light. "What should we do?" the woman asked.

I looked at the weapons they were holding: kitchen knives good for nothing but peeling potatoes. "Go and tell everyone you see the same thing I told you: spears and pitchforks to the east side; archers to the south. If you see someone dressed like me, do what they tell you."

The man stepped forward. "My grandson, Erid, he's just twelve. Could you—?"

"No," I said. It was better they understood what war was, since it had come to their door. "You want the boy to live? Then let's take down those damned Knights." I turned and left them there and ran across the street toward the next group.

It took time, even in a small village, to round up the people. Half of those we managed to get into formation broke their own lines even before we engaged the Knights. Some ran, wild from fear, others out of incoherent rage as they faced the bodies of their friends and families, bleeding out all over the village streets.

"It's almost time," Kest said, coming up behind me. "The Knights have figured out what we're doing and they're going to charge."

"Hold the line, damn you!" I heard Dariana scream from across the square. "You think those Knights are scary? They're just *men*— and they'll just kill you. Me? I'll drag your fucking asses outside the village and feed you piece by piece to your own Saints-damned pigs!"

"She's got an unusual way of motivating her troops," Kest said.

"Just so long as she makes them hold."

"Falcio!" Valiana called out. It took me a moment to spot her, thirty feet away down one of the narrow streets. She was standing with a group of children.

I ran over to her. "Is this all of them?" I asked. Most looked like they were between ten and thirteen. "Where are the younger ones?"

One of the boys spoke up. "My ma teaches the littles on field days—they're in the classroom up there." He pointed to a two-story barn with a flat roof.

"Should I head over there?" Valiana asked.

"No, just get these out of the village. I'll deal with the others as soon as it's safe."

I looked around for another tall building I could climb and spotted a small water tower with a splintery wooden ladder running from the ground to its peak. I made a run for it, swearing as I skidded on the wet ground where a steady leak had created an unseen stream through the grass. I climbed about twenty-five feet up before I turned to look at the scene below me. On one side I saw Dariana, marshaling the men and women carrying the longer weapons and farming implements. Through her unique combination of motivation and terror I could see she'd managed to get them to hold their position. The Knights were waiting for their commander's signal to attack.

On the south side Brasti was shouting orders, clearly ignoring mine; instead of assembling all the archers together, he'd put them in pairs and lodged them between buildings. I had to admit that made more sense as a strategy, since it would be harder for the Knights to use their shields to protect one another. On the other hand, it would be impossible for Brasti to control his archers, so he'd have to hope they'd obey his instructions on when and how to fire.

On the east side of the village, Kest stood facing the Knights in formation. His warsword was drawn, the point resting on the ground as he gripped the pommel with both hands. He looked as if he were leaning against it for support.

For a moment I wondered what it must be like for Kest, to feel the red fire inside eating away at him, then I turned my attention back to the Knights. I had my own job to do.

"I call on the Knight-Captain," I shouted.

One of the Knights standing in the center of the formation lifted the visor of his helm and looked around until he spotted me. He peered up at me. "What is this I see? A strange little brown bird nesting up there on the water tower singing to me."

He spoke with the careful diction of a nobleman—likely he was the second son of a Lord or Margrave. It didn't do much to endear him to me. "And who answers me back but a black crow standing where I should see the bright yellow tabard of Luth—or should that be the green of Aramor? Or perhaps the scarlet of Rijou? I see Knights in black tabards without lawful orders making war on their own people. That's what I see, Knight-Captain."

"It matters not what a little brown bird spies," he replied, "if its wings are properly clipped before he can sing his song for anyone else. Is there a tune you would care to sing for me, perhaps?"

I took a breath and hoped that the others would be able to keep their people in line. "I would sing this, Knight-Captain. We surrender."

There was a brief silence as the Knights looked at their commander.
"You surrender?" the Knight-Captain asked.

"Absolutely and utterly. We ask only for mercy, simple mercy. These people request nothing more than that you spare their lives."

The Knight-Captain roared with laughter. "Simple mercy? For dogs who bite and snap at their masters' feet? The only mercy these brigands will receive will be the good God War's fist crashing down upon their little souls. They have steel weapons, these peasants, taken up against their betters in plain violation of the law."

"And for that, they will pay. But they haven't attacked you, and the penalty for possession of a steel weapon is only a fine or imprisonment, not death. I repeat, Knight-Captain, we surrender. These people are—"

"They are animals," the Knight-Captain said, "and every man, woman, and pig's child among them dies today."

"I repeat a third time, Sir Knight, we surrender and ask mercy." In all the old stories, these things had to be said three times. I thought it best to stick with tradition. A few of the Knights looked troubled, but most didn't. That was fine; I would settle for what I could get. If even a few of them were beginning to doubt their commander's honor then we could use their hesitation to our advantage.

"Surrender a thousand times if it pleases you," the Knight-Captain laughed. "It will make no difference. For a hundred years from today Garniol will be spoken of in terrified whispers by peasants wise enough to know who their betters are."

"Okay, fine," I said. "Just thought I'd ask."

If the Knight-Captain was surprised by my casual response, he didn't show it. Instead he turned to his men. "Will someone with a crossbow kill that brown bird for me?"

I saw two of them setting down their swords to unhitch the leather straps holding crossbows to their backs.

"Before you fire, there's something else you should know," I said.

"Oh? Do you have another song to sing for me?"

"I do," I replied, "and it's a song about Knights, in fact: about the code that the Knights of Tristia once followed. They lived and fought and died by rules that remained unbroken for a thousand years. How many of you, cowering beneath your kite-shields as you prepare to massacre those whom you should be defending, first took up armor and shield dreaming of those better men? Of that better code? How many of you swore you would die heroes one day?" I looked down on them, and though I could not see them clearly, I could imagine their faces. Were they earnest young men here for their first taste of battle, or gray-bearded veterans simply following orders?

"Well?" I shouted. "Tell me, do you feel like heroes today? Do you think those same Knights you heard about in the songs and read about in the stories would call you brother? Or would they instead strike you with their iron-braced gloves and command you to meet them on the dueling field? No, now that I think of it, I don't think they would agree to duel with you at all. I don't believe they would consider you worthy."

The Knights below, secure in their metal carapaces, bristled with rage. I could feel a flood of anger in them, mostly directed at me, of course, but I had to believe that some of them, deep down, had some inkling of how far they'd fallen. Frankly, I didn't care which it was; what mattered far more was that in a battle like this one, every ounce of distraction or confusion I could sow in the enemy would be worth its weight in gold. Now I just had to wait for a man to shoot me with a crossbow.

One of the Knights stood tall as he came out of the formation with a crossbow in hand. He removed his helmet, lifted the weapon and aimed it toward me. There always a decent chance he would miss, of course, or that the bone plates in my coat would keep the bolt from burying itself in my flesh, but I never did trust my luck at dice.

"Brasti!"

From one of the rooftops along the street outside the main square, I saw Brasti stand, aim, and release, and a moment later the Knight had an arrow sticking out of the back of his neck. He slowly toppled to the ground.

The rest of the Knights roared in anger, but so did the villagers in their lines.

"Dariana!" I shouted.

"Forward!" she screamed to her troops: her farmers and plowmen, her beardless boys and young girls in sundresses, holding weapons they'd never been taught to use. And at her command they started to advance, brandishing their spears and halberds and rusty rakes and broken old pitchforks, moving one step at a time toward the fate awaiting them at the practiced hands of hardened military men protected by shining plate-armor.

The Knights advanced too, keeping to their squared-off formation, using their kite-shields to drive the farmers back, until Dariana shouted again, and some of her people in the front line set the bottoms of their weapons and tools against the ground, making it harder for the Knights to press forward, and smaller men and women with swords and hoes and garden rakes ran forward and attacked the kite-shields. Several died, but not all, and some of them managed to pull away the Knights' protection.

"Archers!" Brasti shouted, and arrows flew from high and low, coming from alleys and rooftops around the square. Most hit only those damned shields, but when a few broke through I let out the breath I hadn't realized I'd been holding in. We didn't have to win every strike; we just had to kill a few of them.

As the Knights advanced, they now had to do so over some of their fallen comrades. The Knight-Captain, still barking his orders, nearly fell over, tripping on one of his own lying dead at his feet. He screamed in frustration. This was supposed to have been an easy fight for his soldiers—after all, they were facing farmers, peasants, fuzzy-bearded youths, and barely grown girls with their hair in braids. . . . Even a half-trained Knight should be able to wade through a dozen such pathetic opponents without breaking into a sweat. But there weren't a dozen of them; there were more than a hundred, and every time one of those little girls managed to get a hit, even if she died moments later, spitted on a broadsword or beheaded by a war-ax, the men in armor grew more angry and more anxious.

Saints, what was wrong with me? Was I growing so cold inside that I could so emotionlessly count the bodies of children on a tally?

I raced down the ladder and into the fray.

The Knight-Captain, finally realizing his men were now at serious risk of being overwhelmed, gave the order for five of his Knights to break away from the pack to outflank the villagers and go for Dariana.

That's it, go for the leader. You military men all think the same way, don't you?

Kest, who'd been standing as still as a statue so far, suddenly lifted his blade high in the air and rushed forward, sweeping it down in a great arc that brought the whole north wind with it. He crashed down against the top edge of one of the Knights' shields, very nearly cutting it in half, then without pausing for even an instant, turned his slash into a thrust, pushing straight up into the Knight's gorget. The strike didn't break through the metal plate but it bent it inwards, choking the man. He dropped his sword and with his hands grasping ineffectually at his neck, trying in vain to loosen the armor, he fell back into his comrades.

Two more Knights split off and tried to encircle Kest, but an arrow came down from the sky and landed in the back of one of them.

"No!" Kest screamed, his face red with rage and fever. "*NO!* The next man who takes one of mine meets me on the field when this is done!" He whirled, swinging his sword like a club, and drove it into his opponent even as he dropped down low to avoid attack.

"Falcio!" Dariana shouted, and when I turned I could see her line was breaking. It had held for nearly seven minutes, far longer than I had believed possible, leaving only twelve Knights remaining of the original enemy formation, but these dozen had gathered themselves and reformed and I could see the men and women of the village were fast losing their nerve.

"Disperse!" I yelled back to her, and the moment she gave the order the villagers turned and ran, many dropping their cumbersome weapons as they fled. A few seconds later, only Dariana was left. She put one hand on her hip, gave the Knights a wink, and then turned and ran into one of the side streets.

The attackers were left with no one to attack. They could either stand where they were, doing a great job of guarding each other with their shields but not doing much actual fighting, or they could break up their smart formation and find people to fight. They chose the latter.

Good. If everyone stays out of the square then our archers can attack at will.

Out of the shadows came two figures. *Great, yet again my orders have been ignored. Why do people keep demanding that I come up with brilliant plans if they have no fucking intention of following them?* Brasti, Intemperance in hand, walked toward the Knight with a young boy perhaps twelve years of age in tow. The boy held a quiver in one hand and an arrow in the other.

"Brasti, what are you doing?" I shouted.

If he heard me, he gave no sign. "No more armor," he said firmly, and fired an arrow straight into the chestplate of one of the Knights. The piercing of metal echoed in the large square. The boy had drawn another arrow from the quiver and handed it to Brasti before another Knight started charging them, but Brasti was faster; he nocked, pulled and fired in one smooth motion and the Knight fell to the ground.

"No more armor," he repeated.

The remaining Knights quickly regrouped, trying to get their shield wall up in time to stave off Brasti's attacks, but even as they did, Dariana raced out from the alley between the houses, hammered the point of her sword into the back of one man's knee and fled again before anyone had time to react. The injured Knight went down, screaming like a stuck pig, and crashed into one of his comrades, conveniently opening a gap between the shields.

"No more armor," Brasti said a third time, taking out one of the few Knights still alive.

The rest didn't hang around to be picked off by the madman with the huge bow; as they dispersed, glowering, I ran toward the main square. Sooner or later someone would figure out the ridiculously easy solution to the problem he presented, so I nominated myself to guard Brasti's flank. Sure enough, three Knights—one the Knight-Captain himself—were busy sneaking around to get behind Brasti and the boy holding his arrows. It looked like the Knight-Captain wasn't entirely stupid: his true target was the boy. Once they'd taken him out, Brasti's arrows would fall to the ground and the Knights could overwhelm him before he had time to pick one up.

That was their plan, anyway, and just as I reached them, I saw a warsword come up high and begin its inevitable downward arc toward the boy's head. I crossed my rapiers and jumped toward him, landing hard on my knees but holding my blades up, crossed, just in time to feel the full weight of the warsword crash down on them. The Knight's weapon stopped barely an inch from the boy's head—but neither the boy nor Brasti appeared to have noticed how close he'd come to being headless.

"No more armor," I heard Brasti say again as he nocked and let fly into the square.

"No more Knights," the boy said in answer, handing him another two-and-a-half-foot-long steel-tipped arrow.

The Knight-Captain gave a roar and came for me.

I was still on the ground, on my knees, as the Knight's sword lifted free of my blades. *Get on your feet, damn it,* I told myself sternly, but before I could follow my own orders a red haze appeared on the left-hand side of my peripheral vision, and Kest leapt in front of me, bashing one of my attackers' swords away and squaring off against the other.

For some reason the sight of the blood-red Saint of Swords made the Knight-Captain reconsider his position. *So much for honor,* I had time to think as he grabbed the shoulder of the Knight next to him and pushed him toward Kest before taking off at a run down the square. I rose to my feet to help fight off the two remaining Knights, but Kest swore, "Get the hells out of here and stay away from me, Falcio!"

I ran back into the center of the square. Thanks to Kest's maniacal swordwork, Brasti's single-minded shooting, and Dariana's firm handling of the villagers, the Knights were broken. In front of me a small mob of villagers was moving to overwhelm a single opponent, and to the right, I could see Dariana withdrawing her blade from an opponent's neck. Suddenly there were only two men in armor still standing.

"Surrender!" one of them shouted, and both men dropped their weapons and fell to their knees. "We surrender!"

Brasti walked up to the two men. As if the Gods themselves willed it, he had just two arrows left: one nocked and ready and one left in the hand of the boy. "No more armor," Brasti said. "No more Knights."

"We surrender!" the men repeated, their voices sounding increasingly desperate.

I felt a terrible urge to stand there and watch as Brasti pulled back his arm, sighted and sent his long arrow driving with the force of a gale through the chest of the Knight standing just a few feet away. I wanted to *remember* this. I wanted to be able to play this moment out over and over as these men died for what they'd done.

"Did you say 'we surrender'?" Brasti asked. "Is that what you said?"

"Please!" one of the Knights begged. He was a younger man; I didn't think he was much over twenty years old. He wasn't crying. I wanted him to cry.

"Your armor," Brasti said.

"Please!"

"Take off your armor."

Both Knights frantically began removing their armor, trying clumsily to unfasten the clasps at the shoulder, the buckles at the sides of their chest-plates. It's no simple matter to take off a suit of armor when you're sitting at home after a hard day's fighting. When you're staring at death in the form of a thirty-inch-long fletched shaft tipped with sharp steel, it was even harder.

After a few seconds the two Knights started to help each other.

Too slow, I thought, and suddenly I felt as if I finally understood the Saint's Fever that filled Kest. *Come on*, I silently urged Brasti, *shoot them!*

But there was another voice inside me, a quieter voice, barely a whisper: *I've called out to you*, she said, *always when the victory was won but before the final blow was struck.*

No, I thought, *no. This is right. This is justice.*

But it wasn't. This was vengeance, pure and simple.

It was a sublime, righteous vengeance, admittedly, but still vengeance and not justice.

Why does a trial matter when there are no questions of fact to be determined and no mitigating factors to be considered? What does it matter whether the blade falls now or after a verdict?

Because the law only matters if we hold it higher than ourselves, I thought. My coat suddenly felt very heavy on my shoulders.

The Knights weren't even halfway to removing all their plate when Brasti pulled back on his bowstring.

"Brasti," I said. My voice was quiet. I didn't need to shout because somewhere deep inside himself, he was waiting for me to put a stop to this. "Enough."

At first I wasn't sure what he would do. Had he wanted me to tell him to withdraw just so he could fire the arrow anyway and show me that he no longer followed my orders? The two Knights were still furiously unbuckling and unclasping and prying pieces of their armor from their bodies. The people of the village had begun to assemble around us, more than a hundred of them, packing in closer and closer, waiting to see the arrows fly.

"Brasti," I said. "Stop."

With a slow, almost imperceptible motion, Brasti's bow moved down to his side and the tension of the string eased until the arrow was loose in his hand.

One of the villagers shouted, "Kill them!" at us.

"They get a trial," Brasti said.

A man stepped forward. His bloodied right arm hung by his side, but he was still gripping a small hatchet. "Why? Why should they get a trial after what they've done?"

"I don't know," Brasti said, his eyes on me. "They just do."

There were rumblings within the crowd, bitter growls of out-rage clashing with the moans and weeping of the injured, but I ignored them all. Instead, I looked around for Dariana. "Where's Kest?"

"He took off after the battle ended," she said, pointing to the hill-top behind us.

Someone was missing. I looked around, past the mob gathered at the village square. Bodies littered the ground, Knights and villagers. Thirty Knights had come to Garniol to destroy it; only these two were left. "Valiana?"

"She's with the older children on the other side, near the entrance to the village."

Again I looked at the bodies of the dead Knights, lying there in their black tabards, trying to work out what I was missing—and only then did I realize what it was—or rather, whom. "The Knight-Captain!" I said. "I saw him flee—did you kill him?"

As Dariana shook her head I swore and started, "Go and find Kest. Tell him to look for—"

"Cowards!" a voice bellowed.

At first I thought the shout had come from the crowd, then I heard a woman scream and as I turned to trace the sound some-thing fell from the top of the two-story barn at the far end of the square. Only when it hit the hard ground below did I see it was a young woman. The sound of her neck snapping reverberated through the square.

Oh Gods, let it not be her—I told her not to go there . . . But as I ran toward the woman I saw with a relief that made me ashamed that it wasn't Valiana. The Knight-Captain stood on the roof of the two-story building. He had hastily tied ropes around his arms, his torso, and even legs, and the other end of each rope was attached to a child. Young boys and girls—*the littles*, I realized—sobbed as they tried to pull away, but the Knight-Captain yanked their ropes and drew them back to him. *He's turned the children into a shield—no*, I thought, *into* armor. *He's using them as armor.*

"Cowards!" the Knight-Captain yelled and now it was clear he was screaming at his two men. "Put your armor back on and fight! Knights do not retreat!"

The younger of the two Knights called out, "Sir Learis, stop! This isn't—"

"Silence! We came to pacify this village, and pacify it we will. We must show them our resolve, Sir Vezier." His voice rose as if he were giving a lesson to a group of wayward students. "The peasants need to see this doesn't end until they kneel before us."

Brasti aimed an arrow. "You're a dead man."

"Am I?" The Knight-Captain stepped forward, the children pulled close to him. "Which of these will feel the bite of your arrow as you try to reach me?" He yanked hard on one of the ropes and a small girl slipped and started swinging over the corner edge of the building.

"Eila!" a man yelled. "Please! No!"

"Come on, then!" the Knight-Captain shouted. He hauled the girl back onto the roof next to him. "Fire, archer: maybe you can hit me without hitting the children. Come on. Show your skill."

Brasti's arm pulled back, but I stopped him. "Don't. He's got the children tied to him and he's standing on the corner of the roof on purpose. If you shoot, even if he falls backward, there's a good chance he'll go over the edge and drag the children with him to their deaths."

"Clever little brown bird—smart enough to know these little ducklings won't fly." The Knight-Captain's gaze went across the crowd. "Now," he said, "kneel."

"Do it," I said.

The men and women of Garniol dropped to their knees, and those few who tried to remain defiant, mostly young men, were pulled down. Brasti and I knelt as well, and Dariana hesitated but finally joined us.

"Good," the Knight-Captain said, "very good. Obedient hounds. You see that, Sir Vezier? Sir Orn? This is the power of true command. More than a hundred of them and they bow before one righteous Knight."

"What do you want?" I asked.

The Knight-Captain ignored me. Instead, he spoke once again to his men. "Sir Vezier. Sir Orn. You will take up your swords. You will go from dog to dog in this whining pack of mongrels, and you will strike their heads from their bodies."

The man was grinning from ear to ear as if he truly believed these people would simply kneel and give up their lives, even knowing that those of their children would surely follow.

The older of the two Knights looked around uncertainly but began to rise. The younger—Sir Vezier—grabbed him by the shoulder and held him down. "No, Knight-Captain," he said. "This isn't what we . . . This isn't worthy of a Knight."

"No? Feckless boy. Are you afraid they'll rise up against you? A Knight? Then you don't deserve the title. Sir Orn, you will take up your sword and do as I've commanded. You will begin with Sir Vezier."

This time the older man stayed where he was, his eyes fixed firmly on the ground in front of him.

"We seem to be at an impasse, Knight-Captain," I called out.

"Are we? Very well then, let us see how long this impasse holds. Watch and wait and you will see what true courage looks like: you will see that a true son of War does not flinch when the fire comes."

"What's his game?" Brasti asked.

"I don't know."

Knights don't do well with losing a battle at the best of times, but this man was clearly out of his mind with rage. If he'd planned to throw the children off the roof, he could have done it by now, but that didn't feel like it would be enough for him. He was going to make a point, and he wanted us to watch—

Damn all the Gods, I thought, and I looked at the barn beneath his feet. Sure enough, smoke was beginning to emerge from the wood-slat windows. "He's lit a fire in the barn," I said. "He's going to immolate himself with the children."

A woman rose from her knees and tried to run through the crowd, but a man cried out, "No!" and others grabbed her before she could run into the burning building.

"Come," the Knight-Captain shouted, roaring with laughter, "who will join me?"

Shit. We couldn't kill him and we couldn't wait for the fire to reach them. "Me," I said softly.

"Are you mad?" Dariana asked. "You can't run in there. You'll burn alive."

I flipped up the collar of my coat and tied the straps tight, imagining I looked like a highwayman coming to rob a carriage. "The leather and bone of the coat will protect me from the heat and the silk in the collar will block out some of the smoke," I muttered hopefully.

"And what the hells do you do when you get to the top?" Brasti asked. "If you try to rush him he'll just jump—and besides, even if you do make it to the roof, there's no way you'll get back down through the fire."

"There's a ladder attached to the water tower," I said. "You and Dariana, go and get it."

"Falcio, you don't have a plan! You're going to die for nothing!"

I smiled. Always smile when you're terrified. "I *always* have a plan, Brasti. It's just that sometimes it's not a very good one." I rose to my feet. "On the other hand, I wouldn't be averse to a miracle, so you'd better have that ladder ready just in case."

The first floor of the barn felt oddly peaceful. The flames were still small enough that it looked as if someone had lit braziers to set the scene for a romantic dinner. But I could see the smoldering bales of hay were beginning to catch alight, and the smoke was starting to hang heavy in the air.

I ran up the stairs to the second floor, but the smoke was rising and now it was almost impossible to see more than two feet in front of me. If it hadn't been for the sound of her crying, I never would have known the girl was there.

All I could really see of her as she sat huddled in a corner was her dark brown hair for her head was buried in her knees.

"Run downstairs and out of the barn," I said, my voice low. "Go on!"

The girl sobbed and held her arms out to me.

"I can't go with you—I've got to go up. Please, just run down the stairs and get out now!"

She shook her head and her crying grew louder as her arms kept reaching for me. I started coughing uncontrollably. *Damn it all . . . as if this wasn't difficult enough already.* I put one arm around the child and lifted her to me. "It's time to be very brave," I said to her. "You can stay with me, but you're not going to cry, all right?"

I started up the second set of stairs that led to the roof.

I felt the girl's face nuzzle into my hair. "'m scared," she said.

"I know that, sweetheart, but it's not the time to be scared right now."

"What's your name?" I asked as we were halfway up the stairs.

The girl hesitated, then said, "'m not telling. Da says don't trust no strangers."

"Good plan," I said.

We reached the top and I stepped quietly onto the wooden rooftop. I didn't want to risk startling the madman so I said, "I'm here."

He turned, pulling the children with him. "Ah, my little brown bird—and I see you've brought my wayward duckling. How gracious of you."

I set the girl down and she grabbed at my leg. I gently pried her fingers apart and moved away. "Time to be brave now," I reminded her.

The Knight-Captain scoffed. "Bravery? Without honor what is bravery but the impulses of a dog? The animal has no honor. Whether scared or angry, it simply does as its base instincts command."

"I am getting seriously tired of men who murder children preaching to me about honor," I said.

The Knight-Captain's face grew grim. "And I am weary of watching this country fall to the lesser nature of those who lack honor. The King was a tyrant, the Dukes have failed in their commitment to their own Knights, and the peasants and townsfolk fail to obey us as is our Gods-given right. Only we precious few remain to maintain the strength of this country."

"So you act in defiance of the law, in defiance even of your own Dukes?"

"Some of us have come to the conclusion that the Dukes are false rulers," he said. "It is time for a change."

Well, at least there was one thing we agreed on. The Knight-Captain was looking at me as if he was daring me to debate him. *Saints, he thinks I will! He actually believes we're going to stand here and talk about the will of the Gods and Saints and the nature of honor. Well, sorry, Sir Knight, but I have more pressing concerns.*

I looked at the children tied to the Knight-Captain, all sobbing and wailing, so full of fear that some were even clutching at him as if he were a stout tree. *Ducklings, he called them, as if he's calling out the game we all played as children—or no . . . not all of us*, I suddenly realized. Only *poor* children ever played that game. You didn't need toys or balls or anything to play Ducklings, just a group of children.

"Well now," I said, my voice light, "what a fine looking flock of ducks we have here today! Shall we play then, and see who is the finest duckling of all?" The children barely noticed my presence, let alone heard my question. "Come on," I said, trying my best to make it sound as if they risked missing out on the best thing ever, "when I get scared, I always fancy a game of Ducklings."

"Do you mock me?" the Knight-Captain said, yanking on one of the ropes and setting the little boy on the end screaming.

"I'll be with you in a moment, Sir Knight." I turned my gaze back down to the boys and girls. There were seven in all: that would be enough, I hoped. Just enough.

"Come now, you all remember the rules, don't you?"

"I want to play Ducklings." It was the little girl I'd brought up from the second floor. I looked at her face and saw the wide eyes, the eyebrows pinched up at the center. She was terrified, but she was doing her best to be brave.

"Well then, good ducklings always follow their mama, don't they? When Mama says, 'flock', they 'flock'—remember? And when she says 'slumber', they get down on their bellies and close their eyes, don't they? Now, you never want to be the last duckling to flock or slumber, because if you are, you lose the game, right? Are you ready to play?"

The Knight-Captain looked at me and laughed, sounding so menacing that the children renewed their frantic sobbing. "You seek to calm them? To take away their fear before they die? You are soft, Trattari, just like the rest of this country. What good—?"

"Flock!" I shouted.

All at once the children all ran toward me, and almost instantly, the ropes pulled taut. "Flock!" I repeated, doing my level best to keep my voice cheery and calm, as if we really were just playing. "The last one to flock loses the game," I called.

It was only as the children rushed toward me the second time that the Knight-Captain started to understand. He tried in vain to release some of the ropes he'd tied to himself; one came free, then another, but it was too late to stop the children's momentum and he toppled forward onto his belly.

"Slumber!" I shouted and the children instantly dropped to the floor and closed their eyes. "Now stay sleeping, my ducklings!" I slipped a hand into my coat and withdrew one of my daggers, leapt over their small bodies and landed on the Knight-Captain's back even as he struggled to push himself up. With all my strength I drove the blade of my short knife into the back of his neck, right up into his skull, all the way to the hilt, and then I twisted it viciously, although there was no need by that time; the madman was dead.

For a moment, there was blissful silence, then I heard the soft sound of the breeze and then the crackling of the flames below and I had to accept that the world had not frozen in place. My right hand was trembling and I dimly realized I was still pushing the knife into the back of the Knight-Captain's skull. With more effort than I would have thought possible I managed to stop myself pushing. Slowly I withdrew the blade, then quickly pulled the back of the Knight's tabard up to cover the wound and the blood already flowing from it. I cut each of the ropes tethering the children to his body and then walked over to the edge of the roof.

Brasti and Dariana were waiting below with the ladder.

"Flock," I said, and the children rose up and ran to me, hugging me so fiercely I had to brace myself to keep them from bowling me over the edge of the roof. *That would be a terrible end to this story*, I thought to myself.

"Come on," I said as Brasti's head appeared over the roof, "we have a new mama duck here and he's going to carry you down one at a time."

"Mama duck?" Brasti asked as I handed him one of the girls.

A little boy of maybe five years old walked over to the body of the Knight-Captain. "You're not supposed to still be sleeping," he said firmly. "You didn't flock. You lose the game."

26

THE DEPARTURE

Minutes after we got the last of the children down from the roof, the barn went up like a pyre. Villagers ran to dig trenches and pour water to keep the fire from spreading, though I didn't hold out much hope that they'd be able to save the buildings on either side. Bodies were lying in the streets and the square, most dead, but there were a few alive and needing treatment from those with the skills to help them. And, of course, there was still a monumental anger that risked blazing out of control at any moment.

"Back!" a young voice screamed from behind me, and I turned to see the commotion at the center of the village square: Sir Orn, the elder of the two remaining Knights, was on the ground, his throat slit, and two burly young men, one holding a damned sword, were attempting to get to Sir Vezier past a small figure brandishing a single arrow like a dagger to keep them at bay. It was the boy who'd held Brasti's quiver for him.

"He gets a trial," the boy shouted. "The Archer said so. He gets a trial."

"Get out of the way," one of the men said, reaching out to grab at the boy, and a second later pulled his now-bleeding hand back. "You little bastard!" he shouted and lifted up his sword.

I started running, but I already knew I was moving too damn slowly.

I'm not going to make it—

But Sir Vezier had risen from the ground and now he stepped in front of the boy. Most of his armor was gone, but he still had on his metal gauntlets and he could have caught the clumsy thrust. Instead he spread his arms wide and closed his eyes as the blade drove into his belly.

The Knight stood like that for a moment, his body held up by the sword inside him. The eyes of the burly young man holding the weapon went wide, and then Sir Vezier's body began tipping toward him. Disgusted, he pushed the Knight away and he slipped backward, the blade withdrawing from his body as it hit the ground.

I ran to Sir Vezier and knelt down to examine his wound. The young boy who'd tried to protect him said, "I'll go and get the healer—she'll fix him. There has to be a trial, the Archer said so."

I knew the healer wouldn't come; there were others in need and she'd have little time for a man who'd come here to kill her people.

"It's all right," Sir Vezier said. There was a trickle of blood leaking from the side of his mouth.

"Why?" I asked. "Why did you come here?"

"Orders. A Knight follows orders. We thought . . ." He grabbed my arm and pulled me close. "There are more of us. Hundreds."

"To what purpose? Who leads the black tabards? Is it Trin?"

"No," Sir Vezier said. "The Dukes have failed us—all of them. They treat us like servants . . . and the country gets worse and worse each year. There has to be order. We have to show people that there could be order."

A terrible thought occurred to me. "Sir Vezier, where were you going next?" I asked. "What was your next target?" His eyes closed, so I squeezed hard on his shoulders to bring him back to me. "What was the next target?" I repeated urgently. "Another village like Garniol? Like Carefal?"

He tried to speak, but instead he started spitting up more blood. At last he managed, "Rijou. The Knight-Captain said we would go to Rijou next."

"What village?" I asked.

"Rijou itself," he said. "The capital."

How in all the hells could they ever hope to take the capital city? Duke Jillard had the most secure seat in the world—his own palace was a fortress better protected even than Castle Aramor.

Sir Vezier lifted a hand toward me as if he expected me to take it. I didn't. "What were we supposed to do?" he asked. "There has to be order, doesn't there?" His grip slackened and his hand slid down the arm of my coat. Blood flowed both from the wound in his belly and from his mouth, and Sir Vezier died.

The young man who'd killed him was still standing behind me. He turned to the few people nearby who weren't occupied with the fire. "I . . . I did it," he said. "I killed one of the bastards."

My heart sank at his words and the look of pride slowly emerging on his face. It wasn't that I pitied Sir Vezier for I didn't: he'd been part of this attack and in all likelihood part of the massacre at Carefal. I was glad he'd saved the boy, but how many had he killed before he'd seen the madness inside the man he had followed this far? What broke my spirit was the thought of watching this young villager walk around, his chin high, believing himself a hero: he'd been ready to strike down a boy who was trying to protect an unarmed man—and not just any boy but one of their own. I wondered how his story would change after a few nights and a few beers. I wondered if the other villagers, desperate to embellish their own tales, would come to believe his.

"It's not their fault," a woman's voice said from behind me. Valiana's hair was disheveled and she had dirt on her face and a cut on her cheek. The children she'd protected stood a little way behind her.

"What isn't their fault?" I asked her.

"They don't know how to be like you."

"I don't want them to be like me," I said. "I'm not some—"

"Yes," she said, and knelt down next to me. She put a hand on my chest. "You are. Stop insisting there's nothing special about you, Falcio. It makes the rest of us feel worthless."

I thought about what Dariana had tried to tell me before, and Brasti, too. Hells, probably everyone had been warning me. "You don't have to get yourself killed to be like me, Valiana. In fact, I hardly ever get myself killed."

"Not for lack of trying," she said.

"That's not—"

She held up a hand. "I know—and I'm not trying to die, I promise. But I want to make my life mean something. I want to be—I don't know. Brave. Heroic." She gave me a defiant grin. "And you're the only example I've got in this horrible world. So whether you like it or not, I'm going to live up to the name you gave me." She leaned forward and hugged me fiercely. "I'm Valiana val Mond, damn it, and I'm going to make that count."

I hugged her back. We must have made an odd picture, kneeling on the ground and holding each other over the body of a dead Knight. "Well, then, we're probably all screwed, aren't we?" I said.

The weight of everything suddenly caught up with me, and the terror that had kept me going through the fight and the fire and that mad Knight ready to pull those children with him into his own hell finally overtook my need to pretend I was strong enough to endure. I felt tears dripping down my cheeks and I started to say something, but whatever it was came out as a sob.

Saints, I'm no better than those children were on the roof, terrified out of their minds and paralyzed with fear. I'd spent the last years chasing my own death and now, thanks to the neatha and the paralysis that was pulling me deeper every day, it was coming. "I don't want to die," I said.

We slept that night in Garniol, in the beds of men and women who had died in the battle. Whether our accommodations were simple practicality or a reminder from the villagers that we had failed to save forty-three of their people, I wasn't sure.

I awoke with the increasingly familiar numbness and inability to move. I couldn't feel my fingers or toes, or anything on my skin. My eyes wouldn't open and the world was a boundless gray. At first it was almost a pleasant surprise—usually the morning after a battle is an endless vista of cuts and bruises and vicious aches and pains. But the neatha kept me from feeling any of those things and so for a few brief moments I experienced serenity . . . then I felt the burning inside my chest and a sense of emptiness in my lungs and all I could think was, *I'm not breathing.* It wasn't that my lungs couldn't function, but rather, that whatever part of the mind that is supposed to command the lungs to take in air simply wasn't there.

Breathe, I told myself, though I had no idea what one did to force oneself to do so. *Breathe.* It seems such a simple thing, but only because we never have to think of the steps involved.

I began to see little spots of light winking in and out of existence even though my eyes were still closed. *No,* I tried to shout, *not today. I'm not ready. Please.*

Pressure appeared on my chest and then disappeared. Was I doing something right? *Breathe. You work for me, you stupid lungs. Breathe.*

I heard a loud rasping hiss in my ears like the sound of metal being dragged across a stone floor, and an instant later I tasted air rushing into me like a flood. That sound had been my throat opening up and sucking the air into my lungs. My eyes fluttered open. Above me stood Brasti. He had both his hands on my chest.

"Saints, Falcio! You suddenly stopped breathing—it was like . . . it was like your chest was trying to move, but it was stuck. I tried to push it down and up but—Are you all right?"

I gave a faint nod and he sat down heavily on the chair next to my bed. I was surprised to see him; normally it was Kest or Valiana who tended to watch over me in the mornings.

"Kest?" I asked.

Brasti looked a little stricken. "He's here—I mean, in the village. He's still trying to . . . Actually, I don't know what he's trying to do. It has something to do with that damned red glow of his."

"Others?" I croaked.

"Valiana is out in the fields with Dari, practicing swordplay, if you can believe it. I would have expected them to take a break after yesterday, but Valiana said she misgauged a Knight's attack and took a cut on her cheek for it so now she's got Dari trying all sorts of feints on her."

I was amazed that Valiana had managed to kill a Knight on her own, especially while she was trying to protect the children. She hadn't even mentioned it to me.

"Do you want something to drink?" Brasti asked.

"Min . . . ute," I said, trying to make the word come out as individual syllables. "Few min . . . utes."

Brasti sat back down on the chair and picked something up from the floor. I turned my head and watched as he took a thick iron needle to the shoulder of his greatcoat. At first I thought he must be trying to repair a tear, but after a bit I saw there was no thread on his needle. He was pulling a stitch out.

"Whatreyoudoin?" I asked. *Better*, I thought. *Like a man who's only half-drunk.*

"Fifteen years I've been wearing a greatcoat and that damn right sleeve always gets in the way of my shooting. Taking out these Godsdamned stitches is like trying to pick ore out of a piece of rock, by the way."

I'd never seen Brasti miss so I wondered how much of an impact that sleeve could possibly be having. What bothered me was that it felt like an act of desecration for him to tear out the stitches.

"Stop looking at me like that," he said. "I just want to take off one sleeve. The rest still gives me more than enough protection."

I could feel the prickling sensation that meant my arms and legs were coming back to life and took a chance at pushing myself up to a sitting position in the bed. The result was ungainly, but ultimately successful. When Brasti saw I didn't need help, he turned his attention back to his coat sleeve.

"Whyareyou—?"

"I was wrong," he said suddenly. "In Carefal. I was . . . I don't know what I was. But I took it out on you and it was wrong of me."

"It's fine."

"No, it's not. What you did yesterday . . ." He shook his head. "When we were standing at the top of that hill I thought, 'This is it. Every one of those people is going to die. The damned God of War himself could rise up from the fires of whichever hell he makes his home and all he could do is tell us we were screwed'. But you found a way, Falcio: you gave us our orders and you led us down there and against all the odds we saved most of the village."

It wasn't enough, I was about to say, but he didn't wait for me to speak.

"And even when that mad Knight was up there with those children, I couldn't bring myself to shoot—I was just too damned scared of hitting one of the children or having the Knight fall forward and drag them all to their deaths. But you . . . you just ran up there and by the time you hit the top you had a *plan*." He stopped talking for a while, grimacing as the needle in his hands tore at the threads holding the sleeve on his coat. Finally he stopped and set the coat down on his lap and turned to face me again. "All these years I've always told myself that you and the King and all your little talks about strategy and tactics . . . I always told myself it was just shit. In the end what matters are instincts. I've got good instincts, Falcio, I know I have— but my instincts were all telling me to race down to the village on my horse and just kill as many Knights as I could, and if I'd done that, all those villagers would be dead now." He looked down at the sleeve in his lap, then said, "You . . . I don't know, Falcio. I wish I could think like you."

"You could—"

"Don't," he said. "I'm not complaining, not really. I spent most of my life as a poacher before I became a Magistrate and my instincts served me well for both. I'm an archer, and no matter what anyone else thinks, I know I'm as good with a bow as Kest is with a sword and you are with those clever plans of yours. I don't begrudge you your talent." He smiled at last. "That boy, yesterday? The one who was handing me arrows? He came up to me this morning, him and seven other kids, and they had five adults with them too. Some already had bows themselves and some had picked them up from the dead and they all wanted me to show them how to shoot. Can you believe that? I asked if they wanted to go and learn the sword with Kest instead, but one of them said, 'Why would I want to fight with a stupid old sword?' and the rest all agreed."

I smiled at that as well: Brasti's finest hour, finally having other people agree with him that the bow is better than the sword.

"I'm leaving, Falcio," Brasti said, setting his coat and needle aside.

I smiled again, but I didn't understand. I tried to push myself up. "We've got to go to Rijou, Brasti." I tried to annunciate clearly, though my lips and tongue still felt odd. "That's where this is all headed. I don't know why but—"

Brasti gently pushed me back down. "*You* have to go to Rijou, Falcio, and so do Kest and Valiana and Dari—Kest is readying the horses as we speak, and I pray that whichever Gods don't already have it in for us will help you accomplish whatever it is you set out to do there. But I'm staying here with these people. If I have just a week here in Garniol I can teach the villagers enough to help them fend off an attack."

"You . . ." Could I really tell him not to help these people protect themselves? Of course I couldn't. "All right, Brasti, stay the week, teach these people, then come to Rijou. We'll leave word—"

"No," Brasti said, "no. After I prepare them here, I'm moving on to the next village and then the next town. Hunting bows are everywhere in these parts; the people just don't know how to use them for fighting. There's a man here who knows how to work the forge, so I'm going to have him take the armor from those dead Knights and we're going to melt it down and use it to make steel arrowheads. Just think, Falcio: with just one suit of armor I can make enough arrowheads to take down a hundred Knights. So think of what I can do with thirty suits of armor!"

"Brasti's Law," I whispered.

He nodded. "I know it's not the answer—I know there're other things that have to be done, and you'll do them, you and Kest and Valiana. Watch out for Dari, though. She's amazing, but she's also fucking insane. And for Saints' sake, if she comes to you at night don't—"

"Please," I said, "please don't put that thought in my head."

He laughed. "Poor old Saint Falcio." Brasti tore out one more stitch from the right shoulder of his coat and pulled the sleeve off. He stood up and slipped the coat on. It looked odd, a coat missing an entire sleeve, and yet on him there was something right about it.

"You're a bastard," I said.

Brasti's expression took on a hurt quality. "Don't call me that, Falcio. That's what the King always called me. 'Brasti the Bastard', he'd say. I guess I never quite lived up to his expectations."

I rose unsteadily to my feet. "The King loved you, Brasti."

Brasti's eyes held mine. "No, he didn't, and it's high time you stopped believing that. It's time you stopped thinking the King was this all-loving father figure. He was only two years older than the rest of us. His shit stank like everyone else's. He drank too much, he lied on any number of occasions, and it turns out he fucked half the noblewomen in the country. He was a great man, Falcio, but he was still just a man." He paused for a moment, then said, "He loved you, though, Falcio, and he admired Kest. He cared for a lot of the others, too—Nile, Parrick, Quillata . . . almost everyone. But not me. To him, I was always 'Brasti the Bastard'—just some poacher you insisted a King make into a Greatcoat. I can live with that, and you should too."

"Hells, Brasti, he was a complicated man." I waited to *explain*. "He was scrawny and awkward and trying to save the world, and you, you're handsome and confident and—"

"Stop making excuses for him, Falcio. I know he was brilliant, but what use is brilliance if you don't ever tell anyone your plan? I know you both wanted to save the world, but I don't know how to do that so instead I'm going to spend what time I have left in this dungheap of a country trying to save the people in it."

Brasti turned away from me for a moment and picked up his saddlebags from the floor. Part of me wanted to hit him over the head with the pommel of my rapier and hope that Kest and I could convince him to change his mind, but of course he'd already talked to Kest—his tone, his bearing, the way he'd thought through all of my objections . . . he'd already said his goodbyes to everyone else.

He turned back and gave me a rough hug. When he pulled away, he held me by the shoulders and gave me a wicked smirk. "All right," he said, "now I'm going to smile, and you smile, and then we'll both close our eyes and—"

"Get the hells out of here, Brasti Goodbow," I said, trying to keep the laughter from my eyes and the terrible sadness from my voice.

The last vestiges of the morning paralysis left me stiff and a little numb, but at last I was able to sit atop a horse again. Kest, Valiana, Dari, and I rode slowly through Garniol, reminding ourselves that this had been a victory against whoever was trying to destroy our country. But there was still smoke in the air from the fire of the day before and the blood had yet to soak into the soil. Victory wasn't quite as pretty as I remembered it.

We traveled for three days along one of the narrow roads that led northeast and eventually joined one of the larger trade routes that ran from Pertine to Rijou. Dusty tracks changed to cobbled stone roads and sparse green fields gave way to orchards thick with apple trees, some more than two hundred years old. Their leaves were just beginning to change to red and gold. Like everything else about the duchy of Rijou, the beauty of the landscape was deceptive.

Most of the journey passed in silence. It wasn't that we had nothing to talk about, just that we'd grown used to Brasti being the one to start our conversations, and we felt his absence keenly, each in our own separate ways. Brasti was vain and reckless and, for a Magistrate, remarkably prone to acts of petty larceny, and yet he could also be brave when the moment called for it, and he was faithful beyond measure to his friends. He might not have had the same command of the King's Law that Kest and I shared, but his verdicts made sense to the communities involved, and held just as well as any of ours. Maybe it was because he was so focused on the people living in all those little towns and villages. *You want to save the world, Falcio.*

I want to save the people in it. Of course, those who might oppose Brasti's verdicts heeded them because he was just as deadly with a bow and arrow as Kest was with a sword. In my mind I imagined him looking at me with feigned outrage. *Falcio, that's like complimenting a troubadour by saying he's just as good at playing music as another man is at farting.*

I laughed to myself for a moment and only then realized I'd lost track of time. I let go of my horse's reins so that I could squeeze and release my hands. My fingers were becoming a little numb—too soon, I thought as I tried to will the feeling back. Far, far too soon.

Kest pulled up next to me. "Are you all right?"

"I'm not going to start weeping for Brasti, if that's what you're worried about."

"You know it's not."

"I'm fine," I said. "It's not as bad today as it was yesterday."

Kest stared at me like a man trying to see through a curtain.

"Leave it," I said at last.

We rode a while longer before I remembered to ask, "Did you manage to find out where the villagers got their weapons?"

"No. Everyone we spoke to claimed they were family inheritances—they lied to us with remarkable confidence, given that the swords and spearheads were clearly all new-made, and by the same expert weaponsmith. They must have heard that we'd ordered the people of Carefal to turn over their weapons."

I slowed my horse until Valiana caught up with us. "Did you get anything from the children about where the weapons came from?" I asked.

She rolled her eyes. "Every time I tried talking to them, one of their parents would pull them away, and if I did manage to ask the question, the children just looked baffled. I don't think they knew anything about the weapons."

Saint Dheneph-who-tricks-the-Gods! How many other villages and towns were being fed brand-new swords and spears—and what would happen to them when these mad bands of roving black-tabarded Knights found out?

Valiana's horse started pulling away but she hauled on its reins to keep it next to mine. "Falcio, why not pursue more of those Knights? Do you really want us to risk everything to save Duke Jillard?"

I'd been asking myself the same question ever since we'd left Garniol. Rijou was the very last place on earth I wanted to go—if ever there was a Duke who deserved to be overthrown, it was Jillard. But it wasn't just about him, not anymore. Someone out there was killing off entire Ducal families; someone was arming peasants with steel weapons, and someone was sending groups of rogue Knights in black tabards to massacre them. I could appreciate that there was a certain brilliance to the plan, weakening both the power of the nobility and the will of the common people all at the same time, but the upshot was that Tristia was being torn apart at the seams.

"Falcio?" Valiana asked, and I realized I hadn't answered her question.

"We have to save Jillard," I replied, "not because he deserves it, but because someone wants him dead for the wrong reasons."

"But who?" Kest asked. "To make all of this work, to plan it out so perfectly—?"

I heard Dariana snort from behind us. "Look at all you fancy Greatcoats with your big talk and your conspiracies. It's fucking Trin, obviously."

I really wanted it to be Trin. I knew she had the mind for it, and not a stitch of decency in her heart to stay her from creating chaos, but it wasn't. Trin was entirely selfish, and all of this madness would make the throne she desired so badly all but worthless for a generation or longer. That wouldn't suit her at all.

"It's not Trin," I said, then added, "or at least, it's not all her."

"Well, if it's not, then isn't the most likely candidate the man you're sending us to help?" Dariana asked.

"If it is Jillard—" I stopped. Duke Jillard of Rijou had a history of trying to expand his own territory and I could easily see him looking for ways to annex Luth or even Aramor. But any Duke who tried such a thing would be gambling with his life if the other duchies found out and banded together to take him down. No, this wasn't Jillard, either—and anyway, I was positive he was next on the list.

Rijou sat at the very center of Tristia, and it was the one duchy with enough money and power to hold the country together in a crisis. If someone really wanted to set Tristia afire and send it spiraling down into chaos and civil war, that's where they'd be lighting the spark. Rijou was the next target.

I noticed that Kest and Valiana were staring at me. "What is it?"

"You were speaking, and then you just sort of drifted off," Valiana said.

"Maybe he's losing his mind along with his body," Dari suggested from behind me.

"Are you feeling all right?" Valiana asked.

"Would you all stop asking me that question?"

"I never asked in the first place," Dari said. "But I do have a different question."

"What is it?"

"If you're so bound and determined we should go to Rijou, I assume you've worked out how we're going to get in?" she asked.

Fair question: Rijou has the most carefully guarded gates and walls of any city in the country—and I should know.

She pointed at me. "If there's any truth at all in the stories the troubadours are telling, you publicly humiliated Duke Jillard—and I believe that even before you did so, he badly wanted you dead."

"What's your point?" I asked.

"So if that's the case, how in all the hells are we supposed to get through the city gates? And when we do, how do we get into the palace without being arrested and hanged before we've had a chance to explain why we're there?"

I'd been pondering that very question ever since we'd left Garniol, and in fact I did have a way to get us into Rijou.

Saints forgive me. I'm going to break her heart.

27

HOMECOMING

We were approaching Merisaw. It was an hour or so before sunset. The hilltop town was a few miles from the capital city of Rijou itself, the dark rot at the center of Tristia—and the place where I would make one of the last acts of my life a desperate attempt to save the man who had imprisoned and tortured me, had tried to murder Aline, and who was, even now, quite likely planning to betray us.

Saint Zaghev-who-sings-for-tears, there has to be a better way to throw my life away than this . . .

"There's someone up ahead," Kest said, pointing to the town gates about three hundred yards away, then he added, "It's the town gates, so probably just the city guardsman."

"Merisaw is a peaceful town," Valiana pointed out. "The gates aren't guarded until after sunset."

As we moved nearer I held up a hand to shade my eyes from the late afternoon sun. "Is that a mace he's holding? It looks odd from here."

"It's a woman," Kest said, "and *she* is holding flowers."

For a moment I had visions of Saint Birgid, waiting with white and yellow daisies, ready to chastise me once again, but as we got closer I saw dark, dark hair, smooth white skin, and blue eyes that held mine, even from this distance. The first time I'd seen her she'd been wearing a long white gown made from some gauzy fabric that shimmered in the moonlight. Today she wore a simple red dress, and had a single yellow flower in her hair to match the ones in her arms.

The night Ethalia had saved me in Rijou, her smile had been wise and mysterious. Now it was the simpler smile of a woman filled with joy at the sight of her man.

I stopped my horse when she was still a hundred yards away from me and dismounted. *Birgid-who-weeps-rivers, if you truly are the Saint of Mercy, make her turn back. Make her run into the town and lock her door against me. Have her neighbors lie and tell me she left days ago—or better yet, send a man, a big, strong, and handsome man, to run out of the gate right now with a picnic basket and a jug of wine. Have her turn when she hears him coming and laugh and throw the flowers up into the air as she flings her arms around his neck and showers him with kisses. Let it all have been in my mind: just one night of kindness from a woman who saw a stranger in desperate need.*

Ethalia began running toward me, and I swore. *Damn you, Saint Birgid, damn you and all the other Saints, and damn the Gods. Damn you, King Paelis, with your childish dreams. You want me to break her heart, to betray the hope in her eyes? Well, two can play at betrayal. I swear: if she asks me to set this aside and come with her—if she asks me even once, I'll go, and I'll let this world you've given us fall into the despair and decay it so richly deserves.*

As Ethalia approached, I felt a momentary sense of relief as I watched her smile widen even further. Now I knew what would happen. *She'll come to me and say my name and tell me she's been waiting for me every day. I'll do my duty: I'll tell her why I'm here—that I've traded away what hours and minutes might have been ours in service to a wasted effort to save a man who doesn't deserve to be saved. She'll get angry—of course she will; what kind of fool would do such a thing? She'll give me one last chance, just one. "Come with me," she'll say. "Come and be happy, however briefly."*

And I'll go.

The hells for your dream, Paelis.

But as Ethalia approached, she saw the expression on my face, and she saw Kest and the others behind me. Her pace slowed and her smile faded as her eyes changed, first looking anxious, then fearful, and finally sad. It was as if she had discerned the entire journey of my life since we'd last been together in a glance.

She stood before me, barely a foot away, and yet we had never been further apart. "Ethalia, I—"

She shook her head to stop me from speaking, and we stayed like that for a few moments until finally she took a deep breath, then said, "Very well. But this much for me. This much I have a right to ask." She took the final step toward me and reached up to put her hand behind my neck. She pulled my face down to hers and she kissed me, and I put my arms around her and felt as if all the loneliness and sorrow of my life had suddenly been lifted away. I didn't care about the pain I'd suffered or the death I'd seen, or the neatha eating away inside me, or the violence eating away at the country. All I cared about was her, and that moment, and that kiss.

This much for me.

We stayed like that for a minute or a year, and then she pulled away and spoke. "I am the friend in the dark hour. I am the breeze against the burning sun. I am the water, freely given, and the wine, lovingly shared. I am the rest after the battle, and the healing after the wound. I am the friend in the dark hour," she repeated, "and I am here for you, Falcio val Mond."

It was the formal greeting of her order, not the words spoken to a lover. She held my gaze for a moment more, and then turned to greet the others, who had stayed a little way behind me. "Welcome to Merisaw," she said. "I am Ethalia, a sister of the Merciful Light."

Dariana snorted. "A whore? Your grand plan to get us into Rijou is some—"

"Shut your mouth," Kest said fiercely.

"Peace, swordsman," Ethalia said. "Your anger does me more harm than her words."

"Forgive me," he said, stepping back.

Ethalia went to him and looked into his eyes, searching. "I would help you if I could, Saint of Swords, both for the love you bear Falcio and for your own sake too, but I cannot. You should leave this place and make your way to the sanctuary in Aramor. You are nothing but tinder and spark now."

"I will abide."

"Anyone with eyes can see your strength of will. It isn't enough."

"Nevertheless, lady, I will abide."

Ethalia smiled, and reached out to touch Kest's cheek. She winced as if she were being burned, and finally pulled away.

"Thank you for trying," Kest said.

Ethalia turned to Valiana and curtsied. "My lady. We have met before, though I doubt you remember me."

"Forgive me," Valiana said. "I . . . There were many people then, and I was not the woman I am now."

"All to the good, wouldn't you say? A Greatcoat: the first named since the King died."

"Your information is incorrect, *whore*." Dariana looked at Kest as she emphasized the word. "There are a hundred others."

Ethalia's expression was neither threatening nor afraid, and she looked at Dariana as she might an angry child. "And yet not quite the same, wouldn't you say?"

"You've got that right."

"My—" I stopped myself. I'd been about to call her "my lady," as if she were a stranger. *No*, I thought. *No. Even if our lives must be lived apart, I still get to know that she was here, that she was real, and that in another life she could have*—would *have*—*been mine*. "Ethalia, we need to get into Rijou."

"I know," she said, "but I must warn you that Rijou is an even more dangerous place since last you were there. I have left it behind, as have many from my order."

"But can you get us in?"

"I can," she said, and sighed. "Some still remain, and there are men who guard the gates who feel a . . . a gratitude for the Sisters of the Merciful Light. How soon must you go? You could stay the night in Merisaw and in the morning—"

"Tonight," I said. "It has to be tonight."

Her expression was inscrutable. "As you say, then. Come. I will make the necessary arrangements." She led us into Merisaw, and as we walked she slipped her hand into mine.

This much for me.

That night an absurdly handsome young man dressed in the fine red brocades of a Rijou nobleman escorted us through the first and second gates and into the city. He gave his name as Erastian, which was an alias, unless he really was the Saint of Romantic Love—but he picked his nose quite often and stopped every once in a while to sniff blue and white powder before sneezing into a silk handkerchief, so I assumed it was the former.

Whatever Erastian's connection to Ethalia or the Sisters of the Merciful Light, he didn't speak of it. I worried what the consequences might be for the sisters if their involvement was discovered. I'd done my best to convince Ethalia to leave, to go south to the little island off the coast of Baern she had talked about, but she had refused.

"You'll need to pass the third gate by yourselves," Erastian said, interrupting my train of thought. "I've sent word ahead, and the men there will let you through without question. But I cannot be seen there, not by all of them."

"Thank you," I said, extending my hand, but instead he smiled politely, as if he hadn't seen the gesture, and turned and walked back through the gates behind us.

"Who do you suppose he is?" Valiana asked.

"I don't know," I said, "and I don't think he wanted us to know."

"Then let's hope he hasn't betrayed us," Kest said dryly.

As we continued slowly through the last gate into the city I found myself absurdly gratified that no one poured acid on us from the pipes running through the stone of the archway, or fired crossbow bolts at us through the small holes on the sides.

"What now?" Dariana asked, unable to hide her surprise that we'd made it this far. "We still have to get inside the palace, don't we?"

"I have a plan," I said.

She looked at me as if she were convinced I was lying, but I did actually have a plan: after all, there are always two ways to get inside any Ducal Palace. One is to be invited. The other is to be arrested.

It didn't take long to find one of Shiballe's many informants—the city of Rijou is as riddled with them as a decaying apple is with rotworms. Despite their venal nature, they considered Greatcoats beneath them. Fortunately, we had Valiana.

For the cost of an overpriced gown, a brocade coat, improbably high shoes, and a copper tiara covered in the thinnest layer of white gold imaginable, she had quickly transformed from travel-stained Trattari to the daughter of a Margrave just arrived from the duchy of Baern. If I'd had any concerns that she could still play the part of the haughty noblewoman, they were soon dismissed by the speed and ease with which she terrified one of Shiballe's informants.

"My apologies, my lady—I swear, I meant no offense."

"Get up off the floor," Valiana said, "and if you try to put your filthy lips to my feet again you'll find yourself without teeth."

"Of course, of course," he said, pushing himself back up to his feet and brushing himself down. "But I must be frank with you, my lady. What you're asking for is expensive and difficult to arrange, even for a man like Thesian."

A man like Thesian was, as it turned out, fat, balding, and smelling of far too many scented oils, all a bit on the rancid side. Though I know nothing of the perfumer's art, I was convinced this particular assortment was an unwise combination.

"I'm afraid we have very little money to spare at this time," Valiana said, and tossed five of the gold pieces the Tailor had given me onto Thesian's table. This was, in fact, a princely sum by anyone's measure.

Thesian looked at us as if he was trying to decide just whom we must have robbed on the way to his little shop. "I . . . am sensitive to your plight, gracious lady." He paused for a moment and I could see the little gears of greed grinding his fear to dust. "And yet . . . even with this," he said, lifting and rubbing each of the coins between a thick forefinger and thumb, "I cannot guarantee the safety of your person. Not when it comes to a meeting with the Duke's adviser. Shiballe is . . . ah . . . not always *cooperative*."

"But you'll do everything in your considerable power to persuade him to treat with us fairly, will you not?" she asked, and she placed another two coins on the table.

"Of course—of course, my lady—surely that goes without saying. Thesian has been a great friend to Shiballe, my lady, a *very* great friend. We are as family—closer than family, in fact."

That last part I could believe.

Thesian made the coins vanish into a small red bag that hung from his belt. "If I might be so bold to inquire, how exactly did you manage to find me? Men like me—ah, we are difficult to track down, no?"

"This is indeed the case," Valiana said. In fact, we'd had to walk the full length of a city block before we found a drug seller. "But we persevered and trusted in the Saints."

Thesian smiled. "And the Saints have answered your call." He finished the last touches and blew on the document he'd put together to dry the ink. "Now, are you certain you have chosen the right location for your meeting? If—and I'm not saying this would be possible, even though Thesian is, as everyone knows, a great friend to Shiballe—but if something were to be . . . well, let us say, *misunderstood*, it would be very easy for a hundred Knights to appear, and in that case I fear even so gracious a lady as you, my lady, would have great difficulty in escaping."

There is a protocol to clandestine meetings in Rijou. Negotiations are performed, terms are set, and eventually the two parties meet at a mutually agreed location. In this case, I had chosen the Teyar Rijou, the Rock of Rijou. When last there, I had made a rather negative impression on Duke Jillard's men in general and on Shiballe in particular. It was a wide-open space that would enable him to make quite the demonstration of power if he wanted to, though of course, such an act would be in clear violation of the hastily agreed terms for our meeting.

"It would be unfortunate if any such misunderstanding were to occur," Valiana said firmly. "I presume your influence will . . . reduce any chances of such unfortunate confusion."

"Of course," Thesian said, "and I myself will run to the church and pray the Saints speak in careful, quiet voices on your behalf."

He extended his hand toward Valiana to seal the deal and without missing a beat she turned to me and said haughtily, "Trattari, you will shake hands with this man on my behalf. I would hate to disturb the careful work of my manicurist."

At first I thought she was playing some foolish prank on me—then realized that if Thesian had shaken her hand, he would immediately have felt the rough calluses on her skin, hardly the mark of a noblewoman. *Smart.* Had she always been this clever?

I shook hands with Thesian, which was an even more unpleasant sensation than I'd expected, and we left the back room of his shop and set out for the Teyar Rijou.

"That was nicely done," Kest said to Valiana.

"Yeah," Dari chimed in, "you make a convincingly arrogant bitch."

"Old habits." She favored us with a grin. "Now let me find an alley so I can get out of these ridiculous clothes. I certainly don't want to meet the odious Shiballe without my Greatcoat and sword."

"We're really trusting our lives to that fat slug?" Dariana asked. "And not just a fat slug, but one who works for the other fat slug, Shiballe—the one who tried to have Falcio killed? Aren't you worried he'll just betray you?"

"Yes," I said, "I'm trusting our lives to that fat slug, and yes, of course he's going to betray us."

An hour later we stood in the center of the Teyar Rijou with Shiballe standing in front of us, his soft, fleshy hands planted on his wide hips and an obscenely self-satisfied smirk on his lips. A hundred Ducal Knights surrounded us, their swords drawn.

So my plan had worked.

There were two possible truths currently competing in my mind for dominance. The first was that my King was exactly the man I had always believed him to be: a brilliant strategist who could divine the future by looking at the past; the man who had created the Great-coats and placed them exactly where they should be when the country needed them most. That man had put Dara in Aramor and Nile in Luth to try to protect the Dukes from assassinations that Paelis had somehow predicted.

The other possibility was that King Paelis had been nothing more than a petty tyrant, concerned only with his own lineage; that he had set the pieces in play to ensure that once one of his heirs was discovered, all those who might stand in their way would be destroyed utterly.

And this moment, standing right here with a hundred Ducal Knights encircling us: this was where I would finally determine which King was real; which man I had served.

"I know you're there," I shouted to the men in armor standing there with their swords drawn, turning as I spoke, trying in vain to meet each pair of eyes. "I can't see you under your helmet, but I know you're there."

"What insanity has taken you, Trattari?" Shiballe asked.

"Shut up," I said. "I'm busy."

"I'll have you—"

"It's time," I said, giving my voice as much authority as I could muster. "Whatever mission you've been on, whatever it is you think you're here to do, the Duke is going to be killed unless I help him, and I can't do that if my head is decorating a pike."

Shiballe started laughing, but when Kest and Dariana reached for their swords, I held out a hand to stop them. "Easy," I said.

"I believe we'll have a contest," Shiballe said. "I'll have one of my cooks prepare your flesh, and the man who eats the most fried Trattari without voiding his stomach will win a gold purse. Oh, and your tatty old coat—the winner can take that too, maybe hang it on their wall as a trophy."

Some of the Knights began laughing at that, and I could see
Shiballe was puffing out his chest, readying himself to play to his
audience.

I was running out of time. "Fine," I said, allowing the frustration
to creep into my voice, "I don't usually like to pull rank but you're
starting to piss me off." I paused and looked down at the ground just
a moment. *It's just you and me now, you smart-assed, gangly excuse
for a King.*

Then I lifted my head and said, "My name is Falcio val Mond,
First Cantor of the King's Magisters, and I hereby command the
Greatcoat disguised among you to reveal himself and report. That's
an order." I should have stopped there, but like a fool I added, "I
mean it."

Shiballe nearly fell backward once he realized what I'd just
said. "You really are something, Trattari." He waved to the Knight-
Captain. "Sir Jairn, arrest these fools."

The Knight-Captain came forward, a large man who needed a
prodigious amount of armor to cover his broad shoulders and bar-
rel chest. He stood in front of me as if he were waiting for me to do
something.

"Sir Jairn?" Shiballe said.

The Knight removed his helmet. Underneath was a still-young
face with dusty blond hair and a short beard covering wide-set features. He still bore the scar I remembered him taking in a duel in a
village in Aramor years before. "Parrick Edran, at your command,
First Cantor," he said. He turned to look down at Shiballe with disgust on his face. "If your first command is to kill the slug I would be
very appreciative. But I think we should go and see the Duke first."

28

AN UNUSUAL ALLIANCE

Shiballe tried to have the other Knights arrest Parrick, or Sir Jairn as he was calling himself these days, and that put us at a bit of a stand-off at first. But most of these men had served with "Sir Jairn," and it turned out he made a terrific Knight-Captain: he'd led the fight in dozens of border skirmishes from the front, risking his own life right alongside his fellow Knights.

And Shiballe was clearly loathed; he was reviled as a conniving manipulator who plotted intrigues in the shadows, leaving others to fight and bleed for his machinations. Furthermore, Knights believe wholeheartedly in the chain of command—I'm pretty sure it's bred into them with their mothers' milk—and Shiballe, despite his dark influence at court, was in no way part of that chain.

In the end Parrick surrendered himself to his Knight-Sergeant, Sir Coratisimo, who agreed with him that it would be better to settle any questions of imprisonment and execution at the palace, once the Duke had had a chance hear these revelations. Parrick was nominally under arrest, but despite Shiballe's protestations, no one put handcuffs on him.

"It's a fucking mess, First Cantor," Parrick said as we walked along the wide marble hallways of the Ducal Palace. "We've had reports of problems all around the duchy, even beyond the borders. There are internal complications, too: our Knight-Commander left yesterday with two hundred Knights, apparently to patrol the eastern border."

"What's going on at the eastern border?"

"Nothing—as far as I can tell, he left against the Duke's orders. I know it's unbelievable, but I'm beginning to suspect that there's some kind of mutiny going on."

"What about the north?" I asked. "Has Trin broken through?"

"Duchess Trin has her army stationed in southern Domaris, but she's still getting hammered in sneak attacks by what's left of Duke Hadiermo's forces," he told us with a grin. "The Duke's men have formed up in smaller squads and now they're using really inventive ways to kill off as many of Trin's men as they can—who would ever have thought that Duke Hadiermo had a mind for tactics? I always thought he was a bit of an idiot."

But the Tailor had expected Hadiermo's forces to crumble ... "I doubt he was responsible," I said after a moment. "The Tailor's Greatcoats are likely leading those squads now."

Parrick frowned. "I've heard noises about the Tailor having assembled new Greatcoats. What are they like?"

"Like her," I said, pointing to Dariana. "Excellent fighters with no conscience whatsoever."

Dariana smiled. "Now, Falcio, people are going to think you like me if you keep flattering me like this."

Parrick looked at her. "Not sure how I feel about *new* Greatcoats. Did the Tailor think there was something wrong with the rest of us?"

"Only that you proved to be completely useless," Dariana replied. "And given you've apparently spent the last five years protecting one of the men who killed your King that, I think, is a bit on the generous side."

Parrick looked stricken, and I knew it was more than simply having failed the King—after all, we were all guilty of that. But talking to him now, as if he hadn't stood by and done nothing when—

But no, I wasn't ready to deal with that yet. "Parrick, what exactly did King Paelis tell you—what was his last order?"

Parrick had trouble meeting my eyes—not that I blamed him; after all, the King had ordered him to keep his final mission a secret, just like he had the rest of us.

"Come on," I said. "There's not much point in keeping secrets now."

"That's just it, though," Parrick said. "All he told me was that I should join the Knights of Rijou and guard the Duke's life—that was it; he didn't give me any more information than that. And he made me swear to do it, no matter what. I . . . I nearly broke my promise, Falcio, when I saw you here . . . and then, when the Duke went to Pulnam with five hundred men, he ordered me to stay here and keep the peace—otherwise I'm not sure what I would have done."

"Leave it for now," I said.

"We're here." He pointed at the entrance to the throne room of Rijou. "I hope you have a damned good reason for being here and forcing me to break cover, because I'm fairly sure I'm going to be executed for infiltrating the Ducal Knights of Rijou."

"As a matter of fact, I do have an excellent reason," I said. "I'm here to warn Duke Jillard that someone's planning to assassinate him."

Parrick stopped dead and looked at me as if I'd just walked into a ballroom completely naked. "Falcio—" He took a deep breath before adding, "Saints, that's all you've got? Someone's already tried to kill the Duke—we caught the bastard three days ago."

I looked at the twenty Knights surrounding us and the smirking Shiballe behind them, then into the throne room of the man who'd sworn to see me dead and who now had no reason whatsoever to keep me alive.

Jillard, Duke of Rijou, wasn't handsome so much as well groomed. Like most wealthy nobles he could afford to keep himself fit, dress in the latest fashions, and remain impeccably coifed. Thanks to a sharp barber and the finest imported oils his black hair and short beard were always well groomed, and today he sported a rich purple robe brocaded with silver and gold. He sat on the throne of Rijou, towering above us as if he were waiting to pass judgment. I suppose he was.

"Well, now that I have you, Falcio val Mond, what shall I do with you?" He played with a gaudy red and gold ring, turning it around and around on his finger, an odd, almost anxious mannerism for a man who could have us killed with a single gesture. "You never come alone, do you? You always bring complications to my door." He leaned forward and peered at Valiana. "And I see you've brought the girl Patriana tried to pass off as my daughter. You look rather plain in that tatty coat, my dear. Shall I have Shiballe bring you a nice dress?"

Valiana gave a slight curtsey. "I'm more comfortable as I am, your Grace."

"You might find that coat rather confining in the near future," Jillard said.

Parrick spoke up before I could. "Your Grace, I beg you, listen to Falcio; he's—"

"Silence, Sir Jairn—or, no, it's—what? *Parrick?* Well, whoever you are, you have saved my life, and on more than one occasion, but now I am forced to wonder to what purpose. There is breath instead of blood in your lungs only because I haven't yet decided whether to behead you as a traitor or hang you as a spy."

"With all due respect, your Grace," I said, "I don't see how you could accuse Parrick of being a spy."

"No? Shiballe tells me he's been skulking about under the guise of a Knight here in my home for nearly five years."

"Yes, your Grace, but in fairness, the King was dead *before* Parrick arrived, so there wasn't anyone for him to be spying *for*, if you see what I mean."

"And you believe that now is the time to show off your debating skills?" Jillard smiled. It wasn't a nice smile. And yet underneath his smug expression I could have sworn I saw a slight twitch: a tiny flash of discomfort, maybe even fear.

Shiballe rose. "Your Grace, I will summon my personal guards and deal with this traitor."

"Kneel," the Duke said. "I think I like you better on your knees right now, Shiballe. I'm not entirely sure what I pay you for but I would have thought it included being able to figure out that one of my Knight-Captains is actually a Trattari."

The overstuffed worm immediately dropped to the ground, which pleased me.

"Now you," the Duke said, his eyes on Parrick. "You were one of my best Knights—at least until an hour ago. But despite what you've done for me in the past, why should I trust you now that I know you're a traitor?"

A shadow crossed Parrick's face. "Was I a traitor when I saved your life three years ago, when the ambassador from Avares tried to stick a knife in your throat? Was I a traitor when I kept you from falling to your death in that canyon when your horse broke its leg?" Parrick turned to look at me, his face sick with guilt. "Was I a traitor when I stood by and watched as you—?"

Jillard rose suddenly from his throne. "And all the while doing it under the orders of a dead tyrant and *never* out of loyalty to me!"

The memories of my last stay in Rijou sparked a sudden anger in me, and only Kest's hand on my arm kept me from drawing my rapiers. How could Parrick have served a man like Jillard? How could he have stood by him every day as he carried out one capricious atrocity after another? Why would King Paelis *ever* have given Parrick such an order? And how could he ever have followed it?

And yet, I realized, *Parrick's actions are exactly what's going to save us now.*

"Your Grace," I said, "I believe I can give you an overwhelming reason to trust Parrick."

The Duke sat back down, his eyes still on Parrick. "Really? You think that you of all people can convince me of this Trattari's loyalty?"

I chose my next words very carefully. "When I was last here in the palace, you sent me to your dungeons. You had your men beat me. You let Patriana . . . you let her do things to me, and to Aline."

I turned to Parrick, feeling almost guilty for what I was about to say. *Almost.* "You were here that whole time—when the Duke's men dragged me here in chains, when they took me down to his dungeons and tortured me: you were right here, in this palace."

Parrick's face was ashen. "Saints, Falcio, I'm sorry. I know you must despise me, and I don't blame you. But you have to believe me: the King made me swear . . . he made me swear that no matter what I saw, no matter what the Duke did . . . Falcio I would never—"

I cut him off with a look. I wasn't ready to forgive, not yet. "If this man was going to betray you, Duke Jillard, surely he would have done it then?"

Jillard swirled the wine inside his goblet as if he were trying to shake the answer loose. "I suppose that's true," he said at last. "In the end I was betrayed by a great number of people, including my own torturer." Jillard leaned over to me. "We caught him the next day, you know."

"He had nothing to do with my escape," I said, too quickly to be convincing.

"He unlocked the door and let you out!" the Duke pointed out. "He admitted as much, and then he proceeded to repeat the King's Laws, over, and over, and over—and not one of which he got correct, I should add. He said all this to my face, and proudly, too. Of course, he was a little less proud once we got him on the rack."

"He called out your name a great deal toward the end," Shiballe said from behind me, as if sensing an opportunity to get back into the Duke's good graces. "I imagine many others have done the same over the years."

"Falcio," Kest warned.

"I'm fine," I said, though I wasn't entirely fine, for my hand had apparently drifted rather close to the hilt of one of my rapiers again. "You're a fool, your Grace, to play at these petty games of revenge while the country falls to pieces around you."

"My torturer *betrayed* me," Jillard said, slamming his fist down on the arm of this throne. He quickly regained his composure as his gaze drifted to Parrick. "But not you: you could have freed this

Trattari had you so chosen—in fact, it would have been surprisingly easy to do so without being caught."

Parrick looked like he was going to be sick.

"Very well," he said at last, still turning the ring around and around on his finger, "I will grant that I have some small cause to trust Parrick. But you, Falcio val Mond: why should I believe you? You conceded my freedom after my men failed me in Pulnam, but that was nothing more than a necessary political maneuver on your part. It doesn't put us on the same side."

I'd been waiting for this. I looked back at my Greatcoats, old and new, hoping I wasn't about to condemn them to be buried beneath the heavy stone floors of Jillard's palace. "I'm not on your side, your Grace—how could I be? You're a monster. You ordered the murder of the Tiaren family and countless others, and mostly for spurious reasons. You sent every kind of killer you could after me—and worse, after the King's heir. Even when you lost the Ganath Kalila you tried to break your own laws to end Aline's life. You're a snake, Duke Jillard, and I have every intention of seeing your head severed from your body."

The Duke looked ever so slightly unsettled. "Well then, that simplifies things—"

"But not now, and not today. Your death would be the final straw, the one that would break the back of this country. If whoever killed Duke Isault and Duke Roset gets to you, then civil war—and your darling daughter Trin—will drive us all into whichever of the thousand hells she has planned for us."

Jillard gave a laugh, and this time it actually sounded genuine. "*Trin? That's* what's brought you to your knees in front of me? You baffle me, Trattari, really you do. Trin has her mother's armies and some small portion of her cunning, and she will no doubt amuse herself running around the North playing commander." He leaned forward on his throne and added silkily, "but should she dare to bring her men across Rijou's border, then my soldiers will show her the courtesy I should have shown her unlamented mother long ago."

"You speak boldly for a man who just lost his Knight-Commander and two hundred of his Knights, your Grace," Kest said. Sounding genuinely curious, he asked, "So now who will lead the charge for your soldiers when Trin's forces come calling?"

"Dealing with petty betrayal is the price of my position." He leaned back and waved a hand absently in the air. "Besides, you have solved the problem for me, you and your fellow Trattari."

"How so?" I asked.

"Didn't one of your own Greatcoats—Dara, I believe—didn't she murder the Duke of Aramor? Isault never liked my idea of sharing troops to guard the borders, but this new Ducal Protector of theirs—Sir Shuran? He will need my support if he hopes to hold off the nobles who are even now plotting to break Aramor into little chunks just large enough for them to rule. In fact, I've already sent envoys to negotiate for a thousand of Shuran's best Knights."

Jillard's arrogant tone lacked conviction; his gloating was hiding something underneath. "You seem to have thought of everything," I said. "So why are you so frightened, your Grace?"

"Frightened? You think I'm *frightened*, Trattari?" He laughed. "Frightened of what—an assassin? My Knights, including Sir Jairn—forgive me, of course I mean *Greatcoat Parrick*, here—have already caught the assassin. Of course, I will admit it is a little mortifying to see my relationship with the Dashini has dwindled somewhat since I sent two of them to their deaths chasing you."

I turned to Parrick. "You captured a Dashini assassin? *Alive?* How?"

"With a great deal of luck, and the lives of ten Knights. It was the weight of the dead bodies—all of them in full armor—piling on top of him that held him down long enough for me to knock him out." At my skeptical expression, he added, "I drove the pommel of my sword into his skull."

"And you've got him down in your dungeon, right now?"

"Of course," Shiballe said. "Which is where you shall soon—"

I've got you, you arrogant bastard.

"I don't think so," I said.

"What do you mean?" Jillard asked.

The fact that he'd even asked the question let me know I was right. "If the assassin's been captured and everything is fine, then why didn't you arrest us on the spot? Why go through this whole charade? I think it's because you *are* afraid, your Grace. I think you know there's another attack coming."

Jillard stepped down from his throne and glanced at Shiballe before turning to face me. "Then why don't you tell me how these assassins plan to kill me when this one failed? Look around you, Falcio val Mond. I rule the most heavily armed city in the world. We stand inside a palace that could hold off an army. Five thousand men could lay siege outside my gates and they would get nothing for it but empty bellies."

He was right, of course. Of all the Dukes in Tristia, Jillard would be the hardest to kill. But if the plan was to drive the country into chaos, then Jillard had to be the next target, and if someone wanted him dead, they wouldn't stop at sending one assassin. All the way from Garniol I'd been asking myself how the killers would get to him, and there was still only one answer that made any sense to me. "Your son," I said. "Tommer. They'll find a way to kidnap him and then they'll force you to come for him, and when you do, they'll kill you."

The Duke's face was suddenly very, very still and now I could feel the tension emanating from him. And there was something else there too: despair.

He's hiding something—it's already happened.

"And Tommer," the Duke said, and now I could hear how forced was his flippancy. "In your hypothetical kidnapping, what will happen to him once I'm forced to give myself up?"

I thought about Isault's family: his wife, his two sons, and a little girl who painted pictures of puppies hoping her father would give her one as a present. "I'm sorry, your Grace. They'll kill him, too. If I'm right—I know you may not want to believe me—"

"I believe you," Jillard said, his voice only a little above a whisper. "I believe all of it." His shoulders sank and the air whooshed out of him all at once. It was as if I were watching a performer as he came off the stage, too exhausted to remain in character anymore.

"They've already taken Tommer, haven't they?"

Again Jillard shared a look with Shiballe, and then he turned back to me. "Yes, damn you. The reason I believe you—the only reason you're not already hanging from the apple tree outside my chambers—is that two days ago my son, the only person I love in this world, was kidnapped."

Parrick's face turned so red I thought he might attack Jillard then and there. "Why weren't the Knights told?" he demanded. "We should be searching for him! He's an eleven-year-old boy, damn it! He can't—"

"You weren't told," Jillard said, "because we know exactly where he is."

"Where?" Parrick asked. "I'll get my men—"

"At this very moment Tommer sits fifty feet below us, and the assassin's blade is at his throat, ready to open his neck."

"He's here?" I asked. "*In your own dungeons?* But how—?"

"Tommer said he wanted to see a Dashini assassin for himself. He'd heard the stories—of course it would be a great adventure to him, to see one in the flesh. And of course, I refused him. There are only two keys to the lower dungeon: one is held by the watch-guard and the other is in a secure case in my personal chambers. Tommer snuck in and stole my key."

"What about his personal Knights?" Parrick sounded furious. "Surely they should have been with him at all times—?"

"They were. He convinced them to accompany him—to *protect* him. He's a good boy, but he's not always obedient." The Duke's voice dropped and I realized he was hurting badly. Despite my dislike for Jillard, I believed Tommer really was the one person he truly cared for.

I also remembered what the boy's disobedience had cost Bal Armidor, the troubadour whom he had loved—was he really so callous that he would risk the lives of his Knights, knowing the cost of his father's displeasure?

"Those damned fools!" Parrick said. "I'll beat them to within an inch of their lives when I—" He looked at Jillard, then at me and then at the floor as he suddenly realized how strange his outburst was, given his own particular situation.

"I believe they are already aware of their error," Jillard said.

"So what happened?" I asked.

"The assassin overpowered the Knights, my torturers, and the other guards in the lower dungeon. From the smell down there it would appear he's killed a fair number of them. Once a day he sends a rather damned Sir Toujean to pass on his demands. Sir Toujean is not able to remain with us as he has a very long rope tied around his neck."

"And what are the demands?"

"I should have said 'demand', singular: he wishes me to present myself to him."

"That's it? When?"

"At a time of my convenience." Jillard looked stricken. "He said that Tommer would . . . he said my son would last a number of days yet."

"Why haven't you had your forces break into the lower dungeon?"

"Because, Trattari, quite apart from the fact that the assassin has promised to kill Tommer if I try, we actually can't get in. I believe I told you the last time I had the pleasure of your company that this palace is the most secure building in all of Tristia. Its dungeons are . . . extensive. The walls are solid stone, five feet thick, and the only door, two feet of reinforced iron, is supported by rods set deep into the stone above and below. There are only two keys, both of which are now in the hands of the assassin. The lower dungeon was designed to be inescapable. It appears that we made it impregnable as well."

29

THE BLACK DOOR

The thing I hate most about the Ducal Palace of Rijou is, of course, its current owner. But the original architect comes a close second, as do those who have added to it over the past two hundred years: it's the way they have found no end of inventive ways to make the palace into a perfect representation of Ducal power, from the massive three-tiered central ballroom, cunningly designed to make invited guests feel progressively smaller and less important as they are relegated to the lower tiers, to the rooms and hallways which become narrower, their ceilings lower, depending, the further away they are from the Duke's own chambers. Every door and alcove is designed to remind those passing of their station. And a particular favorite of mine: the unlocked stores of food and supplies are situated on the first floor below the ground, along with most of the servants' quarters—and why tempt ill-treated maids and footmen with mouth-watering delicacies and easily stolen supplies? Because no servant of Jillard would ever be sufficiently desperate—or stupid—to risk the consequences, not when there's a handy architectural reminder of the wisdom of self-restraint in the form of a huge iron door at the end of that hall-way, beyond which lies the twenty-foot-long staircase to the first floor of Jillard's extensive dungeons. And if that's not quite enough to keep underpaid and underfed staff in line, just enough sound reaches the servants' quarters to provide not-so-subtle reminders—day and night—of what will happen if they are caught stealing.

Rijou vae aurut et phaba, the old saying goes. *Rijou runs on money and fear.*

Some time around midnight eight of us made our way down those very stairs. As I had Kest, Dari, and Valiana with me, Jillard had insisted that he should be equally represented, in the form of Shiballe and two Knights—one of whom was Parrick. That struck me as both odd and a little sad: for all his money and power, Jillard could think of no man he trusted more than the one who'd been deceiving him for the past five years. On the other hand, the people of Rijou have always been pragmatic. It was clear Jillard owed his life to Parrick, and several times over.

Parrick had removed his armor and was wearing his greatcoat, and as Jillard and I both stared at him I realized neither of us was pleased.

"It's mine, damn you both," Parrick said. "I earned it twice over and the man who disagrees is welcome to try and take it from me."

The Duke and I looked at each other for a moment. "Wear whatever you want," Jillard said at last. "Just bring me back my son."

The other Knight—the mousey-haired and limp-wristed Sir Istan—was the only other person Shiballe had entrusted with the information that the Duke's son had been kidnapped. I wondered if that was because Sir Istan was so junior he was unlikely to have any ambitious allies yet. He was a nervous young man who descended the stairs in slow, clanking steps, all the while looking as if he had no expectation of returning from the dungeon. I'd spent five days at Jillard's mercy not so long ago—*was it really only five days?*—and I entirely understood the young Knight's fear.

What if this is all an elaborate trick? I thought. *The murders, the story about the assassin—what if it's simply a ruse to get me back here to this perfect little hell Jillard has created?* No, surely not. Even for me, that was taking paranoia to extremes . . . and yet

I'd learned that those who wielded power in Rijou were entirely capable of setting the whole world on fire to achieve even the pettiest of ambitions.

I expect I'm about to find out, one or another, I thought as Shiballe brought us to a halt at the bottom of the stairs.

"We will travel along this main corridor," he announced in a high-pitched, imperious tone, pointing, "and then turn into a smaller one that will bring us to a black-iron door, beyond which lies the stairway down to the bottom level. The black door is the only way to the second level. As Duke Jillard has already made plain, it cannot be breached." He looked at me, not bothering to hide his intense dislike. "So I think this is the right time to ask: how exactly do you plan to get past the door?"

I had no idea, of course, but unless I could find a way into the inner dungeon, Tommer would end up dead, followed shortly thereafter by Jillard, and once the Ducal line of Rijou was wiped out, the duchy would fall apart, and before we knew what had hit us, Tristia would have descended into the chaos of civil war.

"Oh, that's easy," I said. "I'm going to knock."

Shiballe snorted and led us down the wide stone hallway that was the main thoroughfare for the first level of the dungeon. It was intersected by smaller passages illuminated by small bronze braziers hanging from the ceiling.

"How many cells are there?" Dariana asked, peering down one of the passages.

"On this level? One hundred. Each one can hold between three and ten prisoners, depending on how comfortable we wish to make them."

"You can hold *a thousand* prisoners?" She sounded incredulous. "What possible reason could you ever have to lock up that many people?"

Shiballe looked back at me and smiled. "Insurrection."

As the sound of our footsteps reverberated along the halls, I could hear the prisoners moving in their cells and voices calling urgently, "Please, lords—there's been a mistake! I never meant no . . ." The first voice faded into nothingness as we passed but it was immediately replaced by another, and then another.

"How many men do you have here currently?" Kest asked the Duke.

"Not very many at present—fewer than fifty," he said, "along with maybe twenty women and five or six children."

"You have *children* in your dungeons?" Valiana looked ready to pull her sword then and there.

Duke Jillard looked at her with an expression somewhere between bemusement and genuine confusion. "It seemed cruel to separate them from their parents."

I slowed, and without a word Kest matched my pace. I waved the others on and when they were a little way ahead of us I turned to him and murmured, "If we do manage to get Tommer out alive and somehow prevent a civil war and keep Trin off the throne and—by some further miracle—I don't die very soon . . . If we do get there, Kest, you and I are coming back here and we're going to tear this place down stone by stone."

Kest looked around at the walls, the floor and ceiling. "It looks to be hewn out of several thousand tons of rock, Falcio. Just saying. It might be a little difficult."

I drew one of my throwing knives and scratched a line into the stone wall next to us. "We'll find a way."

"'The First Law is that men are free,'" Kest quoted. "Does that apply to criminals as well?"

"No," I replied, "but knowing what I do of Jillard—and however little that might be, it's still *far* too much—I suspect there are plenty of people down here whose punishment does not fit the crime."

A soft, gravelly voice reverberated from somewhere in the dungeon. "First Law is men are free," it said.

I looked around, trying to work out where the sound was coming from.

"Come on," Kest said, "it's just someone repeating what I just said."

"First Law is men are free," the voice sang tunelessly. "Without freedom . . . can't serve heart. Can't serve Gods. Can't serve Kings.

Fuck Kings. Can't serve *heart*. Heart matters. Gods . . . Gods no matter. Heart matters. Man must be free."

My eyes went wide. I knew that voice. *He called out your name a great deal toward the end,* Shiballe had said. Lying little monster.

I started down the hallway, crying, "Kest, help me find that voice."

We ran up and down little passageways, past cells small and large, some filled with ingenious torture devices bristling with spikes and screws and sporting thick leather straps and some with nothing more elaborate than the smell of shit and urine and human suffering. The echoes pulled us in all directions.

"What am I looking for?" Kest asked at last.

"An ugly brute of a man with pepper-gray hair shaved close to his scalp. Just follow the sound."

"Fourth Law is child not being hurt," the voice half-sang, half-hummed. "Child too small, too stupid, no understand. Can't put child in prison. Can't fine child. Can't hurt child. Fourth Law is—"

"Falcio!" I heard Kest shout, and he appeared at the head of a passageway and waved at me to attract my attention.

I joined him in front of a cell some seven feet square separated from the corridor by thick floor-to-ceiling iron bars; between two of them was a small iron door, presumably to let guards in and out. Inside was a man, chained to the back wall. He had pale, mottled skin, small eyes, and thick lips. His big hands were bound halfway up the wall, making it impossible for him to sit. I remembered those hands, the thick fingers, in the hard knuckles that had struck me so many times I had doubted whether any feeling was left in them. Those hands had beat me bloody for hour after hour, and day after day while I was Jillard's prisoner—but they had also lifted me up off the floor of my cell and carried me along the hallway, up the stairs, and out of the dungeon. This man—and I didn't even know his name—had been both my torturer and my liberator. I had called him Ugh.

"Fifth Law is . . . fucking hells! What is Fifth Law? Okay. Okay. First Law. First Law is men are free. If man no free, how can man serve heart? How can—?"

"Ugh!" I called, and was surprised to hear my voice was shaking.

He looked up and slowly his eyes started to focus. "Who you? You come hit again, eh? Okay, okay. Come hit me. Break your hands, fucking girl."

"Ugh, it's me—it's Falcio."

Again he tried to focus his eyes. "Falcio who?" His gaze drifted to my coat. "Greatcoat. Fucking Greatcoat, eh? You back here, stupid, fucking guy? Tough guy, tough like fucking crazy horse. I throw life away for you and you crazy come back here? Should have freed fucking horse instead."

"I'm free, Ugh, look!" I held up my arms so he could see I wasn't shackled. "I'm not a prisoner—but what in all the hells are you doing locked up?"

"Caught me, some fucking Knights, bring me back. Is law torturer no set dumb Greatcoat free, I guess. Like King's First Law only backward, eh?" He gave a hoarse little laugh.

"Falcio, someone's coming," Kest warned.

I looked at Ugh, chained to the wall. Now he was focusing: his tiny eyes in his wide face were staring at me. "I'll be back," I said. "I'm getting you out of here. I swear it."

"Swear? Fucking Greatcoat. You make promises. Shit . . . all shit. Come back, don't come back, is all same. Just . . ."

"What is it?"

"Tell me King's Fifth Law. I forget. Every time, I forget."

I wrapped my hands around the bars of his cell. Ugh had heard me repeating those laws over and over during my captivity here; the King's Laws had held my mind together during my torment—and those same laws had somehow, against all possible reason, changed his heart. "The Fifth Law is that no man shall be punished unjustly without first being proven guilty of a crime sufficient to warrant such punishment," I said softly, and then, louder, "No man shall be tortured."

Ugh grinned. "Ah, yes. Fifth Law: no torture. Now I remember. Funny, this one I forget all the time, eh?"

"I'll come back," I promised.

"Fine, fine, you come back. Stupid fucking tough guy Greatcoats. Probably back in chains, yes?"

Kest and I ran back and found the others waiting at the end of the large hallway. "See anyone you know?" Shiballe asked with a smirk.

I badly wanted to beat him senseless, but his cruelty was just another useless distraction—one of dozens that stood between me and whoever was engineering all this chaos.

"Just take us to the door," I said.

Shiballe ushered us down a smaller corridor that went on for nearly a hundred feet until it ended at the black-iron door. It might be two feet thick but it was less than six feet high; someone as tall as Parrick would need to stoop to pass through. The door must have weighed at least a ton. It had a row of three slits, each about six inches high and two inches wide, set about a foot from the top. Looking through one, I could see a roughly hewn stairway that I guessed must lead down into the depths of the second level. I could also see the remarkable thickness of the door itself; it was clear I'd have as much luck levitating the palace from the ground as I would breaking through that door.

Sir Istan pressed his face to the slits. "It's like . . . it's like the throat of some ancient creature beyond. The rock of the passage is black and red like the inside of—"

"That will suffice, Sir Istan," the Duke said. He turned to me. "Well, we are here and now you have seen the door. Do you have a plan?"

I looked carefully at every single part of the door, from its front face to the edges where it met the stone walls. "There are no hinges," I said. "How does it open?"

"There is a rod, six inches wide, that passes vertically through the left side of the door and into the rock, ceiling and floor and acts as the hinge. When the door is unlocked, it swivels around that rod."

I looked for the place where the rod passed through the door, but couldn't see any signs of it, and in any case, I doubted it would be a weakness. The stone above the door was rough and jutted out in places, forming tiny little ledges, but the rock was carved, not made from individual pieces that might be worked loose.

"Why not just use a battering ram?" Dariana asked. "They can bring down castle walls."

"That's precisely the point," Jillard said. "The door itself is stronger than the rock—even if we had a ram strong enough, *and* we could get it down this passageway, *and* fit in the men needed to lift it, it would take days to even begin to damage the door. But what it would do is destroy the rock, and in the process the ceiling would disintegrate, and it wouldn't be too long before it started to fall and bury everyone, sealing the passageway forever and leaving my son trapped below."

"Pick the lock," I said. "There are specialists with the skills to break into even the most secure of locks, and I imagine there is no shortage of such skilled masters in Rijou."

"This lock is exceedingly complex. If we had one of the keys, it might well be possible for one of those 'specialists' to devise a way of picking the lock—but we don't."

I stared at the lock. It didn't look much different from others I'd seen.

"If you don't believe me, feel free to consult with one of these 'specialists'—we passed a number of them on the way here."

"You locked them up?" Kest asked.

"They failed me—besides, if they really are such 'skilled masters' then I imagine they'll find their own way out."

"I don't understand," Valiana said. "What happens if the guard of the watch loses the key? Do they just come and wake you up so they can borrow your key to attend to the prisoners?"

"If a guard loses the key," Jillard replied, "he loses his life along with it. We hang him here by the door for several weeks; it encourages those who follow him to be more mindful."

"You certainly know how to inspire loyalty," I said.

"I know how to ensure discipline."

"Wait a minute," Dariana interrupted, ignoring his glower. "If you've punished a guard for losing a key, wouldn't that mean there's another key out there somewhere?"

"No," Jillard replied, "both times the key was lost the other guards were ordered to find it or share their comrade's fate. Funnily enough, both times it was soon recovered."

Saints! How does a man like Jillard stay in power, even in a place as corrupt as Rijou?

"Hard to imagine why your Knight-Commander and two hundred other Knights just abandoned you," I said, wondering how his guards dealt with the constant possibility that a single small mistake—even a tiny misfortune like a broken link on the chain that holds their keys—would likely result in not only their own death, but the deaths of those who worked with them?

"What about some kind of acid?" Valiana asked. "Duchess Patriana knew of many—"

Jillard held up a hand. "I am aware of Patriana's experiments in this area, and you're right, such a technique might well work—but it would take acid weeks, even months, to get through the outer shell of the door, let alone the bolts set in the stone surrounding it."

"Well," I said, "that just leaves one way in."

Jillard locked eyes with me.

Glare all you want, you miserable bastard, I thought. *You're the one who let your son get kidnapped.*

The Duke finally dropped his gaze and stepped aside from the door. "Very well. Do it."

I stepped up to the iron door, extended my hand toward it, and knocked.

The sound reverberated throughout the passageway and down the stairs beyond the door. After a few moments, I knocked again, and then again.

The eight of us stood in that narrow stone corridor and waited. With each minute that passed I could see Jillard's face turn paler and paler. *He truly loves Tommer,* I thought. *He's a monster and a tyrant, and yet his heart is trembling in fear at the thought of losing his child. He is oblivious to the fact that he's destroyed the lives of hundreds— maybe even thousands—of other parents and children. What strange creatures this world creates.*

Dariana looked at the door and gave a smirk. "Looks like no one's ho—"

Kest held up a hand to silence her.

"I hear it too," Valiana said.

I put my ear to the slits in the door. A soft shuffling sound was just about discernible, gradually growing louder, and soon I could hear footsteps on the stairs. There was another sound as well: crying. I turned my head and peered through the slits in time to see a man coming up the stairs, apparently struggling with each step. He was naked to the waist and covered in so much blood that he looked as if someone had tried to drown him in a vat of it. From the pained expression on his face and the terror in his eyes it was likely the blood was his own, covering up painful cuts from which it seeped.

As he came up the final step, his head jerked for just an instant, nearly sending him back down the stairs, and that's when I saw the rope tied around his neck. It extended all the way back into the darkness.

Duke Jillard pulled me back so that he could look through the slit himself. "Sir Toujean," he called.

"Your Grace," he started, "forgive me! *Forgive me!*"

The rope pulled taut again and from the depths of the darkness I heard the faintest whisper. It was too soft for me to make out individual words, but Sir Toujean could obviously hear.

"He asks if you have considered his invitation. He says"—more whispering, then—"he says that he begins to worry that Tommer . . . ah, Gods forgive me, your Grace . . ." The rope pulled taut again, and Sir Toujean gave a strangled cough and grabbed at his neck. He pulled himself together and managed, "He says that Tommer fares poorly. They use—They use a kind of dust, your Grace. They blow it in his face and the boy . . . he—"

Sir Toujean began to wail wordlessly.

"Dust?" Sir Istan asked, looking bemused.

"Dashini dust," I said. "They blow it into the faces of their victims. It drives you mad from fear if you're not used to it—even a strong fighter loses his bearings, and that makes it easier for the Dashini to kill."

"He keeps using it on Tommer, sir," Toujean said to me. "He blows it into his face, morning and at night. Tommer . . . Sir, I don't think he can take much more—"

Saints. An eleven-year-old boy and he's being exposed to the Dashini dust, over and over again? He's being killed through fear alone.

"Sir Toujean, tell him that I will give him anything!" the Duke started, "*anything*, if he—"

Toujean's voice became louder, almost annoyed. "He doesn't want *anything*, your Grace! He just wants you!"

"How?" I asked.

The Knight's eyes suddenly focused on me through the slit. "What?"

"How? How is the Duke supposed to go to him?" If the assassin wanted Jillard, then he'd have to open the door at some point—that could be our opening.

"He says the Duke is to stand where he is, on the other side of this door, with two men supporting him. Then . . ." A pause. "Then the duke must take a knife and slit his own throat and let the blood fall down through the gap below the door. There are twenty-seven stairs. When the blood has run down to the bottom, the boy will be freed."

Twenty-seven steps, each one a foot deep. How much blood can a man lose and still survive? I glanced at Kest. He shook his head.

"How then does the assassin hope to escape?" Kest asked.

Sir Toujean's eyes flitted back and forth at us through the thin slit in the door. "I don't think he does. He says he has one mission—to kill the Duke of Rijou—and that he doesn't need to escape to complete this mission."

There is no more perfect trap for your enemy than the one in which you yourself are willing to die. There was no way to win this without the missing key.

I turned to Jillard. "Beg," I whispered.

"What?"

"Beg," I said. "Scream for mercy, as loud as you can, like a man going mad with grief. Beg for mercy for Tommer. *Now*."

Jillard looked at me, his mouth tightening, but after a moment he opened his mouth and began to shout, "Mercy! Mercy for my son—please, I beg you, he is just a boy, an innocent—and he is innocent of *my* crimes. I will give you anything—*anything* you ask, if only you will let me hold him in my arms again!"

As the Duke shouted and screamed and wailed, I stuck my face against the slit. "Sir Toujean," I whispered fiercely, "there are two keys. *Two*. One that Tommer stole, and the one that was held by the watch-guard."

"The watch-guard is dead," he said. "I think . . . I think the assassin has both keys."

"Then you must find a way to steal one from him."

"But I can't," Sir Toujean moaned. "He—don't you understand? He isn't human, he's—"

"Listen to me, Sir Toujean: when you were a boy, you dreamed of being a hero, did you not?" I waited but there was no answer, only Jillard shouting his pleas and Sir Toujean's moaning. "*Answer me! Did you not dream of being a hero?*"

"I . . . I did, sir . . . I wanted to be a Knight like those—"

"That wasn't *real*, Sir Toujean. That was just a story. But *this* is real. *This* is where the hero is called. *This* is when the heart of the warrior pumps blood and iron and unrelenting, mad belligerence through his veins. *You* are the steel, Sir Toujean, not your armor or your sword, but *you*. Your hour is called. The boy you were commands you to be the hero you must become. Get me one of those keys!"

The Knight cried out, a sound half wail, half strangled laugh, then the rope tautened and as I watched, Sir Toujean was pulled back, one step at a time, into the darkness below.

Duke Jillard began to sway and Parrick reached out a hand and steadied him. "Your Grace?"

"I'm . . . I'm all right," he said. "It was just the shouting, that's all."
He turned to me. "This dust . . . I know a little about it. What does it
feel like? What is my son going through?"

What does it feel like to a boy who's trapped and alone? *Like a
hundred hells*, I thought. *Tommer is living through a hundred different hells.*

30

THE DEPTHS

Hours later I was still sitting on the dusty stone floor in front of the black door that stood between me and Tommer. I knew little of the boy except that he had loved the troubadour Bal Armidor, as I had, and that when I called for Jurors at the Rock of Rijou, he had picked up a coin, and in doing so he had saved not just my life but Aline's too.

I can't break you, I said silently to the door. *I can't melt you or drill through you or knock you down. How can something as small as a key be your undoing?*

Duke Jillard sat a few feet away watching me. The others had gone back into one of the wider hallways to discuss ever more elaborate and unlikely means to save Tommer.

"It's hopeless, isn't it?" Jillard asked. "I have built an inescapable prison for my enemies, and now they have trapped my very soul inside it."

There's a way. There has to be a way.

The watch bell echoed through the dungeon, its pitch shifting slightly with each reverberation until the sound became an eerie chorus.

"Four o'clock," Jillard said. "How long, do you suppose, before the assassin torments Tommer again with that infernal dust?" His eyes were full of anguish, mixed with the realization that he himself was responsible for everything that now transpired. He looked up at the narrow slits in the iron door. "I brought in a mage in on the first day of Tommer's capture, an expensive one. Rumor has it he was the one who cast the spell that tore down the castle walls at Neville."

"And what did he say?" I asked.

Jillard gave a hoarse laugh. "He said if I wanted him to tear down the walls of the palace he could, for a fee, do that."

"But not this door?"

"Iron," the Duke said. "Iron is the problem. It weakens the forces the mage draws on and makes them split apart."

"How does that work?" I asked, not really expecting an answer. I hate magic.

"Who knows?" Jillard said. "They speak in riddles and poems, these mages and wizards. There are times when I find myself quite hating magic and those who wield it. I should have imprisoned the smug bastard, but cross one mage and you've crossed them all."

It made sense, I supposed. There were few men who could work real magic in Tristia. Those who did had no doubt learned long ago the necessity of looking out for one another. Too bad the guards in the dungeon weren't smart enough to do the same.

Wait . . . What if they were smart enough? I turned to Jillard. "The other watch-guards—how many are there?"

"Four in total," he replied.

"One down in the dungeon—presumably dead?"

"Sir Toujean said so, yes."

I got to my feet. "I need to see those remaining three watch-guards!"

"Why?" Jillard asked, rising as well. "I already told you—"

"Because you said you killed any guard who lost the key, and that you threatened to kill the others unless it was found."

"I don't see how that—"

"You said they found the key both times after it was lost. What are the odds that on two separate occasions something as small as a key was lost and then found again so quickly?"

Jillard looked at me as if I'd just failed to calculate the sum of two and two. "Since the guards did, in fact, find the key, then I suppose the odds are reasonably good."

"That's the point—they didn't *find* it. Your watch-guards knew they would face death if a key was lost and not recovered, so they took steps to protect each other."

Jillard's eyes narrowed. "How?"

He still couldn't see it. For all his cruel and cunning brilliance, the obvious answer had completely escaped him. "They had another key made."

Shiballe's cheeks jiggled as he shook his head. "Your Grace, I regret . . . I cannot bring you the watch-guards—they fled the city two days ago when they learned that Tommer had been taken."

"Impossible! I'll have them flayed alive for this—I'll see their families—"

"You threaten too many people," I said. "Death for this and death for that—your watch-guards played the odds."

Jillard's expression was defiant for a moment, then he crumbled. "Then that avenue is closed to us and my son will suffer and die for the shortsightedness of his father."

I shared the Duke's despair. If there was a third key, only the watch-guards would likely know about it. Damn the Dashini to a hundred hells for being willing to torture and kill a child. *Fourth Law is child not being hurt.* Ugh's clumsy rendition of the Law echoed in my head.

I grabbed Shiballe by the arm. "Give me the key for the cells on this floor—*now*."

"I will do no such thing!" Shiballe said, doing his best to pull away from me.

"If you're thinking it might be used on this lock somehow, then you're wasting—" Jillard started, but I held up a hand to stop him.

"It's not that—I have a different idea. Tell Shiballe to give me the key."

"Never! A Trattari with the keys of Rijou's—?"

"Do as he asks," the Duke said.

"Your Grace, this is a trick! Whatever lies he's told you, he'll just take the key to set the prisoners free, and then use the confusion to flee the palace."

"And what if he does?" Jillard asked. "Will water no longer flow down to the ground when poured from a jug? Will day no longer give way to night? Will Tommer not die just as quickly? Give him the key, Shiballe."

Shiballe reached into his robes and withdrew a chain of keys. He fiddled with them for a moment until he'd finally removed one. He handed it to me.

"I need the one for the chains in the cells as well," I said.

Shiballe glanced again at the Duke, and then back to me. Hatred in the eyes is, sadly, an easy thing to spot. He pulled a second, smaller key from the ring and reluctantly handed it over.

"Wait here," I said.

I ran back toward Ugh's cell, the others following close behind me. As I arrived I could hear Ugh muttering, "Fourth Law is child not responsible. Child too stupid. Not know difference. Fifth Law is . . . shit . . . Fifth Law is—"

I opened the door to the cell and Ugh looked at me. "Hey, fucking tough guy Greatcoat. You come back? Join me here? Plenty of room. What is Fifth Law again?"

I knelt down and undid the cuffs locking his hands to the walls. "The Fifth Law is there shall be no unjust punishment," I said.

He rubbed at his wrists. "Right, right. Fucking Fifth Law always problem for me."

I put a hand on Ugh's shoulder. "The key to the black door," I said. "Where is it?"

Ugh's eyes focused on me. "Is only two keys for black door. One is watch-guard's. One is Duke's. Go see watch-guard. He less likely have you killed for asking." His eyes swiveled, and he saw Duke

Jillard standing with the others outside the cell. "Ah. Too late, looks like." He started putting his hands back in the cuffs.

"No," I said, pulling his hands away to stop him from chaining himself again, "the *other* key."

"What other key?"

"The one the guards keep in case they lose the watch-key."

Ugh's eyes narrowed for just an instant. *He knows*, I thought.

"Is no other key," he said firmly. "Two keys. One Duke. One watch-guard."

"There's another key," I said, and gently put a hand on his shoulder. "It's all right. You will not be punished." I turned and glared at the Duke to make my point. "Tell us, please."

Ugh shook his head. "Even if other key, watch-guards no talk to rough men like me. Call us dogs."

"But some dogs pay close attention, don't they?" I said. "Some dogs know to keep an eye out in case there's something they might need to know about one day."

Ugh's eyes drifted to the Duke. "No. Dogs sit in corner and shut up. When dog stands, owner kicks. Dog stands again, owner kills."

"That won't happen here," I said. "I won't let it happen."

"Sometimes dog decides, better to die," Ugh said. "Such dog not care about what happens to owner after."

"It's not him—it's Tommer. The boy—he's trapped down in the lower dungeon."

Ugh's expression softened. "Is no place for boy. Is place for . . . ugliness."

"That's right," I said, "it's not a place for a boy. We've got to get him out, Ugh. You and I, we have to get him out of there, now. We need the key."

Ugh looked at me and snorted. "You talk to me like fucking horse, eh? Like you talk to crazy fucking horse. Mad beast covered in scars and hate and you make her think like man. Like man better than me. What you say? You say little girl in cage with horse is little horse. You say, Dam haf fal . . . something like . . ."

"Dan'ha vath fallatu." *I am of your herd.*

"You think I am like horse, eh? You think boy is like me? Like he is my herd? He is rich. Father is rich. I have nothing. He is handsome. I am ugly."

"He is scared," I said. "He is in the dark."

Very slowly, Ugh's eyes began to fill with tears. "Fucking horse. Fucking horse not kill little girl just because you say Damhaf falato. Fucking horse better than me."

"The horse isn't better than you." I said.

"Say it again," Ugh pleaded, tears still streaming down his cheeks. "Say Damhaf—"

"Dan'ha vath fallatu."

He pushed himself up from the floor awkwardly, his legs wavering as he stood. "Fucking horse. Horse no better than me. I go get fucking little boy then you tell horse, eh? You tell horse I save little boy." He stumbled, then pushed past the others to enter the passageway. "Come on," he said. "We get boy now. Fourth Law is child not get hurt . . ."

The eight of us followed Ugh through the passage, down into the main corridor and through a maze of passageways until I was sure we had circled back to the same place. I began to fear he was lost, but at last he turned into one and announced, "Here," he said. "Is here."

We were standing in front of the black door.

"You damned dog," Shiballe shouted, "you worthless piece of excrement! We already *knew* where the door was, you fool! You've wasted our time for nothing."

"You know already?" Ugh asked, turning to the rest of us.

"Of course we know," Shiballe snarled.

Ugh looked to me questioningly and I nodded.

"If you know already, then why you fucking standing here?" He stretched up onto tiptoes and felt around on one of the little stone ledges near the top of the door. Turning back to me, he held out his meaty fist. When he unclenched his fingers, he revealed a six-inch-long iron key. It had nearly twenty different teeth of varying lengths and shapes. "Stupid people. Damhaf falato. We go get boy now, yes?"

31
THE LOWER DUNGEON

We made our way slowly down to the lower dungeon, the dim light of our lanterns illuminating the dust and dried blood that snaked like veins of ore against the rocky surface of the twenty-seven stairs.

"The path becomes narrower as we go down," Kest pointed out. "If an ambush awaits us, it will be difficult to evade it."

I didn't bother to respond; I was too busy trying to deal with the smell. You sometimes hear storytellers trying to frighten their audiences by talking about the scent of despair. They're not being poetic. Fear really does have a smell. If you mix sweat and shit and blood with stale air and dank, musty walls, *like magic!* as a jongleur might say, you get the genuine scent of human despair. That's what greeted us at the bottom of the stairs.

Dariana slid ahead of me and peered down one of the dark passageways that curved away from the stairwell. "What in all the hells is this place?"

"Hell is right fucking word, lady," Ugh replied.

I tried for something clever, but nothing came. I've spent more than my share of time in dungeons, but this place . . . I couldn't begin to imagine how I could ever escape from here.

Shiballe noticed my unease and smiled. "The passages split off in odd directions, like a garden maze," he said proudly. "Even if a man were to escape his cell, he would have great difficulty finding his way back to the stairway. Many of the passageways lead to dead ends, and in some, just to keep things interesting, the shadows hide pits in the floor. When we put a man down here, Trattari, he *never* comes back up into the light."

"Unless he just decides to take control of it instead," Dariana said. "Then what do you do, you fat slug?"

I noted Duke Jillard's wide-eyed gaze as he glanced about the endless dripping walls, as if he'd never seen the place where his orders were carried out. "It was not by my—"

"Shut up," I whispered, trying to shake off my own fear. Damn. This all had to happen fast. We needed to figure out where Tommer and the assassin were before we ourselves were discovered. "We're going to have to split up." I turned to Duke Jillard. "You need to go back, your Grace. If the assassin sees you, he'll try to kill you first, then, his mission complete, he'll turn his blade on Tommer."

Jillard, Duke of Rijou, cast a sideways glance at Ugh. "You think I will let this . . . this *creature* risk himself for my son while I hide upstairs in my room?"

"Fuck you," Ugh said amiably.

"Foul dog!" Shiballe spat. "I'll have your tongue torn from your mouth when this—"

Ugh reached out and put his hand on top of Shiballe's fat head and he squeezed, very slowly. "I may be dog," he said, "but I am fucking tough dog, eh? Fucking strong dog." Shiballe's eyes grew wide as the pressure from Ugh's fingers began pressing hard into the flesh of his skull. "Maybe boy needs a tough guy right now, eh? Not fat worm that slinks along the ground."

"Enough, all of you," Valiana said. Her face was white as a sheet but her voice was firm. "Ugh, let go: Tommer is down here and he needs us to find him, not fight among ourselves."

Ugh released Shiballe's head and smiled. "Pretty girl—you whore? Whores nice to me."

Saint Iphilia-who-cuts-her-own-heart, these are the heroes you send me to help save the boy?

"Let's go," I said. "Kest, you take Sir Istan and Ugh. Valiana, you take Parrick. I'll take his Grace."

"You're leaving me with the slug?" Dariana said, eyeing Shiballe.

"He knows this level better than anyone else. If it helps, it's only of nominal importance that he comes back alive."

She grinned. Shiballe didn't.

"What do we do if we find something?" Valiana asked.

"If you find Tommer, have one person free him while the other stands guard."

"And if we find the assassin?" This time she didn't quite manage to keep the tremor from her voice.

"Scream as loudly as you can. The rest of us will follow the sound. Do whatever you can to keep him at bay. If he's Dashini, don't try to engage him like you would a normal opponent because he's not. It'll be like trying to fight someone lashing at you using a snake with a three-foot steel tongue. Do anything you can to keep him away from you, and for the Saints' sake, don't breathe in any of the dust."

"One more thing," Kest said. "When we find the assassin, step back and let me through."

"Why?" Sir Istan asked, unable to keep the look of relief from his young face.

"Because he is mine and no one else's. *Mine.*" Kest looked at me. "I *need* this," he said.

I could see the reddish glow just starting to push at the edges of his skin and I nodded. "All right. Somewhere in this hell is a man who lives his life in shadow and dances with death. He's never known fear." I drew my rapier from its sheath. "We're going to teach him."

I've tracked killers before. A verdict imposed after a murderer has fled his village doesn't do much good for the family who've just lost a loved one and it does even less for the next family the killer finds. It's not exactly my strong point—Brasti's always been better, and is never slow to remind me of that. So were a few of the other Greatcoats—Quillata could track a man *weeks* after he'd left town.

But neither of them were here.

"Are you blind, Trattari?" Jillard asked, standing over me as I knelt down on the floor. "The tracks are everywhere!"

"Keep your voice down," I whispered, hoping the others were doing a better job of moving silently through the dungeon. "The tracks are the problem."

Normally the problem with following a man is that you're doing it over many miles, searching desperately for the smallest sign of his passing. Here in the bowels of Jillard's dungeon I had the opposite problem: there were tracks *everywhere*, imprinted into the filth that covered the uneven stone floors of the maze.

It didn't help that we had to move so slowly. Sometimes the stone floors were rough and jagged, making it easy to trip, then they would become smooth and slippery—generally right before they gave way to a small man-sized pit with very pointy spikes in the bottom. Even with Jillard's lantern, the shadows were eager to swallow us. In the end, all we could do was move cautiously and try not to circle around too many times.

We're too slow, damn it. We're going too slowly.

Had there been any prisoners alive on the second level we might have been able to trade information in exchange for leniency or even release, but bad luck for us—and them, I suppose, although maybe they saw it as a welcome release—because the only ones we saw were dead. Jillard didn't appear to notice the bodies at all.

"Wait," I said, and stopped to watch a pool of blood on the floor of one of the cells gradually seeping down the cracks in the uneven floor until it eventually met the blood coming from the cell across the way. "You have your men execute prisoners in their cells?" I asked Jillard.

"Do we have time to waste on this?" he asked. "My son is somewhere down here, and so is the assassin."

"Humor me."

Jillard stopped and leaned a hand against the uneven surface of the wall. He looked tired. "If your heart is breaking for the men in these cells, you should save it for someone more deserving. Those who occupy this level of the dungeon are creatures unworthy of pity."

"Eventually we all find ourselves in need of a little pity," I said. *Great. Now I'm quoting Saint Birgid's own admonishment to me.* I set the thought aside. "But that's not my point. How are the prisoners on this level executed?"

Jillard raised an eyebrow. "How many ways are there to die? My Magisters set the punishment to fit the crime. In Rijou a man pays his debts with the coin in which he traded."

"Then we have a problem." I pointed inside one of the cells.

Jillard peered through the iron bars. "The man certainly appears to be dead. What of it?"

"Look at all the blood on the floor. It's hard to see without better light, but he's had his throat slit."

Jillard shrugged. "Then I imagine he—"

"It's not just him. Every body I've seen since we got down here has been slit across the throat."

Jillard's eyes went wide. "But why would—?"

"Because dead men can't reveal what they've seen," a voice called out from further down the passageway. "Or perhaps more importantly, *who* they've seen."

Out of reflex I raised my rapier into guard and took up position in front of the Duke. If I'd stopped to think about it I would have used him as a shield instead.

I peered into the darkness ahead of us, my eyes struggling to focus as I scanned the shadows for any signs of movement. There were none.

"Who is there? Who dares address the Duke—" Jillard started.

"Shut up, you idiot," I hissed. "Don't give anything away. *Your Grace.*"

"Sound advice," the voice replied. "However, I doubt our Lord Duke pays much heed to the wisdom of others, given the situation he finds himself in today."

I started walking forward, keeping my eyes focused on both the shadows in front of us and on the intersection ahead where an enemy might be standing in wait.

"Getting warmer," the voice said.

The proximity of the sound jarred me. *He's here.* I spun around: sitting cross-legged on the cold stone floor at the very back of the darkened chamber opposite me was a man—a *naked* man. Despite the lack of light I could tell that he was somewhere in his twenties, dark-haired and clean-shaven. His nakedness made it clear he was lean but well-muscled. He could have been anyone, except that everything about him was relaxed when it shouldn't be. He looked to be completely unfazed by the madness around him, unafraid of what any sane man should fear. He held up a hand and waved at me, and the graceful way he made that gesture—so *normal*, so simple—told me who he was—or rather, *what* he was. *Dashini.*

32

THE INTERROGATION

"Forgive me if I surprised you," the man sitting in the cell said without irony. "That was impolite of me."

My eyes went to the iron door of the cell and I felt a brief surge of relief to see that it was locked. The internal bolt was pushed well into the iron fixtures welded into the bars.

Jillard caught up with me in front of the cell and saw the man inside. "Who are you?" he demanded.

"You don't recognize me? But of course not—I was wearing my ceremonial garb when I came to see you. No matter. In my heart I am a man like you. Or no, perhaps not like you. Perhaps more like Falcio."

"You know me?" I asked.

"How could I not? You killed two of my brethren and no one has ever done that before. You're a legend to us, Falcio: a story told over and over, like a waterfall pounding away at the rock beneath it."

Hearing the Dashini say my name was just terrifying enough that I felt the need to cover my reaction with false bravado. "Let me know when you've finished erecting my statue, will you? Perhaps it could be a little taller?"

The man in the cell laughed. "I do appreciate your sense of humor—it brings light even to a dark place like this. But it's not a statue they want to build for you, Falcio, it's something much greater. Something the world will remember for a hundred years."

"You say *they* as if you were referring to someone else."

The man's expression didn't change even a fraction, but I sensed something in his stillness, a hesitation. "I have come to question the wisdom of certain agreements that have been made."

"What agreements? With whom? Did you—?"

"Enough!" Jillard interrupted. "Who is this man? Why is he here?"

"He's the assassin," I said. "He's the man who came to kill you."

Jillard looked incredulously into the cell. He must not have had the chance to interrogate the assassin when Parrick and his Knights captured him. The Duke pulled on the door, testing it. "He's locked in. How is this possible?"

"Step back from the bars," I said, pulling Jillard back to the wall with me. "If you want to live, you'll keep away from those bars. You've never been as close to death as you are right now."

The Dashini spread his arms wide. "Such a cautious nature. Look at me. I am alone. My garb has been taken from me. My blades are gone. My dust is gone. I am naked." He leaned forward in his seated position just a hair. "Defenseless."

"On this we agree," Jillard said. He turned to me. "Kill him—stab him through the heart with your sword. Now!"

My eyes stayed on the Dashini. "He's too far back in the cell for me to reach, and if I stick my arm inside the cell to try it, he'll disarm me. Then he'll have a sword."

"Then throw a knife at him, damn you!"

"Then he'll have a knife. He's Dashini, your Grace: even if I hit him, he'll just pull out the knife. It'll be in your throat before a drop of his own blood has dripped from his wound."

Jillard's tone grew angrier. "Then we'll go back up and bring crossbowmen back. They'll—"

"Shut up," I said.

The Dashini and I kept our eyes locked on each other, and though his expression was relaxed, almost indifferent, I knew he was running through the dozens of ways he could kill the Duke while trapped in his cell, even as I considered how I might stop him. He was locked behind strong iron bars, but I was the one who felt trapped and vulnerable.

After a few moments I sheathed both my rapiers.

"What are you doing?" the Duke asked.

"Keeping my hands free," I said.

"Are you mad? He is locked in a cell—even if he is hiding the key, it would take him time to reach around the bars to unlock the door."

"This Duke you guard is foolish as well as feckless," the Dashini said. "Are you sure he's worth keeping alive? I wonder, is his son just as foolish?"

Jillard started toward the bars. "We'll see who's foolish when I have your—"

I reached out and grabbed the back of the Duke's collar just as the Dashini leapt effortlessly from his sitting position. His right arm struck out from between the bars like an arrow, the fingers of his hand bunched together into a single point like a bird's beak aimed right at Jillard's throat.

I hauled the Duke back an instant before the Dashini could reach him and he fell back against the wall next to me. I struck out at the Dashini's wrist with the knuckles of my left hand, but he turned his own hand palm up and slipped under my wrist to take hold of it. But before he could tighten his grip I jerked my arm back and then immediately struck out again with my fist—but his arm had already disappeared and he was standing in the center of his cell looking at me as calmly as if he'd been standing there all day.

Duke Jillard recovered himself. This time he stayed close to the back wall.

The Dashini smiled. "Swiftly done, Falcio. I was expecting you to be slower, what with your recent health difficulties."

"You appear to know a lot about me," I said. "We'd make better friends if I knew your name."

"You know the things that matter: I am Dashini, of a sort, and I was sent here to give the final mercy to Jillard, Duke of Rijou."

"'Of a sort'?" I asked. I looked closer at his face. His features were Tristian, and if I had to guess, he might even have come from Pertine, where I was born. But that wasn't what struck me. I thought back to the faces of the two men I'd fought and killed in Rijou. "You have no markings," I said.

"I am Unblooded. The Duke was to be my first kill." He favored Jillard with a half-bow and a small smile. "It is considered a great honor."

"Why were there no other Dashini with you when you attacked the Duke?" I asked. "Where's your *azu*?"

"He was . . . incapacitated by recent events."

"Then why are you in this cell?" If he had a key, if he had a way out, he could have killed Jillard and me by now. So what was he playing at?

"Like most things in this world, the answer is less intriguing than the question would suggest." He looked up at the ceiling and then around the cell. "I am here because I was captured. The Knights rushed me. I killed three of them too quickly, they fell forward and I was momentarily unbalanced."

"That must be embarrassing for you," I said.

"Quite."

Jillard, despite his fear, could hold back no longer. "Where is my son, damn you?"

"Here," the Dashini replied, "somewhere. I hear him screaming sometimes. He cries, too, mostly at night. It's fascinating . . . he never calls out your name, Duke Jillard. He never screams, 'Daddy, Daddy, come save me.' He calls out for someone named Bal Armidor, who never comes, and so after a while he stops shouting and instead he weeps. Is that the name of a man you've had killed down here in the darkness, your Grace? Oh, and sometimes he calls out for Falcio. Isn't that odd?"

Jillard gave me a glance filled with hatred, but this time at least he wasn't stupid enough to fall for the Dashini's tactics. "Why have your fellow murderers left you in here? What do they hope to gain?"

The Dashini didn't answer. He just looked to me, his smile intact, and yet once again his expression struck me as disquieted.

"The other assassins aren't Dashini," I said.

"Then who?" Jillard asked.

"I don't know—I don't think he knows either."

Jillard's face was a mask of confusion and fear. "But Sir Toujean said the assassins were dosing Tommer with the Dashini dust to drive him mad."

"Your Knights were foolish to confiscate my belongings," the Dashini said. "They would have been safer if they'd left them here with me."

"If they'd done that," Jillard said, "you would have escaped already."

"You see?" the Dashini. "This is how simple creatures think. You see a man in a cell and you assume he is caged. Believe me, I can escape any time I choose." The Dashini looked again around the sparse cell. "Though I grant it will require a little more effort than I feel necessary to expend at this moment, and it is certainly easier to accomplish without the distraction of Falcio here trying to break my fingers."

"Then why didn't you escape earlier?" Jillard asked.

The Dashini smiled. "Because you are not yet dead, your Grace."

Jillard's sudden step back caused him to strike the back of his head against the wall.

"Who sent you to kill the Duke?" I asked.

The Dashini looked at me and tilted his head. "Why would I ever answer such a question? The Dashini have always been tasked with eliminating corruption. The time of the Dukes has passed. Surely you know this by now."

"You filthy—"

I looked at Jillard. "Your Grace, *shut up*. If you want to live, if you want Tommer to live, you need to keep your mouth shut. When he speaks to you, he does so only to make you reckless."

I turned back to the Dashini. "Why are you killing boys and girls barely old enough to understand what it means to be the child of a

Duke? Are they too so corrupt that you have to murder them in their beds under the cover of darkness?"

The Dashini stared back at me through the bars of his cell. Again his face was impassive, but there was tension there, and anger too. "We are Dashini. We kill those who must be killed." The next words came out slowly, one syllable at a time. "We do not kill children."

"And yet you murdered Duke Isault's wife and you murdered his sons, Lucan and Patrin. You murdered his little girl. She was named Avette."

She likes to paint pictures of dogs, Shuran had said. *She hopes if she can make one pleasing enough her father will give her a puppy for her birthday.*

"We were sent to kill Duke Isault," the Dashini said, "not the woman. Not her children."

"So what happened? An accident? One of your brothers slipped and accidentally murdered an entire family?"

The Dashini grimaced. "We are the sharpest of blades, not blunted wooden cudgels." His voice had genuine anger in it now. "*We* did not kill Duke Isault's family."

"Then who?"

"Perhaps it was one of you," he suggested. "The Trattari have great cause to hate the nobility."

He wanted to distract me, play on my uncertainties, and that told me something. "I think you already know it wasn't."

"More's the pity," the Dashini said. "Perhaps your King would still be alive today if he'd had better instincts. Regardless, the death of those in power always brings chaos, Falcio. You above all should know that. And when chaos comes, there are many who would take advantage of it, while laying the blame at the feet of another."

Saint Dheneph-who-tricks-the-Gods! That's why the Dashini was still here, alive, when other prisoners who were still sane had been butchered. "Hells upon hells," I said.

"What is it?" Jillard asked. "What's going on?"

That's what they did to Dara. She'd gotten the wound in her thigh fighting off a Dashini sent to kill Isault, but someone else had killed her and the Duke's family and then made it look as if Dara was responsible. One conspirator was sending the Dashini to kill the Dukes, and another was taking advantage of the chaos to kill their families. But they're not working together, which means we have two players manipulating events from the shadows: one seeking to weaken the Ducal power and the other bent on destroying it entirely.

"Tell me what's going on!" Jillard demanded frantically, "please! Tell me what's happening to my son."

I hesitated before saying my next words, if only because until that day I could never have imagined in my entire life that I would hear myself saying them. "The damned Dashini are being framed."

The men holding Tommer were going to use him to draw in Jillard and kill both of them. Then they were going to kill off the Dashini; they'd make it look as if he were responsible, but that he'd died from a wound before he could escape.

I stared at the man standing in the shadows of his cell. *I see you now. I know what troubles you, no matter how hard you try to hide it. You don't know who's killing these children. You're being played for a fool, you and all your fellow Dashini, and you don't care for it.*

The Dashini nodded, even though I hadn't spoken. Then he said, with words devoid of inflection, "We are lost." I had the strangest sensation he was pleading with me.

"Where are they?" I asked. "Where are they holding the boy? If you and your fellow Dashini aren't the ones killing the Ducal heirs, then you have no need to protect those who are."

"I do not know," he replied, "but I don't think you'll have much trouble finding him now."

"Now? Why now?" Jillard asked.

The only answer that came to my mind was to pray that Kest and the others had already found him.

A strange, high-pitched whine filled the air; at first I thought it might be some kind of flying insect frighteningly close to my ear, but the sound quickly changed, echoing off the walls and down the passageways throughout the dungeon. It became louder, an eerie moan that finally resolved into a scream of such pure terror that I felt as if I might go mad from the sound.

There was the faintest hint of sympathy in the Dashini's eyes when he said, "Because it is morning, and this is the time when they hurt the boy."

The Duke of Rijou ran through his own dungeon shouting and screaming and sounding very much like one of its prisoners. He raced up and down the maze of twisting passageways like a bat who'd lost its sense of direction, trying desperately to navigate by the echoes of his son's cries for help.

"Stop!" I said at last and grabbed him by the shoulder. I pushed him back against the wall, holding him fast even as he struggled against my grip.

"Let me go, damn you! They're torturing my son! They're—"

"Look!" I said, pointing up ahead. The shadows were obscuring the gap in the floor and the deadly spikes waiting below. A guard with experience in these passages, even someone who was just moving carefully, would spot the danger before it was too late—but an escapee running for his life would likely fall in before even realizing the trap was there. "You will not do Tommer any good if you're dead."

The Duke looked around and spotted a side-passage to our right. "There!" he said, pointing, "look! We have to go that way."

"Stop," I said, "think. Look at the ground: those are *our* tracks. We're just going around in circles."

"Saints . . . we're . . ." He twisted his head left and right. "This passage—we were here before, just a few minutes ago . . . But I—" He stopped abruptly, and his face turned into a mummer's mask, so full of despair it looked as if it had been shaped that way by a mad sculptor.

"Come on," I said gently. "I know how to find him now."

I pulled the Duke along the passageway and this time I followed a new one: the virtue of having gone in circles so many times was that I now knew which ways *not* to go. More importantly, I was also getting a sense of how sound traveled in the dungeon and now I stopped concentrating on the *loudest* echo and instead followed the one that was repeating less than the others. I hoped against hope that Kest or one of the others had figured it out before I had.

As we approached the next intersection a shadow flickered on one of the walls and I held my hand up for the Duke to stop.

"Why are—?"

I put a hand over his mouth again. "Quiet," I whispered. "Look." I pointed down the passageway. There was light there, more than we'd seen before. We had found them.

Now I just need the assassins to suffer from sudden blindness so they don't see me coming—

But before I could even begin to formulate a decent plan, Tommer started screaming again, Jillard broke free of my grip and barreled down the passage where we'd seen the light, shouting his son's name at the top of his lungs, and any possibility of a sneak attack vanished into thin air.

Damn your foolishness, Jillard, and damn my own for not knocking you out when I had the chance.

I ran behind him, both rapiers out, trying my best not to let them catch against the walls of the narrow passageway. We turned a final corner and entered a larger open area, with new passages running left and right off it. At the other end was another cell, larger than the others, but instead of vertical bars it was separated from the corridor by a solid iron wall. The large door in the middle was open and inside on the floor I saw three men—Tommer's Knights, I assumed, all covered with blood. I recognized Sir Toujean, who was awkwardly trying to get to his feet. I didn't know the Knight next to him; the third was lying dead in a pool of blood near the door. In the center of the cell, lying on his back and looking almost as if he were asleep, was Tommer, Jillard's son.

"Tommer!" the Duke screamed as he ran down the passage and into the cell.

"Your Grace," Sir Toujean moaned, "Sir Odiard and I heard footsteps and we prayed to Guereste, God of War that it was you."

"The assassins," I said urgently, "where are they?"

The Knight pointed down one of the smaller passageways. "When the Dashini heard the Duke coming they ran down that way."

"How many?"

"Five?"

"*Five* Dashini?"

Now Toujean looked uncertain. "Not . . . I'm not sure exactly, maybe . . . But no, they were wearing masks—they must have been Dashini."

Hells. Even if the assassins weren't Dashini—and I was becoming more and more certain that they weren't—I wouldn't be able to stop five of them by myself, especially when they'd had days to learn these passageways.

The problem solved itself as Kest and Sir Istan arrived. "We followed the Duke's shouts," Kest said in answer to my unspoken question. "How is the boy?"

"I don't know yet. Kest, Toujean says there are five of them."

Kest looked at the dust on the floor. "Too many sets of tracks, going in all directions. How long ago did they leave?"

"Just moments ago," Toujean said, his voice weak and fearful. "They fled as soon as they heard the Duke coming."

"Why would that send them running?" Kest asked, but before Toujean could answer, more heavy footsteps thudded toward us from another passage and Ugh emerged from the passageway with Valiana, Parrick, Dariana, and Shiballe in tow. "Fucking stupid people. Get lost easy," Ugh said. "Fat man so smart, eh?" Ugh pointed his finger toward the ground and circled it around and around.

"Shiballe had us going around in circles," Dariana explained.

Valiana rushed past the others, asking, "Where is Tommer?" and when I pointed, she ran in and knelt down by him. She reached out a hand, but Jillard slapped it away. "Don't touch him!" he said. "No one touches him but me!"

Tommer's eyes blinked open and closed very quickly, like a butterfly's wings flapping against a strong wind. He looked up at his father, and then at Valiana. "Sister?" he asked. "You're wearing a Greatcoat . . . did you come to save me?"

It struck me as odd that Tommer still called Valiana his sister. Apparently Jillard also found the idea discomfiting.

"Tommer!" the Duke said, tears streaming down his face, "I'm here—your father's here. I've got you. I've got you."

Tommer looked to his father. "Yes . . . Father," he murmured, "I'm very sorry, Father . . ."

Jillard cradled Tommer's head. "You stole my key, you silly, silly boy."

"I . . . I didn't—"

"Your Grace," Sir Toujean said weakly, "the assassins . . . they said they had another way into and out of the dungeons—that they could escape and come back to kill you and your son whenever they wanted." He pushed himself awkwardly to his knees, and then clambered to his feet and stood there swaying. "Give me a sword, your Grace, and I will hunt them to the ends of the earth."

"Don't be ridiculous," Jillard said, still trying to rouse Tommer. "You and Sir Odiard can barely stand." He turned to me. "You said you wanted to put a stop to this conspiracy, to end these killings, so go: take these others and find those men and kill them."

A small cloth bag of the darkest blue, barely larger than a baby's fist, caught my eyes. I pulled a knife from my coat and very carefully opened the top of the bag with it. The bag was about a quarter full of blue-black dust. Saints—how much was in there when they started? How much did they use on the boy?

"The boy needs a healer," I said.

"Shiballe!" the Duke shouted, "get my healer! Get Firensi—*now!*"

As he turned and shuffled off down the passageway, Ugh shouted after him, "Try not to get lost, eh?"

Duke Jillard turned to the rest of us. "Sir Istan, Sir Jairn—I mean, Parrick, whatever the hells your damned name is—you stay here and protect my son with me. You others, go and find the assassins before they escape."

"Come on," I said to Valiana.

She started to get up, but Tommer grabbed her arm and cried, "Sister? Stay—? Please . . . ? I'm scared . . ." And again his eyes fluttered open and closed.

"She's not your sister," Jillard said, his voice soft, yet I could clearly hear the tinge of anger. "She's not my daughter, just some—"

The sheer arrogance with which he was dismissing the girl he had believed his daughter for eighteen years made me want to knock him senseless right then and there, but to her credit, Valiana's focus was on Tommer. "He's seen nothing but angry and dangerous men for days, your Grace," she said gently, "so if he finds my face comforting, then—"

"Very well, damn you. But go, now, and get those damned Dashini!"

The rest of us turned and ran back into the open space. "Three hallways," I pointed out, and without another word Kest ran down one, Dariana the next. I took the third, but before I'd gone more than twenty feet I heard Ugh following me.

"I come," he panted, "I come. Fucking mad horse not better than me. Faster though."

We reached the end of the passages and I stared down at the ground, looking for fresh tracks, but I found nothing other than what I'd seen before. "Which way do you think they went?" I asked Ugh.

He pointed to a passageway ahead and to the right of us. "Back upstairs. Back to first level, then to palace. Only way."

"It can't be the only way," I said. "Jillard's got two dozen men waiting at the top of those stairs. No assassin would ever get through, not that way. There must be another exit."

Ugh shook his head. "No other way. One door: black door."

"Listen: Sir Toujean just told us the assassins were talking about another way in and out of these dungeons—"

Ugh said angrily, "You know nothing, fucking Greatcoat tough guy. I come here sometimes, eh? Never know when maybe Duke get angry or bitch Patriana send me here, eh? I look *everywhere*. I go in *every* passage. I look *every* cell. Fucking Knights don't know shit. *I* know. One way out. Black door."

The erstwhile torturer stared at me, daring me to contradict him, his dark little eyes full of such absolute certainty—and yet how could that be possible? How could the assassins hope to get away? For the hundredth time I cursed Jillard and his hideous dungeon, and I cursed Sir Toujean and the other two Knights even more for having stood back as an eleven-year-old boy stole his father's key, for allowing him to drag them down into a dungeon with a Dashini assassin. Were they *trying* to get him killed? Were they—?

"Saint Zaghev-who-sings-for-tears—" I turned and looked into the dim light down the passageway just in time to see two figures rising up from the floor of the cell. One of them was reaching for the blue bag of Dashini powder.

Swearing under my breath I took off at a run back down the hallway, with Ugh chasing after me asking, "What? What—?"

"Tommer didn't make the guards bring him down here," I said, still cursing myself for a fool. "Toujean and the other two Knights dragged him."

33

THE CAPTORS

In the few seconds it took us to run back to the cell we'd already lost the fight. Sir Istan was dying just outside the iron gate, blood gushing from his throat even as he struggled to rise one last time. Parrick was on the ground outside, wrestling with one of the other Knights we'd found lying beside Tommer. The Knight he was fighting hammered a fist against the pommel of the dagger I could see sticking out between Parrick's ribs—he must have found the tiny gap between the bone plates of Parrick's greatcoat—and a heart-rending scream echoed around the cell. Then the Knight climbed on top of Parrick, pulled out his dagger and began to force it down into Parrick's face. Ugh was close enough now to grab the Knight by his long brown hair and he hauled him off and sent him sprawling toward me. I drove the point of my rapier deep into his right shoulder and then again into his left: I needed him to live long enough to find out who had ordered this attack, but that didn't mean he shouldn't *hurt*.

There was a great clanging and I turned to see Sir Toujean pulling the door to the cell shut. He locked himself inside with Valiana, Jillard, and Tommer, and through the vertical slits in the door I could see he had wrapped a cloth around his face that left only his eyes exposed. The boy was still on the ground, but he wasn't moving. Valiana and Jillard were huddled in opposite corners of the room, and both were moaning in terror.

Parrick grabbed at my leg, trying to attract my attention. "The dust," he whispered. "When you left, Toujean threw the dust at us. It's . . . Saints, Falcio, it's worse than I remembered . . ."

I knew what he meant. I would never forget the Dashini dust and what it did to my mind . . .

I went over to search for a way to get in, but just like the black-iron door the only way to see inside was through the three vertical slits, each one barely the width of two fingers. Even as I pulled a knife from a pocket I knew there was practically no chance of throwing it through the narrow slit, let alone hitting someone I wanted to hit. And Toujean wasn't taking any chances; he raced back to his captives and hauling Tommer up, held the boy in front of him like a shield.

"I'd advise against anything too daring, Trattari," the Knight said, reaching an arm around Tommer's neck. "Little boys are surprisingly fragile. *Snap, snap, snap.*"

I stared at Sir Toujean and tried to work out a way to stop him. He was still covered in blood—and now it was obvious it wasn't his own. *Such a simple ruse.* And all the little things that had never quite added up were making sense: he and the other two Knights had stolen the Duke's key and then dragged Tommer down to the dungeon with them. Once safe within the Duke's stony maze they'd been free to kill as many prisoners as they needed to, then they'd sent Toujean up the stairs with a rope tied to his neck pretending to be the terrified victim relaying his kidnappers' demands. The Dashini dust would have kept Tommer docile . . .

But why did they kill the third Knight? I wondered. Had he resisted once he'd realized how far the others were going to go? Was there an ounce of conscience in any of the remaining men?

"What's the matter, Trattari?" Toujean taunted. "Nothing to say? Don't want to know how I'm going to get out of here after I kill Jillard? And the boy, of course."

I ignored him; I was pretty sure once the Duke and his son were dead—and all the rest of us, of course—Toujean would kill the Dashini and play the grieving hero who had managed to avenge his deceased Duke. That would no doubt appeal to his fellow Knights, most of whom likely despised Jillard anyway. He would talk about Knightly honor and the will of the Gods, and the chance for a new, glorious dynasty, and they would lap it all up. I didn't care about any of that; the only one thing that mattered to me at that moment was figuring out how to save the boy and push the tip of my sword right through Toujean's black heart.

Valiana was crouching in the corner. Her eyes were full of terror induced by the Dashini dust but they found mine and for a brief moment she steeled herself and tried to get up—but she immediately fell back down, tears streaming down her face, a horrified moan escaping from her lips. *Damn the Dashini and their damned powders.* There's something obscene about people who can fight so well and yet still use poison to first weaken their opponents.

"Come now, Trattari—surely you're dying to know why Sir Odiard and I decided to kill our own Duke and his only son? Why thrice-honored Knights would—"

"Not really," I said, my mind racing. "I'm just assuming you're an asshole and a coward; I'm perfectly happy to leave it at that."

I couldn't throw my knife—even if I did manage to squeeze my hand and the blade into the slit, the throw wouldn't have enough force to do any damage. He, on the other hand, had only to give one sharp twist and Tommer's neck would break. If Brasti were here he could have put an arrow straight into Toujean's eye—or any other part of his anatomy—but I wasn't anywhere near as good.

Damn you, Brasti, for leaving us when we needed you.

"We are men of honor!" Toujean growled, apparently offended that I wasn't paying sufficient attention to his plan to murder a child in cold blood. "The Dukes have failed the Knights of Tristia. They have failed this country. They—"

"Shut up," I said. "I'm trying to think."

Ugh pushed me out of the way and began throwing himself at the door, over and over again. He was stronger than almost any man I'd ever met and the whole iron wall reverberated with the impact of his body. Perhaps in a hundred years he might just break it open.

"You have plan, tough guy?" he said at last, his breath ragged.

I did have a plan. It just wasn't a very good one. The first time I'd been hit with the dust I'd very nearly choked on my own fear. Quillata had done a little better, though, and so had a few of the other women—so maybe they had better resistance . . . and maybe there was a chance here.

I'm sorry, Valiana. No one should be asked to be this brave.

"You think you're safe in there, Toujean?" I shouted through the slit. "Because *I* think you've just trapped yourself in a room with a Greatcoat."

Toujean laughed. "Her? I tell you, Trattari, the first time I heard that the King was allowing women to become traveling Magisters my friends and I reckoned it must be some kind of joke. After all, there's a reason women don't become Knights, Trattari."

"And there's a reason Knights don't become Greatcoats," I said. I looked at Valiana, trying to catch her eye, but she was busy mumbling something and shaking her head, over and over. "It's scary, isn't it," I called to her. "It's like you're standing on a cliff a hundred miles high and looking over the edge, and then realizing you've just lost your balance—"

"You're wasting your time, Trattari," Toujean interrupted me. "The first time we used it on the boy I got the slightest touch of it on my skin and nearly ran screaming for my life."

Ugh, beside me, chuckled. "Guess you not tough guy, eh?"

"Shut up, dog," Toujean said. "When we bring a righteous purge to Rijou you'll find yourself hanging at the end of a gibbet right alongside the Duke."

"Hanging next to Duke? Big promotion for me, uh?"

"Valiana," I said, "that dust is like breathing hell right into your heart: I know that. It's terrifying. Most people can't take it. But most people haven't been chased across Northern Tristia by an army determined to see them dead—like you have. Most people haven't had to pick up a sword and fight against soldiers twice their size and with ten times the training—like you have."

"I'll snap the boy's neck!" Toujean shouted.

"Then you get knife in chest, eh, smart guy?" Ugh said.

Toujean gripped Tommer tighter. The boy's head moved a little and now I was staring at three sets of eyes. They all looked back at me.

"Valiana," I said, struggling to make my voice as soothing as I could, "most people would just curl up and wait to die rather than fight that dust—but *most* people haven't discovered that their lives were a lie. *Most* people haven't found out that they were not who they believed they were. And *most* people have not stood up and fought back against the world the way *you* have." I pressed up against the iron surface of the door, working on getting my hand through one of the slits. "Valiana, *you* have faced more fear than almost anyone who has ever lived. You're not going to be stopped by some dust cooked up by a bunch of cowards so scared of the world they have to wear masks just to face it—that's not who you are. It's not who you *were*—and that's not who you've *become*."

Toujean twisted his head quickly, just long enough to catch a glimpse of her. When he turned back, I could see his unpleasant sneer, even through the cloth covering his mouth and nose. "It's a nice idea, Trattari, to think you can make someone brave just by haranguing them as if you're some pathetic roadside cleric. I must admit, I found it terribly touching when you tried it with me back at the black door: 'When you were a boy, you dreamed of being a hero, did you not?' Brave words, Trattari—sadly for you, they had as little effect then as they do now. I'm afraid life just doesn't work that way."

He reached down and picked up a sword from the ground. "My friends will be coming soon."

I continued to ignore him. "Valiana, it's time," I said firmly. "You said you wanted to make your life count—so do it, *now*. This is *your* time: so get on your feet and kill this son of a bitch for me."

She looked at me and her mouth opened wide in horror, as if what I was asking her to do was even worse than whatever the dust had shown her. But slowly—so very slowly—she pushed herself to her feet and I could see her hand was reaching for her sword in its sheath.

Toujean heard the sound of her coat creaking as she moved and twisted around—just as I threw my knife. With far more luck than I deserved, the blade struck the Knight in the shoulder, and he bellowed and dropped Tommer to the ground. I reached for another knife but before I could throw it he had grabbed Valiana by the collar and thrown her against the cell's iron wall. She bounced off it and stumbled toward me and I felt her hand briefly touch my fingers poking through one of the slits in the door. She was shaking badly.

"You can do this," I whispered. "There's nothing you need fear but—"

She looked at me through the slits in the door. Her lips trembling on the words, she said, "Falcio, please shut up now." With her hand pressed against the wall, she found her balance before she turned around and faced Toujean. "Su-surrender," she said.

Toujean laughed. "You want to dance with me, little girl?" He flipped the point of his sword up and feinted toward Valiana'a face, and she stumbled back into the door again. But this time she straightened her back and immediately stepped into the center of the cell. Her blade was wavering, but it was out in front of her. I wanted to throw another knife, but Toujean had started skillfully maneuvering her around the cell, ensuring she was always between us.

Valiana thrust her sword at Toujean's chest, although her hand was shaking so badly the blade was almost comically wavering in the air. He shifted his weight and half-turned, smiling victoriously as the awkward lunge missed him, but Valiana didn't stop. She kept attacking, working her way around his guard to strike at his belly, his neck, even his legs. When Toujean counterattacked, she made little effort to parry, instead relying on the bone plates sewn inside her thick leather coat to protect her. I was glad she hadn't seen Parrick, lying there with the sword piercing his own greatcoat. . . . And even though the plates were doing their job, for now at least, Toujean was bigger and stronger than she was, and his sword was heavier. He smashed the edge of his blade against her shoulders, then her ribs, and each time I winced.

Hells, you can't take much more of this. Move him around, girl!

Valiana was trying her best, but every time she tried to position him so I could get a decent shot with my knife he'd do something, like swinging his sword in a wide arc, forcing her to shift her stance just to parry his blade without being pushed over.

"You're going to die, little girl," Toujean said, his blade slapping hers out of line yet again. "How does it feel, knowing that?"

She brought her sword back into line. "Like . . . like a relief."

He laughed again. "This is the story of Tristia, right here: a foolish girl—nothing more than the discarded outcome of the rutting of nameless peasants—dreams herself a warrior—" He broke off, then asked, conversationally, "Do you even have your own name, little girl?" He brought his sword up high and then struck down in a vicious diagonal arc toward her neck.

She managed to get her sword up in time to parry, but Toujean brought his weapon back up and around and almost effortlessly struck her hard in the ribs. "I know," he said gleefully, "*I'll* give you a name! How about—let's see—*Bitch*? Or *Slut*? Or maybe *Whore*? I think I like *Whore* best." Almost lazily, he swung his blade back and forth in wide arcs, all the time forcing Valiana backward toward the iron wall. He wasn't the least bit tired, and she was fading fast.

"You know," the Knight said, as if he had been seriously considering the matter, "now that I think about it, 'Whore' is a bit too short for a proper name, isn't it? So how about '*Dead* Whore'? That's better, isn't it? That has a lovely cadence to it, don't you think?" He swung twice more, and now he was moving much faster, striking her on the leg, then again on her left side. This time I heard a rib crack.

Valiana stumbled back. She was going to die in a few moments.

"Stop," I called out to the Knight. "Please, stop. Don't do this."

Toujean ignored me; he was fired up with self-righteous passion as he moved closer to Valiana.

"You're right about one thing, Sir Knight," Valiana said, shakily recovering her footing. "This *is* the story of Tristia, told right here in this cell deep in the belly of this disgusting palace in the heart of the most corrupt city in the world. It's the story of a Knight so full of dishonor and cowardice that he would murder a young boy to achieve his filthy desire for power."

"Shut up, *Dead Whore*. I'm not some farmer's son you can bray at. I'm a Tristian Knight."

"That you are," she said, her sword dipping down as she struggled to stay on her feet. "And I am . . . I am Valiana val Mond, a peasant and a fool and a Greatcoat all at once." She tightened her grip on her weapon. "And I'm the dead whore who's about to kill you."

She brought her sword up into line and lunged at Toujean's belly, but he parried the sword away and thrust at her chest.

Fast, I thought. *He's too damned fast—she can't parry him.* But she didn't try: she let his blade hit her in the left side of her chest. I heard the bone plates of her coat break, and I could have sworn I heard the leather being pierced, and then the sound of something sick and wet . . .

Toujean's eyes were wide with surprise and delight. "She just . . . she just walked into it!" His smile widened. "You *stupid* whore— don't you know any better? You *never* raise your weapon against a true . . . a trueb—"

The Knight looked down, and only then did he see that the tip of Valiana's sword was resting just under his neck. "Welcome to Tristia," she said, and with both hands on the hilt of her sword she pushed the blade up through his neck and into his head.

They stood there for a moment, eyes locked on one another, two storytellers each convinced their tale was the truest. Then Toujean began to blink furiously, and I saw blood start to seep from the corners of his eyes as the flesh inside his skull began to work its way out. The blood dripped down his face, and just for a moment he looked as if he were crying tears of great sorrow. Valiana pulled her blade out and pushed him away from her and as he fell, the tip of his sword came out of her chest. She dropped her own weapon and fell to her hands and knees next to Tommer's unconscious form.

No, please, no! I thought, pulling uselessly at the handle of the iron door.

Very slowly her right hand slid along the dusty stone floor until her fingers reached the key. Without looking up she threw it toward me and I caught it—just barely, but it was enough. I fumbled at the lock, shaking, until Ugh took the key from me, stuck it in, and opened the cell.

I ran inside and dropped to my knees beside Valiana, lifting her head to rest against my legs and pulling a cloth from my coat to hold against her wound. Her eyes fluttered and the color in her face began to fade. "Valiana!" I screamed, "Don't go! Please—"

She reached up and placed her hand over mine. "M'fine," she said, her voice barely a whisper. She slowly turned her head and looked at Duke Jillard, cowering, still terrified, in the opposite corner of the room. "Bet you wish I was your daughter now."

34

THE BRAVE

"Where in all the hells is the healer?" I screamed, holding Valiana to me with one arm and pressing the cloth from my coat against her chest to keep the blood from flowing freely.

Tommer rose from the floor of the cell, his eyes dreamy as if he'd been awakened from a deep sleep. He walked over to us and peered down at Valiana. "Sister," he said. "You look tired."

Valiana forced her eyes open briefly and smiled at him weakly but said nothing.

Footsteps echoed along the passageway and Kest appeared in the doorway, closely followed by Dariana and Shiballe. Several of the Duke's guards followed them.

"The healer's coming," Kest said. "He was right behind us—he'll be here any moment—"

Shiballe ran into the cell. Jillard's shaking had slowed and now he just sat there, murmuring to himself. I was pretty sure that he would be back to the normal wretch he had always been within the hour.

"The healer will look to the Duke first," Shiballe said, back to his usual bumptious self, "then he will see to Tommer. After that"—he looked with distaste at Valiana—"I will consider requests for assistance."

"Kest," I said, my voice even, "when the healer arrives, direct him to us immediately."

Shiballe turned to look at the guards standing outside the cell. "Arrest the Trattari," he said. "Arrest all of them."

"Oh, and Kest? Feel free to kill as many people as it takes to ensure the healer has a clear passage to Valiana."

Tommer shook his head at me. "Enough," he said. He gestured at the bodies on the floor. "There's been enough death." He turned away from me and walked to Shiballe. "My father will be well. It will take his mind a few hours to clear the dust. My sister is gravely wounded. She will see the healer first."

"She is not your sister," Shiballe said, "She's just a peasant. She's—"

"I am the son of Duke Jillard," Tommer said. "One day, perhaps one day soon, I will be the Duke of Rijou. You would do well to remember that, Shiballe."

For just an instant Tommer was no longer a bruised and terrified eleven-year-old boy. He was the future ruler of the most powerful duchy in all of Tristia. Shiballe's face began to turn a remarkably pale shade of gray. "I . . . Of course, sir."

Tommer turned to Valiana and looked at her with more warmth than I would have thought possible for a boy who'd just gone through such terrors. "She is my sister if I say she is." He sat down next to her, leaned his head on her shoulder and closed his eyes. "She will see the healer first."

"How about we let the one person qualified to make such decisions be the one to determine which of his patients to see and in what order?" a man's voice said from behind the crowd. "Get out of my way, you great fools."

The guards parted to make way for an older man with silver-gray hair carrying a leather healer's case. His elaborate robes of red and gold marked him as a nobleman. He glanced at Tommer, then at Jillard, then knelt down to check Valiana's eyes. He felt her forehead and neck, then put the back of his hand against her cheek. "My name is Firensi," he said. "Does this feel cold or hot?"

"Cold, a little," Valiana replied.

"The wound is in her chest," I said. "Why are you—?"

"I already know where the wound is. I need to know how well her body is coping with it."

"Should I lay her down on her back?"

"Only if you want to kill her." The healer opened his leather case and pulled out a very small wooden box. Inside were some little white pills. "Hold this on your tongue," he told Valiana, placing one in her mouth. "Don't swallow. Let it melt there. The pain will ease and you'll feel a calm come over you."

I thought of Beytina, and her assemblage of fools with tinctures that tasted nice and took away pain but did nothing to prevent the patient from dying. "Is there . . . is there a country healer nearby?" I asked.

Firensi raised an eyebrow but kept his focus on Valiana. "You think I'm some courtly fop who gives out scented potions to wealthy nobles so they can please their wives in bed?"

"I . . ." Antagonizing the man wouldn't help; perhaps for once I should just shut up. "No, I—"

"Because that's exactly what I am," he said. He took out bandages and plasters and needles and some bottles of liquid and arranged them on the side of his case. "I like good food and good wine and I like my bed to be soft, and made by someone else." He turned to me and put a hand on my shoulder. "But my mother was a country healer and she could halfway bring back the dead if she chose. This girl is under my care now and I'll do everything I can for her." He squeezed his fingers into my shoulders, pressing into a nerve that made it feel as if he were pushing six-inch pins into it. "Now get out of my way and let me work."

I eased my arm out from behind Valiana's shoulders and leaned her against the wall, but as I began to rise she grabbed my arm.

"I don't want to die, Falcio."

I stopped and looked down at her, at the strands of dark hair hanging limp and soaking wet against her skin, at the lines of pain creasing her forehead.

"I know it probably looks that way, but I don't," she said. "I'm *scared* of dying—*terrified*. When the Knights . . . Duke Jillard and I were focused on Tommer, and Sir Istan and Parrick were watching the passageway to make sure no one attacked us Sir Toujean and that other man, they were wounded, they looked so bad, but then they just got right up from the floor, and before I knew what was happening poor Sir Istan had his throat slit and Parrick had a sword in his side."

"It's all right," I said, "you can tell me later. You're not going to die." I looked at Firensi, who was cleaning pieces of leather out of her wound even as blood continued to flow from it. If he knew Valiana's fate, his eyes showed nothing of it.

Valiana coughed. "Toujean dug his hand into the blue bag and he flung dust in our faces. I tried not to breathe it in, but—"

"It goes through your skin," I said.

"Odd," Firensi said, now smoothing some kind of sticky salve over the wound; it smelled uncomfortably like the corpses in the room. "That's not something in any of my books."

Valiana flinched as he probed the wound and her hand squeezed my forearm. "When I first met you," she said, "you would just throw yourself into danger to save other people. You . . . I hated you, Falcio. You made me feel like I was a spoiled little girl playing at being a princess. I suppose I was. When you said you were staying in Rijou to protect Aline . . . she was no one of consequence, just some girl from a minor noble's family, and I kept thinking, 'If he dies fighting for that girl, if he sacrifices himself to save one little girl . . . what will people say about him?'"

"That he was an idiot," I said, sitting back down next to her. "Born a peasant, raised a fool, died an idiot."

"That's not true." Valiana's fingers slipped down my arm and slid into my hand. "It's long past time you figured that out. What people remember about us? That *matters*. What are we, really, but acts of courage or cowardice, generosity or greed? I don't want to die, Falcio, but if I do die now, what will they say about me?"

"That you had a very skewed notion of philosophy," I said, my eyes on Firensi's hands as he applied a kind of thick, sinewy bandage I'd never seen before to her chest.

She laughed, just for a moment, wincing at the pain. "No, they'll say the peasant girl with no name picked up a sword and saved the life of the Duke's son even though she knew he wasn't really her brother. They'll say that an orphan's courage can be as great as that of any noble or Knight, and they'll look at the next foolish girl and wonder if she too might be a hero." She squeezed my hand. "That sounds like a good story, doesn't it?"

"A damned good story," I said.

She smiled and closed her eyes. "Good. Now go and put a stop to all of this madness. I'm feeling a little sleepy."

I felt a stab of fear as I watched her breathing slow and become shallow.

"It's the salve," Firensi said, rising up to his feet and stretching. "It's going to keep her out for a while. It'll be a few hours before I can have her moved so I'll have someone clear out these bodies and bring some blankets. She needs to be kept warm."

A thought occurred to me. "There is a woman nearby, in Merisaw. Her name is Ethalia—"

"What, another country healer? Some half-witted apothecary whose parents were brother and sister? Still don't trust me, eh?"

"She's a Sister of the Merciful Light," I said, "and they can—"

"I know who they are." Firensi looked from me to Valiana. "It's not actually the stupidest thing you've said to me so far. It's spiritual hogwash, largely, but there is some evidence that they are sometimes able to make a body heal faster. Ethalia of Merisaw, eh? I'll send someone for her in a day or two." I started to object, but Firensi held up a hand. "Nothing she does will help a sword wound until the body's decided if it's going to live or die. I'll send for her when the time is right."

Some of Shiballe's men jostled me aside as they carried in some eight-foot-long wooden poles wrapped with canvas. Under Firensi's direction they opened them out, revealing the canvas strips to be slings, and carefully lifted Tommer into one of them. While two men gently carried him out of the cell, two more repeated the process for Jillard. Firensi waved the rest of the men away; he obviously intended to stay and watch over Valiana himself.

Toujean and his fellow conspirators were dragged out of the damned dungeon to rot someplace else.

I followed the procession out of the cell and found Kest and Dariana waiting for me.

"Parrick's dead," Kest said. "The knife went into his liver."

I prepared myself for a wave of grief and regret, only to find nothing came. Parrick had stood by and kept his silence as I was being tortured in a cell on the floor above this one. Perhaps it was petty of me—he'd been following the King's last command, after all, and to the letter—but damn him anyway. Damn the King too, for that matter.

"Your friend here tried to stop the bleeding," Kest said, looking at Ugh, who was kneeling over Parrick's body. "But it was too late."

Ugh rose from the floor. His hands were covered in blood and he looked down at them as if he wanted to cut them off. "Fucking useless. Only good for making pain. No good for saving anybody."

The raw grief on the face of this strange brute of a man struck me: he was so full of violence and yet deep down, he was seeking some better tale to make of his life.

I knelt down and removed Parrick's coat, pulling one arm out of its sleeve and then the other, rolling his body around unceremoniously until he was lying on his back, his vacant eyes staring up at me.

"What are you doing?" Dariana asked.

I handed the coat to Ugh. "Put this on."

Ugh's eyes went wide. "I'm no fucking—"

"I know. You're no 'fucking tough-guy Greatcoat'. Put it on anyway."

The big man slid his arms through the sleeves, and I was surprised to see how well it fitted him—it was a little long, but it would do up across the chest and shoulders. He ran his hands across the leather and felt the buttons in the front. He was treating it as if I'd handed him a cleric's holy robes.

"Are you out of your mind?" Dariana demanded. "You're going to make—"

"You have to take the oath," Kest said to Ugh.

Ugh looked up at us. "What is oath?"

Neither Kest nor I answered. This is how it is, how it's always been.

"This is ridiculous," Dariana said, angrier than I would have expected from someone who didn't care about the Greatcoats.

"What would your precious dead King say if he knew you were giving a greatcoat to a damned torturer?"

"I don't know nothing about no King," Ugh said, grimacing at us, his voice thick with angry defiance. "Fuck Kings. Fuck Dukes. Only thing that matters is Law. Fifth law: no unjust punishment for nobody. No torture. No more torture for nobody. You give me coat? I go beat hells out of any man try to torture somebody. You want oath? Fifth Law is my oath. Fuck you if you no like it."

Kest looked at me. "That's . . . original."

"It'll do," I said.

A thin, reedy laugh caught my ears. "Look," Shiballe called out, standing next to Duke Jillard's stretcher, "they put a coat on a pig and called it a Magister. Shall he adjudicate the disputes of cows and chickens?"

Ugh walked over to where Shiballe was standing. "What good is fucking worm, eh? Fucking Duke. Maybe if no more Duke people no need tough guy Greatcoats, eh?"

The Duke, shivering on his back, tried to push himself up on the stretcher. He looked as if he was about to say something but I never heard it. In all the chaos and terror and then the sudden relief of Toujean's death we had all forgotten about one thing. *The Dashini.*

A fight isn't won on strength or speed, nor on the back-and-forth trading of blows and parries. Those are all preamble. A fight is won by the single attack that outwits or overwhelms the opponent's guard and takes his life. If you could devise just one sequence of movements to accomplish this, you wouldn't need to bother with anything else. A single, perfect attack is exactly what the Dashini delivered.

It was Kest who noticed it first. In that strange mind of his the world is made up of angles and trajectories. I felt him tense next to me and only then saw that the line of the Duke's gaze was focused just slightly behind and above us.

We turned and saw the Dashini running naked toward us. His right hand was a ruin, bleeding from the fingers, the bone of his little finger exposed, and my first thought was to wonder if that's how he'd opened the door to his cell. "Dashi—" I began to yell, but even as I reached down to grip my left rapier I knew I'd never draw it in time.

Had the Dashini held a blade in his hand he could have jammed it down my throat. But he didn't, and anyway, I wasn't his target. The instant before he reached us he leapt up and to the right, his foot finding brief purchase on a tiny outcropping two feet above the floor and no more than half an inch deep. He pushed off from it and flipped over and past us.

"Protect the—" shouted one of the guards between us and the Duke, and when I turned I saw that he'd had time to draw his weapon and was bringing it into guard just as the Dashini, tumbling back toward the ground with his knees bent, crashed into the man's chest.

The guard fell backward, collapsing into one of his fellows and knocking him down, but before Kest and I could reach him, the Dashini had used the fallen guard as a platform from which to leap off and this time the light of one of the braziers glinted against steel: the Dashini had the guard's sword in his hand.

The two men holding Jillard's canvas stretcher wisely let it fall to the ground, and the Duke along with it. One tried to get to his sword; the other just crossed his arms in front of his face to protect himself—but funnily enough, neither tactic worked. Both were brought down by a single stroke that took off one man's hands and the other man's head.

Less than seven seconds had passed since I had shouted *Dashi*— and the assassin was now standing over Duke Jillard's helpless body, his appropriated sword coming down for a single, perfect thrust.

The assassin had not just escaped his cell but had watched from the shadows as he devised a complex sequence of movements that none of us would have time to defeat. He had accounted for the narrow walls of the passageway and the dozen guards. He'd factored in my reflexes and Kest's speed. He'd planned for every opponent.

Except one.

Ugh had been standing next to the Duke, but unlike the rest of us he didn't try to draw a weapon or protect himself or get out of the way. As the sword meant to take Jillard's life began its downward plunge, Ugh smashed into the Dashini with the full weight of his body. Any sane man would have tried to disarm his opponent or strike him down, but no one had ever accused the erstwhile torturer-turned-Greatcoat of being sane. Ugh brought his arms around the Dashini and held him.

My rapier was in my hand, but the other guards were too busy getting in our way, trying to create a barrier between the assassin and his intended victim. At first the Dashini tried to ignore Ugh and reach past him with the sword to slit Jillard's neck, but Ugh got him trapped against the rough wall of the passageway. As I pushed past one of the guards in my way I saw a brief flicker in the Dashini's eyes. It wasn't anger or frustration or even fear; I was pretty sure it was regret—a kind of apology, maybe—as he brought his arms up high and then immediately down again. His elbows struck Ugh's neck on either side. The Dashini's eyes went briefly to the Duke, but not even the world's best assassin could get to him now, not with every remaining guard standing over him. And Kest and I were nearly in range. As Ugh's heavy body began to sag to the ground, the Dashini pushed him into the human barrier then, ducking low, he shimmied under the wild slash of a guard's blade.

He sprinted past the guards, past Tommer on his stretcher, past Valiana's cell, to the other end of the passageway, while I shouted, "Stop!" still trying in vain to get past the damned guards who were so determined to form a wall around the Duke that they were making it completely impossible for Kest and me to reach the assassin.

To my immense surprise, the Dashini did stop. He turned to us and said, "I have failed, and we are lost. Come for me, Falcio val Mond, if you would know the answers to your questions, and learn just how empty the world has become." He turned back and disappeared silently into the next passageway.

"Guards!" Shiballe screamed from where he was crouched against the wall, "Capture that man!"

Three of them ran after the assassin, leaving the others to protect the Duke, but they had no chance. Shiballe had brought all his guards down here—if there were any left at the top of the stairs—which I doubted; Shiballe didn't strike me as a man who thought scenarios like this through to the bitter end—they'd be too few and quite unprepared to stop someone as expert in escape as the Dashini.

I couldn't get through the men determined to stop *anyone* reaching the Duke until Jillard, sounding exasperated, shouted from behind his wall of flesh, "Let him through."

Grumbling under their breath, they parted and as I stepped forward I could see Jillard and Ugh, both lying on the ground, their heads less than a foot from each other, their feet pointed in opposite directions.

"You . . . you threw yourself upon the man who'd come to kill me," Jillard said.

"Stupid Duke. I thought he was going after boy," Ugh said. His eyes were unfocused, and almost milky in color.

I knelt down and put a hand on Ugh's arm. "Can you feel my hand?"

"Don't feel nothing."

"Firensi!" I called out, but there was no need; the healer was already coming behind me. He bent down and examined the sides of Ugh's neck, then he looked at me. He didn't even need to shake his head.

I turned to look for Kest, but of course he was already there.

"There's nothing we can do for him, Falcio. It's called the Desert Mercy. It will be done soon."

"Mercy," Ugh chuckled. "Guess so. Feeling nothing is not so bad."

I took his hand even though I knew he couldn't feel mine. "Do you have a family? Someone you want us to—?"

"Tell fucking horse," he said, and then the man I'd called Ugh—though of course that wasn't his name—let out a final sigh and stopped breathing.

He had been a brute for most of his life, but he died a Greatcoat less than five minutes after putting on the coat.

35

DASHINI

Kest, Dariana, and I spent the next six days pursuing the Dashini assassin, following him from the dungeons of Rijou, through the city and south into the northern forests of Aramor. Each day took us down increasingly rough, untraveled roads until the path split into two tracks too narrow for our horses to navigate.

"We'll have to leave them behind," Kest said.

I dismounted and started to tie my reins to a tree when I stopped. Who knew if we'd be coming back this way—or coming back at all? It would be cruel to leave the horse tied up in the middle of nowhere. I left the saddlebags on the ground and pulled out the single small pack of dried foodstuffs and vital supplies I keep prepared for such an eventuality.

"Let's go," I said, hoisting it onto my back and setting out along the forest path.

"Why exactly are we chasing after some traitorous Dashini?" Dariana asked, running to catch up with me. She'd asked the same question half a dozen times already; I was hoping she'd get bored of it at some point. "You said it yourself: it was the Knights who took Tommer, and they're all dead now."

"Toujean and the others were waiting for an opportunity," I replied. "They knew someone would be sending an assassin for the Duke and they used his arrival to take Tommer."

"Why?" she asked.

"*I don't know why!*" I repeated for the sixth time. "All I know is that until I understand how the Dashini are involved in all of this I won't be able to put a stop to the killings."

"We're getting closer," Kest said, looking down at the muddy ground.

"Of course we are, you idiot! He's leading us to our deaths! Falcio is so determined to learn his secrets that he'll see us all dead before we uncover them!"

I stopped for a moment and leaned back against a tree. The path had gradually curved upward and we were now steadily ascending the side of a mountain. I slipped my hand into my pocket and pulled out a little oil-cloth-wrapped package—a considerably smaller package than it had been a week ago—and broke off a piece of hard candy. It was probably a bit bigger than it should have been; I examined it briefly, then popped it into my mouth.

"That's another thing," Dariana said. "How much longer do you think you can fend off sleep with that concoction you keep eating when you don't think anyone's paying attention?"

It wasn't an unreasonable question. Since we'd left Rijou I'd stopped allowing myself to close my eyes for anything more than a few minutes; I was afraid the paralysis would overcome me and we'd lose the trail. So that was six days relying on the hard candy to keep me going: six days of virtually no sleep, which was a day longer than I'd ever gone before and two days longer than the King's apothecary had pronounced safe.

"She's right," Kest said. "You can barely stand on your own, Falcio." He'd been quiet for most of the journey, fighting his own battle inside himself. The urge to draw his blade was so strong that it was burning him up inside.

"I'm fine," I said. "I'm just saving it all up so that I can have a really memorable nap later on. I just need a minute to rest."

"No, you don't 'just need a minute to rest'—you won't last for another day like this, Falcio. You're barely able to keep up—and when we do catch up with the assassin, what if he's not alone?"

"Exactly," Dariana said. "He knew he couldn't beat all of us in Jillard's castle so he's playing on your world-famous need for answers to lure us into a trap."

"He's definitely drawing us on," Kest agreed, pointing to the path through the forest ahead of us.

"What do you mean?" I asked.

"It only stopped raining an hour ago." He picked up a bit of bramble lying beside the footprint in the mud. "Look: the fibers inside the break are dry."

This wasn't the first time this had happened. Each time we thought we were close, the assassin's trail disappeared, and when we eventually picked it up again, it looked days old. There were times when I was certain he'd lost us, and then a few hours later we would suddenly see signs of him again.

I examined the wood. "So that means he only just passed this way. We're close."

"No," Kest said, "look at the depth of the prints. He passed this way yesterday. Then he came back around using another route and walked through again, stepping in his prints again. The second time was when the branch fell in the print." Kest turned to me. "We're not close to him, Falcio: he's close to us. He told you to follow him and now he's making sure we do exactly that. He wants you, Falcio."

I gave a hoarse laugh. "I think you've got an overinflated sense of my importance."

Dariana's hand came out of nowhere and slapped me across the face. "Fucking fool! You still tell yourself these things? Why? Why is it so fucking important for you to convince yourself you're just another Greatcoat out trying to enforce simple laws?"

I was genuinely surprised by her overreaction. I expected her to want nothing more than to kill the Dashini after what they'd done to her mother. Dariana was reckless at the best of times, and this was a chance for her to get revenge. "Because that's what—"

"It's all about *you*, Falcio!" she shouted. "Haven't you figured that out yet? You said the assassin told you he'd stayed in his cell because he was waiting for the chance to kill Jillard—so why didn't he kill him during all that chaos with the Knights in the cell? Or even afterward? He could have slipped through Jillard's guards and put a blade across the bastard's throat like he was supposed to—but instead he betrayed his purpose just so he could lead us on this damn fool chase—and *why*? Why would any Dashini ever do that?" She pushed a finger into my chest. "Because destroying you is even more important to them than their damned oaths, that's why!"

I looked at Kest. "You think we should stop?"

He hesitated for a moment, then said, "No. Everything Dariana's said is likely true, but what you said about the Dashini being connected to the chaos and civil war that's taking over the country? That is also true. That means you are right: until we know their role in this we'll never put a stop to it."

"And just what do you think following his trail is going to do for us?" Dariana asked angrily. "He's playing with us; he's *herding* us like the stupid sheep we are. He loses us, and then he helpfully comes back to make sure we are able to find his trail again. This is just a game to him: a chance to wear us down before he kills us."

"Then it's a game he'll regret," Kest replied.

"Are you well and truly mad, o great 'Saint of Swords'?" she demanded. "What if it's not just one of them who happens to be there, wherever 'there' is? What if there are dozens and dozens, and what if—imagine this!—they decide not to just line up for you and stand there patiently waiting as you defeat them one at a time?"

Kest ignored the question and climbed over a fallen tree that was obstructing the path. Dariana wasn't done with us, though. "They're not fighters, Kest, they're *killers*," she shouted. "Their fucking name means 'the hunt once started ends only in blood'—don't you get it?"

Kest wouldn't let go, though. "Then we'll find another—"

Dariana's words finally struck me.

The hunt once started ends only in blood.

"Shut up," I said.

They both looked at me. "What is it?" Kest asked.

"Just shut up—both of you."

Saint Zaghev-who-sings-for-tears! Is that truly what this is about? Could they really be doing all this just to draw me out? I'd never stopped to consider the implications when I killed those Dashini while Aline and I were trying to survive Blood Week in Rijou all those months ago. I'd just been trying to keep Aline alive—and yes, keeping myself alive was quite high on the agenda too. But Jillard's agents had taken me down right after that fight, so I'd not given it much thought after that, on account of being too busy being tortured. But now I was stopping to give the matter due consideration, I could see that I might have left the Dashini with a bit of a problem. After all, if you're an ancient order of assassins famed the world over for never failing to kill your target, and you've just . . . well, *failed* is probably the right word here . . . It's just that murder isn't just a *job* for them; it's their *religion*.

So I have to ask myself: would they really do all of this just to capture me in some insane elaborate, ritualistic way?

"What do you mean, 'of course they would'?" Dariana asked.

"What?"

"You were mumbling to yourself. You said, 'of course they would.'"

I looked at the path ahead of us, and at the footprint so carefully pressed into the mud. Here we were in the middle of nowhere, at the bottom of a mountain of loose shale, rocks and other hazards that should have made it impassable. "I know where we are," I said. "I know where he's leading us."

Dariana followed my eyes. "Up there? There's no way to get up there."

"There's a path," I said. "One that only a few have walked before us."

"You think it leads to our assassin?" Kest asked.

I nodded.

"Do you think that Dariana's right? Will there be more of them?"

I nodded again.

"How many?"

"All of them."

Kest's eyes narrowed. "That doesn't make any sense. That would mean he's taking us—"

"It's the Dashini monastery," I said. "The assassin's leading us to the place where they're raised, where they're trained, where they're taught to kill."

"But that would be . . . Falcio, the Dashini monastery has been hidden for hundreds of years—no one's ever been able to find it. So why on earth would they give that up?"

"Because they know we'll come," I said, "and they don't plan on us leaving—not alive, at any rate."

"Then we have to run," Dariana said, seizing on the chance to change our course. "We go and collect ourselves an army and then we come back and destroy them, once and for all."

"They'll be long gone by then," I said. "The Dashini don't believe in sacred places. They won't hesitate to destroy a monastery and move if they need to."

"So how do we fight them?" Kest said.

The answer was so feeble I could barely bring myself to say it out loud—but even they had a right to know the bet on which I was about to risk their lives. "Years ago the King began sending Greatcoats to infiltrate the Dashini, one at a time, year after year. He believed there was a chance a handful of us could make it inside: we'd learn their secrets, and ultimately we'd bring them down before they could destroy us—and the country."

Kest didn't look convinced. "That was years ago, Falcio, and we've never heard back from any of them. What evidence do you have that any of them—even one of them—is still alive? The odds are—"

"We're the Greatcoats," I said portentously—it felt like a moment for grand declamations, after all. "Since when do Greatcoats care about the odds?" I gave him a grin, but inside my heart was cold. It wasn't that I believed any of the King's spies really had succeeded in infiltrating the Dashini. I just couldn't see any other way of us surviving what was coming next, and if all I had to cling to was false hope—well, I'd take that over despair any day.

Two Dukes were already dead, the murderers set up to look like Greatcoats. Chaos was growing as the nobility, already nervous of peasant uprisings, were now afraid for their lives—and they had pretty good reason, thanks to the mysterious Knights in black tabards who were wreaking havoc and spreading mayhem through the duchies. There was no doubt in my mind: the Dashini were fomenting civil war and creating hell in Tristia.

So either a dozen Greatcoats were waiting for us inside that monastery, or my world was about to come to its end.

The hunt once started ends only in blood.

You've got that right, you bastards.

As the going got much steeper I needed more and more help from Kest. Though the path looked impassable, with impenetrable walls of vicious thorny vines everywhere the eye could see, we were led us to cunningly concealed hollowed-out paths that slipped beneath the bramble barriers. Other times, we'd find deadly shale beneath our feet that shattered into a million treacherous shards, almost guaranteeing a fall off the edge into the ravine hundreds of feet below—except for a narrow path that had been carefully cut away.

The assassin shepherded us past one danger after another, each step a reminder that without him, we would be lost; it was beginning to look horribly like the Dashini really could do things we mere Greatcoats could not.

I began to feel like I was just too damn *big*; I'd been transformed into a lumbering oaf following awkwardly behind a dancer of unsurpassed skill. How had I ever been fast enough, *precise* enough, that night in Rijou, to kill two of them? Whatever God or Saint had blessed me for those few minutes during that deadly fight had obviously abandoned me now. Even when the neatha wasn't dulling the feeling in my fingers and toes, I knew I was far slower than I had been that day and I started to wonder if I would manage even a few moments when it came to pitting my blades against theirs.

I slipped on a mat of pine needles made slick by frost, but as I lost my balance Kest caught me, stopping me inches before my head collided with a rough-trunked tree.

He'll survive, I thought. So that had to be our plan. *If Dariana and I can blunt their attack for even a moment, Kest will make it back. No matter how skilled or fast the fighter, his opponent is always twice as dangerous if he isn't* trying *to survive.*

The thought of my imminent death, of finally being free of the pain and obligation that shackled me to a dead King's daughter, came as a sudden, enormous relief. *I can't beat them—you can't expect that of me. Better demand that I cut down the mountain with my rapiers than that I fight the Dashini for you.*

Just at the point of sunset we passed single-file through a shattered outcropping of rock rising up from the edge of the mountaintop and there, nearly a quarter of a mile away and yet looking if we could reach out and touch it, was the Dashini monastery.

The very sight made my heart sicken: a blackstone tower in the center of a clearing, as tall and thin as if it had been patterned after a Dashini poignard.

"It's as if someone stabbed a black needle into the country itself," Dariana said.

Kest looked as ill from the sight as I felt. "It's been right here all along, in the middle of Aramor," he whispered.

The Duchy of Aramor had been the seat of the Kings of Tristia for as long as we had had stories of Kings to tell—and for almost as long there have been stories of the Dashini, of their dark mysticism and their dedication to the art of assassination. As Greatcoats we had spent much of our time learning to duel any opponent, and yet every one of us had always feared the Dashini. And here, not fifty miles from Castle Aramor, was the place where the Dashini were trained. Had they wished, every one of their assassins could have marched down the mountain, one at a time, in pairs or all together, and been at our doorstep within a few days.

They could have killed the King any time they'd wanted.

"I asked him to let me go," Kest said.

"What?" I was still transfixed by the tower.

Kest looked at me. "The day the Dukes were coming? When he gave us each our missions? I asked him to let me find the Dashini. But he said no, enough good men and women had died trying, and he would never send another. And anyway, I was the last person in the world he'd send for such a task."

I found myself staring at him in wonder: Kest was my best friend in all the world and yet I kept discovering new ways in which he had never let me in. If any man had a chance to deal with the Dashini, surely it would have been Kest? "Why did he refuse you?"

Kest kept his gaze on the tower. "He said I lacked the patience."

"He didn't want you to die for nothing," I said.

Dariana's eyes went wide and her face contorted with anger. "So Saint Paelis decided you were too important to risk?"

I looked at her. "I'm sorry, Dariana, I know you think the King should have done more after your mother was killed, but he—"

"What you know, Falcio val Mond, is *nothing*! I've spent quite enough time running around after you on your mad fucking quest. You think King Paelis had some master plan? So tell me how that works, because right now I'm pretty sure he was the second dumbest man in all of Tristia."

I ignored the jibe. "Go back down to where we left the horses," I said. "If we haven't returned by morning, go and find the Tailor— and no, I have no damned idea where she is—and tell her the Dashini are behind all of this. If you can't find the Tailor—well, just tell everyone who will listen. The Dashini are attempting their greatest feat ever, to wipe away the stain of the defeat they suffered. They want to assassinate *the country*."

"Fine," Dariana said simply, and she turned and started back down the path. For some reason I'd expected her to argue with me, to refuse to leave us. "Those Greatcoats the King sent are dead, Falcio," she called back after a moment. "You are too."

Kest looked up at the fading sun. "We're losing the light," he said. "We should wait until it's full dark."

"No," I said, pulling one of my rapiers from its sheath, "we go now."

"Now? Why go while there's still light for them to see us coming?"

I pulled one of my rapiers. "Because *they* prefer the dark," I said. "They *like* the dark."

As we set off for the Dashini monastery I started preparing myself for either a quick and brutal death, or a miracle.

It turned out I was wrong. I wasn't at all prepared for what came next.

36

THE MONASTERY

A shift in the wind gave us the first hint of something wrong. We were less than two hundred yards away and fully expecting dozens of assassins in wafty dark blue silk to start swarming all over us. But then the wind shifted and the smell of burning filled my senses.

"I don't understand," I said, peering toward the tower. "Are they cooking something?"

Kest shook his head. "No. Whatever that is, it's not burning anymore. This happened some time ago."

Only when we were very close to the pointy tower did we see the signs of fire. They'd been hidden by the blackness of the stone, but up close I could see the charred edges of rocks. I suppose that's why I didn't immediately notice the old man sitting on a rock waiting for us.

"You're late," he said. His face was turned toward the last dying light of the sun. There were blackened holes where his eyes should have been.

I looked around for any sign of the man we'd followed. "Who are you?" I asked the old man.

"No one of consequence," he replied.

"Are you Dashini?"

"There are no Dashini," the old man said. "There never were. The Dashini were just a story your parents told you to make you say your prayers at night."

"Are you mad? You're sitting right next to their monastery."

The old man laughed. "Really? Wouldn't that be something then? But no, I assure you, there is no monastery, for there are no Dashini."

"Then who are you?"

"A messenger," he said.

"What's your message then?" Kest asked.

"No," I said, "first tell us for whom you are keeping the message, and for how long?"

The old man laughed. "Ah, see, not as dumb as you look, then."

"How would you know how dumb we look? You're blind," I said.

"True, and yet I can say with absolute confidence that you look like a fool. Isn't the universe a wondrous place?"

"Just—"

The old man held up a hand. "For you," he said. "My message is for you."

"And who am I?" I asked.

"Well, we could play this game all night but it's getting cold and I've been waiting a long time. My message is for you, Falcio val Mond, First Cantor of the Greatcoats."

"How long have you been waiting for me?"

"Well now, I haven't really been keeping track. Perhaps you could answer that one yourself."

I thought about that for a moment, then I said, "Perhaps I could, if you can tell me what action of mine required you to give me a message."

"Ah," he said, "see? Clever. Such a clever, clever fool you are. Well, let me answer you this way: my message comes from those who once were, but now are not, nor were they ever."

"We're not interested in games," Kest said. There was an angry tension around his eyes. He'd been expecting a fight, release for the angry fire burning just under his skin. "Not anymore. Are you working for the Dashini or not?"

"The Dashini?" the old man said, barely holding back laughter. "Didn't I tell you? There never were any Dashini."

"Of course there were," Kest said, his voice almost a growl. "Falcio killed two of them in Rijou."

"Ah, you see? That's the proof right there."

"Proof of what?" I asked.

"Every one knows the Dashini never fail, not in the two thousand years of their supposed existence. It would be impossible for the Dashini to fail, for to do so—"

Finally the pieces fell into place for me. "For to fail would mean they were not Dashini, and therefore never were."

The old man picked up his crutch and pushed himself to a standing position. "Now you understand, and now I can deliver my message."

He got up hobbled around the base of the tower and as we followed the smell hit us. There was a great pit dug there. At first the charcoal smoke made it hard to see, but gradually the hazy shadows resolved into the charred remains of corpses. There must have been more than a hundred of them.

"Saint Zaghev-who-sings-for-tears," I said, my hand to my lips— although anyone who thinks this is an effective method for keeping the taste and stench of a hundred dread bodies out of their nose and mouth is deluding themselves. "How could this happen?"

"Falcio, look." Kest pointed to a body on the top of the pile: a lot of the skin was blackened, but he was still recognizable. It was the assassin from Rijou, the man we'd been pursuing across Tristia.

"He killed himself," I said, and I could hear the disbelief in my own voice. "He led us all the way here and then he just killed himself." I turned to the old man. "Why?"

"Because he was not allowed to tell you, so he brought you here to see."

"But how could they have all—?"

"*They*, Trattari? What *they* do you speak of?" the old man asked. "There's nothing there. It's a shame though, isn't it? About the Dashini not having existed? Does it mean, do you suppose, that the Bardatti never existed, either? That the Trattari are simply something we imagined as well? Would that not be the darkest truth? The truth that makes our courage fail and our hearts surrender?"

"The Dashini have nothing to do with us, or the Bardatti," I said, wondering as the words came out of my mouth if I was telling the truth.

"Really? *Trattari—Bardatti—Dashini* . . . Do you truly not see?"

The implications started to grow in my mind. Was there was a connection between the Troubadours, the Greatcoats, and the Dashini? And if that was the case, what did it mean—?

The old man reached into his pocket and pulled out something small and red. He popped it into his mouth and began sucking on it. "Oh my," he said. "I've wanted one of these for so long. I can't begin to tell you how good it tastes."

I took hold of the old man's arm. "Who are you?"

"Who are you talking to?" the old man asked. He shrugged off my hand and walked to the edge of the pit, then he turned so that he was facing us.

"You said you were a messenger—so tell me who you are."

"A messenger? Why, a man would need to have someone to give him a message in order to be a messenger, wouldn't he? And since there's no one to have given the message, there can be no messenger, can there?"

"Look, old man, we—"

"Old man? There's no old man here—there is no one at all, just two fools who climbed a mountain to speak to no one; to find nobody; to learn nothing." He pulled a short black dagger, thin as a needle, from inside his shirt and held it between both his hands. "You know, I feel sorry for you, Falcio val Mond. I really do." Then in one sure motion he stabbed it into his own heart.

"No!" I cried, but even as I reached for him the old man toppled backward into the pit, on top of the charred remains of those who had once called themselves the Dashini. The blood seeping out from his chest was lost in the blackness surrounding him.

I looked into the pit, my eyes searching for something—*any*thing—that would give this meaning. I'd risked everything to come here, only to find the Dashini dead, and apparently long before the murders had begun. But if the Dashini weren't responsible, then who was behind the madness overtaking Tristia?

"We have to go," Kest said.

The strain in his voice was worrying. I turned to see what was wrong.

Kest's skin was as red as fresh blood.

We traveled faster than was safe, sliding on shale and slipping down the muddy paths. Kest was quiet most of the way, though sometimes I could hear him mumbling to himself; I stopped asking him what was wrong as really, it was pretty damn obvious, and I decided I could do without the glaring back at me. Sometimes he refused even to glare back and that was worse.

We lost our way several times, even with the red glow of Kest's skin breaking the shadows in front of us, but in the end, we found our way back, because eventually all things fall to earth. When we reached the bottom of the trail, he stopped suddenly and stood there.

"What is it?" I said, looking around to see what had unnerved him. There was no sign of enemies. The clearing was small, mostly grass, dotted here and there with a few stones and some broken shale. It was surrounded by trees, and there were a few reddish rocks around the very edge. When Kest still didn't speak I said, "Please, tell me what's wrong—I've got enough problems to deal with without you being—"

Kest walked away from me for several paces, then he turned to face me. "Draw," he said.

I realized he was standing ten paces away from me: the exact distance we used when beginning a duel. Worse, he was not just glowing red from head to toe but positively pulsating. "What in all the hells is this about?" I asked, although I was beginning to have a horrible feeling I already knew.

"Draw your sword," he said.

"I won't fight you, Kest. Just stop and think this through."

"No, enough thinking, enough *talk*—enough dragging me around chasing answers that don't exist." His voice was hard as steel, as if every last trace of humanity had drained out of him. "I've followed you on every one of your damn fool's errands and that's enough. I came to the top of that mountain for the promise of worthy opponents—and instead we found *nothing.*"

"The promise of—? Kest, have you lost your mind? Did you think this was all just so you could have an entertaining fight?"

"Draw," he said. "Draw, or else I'll cut you down where you stand."

"I won't fight you, Kest."

"Yes," he said, "you will." He leaped forward, drawing his blade from its sheath in one smooth motion and swinging it in a vertical arc toward my head.

Of course I reacted entirely on reflex. I drew my own rapiers and batted Kest's blade out of the way. "Stop!" I cried, but he ignored me and attacked again, forcing me to back away even as I parried. Kest fights with a warsword, which is a great deal heavier and carries far more force than my rapiers. It's also supposed to be a lot slower, but in Kest's hands the blade was moving so quickly I could barely see it in time to parry.

"Come on, Falcio," he said. "You beat me before so let's see you do it again!"

But that had been years ago, and then I'd won through a trick—one I had no chance of repeating, not now when I could barely stay on my feet. But apparently Kest didn't care about any of that.

His blade whirred by me again and this time I felt something nick my cheek. "Attack me!" he said.

"Please, Kest, stop! Don't make me—"

A woman's voice broke the night air. "What in all the hells are you doing?" Dariana asked.

"Get away!" I shouted. "Get out of here!"

"Yes," Kest said, tossing his sword from hand to hand as if it were weightless, "go away and practice. Practice *lots*. Come back in a few years when you might be able to give me an interesting fight."

Dariana looked uncertain, but she didn't look scared, which surprised me. Anyone facing Kest with a blade in his hand should be as terrified as I was.

He can't stop himself, I realized belatedly, *because he's lost in the red rage.* This was exactly what Birgid had warned me of. And of course she was right: becoming the Saint of Swords wasn't a blessing from the Gods at all. It was a curse—even Trin had said so—and now Kest was suffering from a bloodlust that demanded he find foes good enough to genuinely challenge him.

"What should I do?" Dariana asked. She began to draw her sword, and it struck me yet again that she wasn't frightened.

Why the hells was she not frightened?

"Don't," I said. "He'll kill you."

"Not until I've killed you first, Falcio. Come on, you can beat me. You've always been able to beat me—and yet you prance about pretending I'm better than you, when all the while you're laughing at me behind my back."

He needs to believe that I can beat him so he can fight me. He needs to believe I genuinely have a chance . . . I sighed inwardly. *Hells, this had better work.* I pulled my coat off and threw it to the ground. "If you cut me, Kest, you'll kill me."

He smiled and removed his own coat. "Is that your grand strategy? Is that yet another example of Falcio val Mond's 'masterful tactics'?" Without waiting for a reply he launched himself at me again, swinging his sword in a figure-eight pattern that looked predictable and regular and should have been easy to parry, but every time I tried to beat away his sword I somehow missed by a hair.

He's varying the speed, I realized. *Just slightly, just enough that I can't predict where his blade will end up.* "Kest, you're better than me—you know that. This isn't a fair fight!"

"It's fair enough," he said, and he beat my blade out of line again, forcing me to stumble back.

"The hells for this," Dariana, drawing a throwing knife from her coat. "He's lost his mind. I'm taking him out."

"No," I said, but it was too late; Dariana had thrown the knife at Kest's throat. He barely even varied the pattern of his sword-swinging to knock the knife out of the air.

"Maybe you'd like to fight me both at once," he said.

I tried taking advantage of his attention on Dariana to land a thrust on his leg, and once again he knocked my blade out of the way effortlessly.

"Come on, Dariana," he taunted her even as he pushed me back, "try another knife—who knows? Maybe you'll get lucky this time."

She wouldn't, though. Kest is the best swordsman I've ever seen, and he has been since he was thirteen years old. Now he was inhuman and he could knock knives thrown at him all night long if he wanted and still slice me into pieces in the process. There was no way for either of us to get past his guard. Mine, on the other hand . . .

That's it.

"Another knife," I shouted to Dariana. "Get out another throwing knife!"

Kest smiled at me and took a step closer, sneaking the tip of his blade past my guard and giving me another small cut on my other cheek. It was probably precisely the same length as the first one.

Dariana drew and took aim at Kest. "No!" I said, running backward several steps and cursing myself in advance for what was to come. "At me! You've got to throw it *at me.*"

"What? Are you mad?"

"Just do it," I said, "*now!*"

Kest looked confused for a moment, then he realized what I was planning, but not even he was fast enough to bridge the distance in time. Out of the corner of my eye I saw Dariana pull back and throw, at which point it occurred to me that I probably should have been a little bit more specific about where exactly she should aim for.

The blade came through the air and landed in my left shoulder and I screamed long and loud from the pain. It turns out that knowing what's coming isn't any kind of a pain reliever.

Kest's eyes went wide. "Fool! You damned fool! You haven't got a chance now!" His voice was desperate, almost pleading.

I fell to my knees. *Damn, but a knife in the shoulder hurts.* I hoped it hadn't damaged the muscle—if I somehow managed to live through the next few minutes I would probably need it again soon. "Sorry," I said, pulling the knife out of my shoulder and wincing from the pain, "but I'm not in any shape to give you a fair fight." I dropped the knife to the ground, just in case. "Maybe if you wait a few weeks, then when I'm all healed up I can give you the spanking you sorely deserve."

Kest roared incoherently into the night sky. The red glow around him looked like it was burning him up now, eating away at his soul. He threw his warsword through the air and it flew past me within an inch of my face, stopping only when it impaled the trunk of a tree behind me. I watched as he fell to his knees a few feet away from me and began to pound his fists into the ground, over and over and over, until they came up red, but not from the glow, from the blood on his fingers.

"Stop," I said, and forced myself to my feet. "It's enough."

At first I didn't think he could hear me, but just as I reached him he stopped and his head dropped as if all the strength had left his body. He wasn't screaming or shouting now; he was crying. "What's happened to me?" he moaned. "How do I make this stop?" He began to shiver.

"I don't know," I replied, and knelt down and put my arms around him.

We stayed like that for a while. I could hear Dariana moving around behind us, likely retrieving her knives.

Eventually Kest pushed me away. "I have to go," he said.

"What—? Where?"

"The Saint—Birgid—she told me to come with her, but I refused. I told her I needed to stay with you, to *protect* you." He laughed hollowly.

"How will you even find her?"

"I . . . She told me about this place, a kind of temple. It's called Deos Savath. It's in Aramor—it's where we're supposed to go to complete the ritual and gain control over ourselves. I refused, though. I told her I could resist. Gods, Fal, I'm such a fool."

Part of me wanted to smile. Kest had always quietly insisted that the limitations of normal human beings did not apply to him. But the other part of me realized I was about to lose my best friend. "How long will you need to go?" I asked.

"I don't know. I don't know anything about this. I thought . . . I thought defeating Caveil was a victory. I thought it would make me better, but it hasn't, Falcio. I'm no better a swordsman than I was before. When I first felt the . . . well, whatever it is that passed from Caveil to me, when I beat him, it was like . . . I don't know. It was like being somehow completely drunk and yet completely clear-headed. But something inside me broke then. Before, I fought because I wanted to, or because it was needed. Now I . . . I *have* to . . ."

"I know," I said quietly. I had spent several years of my own life driven by a madness that had nothing to do with courage or necessity. Ethalia had helped heal me of it, but I didn't think she could do the same for Kest. I thought about what the Tailor had done, and what I had to do next, and how much I needed Kest beside me to do it, which made it all the more difficult to say, "You have to go. You have to go to that temple and find Birgid."

Kest looked up at me. "But I don't know if it will work, Falcio—I don't know if I'll be able to come back. If I can't get control over this . . . whatever 'this' is, then—"

"You'll come back," I said firmly, and I walked over to pick up our coats, trying to ignore the dagger wound in my shoulder that was sending spikes of fire through my body with each step. "You'll figure this out and then you'll come and find me and we'll save this shitty world from itself."

"How do you know that?" he asked.

I tossed him his coat. "We're Greatcoats," I said. "It's the only thing we're good at."

He laughed for a moment.

"What's so funny?" I asked.

"Nothing," he said, rising to his feet. "I just thought, if Brasti was here he'd say something funny, but I couldn't think what that would be, and then I thought, this is when Brasti would make fun of me for not knowing, and then I started laughing. Odd, isn't it?" He put on his coat before walking over to the tree and retrieving his sword, and then he walked away into the forest, alone.

"You're doing quite a bit of bleeding there," Dariana said.

I looked down at my shoulder and saw the blood seeping through my shirt. "Not as much as it could have been. You managed to get me without tearing the muscle. Nice shot."

"Couldn't have you dying on me, could I?"

I reached into my coat and pulled a roll of thin gauze from one of the inner pockets and began wrapping it around my shoulder.

"Here," she said, "you're doing it wrong." She took the gauze from me and put it aside.

"What are you doing?"

She pulled a small bottle of salve from her own coat. "Not much point in wrapping the wound just so you can bleed to death a bit more slowly."

She was right: I'd forgotten to put salve on the wound. I watched as she carefully rubbed a thin layer of the black salve on the hole in my flesh, and then wrapped the bandage deftly around my shoulder. She moved slowly, carefully.

The waiting was driving me mad. "Can't you do this any faster?"

"I don't want to go through all this just to have you keel over and die before we even get started," she replied.

"Start what?" I asked.

She finished tying the gauze and helped me put my coat back on. "There, see? All better."

I looked into her eyes and she smiled. "So you're not dead, and you don't seem to be accompanied by twelve secret Greatcoats, so what did you learn up there?"

"The darkest truth," I said, repeating the old man's words.

"What does that mean?"

"There was an old man there and he said something about what we feared most being ourselves."

If the Dashini had all committed suicide after I killed two of them in Rijou, then the assassins tearing Tristia apart aren't Dashini. So who else could they be? And I thought about it, and the answer became clear. It was obvious, really—in fact, people had been trading rumors and gossip about just such a thing for years. My stomach sank, and the sound of my heart became dull and flat in my chest. Who else other the Dashini could sneak into castles, past guards and Knights, to defeat those protecting the Dukes—hells, not just the Dukes but to kill them all, and then get out without being caught? Only one other group of people that I knew of had the skills and training to complete such missions.

"What is it?" Dariana asked.

The truth that makes our courage fail and our hearts surrender. What we fear most is simply ourselves. "The assassins are Greatcoats," I said sadly. "Our own people are doing this."

"What? Are you—? Are you sure?"

I ignored the question. Had I ever been this alone in my life? I'd spent the last weeks fearing being paralyzed, isolated inside my own body—and yet here I was, even without the paralysis, trapped and alone.

I looked at Dariana and felt the sadness threaten to reveal what I knew. "Thanks for the salve," I said. I walked over to my rapiers and picked them up, but I didn't sheathe them.

"Expecting more trouble?" she asked.

I tried lifting both my rapiers into guard but the pain in my left shoulder nearly made me pass out so I had to let that rapier fall back to the ground. "You weren't scared," I said.

"What do you mean?"

"Of Kest. He said he'd take you next and yet you weren't afraid—in fact, you didn't look all that surprised at what happened."

"Are you out of your mind? Of course I was scared! But what good would running around crying do? I saved your life, remember?"

She looked confused and even angry; there was not a sign on her face of deceit. But I'd been at this a while. "You're lying," I said. "You knew he was going to do this." I looked around at the red rocks that surrounded the clearing. I hadn't given them any thought before. "Those rocks—they weren't here when we came by the first time. You put them there to make the Saint's Fever worse, didn't you?"

Her expression didn't change at all, but she held her forefinger just an inch or so away from her thumb. "Just a teensy bit," she said. "He'd been heading for it for some time. We just couldn't be sure he would boil over when we needed him to."

I thought about shouting for Kest, but I knew he was too far away by now. I might have tried it anyway, but there was something else that was bothering me. *She hadn't been scared.* "So how many did you bring with you?" I asked, scanning the trees around the clearing. "They're very good at hiding."

Dariana nodded, as if we'd just come to an agreement of some kind. "There are nine of us," she said. "And Kest is far enough away now."

Figures emerged from the trees, moving silently into the clearing one by one and encircling me. Their swords were drawn. They wore greatcoats.

"It's better this way," Dariana said. "If there were fewer of us you might try to fight, and that wouldn't serve you or the Tailor."

"You think I'm going to just let you kill me?" I asked.

"Kill you? No, First Cantor, that wouldn't solve anyone's problems. You want to confront the Tailor? Yell at her? Threaten her? Fine; we'll take you to her."

I looked at the figures around me. "You know she's going to destroy the entire country, don't you? Assassinating the Dukes? Arming the peasants and pushing them to rebellion? It'll be civil war and chaos for a decade."

Dariana looked at me as if she was trying to decide if I were joking. "See, that's what I don't understand about you, Falcio."

"What's that?"

"You actually care about these things."

37

BLAME

"Well, you've really cocked everything up again, Falcio," the Tailor said, locking eyes with me.

"Yes," I agreed, looking straight back at her. Her so-called Greatcoats were surrounding us, but they hadn't taken away my rapiers and that told me they weren't the slightest bit afraid of me. I tried to pretend that didn't annoy me.

"All you had to do was stay out of the way," she said. "You could have gone away with your little whore—you could have been happy with your 'Sister of Mercy'. Instead you're here, forcing me to do this." Her voice was thick with anger and hurt and something close to indignity—as if I was the one who'd betrayed *her*. She reached a hand out toward me and for just an instant, her expression softened.

I was filled with such a desire for this to all have been some kind of terrible mistake—a misunderstanding between friends that could be solved with words and not weapons, but it took only a quick glance at the murderers standing with her, making a mockery of the coat of office that had meant so much to me for all these years, to remind me that peace between us wasn't possible, not anymore.

"You betrayed my King," I said, my voice and my heart as cold as the neatha running through my veins. I drew my rapiers.

Almost as one, the false Greatcoats drew their swords as well, while Tailor looked at me with eyes so hard I could have sworn the irises were little black rocks ringed by angry copper veins. "He was *my son*, damn you. He might have been your King but he was *my son*—speak of him that way again, First Cantor, say those words again and I'll wring your throat myself."

One of the Greatcoats started to speak but she stopped him. "Keep your mouth shut. I know our agreement."

I didn't need Kest to tell me the odds; my chances of surviving this encounter were slim to none, but I had stopped caring. The neatha poisoning was reaching its inevitable conclusion; my fingers were numb and I was struggling to grip my rapiers. Each thump of my heart felt like it might be the last beat of a drummer too exhausted to continue. But when I closed my eyes, I saw the victims of Carefal before me, lying in smoldering heaps upon the ground, and when I opened them, I saw the traitors of my King's last, best hope.

"To the hells with each and every one of you," I said. I liked to believe I was goading the Tailor to make a mistake, something that would give me the means to get a blade at her throat and take her captive. With that—and an unimaginable amount of luck—I could then effect my escape. But in truth I was just angry and heartbroken. Maybe my death would be as empty as my life, but at least I would see the blood of these false Greatcoats pool on the cold ground next to mine before I was done here.

"Stop!" a thin voice called, and Aline ran out from behind one of the trees and stumbled to the ground between the Tailor and me.

"Stop," she cried again, picking herself up. "Don't do this, Falcio!" Her hair was matted against her scalp; her arms and legs were too thin, her skin too tight on her face. The Tailor took her by the arm and pulled her close.

"You brought her *here*?" I demanded incredulously. "To see this?"

"She has to stay with me." The Tailor's voice was sad, but unapologetic. "Only I can keep her safe."

"*Safe?* Is that how you justify this to yourself?" I turned to the others standing around me with their swords at the ready. "Do any of you know the real reason why she ordered you to kill Duke Isault? To kill Duke Roset? It's not because they were plotting against Aline, I promise you. Isault had given Aline his support."

"Fool. He would have betrayed us to Trin the moment she threatened his borders."

"Then why did you send me to him?" I demanded. "Why make me—?"

"Because I needed to send the person they'd most expect to try to kill the Dukes—all around the countryside people are telling the story of Falsio the Brave; Falsio the Duke-slayer. Falsio the Fool."

"So you sent me there to die? Or just to frame me?"

"No, you great ass—I arranged for the villagers in Carefal to rise up because I knew Isault would want to use you to put down their rebellion. Once he sent you—"

"Your assassin would kill Isault."

"And you would be out there with his Knights, which would keep anyone from believing the Greatcoats responsible. I didn't anticipate you'd be so damned stupid as to actually convince the villagers to put down their weapons."

"And then you went and gave them more," I said, "and you got them killed."

"Don't be such a damned fool. You think I kept *extra* caches of weapons lying around just in case the villagers decided to sell the ones I gave them?"

She sounded sincere, but I remembered the stench of the smoking corpses piled high in the main square, and too many of them had steel sword-hilts branded into the flesh of their palms. So she was lying—but why bother, when I was about to be dead? But if she didn't rearm the people of Carefal, then who did . . . ?

"Isault's troops would have destroyed them," I said.

"And instead it was the Black Tabards. Do you suppose the dead of Carefal take satisfaction in the difference?"

"Then I suppose we must put the blame on the person who put them in that position in the first place."

The Tailor barked a laugh. "For once we agree, Falcio. Do you think for even a second I could've convinced them to rise up if it hadn't been for all your damned heroics in Rijou?" She started slow-clapping. "Congratulations, Falcio. You're the reason this happened, every single part of it. You're the one who made it all possible."

I ignored her and turned my attention to her Greatcoats. "Are you proud of yourselves? This madwoman has turned you into assassins."

A few of them laughed then, but the Tailor silenced them with a gesture. "Boy, you think you're so clever, but you really haven't figured it all out, have you?"

"Why?" I asked. "Why would you do this? You're going to send the country into civil war. How will that put Aline on—?"

The Tailor looked down and patted the matted hair of the girl hugging her leg as she wept piteously. "Aline can't take the throne—isn't that obvious? She's too young—she isn't ready. The *country* isn't ready!" She looked back at me. "And damned Trin is out there, busy securing the all support she'll need, and once she's on the throne, that's it, Falcio, for all of us."

"So you'd rather throw the country into chaos?"

"Aye, I would. Five years, that's what we'll get: five years of the nobility falling all over themselves fighting each other for control while the towns and villages are rising up against them."

"Five years where innocent people will die," I said.

"Innocent people are dying already, Falcio—they always have been. At least this way they die on their feet."

A small, weary part of me—the part that was too tired to fight anymore—wanted to believe there was wisdom in her words, that we might reach some kind of accommodation. "And then what happens?"

"Then the country will remember how much better it was with a proper monarch on the throne. They'll crave someone who can rule with compassion, someone who can keep the country together. And in five years' time Aline will be ready to lead them, and they'll be hungry for her to take the throne."

It was a perfectly logical argument, one built upon the innate political truths that had always governed the people of Tristia. A sensible, pragmatic person would immediately agree. There was only one problem. "The King could have done that," I said, trying to ignore the fact that my vision was growing blurrier by the minute. "He could have spread death and chaos to keep his throne—but instead, he sacrificed himself for the greater peace."

The Tailor's voice was harsh and angry and full of resentment. "'For the greater peace'? Is that what you still tell yourself, Falcio? He was *dying*, you damned *stupid* fool!"

She let the words hang there for a good long while before she said, "He'd been sick his whole life and he was dying then, just as you are now, Falcio. *That's* why he made the Greatcoats step aside—*that's* why he let the Dukes take him." The old woman stepped close to me, ignoring my rapiers, and stuck her face in mine. "It's so easy to be brave and self-sacrificing when death already has you in its clutches—that's why you're always so damned noble, isn't it? You died long ago, back when your wife was slaughtered, and ever since then you have walked the earth praying for someone to put a blade in you. My son was the same." She slapped me hard on the left cheek. "Damn you for trying to make him a Saint when he was only a man."

I tried reaching deep inside me, looking for anger to match the Tailor's own, but all I could find was bitter cold and loneliness. Everything she had said was true. In my heart, Paelis was bold and daring and full of life, and yet in every memory he was coughing and wheezing, his features pale and his voice thin. She was right of course; he was dreadfully sick, so his death could no more be called an act of bravery than a leaf falling from a tree could be said to be aiming for the ground. I had always known that the King was a man like any other. I just couldn't live with it being true.

"So it was all for nothing," I said at last.

"No," the Tailor said, grabbing my chin and looking me in the eye. "There is still the girl. Aline will rule this Kingdom one day. Let that be the King's legacy. Let her—"

"You've committed murder in her name," I said, my voice sounding hollow and tired. "How will she rule when people find out? How will she—?" I looked at Aline, desperate to see her face again.

She wouldn't meet my eyes. "Falcio . . ." she said, her voice almost pleading.

"You *knew*," I whispered. "The Tailor didn't trick you—she didn't lie to you. *You knew.*"

"I . . . what did you want me to do, Falcio?" she cried. "I *told* you I was scared. I *told* you I don't know how to do this. I don't want to die!"

"So instead you let this madwoman send her dogs to assassinate whole families. Did she tell you she was murdering the sons and daughters of the Dukes? Did she tell you they were . . ." My voice caught. "They were *children*, Aline, younger than you. They—"

"I never ordered those children killed," the Tailor said. *"Never."*

"Why should I believe you?" I said, my voice so full of rage that Aline cowered behind the Tailor.

"What good does it do me to have them dead? Alive, the Ducal Concord would have chosen Ducal Protectors, weak men of low ambition who would never think of seizing the thrones for themselves. My plan worked better with the children *alive.*"

"And yet your hounds killed them. I saw the bodies of Isault's children myself."

"And I'm telling you those weren't my orders and it wasn't my Greatcoats."

"Don't call them Greatcoats," I said. "Don't you *dare*—"

"Fine," she said, "they're Queen's Blades. They're what you and Kest and Brasti and all the others should have been."

"They're *murderers*," I said, my eyes on them, "and I will see those coats off their backs and them in chains before this is done."

She let out a hoarse laugh. I was really beginning to tire of her sense of humor. "So much outrage—odd, really, since not one of them would be here without you."

I looked around at them. They were all young, younger than most of us were when we joined the Greatcoats—and yet I had seen them in action and I knew they were already deadly fighters.

The Tailor couldn't have possibly have found enough ordinary men and women and trained them to be so skilled, not in so few years, and that meant they had to have training already, and probably their whole lives. But they didn't fight like Knights, and other than Knights and Greatcoats, no one else studied dueling at this level. No one except . . .

I felt bile rise in my throat even as fear filled my heart. "They're Dashini," I said.

"Aye," the Tailor said. "Of a sort."

"But that's impossible. I was at the monastery. I saw the corpses."

"You saw the Blooded Dashini: those who had taken their final vows and slain their targets. These"—she gestured around her, "are the Unblooded. The ones in training."

"But why aren't they—?"

"Why aren't they dead? Because the Unblooded are not permitted ritual suicide until the Blooded are fully consecrated in the ground. Can you imagine that? They're supposed to sit there for months, waiting for the corpses of their masters to rot way to nothing before they're allowed to kill themselves."

"But you convinced them otherwise."

"I knew what would happen once you killed those two in Rijou— and I suppose I should offer you my congratulations, by the way. You're the only man alive to have defeated Dashini assassins. Now do you believe me? Without you, none of this would be possible."

"So it's true: the entire Order committed ritual suicide just because I got lucky and killed two of them?"

"The Dashini are only Dashini if they are undefeated," she said. "I went to the monastery knowing the Unblooded would be there, knowing they would be leaderless and without direction, so I generously gave them a better opportunity. I offered them a chance at greatness."

"And what did that cost?" I asked.

But I already knew the answer: *I* was the price. I was the gold with which the Tailor had purchased a hundred assassins. *The hunt once begun ends only in blood.* The illusion of self-righteous anger retreated from the Tailor's face, leaving only sadness and shame in its wake. I understood then why the Tailor had felt the need to tell me all this, why it was so important to her that I understood the reasons for her plans. She wanted my forgiveness.

She looked at me for a moment, waiting for me to speak, but for once in my life I found I had no words. Finally she turned to one of the Greatcoats. "Dariana, take Aline away now. It's getting dark, and she should have some supper."

Aline walked up to me and touched my hand, her own trembling. "I'm sorry," she whispered. "I'm sorry I couldn't be braver."

I knelt down for a moment and awkwardly wrapped my arms around her, even as I kept a grip on my rapiers. I could feel the cool, wet skin of her cheek against mine. "It's all right," I said. "You were as brave as anyone could hope. Go on, sweetheart, don't cry. I'll be fine once we work things out here."

Aline stepped back and slowly reached out a small hand. She put it against my face, and then she began to cry. A moment later she turned and ran away, into the dark shadows of the trees. Dariana strode after her.

"That was generous," the Tailor said. For once there was no trace of cynicism in her voice.

"The girl isn't to blame," I said, "and she shouldn't know what comes next."

I closed my eyes and pictured my wife Aline, not as she had been in life, but the way she was when I found her dead upon the floor of that tavern. I reached out for one last surge of stubborn, damned rage, one last rush of fury fueled by the destruction of all my ideals and the ruin I'd made of my own life. I summoned forth every dark and terrible part of myself, and, as I leaped at the monsters who'd blackened the name of the Greatcoats forever, I smiled.

If I could have killed even two of the bastards I would have forgiven the Gods all their injustices. If I'd reached the Tailor, well, then I might even have been grateful. But there were too many, and they were young and fast and fresh, while I was injured and poisoned and tired of living in a world that turned on lies and betrayal. They took me down without my blade touching even one of them.

"I'm sorry, Falcio," the Tailor said as three of the Unblooded held me. "If there had been another road I would have taken it. I hope you can believe that. What comes now—well, I can't say it's for the best, but it's the only chance any of us have, even you."

I had a split lip and I'd been hit in the gut enough times that I could barely take a breath, let alone a deep one. But my arms and legs had gone numb and as I've learned, it's surprisingly easy to be bold and brave when you have no hope of survival.

"I hope you can believe me when I say it's not over until I say it is."

She smiled. It was a soft and compassionate smile that ill suited her face. "That's what I've always loved about you, Falcio, ever since that day you arrived at my cottage, feverish and starved and more than half-dead, carrying Duke Yered's severed head in a sack. You never know when to quit."

"Count on it," I said.

One of the Unblooded turned to the Tailor. "You will go now. What comes now is sacred and not for your eyes."

"I warned you, Falcio. I said I would do anything to put that girl on the throne and I will. *Anything.*" Then she walked off.

As my captors began dragging me away I asked, "Where are we off to? I hope it's all right if I watch. I hate to miss a good sacred ritual."

The two who were dragging me stopped for a minute and another grabbed me by the jaw. "Have no fear on that account, Trattari. You will see and hear and feel every part of what comes next."

"Sounds like a party," I said, but the confidence in his voice, the raw hatred emanating from him, made my guts start to chill.

"Oh, it is." He motioned for the others to continue, and as they dragged me deeper into the forest he asked, "Tell me, First Cantor, have you ever heard of something called the Greatcoat's Lament?"

38

THE LAMENT

The Unblooded had obviously been preparing for this for a while. The clearing they dragged me to, about a hundred yards into the forest, featured a thick yew-tree post standing alone right in the middle. Another tree had been sacrificed to provide two three-foot lengths of post, now attached about five feet up the standing post so that they extended toward the sky. The whole edifice looked like a supplicant begging for mercy from the Gods above.

Or maybe it's just supposed to look like a cactus, I told myself, and I gave a little laugh at my own joke.

The men holding my arms placed me with my back to the post. I was about to say something incredibly cutting and clever when one of them drove his fist into my stomach, and as I doubled over they dragged my arms up and tied my hands to the angled arms.

When they were done, seven of them ranged themselves in front of me. I'd seen most of them at one point or another during the weeks we'd been harrying Trin's forces in Pulnam; I'd even had conversations with them, though you wouldn't have guessed we knew each other, let alone had fought on the same side, because none of them showed any emotion at all. I've had to intimidate people before now, when it was that or get into a fight that might get someone killed. I've even practiced trying to look cold-blooded, much to Kest and Brasti's amusement. But the expressions on the faces of these Unblooded, that was the truest cold I'd ever seen.

There were four men and three women, one of whom was Dariana. "*Deadly Dari*" Brasti had called her. I wondered what he would call her if he could see her now. I kept expecting her to say something or do something—to hit me, or spit in my face, make some remark about how stupid I was or . . . well, anything, really, but she just stood with the others, her face lacking the slightest trace of humanity.

I felt fear seep into me. It swirled underneath my skin and wound its way through my veins. I swear I could feel it creep into my heart.

One of the men stepped forward. He was short, only five and a half feet tall, with close-cropped blond hair; it had a sandy quality that reminded me of the desert. He was young, maybe twenty, and like the others he had no expression on his face—until the moment he came close to me, when his lips curled up into a smile that would have looked friendly, if he hadn't been about to murder me.

"Falcio val Mond, First Cantor of the Greatcoats, King's Heart and Husband of the butchered peasant woman called Aline val Mond, lover of the Rijou whore Ethalia, self-proclaimed father to the woman called Valiana."

"Yes," I said, as two men stepped forward and started strapping my torso to the post, "I am *that* Falcio val Mond. Were you concerned in case you'd captured the wrong one?"

"My name is Heryn. I am . . . Well, it will make no difference to you who I am. Suffice it to say, I will be performing the Lament."

"You make it sound like you're going to pull out a harp and start playing for me. Is that what the 'Lament' is? Because if so, this is working out much worse than I'd feared."

Heryn ignored my flippant remarks as he pulled out a black leather tube and knelt to set it on the ground. As he unrolled it, long six-inch steel needles appeared, along with tiny bottles of various shapes, each with a silver top. Next to each bottle was a little dark blue cloth. Heryn picked up one of the cloths and flattened it, then placed one of the needles, a four-inch-long piece of blackened metal, onto the cloth. He looked at me for a moment, examining me from my head to my chest and then all the way down to my feet. Then he withdrew one of the bottles from the leather case, unstoppered it, and carefully tilted it over the needle. I'd been expecting some kind of fluid but what came out was more of a powder: dried flakes of something dark and red that crumbled as they hit the needle. Heryn carefully picked up the needle and rose to his feet. He pushed my head forward so that my chin was touching my chest. "Are you ready?"

"Let me think about—"

Without the slightest hesitation he drove the needle deep into a spot near the base of my neck. I'd expected pain. I've known pain. I've been tortured before.

But this?

I screamed, and screamed, and screamed.

When I awakened the next morning, everything around me had a reddish tinge, as if my eyes were caked in blood. It took a moment for the shadows to resolve themselves into figures. Heryn and Dariana stood before me.

"That took rather a long time," Heryn said conversationally. "You didn't move at all! And you didn't react when I pulled the needle out—for a moment I thought I'd made a terrible mistake, but Dariana assured me that this is a recent affliction."

My breathing was slow. The air felt heavy and it was several minutes before I could take in a full breath. "Thanks for your concern," I said.

He smiled. "So, not quite chastened yet? You cried and moaned rather a lot yesterday. I'm afraid today will be worse."

The King used to like this phrase he'd found in an old handbook in the royal library, written for spies from a bygone era: *There is no crime in feeling fear, nor any virtue in acknowledging it.*

"You know, something's been bothering me," I said. "Are you still 'Unblooded'? Because that seems unfair to me: you've murdered men and women and children, so surely they can't still make you go around calling yourselves 'Unblooded' when you've caused the deaths of so many innocents, can they? I mean, I realize you haven't had time to tattoo your faces yet, but shouldn't you be full-on Dashini by now?"

Heryn smirked. "There are no Dashini anymore. You can call us Greatcoats."

I pulled at my bonds without thinking, which sent a wave of pain and nausea through my body.

"Careful now," Heryn said. "I don't want you worn out too quickly. Let's set the stage properly, shall we?"

He waved a hand in the air, which was obviously a prearranged signal as two of his men left the clearing for a moment and returned almost immediately dragging a pair of bodies. As they got closer I could see they were a man and a woman, and the bruises around their eyes and reddened cheeks made me think they'd been beaten— though not badly, just enough to make them compliant. It took me a moment more to recognize them as Nehra and Colwyn, the troubadours who'd been following us.

"If you've brought them here to torture them as well, I should warn you the man's singing voice is probably worse than mine," I pointed out helpfully, but my words immediately elicited a howl from the self-styled Bardatti, who started thrashing about.

Colwyn started his begging by immediately distancing himself from me. "Let us go!" he pleaded, "We have nothing to do with this man or his actions. We've done you no wrong—"

I carefully turned my gaze to Dariana. It still hurt. "You see what happens? You go to all this trouble to betray someone and you still get stuck listening to the tone-deaf troubadour."

Dariana said nothing as she helped Heryn's men to position the troubadours upright against a handy tree trunk. She pulled their arms behind them and tied them at the wrist. Nehra, the woman, gritted her teeth from the pain. Colwyn just screamed.

"Careful," Heryn said. "They're not to be harmed."

Really? I thought incredulously. *This is where you decide to draw the line on cruelty? Did someone proclaim it "Be Kind to Troubadours" week when I wasn't paying attention?*

The men let the ropes slacken a little, enough to ensure that Nehra and Colwyn, though not exactly comfortable, were also not in agony.

"There now, that's better." Heryn clapped his hands in approval. "Can't have a performance without an audience, can we?"

"I'm sorry," I said, "but is today's torture that you try to confuse me to death?"

Heryn walked over to the troubadours. He stood in front of Nehra for a moment, then reached out and with a finger traced her jaw-line. She didn't try to twist out of the way, just glared at him and said, "Think on what you do here, Unblooded. You betray your ancestors, and that will not soon be forgotten. What is seen by the Bardatti is ever known to the world."

"I'm counting on it," Heryn said.

He walked back to me and helpfully explained, "I've had these two brought here to witness the Lament, Falcio: to record what takes place here and ensure it is remembered forever."

An absurd thought entered my mind and I couldn't stop myself from chuckling. "Really? I'm afraid that if it's *facts* you want remembered, you've captured the wrong troubadours."

Heryn smiled at my joke. "Well said. This bravado suits you, Falcio val Mond." He turned his head and stared at the troubadours. "Remember him here, like this: his courage; his daring. When you tell this story, make sure everyone knows that Falcio val Mond was valiant in the face of the Lament."

"All this, just because I beat a couple of your Dashini brethren? Heryn, could it be possible that the world's greatest assassins are also history's sorest losers?"

Heryn returned to me. There was no ire in his tone. There was no emotion at all. "You should be grateful, Falcio. Most men live and die and no one remembers their names—but you? For a hundred years your story will be told, over and over. It will be whispered in the dark, and even with the sun high up in the sky it will be spoken of in frightened tones. Idealistic men and women will look around and say, 'The world should be a better place. Injustice should be answered.' They will think about the stories of the Greatcoats, and wonder how a man or woman might fashion such a coat and take up sword and song to make the world a little more fair." He placed a hand on each of my cheeks. "Then they will remember the tale of Falcio val Mond and the agony and terror he endured, how his mouth was struggling to scream even after his heart had stopped beating. And then they will go back to their sad little lives and try their best to forget there ever was such a thing as a Greatcoat."

Heryn knelt down again and opened up his leather bag and pulled out another dark blue cloth, then a bottle made of mottled green glass and finally another needle, this one with a tiny hook at the end. Rising to his feet he said, "A hundred years from now, Falcio val Mond, your greatest contribution to the world will be that from this moment forward, no one ever dreamed of becoming a Greatcoat again." He paused for just a moment, then smiled. "So. Shall we begin again?"

Pain for days on end will, eventually, drive a man to unconsciousness. Turns out the Dashini have found a solution for this aggravating little problem.

"—o, no, First Cantor, you can't miss any of this," Heryn was saying as Dariana waved a blue bottle beneath my nostrils, and suddenly I was completely awake and all the aches and pains that made up my body were magnified a millionfold.

I wondered why I'd stopped screaming, then I dimly realized I still was—it was just that my voice was now so hoarse that it was nothing more than a slight crunchy whisper, like wind passing through dead leaves.

There is no crime in feeling fear, nor any virtue in acknowledging it. "I'm getting bored," I whispered. "Why don't you kill me?"

"There are nine deaths in a Lament, Falcio. You should know by now that it's not about *killing* you. It's about destroying you utterly."

"How many have I had so far?" I asked. I looked over at the troubadours. Nehra was watching me, her jaw clenched as if it took an act of great will to look at me. She was crying.

"We are still on the third death," Heryn said. "Shall we proceed?"

On the fourth day I tried to force myself to stop breathing, and when that didn't work, I tried to bite off my own tongue to stop having to hear myself scream anymore. When I was able to open my eyes again, I realized my vision was blurred and it was hard to see. The world had become a fog made of gray clouds infused with red tendrils that reached out to me, filling my nostrils and my mouth and even my ears.

I thought about the stories of old men who lost their wives and then, for no apparent reason at all, died in the night. They just . . . *ended.* There was nothing ahead for them but solitude, so their hearts simply stopped beating. Like a drunken fool or a madman I started imploring my own heart. *Stop!* I told it. *Stop beating. Your wife is dead. You should have stopped then but you didn't, belligerent child. Your King is dead. Your country is dead. The world has shrunk to this tiny prison.*

"Ah," a voice said. It was Heryn's. "I see you're coming around. Kind of you not to take as long this morning. Perhaps we've made a terrible mistake and you're enjoying the pain?"

Stop. Beating. Stop.

"Shall we proceed?"

Madness. Madness was the answer. I had been trying to make myself die, but that was stupid, a fool's gambit. You can't make yourself die.

Insanity was the answer: insane people don't feel pain—or, well, they *feel* it, but they don't *comprehend* it. They scream and they moan and they laugh and they giggle and they spit and they swallow and they do all the things human beings do, but they don't *understand* any of it.

Understanding was my big problem, it turned out.

Knowing what day it was—that this was the fourth day—and knowing there were still five more before they finally killed me: *that* was the problem.

So insanity was what I needed now.

"Good morning," Heryn said.

My eyes opened and I saw him looking at me. My stomach churned at the sight of him. Nothing in his face or his body or his hair had changed and yet every part of him, everything about him, made my limbs tremble and my eyes shed tears. The stupid part of me, the part people used to call Falcio, tried to hold his gaze, as if that would make anything any better.

Fool.

I forced my head to turn and saw the Bardatti woman was still tied to the tree. She mouthed a word at me.

Fight.

It took me a while to work out what she meant.

Fight.

Fight what? I wondered.

"Are you ready to proceed?"

Her eyes went wide and I wondered why that simple phrase had so bothered her; after all, Heryn had uttered it every day since they took me.

Then I realized why she looked so horrified.

Heryn hadn't said it. I had.

There was something in my mouth: a metal apparatus forcing my jaw open. Small needles set into its frame jabbed me in my gums, my tongue and the roof of my mouth. The apparatus got larger and larger until I realized its metal form was the entire world and I was simply a damned cloth hanging overt it to keep it from rusting in the rain. The apparatus was all there was, and the only sensation was the dull, pulsing pain I felt every place it touched me. The only taste was its metallic flavor in my mouth. The only sound was . . .

. . . something was wrong with the sound of the apparatus. It should have been hard and thin and piercing, and yet . . . The sound in my ears was warm and soothing, and felt like something which must have once existed, maybe before the apparatus . . .

People.

I had it then. *It sounds like a person.* But not a person talking, something else . . .

It's called singing, you fool.

I realized then that the two troubadours were singing. The song was the crackle of fire and the warmth of good winter wool. I didn't understand the words and yet I knew they told of trumpets and horses and a cause worth fighting for. They told of a time—whatever *time* was—a time *after* a battle, a time for relief, for respite. A time for peace.

For a brief moment I became a man again and not a red rag draped over the apparatus, because the troubadours were singing a death song.

They're trying to help me die. The pain didn't lessen; I could still feel every single spike, every burn, every crack and piercing, on my skin, through my flesh, in my bones. But the pain was simply . . . *pain.* You can feel pain, but pain isn't a crime. Pain is in the body, in the mind, in the heart, but there is something else. There's a fire burning inside and the pain can't reach it—the pain doesn't even know it's there. *No one* knows it's there because it's a *secret.* It's just a word written on a boy's hand. He's just learned it; it's part of a story about men and women in long leather coats. The boy didn't understand the word and so he'd asked the storyteller to write it on his hand. "Can you read?" the storyteller asked. "Of course not," the boy said. "But I only need to know the one word."

I was reaching for that word when Heryn's voice broke through the song. "Remarkable," he said. "It appears that there is more to the legends of the Bardatti than I had given credit." The voice changed, as if it were moving in a different direction. "Gag them," he said. I felt a hand on my cheek. It sent a little tremor through the apparatus and the pain magnified again. "This won't do," he said. "We'll have to start again now."

They gave me something on the seventh day—a liquid. I didn't know its color, or its taste. Such things were beyond me now.

I gagged on the liquid at first, but it wormed its way down my throat and into my stomach and from there it traveled along my arms and my legs and into every other part of my body. It radiated outward to my hands and feet and then to my fingers and toes.

My eyes opened. I could see the clearing, and Heryn and Dariana and the two troubadours, and it took me a moment to understand that my sight had returned, and that I knew what "sight" was. The agony was still there, but this time it was worse because I didn't just feel it; I understood it as well. For the past few days I had become enveloped in pain, and in so doing had forgotten anything else existed.

"You tried to escape," Heryn explained. "But you can't. Not yet."

A laugh escaped my throat as my eyes wandered down my chest to examine my body. I was a proper mess: bound to a post with needles sticking out of my face and my naked torso and through my torn and soiled pants into my genitals. I hardly looked as if I'd moved a finger, never mind tried to escape.

But that's not what Heryn meant and I understood that. A part of me liked the fact that Heryn was worried I might be going mad. I would have been content to die like that: the broken, drooling wreckage of something that had once been a man. I imagined it would have infuriated Heryn to find me incoherent and unable to fully absorb the torment he was so patiently exacting on me—after all, what was the sense in a performance without a proper audience?

For perhaps the first time I truly accepted that I was going to die, and not just lose my life; I was going to die alone and in pain, filled to bursting with the sick vapors of a lifetime of failures. *Fine,* I thought. *Let it be just as Heryn said. Let them tell stories of Falcio the fool; of Falcio who, like a child, believed that the world can change just because you want it to.*

I blinked. *Do what you want to me, Dashini or Unblooded or Greatcoats or whatever you want to call yourselves, for I've found a shield you can't penetrate with your needles and your pins.*

Acceptance.

I accept.

What will you do now, Heryn? I accept everything: the pain, the misery, the regret. I want it.

I welcome *it.*

A surge of joy sparked in me. *Let them continue.* Seven days, it's been. Let it go on for seven more, or seventy, or seven hundred.

It would have been a good way to die, I think. It wouldn't have been bravery, exactly, but it didn't need to be. It would have been enough.

I was captive and bound, but I believed that I was becoming free.

Unfortunately, late on the seventh night, something pulled me back and brought me more sorrow than any of Heryn's toxins or potions ever could.

Valiana tried to rescue me.

She did her best to be silent, but she lacked the training and of course they heard her coming. She did her best to be swift, but she lacked the speed to outpace them. She did her best to fight, but she was still suffering from the wounds she'd taken in Rijou.

In the end, the only thing she did well was to be brave. She lasted five strikes before Dariana got around her and held her by the neck.

Heryn walked over and put his hand on Valiana's face. He did that a lot, I'd noticed.

"You were right, Dariana." He turned to me and shook his head in disbelief. "I said we'd need to go out and find the girl, that she'd never be so foolish as to come looking for us—and yet here she is: a pretty bird come to rest in our clearing." He let her go, walked over to me and reached up to the needle stuck between the bones of my wrist.

I screamed.

He removed the needle that was lodged between the bones of my elbow and I suddenly felt as if my arm was no longer there.

He moved one by one to each of the needles he'd placed so carefully at the nerve endings on each of my limbs, chatting away as he worked. "Congratulations, Falcio val Mond," he said, "we finally have what we need to give you your ninth and final death."

They're going to kill her, I realized. *This is how they do it. This is how they break through the shield of my acceptance.*

And yet something was off.

"I think you skipped a day," I whispered.

"You're quite right," Heryn said. "The girl is a vital participant in your final death, but one thing remains first."

"You should probably get on with it then," I said, more eager to die than I had ever been to live.

"He's right," Dariana said, examining my face. "He's not long for this world."

Heryn shook his head. "No, we will wait. We have an agreement. It must be honored."

"She should have been here by now," Dariana said, eyeing the night stars above us.

"We will wait," Heryn repeated. He turned to the troubadours. Nehra and Colwyn were hanging limply from the ropes holding them to the tree and I realized suddenly that Colwyn had died at some point, but they'd just left him there. So much for "They must not be harmed."

"Stay vigilant, little Bardatti. She will be here soon, and what happens then will be something no one has witnessed for a hundred years."

It was still the seventh night, just on the edge of morning, when she came to me. My sense of time came from the coolness of the air fighting against the burning sensation that emanated from the ropes and radiated across the damaged canvas of my skin. I could hear the buzzing and whirring of insects and the rustling of the small animals of the forest, louder than normal, as if they were trying, through their normal and natural behaviors, to cover the atrocities being committed in their habitat.

My eyes were closed, but I could see her.

"It's nearly time, Falcio." The night breeze was playing in her hair. I'd forgotten how curly it was. I don't think I should be blamed for this, though. She'd been dead for more than fifteen years.

"Time for what, sweetheart?" I asked, though the sound that came from my lips was barely more than a moan.

"Time to be brave," Aline said.

I felt the faintest touch of tears underneath the lower lashes of my eyes. The sensation was so small, and yet I felt it just as strongly as the splitting pain in my bones and the stabbing ache in my flesh.

"I've been brave," I said plaintively, like a child being accused.

She brought her hand close to my face. I so longed to feel her skin against mine. I had forgotten the lines of her face but I could remember every callus on those hands, every curve of her fingers; that the first joint of the third finger on her left hand had a slight bend in it which always made it hard for her to put on her wedding ring. Better to simply keep it on forever, she'd said to me one day, and I'd agreed, *forever*. Forever and ever. But though I remembered every part of her body, all I had was the memory, and even in my hallucination I couldn't feel her hand against my face.

"Why won't you touch me, Aline?" I asked. "Should a woman not touch her husband when they've been so long apart?"

"I can't," she said. "They've taken that from us." I imagined her dark eyes to be sad, though not full of tears. Aline was never one for crying.

"That's unfair," I said. "The torture I can understand. The murder is inevitable. But a man should at least be able to hallucinate his wife stroking his face, don't you think?"

She gave a little laugh. I'd always been able to make her laugh, although I didn't think the things I'd said had always been very funny, so it made me wonder if all those times she'd only laughed to make me feel better.

"You're going to have to be very brave now," she said.

"You said that already. Haven't I been brave enough for this world yet? Haven't I stood my ground all those times, even when outnumbered by Knights and bully-boys and assassins? Haven't I tried to do right even when the trying was hopeless? Didn't I put a knife in my King when he asked me to? I've *been* brave, Aline. I'm not afraid to die."

"You've been so brave, my darling. And now you must be braver still."

"But why?" This time I heard the slight creaking sound of my words in my ears and not just in my mind.

"Because she is here."

My eyes began fluttering open and though I expected Aline to disappear, her body instead shifted back and forth, interchanging with that of another. The seconds ticked by and my wife faded away completely until standing in front of me was another woman, one whose physical beauty exceeded Aline's, but whose black heart made mine freeze inside my chest. Aline's hand could not reach me, but I could feel this other hand, with its smooth skin and perfectly straight fingers, gently stroking my cheek.

"Hello, my lovely tatter-cloak," Trin said. "What delightful moments we are going to share."

39

THE EIGHTH DEATH

It might sound strange, but when I realized Trin was there, I felt relieved. Aline had told me I needed to be brave but she hadn't understood how far down into the depths of despair I had already sunk; there was nowhere left to fall.

It's nearly over, I promised myself. *She will torture me and taunt me and when she grows bored, as she surely will, it will be over.*

"Tell me how it works," Trin said, but she wasn't talking to me.

Heryn was preparing more needles, this time dipping them first in a viscous black liquid, and then into a dark blue powder. "There is the *compound*, of course," he said, "but it is only a conveyance for the magic. It calls an ancient thing that is quite wonderful in its workings." He looked up at her. "Have you your part?"

As Trin pulled a little leather bag from inside her shirt Heryn picked up one of his little dark blue cloths and held it out to her. She up-ended the bag and something small and brittle and yellowed fell out. A tooth.

"I told you I had another, Falcio," she said, turning to me. "It took a great deal of pain and effort to acquire that first one, the one you so churlishly threw away. Fortunately, there was more than one."

She turned back to Heryn. "Is it enough? To make him—?"

He nodded.

"And for me?" she asked.

"Yes, but your skin must touch his skin."

Trin began removing her clothes. She first took off her long brown coat and then quickly unbuttoned the top of the spotless white shirt underneath. Then she winked at me and, moving more slowly, unfastened one button at a time, lifting her chin just a little, carefully parting the fabric to reveal her breasts, running the backs of her fingers down her torso until they reached the waistband of her pants. She slipped out of them too, then removed her underclothes until she stood naked in front of me.

"You only need a bit of skin, you know," Dariana said.

Trin turned to her. "What fun would that be?"

"We should begin soon," Heryn said. "The preparation is ready."

Trin came to me and slid the tattered remains of my shirt off my shoulders, then removed my pants before taking a knife to what was left of my underclothes, which was probably for the best, as they were soiled.

"Again, not necessary," Dariana said.

"Are you jealous you didn't think of it first?" Trin asked. Her hand slid down to my crotch and I felt her fingers lightly graze back and forth. "Can you make him hard?" she asked. "I want him to be hard."

Heryn shook his head. "Lady, he is paralyzed. We have made a ruin of the nerves in his body. He can feel pain and nothing else. There is only a very little piece of his mind left to destroy."

"And his heart," Trin said. "Let's not forget my darling tatter-cloak's heart." She reached around me with her arms, one hand on the small of my back and the other behind my neck, then wrapped her right leg around my left and held herself tightly against me, as if I were the mast of a ship in the midst of a great storm.

"You're ambitious," I muttered. I had something funnier in mind, but I lacked the strength to say it.

"It is time," Heryn said. He held up the two long needles and walked behind me. "I must place the instruments precisely, Lady

Trin," he said, and I felt him move Trin's hand from the small of my back.

I felt the stab of the needle through my skin, through the muscle and into my spine. There was pain, of course, but it was no more or less than what I'd already been through. Even as Heryn stabbed the second one up through the back of my neck and into my skull I felt relieved. *It's almost over,* I reminded myself. I looked over at the Bardatti. Colwyn's dead eyes looked at me, full of condemnation. Nehra's were horrified.

"Poor Falcio," Trin said, kissing my neck. "Don't worry, you won't be alone. I will be with you the entire journey. I will see what you see and feel what you feel, and every moment will be shared and precious between you and me. Oh, and her, of course."

Before I could even begin to wonder what she'd meant, my eyes sagged closed and my breathing slowed. I saw a light, but it wasn't the light they say comes to a man at the moment of his death. Instead, it was the mundane light of oil lanterns hanging from the wooden beams across a low ceiling, illuminating the common room of an ordinary tavern. Long wooden benches were arrayed around a central fire. There was a bar at the end and a man in his early forties was washing cups, apparently in preparation for the evening crowd to arrive. The place was familiar.

"Oh my." I heard Trin's voice deep inside me. "It's perfect."

I heard the sound of doors bursting open and four men came into view: Ducal guardsmen. The thickset men were barely two steps up from bully-boys. One was taller than the others and he carried an ax, and because of that ax I recognized him instantly. His name was Fost. Then I saw that the other three were carrying something between them, and that *something* was writhing and scratching and trying to bite. The woman screamed and struggled and in a glint of the light I caught sight of her face.

And at that moment I finally understood what was happening and what I was about to witness, and only then did I understand Aline's words. *You must be very brave now, Falcio.*

But I couldn't. *I couldn't . . .*

They held Aline down against the rough wooden table and tore the pale gray dress from her body, and though I tried to force my eyes shut, I couldn't, because my eyes were already shut. I could see everything with perfect clarity, so sharply delineated it was as if a knife was carving the images on the surface of each eye.

Aline tried to kick them, but two men grabbed her legs while the third held her arms up, as if they were trying to stretch her two sizes taller. I begged for my heart to stop beating, but instead I felt it pounding faster, and lightly, like a bird's, and I realized I was feeling Trin's heart against mine.

The men started laughing, and they said something about a cow giving milk, then Fost pulled his pants down around his knees and said something else, though I couldn't hear him because the men were laughing too loudly and Trin was giggling in my ears.

Aline swore at them. She said there was a curse she could utter that would shatter them, and all men like them. She said there were darker things that could be unleashed in this world than the foul desires of rapists and murderers. She said her husband would come for them. And still they laughed, and when Fost was done his first turn, he went to change positions with one of the men holding her legs—a fat man with a fringe of red hair around his otherwise bald head—but in the instant before Fost could grab hold she pulled her leg back and kicked the fat man in the face. Blood spurted from his nose and he leaned forward across her body and punched her in the mouth. She used the momentary distraction to free one of her hands from the man gripping her arms and struck out, her fingertips held tight together as if she were holding a pen, and drove them into the man's eye.

Even as Aline fought she was screaming. She screamed for the innkeeper to help her; she told lies and said men with swords were coming even now, that she would see any man spared who helped her. But the innkeeper didn't help her. I watched as he turned and quietly walked away out the back.

Fost and his men got a grip on her again, but she spat something bloody from her mouth, into the eye of the man who'd taken her arms. It was a tooth, I realized: when the fat one had punched her, he'd broken several of her teeth, and my brave, beautiful girl had managed not to swallow them so she could use them as weapons. But teeth are not swords, and an unarmed lass, no matter how brave, will never win against four strong soldiers. Fost struck her hard in the side of her ribs, saying something about knocking the wind out of her sails, and there was a loud crack that filled the room, followed by peals of laughter from the others.

The fat man forced himself inside her and pounded against her in a rage, and I watched her eyes dart back and forth as she looked for a weapon or a way to distract her attackers, even for an instant. For a moment I thought her eyes met mine. But of course that was impossible.

The fat man pulled out from her and said something, but I couldn't hear it. Instead I heard a terrible wrenching sound: Aline had pulled her own arm from its socket. The sick wet sound caused the man holding her arms to let go in shock, just for a moment, and my brave girl bit her lip bloody through the pain and rose up to jab at Fost with the elbow of her good arm. She struck him in the throat and he stumbled back, then he grunted an order at his men. I couldn't hear the replies; all sound was lost in the rushing of blood in my ears. The three remaining men, bloodied and bruised and scratched, took hold of Aline once more.

Fost reached for his ax. "Enough," he said. And this I could hear as clearly as the roar of thunder on a dry night. "All she needs is two tits and a cunt for my needs."

As he lifted the ax high above him, Aline's eyes went wide, full of terror and anguish, and her endless courage drained at last down to the last drips of the bottle. She was looking at me then, I swear it, and I could hear her screaming my name: "Falcio! Falcio! *Falcio!*"

I prayed that when the ax fell I would feel it too, but I didn't. She had been alone, after all.

There was more laughter as the lights in the tavern began to flicker and fade and I opened my eyes to see Trin's face laden with sweat, her gaze unfocused, her lips slightly parted. She was still entangled with me. Her breathing was heavy and she gave a small moan. She was climaxing.

"It is done," Heryn said, and I felt the needle at the base of my skull slowly pulled away, then the one in my back. The others he left in place.

Trin finally removed her leg from around mine, then one hand, then the other.

"Was it satisfactory?" Dariana asked. There wasn't a trace of emotion in her voice.

Trin's eyes were still on mine. "I want to do it again," she said.

Heryn gave a small laugh. "I'm afraid that isn't possible, Lady, nor would it increase his suffering, if that's what you seek. He is broken now, and almost ready for the ninth death."

"Pity," Trin said, and I watched as she dressed herself.

When she was done, Heryn stepped in front of her. "The agreement was—"

"Yes, yes, my dear Unblooded, our agreement is fulfilled."

"Good, then—"

"But I would like to make a small adjustment," she said, pulling a dagger from her belt, "with regard to the nameless bitch you have tied up over there." She stepped around Heryn and walked toward Valiana, but Dariana positioned herself in front of her.

"That wasn't the agreement."

"She's right," Heryn said, and when Trin turned to him, a darkness in her eyes, he shook his head. "It would be unwise to break faith with us."

For a moment they were still, all three of them, and then Trin put the dagger back in her belt and came back to me and smiled. "I will have to make do with the memory, my lovely tatter-cloak." She kissed me on the cheek. "Thank you, Falcio. I will always love you for this."

Oddly, impossibly, I began to cry. *How was there room for misery inside me still?* I told myself it must be the pins and the needles and the oils and the ointments they were using on me. Falcio, that foolish man, had died, days ago, most likely, and it was only these strange

Dashini secrets keeping the remains of his body together. *It's over*, I told myself. *Stop breathing. Just stop breathing.*

But still I couldn't: air came into my mouth and left the same way. Pain came in from the world and grew inside me. I wasn't dead. I was a garden for shame and regret. But Aline had said something, hadn't she? It couldn't have been long ago. It was something about bravery. *You must be braver than ever now, Falcio.* That's what she'd said. *But I can't be brave*, I thought, not like she had been. *I'm too busy growing failure inside my heart. It's taken root now, and it grows and grows and grows.* Yet still her words kept coming back: *You must be brave now. Braver than ever.*

I thought about trying to scream my frustration. I thought about how I would threaten them all. I would list every torment that my rage would inflict on them, as Aline had done. I would make promises of revenge that would make the Gods and the Saints turn their gaze away from Tristia for fear of what they might see when Falcio was finally free. But that wasn't bravery; that was simply bravado. What good are the threats of a corpse, even when it hasn't discovered its own death yet? But there had to be an answer. Aline had commanded me to be brave: *very* brave. *Braver than ever before.* What was it the King used to say? Our greatest strength is our judgment; our finest weapon is our knowledge of the laws. It sounded so trite, but what else was left?

Fine, I thought to myself. *Let the last thing they hear from me be the thing that hurts them most. Let the last knife I wield be the one with the truest edge.* And so I began to recite the laws my King had taught me, one after another, as I had done in my proudest moments at the side of my fellow Greatcoats, and as I had done when I had last believed myself to be near the end, in the dungeons of Rijou. I began with the first law. *A hundred times I'll say it*, I told myself. *And then I will move on to the second.*

"The First Law is that men are free," I sang softly, "for without the freedom to choose, men cannot serve their heart, and without heart they cannot serve their Gods, their Saints, or their King."

My voice was so light that neither Heryn nor Dariana were close enough to hear me. Trin looked up and leaned toward me as if she was trying to make out what I was saying.

"The First Law is that men are free," I repeated. My voice was a little stronger, I thought. I sang it again, and again, and Trin came even closer until her ear was nearly touching my mouth and so I kept singing. I repeated the words over and over, knowing in my heart that the words were magic, that if I just kept saying them they would break through the corruption inside me and all around me.

Finally Trin stepped back. "I think he's ready for your ninth death," she said, her eyes still on me. She looked genuinely surprised.

"Why do you say that?" Heryn asked.

"Because he just keeps saying 'kill me, kill me' over and over again."

40

THE KING'S PATIENCE

"Are you going to tell me what it says?" I asked.

King Paelis and I were having lunch in the solarium that he'd had built on one of the great lawns outside the walls of Castle Aramor. We were discussing a recent property dispute. The weather was pleasant, with a few clouds in the sky, "just enough for decoration," as my mother used to say. One of the royal retainers had come out with a note, and as soon as the King had opened it his face had gone pale and for the next several minutes he'd just sat there staring at it.

"I did something, Falcio," he said finally. His hands were trembling as he picked up the silver wine goblet and brought it to his lips.

"Your Majesty?"

"It was . . ." He took a sip, then stopped and carefully put the goblet back down, almost as if he felt he didn't have the right to drink the wine. He rose from his chair and walked over to the tall windows with the stained-glass arches that looked out at the courtyard where the Greatcoats trained. "Kings *use* people, Falcio."

I wasn't sure what to say to that so I tried to make light of it. "Is that not the function of Kings? Those who can, do, those who can't, rule?"

But he didn't rise to the bait, nor did he laugh. "It's necessary," he said, as if it needed explaining. "Sometimes you know you have to send people to fight, and likely to die. I can live with that. But there are other times when you spend someone's life not on a certainty— not on the assured right thing to do—but on a probability . . . not even that. A bet. A whim, even."

I didn't understand what he was going on about. The King hated violence; he hated taking risks with our lives. We all knew that.

"We volunteer," I said. "None of us Greatcoats are conscripted. It's not like the Dukes—"

"The Knights aren't conscripted either," he said.

I nearly spat—in those days, any mention of Knights was enough to set me off. "Forgive me, your Majesty, but Knights take up arms to satisfy their egos, believing that their wealth and training and armor and Gods-know-what-else make them too important to die. When a Knight is killed in battle, it's always with a look of surprise on his face."

"And the Greatcoats?"

"We spend our lives in service of a just country—a just *world*."

The King gave a rueful laugh. "We are a very small country, Falcio. One day you will set foot outside our borders and discover just how small we are."

"Well, I'll start by spreading justice here and get around to those other countries when I have a bit more time."

He turned and looked at me with that sideways smile of his. "You are very sure of yourself, First Cantor."

"No. I'm very sure of you."

His face settled into a flatter, sadder expression and he turned away. "There are days, Falcio, when the weight of your faith is almost more than I can bear."

"I—"

He waved a hand at me and I shut up and we sat like that for a while, the King standing staring out of the window while I sat silently a few feet away. The King hadn't dismissed me, and after a while I decided to presume on our friendship. "What did you do?"

"Hmm?"

"I asked, what did you do?" If one of the other Greatcoats had been sent on a mission from which they weren't going to return, I wanted to know. "You've clearly done something that's weighing on your conscience. Who did you send?"

He shook his head. "No one you know."

For some reason, the answer surprised me. The Greatcoats were the most capable duelists in the country, and in those days I knew every one of them by name. To send someone who wasn't as able seemed . . . callous. "If the mission was so important, then why not send one of us?"

"Because I needed someone who could be corrupted." He turned back to me. "And I needed to hope that they could overcome such corruption as would destroy any man's soul."

"How would—?"

"That's enough," Paelis said. "I'm tired of your questions, Falcio. I'm tired of having you sit there and look at me like . . ."

He crumpled the note in his hand and let it drop to the floor. "The hells for your faith, Falcio." He walked through the open door and back across the grass toward the castle, leaving me there with the food and the wine and my notes on the property case. After a few minutes I reached down and picked up the crumpled note. I straightened it out and read it.

On a single line, in a feminine hand, were the words: *I am lost.*

On the morning of the ninth day I no longer cared about pain, nor for my life, nor even my soul. The Dashini had lost that much at least.

Dariana, Heryn, and two other Dashini remained. On one side of the clearing was Valiana, bound hand and foot, sitting on the ground. On the other side, the Bardatti, one living, one very dead— Colwyn's body had begun to stink so badly that even I could smell him—were still tied to the trees. Nehra watched me, as always. The gag was still covering her mouth. I felt guilty under her gaze.

They needed the troubadour to witness what they did to me and to spread the story of my death, but they would kill Valiana, for she had no value to them. She was just a small, ugly piece of my death.

Even through my agonizing exhaustion I could see the irony in the situation. At first I blamed the healer. Why had Firensi let her go? She'd taken a sword-thrust to the chest; surely he should have bound her to a bed for a month? So I tried to curse him, but I found I couldn't muster the will.

Valiana had been trying to get herself killed since she first put on that damned coat to prove to the world that heroism could be found in anyone. *I'm Valiana val Mond, damn it. I'm going to make that count.* And it would count. They would use her to make my death just a little worse, so instead of inspiring others, her contribution to history would be showing once and for all that there is no such thing as a noble death.

Heryn was in excellent spirits this morning. "Do you know how many times your feckless King tried to send men to infiltrate our order, Falcio?"

"One too few?" I suggested. But no, I hadn't actually said that. I thought I had, but what actually came from my lips was a whimpered, *"Please . . ."*

"Twelve. Twelve times he sent Greatcoats to try to join the order." He pulled out a small cloth from his coat. "I kept souvenirs." He opened the bag and revealed a jumble of finger-bones. "Twelve men. Twelve little fingers."

I suppose Heryn wanted me to feel terror at that moment, or anger for my fallen comrades, but the sight of the fingers only made me wonder about their families. Each of those dead Greatcoats must have had someone who had cared about them, who had wondered where they were. Those people had nothing left of their loved ones.

Absurdly, momentarily forgetting my bonds, I reached out to take the little bones from him, but by the time I realized I hadn't moved I saw that Heryn was kneeling by his black leather roll, setting out the needles and bottles.

Something harsh and vaguely clever came to my mind, but yet again the words from my lips were a betrayal: "Yes," I said, "please. Please. Now." I wondered if it would help if I called him master.

Heryn looked up at me and grinned. "Oh no, this needle isn't for you. It would hardly be very elegant, would it, if in the end we just killed you with a piece of steel jammed into your skull? No, no: have you not understood yet? The whole *point* of the Lament is that you die from grief, First Cantor. It's in the *name*, don't you see?"

He came over and flicked one of the needles he had left in my chest and the sudden burst of pain made me stiffen, which made all the other needles feel like they were breaking off inside of me.

"All of these are to just to prepare your body, Falcio. Do you know that even now, even with all the pain you've experienced, you could still live? You stand at the very edge of death's door—you need to pass through it by yourself."

He walked over to Valiana. His mere presence roused her and she began squirming. Dariana knelt down and held Valiana in place as Heryn very carefully inserted the needle into her cheek, just below her eye. She sucked in a breath and tried to scream, but she couldn't. I could see her eyes flooding with tears as she moaned, and her agony was so acute that I could feel it myself: a new pain, and one from which neither my broken body nor my broken heart could shield me.

So this was how they wanted me to die. *This* was the Greatcoat's Lament. My mind turned not to words of anger, nor to the acts of violence I so desired to inflict on Heryn and Dariana; instead all I could think of was how much I wanted to be dead. I wanted to bash my head back against the post to knock myself unconscious, or swallow my tongue so that I could choke. I wanted to walk through death's door, right then and there.

Do what you want to her, but let me die rather than see it, I thought, but that wasn't what came from my lips.

"Stop," I said, the treasonous word forcing its way between my clenched teeth. "Stop now."

Heryn's grin widened. "You've found your voice again? Excellent." He twisted the needle, and Valiana's body began to spasm.

"Stop," I repeated, straining against my bonds, feeling the knotted cords push deeper into the pressure points in my flesh.

Dariana was looking at me, her eyes troubled, but Heryn wasn't paying attention. "Don't die now, Falcio, I still have—"

Dariana glanced around. "Someone comes," she said.

Heryn was annoyed. "I hear no one."

"Regardless of what you hear, someone comes."

"Very well." Heryn turned to the other two Unblooded. "Go—find whomever it is and kill them. Dariana and I will complete the ritual." He turned to me, his hand still on the needle in Valiana's cheek. "Imagine, Falcio: imagine that someone is coming to save you. Let hope enter your heart, just for a moment—it will make the final fall all the sweeter."

His Unblooded left, but despite Heryn's urging, I felt no hope. I knew Kest wasn't there. I knew Brasti hadn't miraculously come back for me. I was completely alone.

I expected the thought to make me despair, but somehow, it did the opposite: the equation was so simple that I wondered why I had lacked this clarity every day of my life.

I was alone.

Valiana was being killed.

I could not allow it.

It is so simple. Why hadn't I thought of it before? I would simply break free from my bonds and kill the Unblooded and then she would be safe.

Simple.

An eight-year-old boy shakes his fist at the sky and earth and vows, *My name is Falcio val Mond and I am going to be a Greatcoat.* The boy has nothing, though. His father is gone and his mother is slowly withering away from solitude. He doesn't know how to fight, or how to swing a sword. *And yet.*

And yet there's something inside him.

It's in you, too, he says to me. *It's the one thing we never lost. It's the thing they can't take from us.*

What is it? I ask.

The boy Falcio looks at me like I'm a fool. *You want a word for it? What will giving it a name do?*

I don't know. Something. Names mean *something.*

Fine, he says, and he looks down at his palm. There's something written there. After a moment he looks up at me and grins. *There is a word for it. Imagine that!*

So what's the word? I ask.

I don't know. I haven't learned to read yet, stupid.

Show me, I say, and he thinks about it for a while, as if maybe he wants to keep it his secret, but finally he holds up his palm.

Can you read it for me? he asks.

The boy's hand is blurry, as is the world around him, but the word isn't. The word is clear. *Yes,* I say. *Yes. I can read it.*

It's the only thing we have left, isn't it? It's the thing they can't take from us.

Yes, I agree, *it's the one thing they can't take. Do you want me to tell you the word?*

He shakes his head. *No. It's not something that needs to be said. It's something that needs to be* shown. *You need to show them the word.*

All right, I say. *But I want to say the word anyway.*

Will it make a difference? the boy asks.

It will to me, I reply. *Words* matter. *Without words you can't have stories and without stories we would never have heard of the Greatcoats.*

Fine, he says, *tell me the word, but hurry up. It's time to show them what's inside us, underneath all the stupid stuff.*

I hesitate for just a moment, both because I'm scared and because I want to make him ask again.

What's the word? he asks impatiently.

"Valor. The word is valor."

The boy smiles. *That's a good word,* he says. *Can you forget a word like that?*

Yes, I say. *You shouldn't, but I think I might have forgotten it for a while.*

You won't forget it again, right?

Never. I'll never forget it again. They'll never break us again.

So show them, he urges me now. *Show them what valor looks like.*

The boy wants me to break free of the bonds and duel with Heryn. He still thinks like a boy. *That's really not how it works*, I want to tell him, but I don't want to disappoint him so I keep that to myself.

"Remarkable," I hear Heryn say as he and Dariana come close. "Look at him. He should be completely paralyzed. He can't feel his arms or his legs or anything except the pain emanating from his broken nerves, and yet look how he strains against the bonds. I think he might even break free if he had time."

Dariana's face is troubled. "Is that even possible?"

Of course it is, you fool. There are things stronger than hate and more deadly than fear, and this is one of them. The world demands a response to corruption and decay.

Heryn is silent, his eyes narrowed, but then suddenly he smiles. "Ah, the neatha—it's the neatha."

"Shouldn't that make it worse?" Dariana asks.

"You would think, but it looks like it's harder for our toxins to bind to his nerves. I suspect the two poisons are fighting each other inside him. All the same, the pain and grief alone should mean he can't move—so why does he continue?" he wondered aloud.

Dariana looks at me for a long time. Her eyes are strange. Sad. "For her," she says at last.

Heryn glances back at Valiana. "The girl?"

Dariana nods, and her voice breaks, just a little. "There is no pain he will not experience to stop us from hurting her."

"Such folly. He still thinks himself one of those heroes woven into old tapestries," he says, waving a hand airily. "If he could see himself, so pathetic and broken, he would not dream of moving. He would simply await the ninth death with what little dignity is left him."

Inside me, the boy is holding up his hand, as if he can force them to see the word written there.

"He has no dignity," Dariana says, "only valor. This is what valor looks like." She pauses. "It isn't like in the stories at all."

"You sound sentimental." Heryn laughs, but behind his sneer, I see fear.

"I . . ."

The sound of their voices drifts in and out as blood and fire rush through my ears. I feel the bonds begin to give way, but only to the slightest degree. *Another year or two*, I tell myself, *and I'd break out of here and really show them something.*

"Enough," Heryn says at last. "You disappoint me, Falcio val Mond. Your heart is broken; your spirit fades, and yet this empty shell still fights on." He motions to Dariana and says, "Bring me the last needle. We will use simpler means to usher the First Cantor to his final death." He looks at me. "Take what consolation you can from this, Falcio val Mond; you have thwarted us, if only in the slightest degree."

Dariana hesitates, and I wonder why. She has stood by and watched as Heryn inflicted on me every torment the world has ever seen. She hasn't spoken out for mercy, not once. If my hands were free I would probably kill her first. *Vengeance isn't bravery*, I think. Or do I hear it? Was it something Aline said? No, she didn't speak in pronouncements. Paelis—the King—he said that once. To me? No, I remember now. *Patience*, he said. *Vengeance isn't bravery. Patience is what is needed now. Even a King needs patience. A King needs patience above all.* When had I heard him saying that? It was ten—no, not ten, twelve years ago, shortly after Shanilla had been killed by the Dashini. There was a girl there too. I saw her running from the room.

I look into Dariana's eyes, deeper than she would ever want, and in that moment I finally understand.

I've done something, Falcio.

A girl, running from the room.

A King needs patience above all.

A crumpled note on the floor: *I am lost.*

How could you, my King? Kings *use* people. Plans within plans: men and women sent far and wide, no one understanding the last command you gave them, but all of them in some greater purpose, some deeper strategy. *A King needs patience above all.*

"It's time," I say to Dariana.

For a moment there's nothing. She looks confused, uncertain, as if she'd heard a voice but wasn't sure whose it was. How had this been done to her? How had the King locked her knowledge of who she was inside her? How deeply buried was she?

"I am Falcio val Mond of Pertine, First Cantor of the King's Great-coats," I say to her, my voice a hoarse whisper. I take in a little breath, because this next part is everything. *"And I am the King's Heart."*

Heryn is annoyed. "Do you think we don't know who you are? Do you think we did not know the name of everyone your weak little King sent to be captured by us? To be killed by us? The King's Eye was the first. The King's Mace suffered magnificently. Shall I tell you what we did to the King's Laughter? We cut out his—"

I turn my attention to Heryn, just for a moment. "How many men did you say the King sent to infiltrate the Dashini?" I ask.

"Twelve. Would you like to count their finger-bones again?"

"Twelve men," Dariana echoes, her voice at once that of a grown woman but also that of a young girl.

Heryn turns to look at her. Too late.

"And then he got smart," she says, "and he sent a woman."

She drives the needle straight into the center of Heryn's forehead. The point passes so cleanly and perfectly into his brow that only a single drop of blood emerges at the place where it enters. Heryn's mouth opens wide, but the only sound that escapes is a soft hiss. Then it opens wider still, as if what Heryn wants to say is too big to come from so small an opening.

His hands begin to move up toward his face and I see his fingertips twitching. He brings them up along his cheeks and toward his brow as they seek out the needle in his forehead. Only then do I realize he can't see. Somehow Heryn's legs are keeping him upright, and he stands there, eyes wide, dying but not yet dead. After a few moments, his hands slowly drop to his sides again and he gives a long sigh.

Just before he falls backward, Dariana grabs him by the lapels of his coat and holds him up. "I am Dariana, daughter of Shanilla, Thirteenth Cantor of the Greatcoats," she says. "And I am the King's Patience."

41

FRAGMENTS

At first, the world is made only of dust. Tiny specks of light, of sound. The briefest flicker of sunshine reflecting off the blade of a small knife. The scratch of thin strands of rope resisting and then giving way. The sensation of falling . . .

Voices.

". . . needs . . ."

". . . no time . . ."

". . . he'll die . . ."

". . . anyway . . ."

The dust begins to disappear, replaced by a seamless gray that goes on forever and ever. This absence of sights and sounds and sensations has a name. *Sleep.* I think I like sleep. I want to hang onto it, but I can't.

The world becomes slivers: sharp, nasty seconds that cut through the peaceful gray.

"Stay away from him! You don't touch him or me again!"

"I'm . . . little bird, I swear, I'm so sor . . ." The word melts into a single heartrending sob. And that too dissolves, replaced with iron. "We don't have a choice, damn you! We can't fight them all at once. If they catch him—"

Cold, and wet. Something against my neck and back. Messy. Dirt. Pressure against my arms and shoulders. I'm sinking, but not very far, just a few inches. *I know what "inches" are.* Something sprays on my chest, my face, into my mouth. Dirt.

Oh Gods, don't bury me.

Don't. Just. Don't.

Gray. Sleep.

The world is made of shards, broken bits of smells and tastes; of coughing and choking, of water, of crying, of something soft, like silk—no, not silk, hair. Hair on my face. Valiana's, I think. Her head is on my chest. Is she listening to my heart? Or sleeping?

Sleep. Gray.

The world is a single cold and callous voice.

"Your body is healing," Dariana said, "but it isn't healing fast enough to outrun the fever inside you."

There is a great deal of heat, yes, but who cares? I taste something wet and salty around my lips: sweat. I'm sweating all over. Everything around me is soft, though, so I don't mind. There are blankets under my body, a pillow under my head.

"I have to bring you a healer," she said.

Wouldn't it have been easier just not to have tortured me to death? I wondered—no, I actually heard the words. The voice was familiar. It was *my* voice.

"It's better if you rest. We're in a forest near the border of Aramor—we're safe. Valiana and Nehra stand guard for you. I'll get a healer now. Rest."

Good advice. Excellent advice. Exactly what I'm going to do. Rest. No words. No questions.

"Why?" my voice asked. "He . . . for eight days, he . . . Why did you wait until the last moment?"

I tried opening my eyes, but the light was harsh. *Just sleep*, I told myself. *Go back into the gray.*

You've probably realized by now that I've never been good at taking advice, least of all my own.

A room came into view, only it wasn't a room. The walls were wooden, but they were logs, and someone had stuck them into the ground at slightly odd angles. *Trees, stupid.* The ceiling was a canopy of leaves. I was outside, of course. There was a fire behind me.

I hope it doesn't burn down the rest of the room.

Dariana, on my right, was leaning over me. "Now isn't the time," she said, and started to turn.

I grabbed her wrist, surprised that my arm could even move. "No," I said, "now."

She shook off my hand. "The neatha is gone from your body. That's why you aren't waking up paralyzed. If I'd stopped Heryn any sooner, you would be dead by now."

It took a few seconds for my mind to make sense of the words because there were so many of them. I separated each one, looked at it by itself, and then joined it to the others until what she said made sense. It was logical. And yet . . . "You're lying—you didn't know . . . You *couldn't* have known."

"Maybe you're right. Maybe it's just that I didn't remember who I was. I knew my name, I knew my history, but none of it was real . . . not until—"

"You're lying again," I said. *Doesn't this woman know I'm a Great-coat? We interrogate people for a living, lady. You think I can't tell that this is just another lie, too? I mean, of course it's true, but it's not the real reason, is it?*

The way Dariana looked at me hardened. "Fine. You want to know *why*? I was fourteen years old when King Paelis sent me to infiltrate the Dashini. I spent nearly twelve years in that monastery. I was beaten—no, not just beaten, *tortured*. I was trained—*tempered*. I'm a sword made from sorrow and grief and the stupid, useless anger of a fourteen-year-old girl too innocent to know what she was volunteering for. And yet your fucking King Paelis sent me to that place, to those men. You want to know why I waited so long to save you, Falcio? It's because until that exact moment I couldn't decide which side I was on."

She left.

The world is made of fragments.

* * *

There have been three moments in my life when I have experienced true joy: a sensation so strong it breaks through every ache or pain or regret.

The day Kest's father called me "son" was one of those. The day I married Aline was another. The day I took up my Greatcoat was a third. Happiness is a series of grains of sand spread out in a desert of violence and anguish.

When I woke up in the forest the next day with the last embers of the fire reaching up to greet the dim light coming down through the leaves above me, I had my fourth such moment.

"Ethalia," I said.

She was kneeling down, looking into my eyes, and she was crying, which I assumed meant I didn't look very good. But she was there, which made me complete. I wanted the moment to go on for as long as I drew breath, but after a few seconds she wiped away the tears and turned to someone I couldn't see. "Get my bag. We have work to do."

I strained to turn my head and see who she'd been speaking to. It took a moment to make out his features, lit as he was by the light of the rising dawn. After a second I realized it was Kest.

And that was the fifth moment.

For a while I just lay there looking at him. He had a thick growth of beard, which was unusual for him, and without conscious thought I stretched out my hand and felt my own face. A thick, scratchy covering of coarse hair greeted my fingers and I wondered what I must look like. I thought I might have something funny to say about that, but Kest shook his head before I could speak.

He stood over me a few moments longer, then looked around for something to sit on. His eyes settled on a flat stone that he lugged over and positioned by the side of my bedding. He sat down next to me and stared at what was left of the fire.

Ethalia held a small jar in her hand. She dipped a finger in it and gently ran her finger along my lips. "Try not to swallow it," she said. Then she turned to Kest. "I have preparations to make. You can speak with him for a few minutes, no more."

"She sounds worried," I said. "You must look really bad."

Kest smiled, but still he stared at the fire. "Ah, Falcio," he said at last, his voice deep and resonant, and yet I thought I could hear a note of fragility. That's when I noticed he had tears in his eyes.

"Hey," I said, "I'm fine. Really. Just a little miscommunication with—"

"The entire world?"

"Dead people like me just fine, you know. They all say nice things about me."

"That's because they think you're one of them," Kest said. "How's your fever?"

Awkwardly I reached a hand up to my forehead. It came away slick with sweat. "My fever seems to be doing extremely well, thank you. How's yours? Because if you're planning on glowing red and trying to kill me, you should know that I'm considered quite handy with a sword."

"I'll keep that in mind," he said.

I waited a while before asking the question, but in the end I had to. "I take it you found the sanctuary."

"I did."

What was it like?'

"Peaceful," he said. "Humbling. After a few days, extremely boring."

"Boring sounds better to me these days than it used to. Did it work?"

He nodded. "When the Sainthood passed from Caveil to me at the end of our duel, it was like . . . it was like I could suddenly see everything in front of me with perfect clarity. I could feel the balance of my sword in ways I'd never understood before. It was . . . overwhelming." He chuckled. "It also made me completely defenseless, by the way."

"What do you mean?" I asked.

"Just then? At that precise moment? I was so enthralled that if a six-year-old with a rusty kitchen knife had attacked me he could have cut out my liver before I'd worked out what was happening."

"Think how surprised that six-year-old would be once he started glowing red because he'd just become the Saint of Swords."

"I understand it better now, Falcio. It's not what I expected. It's like . . . like having a question you have to answer, but you don't have all the information, even though the question is always there, burning inside you."

"So how do you answer it?" I asked, genuinely interested.

"I'm not sure. But everyone you meet holds a piece of it. Some just have the tiniest sliver, others . . ." He paused and looked at me. "Others have more."

"That's not a reassuring look you're giving me. That reminds me, how did Dariana find you?"

"She didn't."

"Then how?"

"A troubadour told me, if you can believe it." He held up a hand. "It's too long a story. Suffice it to say, the Bardatti are every bit as strange and mysterious as the stories suggest." He looked at me again. "As are you, apparently."

"Me? I'm just your everyday, bog-standard traveling Magistrate."

"Who survived the Greatcoat's Lament. Falcio . . ." His eyes filled with an infinite sadness. "I'm sorry I wasn't there when they—"

"Stop," I said. I understood what he wanted to tell me; I just couldn't stand to hear it, not yet. "If Brasti were here he'd say, 'Stop fawning over everything Falcio does! Sure, it was torture, but you know what else is torture? Having to hear about it, that's torture!'"

Kest laughed for a moment, then he touched me gently on the arm to let me know he understood. Some things we don't talk about.

"I don't suppose you've heard anything about Brasti?" I asked.

He smiled, and this time it was genuine. "As a matter of fact, I heard two separate stories on the way here, of someone people are calling 'The Archer', who's apparently defeated several bands of the Black Tabards. He picks up five or ten decent bowmen from a village, takes them out, and ambushes groups of these Knights before they can cause too much trouble."

I grinned at the thought of Brasti and his archers. "Five or ten bowmen? Isn't that just like Brasti to think in terms of drips of water when the enemy has an ocean?"

"I don't know," Kest said. "I suspect that if Brasti were here he'd say, 'Five drips here, five there, pretty soon you've got a whole cup.'"

I started laughing, ignoring the pain that came along with it. "Kest, that is by far the worst Brasti impression I have ever heard." I began to feel tired. "I could use a little gray right now," I said.

"I don't understand," Kest said, looking around the room.

"Sleep, I said sleep."

"You said gray."

"Really? That's . . ."

The world began to shrink down again, from fragments to shards, from shards to slivers, from slivers to a single mote of dust. I heard a woman's voice calling out. "Quickly . . . water . . . heat . . . Falcio, listen to . . . need t . . ."

Gray.

42

SOLACE

It took days for my fever to break. Ethalia ministered to me with potions and salves, but more often with simpler things: damp cloths to wipe the hot sweat away and cool me down, a gentle touch of her hand across my cheek. She would whisper into my ear; not talking to *me*, but instead trying to coax my heart to beat and my lungs to breathe, like a general issuing carefully thought-out commands to her army. And sometimes she would kiss me. That was just for me, I think.

We were traveling most of the time, I think. In the mornings, they loaded me onto the back of a narrow cart and hauled me along the back roads of Aramor. At night, they'd hide the cart and bring me and the horses deep into the forest. Kest would carry me in his arms and then lay me down on the ground so Ethalia could check me over while someone else built a fire.

I slept most of the time, though at night I'd often wake to hear voices arguing. Kest and Dariana appeared to be on one side of the argument, Ethalia and Valiana on the other. Nehra never spoke, but sometimes she would play her guitar. There were times I thought I could understand what the notes were saying. It was a love song for someone who'd died, but I couldn't make out the name, and whenever I thought I was close to understanding the song, or when the arguments became too heated, Nehra would change the notes, just a little, and I'd fall asleep again.

I felt a great deal of pain during the days after my fever broke, every minute of which I treasured. Though I was weak, whenever I woke up in the morning I could see and hear and feel right away. I would open my eyes and will my hand to come close to my face so that I could wiggle my fingers. Fingers are funny things. They made me laugh.

"Is he mad?" I heard Dariana say one morning. "He keeps doing that and giggling like a half-witted child."

"Shush," Ethalia said. "Go and fetch some water for tea. Someone is coming and I suggest you don't try to kill her. The Saint of Swords would take it poorly."

I listened to Dariana rising, sheathing her sword, and opening the door. We were in a cabin, though I had no idea when we'd arrived or where the cabin was.

"If I decide to kill her," Dariana said, "she'll be dead. And don't shush me, you stupid cow."

I turned my head away from my wiggling fingers because I knew Dariana's words would make Ethalia smile and I wanted to see the little lines crease around her eyes.

"You'll be well soon," she said.

"Really? You have an awfully optimistic view of the world."

She slid her fingers along the side of my cheek and into my hair. "The neatha is gone."

"The poisons that Heryn used, did they—?"

"That's part of it," she said. "The Dashini toxins were meant to drive your nerves past breaking point and in so doing, destroy your mind. But neatha is different: it binds itself to your nerves, preventing sensation and movement of the body, so it blocked the toxins, even as the toxins eventually destroyed it. In a way, the neatha saved you from the Dashini toxins, while they in turn saved you from being killed by the neatha."

A thought occurred to me and I started laughing so hard I couldn't speak. By the time I could, I realized I was crying. "So I should be grateful to both Duchess Patriana *and* the Dashini for saving my life."

Ethalia kissed me, which calmed me. "That is part of it, and it would serve you well to see it that way. But something else burns inside you and that cannot be quenched by any poison."

"My sense of humor?" I asked.

She smiled and kissed me again, not because what I had said was particularly funny but because she knew I wanted her to kiss me. I felt something stirring inside me and reached out to pull Ethalia into the blankets with me. *Saints, maybe I am getting better,* I thought.

"Please don't corrupt my disciple any more than absolutely necessary," a voice said from the door. "She's already terribly wanton."

Ethalia smiled at me and rose from the blankets, tugging down her skirts as if she were a teenager caught fooling around with one of the local farm boys in the hay barn. "Oh my," she said, "I'm ever so sorry, ma'am. T'weren't no wrong 'appenin' here, we was just—"

"Are you making fun of me?" Birgid-who-weeps-rivers, Saint of Mercy, asked.

"Perhaps just a little," Ethalia replied, and ran to hug her.

"There now, child, it hasn't been that long since we've seen each other, has it?" The way Birgid spoke struck me as odd, especially as she looked younger than Ethalia, with her white-blond hair framing her pale, radiant face.

Ethalia stood back. "It's been three years!"

"Ah well, I've been busy." She sounded sheepish. She hugged Ethalia again, then came and sat down next to me. "So."

"So," I said, not sure what other response I could offer.

She checked me over, and for a woman who looked fifteen years younger than me, did a very fine impression of a disapproving grandmother. "I see that my efforts to sway you from the path of violence had little effect."

"In my own defense, people were trying to kill me."

"That's just an excuse," she said. "And now? What will you do?"

I knew what she was asking, or rather, what she was offering: another chance—my third and maybe my last. Ethalia and I could make our way to Baern and find a boat to take us to the Southern Islands, where we'd be free of violence and rid of duty. We'd be happy there. I could let someone else take a turn at trying to fix the world. After all, I'm just one man, with no army, no influence, no power . . .

You don't need any of those things, a voice inside me said, the voice of a boy still clinging to his childhood ideals. *You're a Greatcoat.*

Birgid sighed. "Hopeless," she said.

"Not hopeless," Ethalia said, "and not foolish, either. Something else—something good."

Birgid turned to her and smiled. "You're just as bad," she said. "Go and wait outside for me. Keep the angry girl from coming in here—oh, and try not to have sex with men for money while you're there."

Ethalia gave her a wicked grin and then left.

"Such a foolish child," Birgid said.

I reached out and grabbed the Saint's arm. "Don't," I said. "You don't get to call her that."

Birgid's eyes bore into mine and I felt something there, something old and powerful and far, far stronger than me. "Would you challenge a Saint, Falcio val Mond?"

There was something terrifying in that gaze, but I'd seen a lot of terrifying things lately. "Lady, if you're trying to threaten me you probably should have gotten to me before I spent nine days being tortured by Dashini assassins."

"There are worse things than—"

"No," I said, my mind turning back to the eighth death, "there aren't."

Birgid sighed. "No, I suppose there aren't." She was silent for a moment, then finally said, "She argues for you, at night, when she and the others think you're asleep."

I'd heard the angry whispers back and forth at night, but I'd never been able to make out what they were fighting about.

"The Duke of Rijou has called a Ducal Concord at Castle Aramor. He intends to work with the remaining Dukes to put an end to the murder and mayhem that has beset the country."

A bitter laugh escaped my throat. The last time the Dukes had held a concord was when they'd decided that the only way to save the country was to depose King Paelis. *Hells.* "The Tailor—"

Saint Birgid smiled grimly. "Indeed. She's taking her forces to Castle Aramor. She knows the Dukes have lost faith in most of their Knights and will go with only those few they know they can trust."

"She'll kill every last Duke," I said. "She thinks—"

"I already know what she thinks, Falcio."

I felt the weight of the world descend on my chest, pushing me down, making it hard to breathe. All I wanted was to go back into that deep gray sleep and wake up somewhere else—somewhere peaceful. *That's what they argue about at night.*

"That's it, isn't it: it's about where to take me. Dariana and Kest want to go to Aramor. Ethalia and Valiana want to take me away somewhere safe."

The Saint of Mercy laughed. "Is that what you think? Ethalia loves you and so she tries to sneak you away against your will to be with her?"

"But then—"

"Kest and Dariana are the ones trying to get you *away* from this, Falcio. They don't believe you can take any more—no one could. Valiana is foolish and idealistic; she doesn't think you can be stopped. Ethalia is wiser, though you wouldn't know it from how powerfully she argues your cause. She knows you will likely fail, and die."

"Then why does she argue for me to go to Aramor?"

"Because love isn't a cage." She reached out a hand and stroked my cheek, a soft and intimate gesture that masked something underneath.

"You're angry with me," I said. "Why?"

Birgid turned to gaze at the cabin's door. "She could take my place, you know. It's what I'd hoped for her."

That surprised me for a moment, though I could see very clearly that Ethalia could well be the Saint of Mercy. Then I thought about what Kest had been going through. "It doesn't sound like a very good job."

"Like most things in life, it is what we choose to make of it." She turned back to me. "You've ruined her, Falcio. She loves you, and that love will forever hold her back."

I felt a sharp pain, deep in my stomach. What if Birgid was right and Ethalia's purpose was to become the Saint of Mercy? What did I have to offer her in return? The chance to spend her days and nights waiting alone, wondering if I was alive or dead? Or, worse, the possibility that someone would hurt her to get back at me? No, I couldn't live with that—not again—

Suddenly my right cheek burned and I realized Birgid had just slapped me, hard, across the face. "That's not exactly merciful," I said, holding my hand to my cheek.

"It's merciful compared to what I wanted to do. You don't *own* her, Falcio val Mond."

"I'm not—"

"It's not your place to tell Ethalia what she will or will not become, nor what dangers she can or cannot face."

For a moment I wasn't sure what to say, but then I thought about Aline, my wife, and I knew exactly how to respond. "You're wrong," I said. "If I can't protect her from harm, then what's the point of love?"

Birgid gave a small laugh. "I was wrong about you, Falcio, and about Ethalia too, I suppose. I thought you were just a man of violence, and she a Sister of Mercy, but I saw only one side of the coin. Of course she loves you, for she is compassion and you are valor itself, and compassion is ever drawn to valor."

She put a hand on my chest and patted me twice as if I were a sick child, then she rose and walked to the door. "If you wish to make her happy, Falcio, then turn away from this path and let the world solve its own problems."

I pushed myself up onto unsteady legs. "And if I can't?"

"Then know that you are still weak, that you have no army, and that the Ducal Concord begins in three days."

43

A FINAL JOURNEY

"You've got to rest," Valiana said, pulling on my arm to try to keep me from mounting my horse. "We've been riding for two days without stopping—you're going to kill yourself."

"I'm fine," I said, trying for the third time to get my foot into the stirrup.

Horses can last only so long when they're ridden hard and so we sold ours after the first day when we reached a town large enough to buy fresh ones, and then again early on the second day. But the horses weren't the problem. I was.

"Here," Kest said, holding out a small square packet the size of a man's thumb. "You must be out of the hard candy by now."

I pushed his hand away and reached into my pocket. "I'm fine," I said as I withdrew my own packet and popped the last remaining sliver into my mouth. Almost immediately I felt that strange sharp focus coming to my eyes and my heart beating faster. "You should save yours. It won't do for you to be tired while you're fighting all those people."

"What will you be doing?" Kest asked.

I leaned my head against my horse's saddle, waiting for the dizziness to pass. "Watching, mostly. I might cheer you on occasionally, if you think it will help."

Nehra, sitting astride her horse, nudged closer to us. "What precisely will you do when you get there?"

"Writing a story, are you?"

"I'm Bardatti. It's what I do."

"Well," I said, humoring her, "if all goes to plan, we'll arrive before the Dukes have assembled so that when they get there with whatever Knights and guardsmen they still trust, I'll be able to warn them that a group of Greatcoats are about to arrive with the sole purpose of assassinating them all."

"Won't they send their Knights and guardsmen to arrest you? Especially as you're wearing greatcoats?"

"I'll do my best to explain the difference."

Nehra frowned. "Do you always run headlong into certain death?"

"Sometimes he walks," Dariana said. "Occasionally he shuffles. Once I'm pretty sure I saw him amble into certain death."

Nehra rolled her eyes. "You risk your lives on foolish odds."

"We risk our lives to make them count," Valiana said. "It's what *we* do."

I lifted my head and smiled at her. Saints, but I loved how brave she was. What happened to the princess who saw everyone else as a servant? Where was the mad orphan child, desperate to die before anyone could tell her she didn't have a right to live? All I saw before me now was a Greatcoat. *King Paelis would have adored her*, I thought.

Dariana mounted and set off, followed by Valiana, Nehra, and Kest. I put a hand on Ethalia's arm before she could do the same. "Wait," I said.

She turned and I saw the sadness and resignation in her eyes. *She knows what I'm about to do.* I pointed to the fork in the road ahead of us. "That road goes south through Aramor and then into Baern."

"Oh? And have you decided to leave behind this madness and come with me?"

"I can't, Ethalia. I just can't sit back and let the country be destroyed. I can't have the last thing people remember about the Greatcoats be that they came and committed murder to throw the country into civil war."

She turned away from me. "So you ride into danger, yet you ask me to stay behind like some poor fisherman's wife hoping the storm won't drag your boat under?"

"I'm going to have to fight," I said. "I have to . . . And I can't do it if you're there, Ethalia. I need to—"

"You need to throw away your life recklessly," she said, "and you're afraid that my presence will make it that much more difficult."

"No, damn it." I reached out to her and pulled her toward me, although I expected her to pull away—it's what I would have done if I'd been her. But Ethalia always had a deeper wisdom than me; she'd known from the start that our time together was a gift and anger the thief who would steal its most precious moments. "I don't want to die," I said. "Not anymore."

"There is one path that leads to life and happiness, and another that leads to pain and death. You've got a pretty poor sense of direction, Falcio."

I laughed. We'd known each other a short time, really; I don't think I'd realized how funny she could be. "Of that you can be certain. But let's not forget it was that same poor sense of direction that led me to you in the first place."

She tilted her head up and kissed me. "Nonsense," she said with a wry grin. "Some loves are foretold by the stars and demanded by the world, and not even the Gods dare stand in their way."

"It's not the Gods I'm worried about—although the way things have been going recently, I probably shouldn't speak too soon." I stepped back and held her at arm's length, trying to imprint the memory of her face in my mind forever. "You know I have to do this. I can't sit back and let everything the King fought for become corrupted, the way everything else is in this damned world."

"I haven't asked you to stop being who you are, Falcio—I would never do that."

"Then go south and find happiness, if for no other reason than I'll fight better knowing you're in the world."

"And what world is left for me if you're not in it?" she asked.

"The one where I loved you."

She kissed me then, on the cheek. "Go then—but love is not a cage, Falcio. You have to remember that when the time comes."

I walked back to my horse and set off to follow the others, leaving Ethalia and all she represented—all she *promised*—behind me. She was wrong, and so was Birgid: love *was* a cage, and I couldn't do what I had to do next while locked inside it. *Another few hours*, I thought, and then the Tailor and I were going to have a very long conversation about the direction of the country. Unless she killed me first, of course.

The five of us galloped along the back roads that ran through central Aramor, using every shortcut Kest and I could remember from the days we'd spent exploring with the King. Finally, just before nightfall, we came to a small hill a few hundred yards from Castle Aramor. We dismounted and made our way to a vantage point near a copse of trees that looked down on the castle.

"Just a few minutes rest," I said, doing my best not to fall to the ground. "Then we go down there and do what we came to do."

Kest walked up the rest of the hill, Dariana and Valiana following close behind. Nehra came and stood beside me. At least she had the decency to pretend she was tired too.

"I won't be fighting with you," she said.

I turned my head to look at her. She had made no complaint since the moment she'd been captured by Heryn's men. Colwyn had died, and yet she hadn't even once sought revenge from Dariana. "I'm sorry about Colwyn," I said. "I didn't know him, but—"

"Please don't say stupid things, Falcio. That's not the reason."

"You don't agree with what we're trying to do? You think civil war and chaos are legitimate ways to—"

"And a second time you show your ignorance, First Cantor of the Greatcoats," Nehra said. "Come, give us a third, for the Gods love things in threes."

I looked at this strange woman who was so plain in herself and yet who could make music that transformed everyone around her; who said little, yet knew every story there was . . .

"It's about the story, isn't it?" I asked. "You have to witness the story of what happens here today."

She slapped me on the back. "You see? It appears you're not entirely without wits. I'll be there when whatever happens, happens, but I can't be part of it, not now, not when the tale must be heard, for it must be told."

I stood up and stretched my back and rotated my shoulders. *Stiff,* I thought. *Still too stiff.* "I'll do my best to give you a good story, then," I said. "Try to get my name right, will you?"

She looked at me then without a trace of ire or sarcasm in her expression, then leaned over and gave me a soft kiss on the cheek. "I will, Falcio val Mond of the Trattari," she said, and then walked away down the hill.

I winced. "Please stop calling us Trattari."

I heard the sound of steel being drawn and looked up the hill. The three of them had their swords in hand and I raced toward them, drawing my own rapiers. "What is it?" I asked. "Are they here already?"

Valiana turned to me, looking sick. "We're too late."

I moved past her and looked down the hill. The lawn in front of Castle Aramor was designed to hold great assemblies. It had been created more than a hundred years ago by uprooting several acres of trees from the forest at the edge of the castle's walls. The King used to call it "the green gauntlet" because it looked as if a giant had left an eight-hundred-yard-long glove on the ground, with the castle on one side and thick forest on the other. And there, lying all over that lush green grass, were dozens and dozens of dead bodies, scattered as if that same giant had dropped them all from a great height.

The bodies wore greatcoats.

44

CASTLE ARAMOR

We stared in horror at the carnage staining the green grass of Castle Aramor below. The dead lay sprawled around the field, the wreckage of their bodies partially covered by their long leather coats, looking like derelict ships filling a harbor after a storm. The wind picked up and the coats flapped in the wind and the smells of blood and death and great fear rose up to us.

Further along the gauntlet I saw row upon row of mounted Knights. There were too great to count, but they numbered perhaps close to a thousand. They sat their horses as if preparing for a parade. Some were armed with warswords, some with lances, but they all wore black tabards.

Valiana turned to me. "I don't understand . . . they're all dead. How could they—?"

"The Dashini are killers," Dariana said. "We fight in the shadows, in dark alleyways and narrow streets. We fight with stealth and speed, not the brute force of a cavalry charge on an open battlefield."

"Then why—? Why would the Tailor try to fight here?"

"Because we had no choice," a woman's voice said.

The Tailor stumbled out from the copse of trees, her own leather coat covered in blood. She held a broken sword with one hand and pressed a dark red cloth to her side with the other. Her gray hair was flying wild in the wind; her face showed the bruising and cuts of battle. She took two steps toward us and began to topple, but Kest reached her in time and took hold of her shoulders.

"Just help me sit down," she said, tossing the sword away.

Kest helped her as she sat heavily on the grass, then he knelt down to examine the wound in her side.

"It's nothing," she said, pushing him away. "I got nicked by the tip of a Knight's lance when my horse went out from under me. Most of the blood isn't mine." She looked up at me. "I see you survived the Lament. Must be pleased with yourself."

For just a moment I was back there, tied to that post, with Heryn holding a needle and saying, *"Shall we proceed?"* It took every ounce of self-control not to stab the Tailor in the throat with one of my rapiers.

She laughed. "Ah, Falcio. Look at that face of yours. So much righteous indignation. Well? Come on then. I failed. My Greatcoats are all dead down there. If you're planning to kill me, now would be a good time."

"How?"

"What do I care? A thrust to the heart would be humane, but at this point you could carve me into pieces and turn me into stew and I'd be grateful."

"No," I said, "how did *this* happen?"

"We came to fight the Dukes and their retainers and a few personal guards. We expected a hundred men and instead we found a thousand." She waved a hand out at the wide-open space below us. "Instead we got that."

"Where's Aline?" Valiana asked. "Is she—?"

"Captured," the Tailor said.

"We've got to—"

"Keep your sword in its sheath, girly. There's nothing you can do. They won't kill her, not now, not with a Ducal Concord in session.

They'll just make her renounce her claim to the throne—she'll be no threat to them then." The Tailor looked at me. "Aline's life is all that's left to fight for now. You're going to go down there, First Cantor, and you're going to beg Jillard to let you take Aline away from here. Promise to take her out of the country, if that helps. You saved his life. Maybe some small good can come from your betrayal."

Valiana began to draw her sword again, this time for me, but I reached over and put my hand on hers. "Stop. It doesn't matter."

"I'm not going to let her accuse you of treason, not after what she's done to all of us!"

I looked at the old woman with her iron-gray hair and eyes as hard as steel, her skin like leather and a tongue as sharp as a needle. I had loved her once, I realized, back in those early days with King Paelis. She'd been like one of those sages in the stories, the one who guides the hero to some secret magic that will save the day, only with more swearing and insults. I so wished she really was that foul-mouthed sage I'd believed her to be—or if not, then at least the exact opposite, the vile traitor who seeks the hero's destruction from the darkness. But it'd taken me a long time to see that she was neither; she was just a mother who had lost her son and a grandmother about to lose her granddaughter. She was brilliant and powerful and devious and cold, but she was human and every bit as flawed and broken as the country that had spawned her.

"The Tailor's right," I said. "All that's left now is to get Aline her life, if we can."

"What's the plan?" Kest asked.

"No plan," I said. "You take the others and get out of here. I'll go and see what kind of deal I can make."

"They have Aline—what have you to trade?"

I knelt down and picked up the sword the Tailor had tossed on the ground. "Whatever I have to offer that they want." I stared at the sword's wide steel blade, broken less than a foot from the hilt. Such a simple thing, and yet capable of so much destruction. Rolled steel, tempered in a fire, beaten with a hammer until it held onto all the violence of its birth, waiting to unleash it on human flesh. I wondered if blacksmiths ever felt regret as they finished their work and stamped their mark on the sword. I held the one in my hand up to the light. The maker's mark was a simple circle with a cross inside and three dots spread out above, like a crown. Did the man who made this sword have any idea how much chaos he brought into the world?

I looked at the maker's mark again. It felt familiar, somehow.

Oh, hells . . .

I stepped back so quickly I nearly fell into Kest.

"What's wrong?" he asked.

"The swords," I said, "the steel weapons in Carefal." I went over to the Tailor. "You gave the villagers those weapons."

"Of course, and you already know why, so don't—"

"No, I mean, *after* we confiscated them—after Duke Isault's men bought them and took them away—did you go back and give them more?"

"I already told you I didn't. How could I, you fool? I'm not made of gold. I had to spread my resources among all nine duchies."

I turned to Valiana. "Give me your sword—the one you picked up in Carefal after the massacre."

"Why—?"

"Just give it to me."

She drew the blade and handed it to me. I held it up next to the Tailor's broken blade.

"What is it?" Kest asked.

I flipped the blades around and held them up for him.

Kest leaned in and inspected the blades where they met the hilt. Both had the same maker's mark cut into the blade: a cross inside a circle with three small dots above it.

"They have the same maker's mark—but that means the swords the villagers had the second time—"

"—were the same ones we confiscated," I agreed.

"But wouldn't that mean—?"

"Shuran," I said. "The Knight-Commander of Aramor had someone give those very same weapons back to the villagers in Carefal."

"But why?"

"So he could create fear among the nobles. Think. What's the one thing everyone has in common right now—the Dukes, the peasants, everyone . . . ?"

"They're afraid," Dariana said.

"Not even just afraid: they're *terrified*: noble families are being murdered in their beds, villagers are rebelling, Knights in black tabards are running around massacring people. And what does everyone want when they're afraid?"

"A protector: someone who will keep them safe," she replied.

"And who better than a loyal Knight of Tristia to be their protector?" said a voice behind us, and I turned to see Sir Shuran, Knight-Commander of Aramor, walking up to us from where we'd left our horses. "You know, I told my men there was an old woman among the assassins and they didn't believe me. And yet here I find you, madam, sitting on this little hill as if you were about to have a picnic."

The Tailor rose to her feet and put a hand out to grab Dariana's arm. "Kill him," she said. "Kill him now."

"That would be a terrible idea," Shuran said. "For one thing, if you look down there—at the bottom of the hill—yes, right there—you'll see I've brought my own friends with me so we can have a little picnic as well."

When I looked down below as bidden I saw twenty men on horseback coming up the path toward Shuran.

"We also have a little girl back at the castle who is very afraid right now; I expect she would probably like to see some friendly faces—let's all go down and get better acquainted, shall we?"

"I'll come with you," I said. "The others go free." Of course I didn't expect a positive response, but I wanted to keep him talking while I tried to figure out a way around him and his men.

"I don't think the Dukes would appreciate me letting them go, Falcio." Shuran smiled. "On the other hand, what do I care about the Dukes and their wishes?"

I was stunned. "You'll let the others leave unharmed?"

Shuran reached out and put a hand on my shoulder. "I hold no ill will toward you, Falcio." He looked at the others. "Nor to any of you. Although I can't very well let the old woman go. My apologies, madam, but assassinating Ducal families is generally frowned upon. We'll find you a nice comfortable cell while we work things out."

"Take the deal," the Tailor said to me.

"Go," I told the others. "Get on the horses and go now."

Valiana started to object. "We can't leave—"

"For once, please, will you do as I ask and just go?"

I felt Shuran's fingers squeeze into my shoulder. "I do have one favor to ask in return."

"What is it?"

"Oh, not from you, Falcio." He released my shoulder and turned to Kest. "I want the Saint of Swords to finally favor me with that bout."

Shuran and his men escorted Kest, the Tailor, and me down the hill and made us march through the dozens of dead Dashini Unblooded in their torn leather coats sprawled across the churned-up green gauntlet. After the King had died, Castle Aramor had been closed, by order of the Ducal Concord. It had been empty for more than five years. The grasses had grown and weeds had begun to take over, but now I could see that someone had taken the time to trim the grass in a patch in front of the castle and had set out chairs and a large white table. The Dukes might be facing the worst crisis to afflict Tristia in a hundred years, but it was nonetheless vital to ensure a pleasant environment for their deliberations. Several of them were sitting around the table, sipping wine from delicate glasses decorated with golden swans that I recognized; they were from King Paelis's own collection.

Three of them stood as they saw us approach, no doubt uncomfortable to see more Greatcoats.

Duke Jillard was the first to step forward. "You look a little the worse for wear since last I saw you, Falcio."

"The result of an unfortunate misunderstanding, your Grace. You, on the other hand, look much improved since my last visit to Rijou."

"Quite. That Dashini dust really is a terror, though." He looked at me and then at Shuran's Knights, behind us. "I do hope you didn't come here to try to assassinate me, Falcio. It hardly seems appropriate, not given how hard you worked to keep me alive."

"I was hoping you might return the favor."

Jillard smiled. "I rather thought you were. Very well. Shuran? Let the two men go. The woman stays, of course." He turned as if the conversation were over.

"I want Aline," I said, "alive and unharmed. And I want oaths from you and your fellow Dukes that you will leave her to live in peace."

He held out his goblet as if expecting wine to fall from the sky. Weirdly, it did—well, all right, one of the servants immediately rushed forward to refill it, but the effect was the same. "Really, Falcio? I gave you your life, so our debt is paid. Why would I also give you the girl?"

"I'll get her to renounce her claim to the throne."

"She'll do that anyway. Give me something else."

The other Dukes were looking at us as if we were unsightly weeds growing in their garden. The very last thing I wanted to do was save their lives: they had set Tristia on this path when they had killed the King five years ago and now they wanted me to barter for the life of his daughter. Ethalia was wrong: love *is* a cage.

"I'll give you your lives," I said at last. "Or at least, I'll try my very best to do so."

Jillard raised an eyebrow. "Are you threatening to kill us, Falcio? Because I am pretty sure that Sir Shuran and his thousand Knights will be able to protect us. I feel quite safe in their presence."

"Then you are shortsighted, your Grace. Sir Shuran is the one planning to kill you."

The assembled Dukes and their retainers laughed heartily at that.

Jillard set his goblet down on the table. "You do realize you're accusing the Knight-Commander of Aramor? The very man whose forces saved us from being assassinated just a few hours ago?"

"And also—and I'm taking a wild guess here—the man you're about to elevate to the rank of Realm's Protector?"

Jillard's eyes widened and he opened his mouth to speak, but I went on, "You're going to put the rest of the Ducal armies under his command and send him north to destroy Trin's forces. He's an able commander, and the most respected Knight in the country. He'll tear her soldiers apart, always assuming they don't immediately abandon her when they see him and his Knights coming."

"And when he does," Jillard said, his eyes on Shuran, "he will help us set the rest of the country to rights, and then step down from his post."

"Somehow I doubt that," I said. "Shuran is the one who's been both arming villages against your duchies and then sending out the Black Tabards to massacre them. He orchestrated the fear of rebellion so you'd need to turn to the Knights—many of whom he's already bought off with not inconsiderable sums, and the rest of whom . . . well, forgive me your Graces, and I'd like to say it hurts me to say this . . . but the rest of whom respect him more than you anyway. It was Shuran who had Duke Isault's children murdered, and he who ensured the other Dukes' families would die."

"Why?" Jillard asked. "What possible reason could he have for doing such a thing?"

"A Knight could never ascend a Ducal throne, not even a Knight-Commander," the Tailor replied, her eyes on me as she finally realized that she too had been played for a fool. "It would never be allowed. But what if all the Ducal lines were destroyed, the families annihilated? What if people were scared enough? What if every other noble feared being assassinated in their sleep? They might well be willing to see a Knight take control, for a while at least."

Jillard shook his head. "What you're suggesting—arming the peasants, bribing Knights, arranging murders—such a thing would

require untold sums of money. Where would a common Knight—
even a Knight-Commander—ever secure such funds?"

I looked at Shuran. "Do you want to tell him or should I?"

"Please," he answered, smiling. "Do as you see fit. It's your story."

"Will there be a wedding announcement soon?" I asked, then
added, "No, don't bother answering that." I turned back to Jillard.
"You were right all along, your Grace: Trin could never have kept
the throne. Oh, she could kill Aline, which I doubt any of you would
have much minded. She could sweep in with her armies, maybe even
win a war with the south if you failed to unite. But in the end, you'd
have found a way to have her killed and she's always known that. Her
mother, Duchess Patriana, knew that too, and that's why they spent
so many years building up an extremely impressive infrastructure
within your duchies. You make Shuran here the Realm's Protector,
he kills off the rest of you, he and Trin form a pact—or even marry—
and now they have an entirely new nobility to take hold of Tristia. In
truth, it might not even be worse than the one we're stuck with now."

"That's . . . Gods . . ." Jillard looked at Shuran with morbid curiosity. "It all makes sense now . . . the killing of the children, the way
you were able to . . . But how could a Knight ever be so dishonorable?
And not just a Knight, but a *Knight-Commander*? How could you do
such things to your lord?"

Sir Shuran's expression remained placid as he backhanded Jillard
with his metal gauntlet, knocking the Duke of Rijou to the ground.

"She did say you were clever, Falcio," Shuran said, "but I'm clever
too. I've got a thousand men here, and more will be on the way
once Jillard is dead and his former Knight-Commander returns to
Rijou to take control of the armies." He looked back toward his men,
waiting patiently on the field. "Marvelous, aren't they? Most soldiers
these days are unruly and ill-disciplined, but these men are *committed*. They are true Knights." He turned back to me. "I've given them
strict orders to attack when the last light of the sun dies over the
horizon, Falcio. Until that precise moment they'll wait there on their
horses, in perfect formation. They'll sit there even if the mountains

themselves begin to fall on them. That's what Tristia is crying out for: discipline. Order. And that's what Trin and I will bring."

"You murdered the very children you were sworn to protect," I said. "You gave the country chaos and bloodshed. If there's one thing I take comfort in, it's that any man who ties his fate to Trin is already dead and simply doesn't know it yet."

"Now is that any way to talk about your Queen?"

I recognized the voice as Trin's, but when I turned it was Aline I saw stumbling toward us, her head in a wooden oval frame attached with thick bolts. Inside the frame was Trin's face.

"You see the wonderful solution I've worked out, Falcio? You wanted Aline to be Queen but I want to be Queen too—so now we can both be Queen. Well, after a fashion—"

"No!" the Tailor screamed, reaching out for the girl, but I grabbed her and dragged her back.

"*Stop!* She can kill Aline from inside her own body if she wants and there is nothing we can do to prevent her."

"It's not my intention to hurt the girl permanently," Shuran said.

"The girl dies tonight," Trin declared, her eyes fixed on the Knight-Commander.

There was a pause, then Shuran gave me a rueful smile. "Well, as you can see, that's out of my hands. I'll be happy to return her to you as soon as we're done, though."

"Don't do this, Shuran," I begged. "Don't—"

"It's all right, Falcio," Kest said. "He's not doing this because of Aline. I don't think he's even doing it because he wants to rule Tristia, or, at least, that's only part of it."

"Then what—?"

"He wants something that only I can give him," he said, and turned to Shuran. "Let's have that bout then, shall we?"

45

THE BLACK TABARD

The Saint of Swords and the Knight-Commander of Aramor stared at each other across a patch of muddy grass. They were no further apart than if they had been standing at opposite ends of a Lord's bathtub. If one man were to draw his sword and attack and the other hesitated for the blink of an eye, a head would fall to the ground.

"I seem to recall," Shuran said casually, "that when we first met you numbered the moves it would require to defeat me."

"Ten," Kest said.

"And do you stand by that assessment?"

Neither man moved an inch, but Kest's gaze slid briefly over Shuran's shoulder to the path in the dirt he had made when he approached. "Your footsteps are even now. You walked more heavily on your left before. You were favoring your right side when we first met. Was that from a wound, or were you pretending?"

Shuran smiled. "If I told you it was from a wound I sustained when my horse was shot with an arrow, how would you judge our fight now?"

"Seventeen moves," Kest said without hesitation.

"Really? So I've gained seven more strikes in which to savor life. And how many if I were to tell you that even then I was pretending, so as to hide my abilities?"

Nothing about Kest moved and yet I could tell his mind was working. "Twenty-two," he said finally.

"Prodigious," Shuran said. "Now since you've been so kind in indulging me thus far, let me press further upon your patience."

Shuran began moving his left hand lightly, smoothly, in the air, making no effort to threaten or surprise. He looked like a man listening to beautiful music, the motion of his hand matching the rhythm of the instruments as his fingers pretended to play the melody. For an instant I thought it might be some trick or spell, but then I saw Kest's eyes as he followed the movements and only then did I glean that Shuran was revealing himself.

"Thirty-one," Kest said. "No. Thirty-nine."

Shuran kept moving his hand gently in the air, changing direction and tempo. It looked like empty posturing—except that I knew I could never move so smoothly, so accurately, with such perfect control.

"Fifty-four," Kest said.

"Really? Is that all?" Shuran asked.

Kest stared at Shuran's smile, which hadn't affected the perfection of his movements in the slightest.

"Seventy," Kest said.

Shuran laughed. It was a surprisingly beautiful sound, and perfectly controlled. His laughter did not affect any other part of his body.

"Ninety-four," Kest said.

"Careful now," Shuran said. "If we keep this up you'll soon tell me you can't defeat me at all."

"Ninety-four," Kest repeated.

"Who taught you the sword?" Shuran asked.

"My father. My friends. My enemies," Kest replied.

"Elegantly put," Shuran said. "I think it's important to learn from the best, don't you?"

Something in the small twist of Shuran's smile bothered me: it wasn't that it was crazed or even menacing, but it was familiar—not in the way that made me think I'd seen it before; rather, that I felt as if I'd seen its mate somewhere. It was like seeing a beautiful woman and being absolutely sure you'd met her before, only to learn that you hadn't, but you once met a man who'd described the love of his life while spinning a wild tale in a tavern over drinks and now you realize you've found her.

"Kest, something's wrong," I said.

"Come now," Shuran said, "are we still stuck on ninety-four? Can I do no better than that?"

"Who taught you?" Kest asked.

"Hmm?"

"You asked who my teachers were. Who were yours?"

"Ah, well, I really had only one of note. My father—he was quite good, though, or so I'm told. Frankly, I'm surprised he agreed to teach me at all, as he had little use for children. I was something of an embarrassment to him, at least from his point of view. He beat me with the flat of his sword, quite badly, the first seven times I begged him to teach me."

"I take it he eventually took pity on you?" Kest asked.

"Pity? I suppose. I think he found it entertaining at first. He was a cold man, really. He liked to watch me bleed. It upset my mother no end."

The motion of Shuran's hand, the tone of his voice, his smile . . .

The pieces fell together. "Gods, Kest! I know who taught him—I know who his father was—"

"Saints," Shuran said as his smile broadened and his hand finally came to rest. "The correct oath in this instance is 'Saints.'"

It had never occurred to me, the one time I'd met the man who must have been Shuran's father, that he might have a family. I had been so sure that our lives were about to end that all that had mattered to me was that my best friend in the entire world was about to throw away his life to give Aline, Valiana, Brasti, and me a head start—just a few minutes—so we could try to escape. Who would have thought that such a creature as that, so focused on the singular enterprise of perfecting the art of the sword, would ever bother with such a mundane thing as making love to a woman—or having a son?

"Caveil," I said out loud. I felt as if I had to say the name to prove it didn't fill me with fear. "Your father was Caveil-whose-sword-cuts-water."

Shuran's eyes drifted to mine. "I always prefer to think of him as my teacher. He was never very good at being my father."

"But how . . . ?" My voice sounded weak and strained to my ears.

"Even a Saint as—well, shall we say *limited in his interests*? Even one such as Caveil beds a woman once in a while."

"But I thought the Saints could produce no offspring—"

Shuran laughed. "Really? Falcio, you must learn to be more discriminating in which old stories you choose to believe. Although I suppose that might be true if they're bedding normal people. Fortunately for me, the issue was moot: apparently two Saints can do just fine together where producing children is concerned."

Birgid: his mother was Saint Birgid-who-weeps-rivers. *The union of mercy and violence is only more violence.* She'd tried to temper Caveil's violence with her own mercy and instead their offspring was Shuran, a man of pure violence. His whole life he'd trained to become the Saint of Swords, and he would have been, except that Kest, against all probability, had managed to defeat Caveil to save our lives.

But Shuran had been born for this.

"So," Shuran said, turning his gaze back to Kest, "how many moves do you think it will take to defeat me now?"

I've been a swordsman since I was a child. I've practiced nearly every day since I first picked up a rapier. I've read every book on fencing, no matter how old or obscure or esoteric, ever written. I've fought with swords, been bruised by swords, cut by swords, and on many occasions, nearly died by the sword. When you spend your life in this manner, you become accustomed to the fact that you can't hope to see an experienced opponent's blade move; it's simply too fast for the eye to catch. So you watch other things: the bend in their elbows, the stance of their feet, the tension in their shoulders. It's these things that tell you where they'll move next. And if you're a *real* expert you can simply watch your opponent's eyes. That's what Kest and Shuran were doing.

Their swords flashed briefly in the air, only to return to a guard position before my ears had even heard the *tink* of the blades in contact. When they attacked it was like a mockingbird swooping in for a red berry; not much, just a tiny cut here, a few drops of blood shed there: enough to slow the other down, if only by a fraction of a second.

"Do you find it makes you faster?" Shuran asked as their blades settled after what I'd counted to be five exchanges but might as easily have been fifty.

"Does what make me faster?" Kest asked.

"Your Sainthood: you've started to glow red. Does it give you greater speed?"

"Not that I'm aware of."

Shuran tilted his head—a natural act, but not a wise one, for Kest's blade spun in and the tip reached for the big Knight-Commander's throat. Shuran whirled his blade to knock Kest's away, but by then it was no longer there.

"Does it make you stronger?" Shuran asked, as if nothing had happened.

"I haven't noticed any increase in the strength of my sword arm."

"Well then—?"

"To be honest with you, I haven't noticed that Sainthood makes much difference one way or another. Perhaps it's because I'm still new to it . . . but I didn't get the impression it did all that much good for Caveil either."

A flicker of anger crossed Shuran's face, and he launched his attack, delivering a flurry of blows that, despite the force behind them, were surprisingly graceful. He shifted effortlessly—or at least that's how it looked—between a diagonal slash that would have severed Kest's jaw from his head to a powerful thrust to his kneecap. His blade swept high, then low, at one moment flicking for a small cut and at the next coming down from on high with enough force to cut his opponent's body in half. Kest evaded each blow, sometimes parrying, sometimes neatly sidestepping the strike, letting the blade pass a hair's-breadth from his face.

"That won't work, you know," Kest said.

"What's that?" Shuran's reply didn't betray even the slightest bit of strain, let alone the exhaustion most men would feel after so much effort.

"You won't trick me into giving you the extra two inches of ground you want."

Though both men were fighting with broadswords, Shuran's was the longer, by three inches. If he could widen the distance between them, just slightly, he would have the advantage.

Shuran smiled. "Well then, we'll just have to try something else, won't we?" He feinted toward Kest's exposed left side and I knew it was a feint because it was far too obvious a move. Kest parried the attack anyway, because an expert swordsman can turn a feint into a genuine attack if he senses at the last instant that his opponent isn't going to block the strike. In this instance Kest thrust his blade toward Shuran's right hip, forcing him to step back, then Shuran brought his sword back into guard just a little too stiffly; tightening his grip he exposed his own left side, just a fraction—all Kest needed to do was advance half a step and strike him down—

"That won't work either," Kest said, remaining exactly where he was.

"What was I doing now?" Shuran asked innocently.

"The pebble on the ground, balanced on top of that stone? You think by pushing to get me to step there, I will lose my balance."

"I am just full of devious ploys today, apparently."

Now Kest began his own attacks, each one varying not only in target and tempo but in style as well, and he slid seamlessly from classical fencing styles to the harsher forms used by warriors on the battlefield. Sometimes he even threw in one of those back-alley brawler moves that works not because of its efficiency but because of its sudden and unexpected ferocity—but Shuran evaded and parried and anticipated and counterattacked, and all in all, the exchange lasted barely twenty seconds and at the end of it they had moved less than two feet in the dirt.

When they both returned to guard positions there was a tiny bead of blood, just above Shuran's brow. "Bravo," he said.

Slowly, ever so slowly, the drop of blood enlarged and began to move down Shuran's forehead. In a matter of moments it would drip into his right eye, and he would be forced to blink. In that instant he would die.

"I was close that time," Shuran said conversationally. "In the fourth movement? I nearly had you. Just for a second your weight shifted."

"There was a patch of loose dirt. I expect you knew that."

"And yet you noted it and adjusted for it," Shuran said. "You're remarkable."

"You're good yourself," Kest acknowledged. "But you're no Saint."

The Knight-Commander smiled. "That's for certain. I could never beat you fairly. I know that now."

The word *fairly* set me off. I looked around to see if this was some trap—if one of Shuran's men might be hiding out of sight, readying a crossbow, but I could see nothing. Perhaps this was simply the final, magnanimous admission of a man who has truly met his better.

A drop of blood was resting on Shuran's eyebrow. In a second it would be over.

The talk of pebbles and loose dirt made my gaze drift down to the ground, just to see if there might be anything else that might impede Kest finishing Shuran, but I saw nothing. Despite Shuran's manipulations, Kest had always moved carefully, ensuring he stayed on solid ground—every time he had tried to lead Kest onto poor footing, Kest had worked around the hazard. My brain started itching. Why then had Shuran kept following a failed strategy? And for that matter, how had he known so well where every single rock and pebble was sitting? It was as if—

Of course he'd placed them all there himself, I realized. The sneaky bastard had studied every miniscule pebble, every mote of dust on the ground before the duel so he'd know exactly where to move. But Kest was too smart—and too observant—for Shuran; he'd moved between and over everything the Knight-Commander had set in his path, and now he stood on . . .

Oh, Hells . . .

"Kest," I said, "move back—"

"Too late," Shuran said. He shook his head, just slightly, and beads of blood sprayed from his forehead. Kest brought up his sword to strike Shuran's head free from his neck. Blood droplets hit the ground—and Kest's blade stopped where it was.

Kest tried to move but couldn't. His legs were shaking as if a giant hand were trying to push him down to the ground.

"I had a cleric consecrate the ground." The Knight-Commander scuffed away the dirt in front of him to reveal a carefully drawn circle. Kest was standing in the middle of it. "It needed only a drop of blood to complete the magic. I would have preferred for it to have been yours, of course, but mine will work just as well. You should probably bow down: that's what the Gods expect from a Saint standing on consecrated earth."

I raced toward them, intent on knocking Kest out of the circle, but Shuran's sword was up and out. I only just managed to stop myself from impaling myself on the sharp end.

"I think not," Shuran said, his attention still focused on Kest. "If it makes you feel better, I can't kill you while you're in the consecrated circle, Kest." He took an idle swing at Kest's head and his blade bounced back as if it had hit a stone wall. "All this religion is so bothersome, don't you think?"

Kest fell to his knees, his head involuntarily bowed. "You couldn't beat me before, Shuran. Whatever you do now, I'll kill you when this is done. You will never be the Saint of Swords."

"Of course I will." Shuran flicked his sword toward me and I lurched back, but not quite far enough: I felt a slight sting on my cheek and when I pressed my hand to it, my fingers came back with a trace of blood.

With great difficulty, Kest managed to turn his head toward me and I saw the fear and concern in his eyes.

"You're so controlled, Kest," Shuran said. "You're so very logical. You think *everything* through, every move. I don't think anyone can beat you when your mind's on the game." At last he turned his gaze to me. "That's why I'm going to kill your friend Falcio here, right in front of you, and quite horribly."

"If you really wanted to shock Kest then you probably should have tried this plan *before* the Dashini tortured me for nine days," I said.

Shuran ignored me. People were doing that a lot lately. "And after I'm done with him I'll have my men go and retrieve the others. I'll kill Valiana first. I think she's a lovely girl, so that will be a great pity. I'm not sure how much you care about Dariana—if at all; she doesn't appear to be all that likable, does she?—but whatever your opinion of her, I'm going to do the same to her."

He stepped forward and looked down the line of his blade, which was still aimed at me. "Then I'm going to bring little Aline over here and Trin and I are going to—Well, to be honest, she's only a young girl and I would really rather not have to do such things, but needs must."

"You would commit such acts of useless cruelty," Kest said, struggling against the unseen weight holding him down, "and yet none of this will make you a Saint."

Shuran smiled. "And that's where you're wrong, because after destroying your friends and letting Trin desecrate innocent little Aline right in front of you I'm going to get my cleric to deconsecrate the circle. And do you know what's going to happen then, Kest? You're going to come at me with black rage in your heart. You're not used to fighting with anger, are you? So that's how I'm going to beat you; that's how I'm going to kill you—that's how I'm going to become the Saint of Swords."

46

THE DUEL

There's an old saying—and, very handily, it's written inside the front cover of one of the many books on fencing that King Paelis kept in his personal library—and it says, *The most important fights are never won on skill.* This is considered by most master swordsmen to be a bit of a mistranslation, since the whole point of spending a lifetime studying the sword is precisely that: to develop your skill until you're unbeatable.

Some have argued that the quote is missing a word, like "*alone*": as in, *The most important fights are never won on skill alone.* I'm sure this would be enormously reassuring to swordmasters everywhere, but I'm afraid it's simply not true.

Kest and I used to sit and stare at that quotation for hours on end, trying to figure out what it really meant. Did the author truly believe that a combination of greater strength and speed and a longer reach—all of which are obviously hugely important factors in sword-fighting—could overcome skill? If so, that was obviously going to do me no good at all, since Shuran was not only stronger and faster than me but he also had several extra inches of reach on me too.

I couldn't help but keep repeating that quote in my head as Shuran stood before me, his sword in a high guard, waiting to cut off my head. He looked over at Kest, who was still kneeling on the ground. "Well, Saint of Swords, how many moves do you judge it will require me to take your friend's head off?"

Kest tried to rise to his feet, but instead fell back to his knees, looking for all the world like a bent-backed old man who'd had too much to drink. He looked at Shuran and then at me. "Seven," he said.

"Seven moves," Shuran repeated. "What a shame your Tailor betrayed you to those Dashini; they must have done some real damage. Come, Falcio, my friend—how much value do those seven moves really hold for you? Wouldn't it be better to make it easy on yourself, just for once? Maybe you could sit and make peace with the Gods? Or, if you prefer, I can have the Tailor brought here, and you can kill her for her betrayal. Either way, isn't it better to enjoy these final moments, just let death come for you?"

"No," I said.

Shuran looked genuinely confused. "Why not?"

For once in my life I had no ready answer. Even if, by some extremely timely miracle, a very large tree fell out of the sky and landed on Shuran, killing him instantly, I would still lose, for a few hundred yards away a thousand Knights were waiting for us. The battle had already been lost.

The fights that matter most aren't won on skill.

Then how in all the hells are they won?

I heard footsteps behind me. "Stay back," I said, assuming it was Valiana or Dariana.

"Well, now, and who's this then?" Shuran asked, and when I turned my head to see who he was looking at I felt my heart break in my chest. She looked exactly as she had the first time I saw her, with her long dark hair framing her pale face, her otherworldly beauty set off by a long dress made of gauzy material that caught the last feeble rays of sunlight and reflected them like a thousand little stars.

Ethalia.

I reached out to her, but she evaded my touch. She ignored Shuran's blade too, instead walking past us to stand just a few feet away from him. She clasped her hands in front of her.

"And who are you?" Shuran asked.

"I am the friend in the dark hour," Ethalia said. "I am the breeze against the burning sun. I am the water, freely given, and the wine, lovingly shared. I am the rest after the battle and the healing after the wound. I am the friend in the dark hour," she repeated. "And I am here for you, Shuran, son of Caveil."

Trin ran Aline's body, with her black heart deep inside Aline's soul, forward and tilted her head sideways. The vicious wooden frame around Aline's head listed as she did it. "She's his whore," she announced helpfully. "One of those Sisters of Mercy Fucking, I believe they're called."

Shuran smiled. "Have you come to offer yourself to me? Have you come to beg for Falcio's life?"

Of course she has, you bastard. She's all love and compassion and sacrifice, and she has no idea what she's doing! "Ethalia, come back to me, very slowly," I called softly.

She ignored me and kept her focus on Shuran. "I have indeed come to offer myself to you—but not to beg for Falcio's life."

Shuran looked at her for a moment, his eyes wide, and then his head went back and he laughed so loudly it filled the whole of the green gauntlet. "Oh, my sweet lady. I am very nearly overwhelmed by your offer. But alas, even I can't do that to Falcio. Hasn't he suffered enough?"

"No," Ethalia said, her voice as calm and quiet as still water, "I wish it were not so, but he needs to suffer just a bit more yet."

"You stupid bitch," Dariana said, and stepped forward to grab her, but quick as lightning Shuran brought his blade up and struck Dariana with the flat of the blade, first on one side of her face and then the other.

As she reeled backward, as much from the shock as from the pain, Shuran said, "That is no way to talk to a lady."

Trin was still looking at Ethalia. "I want to know what the whore wants," she demanded.

"My offer is simple," Ethalia said, turning her attention to Trin. "You performed a ritual with the Dashini to make him relive the death of his wife. You were with him in those moments, weren't you?"

"I was," Trin said, her lips twisting into a smile that was hideous to my eyes. "It was . . . *invigorating*. I recall every second; I can still feel every time she was beaten; I can still see every bone breaking, and her flesh coming apart, her teeth falling from her mouth . . . I remember the feel of each of those men's—"

"You needn't continue," Ethalia said. "You've made my point."

"Oh? And what point is that?" Shuran asked. "You said you had an offer."

"I do." Ethalia turned to me, her eyes on mine even as she spoke to Shuran. "If you can defeat Falcio in battle you may do to me all those terrible things Duchess Trin felt: every bone breaking, every piece of flesh tearing."

"Are you *mad*?" I shouted. "Get out of here! *Run!*"

But Trin had beaten me to it, for she was already crowing, "We accept!" Her voice was full of excitement and laughter, as if she had just been promised a high treat "What a delight!"

"Very well," Shuran said. "You have sealed your own fate with this foolishness, my lady."

"I have," Ethalia said, her voice full of defiant sorrow. Her eyes went to the big Knight. "My path was that of mercy, until today; my destiny was one of—But I suppose none of that matters now."

He smiled. "Fret not, my lady. I promise you—"

Ethalia cut him off. "There is nothing you can do for me, Shuran, son of Caveil. You are already dead. I have killed you."

She left him standing there with his mouth open. As she passed me, she said, "Be merciful, if you can, and when the time comes, make it quick."

My chest hurt. I couldn't breathe. I could feel the eighth death coming back. Every sight, every sound, the taste of blood in my mouth, the feeling of—

No—No, please—

I opened my eyes and looked at Kest. *Save me*, I thought. *Get up out of that damned circle and save me from this. I can't do this, Kest. I can't do it without you.* I watched as he strained against an invisible weight heavier than all the guilt he felt inside. He pushed and pushed and pushed, but no matter how hard he fought, still he failed.

It's time to be brave, Falcio.

When I closed my eyes, my Aline was there, but I *still* couldn't work out why she would do this to me again. *Don't make me see this,* I begged, *not again . . .* and then, *Why?*

Because it's time you stopped running away.

When? When have I run away? Ever since you died I just keep fighting and fighting and it doesn't get any better. I'm not running, Aline.

You keep running away from my death and I need you to let it go. You need to see it one more time. You need to let it flow through you. Because the fights that matter aren't won on skill.

I opened my eyes and looked at Ethalia and all at once I understood. I looked at Kest and I saw that he too knew what had to happen next. Shuran was better than me. He was the second-best swordsman in the world and no matter what I did, he was going to win.

"I do feel genuinely sorry for you, Falcio," Shuran said as he began to move in lazy circles around me. "You never did a single thing wrong, other than to follow a dream that wasn't yours, a set of ideals that you didn't understand and that in the end were never meant to be."

I thrust both my rapiers out at once, the blade in my right hand feinting toward Shuran's right eye, hoping he'd parry instinctively and then I could evade his counter and thrust to his neck, while I prepared the blade in my left hand to slash across his armored left leg. I knew the big Knight wouldn't fall for the thrust to his eye, and the slash would do nothing but produce a few sparks, but sometimes these can draw the opponent's gaze and give an opening for a thrust to the face.

But Shuran did neither; instead he moved so quickly that with his single broadsword he knocked out first my left rapier and then my right before I'd even worked out what was happening. They fell several feet away from me.

It was a masterful trick—one you would never, ever risk if you had even the slightest concern for your opponent's skill. Was I really such a pathetic sight?

"That's one," he said to Kest. He stood aside for me and gestured to go past. "You should probably pick those up."

Having no better option, I went and stopped by my swords, waiting for a moment to see if he really was going to let me pick them up.

The Knight-Commander stopped moving for a moment. "Saints, Falcio! You do understand, don't you? You must *know*."

"Know what?" I asked.

"That on your best day—on your *very* best day—you could never beat me."

"I do know that," I said, "and thanks very much for reminding me."

"Then why all this pretense? Why go through the motions?" He sounded genuinely interested.

"Because, you . . ." I reached for the worst insult I could think of and settled on, "you stupid son-of-a-Saint, I've been beaten and tortured and killed eight times. I'm tired and weak. My best friend sits trapped in that stupid circle, despising himself. The daughter of my King is possessed by Trin through magic, which I hate, by the way, and the woman I love has just set herself up to be killed horribly in a manner that I can't stop replaying in my head, over and over."

"I don't understand your point."

"My point is, you feckless thug, this isn't my *best* day. It's my *worst*. So I'm going to use it to put you down."

I retrieved one of the rapiers and reached down for the second. The instant it was in my hand, I threw it at Shuran so that he'd be forced to either duck or bat it out of the way with his blade, leaving an opening for my other rapier to thrust into his groin. He moved, but barely an inch as he reached out and caught the rapier in his gloved left hand while again slamming the flat of his broadsword against the guard of my other weapon and knocking it to the ground. He looked at the blade held in his left hand for a moment, then flipped it in the air and grabbed it by the grip.

"Here," he said, handing it to me. "I'm absolutely positive you'll want this."

I took a step backward and just for a moment, I closed my eyes.

It's time, Aline said.

I know.

You can't hide from it.

I won't. I'm here. I closed my eyes and I saw the light from the lantern hung from the ceiling; I saw the rough wooden tables spaced out across a dirt floor covered in crap. I saw men with rough hands and black hearts, and men in armor, smiling.

I threw myself at Shuran, my blades only barely in line, and he knocked them aside effortlessly, then struck my head with the flat of his sword. I saw stars and cursed at him, swearing like a madman, and he tried to push me back to proper fencing distance, but now I just kept running at him. When he pushed me away, I kicked out at him wildly and I felt my foot connect with something soft. He gave a yelp, his blade whipped out and I felt a cut on my cheek.

"What's wrong with him?" Trin asked. "Why is he acting like that?"

"I don't know," Shuran said, pushing me back. "Perhaps he's gone mad."

I threw my right rapier at him, he beat it out of the air with his sword, and as he did I ran in again. He brought his blade around in a smooth arc and struck me in the belly. The bone plates in my greatcoat held, but he knocked the wind out of me.

"Gods of Love and Death," Trin said suddenly, "I know what he's doing now."

"What? Is this some kind of magic?" Shuran asked as he forced the point of my blade down to the ground. I struck out at his face with the elbow of my other arm again, and then again, and twice I connected.

SEBASTIEN DE CASTELL

He paid me back by hitting me in the cheek with the pommel of his sword. I felt a tooth break loose.

Trin's voice was a mixture of shock and fascination. "No, it's not magic at all. He's . . . he's fighting like *her*. Like his wife—he's reliving her death."

You've got that right, you fucking lunatic. I spat the tooth as hard as I could into Shuran's face and it struck him in the eye and he yelled, though more from anger than any pain. Now I stayed in too close for him to use the edge of his sword. He struck me in the side with the pommel of his weapon, and kept doing it and I heard one of my ribs crack, but in exchange I smashed my forehead into his face and I must have hit his bottom teeth because I felt something hard and sharp cut into my skin.

I dropped my other sword on the ground and brawled with Shuran, striking out at him with every part of me: I kicked, I punched, I bit, and while Shuran fought with consummate skill, I fought like an animal. The difference was that he was trying to win—I wasn't. I didn't need to. I just needed to keep everyone distracted a little longer.

I screamed, over and over again, with no idea what words were coming out of my mouth, but it didn't matter. I was there, with her, in that damned tavern with those damned men, and yes, they were going to kill me, but I was going to take with me every piece of them that I could.

Time to be brave, sweetheart. The fights that matter most aren't won on skill.

Shuran was yelling as well now, for he'd found himself fighting for his life despite his superior strength, despite his matchless speed and his consummate skill.

You brought Aline back, you bastards, and it's time you met her properly.

And now the Knight-Commander was towering over me, his face red with sweat and blood and rage. He reached down, picked up one of my rapiers and tossed it to me. "Take it," he growled. "I want you to die with a blade in your hand." He'd been trying to win elegantly before and that had been his mistake. But he was done with that; now it was going to be about sheer power and speed. Shuran was going to kill me.

But the fights that matter most aren't won on skill, and I had kept everyone's eyes on me long enough.

"Kest," I said, "now."

And Shuran looked past me to see Kest on his knees inside the circle, his right hand pushing against the invisible wall that separated us as it had since my fight with Shuran had started. The Knight began laughing. "Is that what this was about? All that kicking and screaming? Did you think it would somehow set Kest free? I'm afraid the world doesn't work that way."

Kest, still on his knees in the circle, kept pushing slowly with his right hand, trying to reach us. "You're a master swordsman, Shuran."

The Knight-Commander raised an eyebrow. "Really, Kest? That's what you have to say? 'You're good'?"

"Better than good—better than Falcio."

"That much is evident to all concerned, I think."

I didn't think he needed to sound quite so sneery.

Kest's fingertips were shaking and sweat was dripping from all his pores. It looked as if his fingers weren't getting any closer at all, and yet I knew they were. "You know," Kest said, "the moment I killed Caveil, his sainthood passed to the next most skilled swordsman in the world. Me."

"Yes," Shuran said, "I already knew that."

Kest's eyes were far away. I heard a cracking sound and wondered if the bones of his right hand were breaking. "It was like . . . it was as if all the power of a raging river was flowing from inside me. The sensation was . . . intoxicating . . . overwhelming." His hand was closer now, and I could see it was nearly past the circle.

I tensed, and Shuran noticed and smiled warmly at me. "Ah, ready for our seventh exchange? I believe that will be the last one."

Kest shook his head, still pushing with all his might. Blood was dripping from his right hand. "Two. There are two movements left."

Shuran's expression was confused.

With a last, soul-breaking effort, Kest extended his right arm out, his wrist just past the circle binding him. For just an instant I looked into his eyes and saw tears of sorrow and fear. His lips barely moved as he mouthed the word, "Now."

I lifted my sword and in a single strike I brought it down against his exposed wrist. The blade cut through skin and muscle and bone, and Kest's right hand fell to the ground.

"Why . . . why would you do that? How—?"

Shuran's eyes took on an unnatural color. Red.

"That was one," Kest growled, gripping his wrist with his remaining hand.

Shuran looked over himself. He was beginning to glow crimson.

"Congratulations, Sir Shuran," I said. "You're the new Saint of Swords."

"I . . . the sensations . . . Gods, *I am the Saint of Swords.* I can see . . . I can see . . ." Shuran was smiling, an incandescent smile that lit up his face. "I felt that . . . even before you moved, I felt it. I see how every movement of the air—! Kest, you're right, the sensation is like nothing else. I—"

It was only then that Sir Shuran, Knight-Commander of Aramor, bothered to take note that my rapier was thrust deep into his belly.

"That's two," Kest said, and then he fell to the ground.

Shuran looked at me and then at Kest. "He had . . . he gave this up? For *you*? Why?"

"Because the fights that matter most aren't won on skill," I said. They're won on sacrifice.

47

THE WAR

Just before the world went mad, it went quiet.

It begins with Shuran staring at me, his eyes wide, his mouth pleading wordlessly. There is a foul odor in the air, and I realize I must have punctured his bowels when I ran him through with my sword. His body slides, very slowly, toward the ground, taking my rapier with it.

My now empty hands begin to shake, and at first I think it's from exhaustion and fear but then the faint red glow starts moving slowly across the surface of my skin and I look up to see the world in front of me, full of color and detail: a repository of never-ending challengers for me to defeat. I glance at the Knights, standing two hundred yards in front of me, and I can see the flaws inside them. I feel my friends behind me, with their own strengths and their weaknesses, and I feel a sudden burst of excitement at the chance to test them, to defeat them, to watch their blood slip down the length of my blade and onto my already red hands . . .

He isn't yours, *a voice inside me says. It's Aline, my wife, and she's standing in front of me. She's holding back the red.*

He is called, *the red voice replies.*

She doesn't answer; instead, she takes my hand and holds it up. There's a word inscribed on it. I can't make it out and yet between the lines and curves of the letters I see pieces of myself, and those I love.

Think of what you could accomplish with me, *the red voice calls.*

I believe it—I can see it. How much better would the world be if I could walk up to my enemies and just kill them? How much faster and easier life would become without any foolish notions of justice and law, which are nothing but excuses weak men make to hide their fear of doing what must be done.

I want to listen to the red voice. I want its whisper to fill me up inside.

Aline has not even a trace of concern on her face. She shows me that damned pernicious word, and again, and over again, and I know with absolute clarity why I will never, ever become the Saint of Swords, even though I was once the third-best swordsman in Tristia. Go, I say to the red voice, go and find some other fool. I'm already spoken for.

I look back down at my hands and they are my own again, pale and white and trembling, but this time shaking not with anticipation but because of fatigue.

The flat thump of Shuran's body hitting the ground reaches my ears and whatever combination of desperation and need that has been keeping me on my feet until that moment disappears and I drop to my knees. I can hear only the sound of my own breathing; the beat of my heart pounding faster than it should in my chest, but after a moment, even that begins to fade as the last vestiges of Shuran's impact against the dirt dies away and time starts to demand her proper pace once again.

For an instant, there was absolute silence.

Then Trin screamed.

She ran—or rather, *Aline* ran—to Shuran's corpse. Trin beat his chest with Aline's fists and cried with Aline's tears, but the rage and hatred in her eyes was all Trin's own. Then the corners of her mouth moved very slowly up as she smiled. "Yours for mine," she whispered.

Damn you, I thought helplessly, and even as I reached toward her I knew I could never get to her in time. Trin was going to kill Aline and there was nothing I could do.

A voice yelled from behind me, "Now!" and out of the corner of my eye I saw someone run past me, and before I had even finished processing the image, Valiana and Dari had grabbed a firm hold of each of Aline's arms, stopping Trin from making Aline reach up and twist the wooden handles to drive the iron screws deep into her skull. They pulled Aline's body to the ground and Ethalia knelt in front of her. Trin spat in her face, screaming incoherently, still struggling to free her hands, but they were sitting on her now and she wasn't going anywhere fast.

Ethalia reached down and very carefully undid the bolts fastening the contraption around Aline's head so she could remove it. Then with a sudden angry movement she smashed the wooden frame over her knee, and immediately Aline was herself once more.

It had all happened so fast. The three of them had orchestrated this while I was fighting Shuran . . . before any of us knew if there was any hope at all for our survival.

Damn, but I've known some smart women in my time . . .

Aline's eyes fluttered open and almost instantly flooded with tears, but Valiana held her close even as Ethalia got to her feet and ran to Kest, Dariana close behind her.

"Quickly now," she said, and her voice was astonishingly calm under the circumstances. "We must staunch the bleeding." She pulled a small jar of salve from a pocket in her dress as Dariana stripped off Kest's shirt and started tearing it into bandages.

I wanted to help them, but I discovered that I hadn't the strength to rise. I knelt there on the ground, completely useless, desperately trying to keep myself from tipping forward. I had never felt so tired before, not even when the neatha was at its most virulent inside me. I closed my eyes, just for a moment.

My wife stared back at me.

I think I like this Ethalia well enough, Falcio. She seems competent. And sensible.

I'll tell her you think so, I said.

She laughed. *So you really don't know any more about women now than you did when I was alive.*

Perhaps you could educate me. I reached a hand out toward her face.

She shook her head. *No. It's enough now: enough of living with memories, and enough of guilt. Time to leave me be, Falcio. And leave that foolish King of yours alone, too. Stop using the dead to justify the living.*

Her words hurt me, but Aline had always been a woman who said what needed to be said, not what I wanted to hear. The world around me was falling to pieces but I still wanted to spend a few more moments with my pragmatic, beautiful, brave—

No, she was right. It's enough now.

Then say it, Falcio.

I took one last look at Aline, my wife, my first love, the woman who made me the man I was. She really was right: it was past time for me to become the man I *should* be.

"Goodbye," I said.

I opened my eyes and looked down at Kest, but something was wrong because the ground looked suspiciously like the sky.

"Now why is it that the man who just lost his hand is standing on his own two feet and the one who chopped it off is lying flat on his back?" Dariana asked.

"You should get up now," Kest said. His face was pale but his eyes were clear. I wondered how much of the hard candy he had taken to keep himself from passing out.

"Kest, you need to—"

The bandage wrapped over the stump where his right hand should have been was already a little bloody. "A thousand Knights are about to overrun us, Falcio."

Dariana helped me to my feet and I looked out at the field in front of us. Some small, foolish part of me had hoped that Shuran's death would make the Black Tabards reconsider their position.

Any minute now one of them is going to come and offer their unconditional surrender to me.

At least, that's what would have happened in the old stories.

Disappointingly—and I really hated to admit it, but this kept happening to me—life failed to live up to my expectations.

Rather than falling to their knees and begging for their miserable lives, the Knights began to straighten their lines. I looked toward the sun, which was close to the horizon now, and wondered idly how much time we had before they killed us all? An hour? A few minutes? And part of me couldn't help but wonder why they were even bothering—would a thousand Knights really ride down the field to overrun the six of us? It hardly seemed worth the effort.

I looked around at Castle Aramor, where I could see the Dukes, standing just inside the castle entrance with their guards in close formation around them. When the battle started they'd close that gate—it had been built to withstand a siege, after all, so it would be nice to see if it was really up to the job—and cower inside, awaiting a later death. I noticed that all of them—the Dukes, their guards, and what family they'd foolishly brought with them—were staring not at the Black Tabards, but at us.

"What are they doing?" Dariana asked.

"They're hoping," I said.

"Hoping what?"

I turned to look at her. There was something fiendishly compelling about her hawkish features and the prideful way she stood. Her arms were crossed and she had one eyebrow raised; she looked as if she was about to launch into her usual litany of reasons explaining why everyone except her was a fool. It made me smile.

I turned my attention back to her question. "They're hoping that the old stories are true."

"Which ones are those?"

"The ones where we save everybody."

"Then maybe we should do it," Valiana said. An angry little red scar on her cheek drew my gaze: it was where Heryn had inserted his needle. For the first time I realized how many cuts and wounds

Valiana had taken over the past months. She was still beautiful, but that beauty was marred—no, I was wrong; her beauty was *accented* by the proofs of her courage and her determination.

It wasn't just her, though; it was all of them. Kest had sacrificed his hand. Ethalia had given up any chance for peace and happiness. Aline crept over to us and clung to Ethalia. Her hair was in disarray, messed up by that loathsome frame, and her face was tracked with tears. Betrayal, terror, and violence had destroyed her innocence and she more than any of us deserved better than this. I had spent so much time concerned with the dead and dying that I'd never truly understood how much I loved the people who stood right in front of me. They all deserved a better end than to be mowed down by cowards in masks and black tabards.

And now they all looked at me: my friends, my enemies, even the craven Dukes hiding at the entrance to the castle, and for a moment the weight of their gazes nearly drove me back to my knees.

I can't bear this weight, my King. Tell me what to do. Despite my promise to my wife I closed my eyes, hoping to see his cocky smile, his winking eyes. I wanted to hear him give me one final command, or at least tell me one more of those stories he always loved—the ones about courage and honor and virtue that all managed somehow to end up in a dirty joke.

But Paelis wasn't there and I knew that it was my turn to tell the story.

I think I was finally beginning to understand why he'd created the Greatcoats, or at least a small part of his intention. It wasn't about imposing his laws on the corrupt Dukes, or keeping thugs under control by beating them senseless in duels; it wasn't even about putting his daughter on the throne. My King wanted us to be an *example*—that's why each Greatcoat was given a mission. Dara and Nile and Parrick were sent to protect the Dukes who'd killed him to show that we stood for something beyond the King himself. And that was why Trin and all the rest of them were so keen to see us ruined, even when there were so few left, and that was why the Dashini created the Lament, so they could twist the *story* of the Greatcoats into one of despair.

No. You can take everything else away from us, but not that.
I forced myself to walk as normally as I could toward to the
Knights assembled at the other end of the field. I took a deep breath,
trying not to show how much that hurt with half my ribs broken,
and projected my hoarse voice, hoping I could make it loud enough
to be heard. "Look at you: a thousand men on horseback, clothed
in armor and shielded by the lies you've told yourselves. You think
you've come here to change the world, but all you're here to do is
commit murder."

I could see some of them bristling at the word *murder*. Their
nervousness was making their horses uneasy, but the commanders
quickly restored order.

I didn't give them time to enjoy it. "I said, *look at yourselves!* You
wear black tabards to hide from your origins. You wear helmets to
hide from your faces. You give no names so that when this black,
bloody work is done no one will remember who you were and what
you did here."

I paused to breathe in again. Damn, but I'd forgotten how much
broken ribs could hurt.

"You want to hide behind your masks?" I cried. "You want your
names to be forgotten? Then I say: *Be forgotten.*"

I turned and directed my voice to the castle gates where the
Dukes and their families and their guards cowered in safety . . . well,
temporary safety.

"There will be stories told about this day: tales about anonymous
men in black garb who came to commit murder. And there will be
stories about those who died fighting them—those who *stood up to
them.* For a hundred years and more, people will talk about what
happened at Aramor."

I turned back to the Knights. "Your own children will grow up
hearing those stories. So have your way: let the world forget your
names." I took a step forward. "But they will remember *ours.* Every
child of yours, every grandchild and great-grandchild will hear of
the day men in armor and black tabards came a-thousand-strong
against four Greatcoats, an unarmed woman, and a little girl, and

our names will be repeated, over and over again, until the day you lie on your deathbed waiting for the last shadow to fall across your face. And your last fumbling words? *They will be our names.*"

I thought about what I was going to say next, and for the briefest moment I laughed to myself. *Damn you, you sickly wretch. If you'd told me any of this I never would have volunteered!*

I raised my sword as high as I could and announced, "I am Falcio val Mond, First Cantor of the Greatcoats, and I am the King's Heart. I fought at Aramor."

Kest stepped forward to stand next to me, his sword in his left hand. "I am Kest, son of Murrow. I am the King's Blade, and I was at Aramor."

Dariana surprised me by appearing on my other side, her sword in the air. She shocked me more with the tears in her eyes. "I am Dariana, daughter of Shanilla. I am the King's Patience, and damn you all, I was here, in Aramor."

Valiana, who, more than any of us, showed the promise of what the Greatcoats could be, took her rightful place next to us. "I am Valiana val Mond," she called out, "and I am the Heart's Answer. I was at Aramor."

"I am the friend in the dark hour," Ethalia said. Her voice was no louder than a whisper, and yet it seemed to ripple across the field, "and I stood with my love at Aramor."

I felt a small hand reach for mine and I looked down to see Aline's face. She was terrified.

"I'm sorry, Falcio . . . I'm so sorry, about the Tailor's Greatcoats and the Dashini and all of it. I was so—"

"It's all right," I said, and I squeezed her right hand in my left.

Valiana took her other hand. "Just tell them who you are."

Aline shook her head. "I can't, I just—I can't anymore. I can't watch you die trying to protect me, Falcio. If I have to die, then—" She pulled away from me and started running toward the Knights.

"Aline, no!" I raced for her, trying to stop her running headlong to her death, though my legs were barely strong enough to carry me more than a few paces. Thank the Gods, my legs might be feeble, but they were still longer, and I caught up with her before she'd gone more than a dozen yards.

"Let me go, Falcio!" she screamed. "Let me—"

I saw another figure out of my peripheral vision, running toward us from the castle. Tommer, the eleven-year-old son of Duke Jillard, stopped in front of Aline and gave a small, oddly formal bow. "It's best if you stay behind me, my lady."

"Tommer! Tommer, come back!" Jillard was shouting from the entrance of the castle, but the boy ignored his father's call. Instead, he turned and stared at the Knights arrayed down the field. "I am Tommer," he shouted, his high tenor voice drifting like a tiny boat across the vast ocean of the field, "heir to Rijou and the last student of Bal Armidor. I am the Minstrel's Voice at Aramor, and you will not touch her while I live."

I looked back at the Knights, sure that they must have started their charge, but they remained still.

"What are they doing?" Kest asked, joining me.

"Waiting. Waiting for the appointed hour, just as Shuran said."

From the castle another man came forward: a big man with black hair flecked with gray. He was carrying a long spear and wearing the red and gold of Rijou. "Your father commanded me to bring you back," he told Tommer.

"And I command you to leave me here," Tommer replied.

The guard smiled. "I thought you might. Well, the hells for the both of you." He turned to the Knights and shouted, "I am Voras of Chantille. I'm—" He stopped and looked around as if he'd lost something, then he grinned and finished, "I'm the fucking spear that's going into your asses, you black-shirted bastards. How's that for a name, eh? Hah!"

A woman came toward us from the castle. She wore the clothes of a servant and held a rock in her hand. "I'm Kemma," she shouted to the Knights. "My father was the blacksmith of a small village that once was and is no more. You can call me the Hammer of Carefal. I wasn't there when you destroyed my home, but I was at Aramor when you met your fates."

Another came forward, then another, and each one called out their name and their village; every one was ready to die when the onslaught began.

And after a few minutes, one of the Dukes came out. I recognized the big man as Meillard, Duke of Pertine. He turned to me with a rueful grin. "Well, boy, at least you've put our duchy on the map." He turned and bellowed so loudly I thought the earth itself would shake, "I'm Meillard and I'm the Gods-damned Duke of Pertine. I need no better name than that and I swear by Saint Shiulla-who-bathes-with-beasts that I'll rip the head off any Knight in a black tabard who came from my duchy!"

We stood there, nearly fifty of us, facing off against a thousand Knights who didn't move, didn't speak. If they were impressed by our daring, they didn't show it. I looked up at the sky. Sunset was nearly upon us.

A voice called out to me, "So *that's* your great plan? Stand there and shout your names at a bunch of black-hearted bastards in armor and hope they fall over laughing at you?"

I tried to see who had shouted, but it was only when I felt Kest's hand on my shoulder that I realized the sound had come from behind us, and my heart soared as I turned to see a man riding casually toward us on a gray horse, wearing a brown greatcoat with one of the sleeves missing. "Well, aren't you a sorry collection of half-hearted heroes," Brasti said, sliding off his mount. "And what in all the hells have you done with Kest's hand?"

I felt such an odd joy at the sight of him: if I had to die, let it be here and now, surrounded by the people I loved best in all the world. "I thought you were done with us," I said. "'You go save the world, I'm going to save the people in it'—isn't that what you told me?"

"Changed my mind," he said, grinning.

"Any particular reason?"

He looked around. "I love autumn in Aramor, don't you?"

I grabbed him and embraced him. "Come on, Brasti, admit it—we're all about to die anyway. Deep down inside you believed in the King's dream as much as I did."

He pulled back from me, his face serious all of a sudden. "That's what you never understood, Falcio: I never followed the King—hells, I never even followed the Greatcoats. I'm a simple man at heart. I don't go in for Dukes or Gods or Saints, and nor does Kest for that matter, or anyone else."

"Then why—?"

"You, Falcio, you idiot. I followed *you*. We all did."

I looked around, at Kest and Dariana and Valiana and Ethalia, and as each one in turn nodded their agreement, I wanted to ask *Why?* They'd all come with me here to die today, but I didn't know who I was that they would all come to this for me. I've never done anything more than try to follow the dreams of the one man I've ever met in this world who believed things could be better. But . . . *Maybe I'm following you*, the King had said to me that day.

"Is that the entirety of your plan?" Brasti asked again. "To stand here while those dogs in black tabards come and kill us? Because I have to say it sounds a lot like all your previous plans."

"You have to admit," I said, "it'll make a hell of a story. We've even got a real Bardatti out there somewhere to make sure it gets heard."

He grinned. "Well, we could go with your approach—I mean, it sounds very noble and I'm sure the tale of *Falsio at the Battle of Aramor* will be both romantic and tragic at the same time. On the other hand, I have a different plan."

"Really?" Dariana said. "Brasti Goodbow has a *plan*? The stars must be tumbling right out of the sky."

Brasti ignored her and walked past us and out onto the muddy expanse between us and the Knights. "I never did tell you what the King commanded me to do that day five years ago, did I, Falcio?"

I looked at the two-hundred-yard gap that separated us from the row upon row of armored Knights. The sun was fast sinking below the horizon and by the stamping of the hooves and the jangling of the harnesses I could tell they were readying their lines to charge us.

"Obviously I'd love to know, but I'm not sure now's exactly the right time, Brasti."

He glanced over at the Knights too. "Really? I should think now's as good a time as we're going to get."

"Good point. Fine. What did he tell you?"

Brasti smiled. "I was one of the last he called in, remember? He was pretty tired by then, and he was getting irritable—you remember the way he was sometimes?—and I knew that because when I entered the throne room I made a joke, and he said, 'You know what, Brasti? You're a real bastard. You think that bow of yours makes you so special, but I know it's just your way of sticking your finger up the backside of the world.'"

Brasti laughed, and so did Kest. The King had rarely sworn, and no one could get him going quite as well as Brasti could.

But something was bothering me. "Well?" I asked.

"Well what?"

"What was his final command for you?"

"Ah, that. He was clearly in a pissy mood, which I suppose wasn't all that surprising since the Dukes were about to have him killed. At first I started walking away but then it irked me that he hadn't given me a final command. He always acted as if I was somehow less than the rest of you just because I didn't look at him all moon-eyed as if he were the light of the world."

"I think we're out of time," Kest said, pointing to the Knights. The first lines were kicking their horses into motion.

"Right, okay, so, I turned back and asked the King, 'What? No divine command for me, your Majesty? No grand mission?' Then he gives me this ugly grin and says, 'You? You've always been a bastard and now on this of all days you've convinced me that from now until the day you die you'll still be a bastard, Brasti. You and that stupid bow of yours. But you know what? The world needs more bastards. There. That's my command. Now get out of here.'"

"That's it?" I asked. "The world needs more bastards?"

Brasti nodded.

"So in effect, these past five years that you've been a pain in my ass have been . . . what?"

He smiled. "Just following the King's orders."

The King had a sense of humor all right. It never had manifested at an appropriate time.

But Brasti hadn't finished. "I have an admission to make: it turns out I was wrong about what the King meant."

"How so?" Kest asked.

Brasti picked up Intemperance and set a black arrow to her string. He turned briefly to the rest of us and announced, "A thousand armored Knights are coming for us." Then he aimed the arrow high into the air, pulled back the bowstring and released.

We watched as the arrow rose high up into the sky, as if it were trying to reach toward the sun, then, slowly turned into its tight elliptical arc, making its inexorable way back to earth, some five hundred yards from where we stood.

Too late the Knights realized what was happening, and a few scrambled to get out of the way as the two-foot-long shaft came toward them, but they were too tightly packed and when the arrow finally reached them it lanced straight through a metal helm, instantly killing the man wearing it.

Brasti turned back to us. "One down. Nine hundred and ninety-nine to go."

One of the commanders barked an order and the Knights began to charge in earnest. They would be upon us within moments.

"I suppose if we have to die it's nice to have made a statement," Kest said, holding his warsword in his left hand.

Brasti snorted. "Still with the swords? Haven't I shown you the superiority of the bow?"

"Unless you can do that again nine hundred and ninety-nine times in the next couple of minutes, I don't think it much matters now, does it?"

He smiled. He was looking altogether too cocky for a man facing imminent death. "Watch this."

The Knights had covered half the distance between us, passing between the thick lines of hedges that lined the gauntlet on either side, when suddenly arrows flew from those hedges, arching through the air and cutting into the front lines of the Knights' charge. Men and horses fell screaming, and the horses behind them stumbled onto the fallen in front of them. There must have been a hundred arrows in that first flight, and a few seconds later, a hundred more.

I had had no idea there were men hiding in the trees and hedges, let alone enough to send volley after volley of steel-tipped arrows down on the Knights.

"How—?" I was as near speechless as I'd ever been.

Brasti had always been too handsome for his own good, too much in love with looking clever and being wanted. He'd never looked beyond the night's carousing—or the most recent pretty girl—in all the years I'd known him. Now he looked at me with a different smile on his face, one I'd never seen before, and there was a very different look in his eyes.

"I call them 'Brasti's Bastards,'" he said proudly.

"'The world needs more bastards,'" Kest said, his voice full of awe.

Brasti mounted his horse.

"What are you doing?" I asked.

He placed Intemperance in her holder below the saddle and drew *Insult*, his horse-bow. "Why, I'm adding insult to injury, of course."

With that he took off and began firing arrows at those few Knights who were managing to get through the crossfire his men were creating. Valiana and Dariana chased after him, songs and war cries on their lips.

Ethalia took Aline and began pulling medicines from her bag.

Kest and I just leaned on each other for support.

"Gods. What has he done?" I asked.

"He's broken them," Kest said. "He's broken the Knighthood. They'll never be the same."

No more Knights.

48

THE CONCORD

"You know what I find amusing?" Brasti asked.

I opened my eyes to find only darkness waiting for me and I panicked. *I'm paralyzed—Gods, no, not now! You can't do this to me, not again—not after all I've been through—*

"It's all right," I heard Ethalia say gently. "It's just dark."

I had fallen asleep on one of the long benches in the wide hallway outside the throne room of Aramor with my head in her lap. I felt the warmth of her hand against my cheek and took a deep breath, and only then did I hear a guitar playing softly, the notes echoing from wall to wall.

"Nehra?" I asked.

"Over here, Trattari," she answered. "You've given me the beginnings of a fine story to tell, but it'll need the right melody to accompany it."

"What time is it?" I asked.

"Late," Dariana replied. She was sitting on the floor running a whetstone back and forth against the blade of her sword. "I would guess we're two hours from sunrise. No one bothered to light torches for us. I fear you and your Greatcoats are just as beloved now as you were before this whole thing started."

I peered through the darkness, trying to find Kest, and made out his vague outline across the hall. Just for an instant I could have sworn he flickered red, as if he were standing in front of a fire, but a moment later everything was dark again.

"Would you please stop doing that?" Brasti asked from a few feet to my right. "Either *be* the Saint of Swords or don't, but make up your damned mind."

"It's not something I can control," Kest replied plaintively.

"Your hand," I said, lifting my head from Ethalia's lap and instantly regretting the decision, "is it—?"

The shadow of Kest's head nodded. "A healer treated the wound with some kind of acid to prevent infection and bandaged me up so I won't bleed to death. The pain is . . . *significant.*"

He flickered again, a brief flash of red against the blackness of the unlit room.

Brasti coughed. "As I was saying, do you know what I find amusing?"

"Hang on," I said, "how long have we been waiting here?"

"Several hours," Kest replied. "The Dukes have been meeting continuously since the battle ended. One of their retainers came out an hour ago to 'remind us' to stay here."

"Ducal Concords have very strict protocols," Valiana said. Her voice came from the deep shadows on the other side of the room.

"Where's Aline?"

"She's in there with them."

I started to rise, but Kest stepped out of the shadows and stopped me. "They assured me that regardless of the outcome of their deliberations, they would not harm her. I did my best to explain what would happen to them if they did."

"We should be in there with her," I said.

I heard the soft sound of Valiana's footsteps. "They won't harm her, Falcio. I was trained in Concord protocol and I can promise you: the rules are clear and the safety of the participants is inviolate.

The process is complex—even if you were in there, I doubt you'd understand what was happening."

I let pass the fact that she'd just told me I was too stupid to understand affairs of state. "Then you should be in there—you know how all this works. You could look out for her interests."

"I'm not a Duchess, Falcio—I'm not even a noble. I'm no one of consequence."

"You're as good as any Duke or Duchess, pretty bird. Better, from what I've seen of them," Dariana said, and for once I agreed with her.

"No one of consequence? You might just be the only noble person in this whole sorry affair."

"Look," Brasti shouted, "is anyone going to ask me what I find amusing?"

I turned in the general direction of where he was sitting, across the hallway from me, and said, "Fine. Brasti, what is it that you find so desperately amusing?"

"This castle."

"You find the castle amusing?" Kest asked.

"Well, not the castle so much as the fact that there are cobwebs all over it."

"I don't understand," I said. I wasn't just humoring him; I really didn't.

Brasti rose and spread his arms. "Look at this place: It's Castle Aramor, for Saints' sake. It's the seat of power for Tristia and yet it's been sitting here completely empty for more than five years. The Dukes took it from the King—and then they just left it. No one's even entered the place until now."

"It had to be kept empty," Valiana said, as if the reason was obvious. "If one of the Dukes had come here it would have been seen as an act of war against the others."

"I know, but here's the thing, see? Castle Aramor is the single most defensible fortress in all of Tristia. You could probably hold the thing with—how many, Kest?"

"Fifty soldiers," Kest replied.

"Fifty soldiers. So with fifty soldiers and enough supplies, you could hold this place for a year."

"What's your point?" I asked.

"I'm just saying, all these intrigues and really the best way to take over the country would've been for Trin to just come here with her Knights and declare herself Queen. I'm surprised some goat-herder didn't just move in with forty-nine of his friends and nominate himself Emperor!"

Despite myself, I started thinking about the men at the Inn at the End of the World sitting at a table contemplating making themselves rulers of the country. King Jost. I started to laugh uncontrollably.

"I'm not sure it was that funny," Kest said.

"It's not that," I said, holding my ribs and trying to stop laughing because it hurt too much. "I'm thinking the next time we run into this problem of the lack of a ruler I'm going straight into the nearest village and the first man or woman who can sign their name can come back here to the castle and be crowned monarch."

The others began laughing too, and we spent the next hour expanding on the virtues of choosing a King through random selection, until the great double doors of the throne room opened and one of the Ducal retainers came out. He pointed to Kest and Brasti and finally me.

"The Dukes are ready for the three of you now," he said importantly. "The others must wait here."

I squeezed Ethalia's hand and rose. "Come on then," I said to the others. Valiana didn't move, so I took her firmly by the hand and began leading her in.

"The girl's presence is not required," the retainer started.

"It's required by me," I replied, and we all walked past him and into the throne room.

The Dukes were sitting around a large dining table someone had placed a discreet distance from the throne. It had been five years or more since I'd been in the throne room of Castle Aramor, and weirdly, it felt smaller than I remembered, and the Tristian seat of power itself much less ornate than the thrones used by the Dukes in their own castles.

Food had been served, and most of the people around the table had plates in front of them. A multitude of servants in assorted livery representing the various duchies were busy refilling goblets of wine. *They brought more servants with them than guardsmen.* I shouldn't have been shocked, but somehow I was.

Aline was sitting on a chair a short distance away from the table, her hands resting on her knees, a small plate of food, barely touched, sitting on her lap. The Dukes themselves, occupied with eating and drinking, paid no attention to the four of us.

"Anything left for us?" Brasti asked casually.

I felt Valiana tense next to me, no doubt expecting, as I did, a scathing retort from either the Dukes or the retainers who stood around them—after all, Dukes do not eat with commoners. To my surprise, Duke Meillard of Pertine grunted, "There's some chicken left. It's dry and I can't speak to its provenance, but you might as well eat as stand there looking like fools."

Some of the others looked shocked, which comforted me somewhat, but after a moment Duke Jillard signaled to one of the retainers, who brought out plates and placed them in front of empty chairs at the far end of the table. Not knowing quite what else to do, I sat down, and the others joined me.

When a leg of chicken was placed on my plate I very nearly passed out from the smell. I'd forgotten how long it had been since I'd eaten, let alone sat down to a proper meal at a table. However mediocre Duke Meillard might have found it, to me that chicken was the most succulent flesh I could ever remember tasting. A silver goblet was placed near my right hand and wine was poured into it.

"Could I trouble you for some water?" I asked the retainer. It wouldn't do to drink now, not when I was so tired and hurt and there was dangerous business to deal with.

Brasti had no such concerns. "See, now, this is nice," Brasti said, placing his already empty goblet back on the table and motioning for the retainer carrying the jug of wine to return. "We should do this more often, you know, have dinner together and sort out our problems like gentlemen."

"Brasti, shut up," Kest said.

Duke Meillard stood. "All right, so let's call this open session of the Ducal Concord back to order. Let it be noted that we have agreed to continue despite the lack of representation from the duchies of Orison, Luth, and Aramor, as well as from the Duchess of Hervor."

The Duchess of Hervor?

"Um, excuse me," I said, "but—"

Meillard held up a hand. "First, Trattari, you'll speak only when recognized by the head of the Concord, which is me. Second, to answer your unspoken question, Trin is, despite the current disputes, still the lawful Duchess of Hervor."

"Might I be recognized, then?" I asked.

"Hells. Fine. What do you want to say?"

I rose. "Well, first of all, I'd like to say that this is excellent chicken."

"So noted. Moving on now—"

"Second, my friend Brasti seems to be out of wine again."

Hadiermo, the Iron Duke of Domaris, slammed his fist down on the table. "This is the Ducal Concord, not some country wedding. Do you think this is a joke, Trattari?"

"I think it must be. A few hours ago most of you were cowering by the front door waiting to be slaughtered by your own men while Shuran was preparing to take over the entire Kingdom. You yourself, Duke Hadiermo—you gave up the battle against Trin's forces after— what? A week of fighting?"

"There were—"

"Silence!" Brasti said with mock imperiousness. "You haven't been recognized!"

"You do realize we're outnumbered by a goodly amount, and injured besides, don't you?" Kest asked me.

I kept my attention focused on the nobles seated around the table. "The country is teetering on the brink of civil war because the lot of you have not just driven the countryside into rebellion, but you have allowed your Ducal Knights to become renegades."

"And you think you're the one to tell us our faults?" Meillard growled.

"Who else will? The four of us, along with so many others who have given their lives—and that, I should note, despite many of you doing your best to have us killed these past five years despite oaths sworn—where was I? Oh yes, so we have managed to defeat your enemies and keep you alive: and now you all sit there apparently believing you can set the country in whatever direction suits you while the King's heir sits in the corner like a scolded schoolgirl. So yes, your Graces, I do believe this must be a joke."

The room was silent for a moment and then someone clapped. Unfortunately, it was Jillard, Duke of Rijou. "That does sound like a rather substantial amount of upheaval."

"It is," Brasti said, putting both his feet up on the table. "And since we saved your worthless lives, we'd expect at least some degree of contrition."

"Does water still fall downward when poured from a jug?" he asked.

"Does what?" Brasti asked.

"Water. When you pour it, does it still fall downward?"

"I've only been pouring wine thus far, your Grace, and that mostly down my gullet, but I expect water behaves in a similar fashion."

He smiled and nodded. "Good. So in fact the world still functions according to the laws of nature and of the Gods. Understand?"

"Not really," Brasti said, "but I have had rather a lot to drink in a very short time."

"He means," Kest said, "that despite everything that's happened, the Dukes believe the natural order remains the same: that they are masters of this country and we their servants or their enemies."

"You show excellent clarity of thought for a Trattari," Jillard said.

"Thank you, your Grace," I said. "And now I believe the four of us should leave. We'll take Aline with us." I reached out a hand for her.

"What's the meaning of this?" Meillard demanded.

"I'd like to know that, too," Kest said quietly.

I kept my eyes on the Dukes. "We leave here. We bring Brasti's troops—"

"Brasti's Bastards!" Brasti shouted, and then started giggling.

"—and we make war," I shouted, my voice echoing through the room. Then more conversationally, I said to Kest, "It's the only thing they understand."

"You can't be serious!" Hadiermo said. "You've got—what? A hundred country bumpkins with longbows?"

"A hundred country bumpkins just destroyed a thousand Ducal Knights," I pointed out. "*Your* Knights. Imagine what happens when that story spreads through the countryside."

Ossia, Duchess of Baern, a woman in her sixties who had always been at least a little decent toward the King and his Greatcoats, coughed delicately. "I believe we have seen trying times, all of us. Perhaps it is time for us all to withdraw—surely we can pursue this matter over the coming months? And I'm sure we can agree to a cessation of any hostilities while we get our homes in order?"

I thought about what that would mean: more fear, more uncertainty, more maneuvering by the Dukes.

"No," I said. "Those aren't the terms."

"'Terms'?" Duke Hadiermo asked. "Do you think you're here to negotiate *terms* with us?"

"No, your Grace," I said. "I'm sorry, was this not clear? I'm here to *dictate* them."

Several people started to rise, but it was my turn to slam my fist on the table. I'd been wanting to do that for ages; shame I hadn't realized it was going to hurt quite so much. Ah well. "You've had your way with this country long enough. Since the King's death, you have taxed the common folk beyond measure. You have allowed the trade routes to fall into disrepair until bandits have become richer than merchants. You have plotted and intrigued and poisoned everything the King tried to build."

"That," Jillard said, "is how you see it."

"No," I said, "that's how you see it—all of you. You know that what I'm saying is true. The King might have offended you with his laws, but he also gave you certainty. He gave you reliable trade and safe borders."

"He gave us the Greatcoats, too, coming in and interfering in our own lands," Meillard said.

"Yes, he did: and for nearly a decade we traveled the long roads and heard cases in every town in the country. And tell me"—I looked around the table—"how many uprisings did you have in those years? How many times did the common folk try to assassinate you?"

"So that's what this is about?" Jillard asked. "You want us to reinstate the Greatcoats?"

"Give us a year," I said, "one year to set this country back to rights. One year to show people that there is still some measure of justice and fairness in the world."

"And then?" Jillard asked.

"And then you can go back to plotting each other's deaths if you like. You can refuse us entry to your duchies after that. You can go back to trying to kill us. But I don't think you will. I think you and your families and above all your people are sick and tired of watching decay and corruption reign over Tristia."

"Give me one year. I'll give you a country."

There was silence in the room for a few minutes, but then Meillard shook his head. "I don't see how any of that is going to work, not without a monarch on the throne. I don't dispute your skill or your courage, but there are very few Trattari left. We can't continue like this. We need a monarch."

Jillard turned to Meillard. "Are you mad? You want to put this *child* on the throne?"

Meillard shrugged. "She's the King's daughter. I don't see how we can find a way around that."

"She knows *nothing!*" Jillard went on. "She's a little girl with no training and no experience—and you want to make her Queen now? While we're trying to rebuild the country? What happens the moment she finds it all too overwhelming? Who will her councillors be? What happens when someone suggests she haves us all assassinated? She approved the plan to have us murdered! Rijou would sooner have no monarch on the throne."

"You did have her family killed," Brasti pointed out.

"And you tried really quite hard to have her murdered as well," Kest added.

Meillard looked tired. "I . . . The Duke of Rijou has a point. I can't see how this untrained child is going to hold the throne for a week, never mind a year. It takes resolve to rule a kingdom. It takes breeding and experience."

His words were firm and final, but I saw something in his eyes, and when I looked around at the other Dukes I saw it echoed, again and again: fear and need.

They need the Greatcoats, I realized. If I tell them Aline must take the throne, they'll do it—they'll threaten and they'll complain, but in the end even Jillard will say yes because the Dukes need us and because if nothing else, Aline has the *breeding* they care so much about.

That word, *breeding*, stuck in the pit of my stomach. *That's all this whole country cares about: which family you were born into.* I despised every person seated around that table because, whether friend or foe, they all thought life should be dictated by bloodlines— and was my King any different? After all, he expected me to put his daughter on the throne.

Aline was watching me, and though she sat still and upright on her chair, her eyes were full of quiet terror, just as they had been ever since this had began. Meillard was right: she wouldn't last a week on the throne. She had tried to be brave, but trying wasn't enough, not for Tristia.

"Well?" Meillard asked, breaking my train of thought. "Are you still demanding that we put this child on the throne?"

I thought back to all those moments, trapped in the paralysis brought on by the neatha, with my King standing there in front of me. *You will betray her.* It was only then that I realized he'd never said it angrily, only with certainty.

"No," I said at last, "Aline can't take the throne today."

Chaos ensued as a number of the Dukes immediately assumed I was going to try to take the throne for myself. Even Valiana, standing next to me, put her hand on the hilt of her sword, ready to fight to the death to protect Aline, and I smiled because she had proved me right. I looked over to Aline and saw tears of confusion in her eyes. *I'm sorry, sweetheart. Maybe you'll thank me for this; maybe you'll curse me.*

I held up a hand for quiet. "You say it takes breeding to rule a country. I say it takes courage: courage and compassion and the willingness to sacrifice. Your Graces, you were going to appoint a Realm's Protector—someone to run the Kingdom, to give time to select a new monarch. So do that: appoint a Realm's Protector while Aline learns the ways of a monarch—and you have time to satisfy yourselves that she has no homicidal tendencies toward you."

That shut them up them for a few seconds. It was Meillard who spoke first. "It's not the worst idea I've ever heard. We do it in the duchies when the heir is too young to rule."

"And who would this Realm's Protector be?" Jillard asked. "You, Falcio val Mond? Will you now finally reveal your purpose? Would you see yourself—?"

"Not me."

"Thank the Saints," Brasti said.

I pointed to Valiana. "Her."

Several voices began objecting at once.

Jillard, oddly, was silent.

Meillard signaled for silence. "The *peasant*? You'd put a peasant in command of the country?"

"Not so long ago the lot of you planned to make her Queen," I said.

"We thought she had noble blood," Meillard said, his voice full of self-righteous anger. "That bitch Patriana lied to us."

"Of course she did," I said, "and what a surprise that must have been to you all! But it doesn't change the fact that for eighteen years Valiana was raised to rule. She's learned the laws, both King's and Ducal Laws. She's learned protocol, and the ways of the court—and she's learned them from all of you."

Almost everyone in the room began to shout their objections all at once, not just Dukes, but their noble retainers, calling Valiana—and me too—some very unpleasant names. Hadiermo went so far as to suggest that he would lead the Northern duchies in secession from

Tristia, though that ended quickly enough when Ossia pointed out that Trin would likely have something to say about that.

Finally Jillard raised a hand for quiet. His eyes found Valiana's. "If we do as the Trattari asks—if we name you Realm's Protector for the next year—would you hold to the agreements made here today and swear no retribution against the Ducal Concord? Would you set aside all past . . . disagreements?"

Some of the other Dukes began to renew their objections, but Jillard shouted, "Silence!" so loudly that the plates and goblets rattled. Once the hubbub had quieted, he said, "Let us play no more games. We all know we need someone on the throne and it can't be any of us. Who better than her? When my son's life was in danger she . . ."

He paused, and just for a moment I saw the man who had screamed in terror over Tommer's life down in the black pit of Rijou's dungeons.

"This girl stood and fought for my son. Would any of you have done that for me? Would you—?"

"So now you've gone all soft because someone threatened your boy? Rijou doesn't lead the Concord," Hadiermo shouted.

Meillard stood. "But I do." He shook his head in disgust. "I never held with that nonsense the rest of you had cooking to put a puppet on the throne, but you did it anyway. Now we need someone who knows how the country works and understands all of it—the good *and* the bad." He turned back to Valiana. "Come on, girl, speak. Do you want to be the Realm's Protector or not?"

Valiana stood shakily. "I . . . no, your Grace. I do not want to rule, nor do I wish to hold the throne in any way."

"Good," Meillard said. "Then you're perfect for the job."

That wasn't the end of all the yelling and shouting, not by a long shot, and I was surprised at how quickly all of their precious protocol slipped away. But in the end Meillard and Jillard prevailed.

Valiana walked from the table to kneel before Aline. "I swore an oath to you," she said. "I swore to protect you, no matter what."

Aline nodded. The tears had stopped and now she just looked tired—too tired for such a young soul.

"I . . . Things will be different if I do this," Valiana said. "I won't take the role unless you agree to it, but if you do, things will be different between us. I will have to put the country's needs ahead of your own."

Aline remained silent.

Valiana took one of Aline's hands in hers. "You have to say it: you have to release me from my oath, or I won't do it."

"This is foolish," Duke Hadiermo complained.

"There are worse things than a ruler who holds to their oaths," Meillard replied.

Aline stood up and placed her hand on Valiana's head. "I am Aline, daughter of Paelis. I am heir to the throne of Tristia and I release you from your oath, Valiana val Mond of the Greatcoats."

And just like that, I had betrayed the last command of the King whom I loved more than the world itself.

EPILOGUE

I stood staring through the iron bars at the Tailor, who was sitting on a stool in the very center of her cell. "You asked to see me, and here I am."

The King never liked prisons much, having spent a good deal of his life locked in one, so he'd seen to it that the cells beneath Castle Aramor were only partially underground, and had light coming from small windows—too high above the floor for prisoners to reach, but angled so they could still see the sky during the day.

"I see they found you appropriate accommodations," I added.

"It suits me well enough," she said. Then she smiled. "Besides, it's only temporary."

"I doubt you'll find your way out of this. An awful lot of people died because of you."

"People would have died anyway. I think things turned out as well as we could have hoped. They never would have accepted a proper Queen on the throne unless they absolutely had to. They never would have allowed you and your Greatcoats to take control, not unless there was something far more dangerous to fear—and I gave them that, Falcio. I gave them a glimpse of civil war and chaos.

I showed them an army of assassins who made their worst fears of the Greatcoats nothing more dangerous than soft rain on a warm summer night."

"You turned into a monster as bad—no, worse—than Patriana."

"No, I became exactly what the world needed me to be, nothing more—and nothing less." Then she reached out a hand and took my jaw. "Just as you have, Falcio."

I pushed her hand away. "I stayed true to my oaths."

"Oaths." She spat the word. "And where did this great oath come from? It came from the death of your wife, from a long, dark journey that began in blood and ended with steel. Your *oath*, Falcio val Mond, First Cantor of the Greatcoats, came from every evil thing that has ever been done to you. The world required a man of valor and so it gave you pain and misery to turn you into what it needed." She smiled then and reached out for me once more, but I stepped back. "And it needed courage and decency. The world needed a hero, and you were the clay it molded for that purpose."

"It's too bad Nehra isn't here," I said. "She might know the proper word for whatever it is you've become. You and I are through," I said as I began to walk away.

"You were dying."

I stopped. I had known she might say what she was about to and I had promised myself I would leave before she took the chance, and yet I stayed—if only because profound irony deserves an audience.

"The neatha was killing you," the Tailor continued. "Nothing I nor any healer could have done would have stopped it from reaching your heart. What the Dashini did to you—it burned out the poison. It saved your life."

I turned and did my very best to look surprised. "And you knew this?"

I don't know if she fell for my performance or merely tolerated it for the sake of her own act of self-deception.

"I suspected. I've told you before, boy: life is pain. What the Unblooded inflicted on you . . . I cannot begin imagine—but I do know that without it you would surely be dead."

I smiled grimly, unable to keep up the pretense any longer. "So really, you only betrayed me to the Dashini so that you could save my life."

Her expression remained as hard and impassive as ever.

"In that case, next time, Tailor, I would consider it an enormous favor if you would just let me die."

She snorted. "Really? You still think I care about your pride? Or your pain? I told you—I told you *over and over*: there is *nothing* I won't do to protect Aline. *Nothing.* Everything I did, I did to put her on the throne."

"You brought mayhem and murder to all of our lives."

"Aye. I did, and I'll do it again, if needs be. I'll see this country turned into a river of blood if that's what it takes. Aline will be Queen."

I knew what I wanted to say, but I hesitated. I imagined Saint Birgid, whispering in my ear: *I've called out to you, always when the victory was won but before the final blow was struck.* I did believe in mercy, in compassion—now more than ever, I believed it was vital.

But there is also justice, *Birgid. And besides, I'm no fucking Saint.*

"Your son would hate you for what you've become," I said.

At first, I thought the Tailor would grow angry and rage at me, or maybe she might even break down and cry, but she didn't, of course. She said only, "Of course he would hate me for what I've done, Falcio. In a thousand years he could never forgive me for all of this, even in the name of putting his daughter on the throne. That's why you and I loved him so much, isn't it?"

Later that night six of us stood upon the ramparts of Castle Aramor under stars so bright I could almost trick myself into believing I was on one of the southern islands. Strangely, the two people who would most have understood what I felt weren't with us. Aline was in a room in the castle, safe from harm, though not safe from her own fears. *Not yet, but soon,* I promised her. And Ethalia was staying with her until she fell asleep. Aline had trouble looking at me now, though I couldn't say whether it was from guilt or out of a deep sense of betrayal that I had failed to make her Queen.

"I could do with being King, you know?" Brasti said, one foot on the low stone rampart, looking out over the countryside as if it belonged to him.

"You'd make a terrible King," Kest said. His arm had been rebandaged at the point where I'd cut off his hand. It no longer showed that bloom of red.

"Doesn't that hurt?" Brasti asked.

"It's agony," Kest replied. "It feels as if it's still being sawed through, very, very slowly."

"Then why aren't you . . . you know . . . ?"

"What?"

"Screaming!" Brasti shouted. "Or crying. Or moaning or . . . anything that human beings do when they've had their hand cut off!"

Kest looked at him for a moment, the faint smile on his face somewhere between bemused and genuinely curious. "Would that help?"

Brasti threw up his hands. "You're hopeless."

Valiana started laughing, and so did Nehra, who brought out her guitar and began to play a soft melody that went well with the bright stars. I turned to Dariana, who was standing a little way apart from us.

"What are you doing over there?" I asked.

She turned to me. "What? Nehra said I had to be here, and here I am."

"If you stood any further away you'd fall off the castle."

"I'm not one of you," she said. "I never have been."

"And how's that been working out for you?" Brasti asked.

She looked at him and for a moment, her eyes narrowed, but then a smirk appeared on her lips. "You do realize that I only slept with you because I was planning on cutting off your balls afterward and keeping them as trophies, don't you?"

"Dariana, if you really want to hurt me, all you need to do is have sex with me again. Frankly, cutting off my balls would be more merciful."

"Enough," I said. "Some of us have had painfully close brushes with such things recently."

Brasti looked horrified. "Hells, Falcio, I'm sorry—I didn't mean—"

"It's time," Nehra interrupted.

"Time for what?" I asked. "Are you going to tell us why we all had to come up here? It's damned cold."

"Perhaps you should have worn your coat," Kest said, and though none of the others noticed it, there was a note of sadness mixed with resignation in his voice.

I hadn't worn my coat because earlier that night I'd found the old wooden chest that the King had taken our coats from, the day he'd given them to us. Mine was inside it now, and the lid was closed. I was done. I'd served my King as well as any peasant boy from Pertine could ever have been expected to do, and when I left the ramparts later that night, I would go downstairs to my room and find Ethalia, who would be waiting for me. She would stand in front of me and smile that smile of hers and she would ask me one final time to leave this place behind. She would tell me once more about a particular small island off the coast of Baern that had no Dukes, nor Knights, nor Greatcoats, for that matter. She would ask me to come with her.

I would say yes.

Nehra's voice pulled me from my thoughts. "There's a story that will be told in the coming days and years. I intend to get it right."

Brasti grinned. "Well, it all started with a young poacher: a brave and hardy soul, born to humble beginnings but destined for—"

"I don't mean the story of what happened," Nehra said, "and I especially don't want your version of it. I mean the story that comes after."

"I don't—"

Valiana spoke up. "I think I understand."

Nehra smiled, then she looked at me. "You see, Falcio? There's at least one thing in this world you got right."

"I'm not sure I had much to do with it."

"Still the fool, then." She turned back to Valiana. "Go on, Realm's Protector. You might as well begin."

Valiana pulled her shoulders back.

Saints, I thought, *I used to think she looked like one of those princesses rescued by heroes and woven into tapestries. But she doesn't anymore.* She's *the hero.*

"The Dukes aren't done with their schemes," she said. "They've got a year in which to find some new treachery which will enable them to take power—Jillard, Hadiermo, all of them: they've still got money and influence. And then there's Trin—she won't stop, not ever. She'll bide her time, lick her wounds for a bit, and then, slowly but surely, she'll start making plans again. She thinks she knows me—they all do. They think I'm still the same vain, foolish child who smiled prettily and knew how to curtsey at all the right times. They'll all believe they can destroy Aline, because they think they're so much more cunning than I am." She turned to the rest of us. "*They* don't know me at all."

I thought I should say something next but before I could, Brasti leapt up onto the rampart. "There are still Knights out there," he said, "men in armor who think their warped sense of honor means the Gods and the Saints are on their side and that puts them above the law. I mean to prove them wrong."

"The Gods *are* on their side," Kest said, "or they seem to be, at least."

I smiled. "You planning on dueling more Saints? Didn't you notice how that turned out last time?"

"No," Kest said, "I thought I might try my hand at a God next time."

And then I saw he was smiling, too.

"No!" Brasti said. "Absolutely fucking not."

"What's the matter?" Kest asked innocently.

Brasti jumped down from the rampart and held out an accusatory finger. "You are *not* going to become a God before I've even made Saint! I'm sick of doing all the real work while the two of you become legends! Did anyone happen to notice that it was *me* who killed off a thousand charging Knights? Saint Zaghev-who-sings-for-tears! There is no fucking justice in this world."

Kest, Valiana, and I started laughing, and after a moment even Brasti couldn't hold onto his righteous indignation and joined us. I loved the feeling of being surrounded by these strange, brave men and women, but I also knew I had to tell them.

"I've got something to say," Dariana said. "I mean, if it's all right."

We waited for her to speak, but she remained silent and after a moment Nehra looked at me and mouthed the word "idiot."

Fine, I thought. "You were meant to be here," I said firmly. "I'm not sure I'll ever understand why or how, but I know you belong here. With us."

Valiana walked over and embraced her. "Say what you need to say."

Dari took in a deep breath before gently pushing Valiana back. "I hated the Dashini. They were scary, sadistic monsters and they— Well, I hated them so much I became just like them."

"You're free now."

"I know that, but . . . There was something, I don't know—the old man, the one you met at the monastery?—he talked of a time when the Dashini were, well, not *good*, exactly, but *necessary*: that there were times when someone who committed a crime was too powerful to be stopped any other way. There was something *right* about the Dashini once, something that got corrupted." She turned to the rest of us. "I mean, what does happen if a Lord or a Duke or, hells, even a King becomes so powerful they can't be stopped? Trin's even got magic none of us have seen before."

"Are you really saying—?"

"Yes, I think I am. Someone has to find out what the Dashini used to be—what they were *meant* to be, and maybe . . . maybe put that back somehow. I'm sorry . . . I know you'd all rather I put on a pretty dress and start acting like some virtuous maiden—"

Brasti laughed out loud at that. "For all the Gods' sakes," said he begged, "*please*, don't put on a pretty dress and start acting like a virtuous maiden! The world's seen quite enough chaos already."

She smiled, and it was the first time I'd seen her do it without it being just a smirk. "On that score, you don't need to worry, Brasti Goodbow."

I wanted to stay in that moment forever, but Nehra's tune on the guitar, repeating over and over, told me she was still waiting for me to speak.

I was only just beginning to understand how much I loved them, and what I had to say would break these wild and idealistic hearts. I was going to cut the last thread binding us all together. *I won't give up Ethalia—I can't refuse her again.*

"I'm not . . . I need to . . . hells. I do have something to say, damn it, though I don't think you're going to—"

"Promise me you're going to tell this story differently than Falcio does," Brasti begged Nehra.

"Shut up," she said. "This is where it begins."

I felt a touch at my arm. I'd been so lost in my own thoughts I hadn't heard anyone approach. I turned and Ethalia was there, her face close to mine. *She's meant for moonlight*, I thought. Unfortunately, what I said was, "You look nice in the dark."

Brasti and Dariana snorted in perfect synchronicity, but Ethalia just smiled and ignored my stupidity, which she'd been doing for some time now, probably since the day we met, if I was being honest with myself.

"I brought you this," she said, and handed a bundle to me.

I looked down at the thick leather material, the clasps and straps; the stains and nicks I knew as well as I knew my own skin.

"I don't understand."

Ethalia stood in silence, waiting for me to put the coat on, and when I'd finished she pulled on the lapels and drew me to her. She kissed me deeply, and when she'd finished, she brushed imaginary dust off my shoulders.

"That's better," she said at last. "The night is cold and it comforts me to know you are warm." She let me go and walked back toward the stairs, but before she took the first step she turned and said, "Don't stay up too late. It's cold down there as well, and I too deserve to be warm."

I listened to the sound of her footsteps as she descended the stairs.

"Will someone tell me what that was all about?" Brasti asked.

It means love is not a cage, I thought. I turned to the others, and for once I knew exactly what to say.

"What's wrong with his face?" Dariana asked.

"He's smiling," Brasti replied. "It's a rare and altogether terrifying—"

"Shut up, Brasti," Kest said.

I turned to Nehra and even though she wasn't playing any louder, the melody coming from her guitar filled my ears. I felt as if I needed to shout to be heard over it. *No, I don't need to shout. I want to let them all hear it—let the whole world hear it.* "When you tell the story of what happened here, Nehra, tell it however you like. Have me standing atop a mountain pushing back the clouds if you want. But when you reach the end, there's something I want you to tell those listening."

Nehra paused in her playing and let the last notes ride out into the night sky. "What would you have me say?"

"Tell them the Greatcoats are coming."

The story of Falcio, Kest, Brasti, and
the Greatcoats continues in

TYRANT'S
THRONE

ACKNOWLEDGMENTS

The Greatcoats of
Knight's Shadow

I was in a bar in Toronto in 2012 with my new publisher, Jo Fletcher, with whom I had just signed a four-book deal for the Greatcoats series, when I confessed that I was terrified of writing the sequel to *Traitor's Blade*. She was very understanding and proceeded to say a number of very reassuring things, none of which I can remember because I was too busy telling myself that I was completely screwed.

When you find yourself in this kind of situation, it helps to have an army of Greatcoats at your back . . .

The Trio

Falcio, Kest and Brasti are the stars of the Greatcoats series but I turn to a different set of heroes when I'm writing my books.

Christina de Castell—in addition to being a constant source of inspiration, my darling wife helped me break through several huge blocks as I was writing *Knight's Shadow*.

Eric Torin—my frequent writing partner and a true friend, who always challenges me to go deeper with my writing. I can't wait for you to one day read one of the books that Eric and I have written together.

Heather Adams—go and find a book about agents, read all the sections about how you can't bother your agent, shouldn't expect them to help you with writing problems and they absolutely won't listen to you whine. Heather's the opposite of all that.

THE SAINTS

It's common for Falcio to utter the names of Saints when in dire need (and sometimes just when he's swearing at the world). Unlike his Saints, mine always reply to my e-mails.

Jo Fletcher-who-obliterates-clichés, Saint of Editing
Adrienne Kerr-who-faces-the-oceans, Saint of Supporting Authors
Nathaniel Marunas-who-knows-all-markets, Saint of Navigating
    Strange Waters
Andrew Turner-who-tweets-the-world, Saint of Publicity
Nicola Budd-who-hammers-the-details, Saint of Getting Things Done

THE SECRET GREATCOATS

Then, of course, there are people whom I almost never, ever get to see but who work tirelessly to make this book and so many others possible.

My thanks goes to Patrick Carpenter, Keith Bambury, Melanie Thompson and the sales, marketing and rights teams, and buerosued .de for the cover design and illustration.

MY FELLOW SWASHBUCKLERS

The folks in my critique group are more than just fellow writers— they are fencing partners who (thankfully) are willing to skewer me every time my chapters aren't sharp enough: Wil Arndt, Brad Dehnert

(@BradDehnert), Sarah Figueroa, Claire Ryan (www. ryanfall.com) and Kim Tough.

Kat Zeller, Mike Church and Sam Chandola were kind enough to read this book at various stages and help point out ways to make it a better story.

THE BARDATTI

Books and stories need champions to help people find them. The heroes of the publishing world in the twenty-first century are the bloggers, booksellers, librarians and readers who go out of their way to share books they've discovered with the world. I couldn't hope to name all of the wonderful people who've helped get the Greatcoats noticed here, but I thank you all and wanted to share a few stories:

Book Bloggers, in case you haven't met any, are these rather amazing people who give up their own free time not just to find books they love but to write with eloquence and passion so that others can discover new stories and adventures. Folks like:

Marc Aplin of Fantasy-Faction.com

Stefan Fergus of Civilian-Reader.blogspot.co.uk

Tabitha Jensen of NotYetRead.com are just a few of the wonderful people I've connected with recently. I very much hope to meet many more of you over the next few years.

Goldsboro Books took a risk on *Traitor's Blade*, issuing a special first edition that helped to get the book noticed even before it was released. I had the pleasure of meeting Harry Illingworth who probably hand-sold half of them. Thanks, Harry!

Some of the most wonderfully supportive people have turned out to be the folks who work in bookstores, like Nazia Khatun from Waterstones in London, who I had the pleasure of meeting in person.

Walter and Jill of White Dwarf Books in Vancouver have also been incredibly supportive, as they have been of so many fantasy and science fiction writers over the years. If you ever come to Vancouver, you owe it to yourself to check out their store and meet them.

Finally, to those of you who read the Greatcoats series and make it such a joy to write, thank you so much for your e-mails, tweets and other good vibes that make being an author anything but a lonely profession.

With gratitude,

Sebastien de Castell
twitter: @decastell
web: www.decastell.com
Vancouver, Canada
November 2014

P.S. If you've read this far then you are a true lover of books and those who make them. For you alone do I give the following secret of the Greatcoats: Ugh's real name, which is not revealed anywhere else in the series, is Vadren Graff. As a young man he wanted to study philosophy, but his size and strength soon got him pressed into the Ducal guards. His captain called him Dog and considered him too stupid (and scary) to be kept with the other men, and so Vadren was sent to work in the dungeons of Rijou and later forced to become a torturer. No one ever asked him his name—they simply called him "the Dog," which suited Vadren fine. Until he met Falcio he'd convinced himself that he could live with his role because even the worst torturer is unlikely ever to kill as many innocent people as a soldier does. Vadren would have made a decent, if controversial, philosopher.

ABOUT THE TYPE

Typeset in Minion Pro Regular, 11/14.25pt.

Minion Pro was designed for Adobe Systems by
Robert Slimbach in 1990. Inspired by typefaces of the Renaissance,
it is both is easily readable and extremely functional
without compromising its inherent beauty.

Typeset by Scribe Inc., Philadelphia, Pennsylvania.